Night Embra...

"With her steamy, action-packed *Dark-Hun*...
ing in a whole new class of night dwellers...
and snappy dialogue keep the plot both acc...
its courageous, unconventional characters, and wry humor, this fast-moving fantasy will fill the void left by the end of the *Buffy the Vampire Slayer* series."

—*Publishers Weekly*

"The second novel in Sherrilyn Kenyon's hot series is just as exciting, sexy, and thrilling as the first. Kenyon has hit on a fabulous premise that promises to be fodder for many more outstanding page-turners."

—*RT Bookclub*

"Her heroes are not only the ultimate alpha men, but are also the embodiment of every female fantasy . . . well rounded, with romance as its cornerstone, and plenty of action, suspense, humor, and sorrow."

—*The Road to Romance*

"A marathon of discoveries and pleasures—a wonderful addition to the *Dark-Hunter* series. Ms. Kenyon delivers another exciting, heart-pumping, virile male to titillate us . . . it's full of surprises, but this author's great storytelling talent is no surprise at all."

—*Old Book Barn Gazette*

Night Pleasures

"A perfect ten!"

—*Rendezvous Reviews*

"If you love *Buffy the Vampire Slayer* or *Angel,* then boy, is this the book for you . . . original and complex . . . the characters are unforgettable and the action thrilling."

—*RT Bookclub* (top pick)

"A wild, wicked delight . . . no one does sexy, tormented heroes better—or more inventively—than Sherrilyn Kenyon."

—Nicole Jordan, author of *The Warrior,* on *Night Pleasures*

NIGHT PLEASURES

NIGHT EMBRACE

ALSO BY SHERRILYN KENYON
IN READING ORDER

Fantasy Lover
Night Pleasures
Night Embrace
Dance with the Devil
Kiss of the Night
Night Play
Seize the Night
Sins of the Night

AND COMING SOON

Unleash the Night

FROM ST. MARTIN'S PAPERBACKS

NIGHT PLEASURES

NIGHT EMBRACE

Sherrilyn Kenyon

St. Martin's Griffin ✠ New York

www.stmartins.com

ISBN 0-312-35563-7
EAN 978-0-312-35563-0

Night Pleasures was originally published
by St. Martin's Paperbacks in October 2002

Night Embrace was originally published
by St. Martin's Paperbacks in July 2003

First St. Martin's Griffin Edition: October 2005

10 9 8 7 6 5 4 3 2 1

NIGHT PLEASURES

For Kim Cardascia, who gives me the freedom to push past the boundaries of my imagination, and Nancy Yost, who keeps me sane while I do it.

To the Ladies of Sanctuary and the RBL Romanticans for all the laughs and support you guys have given me and the Dark-Hunter series. I lub all of you. Thanks for just being you and for loving romance novels as much as I do!

For my friends without whom I would be eternally lost: Rickey, Lo, Janet, Cathy-Max, Deb, Rebecca and Kim Williamon.

To my husband and sons for your patience, your love, and all the incredible happiness the four of you have added to my life. And last but never least, for my family for being an incredible source of support.

NIGHT
PLEASURES

AN ANCIENT GREEK LEGEND

Born to extreme wealth, Kyrian of Thrace wielded charm and charisma as powerfully as he wielded his sword. Courageous and bold, he ruled the world around him, and knew nothing save the very passionate side of his nature.

Ardent, wild, and restless, he lived his life recklessly. He knew no danger, no limitations. The world was his oyster and he vowed to feed fully from it.

With the strength of Ares, the body and face of Adonis, and the sensuous gifts of Aphrodite, he was sought by all women who saw him. They wanted him for their own, dreamed of possessing the proud warrior prince whose touch was said to be the closest a woman could ever come to paradise.

But he was not a man whose heart was easily tamed.

He was a man who lived for the moment, lived for his senses, and for the wild fulfillment of all his desires. He loved pleasure, both the giving and the receiving.

The few women who had claimed him for a night of ecstasy lorded it over those who could only dream of touching his exquisite body.

For he *was* passion. Desire. All things sensual and hot.

A born warrior, he was respected and feared by all who knew of him. And at a time when the Roman Empire was invincible, he, alone, beat the Romans back with a hero's glee, and brought riches and glory to his name and homeland.

For a while, 'twas said he would be ruler of the known world.

Until an act of brutal betrayal made him the Ruler of the Night.

Now he walks the shadowy realm between Life and the Underworld. Neither man nor beast, he is something else entirely.

He is Solitude. He is Darkness.

He is a shadow in the night.

A restless, lonely spirit whose destiny is to save the very mortals who despise and fear him. He will never know rest or peace until he can find the one woman who will not betray him. The one pure heart who can see past his dark side and bring him back into the light.

CHAPTER 1

"I say we should stake him to an anthill and throw little pickles at him."

Amanda Devereaux laughed at Selena's suggestion. Leave it to her big sister to make her laugh, no matter the tragedy. Which was exactly what had her sitting at Selena's tarot card and palm-reading table in Jackson Square on a cold Sunday afternoon, instead of lying in bed with the covers pulled over her head.

Still smiling at the thought of a million ants biting Cliff's pasty, dough-boy body, Amanda glanced around at the tourists who were thronging the New Orleans landmark even on this drab November day.

The smell of warm chicory coffee and beignets floated from the Cafe Du Monde across the street, while cars zoomed past a few feet away. The clouds and the sky were an eerie gray that matched Amanda's dour mood.

Most of the Jackson Square peddlers didn't bother setting up booths during the winter season, but her sister Selena considered her psychic stand as much a New Orleans treasure as the St. Louis Cathedral behind them.

And what a treasure Selena's stand was . . .

The cheap card table was disguised by a thick purple cloth their mother had sewn with "special" incantations known only to their family.

Madam Selene, the Moon Mistress, as Selena was known,

sat behind it wearing a flowing green suede skirt, purple knit sweater, and a large black and silver overcoat.

Her sister's strange outfit was quite a contrast to Amanda's faded jeans, pink cable-knit sweater, and tan ski jacket. But then, Amanda had always preferred to dress in an understated way. Unlike her flamboyant family, she hated to stand out. She much preferred to blend into the background.

"I'm through with men," Amanda said. "Cliff was the last stop on the bus to nowhere. I'm tired of wasting my time and energy on them. From now on, I'm going to focus all my attention on accounting."

Selena curled her lips in distaste as she shuffled her tarot cards. "Accounting? Are you sure you're not a changeling?"

Amanda gave a halfhearted laugh. "Actually, I'm sure I am a changeling. I just wish my real family would come claim me before it's too late and some of the weirdness rubs off."

Selena laughed at her while she set her tarot cards out in a game of psychic solitaire. "You know what your problem is?"

"I'm too straitlaced and uptight," Amanda said, using the words her mother and eight older sisters most often applied to her.

"Well, yeah, that too. But I'm thinking you need to branch out with your tastes. Stop going after these tie-wearing, ho-hum, cry-to-my-mama-'cause-I-have-no-life geeks. You, my baby sister, need a sexcapade with a man who can make your heart race. I'm talking truly reckless and wild."

"Someone like Bill?" Amanda asked with a smile, thinking of Selena's husband, who was even more straitlaced than Amanda was.

Selena shook her head. "Oh no, that's different. See, I'm the reckless and wild one who saves him from being boring. It's why we're perfect for each other. We balance. You have no balance. You and your boyfriends tip the scale way into Boredom City."

"Hey, I like my men boring. They're reliable, and you don't have to worry about them having major testosterone moments. I'm a beta girl, all the way."

Selena snorted as she played with her cards. "Sounds to me

like you need a few therapy sessions with Grace."

Amanda scoffed. "Right, like I need dating advice from a sex therapist who married a Greek sex slave she conjured out of a book. No, thanks."

In spite of her words, Amanda really did like Grace Alexander. Unlike Selena's usual crew of insane friends, Grace had always been grounded, and blessedly normal. "How's she doing, by the way?"

"Fine. Niklos started walking two days ago and now he's into everything."

Amanda smiled as she imagined the adorable blond toddler and his twin sister. She loved it when Grace and Julian let her baby-sit for them. "When's her new baby due?"

"March first."

"I'll bet they're excited," Amanda said, struck by a tiny stab of jealousy. She'd always wanted a house full of kids, but at twenty-six her prospects appeared bleak. Especially since she couldn't find any man willing to procreate with a woman whose entire family was certifiable.

"You know," Selena said with that speculative look that made Amanda cringe. "Julian has a brother who was cursed into a book, too. You could try—"

"Big no, thanks! Remember, I'm the one who hates all this paranormal junk. I want a nice, normal, *human* male, not some demon."

"Priapus is a Greek god, not a demon."

"Close enough in my book. Believe me, I had my fill while living at home with the nine of you casting spells and doing all that hocus-pocus. I want normality in my life."

"Normality is boring."

"Why don't you try it before you knock it?"

Selena laughed. "One day, little sister, you're going to have to accept the other half of your blood."

Amanda disregarded her words as her thoughts turned back to her ex-fiancé. She'd really thought Cliff was the one for her. A nice, quiet, average-looking data entry clerk, he had been just her cup of tea.

Until he had met her family.

Ugh! For the last six months, she had put off introducing him to them, knowing what would happen. But he had insisted and last night she had finally caved.

Closing her eyes, Amanda winced at the memory of her twin sister, Tabitha, meeting him at the door all decked out in the Goth clothes she used for stalking the undead. The outfit came complete with a crossbow Tabitha just had to show him, and her entire collection of throwing stars. *"This one is special. It can cleave the head off a vampire at three hundred yards."*

If that wasn't bad enough, her mother and three of her older sisters had been conjuring a protection spell for Tabitha in the kitchen.

But the absolute worst had come when Cliff had mistakenly drunk from Tabitha's cup, which had been filled with her strength potion of curdled milk, Tabasco sauce, egg yolks, and tea leaves.

He had heaved for an hour.

Afterward, Cliff had driven her home. *"I can't marry a woman with a family like that,"* he'd said as she handed her engagement ring back to him. *"Good God, what if we had kids? Can you imagine what would happen if some of that rubbed off?"*

Leaning her head back, Amanda could still kill her family for the embarrassment. Was it too much for them to be normal for one dinner?

Why, oh why, couldn't she have been born to a regular family where no one believed in ghosts, goblins, demons, and witches?

Come to think of it, two of them still believed in Santa Claus!

How could her wonderfully normal father stand all their nonsense? He definitely deserved to be sainted for his patience.

"Hey, guys!"

Amanda opened her eyes to see Tabitha approaching. *Well now, isn't this just peachy keen?* What would happen next? Would a bus run her over?

This day just gets better and better.

She loved her identical twin, but not at this moment. At this moment, she wished very vile things on Tabitha's head. Painful nasty things.

As usual, Tabitha was dressed all in black. Black leather pants, turtleneck, and long black leather coat. Her thick, wavy dark auburn hair was pulled into a long ponytail, and her pale blue eyes glowed. Tabitha's cheeks were flushed and she had a chipper step.

Oh no, she was on a hunt!

Amanda sighed. How on earth could they have come from the same single egg?

Tabitha reached into her coat pocket and pulled out a scrap of paper, then placed it on the table in front of Selena. "I need your expertise. It's Greek, isn't it?"

Without answering the question, Selena set her cards aside, and looked the paper over. She frowned. "Where did you get this?"

"It was on a vampire we dusted last night. What does it say?"

" 'The Dark-Hunter is close. Desiderius must prepare.' "

Tabitha put her hands in her pockets as she considered the words. "Any idea what that means?"

Selena shrugged as she handed the paper back to Tabitha. "I've never heard of either this Dark-Hunter or Desiderius."

"Eric said 'Dark-Hunter' was a code name for one of us. What do you think?" Tabitha asked.

Amanda had heard enough. Ye gods, how she hated it when they began with the whole vampire-demon-occult garbage. Why couldn't they grow up and live in the regular world?

"Look," Amanda said, rising. "I'll catch you two later."

Tabitha grabbed her hand as she started to walk off. "Hey, you're not still sore about Cliff, are you?"

"Of course I am. I know you did all that on purpose."

Completely unabashed about the fact she'd broken Amanda's engagement, Tabitha released her hand. "We did it for your own good."

"Oh yeah, right." She beamed a false smile. "Thank you so

much for watching out for me. Wanna poke my eye out while you're at it, just for fun?"

"C'mon, Mandy," Tabitha said with that cutesy face that made their dad forgive her anything. It didn't do anything to Amanda, except irritate her more. "You might not like what we do, but you do love us. And you can't marry some uptight jerk who can't accept what all of us are."

"Us?" Amanda asked incredulously. "Don't include me in the madness. I'm the one with the recessive normal genes. You guys are the ones—"

"Tabby!"

Amanda broke off as Tabitha's Goth boyfriend ran up to them. Eric St. James was only an inch taller than the two of them, but since they were five-foot-ten, that wasn't unusual. His short black hair had a purple stripe in it and he wore it spiked. He would have been very cute if his nose wasn't pierced, and if he would actually find and keep a full-time job.

And lay off the vampire-hunting. Sheez!

"Gary got a lead on that vamp pack," Eric said to Tabitha. "We're going to try and get the vampires before it gets dark. You ready?"

If Amanda rolled her eyes any harder back into her head, she'd go blind from it. "One day, you guys are going to inadvertently kill a human being acting this way. Remember that time you attacked the Anne Rice–Lestat reenactment group in the cemetery?"

Eric smirked at her. "No one was hurt, and the tourists loved it."

Tabitha looked back at Selena. "Can you do some research for me, and see if you can find anything on this Desiderius and Dark-Hunter?"

"C'mon, Tabby, how many times do I have to tell you to lay off it?" Eric said irritably. "The vamps are just playing with us. 'Dark-Hunter' is just a bogeyman term that means nothing."

Selena and Tabitha ignored him.

"Sure," Selena said, "but Gary would probably be your best bet."

Eric let out a disgusted breath. "He said he'd never heard of it, either"—Eric looked at Tabitha heatedly—"which means it's nothing."

Tabitha shrugged his hand off her shoulder, and continued to ignore him. "Since it's written in Greek, I'm betting one of your college professor friends might be more up on it."

Selena nodded. "I'll ask Julian tonight when I go over to Grace's."

"Thanks." Tabitha looked back at Amanda. "Don't worry about Cliff. I know just the guy for you. We met him a couple of weeks ago."

"Oh Lord," Amanda gasped. "No more blind dates from you. I still haven't recovered from the last one and that was four years ago."

Selena laughed. "Was that the alligator wrestler?"

"Yes," Amanda said. "Crocodile Mitch, who tried to feed me to his pet, Big Marthe."

Tabitha snorted. "He did not. He was just trying to show you what he did for a living."

"Tell you what, the day you let Eric hold your head inside a live alligator, then you can make a comment. Until then, being the expert on alligator halitosis, I'll stick with my opinion that Mitch was just looking for a cheap Scooby snack."

Tabitha stuck her tongue out at her before grabbing Eric's hand and dashing down the street with him in tow.

Amanda rubbed her head as she watched the two of them make goo-goo eyes at each other, thus proving that there was someone out there for everyone. No matter how bizarre the person.

Too bad she couldn't find someone for herself.

"I'm going home to sulk."

"Listen," Selena said before she could leave. "Why don't I cancel with Grace tonight and the two of us can go do something? Have a symbolic itty-bitty weenie roast for Cliff?"

Amanda smiled in appreciation of the thought. No wonder she loved her family. In spite of the chaos, they were dear hearts who cared for her. "No, thanks. I can roast the Vienna sausages on my own. Besides, Tabitha will stroke out and die if you don't ask Julian about her Dark-Hunter."

"Okay, but if you change your mind, let me know. Oh, and while you're home, why not call Tiyana and have her do a penis-shrinking spell on Cliff?"

Amanda laughed. Okay, there were times when having a voodoo high priestess as an older sister came in handy. "Trust me, he can't afford it." She winked at Selena. "Later."

That evening, Amanda jumped as the phone rang, startling her out of her daydreams. Laying her book aside, she picked the phone up.

It was Tabitha.

"Hey, sis, can you go by my house and let Terminator out?"

Amanda ground her teeth at the familiar request that came at least twice a week. "Oh, come on, Tabby. Why didn't you do it?"

"I didn't know we'd be gone so long. Please. He'll wet on my bed in protest if you don't."

"You know, Tabby, I do have a life."

"Yeah, right, like you're not sitting alone on the sofa, reading Kinley MacGregor's latest romance, and scarfing down chocolate truffles like there's no tomorrow."

Amanda arched her brow as she looked at the multitude of truffle wrappers scattered on the coffee table in front of her, and her copy of *Claiming the Highlander* on the end table.

Damn, she hated it when her sisters did that.

"C'mon," Tabitha begged. "I promise I'll be nice to your next boyfriend."

Sighing, Amanda knew she couldn't really say no to her sisters. It was her biggest weakness. "It's a good thing you only live down the street or I'd have to kill you over this."

"I know. I love you, too."

Growling low in her throat, Amanda hung up. She cast a wistful look at her book. Doggone it, she was just starting to get into it.

She sighed. Oh well, at least Terminator would be company

for a few minutes. He was one seriously ugly pit bull, but he was currently the only male she could stand.

She grabbed her tan ski jacket off her armchair and exited out the front door. Tabitha lived two blocks over, and though the night was extremely dark and cold, Amanda didn't feel like driving.

Pulling her gloves on, she headed down the sidewalk, wishing Cliff were here to do this chore. She couldn't count the times she had suckered him into letting Terminator out of Tabitha's house on his way home.

Amanda stumbled over a broken piece of the sidewalk as Cliff crossed her mind for the first time in hours. What really made her feel bad about their breakup was the fact she didn't miss him. Not really, anyway.

She missed having someone to talk to at night. She missed having a TV-watching buddy, but she couldn't honestly say she missed *him*.

And that was what depressed her most of all.

If not for her whacked-out family, she might have actually married him, and then found out too late that she didn't truly love him.

The thought chilled her more than the cold November winds.

Pushing Cliff out of her thoughts, she focused on her surroundings. At eight-thirty, the neighborhood was amazingly quiet, even for a Sunday night. Cars were parked along the street, and most of the houses were lit up as she walked down the old jagged sidewalk.

Everything was normal, but still it was eerie out. The partial moon hung high above, casting twisted shadows around her. Every now and again, she'd catch the faint sound of laughter or voices on the wind.

This was a perfect night for evil to—

"Get out of my head," she said out loud.

Now Tabitha had *her* doing it! Jeez!

What next? Would she find herself walking the bayou with her sisters looking for weird voodoo plants and alligators?

Shivering at the thought, she finally reached the creepy old house Tabitha and her roommate rented on the corner. A garish purple color, it was one of the smallest houses on the street. Amanda was amazed no one in the neighborhood complained about the unsightly hue. Of course, Tabby loved it since it made giving directions easy.

"Just look for the little purple Victorian with the black iron fence. You can't miss it."

Not unless you were blind.

After opening the low, wrought-iron gate, Amanda headed up the walkway to the porch where a huge, sinister stone gargoyle stood watch.

"Hi, Ted," she said to the gargoyle Tabitha swore could read minds. "I'm just letting the pooch out, okay?"

Amanda pulled the keys out of her coat pocket and opened the front door. Entering the foyer, she wrinkled her nose as she caught a whiff of a nasty-smelling something. One of Tabby's potions must have gone bad.

Either that, or her sister had tried to cook dinner again.

She heard Terminator barking in the bedroom.

"I'm coming," she said to the dog as she closed the door, turned on the lights, and headed across the living room.

Amanda was one step away from the hallway when she heard the voice in her head telling her to run.

Before she could blink, the lights went out and someone grabbed her from behind.

"Well, well," a silken voice said in her ear. "At last I have you, little witch." His hold tightened. "Now it's time to make you suffer."

Something hit her head a second before the floor rose up to meet her.

CHAPTER 2

Amanda came awake to an awful throbbing in her head. She felt terrible.

What had hap—

She tensed as she remembered the unseen man.

His words.

Terrified, she pushed herself up, and quickly learned she was on a cold concrete floor, in a very small, dust-covered room . . .

And *handcuffed* to an unknown blond man.

A scream wedged itself in her throat, but she held it back.

Don't panic. Not until you have all the facts.

For all you know, Tabitha is making good her threat for a blind date—just like the time she "accidentally" locked you in the supply closet with Randy Davis for three hours.

Or "kidnapped" you in the trunk of her car with that weird musician.

Tabitha was always trying unorthodox ways to set her up with guys. Although, to be fair to her sister, Tabitha didn't usually knock the guy unconscious before she forced them together.

Still, with Tabitha there was a first time for just about anything. And extreme blind-dating was very vintage T.

Forcing herself to remain calm until she had more information, Amanda took in her surroundings. The two of them were in a small room with no windows and one rusty iron door. A door she couldn't reach without dragging her "friend" across the floor.

There was no furniture or anything else. The only light came from a small bulb in the center of the ceiling.

Okay, so she wasn't in immediate danger.

Still far from comforted, she looked at the body beside her. He lay with his back to her, and he was either dead or unconscious.

Preferring the latter, she inched toward him. He appeared rather tall, and he was positioned as if he had been dumped roughly onto the floor.

Her legs shaking, Amanda rose slowly to her knees and moved over him to keep his arm from being twisted any more.

He didn't move.

She trailed her gaze over his body. A long black leather coat, black jeans, and a black crew-neck shirt combined to give him an extremely dangerous appearance even while lying on the floor. His feet were covered by a pair of black biker boots with strange silver inlays in the heels.

His wavy blond hair fell over his face and met the collar of his coat, obscuring his features from her view.

"Excuse me?" she whispered, reaching out to touch his arm. "Are you alive?"

As soon as her hand touched the hard, lean muscle of his biceps, her breath faltered. His prone body was like coiled steel. There wasn't a bit of a fleshy feel to him. He was all lithe, strong power.

Oh my, my.

Before she could stop herself, Amanda ran her hand down his arm. The feel of it!

She let out a slow, appreciative breath.

"Guy? Mister?" she tried again, shaking his hard, muscular shoulder. "Mr. Goth man, would you please wake up so I can leave? I really don't want to hang out in a closet with a dead man any longer than I have to, okay? C'mon, please, don't make this a *Weekend at Bernie's* thing. There's only one of me and you're a really big, *big* guy."

He didn't budge.

Okay, I'll have to try something else.

Biting her lip, Amanda rolled him onto his back. His hair fell away from his face at the same moment his collar did.

Her breath caught in her throat. Okay, now she was majorly impressed.

He was gorgeous. His jaw was strong and defined, his cheekbones high. His face was aristocratically boned, and he had just the tiniest hint of a cleft in his chin.

Oh baby, this man possessed that rare masculine beauty that only a few, *very* lucky women ever saw in the flesh.

Better still, he had the best looking lips she'd ever seen. Full and expressive, that mouth had been made for long, hot kisses.

In fact, the only flaw on his face was a hairline scar that ran across the lower edge of his jaw, from his ear to his chin.

He could easily rival Grace's husband for handsomeness. And Julian the Demigod was a hard man to compete with.

But then, Amanda had never been all that impressed with the way men looked. She preferred their minds over their bodies. Especially since most of the men she knew who looked even half this good generally had IQs that were smaller than her combined shoe size.

Unlike Tabitha, it took more than a cute butt and wide shoulders to turn her head.

Although . . .

Amanda ran her gaze over his lean, muscular body. In the case of this man, she might be willing to make an exception.

Provided he wasn't dead, anyway.

Hesitantly, she reached out and placed her hand against his tawny neck to check his pulse. A strong, heavy heartbeat thumped against her fingertips.

Relieved he was alive, she tried to shake him again. "Hey, yummy leather guy? Can you hear me?"

He moaned low in his throat, then slowly blinked his eyes open. Amanda started at the sight of those eyes. They were so dark they appeared black, and when they focused on her, they dilated menacingly.

With a curse, he grabbed her by the shoulders.

Before she could move, he rolled over with her, pinning her against the floor beneath his body as he held her wrists above her head.

Those dark, captivating eyes searched hers suspiciously.

Amanda couldn't breathe. Every inch of him was pressed intimately against her and she became instantly aware of the fact that his arms weren't the only part of his body that was rock-hard and solid. The man was a wall of sleek, strong muscle.

His hips rested dead center between her legs while his hard, taut stomach leaned against her in a way that brought a flush to her cheeks. Made her feel hot and tingly. Breathless.

For the first time in her life, she wanted to lift her head and kiss a man whom she knew absolutely *nothing* about.

Who was he?

To her complete shock, he lowered his head down to the side of her face and took a deep breath in her hair.

Amanda went rigid. "Are you *sniffing* me?"

A deep, melodious laugh rumbled through his body, sending an odd tingly surge through her.

"Only admiring your perfume, *ma fleur,*" he whispered softly in her ear with a strange, provocative accent that melted her. His voice was so deep it reminded her of thunder and it rumbled through her with a devastating effect.

Okay, so the man was incredibly hot, and his breath on her neck sent thousands of needlelike chills over her body.

"You are not Tabitha Devereaux." He whispered the words so softly that even with his mouth brushing her ear she had to strain to hear him.

She swallowed. "You know T—"

"Shh," he whispered in her ear as his thumbs caressed her captured wrists in a rhythm that sent electric surges through her. Her breasts drew tight as desire scorched her.

He moved his face against hers, scraping her cheek gently with his whiskers and causing another wave of chills to consume her. Never in her life had she felt anything more arousing than his weight on her or smelled anything more exciting than the spicy, manly scent of him.

"They are listening." Kyrian drew a deep, appreciative breath.

Now that he was certain she posed no immediate threat, he knew he should move away from the woman beneath him, and yet . . .

It had been a long time since he'd lain between a woman's thighs. An eternity since he had dared be this close to a female. He had forgotten the warm softness of breasts pressed against his chest. The feel of hot, sweet breath on his neck.

But now that she was under him . . .

Oh yes, he remembered this. He remembered the way a woman's hands felt as they roamed his naked back. The way a woman felt as she writhed to his expert touch.

For a minute, Kyrian actually lost himself to the sensation of it as he imagined removing their clothes and exploring her curves more fully.

And *much* more intimately.

He closed his eyes at the thought of running his tongue over her breast, of toying with the swollen nipple while she buried her hands in his hair.

She squirmed beneath him, only adding to his fantasy.

Hmmm . . .

Of course, if she ever found out who and what he was, she would pale in terror. And if she were anything like her sister, she would attack until one of them was dead.

Such a pity, really. But then, he was used to people being terrified of him. It was the curse and the salvation of his breed.

"Who's listening?" she whispered.

Opening his eyes, he relished the sound of her gentle, lilting voice. How he loved a smooth Southern drawl, and this woman had one that rolled off her tongue like exquisite silk.

Against his iron will, his body stirred viciously in response to her. The need rose in him to taste those full, parted lips as he spread her thighs wide and buried himself deep inside her heat.

Oh yes, he could savor this woman.

All of her.

He pulled back slightly to better study her face. Her dark

brown hair was liberally laced with auburn strands that caught the light. Her deep blue eyes showed her confusion, her anger, and her spirit. They were set in a beguiling face that had one tiny freckle just below her right eye. That mark alone distinguished her from her sister.

That and her scent.

Tabitha wore expensive perfumes that overwhelmed his highly developed senses, while this woman smelled of roses and softness.

Right then Kyrian wanted her with a need so demanding that it momentarily stunned him. It had been centuries since he last craved a woman this way.

Centuries since he had felt anything at all.

Amanda's face burned as his erection bulged disturbingly against her pelvis. The man might not be dead, but he was certainly stiff. And this had *nothing* to do with rigor mortis. "Look, buster, I really think you need to find someplace else to rest."

His gaze focused hungrily on her lips and she saw the raw longing in the depths of those midnight eyes. His jaw flexed rigidly as if he were fighting himself.

His masculine power and overt sexuality overwhelmed her.

As she lay there beneath him, she realized just how vulnerable she was to him. And how much she truly wanted a taste of those well-shaped lips.

That thought both scared and excited her.

He blinked and a veil came over his face, disguising his mood from her. He released her.

As he moved away, she saw the blood on her pink sweater. "Oh, my God!" she gasped. "You're bleeding?"

He took a deep breath as he sat next to her. "The wound will heal."

Amanda couldn't believe his nonchalant tone. Judging from the amount of blood on her clothes, she would say he was deeply injured and yet he showed no other signs of it. "Where are you hurt?"

He didn't answer. Instead, he ran his left hand through his tawny hair. He paused to glare at the large silver handcuff on his right wrist, then he started pulling angrily at it.

By the deadly, cold light in his eyes, she could tell the handcuffs bothered him even more than they did her.

Now that he was awake and not on top of her, Amanda was struck by the dark moodiness of his features. There was something very romantic and compelling about his face.

Something heroic.

All too easily, she could see him dressed like a Regency rake or medieval knight. His classical features held an indefinable quality that seemed oddly out of place in this modern world.

"Well, well," a disembodied voice said. "The Dark-Hunter is awake."

Amanda recognized the evil voice as the one belonging to whoever had clobbered her at Tabitha's house.

"Desi, babe," the man beside her said in a chiding tone as he looked about the brown walls. "Still playing your little games, I see. Now why don't you be a good Daimon and show yourself to me?"

"All in good time, Dark-Hunter, all in good time. You see, I am not like the others who run and cower from the big, bad wolf. I am the big, bad woodsman who executes that wolf."

The disembodied voice gave a dramatic pause. "You and Tabitha Devereaux have been merciless in your pursuit of my brethren and the time has come for you to know fear. By the time I finish with the two of you, you will be begging me to let you die."

The Dark-Hunter lowered his head and laughed. "Desi dearest, I have never begged a day in my life, and the sun will surely splinter before I *ever* plead for anything from the likes of you."

"Hubris," Desi said. "I so love punishing that crime."

The Dark-Hunter pushed himself to his feet, and Amanda saw the wound in his side. His shirt was slightly torn and blood stained the floor where he had been sitting.

But he didn't seem to notice the injury.

"Tell me, do you like your handcuffs?" Desi asked. "Those shackles are from the forge of Hephaestus. Only a god or a key fashioned by Hephaestus can open them. And since the gods have abandoned you . . ."

The Dark-Hunter glanced around the room. The fierce look on his face would have scared the devil himself. "I am so going to enjoy killing you."

Desiderius laughed. "I doubt you'll get the chance once your little friend learns what you are."

The Dark-Hunter cast a look at her that told her to keep her identity quiet. Not that he needed to. The last thing she would ever do was betray her sister.

"Is that why you chained us together?" the Dark-Hunter asked. "You wanted to watch us fight?"

"Oh no," Desiderius said. "Not my plan at all. If you kill each other, that would be fine by me, but what I intend to do is release you come the dawn. You see, the Dark-Hunter is about to become the hunted and I am going to *thoroughly* enjoy tracking you down and making you suffer. There is no place you can hide where I won't find you."

The Dark-Hunter smirked. "You think you're capable of hunting me?"

"Oh yes. Yes, I do. You see, I know your weakness even better than you do."

"I have no weakness."

Desiderius laughed. "Spoken like a true Dark-Hunter. But all of us have an Achilles' heel, especially those who serve Artemis. You are no exception."

Amanda swore she could almost hear Desiderius lick his lips in satisfaction. "Your greatest weakness is your nobility. That woman hates you, yet you won't kill her to be safe. While she tries to kill you, you'll guard her from me with your life." Desiderius laughed evilly. "You just can't resist a human in peril, can you?"

"Desi, Desi, Desi," the Dark-Hunter tsked. "What am I going to do with you?"

"Don't you *dare* take that flippant tone with me."

"Why ever not?"

"Because I am not some scared little Daimon to run cringing from you. I am your worst nightmare."

The Dark-Hunter scoffed. "Must you resort to clichés? C'mon, Desidisastrous, couldn't you think of anything more original than that B-movie dialogue staple?"

A furious snarl echoed in the room. "Stop mocking my name."

"Sorry, you're right. The least I could do is show you respect before I expire you."

"Oh, you won't *expire* me, Dark-Hunter. You are the one who will die this time. Have you given thought to how much she's going to slow you down? Not to mention the existence of her little friends. They will take you down like a pack of wild dogs. And if I were you, I'd pray for that. You have never known the suffering I will inflict upon you when next we meet."

His lips in a tight, firm line, the Dark-Hunter smiled at Desiderius's threats. "You seriously overestimate your abilities."

"We shall see."

Amanda heard a mike click off.

The Dark-Hunter jerked again at the cuffs. "I am going to kill that horror-movie reject."

"Hey, hey, hey!" she said as he flapped her arm around while trying to free himself. "That arm *is* attached."

He paused and looked down at her. His gaze softened. "Twins. It never occurred to him. Have you any idea where your sister is?"

"I don't even know where *I* am or what time it is. For that matter, I don't know what's going on here. Who are you and who is that guy?" Then, she lowered her voice and added, "Can he hear us?"

Kyrian shook his head. "No, the mike channel is closed. For the moment, he's off plotting his Igoresque revenge. I don't know about you, but I have this image of him rubbing his hands together and laughing like Dexter from *Dexter's Laboratory.*"

Kyrian took a minute to study her. She didn't appear hysterical . . . yet, and he wanted to keep it that way. Telling her Desiderius was a soul-sucking demon who was after her sister didn't seem like the best way to accomplish that.

Of course, given her sister's penchant for vampire-hunting, it shouldn't really come as a surprise to her, either.

Closing his eyes, he reached into her mind with his and found confirmation of his suspicions. There was a healthy dose of fear in her.

Unlike her sister Tabitha, she wasn't one to jump to conclusions, but she was curious and angry over their situation. It was possible he could tell her everything without freaking her out, but the Dark-Hunter in him operated on a need-to-know basis.

Right now all she needed to know was the bare minimum. With any luck he would be able to separate them without having to reveal anything more about himself to her.

"I am called Hunter," he said solemnly. "And *that guy* is a man out to harm your sister."

"Thanks, but that much I already got." Amanda frowned. She should be frightened by all this, but she wasn't. Her anger over it was too great. Leave it to her to get mixed up in her sister's crazy life.

In fact, she was glad they had captured her by mistake, since Tabitha would no doubt have pulled some kamikaze stunt and gotten herself killed.

She looked up at the Dark-Hunter and her frown deepened. How did he know about Tabitha? For that matter, how had he been able to tell them apart when even their own mother had trouble at times? "Are you one of my sister's friends?"

He looked at her blankly, before pulling her to her feet. "No," he said as he patted his chest, hips, rear, and legs.

Amanda tried not to notice just how incredibly toned that body was as her hand was dragged in the wake of his. And when her hand brushed his hard inner thigh, she thought she would moan.

He was built for sex and for speed. Too bad he wasn't her type. In fact, he was the total antithesis to everything she found desirable in a man.

Wasn't he?

He cursed. "Of course, he has my phone," he muttered, before leading her to the door.

After trying the knob, he studied the hinges.

When he unbuckled his left boot and toed it off, Amanda arched a brow. "What are you doing? Going for a swim?"

He gave her a cocky smirk before leaning down to pick the boot up off the floor. "Trying to get us out of here. You?"

"I'm trying not to get irritated at you."

Amusement flashed in his eyes, then he returned his attention to the door.

Amanda watched as he pressed one of the silver inlays on the boot heel and a vicious five-inch blade shot out of the toe. He was definitely Tabitha's type. She wondered if he had throwing stars inside his pockets, too.

"Oooo," she commented dryly. *Very scary.*"

He gave her an unamused look. "Baby, you ain't seen scary yet."

Amanda smirked at his Ford Fairlane, tough-guy demeanor and gave a very unfeminine snort.

He ignored her. Using the jagged blade, he tried to pry loose the rusted hinges.

"You're going to break that blade if you're not careful," she warned him.

He gave her an arched look. "Nothing on this earth could break this blade." He ground his teeth while hammering the boot with his fist. "Much like nothing on this earth appears able to move this hinge." He tried for several more minutes.

"Damn," he snarled when the hinge refused to budge. He retracted the blade, then bent over to put the boot back on. The back of his coat parted with his movements, gifting her with a nice view of him.

Oh yeah, *nice* butt.

Amanda's mouth went dry as he finally straightened to his full six-foot-five-inch height.

Oh my, my, my.

Okay, she took it back, he did have one feature she found irresistible. His height. She'd always been a sucker for any man taller than her. And with this guy, she could easily wear three-inch heels and not offend his male ego.

He towered over her.

And she liked it.

"How do you know my sister?" she asked, trying to keep her thoughts focused on the matter at hand and not on the matter of how much she wanted to taste those lips of his.

"I know her because she keeps getting in my way." He snatched at the cuffs again. "What is it with you humans that you feel this incessant need to delve into things you should leave alone?"

"I don't delve into . . ." Her voice trailed off as his words penetrated her mind. "You *humans*? Why would you say that?"

He didn't answer.

"Look," she said, holding up her arm to show the handcuff. "I'm stuck with you right now, and I want an answer."

"No you don't."

That did it. She hated alpha men in the worst sort of way. Those domineering, I'm-the-man-baby-let-me-drive types nauseated her.

"All right, macho babe boy," she said irritably. "I'm not some little ditz to bat my eyelashes at the buff stud in black leather. Don't try your he-man tactics with me. I'll have you know, in my office I'm known as the ball-breaker."

Kyrian frowned at her. "Macho babe boy?" he repeated in disbelief.

There had never been a time in his extremely long life that anyone had had the mettle to stand up to him. As a mortal, he had made entire Roman armies flee in stark terror of his approach. Few men had ever dared meet him eye to eye.

As a Dark-Hunter, he made legions of Daimons and Apollites quake in his presence. His name was whispered in awe and with reverence, and this woman had called him . . .

"Buff stud in black leather," he repeated out loud. "I don't think I've ever been more insulted."

"Then you must have been an only child."

He laughed at that. In truth, he'd once had three sisters, but none of them had ever dared insult him.

He swept a look over her. She wasn't classically beautiful, but there was an exotic quality to her almond-shaped eyes that lent her a fey charm.

Her long, mahogany hair was loose, spilling about her slender shoulders. But it was her blue eyes that were captivating. Warm and intelligent, they were narrowed on him now with malice.

A faint blush stained her cheeks, making her eyes a full shade darker. In spite of the danger they were in, he wondered what she would look like after a full night of raw, exhausting sex. He could just see her eyes dark with passion, her hair mussed, her cheeks red from his whiskers, and her lips moist and swollen from his kisses.

The thought made his entire body burn.

Until Kyrian felt the familiar prickling on the back of his neck. "It will be dawn soon."

"How do you know?"

"I just do." He pulled her to the left, then began examining the rust-covered walls for an escape. "Once we're released, we'll have to find a way to break out of these cuffs."

"Nice of you to state the obvious." Amanda glanced down his body and saw the jagged wound through the torn material. "You really need to tend that."

"God forbid I should bleed to death, eh?" he asked sardonically. "Then you'd have to cart around my rotting corpse."

She wrinkled her nose in distaste. "Could you be any more morbid? Jeez. Who was your idol growing up? Boris Karloff?"

"Hannibal, actually."

"You're trying to scare me, aren't you?" she asked. "Well, it won't work. I grew up in a house with an angry poltergeist and two sisters who used to conjure demons just to fight them. Buster, I've seen it all, and your gallows humor isn't working on me."

Before he realized what she was doing, she grabbed the bottom of his shirt and lifted it.

Amanda froze at the sight of his bare stomach. It was lean, hard, and flat, and he had a rippling six-pack of abs that any gymnast would envy. But what made her gasp was the multitude of scars covering his flesh.

Worse, she saw the terrible gash in his side that ran along his lowest rib.

"Good Lord, what happened to you?"

He jerked his shirt down and took a step back. "If you mean the scars, it would take me years to account for all of them. If you mean the gash, it came from a thirteen-year-old Apollite I mistook for a child in need of help."

"You walked into a trap?"

He shrugged. "It's not the first time."

Amanda swallowed as she swept her gaze over him. An aura of danger and death surrounded him. He moved like a sleek, graceful predator, and those eyes . . .

They seemed to be able to take in more than just his basic surroundings. Those wicked jet eyes held an indescribable ethereal glint to them.

And they stole her breath every time he looked at her.

She'd never seen a blond man with eyes like that. Nor had she seen any man so incredibly handsome. His features were chiseled and perfect.

He oozed an almost unnatural masculine sexuality. She'd seen plenty of men who had tried their best to project what nature had dumped by the truckload onto this man.

"What is a Dark-Hunter?" she asked. "Is it like *Buffy the Vampire Slayer?*"

He laughed at that. "Yes, I'm a small, emaciated teenage girl who struts around fighting vampires in earrings they would rip out of my ears and shove up my—"

"I know you're not a girl. But what is a Dark-Hunter?"

He sighed as he led her around the room, looking at the walls as if searching for a secret door. "In short, I execute the things that go bump in the night."

A chill went up her spine at his words, and yet she sensed there was something more than just his simple explanation. He appeared deadly, but not twisted, or even cruel. "Why do you want to kill Desiderius?"

He glanced at her before trying to open the steel door again.

He wrenched the handle so forcefully, she was amazed he didn't rip the doorknob off. "Because he not only kills humans, he steals their souls."

She tensed at his words. "Can he do that?"

"You said you've seen it all," he said in a mocking tone. "You tell me."

Amanda wanted to choke him. Never in her life had she met a more arrogant, or infuriating man.

"Why do I always get sucked into this supernatural mumbo jumbo?" she muttered. "Is it too much to ask that I have one average day?"

"Life is seldom what we want it to be."

She frowned at his words, and at the odd note in his voice.

Kyrian tilted his head, and held his hand up to signal her for silence.

Out of nowhere, the doorknob clicked.

"Knock, knock," Desiderius said. "You have the day to hide. Come nightfall, we hunt."

"Yeah, yeah," Hunter said. "You and your little dog, too."

His blithe tone amazed her. The chilling words had absolutely no effect on him. "You're not scared of his threats?"

He looked at her dryly. "Chère, the day I fear something like him is the day I lie down at his feet and hand him the knife to cut my heart out. The only fear I have is getting you back to your sister and convincing High Queen Hardhead to leave off this matter until I can locate Desiderius and send his soul into oblivion where it belongs."

In spite of herself and the danger they were in, Amanda laughed at his words. "High Queen Hardhead? You know Tabitha well."

He disregarded her comment as he carefully shielded her with his body, then opened the door slowly. He paused to look around.

Outside the door was a narrow hallway with large, dust-covered windows that showed the dawning sun.

"Damn," Hunter snarled under his breath as he took a step back into the room.

"What?" she asked, her heart skipping a beat in terror. "Is someone out there?"

"No."

"Then let's go." She started out the door.

He didn't budge.

Clenching his teeth, he looked down the hallway again and said something in a language she didn't know.

"What's the problem?" Amanda asked. "It's dawn, and no one's out there. Let's leave."

He took a deep, aggravated breath. "The problem isn't the people. The problem is the sun."

"And the problem with that is . . . ?"

He hesitated for a few heartbeats, then opened his mouth and ran his tongue over his long, *pointed* canine teeth.

CHAPTER 3

Mr. "Do Me" Gorgeous Man is a vampire!

"Oh no, no, no." Amanda's entire body shook from terror and it took every piece of self-control she possessed not to launch into a screaming fit. "Are you going to suck my blood?"

He arched a sardonic brow. "Do I look like a lawyer to you?"

She ignored his sarcasm. "Are you going to kill me?"

His face completely unamused, Hunter sighed irritably. "If I intended to kill you, don't you think you'd already be dead?"

He stepped closer to her and offered her a wry, evil grin she knew was meant to intimidate her. And boy howdy did it work.

He lifted his free hand up to stroke the skin of her neck where her jugular was. The feather-light touch sent chills over her. "Come to think of it, I could just suck you dry, then gnaw your hand off with my fangs and be free."

Her eyes widened in terror.

"But lucky you, I have no intention of doing that, either."

"Don't be sarcastic, okay?" she breathed, her heart still pounding because she wasn't sure if he was joking with her or if he really would turn all grisly on her and start feeding off her blood. "I can't cope with it. Imagine if you were in my shoes. I just went to let Tabitha's dog out so he wouldn't mess on her bed. I went from that to being knocked on the head, and chained to a vampire. Excuse *me* if I'm a little freaky at the moment."

To her amazement, he dropped his hand and backed off. "You're right. I imagine you're not used to having people attack you for no apparent reason."

By his tone, she could tell he, on the other hand, was rather experienced at finding himself in the middle of such situations.

He offered her a tight-lipped smile that didn't quite reach his eyes. "If it makes you feel better, I don't feed on humans."

For some reason, it did make her feel better to hear him say that. Not that she believed it. But still, it was a little re-assuring. "So, you're like Angel?"

He rolled his eyes at her. "You watch way too much tele-vision," he muttered. Then louder, he said, "Angel has a soul. I don't."

"Now you're back to being scary again."

The look on his face reiterated his earlier words: *Baby, you ain't seen scary yet*.

He glanced back out the door. "All right. We're going to have to run for it before the sun rises any higher."

Hunter gave her a penetrating stare. "The main problem is that I don't know where that hallway leads. In the event it leads out into the open and I die a particularly agonizing death where I spontaneously combust into flames, I need a favor from you."

"A favor?" she asked in disbelief. The man had one serious set of cojones on him. He bullied her, threatened her, then dared to ask a favor?

"Sure, why not?" she asked.

He took the ring off his right hand and gave it to her. "I need you to take that and find a tree."

Amanda frowned at the ring in her hand. The gold was scuffed and nicked in a number of places as if it had been seriously mistreated. Or rather the hand that bore it had been through a lot of damage.

The top of the ring was made of flat rubies and held the design of a sword of diamonds surrounded by emerald laurel leaves and topped with a sapphire crown. She could tell it was a valuable antique.

Why would he entrust it to her?

Unsure of what to make of him, she placed it in her jeans pocket. "Any tree?" she asked.

"Any tree. Then say the words 'Artemis, I summon you to human form.' "

"Artemis—"

He put his hand over her mouth. "For the love of Zeus, only say it once I'm gone. After you utter the words, wait until a very tall, red-haired woman appears and tell her you need protection from Desiderius."

Amanda arched a brow. "You want me to summon a goddess to protect me?"

"If you don't, he will get you and your sister."

"Why do you care?"

"It's my job to protect the humans from the Daimons. That's what a Dark-Hunter does." Though his face was harsh, there was a light in his eyes that told her there was much more to the story than that.

"What are Daimons?" she asked.

"They're vampires on steroids with a God complex. Now, promise me you'll do it."

Why not? It was a strange request, but then, considering the fact she was handcuffed to a vampire, who was she to say what was or wasn't strange? "Okay."

"Good. Now, let's run for it."

Before she could protest, he grabbed the handcuff over her wrist, and ran out the door to the right and down the hallway.

As they ran along the rusty floor, Amanda realized they were inside an abandoned factory of some sort.

At the end of the hallway were stairs that led down.

Hunter pulled her along after him until they reached the bottom of the stairs that opened into an enormous empty room with a cement floor. The old steel walls were cracked, with rays of the dawning sun streaming through.

The Dark-Hunter fell back into the shadows, away from the sunlight. His face looked a bit sunburned, but overall he didn't appear too much the worse from their mad dash.

"Now what?" she asked as she tried to catch her breath.

The Dark-Hunter wasn't even breathing hard. But his gaze was just a little too hot as he stared at her breasts with interest.

Amanda crossed her arms over her chest.

For the first time, she saw a real smile from him as she realized his hand was dangerously close to her breast. So close, his fingertips brushed the nipple, making fire rip through her veins.

She immediately dropped her hands to her sides while his smile taunted her. Though tight-lipped and devilish, it was still devastating. The amused gleam in his eyes was breathtaking, and his features softened into a boyish charm that could melt the heart of anything female.

He glanced around the empty factory. "Now I wish we either had a cell phone or subway system. I knew I should have taken that open position in New York."

Confused, Amanda looked up at him. "Open position? What? Is hunting really a job?"

"Yes. They even pay me to do it."

"*Who* pays you?"

Instead of answering, he held up a hand for silence in a gesture that was starting to piss her off—the main reason being because it seemed to herald trouble. And she was tired of finding trouble meant for Tabitha.

Two seconds later, Amanda heard someone walking around outside. Hunter pulled her deeper into the shadows with him while they listened. He had his free arm draped over her shoulders, pinning her to his body.

Amanda went stock-still as her back connected fully with his chest and a wave of misplaced desire tore through her. The heat of him warmed her and that raw, masculine aura of power overwhelmed her. Even more disturbing, his welcoming scent of leather and sandalwood invaded her head.

She wanted this man.

What are you, nuts? The man's a vampire!

Yeah, but he's a really, really sexy one.

Kyrian couldn't breathe with her so close to him. His

heightened senses felt her all the way through his entire body. He heard her heartbeat speed up, felt the dryness of her throat, but even worse, he could taste her desire.

It whetted his appetite for her even more. And it reminded him why he had made it his habit to avoid being around women as much as possible.

Damn you, Desiderius.

Because right then it was hard to remember he couldn't have her. And even harder to forget the way she smelled. The way she moved—like a confident dancer. Her lithe body was a symphony of grace and all too easily he could imagine her sitting on top of him as he showed her a sexual pleasure he was quite certain no other man had ever given her.

His loins tightened to the point of pain. He couldn't even remember the last time he had been this hard for a woman. And it took all his willpower not to kiss her. Not to bury his lips against her throat and inhale her warm sweetness as he . . .

Kyrian flexed his hand on her shoulder as he realized all he had to do was lower his hand three inches and he would be cupping her breast.

Just three *tiny* inches . . .

Suddenly, the sound of a walkie-talkie broke the silence.

"It's a construction worker," she whispered, bolting to a window.

Kyrian hissed as she pulled him into the sunlight. He jerked her back into the darkness.

"Sorry," she whispered. She edged closer to the window, making sure to keep him out of the sun.

"Hey!" Amanda called as she saw the man a few feet away, poking around an old tractor.

The construction worker looked up at her and did a double-take. Scowling, he walked over to the window and looked inside. His eyes narrowed on them. "What are you doing in there? This area is off-limits to the public."

"It's a long story," Amanda said. "The short version is I got left here. You wouldn't happen to have a cell phone I could borrow, would you?"

Still scowling, he handed his cell phone to her through the open window.

Hunter immediately took it from her hand.

"Hey!" she snapped, reaching for it.

Moving it out of her reach, he ignored her while he dialed a number.

"Where are we?" Hunter asked the construction worker as he placed the phone to his ear.

"The old Olson Plant."

"In Slidell?"

Amanda arched a brow that the Dark-Hunter would recognize it. She'd lived in New Orleans all her life and had no idea this place existed.

"Yeah," the worker said.

Hunter nodded.

"Hey," he said into the phone, "it's me. I'm at the Olson Plant in Slidell. Do you know where it is?"

He paused as he listened to whoever was on the other end.

Amanda watched him closely. It amazed her that he was able to talk without showing his fangs, but he disguised them well.

And now that she thought about it, how could a vampire be so tanned and warm? How could he have a pulse and a heartbeat?

Weren't vampires supposed to be the cold, pale undead?

"Yes," Hunter said. "I need a ride out of here, preferably before the sun gets any higher."

The Dark-Hunter turned the phone off and tossed it out the window to the construction worker.

"Hey!" she snapped, reaching out of the window to reclaim the phone. "I need that."

"Who are you going to call?" Hunter asked menacingly.

"None of your damn business."

Hunter took the phone out of her hand. "As long as we're attached, it is my business."

She narrowed her eyes on him as she grabbed the phone. "Mess with me, buster, and I'll take another two steps to my right."

His heated glare sent a shiver over her. "Don't you dare call your sister."

The seething look on his face made her rethink pushing her luck. She handed the phone back to the worker. "Thanks," she said.

The construction worker clipped the phone to his belt and gave them a chiding stare. "You know, you two need to get out of there. This b—"

The Dark-Hunter held his hand up and the man's eyes went blank, empty. "There's no one in the building. Go do whatever you need to do."

The man walked off without another word.

Mind control? Amanda gaped at Hunter.

Of course he had mind control. He was a vampire.

"You better not use that on me," Amanda said.

"Don't worry. You're too strong-willed for it to work."

"Good."

"Not from where I'm standing, it isn't."

Though the words were edged, there was an amused light in the depths of his eyes that said he wasn't as peeved as he sounded.

She looked askance at him. He was leaning nonchalantly against a post with his eyes closed, and yet she had the distinct impression that he was alert to everything around them, both inside the building and out.

"Why did you become a vampire?" she asked before she could think better of it. "Did someone turn you against your will?"

He opened his eyes and cocked a brow at that. "No one becomes a Dark-Hunter unless they are willing."

"And you were willing to . . ." Her voice trailed off as she expectantly waited for him to explain.

"To sacrifice a nosy little human if she doesn't stop pestering me."

She should be frightened of him and yet she kept hearing Desiderius's words in her mind telling her that he would never harm a human.

Was it true?

She ran her gaze over his scrumptious body wishing she knew for certain.

They stood without speaking for quite a bit, until Amanda couldn't stand it any longer.

"So," she said, trying to break the awkward silence. "How long do you think we'll have to wait?"

"I don't know."

"Who did you call?" she tried again.

"No one."

Amanda took a deep breath and fought the urge to strangle him. "You don't like to answer questions, do you?"

"Honestly? I don't like to talk at all. I'd rather just stand here in silence."

"And brood?"

"Yes."

She blew her hair out of her face. "Well, I happen to be bored and if I have to stand here waiting for your ride, I'd like to do something to pass the time."

His gaze dropped to her lips, then slid slowly down to her breasts and hips. He shuttered his eyes, but even so she saw the raw hunger in the midnight depths. She felt it, hot and demanding.

"I can think of one way to pass time . . ."

She widened her eyes. "You're not going to bite me, are you?"

He smiled wickedly. "I don't want to bite you, *agapee-menee.* I want to nibble every inch of your bare flesh, especially your bre—"

She reached up and stopped his words by placing her hand over his lips. The softness of them contrasting with his whiskers stunned her. And the sensation of his skin under her hand jolted her with electricity. Swallowing hard, she dropped her hand. "I didn't think vampires could have sex."

He arched a taunting brow at her. "Why don't you and I conduct a little experiment and see?"

Amanda knew she should be offended. She should be angry. She should be anything other than turned on by his words.

But the idea actually appealed to her as she ran her gaze down his lean, perfect body.

Kyrian felt her confusion. She was actually considering his offer. Had the fire in his groin not been so fierce, he would have laughed. But as it was, he wasn't sure whether or not he was toying with her, or truly propositioning her.

All he knew was that the sight of her parted lips tempted him in a way he'd never been tempted before.

Not that he should be surprised by the way his body responded to her. She was just the type of woman who had always appealed to him. Intelligent. Brave.

And simply beguiling.

He glanced to the wall behind her, and imagined what it would feel like to press her against it while he took her hard, fast, and furious.

He swore he could feel himself already inside her. Could hear her moaning in his ear as he . . .

Kyrian shook his head to dispel the image. There were times when he hated his psychic abilities. Right now was definitely one of them.

Licking his dry lips, he remembered a time when he wouldn't have hesitated to take a woman such as this to his bed. A time when he would have peeled those safe, conservative clothes off her body and kissed every single inch of her bare flesh until she was wild with unbridled desire. Touched her until he brought her to the edge again and again as she clung to him and begged for more.

Kyrian clenched his teeth at the heat searing his blood. How he wished he could relive those days.

But that was a long time ago. And no matter how much he might want her, she was not his to take.

He would never know her body.

He would never know *her*. Period. It was why he hadn't asked her name or given her his. He had no intention of using it. She was nothing more than another nameless person he had sworn to protect. That was as close as he intended to get.

He was a Dark-Hunter, and she was an uninitiated human. The two were not to mix.

Kyrian looked up as he heard the faint sound of a siren approaching. Silently, he thanked Tate's timing.

Amanda glanced out the window as she heard an ambulance. Oddly enough, it stopped in front of the factory.

After a brief pause, the two front factory doors opened and the ambulance pulled inside.

"Your ride?" she asked.

The Dark-Hunter nodded.

Once the ambulance was deep enough inside the factory so that the sunlight didn't reach it, a tall African-American man got out and approached them. He gave a low whistle as he caught sight of Hunter's sunburned face. "Man, you look like hell. Should I ask about the handcuffs?"

Hunter led her toward the driver. "Not unless you want to die."

"Okay," the driver said good-naturedly. "I can take a hint, but here's the next problem. You're not going to be inconspicuous in a body bag wearing those. People are definitely going to notice."

"I already thought of that," Hunter said. "If anyone asks, tell them I died of a heart attack during a wild sexcapade with her."

An eerie chill went up Amanda's spine as she recalled Selena's words the day before. "I beg your pardon?"

Hunter cast an amused look to her that let her know he was thoroughly enjoying her torment. "And she can't find the key."

Tate laughed.

"I don't think so," Amanda said heatedly.

Hunter gave her that devilish grin that warmed her all over, and the look he swept over her made her tingle. "Look on the bright side; you'll have men lining up to date you."

"You're not funny."

Hunter shrugged. "It's the only way out of here."

"For you maybe," she said. "I can walk right out of here on my own, and dust you."

He cocked a taunting brow at her. "Try it."

She did, and quickly learned that tall, dangerous vampires didn't budge unless they wanted to.

"Okay," Amanda said, rubbing her wrist where the cuff was biting into it. "We'll be getting in the ambulance, then."

Hunter led the way.

When he got to the back of the ambulance, Hunter lifted her up with such ease that it startled her. She moved to the left, trying to make room for him, but he was so tall, he was doubled over. In one fluid motion, he lay down on the stretcher, inside the black body bag that was on top of it.

Without a word, Tate zipped it closed.

"You two do this a lot?" she asked.

Tate smiled in easygoing friendship. "Every now and again."

Amanda frowned as Tate adjusted the bag so that her hand was on the outside and Hunter's inside it. It seemed strange to her that Tate was so willing to help a vampire.

"How did you two meet?" she asked Tate.

"I was feeding off a body when he found me," Hunter said from inside the bag.

Tate laughed as he straightened. "One night while I was on call, I went to pick up a body that wasn't dead. If not for Hunter, I'd be the one in the body bag."

"Shut up, Tate," Hunter snapped, "and drive."

"I'm going," Tate said as if completely unoffended by the high-handed way Hunter treated him.

"You know," Amanda said to Hunter as Tate got up front and started the ambulance. "You could try being nicer to people. Especially when they're helping you."

She heard his aggravated sigh even through the plastic. "Shouldn't that advice apply to you, as well?"

Amanda opened her mouth to respond, then closed it. He was right. She had been rather testy with him since all this started. "I guess you're right. Maybe we should both try and make the best of this."

If he responded, she didn't hear it since the siren blared again. Tate drove them to the hospital in record time, but the ride was far from smooth.

By the time they arrived, she felt as if she had been tossed around like sweatsocks in a dryer.

Tate pulled up to the rear of the hospital, under an awning that kept the sunlight from touching them. With a warning to her to remain quiet, he carefully pulled the stretcher out of the back so that he wouldn't hurt her arm as they descended out of the ambulance.

Once inside the hospital doors, Amanda held her jacket closed to hide the bloodstains on her sweater.

Hunter remained completely still and silent as Tate pushed the stretcher through the bustling areas. Amanda walked along beside them, and wanted to cringe and die given how obvious the handcuffs were.

Did they have to gleam so brightly under the fluorescent lights? Couldn't Desiderius have found nice, small police-sized cuffs?

Oh no, these had to be five inches thick with some kind of weird Greek design all over them. And a chain that ran a good four inches in length. Anyone who saw them would definitely think they came from one of Tabitha's weird sex catalogues.

The horror of it! Amanda had never even been inside a Frederick's of Hollywood. For that matter, she'd blushed profusely the handful of times she'd been in Victoria's Secret.

And everyone they passed turned to gawk at them.

"I haven't seen *that* in at least six months," an orderly said as they passed the admissions desk.

"I heard that," another orderly responded. "Wonder how old the poor guy was?"

"I dunno, but by the looks of her, I'd say sign me up."

Their laughter made her entire face burn. By the interested looks the men were raking over her body, she could surmise Hunter's words about her having dates might not have been too far off the mark.

"Hey, Tate?" a young doctor asked as they drew near the elevators. "Should I ask?"

Tate shook his head. "You know all the weird shit comes through my office."

The doctor laughed while Amanda covered her face with her hand.

As soon as the elevator doors closed behind them, Amanda

whispered under her breath, "Hunter, I swear, I'm going to kill you for this."

"Dearie," an elderly hospital volunteer said from beside her. "It looks to me like you already did." She patted Amanda lightly on the arm. "The same thing happened to me and my Harvey. Poor thing. I sure do miss him, too."

Tate choked on his laughter.

Amanda groaned and prayed for this ordeal to end.

Once they reached the morgue, Tate took them into a dim, metallic lab and locked the door. Hunter unzipped the bag from the inside.

"Thanks," he said to Tate as he sat up and removed the bag from his body. He folded it and placed it on a table.

Tate opened a drawer in the small cabinet next to the door. "No problem. Now, take your coat and shirt off and let me see what happened to you."

"It will heal."

Tate set his jaw stubbornly. "What of infection?"

Kyrian laughed. "Immortals don't die from infections. I am completely incapable of carrying *any* disease."

"You may not die from it, but it doesn't mean it won't hurt and it'll heal faster if treated." He gave Kyrian a look that said he would not be swayed. "I'm not going to take no for an answer. Let me treat that wound."

Kyrian opened his mouth to argue more, but if he knew anything about Tate, it was that the man was stubborn. Deciding not to waste his time, Kyrian obeyed before he remembered the coat and shirt wouldn't come completely off, thanks to the handcuffs.

He gave an exasperated sigh and left his clothes to hang against his forearm, then got back on the stretcher and leaned back on his elbows to wait for Tate.

As he watched Tate gather supplies, he heard Amanda's heart pounding and her breathing speed up. Felt her keen interest as she raked her gaze over his body. She wanted him, and her hot desire played havoc with him.

Kyrian shifted and wished his jeans were a couple of sizes

bigger, since the black denim started biting fiercely into his erection.

Damn, he'd forgotten what a literal and figurative pain his body could be when an attractive woman was around.

And she *was* attractive. What with that charming, elfish face and those big, blue eyes . . .

He'd always been a fool for blue eyes.

Even without looking at her, he knew she was licking those plump, full lips, and his throat went dry as he imagined the taste of them. The feel of her breath on his face and her tongue against his as he kissed her.

Dear gods, and he had thought the Romans had tortured him! Their best interrogator had been an amateur compared to the physical and mental agony her nearness caused him now.

Even more disturbing than her looks was the fact that she had been an amazingly good sport about all of this. Most women would have been screaming in terror of him or crying.

Or both.

But she had met the entire ordeal with a courage and strength of heart he'd not seen in a long time.

He actually liked her, and that surprised him most of all.

Amanda jumped when Hunter met her gaze. Those deep, black eyes bored into hers and made her hot and breathless.

He lay on the stretcher with one leg bent up and the other hanging over the edge. The black denim hugged his long, powerful body.

And those muscled arms . . .

Lean and defined, he was all masculine beauty. His biceps were flexed as he leaned back on his elbows. She wanted to reach out and touch him so badly that she ached from it. No doubt, he would be rock-hard and satiny underneath her hand.

His shoulders were incredibly broad, with sculpted muscles that promised strength, speed, and agility. His pecs and arms were every bit as well-formed and tight.

And his stomach, oh heaven! Those flat abs had been made for nibbling.

Unbidden, her gaze followed the thin trail of coffee-colored hairs that started at his navel and vanished under the tight denim. By the size of the bulge in his jeans, she could tell he was amply endowed, and more than passingly interested in her.

The thought made her even hotter.

The deep, golden tan of his flesh defied what she knew him to be. How could a vampire have skin so tawny and inviting?

But even more tantalizing than the lean muscles that beckoned for caresses were the multitude of scars that crossed his flesh. He looked as if he had been clawed by a huge tiger, or beaten within an inch of his life with a whip.

Or both.

Hunter lay down as Tate approached, and she saw a small double-bow-and-arrow symbol *branded* into his left shoulder. She cringed at the thought of how much such a thing must have hurt, and she wondered if he had agreed to it, or if someone had put it there against his will.

"I take it from your scars that your vampire friends don't think much of you," she said.

"You think?" he retorted.

"Is he always this sarcastic?" she asked Tate.

"Actually, I thought he was being rather nice to you." Tate cleansed the vicious-looking wound with alcohol. He prepared to give Hunter a local.

Hunter caught his hand before Tate could inject him. "Don't bother."

"Why?" Tate asked with a frown.

"I'm immune to it."

Amanda's jaw dropped.

Tate just reached for the sutures.

"You can't do that," she said, interrupting him. "He'll feel it."

"He needs that wound closed," Tate insisted. "Jeez, you can see his bones through it."

"Go ahead," Hunter said with a calmness that astounded her.

Stunned, she cringed while Tate made the first suture.

Hunter kept his jaw locked and said nothing.

Amanda watched Tate tend Hunter. Her heart wrenched at the thought of how much pain Hunter must be feeling.

"Doesn't that hurt?" she asked him.

"No," Hunter said between clenched teeth.

Amanda could tell by the way the veins stood out on his neck and the way he clenched his fists that he was lying.

"Here," she said, taking his hand in hers. "Just hold tight."

Kyrian started at the softness of her hand in his. He couldn't remember the last time someone had touched him like that. He'd been a Dark-Hunter for so long that he had all but forgotten simple kindness.

Tate acted out of gratitude and a sense of obligation.

But her . . .

There was no reason for her to hold his hand. He'd barely spoken a civil word to her, and yet she reached out to him when no one else would have. It made him feel strange toward her. Protective. Tender.

More than that, her simple touch scorched him all the way to his caged heart. He swallowed, then stiffened. He couldn't let her close to him. She was a creature of light and he was one of darkness.

The two were not compatible.

"So, how long have you been a vampire?" she asked.

"I told you," he said, his jaw tight, "I'm not a vampire. I'm a Dark-Hunter."

"What's the difference?"

Kyrian gave her a hard glare. "The difference is I normally don't kill humans, but if you don't stop quizzing me, I might make an exception."

"You are one seriously testy Creature of the Night."

"I love you, too."

Amanda dropped his hand. "Oh, that's it," she said. "I was just trying to comfort you. God forbid, you should let anyone actually be nice to you."

Irritated, she met Tate's surprised gaze. "Can you just saw his arm off while we're here and get me loose?"

Tate snorted. "I could do that, but he needs his more. I'd cut yours off before I did his."

"Oh, great, what are you, his Igor?"

"Wrong movie," Tate corrected. "Igor was Frankenstein's flunky. Renfield is the one you're thinking of, and no, I'm not Renfield. Name's Tate Bennett. Parish coroner."

"I'd already guessed the coroner part. Rather obvious since we're in a cold lab full of *dead* people."

Tate arched a brow at her. "And you call *him* sarcastic."

Hunter jerked as Tate pulled too hard on the sutures.

"Sorry," Amanda said. "I won't distract him anymore."

"I would appreciate it."

Once Tate finished, Hunter put his shirt and coat back on. He slid off the stretcher with only the slightest hiss to reveal his side was sore.

Tate's pager went off. "I'll be back in a few minutes. You kids need anything?"

"I'm fine," Hunter said. "But she probably needs breakfast and a phone."

Amanda quirked a brow at his words. Why would he let her have a phone now?

Tate quickly cleaned up the mess. "The phone is against the far wall, just dial nine to get out. I'll grab something in the cafeteria and be back as soon as I can. Stay in here and keep the door locked."

As soon as they were alone, Hunter moved so that she could sit on the small stool by the phone.

Blinking, Hunter rubbed his hand over his eyes as if they were sensitive to the fluorescent lights. "We need to make plans," he said quietly. "You wouldn't happen to know anyone in this city who might have a way to break handcuffs made by a Greek god?"

Getting used to his sarcasm, she smiled. "Actually, I think I do."

His face instantly lightened. Gracious, the man was gorgeous when not scowling or barking. "One of your sisters?"

"One of their friends."

He nodded. "Good. We need to do that, preferably before sunset, or at least not long after it. You also have to call Tabitha and tell her to lie low for a few days."

"You know, for the record, I hate to take orders. But!" Amanda said interrupting him before he could pull rank. "I realize I'm in over my head. You have no idea how much I hate all this supernatural garbage. So I'm willing to listen to you, but you better start acting like I'm a person and not some mindless blow-up doll."

She pulled his ring out of her pocket and returned it to him. "And another thing, I really have to go to the bathroom."

Hunter laughed out loud.

"It's not funny," she snapped at him as he put the ring back on his finger. "Any idea how we can do this without my dying of embarrassment?"

"More than that, any idea on how to do that without my getting arrested for being in the ladies' room?"

She cut a sharp glare at him. "If you think I'm going into the men's room, forget it."

"Then I hope you can hold it."

"I am not going into the men's room!"

Five minutes later, she was in the men's room and cursing Hunter under her breath. "You really get off on being a bully, don't you?"

"It's what I live for," he said in a bored voice as he stood with his back to her. He had his arm bent behind his back to allow her more latitude with the handcuffs.

Amanda glared at him. Her bladder felt as if were going to burst, but she was having a very difficult time going with him sandwiched between her and the stall door.

And all because Tabitha couldn't remember to let her damn dog out! If she ever got out of this, she was going to kill her sister. Dead. Dismantled!

"What's taking so long?" he asked in an aggravated tone.

"I can't go with you standing there."

"Would you just go?"

"Just you wait! Sooner or later, it'll be your turn and I'm going to enjoy watching you squirm."

He went rigidly still at her words. "Baby, you could never make me squirm."

The coldness in his voice scared her.

It took her a few minutes, but she finally finished and her face was hotter than a summer afternoon at the equator. She washed her hands, all the while trying not to look at Hunter.

"You have toilet paper on your shoe," he said, glancing down at her foot.

"Oh, of course," she said. "Anything to make this more embarrassing for me. Could you get any more personal?"

A devilish gleam entered his eyes. Then that dark, penetrating stare dropped to her lips. She swore she could feel his hunger, feel his inner need to touch her.

Before she knew what he was doing, he cupped her head with his free hand, brushed her bottom lip with his thumb, and bent his head down to capture her lips with his.

Stunned, Amanda couldn't think, couldn't move, as his warm lips parted hers.

The scent of leather and taste of vampire invaded her senses. Never in her life had she felt anything like his mouth on hers. His kiss was fierce and hot as he pulled her into his arms and ravished her mouth like a marauder.

Every hormone in her body fired. She moaned low in her throat. Oh heaven, the man could kiss. And the feel of his hard body against hers was so incredible that she clutched at his shoulders wanting desperately to taste more of him.

His tongue danced with hers as his honed muscles rippled under her hands, and when her tongue accidentally brushed against his fangs, an unexpected shudder of pleasure ran through her.

For the first time since she had learned what he was, the thought of him biting her neck actually appealed to her.

But not nearly as much as the thought of laying him down on the cold, hard floor and having her way with all that lean, mean strength until they were both hot, sweaty, and spent.

Kyrian tensed as he tasted the first bit of paradise he'd been allowed in over two thousand years. He was instantly aware of her soft, feminine curves pressing against his hardness. Aware of the way she smelled like flowers and sunshine— things that had been taken from him centuries before.

There was magic in her kiss. A raw, untapped passion. She

might have been kissed before, but he could tell no man had ever made her feel like this.

His body on fire, he ran his hand down her back, pressing her closer to him. He wanted her in a way he'd not wanted a woman since his days as a mortal man. He ached to touch her all over, to gently scrape his fangs over her neck, her breasts.

To feel her writhing in his arms . . .

Closing his eyes, he breathed her sweet, feminine scent as his body throbbed and ached for her with a primitive need.

Amanda gasped as he slid his hand down the side of her breast to her waist, then down to cup her buttocks. She'd never been the kind of woman to let a man handle her this way, and yet there was something about the Dark-Hunter she couldn't resist.

When he pulled her heatedly toward the wall and pinned her to it, she thought she would literally melt.

His chest pressed against hers, making her even more aware of his lean, hard muscles. He separated her legs with his powerful thigh, and raised it to collide with the center of her body in a way that made her throb even more. Amanda hissed in pleasure as he deepened his fiery kiss.

She wrapped her free arm around his neck, pulling him closer as her head swam.

What would it be like to make love to such an untamed predator? To run her hands over all those sleek, taut muscles that rippled with every move he made?

He left her lips and seared a trail with his tongue from her mouth to her ear. She felt the barest scrape of his fangs on her neck.

Amanda shook all over in response to him as her breasts swelled, longing for his caress. And all the while his thigh stroked her between her legs, making her burn even more. Her knees weakened and she sank deeper onto him.

Suddenly, a knock sounded on the door. "Hey, you two," Tate said, cracking it open. "Someone's coming."

The Dark-Hunter pulled back with a growl. It was then she realized what she'd done.

"Oh God," she breathed. "I just kissed a vampire!"

"Oh gods, I just kissed a human!"

Amanda narrowed her eyes at him. "Are you mocking me?"

"Guys!" Tate called again.

Hunter took her arm and led her out the door. The janitor gave them a strange look, but said nothing as he entered the bathroom behind them.

Tate led them to his small office outside the morgue.

An old wooden desk was set against the far wall, with two chairs in front of it. A sofa with a neatly folded blanket and pillow on top of it was to her right and a set of metal filing cabinets to her left. Tate showed her to the phone on the desk, then left them to attend his business.

Trying her best to forget what had just happened in the bathroom and how good Hunter had felt in her arms, Amanda called Tabitha while Hunter stood over her.

Of course, Tabitha immediately started in on her for not letting the dog out.

"Okay," Amanda said irritably. "I'm sorry Terminator scored on your new comforter."

"Sure you are," Tabitha said. "So, what happened to you last night?"

"What? Are your psychic abilities failing you? I got way-laid in your house by one of your vampire buds."

"What!" Tabitha shrieked. "Are you okay?"

Amanda looked up at Hunter and wasn't sure how to answer. Physically, she was fine, but he did something strange to her that she couldn't even begin to define. "I survived it. But they're looking for you, so you need to hide out someplace safe for a few days."

"I don't think so."

Hunter grabbed the phone from her hands. "Listen to me, little girl. I have your sister with me, and if you don't leave your house and vanish for the next three days, I will make your sister wish you had listened to me."

"You touch her and I'll stake you."

He laughed bitterly. "Been there, done that. Now get out of your house and let me handle this."

"And Amanda?"

"She is safe as long as you listen to me."

He handed the phone back to Amanda.

"Hey, Tabby," Amanda said sheepishly.

"What has he done to you?" Tabitha demanded.

"Nothing," she said, her face growing hot as she remembered his kiss. Nothing other than make her incredibly horny.

"Okay, listen," Tabitha said. "I'm going to Eric's, and we'll gather the gang, then head out to find you."

"No!" Amanda said as she saw the dark, angry look descend on Hunter's face. Her heart stopped as she realized he could hear through the phone line.

You can hear her? she mouthed to him.

He nodded.

A chill went over her. "Listen, Tabby, I'm safe. Just do what he wants. Okay?"

"I don't know."

"Please trust me."

"You, I trust. Him? Hell, I don't even know who he is."

"I know," Amanda said. "You head over to Mom's and I'll stay in touch. Okay?"

"Okay," Tabitha groused, "but if I don't hear from you by eight o'clock tonight, I'm going hunting."

"All right, I'll talk to you later. Love you."

"You, too."

Amanda hung up the phone. "You heard all that?"

Hunter leaned over her, his body so close that she could feel his heat. His gaze bored into hers. "All my senses are *highly* developed."

His gaze dropped to her chest where her nipples drew tight from the intense stare. "I can hear your heart beating faster, your blood flowing through your veins as you sit there wondering whether or not I would really hurt you."

The man was truly frightening. "Would you?" she whispered.

He locked gazes with her. "What do you think?"

She stared at him, trying to get a reading on his mood and feelings, but the man was a brick wall. "I honestly don't know."

"You're smarter than I thought," he said as he took a step back.

Amanda didn't know what to say to that. So she called work and told them she was sick for the day.

Hunter rubbed his eyes again.

"Do the lights bother you?" she asked.

He dropped his hand. "Yes."

She remembered what he said about his senses.

Before she could ask him anything else, he picked up the phone and dialed a number.

"Hola, Rosa. Cómo está?"

Spanish? she thought with a start. He spoke flawless Spanish?

Even more intriguing was the incredibly sexy sound of the words in that strange accent of his.

"Sí, bien. Necesito hablar con Nick, por favor."

Hunter cradled the phone between his cheek and shoulder as he massaged the wrist where the cuff was making a red mark. She wondered if he realized the feral intensity that came into his eyes every time he saw the cuffs.

"Hey, Nick," he said after a minute. "I need you to retrieve my car from the corner of Iberville and Clay, and bring it to St. Claude. You can leave it in the doctors' lot."

He let go of the cuff and took the phone back in his hand. "Yeah, I know I'm a real asshole to work for, but you can't knock the pay and perks. Head out at three, and after you drop my car off, you can go home early."

He paused as he listened for a few seconds. "Also grab the backup case out of the cabinet . . . yeah, *that* one. I need you to bring it and my spare keys to the hospital and leave them for Dr. Tate Bennett."

He stiffened as if Nick said something that irked him. "Yes, you can take tomorrow off, but keep your beeper and phone on in case I need something."

Hunter growled. "Boy, don't make me change my tone with you. You forget, I know where you sleep." Though the words were harsh, there was an underlying note of humor in his voice. "All right, but don't burn out the clutch again. I'll see you later."

Amanda arched a brow as he hung up the phone. "So who's Nick?"

"My gofer."

She gaped at him. "My God, can it be you actually answered a question? Holy cow, we'd better call Tate in here quick before you keel over dead or undead or whatever it is you vampires do."

"Ha, ha," he said with a smile.

Good night, this is one sexy vampire when he smiles . . .

"Does Nick know what you are?" she asked.

"Only the people who need to know, know what I am."

She thought about that for a minute. "I guess I'm privileged, then."

" 'Cursed' would be more appropriate."

"No," she said as she thought more about it. "When you're not being sarcastic, scary, or bullish, you're actually not bad to be around." Impishly, she added, "Of course, I've only been around you for about two minutes when you weren't one of those three things, so who am I to judge?"

His face softened. "I don't know about you, but I have to sleep. I had a long night and I'm exhausted."

She was rather tired, too. But as she slid her gaze to the fake leather sofa, she realized it would never fit both of them.

Hunter grinned at her. "You take the couch, I'll sleep on the floor."

"Can you do that?"

"I've slept in worse places."

"Yeah, but don't you need a coffin?"

He gave her a droll stare, but said nothing as he led her to the sofa.

No sooner had Amanda lain down than she realized it wasn't going to work. "This isn't comfortable. I can't sleep with my arm hanging over the edge and I'm twice as long as the couch is."

"What do you suggest?"

She grabbed the blanket and pillow and lay down on the floor beside him.

Kyrian flinched as she lay so close to him that he could feel her body heat. Worse, the only way to comfortably sleep would be to drape his arm over her.

Like lovers.

The thought tore through him, lancing his heart so deep that for a minute, he couldn't breathe as he remembered the last time he had made the mistake of being with a woman and letting his guard down.

Unbidden, the sight of blood, and the memory of grueling, unrelenting pain ripped through him with such ferocity that it made him flinch.

That was the past, he told himself. Ancient history. Still, some things were impossible to forget. And not even a man with super psychic powers could bury them.

Don't think about it.

This wasn't the time for memories. It was a time to be practical.

Desiderius would be after him tonight and if he was to save her and her sister, he would have to be awake, and fully alert.

Closing his eyes, he made himself relax.

Until she shifted, and her buttocks collided with his groin.

Kyrian ground his teeth. He was on fire as he inhaled the sweet rosy scent of her. It had been so incredibly long since he had last taken a woman. So long since he had dared close his eyes with one by his side.

Necessity was a bitch. But then he had learned that lesson the hard way when he had fought against the Romans.

Swallowing, he forced his mind to blankness. There was nothing in the past worth remembering. Nothing back there except pain so profound that even after two thousand years it could still bring him to his knees.

Focus, he told himself, relying on his staunch military training. *Now is the time to rest.*

Amanda tensed as he moved to spoon up against her spine. And when he put his arm over her, her heart pounded.

All that lean, hard strength was pressed against her back in a most distracting way.

She stared at his hand in front of her face. He had long, graceful fingers that looked as though they should belong to an artist or musician. Goodness, but it was hard to remember this man wasn't really a man.

You're lying with a vampire!

No, he's a Dark-Hunter. Not that she really understood the difference, yet.

But she would. One way or another.

Amanda lay for hours listening to Hunter breathe. She could tell when he had finally fallen asleep because his arm relaxed against her and the breath on her neck evened out.

Outside Tate's office, she heard people coming and going, the hospital paging system calling out for different doctors and orders.

A little after noon, Tate brought them lunch, but she wouldn't let him wake Hunter. She ate half of her sandwich and continued to lie there, all the while wondering how she could feel so strangely safe with a vampire she barely knew.

She rolled over slightly to look at him. He really was scrumptious. His hair fell over his eyes as he slept and his relaxed features held a boyish charm to them.

As she stared at his perfect lips, she remembered the way they had tasted. The raw, powerful feel of them on her neck.

The remnants of that kiss made her lips burn, her body quiver.

She'd been kissed more times than she could count, but no man had ever made her feel the way he did. The touch of his mouth on hers had set her on fire.

How had he done it? What was it about Hunter that made her ache to have him in spite of herself?

Was it part of his immortal powers?

She wasn't a nymphomaniac. She had a normal, healthy sex drive that wasn't too low or too high. Yet every time she looked at him, she wanted to touch his skin, his lips, his hair.

What was wrong with her?

Put it out of your mind. Closing her eyes, she started counting backward from one hundred.

When she reached negative sixty, she realized it was futile.

Sighing, she absently reached out and toyed with the ring on his hand. Before she realized it, she was holding his hand in hers.

Hunter murmured dreamily as he snuggled closer. Amanda's eyes widened as his hot breath fell against her cheek and his erection pressed disturbingly against her hip. His grip tightened on her hand an instant before he gathered her in his arms and cradled her body protectively with his.

He whispered something in a foreign language, then settled again, still fast asleep.

Her heart hammered. No one had ever held her like this. So possessively. So completely. It felt as if she were cocooned by his strength. The weirdest part of all was that deep down she liked the feeling a whole lot more than she ever wanted to admit.

Nestled in his arms, she finally drifted to sleep.

Amanda came awake to a hard thigh wedged between her legs and to a hot hand beneath her sweater, skimming the flesh of her stomach. Hunter's arm held her so close to him that she could barely breathe.

"I've missed you," he whispered tenderly an instant before he slid his hand under her bra and cupped her breast.

Amanda hissed in pleasure as his warm fingers brushed against her flesh in slow, simmering circles. That touch branded her with desire and it was all she could do not to turn her head to his and kiss him.

"Theone," he breathed lovingly.

"Hey!" she snapped at him. It offended her to the core of her soul that he would dare call her by someone else's name. If he was going to grope, then he better damn well remember who it was he groped. "What are you doing?"

Kyrian tensed as he came fully awake and opened his eyes wide. The first thing he felt was the warm, soft breast that overfilled his palm. The second was the throbbing ache in his body that demanded release.

Oh shit! He jerked his hand away as if it were on fire.

What the hell was he doing?

His job was to protect her, *not* touch her. Especially not when she felt this good in his arms. The last time he'd made that mistake with a woman, it had cost him his very soul.

Amanda saw the confusion on his face as he pulled away from her and sat up.

"Who's Theone?" she asked.

Hatred flared in his eyes. "No one."

Okay, he didn't like Theone while conscious, but there for a minute . . .

He rose slowly to his feet and helped her up. "I slept longer than I meant to. The sun is already setting."

"Is this some weird psychic thing you have with the sun?"

"Since I live and die by when it sets and rises, yes." He pulled her toward the door. "Now then, you said you know someone we can see about getting free?"

"Yeah, they should be home. Want me to call and make sure?"

"Yes."

Amanda went to the desk, picked up the phone, then called Grace Alexander.

"Hey, Gracie," she said as soon as Grace answered. "This is Amanda. I was wondering if you guys would be home tonight? I have a bit of a favor to ask."

"Sure. My in-laws are over for a bit, but that'll keep the babies occupied. You want to tell me—"

"Not over the phone. We'll be there as soon as we can."

"We?" Grace asked.

"I have a friend in tow, if you don't mind."

"No, not at all."

"Thanks. I'll see you in a bit." Amanda hung up the phone.

"Okay," she said to Hunter. "She lives off St. Charles. You know the way?"

Before he could answer, Tate came in with a black brief-case in his hand. "Hey," he said to Hunter, "I figured you'd

be getting up about now. A guy named Nick came by a couple
of hours ago and left this for you."

"Thanks," Hunter said as he took the briefcase from him.
He placed it on the desk and opened it.

Amanda's eyes bulged at the sight of two small handguns,
a recoiling gun, a holster, a cell phone, three wicked-looking
knives, and a pair of small, dark, round sunglasses.

"Tate," Hunter said with a friendly note in his voice she
wouldn't have thought him capable of. "You're the man."

"I just hope Nick didn't forget anything."

"Nope, he nailed it."

Amanda arched a brow at the strangeness of hearing modern American slang coming out of a man with such a heavy,
seductive accent.

Tate nodded to them, then left.

She watched as Hunter strapped the holster to his hips, then
he slid the plate back to lock a bullet in the chamber of each
gun. He flicked on the safety, twirled them around, then hol-
stered them so that his coat concealed them.

Next, he picked up a butterfly knife and shoved it in his
back pocket. The other two knives went into his coat pockets
and he clipped the cell phone and his PDA to his belt.

Amanda arched a brow at his weapons. "I thought only a
wooden stake through the heart killed a vampire."

"A wooden stake through the heart will kill just about anything. And if it doesn't, run like hell," Hunter said blandly.
"Again, my lady, you watch too much television. Don't you
have a life?"

"Yes, unlike you, I have a blessedly boring life where no
one tries to kill me. And you know what? I like it, and I really
want to get back to it."

His eyes glowed with humor. "All right, then, let's go find
your friend to separate us so that you can get back to your
boring life and I can lead my dangerous one."

Raking her with a hot, lustful stare, he ran his tongue over
his fangs. Then he placed the sunglasses on his face.

Amanda's pulse quickened. With those dark glasses on, he
looked even more like a soulful poet than ever before. It was

all she could do not to step back into his arms and demand he kiss her again.

He tucked her hand into his coat pocket with his to conceal the handcuffs, then led her out of Tate's office and through the hospital corridor.

As he walked, she noticed his smooth, predatorial gait. His air of refinement. The man was pure, fluid grace. And that was a seriously dangerous swagger he had developed. One that drew the attention of every woman they passed.

But Hunter didn't seem to notice as he headed out the back exit.

Once they reached the dark parking lot, Amanda gave a low whistle as she saw a Lamborghini Diablo in one of the employee spaces. The light above it glinted across the sleek black paint much like a halo. Normally, she didn't give a whit about cars, but the Lamborghini had always been her one exception.

It must belong to a surgeon.

Or so she thought until Hunter approached it.

"What are you doing?" she asked.

"I'm getting into my car."

Her jaw dropped. "You own this?"

"No," he said sarcastically. "I'm stealing it with the key in my hand."

"Good Lord," she gasped, "you must be loaded!"

He pulled the sunglasses down the bridge of his nose to give her a peeved glare. "It's amazing how much savings you can accumulate in two thousand years."

Amanda blinked as his words registered. Could he honestly be . . .

"Is that *really* how old you are?" she asked skeptically.

He nodded. "Two thousand one hundred and eighty-two years old last July, to be precise."

She bit her bottom lip as she swept her gaze over his gorgeous body. "You look good for an old man. I wouldn't have put you a day over three hundred myself."

Laughing, he placed the key in the lock.

As Amanda waited for him to open the door, the imp in

her couldn't resist teasing him. "You know, they say men who drive cars like this are compensating for little"—she let her gaze roam meaningfully down the front of his body, pausing at the bulge in his jeans—"packages."

He cocked an eyebrow at her, then gave her a crooked smile that was teasing, warm, and wicked as he pulled the door up.

Before she knew what he was about, he stepped forward, overwhelming her with his masculine scent and power, then he took her hand that was cuffed to him and pressed it against his swollen groin.

Nope. No compensating there.

He dipped his head down to whisper in her ear. "If you need more convincing . . ."

Her breath faltered at the incredible feel of him in her palm. That was *not* a tube sock in his jeans.

He stared at her lips and cupped her face with his free hand. She knew in that instant he was going to kiss her again.

Yes, please!

"Knock, knock," Desiderius said from the darkness.

CHAPTER 4

"Now, ain't this a bitch," Hunter said in an even tone as he pulled the sunglasses off and tucked them into his coat pocket. He moved with such deliberate slowness that Amanda knew it was his way of letting Desiderius know just how small of a threat the Dark-Hunter perceived him to be.

"Here I am, trying to kiss my girl, and you have to interrupt us. What, were you raised in a barn?"

With a calmness that astounded her, Hunter turned around to face Desiderius. "By the way, touch the woman—or the Lamborghini—and you're a dead man."

Desiderius came out of the shadows to stand beneath a circle of white moonlight. The contrasting buttery lamplight fell behind him at an odd angle, giving him a sinister appearance despite his angelic beauty.

"Nice car you have there, Dark-Hunter," Desiderius said. "It makes trailing it to you so much easier. As for your threat, I'm already a dead man." His perfect lips twitched into a mocking smile. "And so are you."

Dressed in a fashionable blue pin-striped suit, Desiderius looked like a highly paid male model. His skin was golden and unblemished, his blond hair a shade lighter than the Dark-Hunter's. His beauty was so flawless, it was almost surreal.

He didn't appear any older than his mid-twenties. A man at the height of his sexual appeal and strength.

Amanda swallowed as a shiver of fear went up her spine.

There was something insidious about a man so evil looking so sublime. The only giveaway to his real nature was the long canine teeth he didn't bother to conceal when he spoke.

"I almost hate to kill you, Dark-Hunter. Unlike the others I've bested, you have such an amusing sense of humor."

"Well, I try." Hunter placed himself between them. "Now, why don't you make this a bit more interesting and let the woman go?"

"No."

Out of nowhere, they were attacked.

Amanda heard a sharp click.

Grabbing her hand that was bound to his so that he wouldn't hurt her during the fight, Hunter caught the first golden vampire with the toe of his boot. As the vampire vaporized into a cloud of dust, she realized the click had been the blade in his boot being released.

The blade instantly retracted.

With a move straight out of Hollywood, Hunter clipped another vampire with his elbow, then sent him flipping head over heels onto the ground. In one lightning-fast action, he knelt, twirled open a butterfly knife, embedded it into the Daimon's chest, then twirled it closed as the vampire evaporated.

Hunter rose to his feet.

A third one came from the shadows.

Acting on instinct, Amanda whirled and kicked him back with her leg. She caught him in the groin and sent him to the ground, whimpering.

Hunter arched a brow at her.

"Black belt in aikido," she said.

"Any other time, I'd kiss you for that." He smiled, then looked past her shoulder. "Duck."

She did and he tossed a knife straight into the chest of another vampire. The vampire vanished into black vapor.

Hunter pulled the gun out of its holster. "Get in the car," he ordered, pushing her toward the driver's seat.

Her entire body quaking from adrenaline, Amanda got in as fast as the handcuffs and his hold on her hand would allow.

She climbed over the gearshift, into the passenger seat, while Hunter fired at the vampires.

He got in behind her, closed the door, and started the car.

Good Lord, Hunter was amazing, and perfectly calm. She'd never seen anything like it in her life. He was totally unruffled.

Another beautiful, blond vampire jumped on the hood as Hunter put the car in reverse and hit the gas. His fangs bared, the vampire tried to punch through the windshield.

"Didn't I tell you *not* to touch the Lamborghini?" Hunter groused an instant before he cut the wheel and sent the vampire flying through the air.

"And they told me you guys couldn't fly," Hunter said, straightening out the car and heading for the street. "I guess Acheron needs to update the handbook."

Amanda realized there were two cars after them.

"Oh, my God," she breathed, placing her hand on his thick, masculine wrist to allow him as much mobility as she could while he shifted gears. This was getting ugly and the last thing she wanted was to interfere with whatever he had to do to get her safely out of this.

"Hold tight," Hunter said as he turned the radio on, and accelerated.

Lynyrd Skynyrd's "That Smell" blared as they whipped out of the parking lot, into traffic.

Her entire body rigid, Amanda started praying the Rosary even though she wasn't Catholic.

"Lights!" Amanda shouted as she realized he was driving in total darkness and his windows were tinted far past the legal limit. "Lights would be very good right now!"

"Since they hurt my eyes to the point I can barely see, no they wouldn't. Trust me."

"Trust you, my left foot," she snapped, using her free hand to hold on to the seat belt like a lifeline. "I'm not immortal over here."

He laughed at that. "Yeah, well, in a bad enough car wreck, neither am I."

Amanda gaped. "I really hate your sense of humor."

His smile widened.

They went speeding through the crowded New Orleans streets, weaving in and out of lanes until she thought she'd be sick with fear. Not to mention a couple of times when she was sure her hand would be wrenched off by his movements.

Swallowing, she did her best to keep her nausea at bay while she braced herself against the dash.

A huge black Chevy pulled up beside them and tried to run them into a tractor-trailer. Grinding her teeth, Amanda bit back a scream.

"Don't panic," Hunter said over the music as he cut the wheel to move underneath the semi. He gunned the engine. "I've done this a lot."

Amanda couldn't breathe as they entered another lane where a red Firebird waited to try and ram them. The Dark-Hunter narrowly missed a parked car.

Amanda's panic was so severe all she could do was gape. And pray. She did lots and lots of praying.

By the time they reached the interstate, Amanda had seen her entire boring life flash before her eyes. And she didn't like what she saw.

It was way too brief. There were a lot of things she wanted to do before she died—including getting her hands on Tabitha and beating the snot out of her.

Suddenly, the black Chevy was back, trying to run them off the road. Hunter hit the brakes and jerked his car over. They skidded sideways.

Her stomach lurched.

"You know," Hunter said calmly. "I really hate Romans, but I have to say their descendants make one fine automobile."

He shifted and accelerated again, flying past the Chevy. They jumped the median, drove across oncoming traffic, and went down an exit so fast that all she could see was a flashing blur of lights.

The sounds of horns and screaming brakes filled her ears. It was followed by grinding metal and a loud pop and crunch as the Firebird full of Daimons hit the black Chevy. The Firebird drove the other car of Daimons into the retaining wall where it flipped over the traffic.

Amanda still couldn't breathe as the Daimons' Chevy came to rest beside the highway without striking another car.

Hunter actually whooped as he cut the wheel to turn the Lamborghini around in the street to face the opposite direction. He slammed on the brakes and took a look at the chaos they had left in their wake.

Her entire body shaking, Amanda gaped.

Hunter turned the radio off and smiled triumphantly. "And not a single mark on the Lamborghini. Ha! Eat steel, you soul-sucking bastards."

Downshifting, he stomped the gas, turned a tight, squealing circle in the street, and headed back toward the Quarter.

Amanda sat in stunned disbelief as she did her best to take long, deep, soothing breaths. "You actually enjoyed that, didn't you?"

"Oh, hell yes. Did you see the look on their faces?" He laughed. "Man, I love this car."

She looked up at the sky, and implored divine aid. "Dear God, please separate me from this maniac before I die of fright."

"Oh, c'mon," he said, his voice teasing. "Don't tell me that didn't get your blood pumping."

"Yes, yes, it did. In fact, my blood is pumping so fast that I'm not really sure why my heart hasn't exploded." She stared at him. "You are one crazy human being."

The laughter died instantly. "I used to be, anyway."

She swallowed at the hollowness of his voice. Without meaning to, she must have struck a nerve.

Their mood subdued, Amanda gave him directions to Grace's bungalow off St. Charles.

A few minutes later, they pulled into the driveway behind Julian Alexander's black Range Rover. The back fender was slightly crushed in from his latest collision with a lamppost.

Poor Julian, he really was a menace on the road. She slid a sideways glance to the Dark-Hunter. Then again, comparatively speaking, Julian wasn't so bad after all. At least he'd never given her a heart attack.

Hunter helped her out of his side of the car, then led the

way to the door. The old-fashioned bungalow was completely lit up, and through the sheer curtains over the windows, Amanda could see Grace sitting in an armchair in the living room.

The petite brunette had her long hair in a ponytail, and her stomach was twice as round as it had been the last time Amanda had seen her. Even though the baby wasn't due for another nine weeks, poor Grace looked as if she could give birth at any moment.

Grace was laughing at something, but there was no sign of Julian or their guests.

Amanda paused to brush her hair with her hand, straighten her dirty clothes, and button her coat over the bloodstains. "Grace said they have company, so I think we should try and be a little inconspicuous, okay?"

He nodded as she rang the bell.

After a brief wait, the door opened to show Julian Alexander in the foyer. At six three, Julian was every bit as striking as Hunter. He had hair the same shade of blond and the bluest eyes Amanda had ever seen. His face was perfectly sculpted, but considering that he was the son of the Greek goddess Aphrodite, it was to be expected.

The welcoming smile on Julian's face faded as he caught sight of Hunter.

His jaw went slack.

Amanda turned to see a very similar reaction from Hunter, who stood stock-still.

"Julian of Macedon?" Hunter asked in disbelief.

"Kyrian of Thrace?"

Before she could move, the two men grabbed each other like long-lost brothers. Her arm was snatched upward as Kyrian hugged him.

"Oh gods!" Julian gasped. "Is it really you?"

"I can't believe it," Hunter said as he pulled back and ran a shocked look up and down Julian's body. "I thought you were dead."

"Me?" Julian asked. "What about you? I heard the Romans executed you. Dear Zeus, how can you be here?" Julian glanced down and saw the handcuffs. His frown deepened. "What the . . . ?"

"That's why we're here," Amanda said. "We got latched together, and I was hoping you could separate us."

"They were made by your stepfather," Hunter added. "Any chance you have a key lying around?"

Julian laughed. "I guess I shouldn't be surprised. At least this time she's not an Amazon princess with an irate mother demanding parts of your body be removed." Julian shook his head like a father scolding a son. "Two thousand years later, and you're still getting into unbelievable messes."

Hunter gave him a tight-lipped smile. "Some things never change. Care to indebt me to you again?"

Julian cocked his head. "Last time I counted, I was two favors down to you."

"Oh yeah, I forgot about Prymaria."

By the expression on Julian's face, Amanda could tell he hadn't and she was dying to know what had happened. But there would be time for that later.

First, she wanted her arm free. She jingled the chain, hinting.

Julian stepped back and let them enter his house. "You're actually in luck," he said as he led them into the living room.

Grace hadn't moved from her chair where she now held Vanessa on her lap while Julian's gorgeous, blond mother sat on the sofa teasing Niklos with a stuffed doll. A tall, dark-haired man sat beside Aphrodite, holding Niklos in his arms and laughing at the two of them.

The Dark-Hunter sucked his breath in sharply at the quaint family scene. Roughly, he pushed Amanda away from him an instant before Aphrodite looked up and cursed.

Before Amanda could process what was going on, Aphrodite threw her arm out and what appeared to be a bolt of lightning came out of her hand and struck Hunter. The blast knocked him off his feet and threw him to the floor, pulling her along with him.

Amanda landed on top of his chest. She saw the burn on his shoulder and smelled the smoldering leather and skin.

She knew his wound had to be excruciating, but he didn't even react to it. Instead, Hunter quickly removed his sunglasses, pushed her off his chest, and tried to get her as far away from him as he could.

Rising to his feet, he placed himself between her and Aphrodite.

"How dare you!" Aphrodite shrieked while fury contorted her beautiful face. Her eyes narrowed, she left the couch and stalked toward Hunter like a deadly beast of prey. "You know you are not to be in our presence."

Julian grabbed Aphrodite before she could reach them. "Mother, stop! What are you doing?"

She glared at Julian. "You dare bring a Dark-Hunter before me? You know it is forbidden!"

Frowning, Julian turned to look at Hunter. Disbelief was etched on his face.

Hunter glanced at Amanda over his shoulder. "You're about to be free, little one," he whispered.

Aphrodite raised her hand.

Terrified, Amanda realized Aphrodite meant to kill him. No! The word caught in her throat while her heart raced in panic.

Julian caught his mother's wrist before she could blast Hunter again.

"No, Mom," Julian snapped. "Dark-Hunter or not, he happens to be the only man who ever stood guard at my back while everyone else prayed for my death. You kill him, and I will *never* forgive you for it."

Aphrodite's face turned to stone.

Julian let go of her hand. "I have never, in my entire life, asked you for anything. But I'm asking you now, as your son, help him. Please."

Aphrodite looked from Julian to Hunter. The indecision in her eyes was tangible.

"Hephaestus?" Julian asked the man on the couch. "Will you free them?"

"It is forbidden," he said gruffly, "and you know it. Dark-Hunters are soulless and beyond us."

"It's all right, Julian," Hunter said quietly. "Just ask her not to let the blast go through me and hit the woman."

It was only then Aphrodite noticed Amanda. Her gaze fell to the cuffs.

"Mom?" Julian asked again.

Aphrodite snapped her fingers and the handcuffs disappeared.

"Thank you," Julian said.

"I did it only to help the human female," Aphrodite said grimly before returning to the sofa. "The Dark-Hunter is on its own."

Hunter said a quiet thanks to Julian. Then, he turned and started for the door.

"Kyrian, wait," Julian said, stopping him. "You can't go out there hurt."

The Dark-Hunter's face was stoic. "You know the Code, *adelfos*. I walk alone."

"Not tonight, you don't."

"If he stays," Aphrodite said, "we have to leave."

Julian looked back at his mother and nodded. "I know, Mom. Thanks again for helping him. I'll see you later."

Aphrodite vanished in a flash of light. Hephaestus set Niklos down, then evaporated, too.

"Julian?" Grace called from her chair. "Is it safe to let go of Vanessa now?"

"Yes," he said.

Amanda watched the sad look on Hunter's face as the twins came running toward their father.

Niklos took a happy detour to her, jabbering as he held his arms out. Amanda picked him up and cuddled him close before kissing the top of his soft, blond curls.

Bouncing in her arms, he laughed and hugged her.

Vanessa made straight for Hunter in true Vanessa form. The little darling knew no strangers. She handed him the half-eaten cookie in her hand. "Cook-ie?" she asked in her broken, baby speech.

Kneeling before her, Hunter smiled tenderly as he took it

from her outstretched hand. He brushed a gentle palm over the toddler's dark hair.

"Thank you, sweeting," he said softly before handing the cookie back to her. "But I'm not hungry."

Vanessa squealed and threw herself into his arms.

If Amanda lived an eternity, she would never forget the desperate, aching look on Hunter's face as he held Vanessa to his chest. It was one of such longing. Of pain. The look of a man who knew he held something precious in his arms that he never wanted to let go of.

He closed his eyes and leaned his cheek against the top of Vanessa's head as he balled his fist against her back and held her tight. "Gods, Julian, you always made such beautiful babies."

Julian didn't say anything as Grace came forward. But Amanda saw the anguish in Julian's eyes while he watched his friend and his daughter.

The two of them locked gazes.

Something passed between them, some shared nightmare Amanda knew nothing about.

Julian took Grace's hand. "Grace, this is my friend Kyrian of Thrace. Kyrian, this is my wife."

Like a graceful black panther coming out of its deadly crouch, Hunter rose to his feet with Vanessa cradled gently in his arms. "I'm honored to meet you, Grace."

"Thank you," Grace said. "I have to say the same about you. Julian's talked about you so much that I feel like I know you."

Hunter narrowed his eyes on Julian. "Considering how often he censured my behavior, I shudder to think what he's told you about me."

Grace laughed. "Nothing too bad. Is it true you once incited an entire bordello into—"

"Julian!" Hunter snapped. "I can't believe you told her that."

Completely unabashed, Julian shrugged Hunter's irritability off. "Ingenuity under pressure was always your forte."

Grace gasped, then put her hand against her distended

stomach. Julian reached out and took her arm, watching her worriedly.

Taking deep breaths, Grace rubbed her stomach and offered them a tentative smile. "Sorry, the baby kicks like a mule."

Hunter stared at Grace's belly, and a strange light came into his eyes. For an instant, Amanda could swear they glowed.

"It's another boy," he said quietly, his voice distant.

"How did you know?" Grace asked in surprise as she continued to run her hand over her stomach. "I just found out yesterday."

"He can feel the baby's soul," Julian said quietly. "It's one of the protective powers of a Dark-Hunter."

Hunter looked to Julian. "This one is going to be strong-willed. He's loving and giving, but completely reckless."

"Reminds me of someone else I once knew," Julian said.

The words seemed to haunt Hunter.

"C'mon," Julian said, taking Vanessa from Hunter and setting her down even though she squealed in protest. "I need to get you upstairs and tend that wound."

Amanda stood in the hallway, unsure of what she should do. She had a million questions she wanted answered, and if not for Hunter's wound, she'd be on her way upstairs right now asking them all. But Julian was right. That vicious-looking wound needed tending.

With a wistful glance to the stairs, she turned back to Grace. "You're amazingly calm given all this chaos. Gods poofing out, people coming in wearing bloody clothes, and getting blasted in your foyer. I would think by now you'd be freaking out, especially given your condition."

Grace laughed as she herded the crying Vanessa back into the living room. "Well, over the last few years, I've gotten rather used to Greek gods poofing in and out. As well as other things I don't want to think about. Being married to Julian has definitely been an education in staying calm."

Amanda laughed halfheartedly as she glanced toward the stairs and again wondered about her enigmatic Dark-Hunter. "Is Hunter—or Kyrian—a god, too?"

"I don't know. From the things Julian has said, I always assumed Kyrian was a man, but I'm as much in the dark as you are."

As Grace sat down, Amanda heard the men talking through the baby monitor.

Grace reached to turn it off.

"Please, wait."

Amanda took a seat and played with Niklos while she listened to the men above.

"Damn, Kyrian," Julian said as soon as Kyrian handed him his shirt. "You've got more scars on you than my father had."

Kyrian let out a deep breath while he gently probed the burn on his shoulder from Aphrodite's blast.

The two of them were alone in the twins' nursery at the end of the upstairs hallway. Kyrian squinted against the bright yellow teddy-bear wallpaper that hurt his light-sensitive eyes and reached for his sunglasses.

Julian must have remembered his ancient Greek mythology because he turned out the overhead lights and turned on the small nursery lamp that bathed the room in a soothing dull glow.

Weak from his pain, Kyrian noticed that his reflection in the mirror was only barely there. An inability to cast reflections was one of the camouflage benefits bestowed on all Dark-Hunters. The only way for them to have a reflection was to force it from within their own mind. Something that was hard to do when they were wounded or excessively tired.

He stepped back from the white-painted dresser and met Julian's curious gaze. "Two thousand years of combat tend to take a toll on the body."

"You always had more balls than brains."

An eerie chill went up Kyrian's spine at those familiar words. He couldn't count the times Julian had said that to him in Classical Greek.

How he had missed his friend and mentor over the centuries. Julian had been the only man he'd ever listened to. One of the few men he'd actually respected.

Kyrian rubbed his arm. "I know, but the funny thing is I can always hear your voice in my head begging me for patience." He deepened his tone and adopted Julian's rougher-edged Spartan accent. " 'Damn, Kyrian, can't you ever think before you react?' "

Julian fell silent.

Kyrian knew what was going through Julian's mind. The same bittersweet memories that tugged at him at night whenever he paused long enough to dwell on the past.

They were images of a world that had long ago ceased to exist. Of people and family who were nothing more than vague memories and lost feelings.

Their world had been a special one. Its primitive grace a warmth in their hearts. Even now, Kyrian could smell the oil from the lamps that had once lit his home. Feel the cool, fragrant Mediterranean breeze blowing through his villa.

In an odd contrast to Kyrian's thoughts, Julian dug around the small first-aid kit for a modern ice pack.

Finding it, Julian popped the seal to release the cooling gel, then held it against Kyrian's shoulder.

Kyrian hissed as the ice touched his throbbing skin.

"I'm sorry about that blast," Julian said. "Had I known . . ."

"It's not your fault. You had no way of knowing I'd traded my soul. It's not exactly how I start out conversations. Hi, I'm Kyrian. I have no soul. What about you?"

"You're not funny."

"Sure I am, you just never appreciated my sense of humor."

"That's because you would only let it out when we were one step away from death."

Kyrian shrugged, then wished he hadn't as pain sliced down his arm. "What can I say? I live to tease old Apollyon." Kyrian took the pack out of Julian's hand and stepped back. "So what happened to you? I was told Scipio had you and your family assassinated."

Julian scoffed. "You know better. It was Priapus who killed my family. After I found them dead, I had a 'Kyrian' moment where I went after him."

Kyrian arched a brow at that. To his knowledge, Julian had

never had an impulsive moment in his entire life. The man
was forever calm and collected, no matter the turmoil. It had
been one of the things Kyrian liked best about him. "*You* did
something rash?"

"Yes, and I paid for it." He folded his arms over his chest
and he met Kyrian's gaze. "Priapus cursed me into a scroll. I
spent two thousand years as a sex slave before my wife freed
me."

Kyrian exhaled in disbelief. He had heard of such curses.
The pain of them was excruciating and his proud friend must
have had a hard time of it. Julian had never been one to let
anyone rule his life. Not even the gods.

"And you called me insane," Kyrian said. "At least I only
antagonized the Romans. You went after the pantheon."

Julian handed him a tube of burn ointment. When he spoke,
his voice was low and thick. "I was wondering, after I left,
what happened to . . ."

Kyrian looked up and saw the agony in Julian's eyes, and
he knew what was too painful for his friend to even mention.

Even now, he could feel his own grief over the death of
Julian's son and daughter. With blond hair and rosy cheeks,
they had been beautiful and vivacious beyond description.

They alone had made Kyrian's heart ache with envy.

Gods, how he'd wanted his own children, his own family.
Every time he'd seen Julian at home, he had yearned to have
such a life.

It was all he'd ever truly wanted. A peaceful hearth, children to love, and a wife who loved him. Such simple things,
really. Yet they had forever eluded his grasp.

Now, as a Dark-Hunter, such wishes were an impossibility.

Kyrian couldn't imagine the horror Julian must still feel
every time he thought of his children. He doubted if any man
had ever loved his children more than Julian had. Indeed, he
remembered the time five-year-old Atolycus had replaced the
horsehair in Julian's helm with feathers as a gift for his father
before they rode out to battle.

Julian had been one of the most feared commanders of the
Macedonian army, yet rather than hurt his son's feelings, he

had proudly worn his son's gift in front of all his men.

No one had dared laugh. Not even Kyrian.

He cleared his throat and averted his gaze from Julian's. "I buried Callista and Atolycus in the orchard overlooking the sea where they used to play. Penelope's family took care of her, and I sent Iason's body back to his father."

"Thank you."

Kyrian nodded. "It was the least I could do. You were like a brother to me."

Julian gave a halfhearted laugh. "I guess that explains why you went out of your way to annoy me all the time."

"Someone had to. Even at twenty-three, you were too serious and stern."

"Unlike you."

Kyrian could only vaguely remember being the man Julian had known all those centuries before. He'd been carefree and battle-ready. Hot-blooded and pigheaded.

It was a wonder Julian hadn't killed him. The man's patience knew no limits.

"My glorious days of misspent youth," Kyrian said wistfully.

Looking at his shoulder, Kyrian spread the soothing salve over the burn. It stung, but he was used to physical pain, and he had suffered worse injuries than this tiny ache.

Julian leveled a probing stare at him. "The Romans took you because of me, didn't they?"

Kyrian paused at the remorse in Julian's eyes. Then he returned to spreading the ointment over the burn. "You were always too hard on yourself, Julian. It wasn't your fault. After you were gone, I went on a bloodthirsty crusade against their forces. I made my own destiny in that regard, and it had nothing to do with you."

"But had I been there, I could have kept them from taking you."

Kyrian snorted at that. "You were good at pulling me out of trouble, no doubt about it. But not even you could have saved me from myself. Had you been there, the Romans would have just had another Macedonian commander to crucify.

Trust me. You were much better off in that scroll than meeting the fate Scipio and Valerius had in mind for us."

Still, Kyrian saw his friend's guilt and he wished he could give Julian absolution.

"What happened?" Julian asked. "Historical accounts say Valerius captured you in battle. But I can't believe that. Not the way you fought."

"And history says you were killed by Scipio's assassins. Victors make their own versions of truth."

For the first time in centuries, Kyrian allowed his thoughts to turn to that fateful day in the past.

He clenched his teeth as a wave of rage and agony washed over him anew and he remembered all too well why he had banished those memories to the farthest corner of his mind. "You know, the Fates are treacherous bitches. I wasn't taken by Valerius, I was handed over, gift-wrapped."

Julian frowned. "How?"

"My little Clytemnestra. While you and I were out fighting the Romans, my wife was at home welcoming them into her bed."

Julian's face paled. "I can't believe Theone would do that to you after all you did for her."

"No good deed goes unpunished."

Julian scowled at the bitterness he heard in Kyrian's voice. This wasn't the same man he'd known in Macedonia. Kyrian of Thrace had always been fun-loving and lighthearted.

The man before him now was jaded. Guarded. Suspicious and almost cold.

"Is her betrayal why you became a Dark-Hunter?" Julian asked.

"Yes."

Julian closed his eyes as he felt compassion and anger for his friend. Over and over in his mind, he could see Kyrian the way he'd been all those centuries before. His human eyes had always been laughing, mischievous. Kyrian had loved life in a way very few people ever did.

Generous in spirit, kind in nature, and courageous of heart,

Kyrian had even managed to win Julian over and he had truly wanted to hate the spoiled, arrogant brat.

But hating Kyrian had been impossible.

"What did Valerius do to you?" Julian asked.

Kyrian drew a deep breath. "Trust me, you don't ever want the exact details."

Julian saw Kyrian flinch as if some memory flashed in his mind. "What?"

"Nothing," Kyrian said sharply.

Julian's thoughts turned to Kyrian's wife. Small and blond, Theone had been more beautiful than Helen of Troy. Julian had seen her only once, and then at a distance. Even so, he had known instantly what attracted Kyrian to her. She had possessed an irresistible aura of grace and sexual expertise.

Barely twenty-two when he met her, Kyrian had fallen in love instantly with the woman who was eight years his senior. No matter what any of them said about her, Kyrian had never listened. He'd loved that woman with every fiber of his body and soul.

"What of Theone?" Julian asked. "Did you ever find out why she did it?"

Kyrian tossed the salve back into the bag. "She said she did it because she was afraid I couldn't protect her."

Julian cursed.

"My thoughts were somewhat stronger," Kyrian said quietly. "You know, I lay there for weeks trying to figure out what it was about me she hated so much that she could hand me over to my worst enemy. I never knew I was *that* big an asshole."

Kyrian clenched his teeth as he remembered the way his wife had looked when they had started his execution. She had met his gaze levelly, without even the tiniest bit of remorse.

It had been then he'd known that even though he had given her only the very best of himself, the whole of his heart and soul, she had never given him anything of her. Not even her kindness. If only she'd had one flash of regret in her eyes, one tiny bit of sorrow . . .

But only morbid curiosity had darkened her face.

It had torn his heart asunder. If she couldn't love him after all he had given, then he must truly be unlovable.

His father had been right all along.

"No woman can ever love a man of your standing and wealth. Face it. All you will ever be, boy, is a hefty purse."

To this day, his heart wept from the truth of it. Never again would he allow a woman that much hold over him. He refused to let love or anything else blind him from what he needed to do. His duty was all that mattered.

Now more than ever before.

"I am so sorry," Julian breathed.

Kyrian shrugged. "We're all sorry for something." He reached for his torn, bloodied shirt.

"Listen," Julian said, stopping him, "why don't you take a shower and let me loan you some clothes?"

"I have a hunt to finish."

"No offense, Kyrian, but you look like hell. Granted it's been a long time since I fought, but I know how much easier it is with a full stomach and a hot bath."

Kyrian hesitated.

"Fifteen minutes?"

"Make it quick."

Kyrian let the soothing water slide over his battered body. The night was still young, but he was tired already. His shoulder throbbed and ached and his side wasn't much better.

Yet what held his attention was the woman downstairs.

Why was he so attracted to her? He had saved countless humans over the centuries. He had felt nothing for them other than a passing curiosity.

And yet this woman with open, honest eyes and a beguiling smile tugged at a heart he had banished centuries ago. He didn't need that. Dark-Hunters were forbidden to take steady lovers. Out of necessity, their sexual encounters were relegated to one-night stands.

They were reborn to walk alone through time. Each of them knew it. They had sworn themselves to it.

Never before had it bothered him.

There had only been one other time in his long life that he had felt this strange giddy feeling in the pit of his stomach when a woman smiled at him.

He cursed at the reminder.

"Oh, come on, Kyrian," he said as he bathed himself. "Get out of the house, kill Desiderius, and go home. Forget you ever saw her."

Pain cut through him at the very thought of never seeing her again.

Still, he knew what he had to do. This was his life and he loved the night he was bound by oath to. His duties were his family. His loyal oath his heart.

His job was his love, and it would remain that way for eternity.

"Amanda?"

Forcing her thoughts away from her handsome Dark-Hunter, Amanda looked to where Grace was seated in the armchair.

"Would you mind going up to the babies' room and getting a diaper for me?" Grace asked. "If I walk up those stairs again, I might not come back down."

She laughed. "Sure. Be right back."

Amanda went up the stairs, then headed down the hallway. She passed the bathroom at the same time Hunter came out of it, wrapping a towel about his waist.

They collided. Hunter put his hands on her shoulders to steady her, his eyes widening a degree as he recognized her.

Amanda froze as she realized her silver charm bracelet had gotten tangled in one of the terry-cloth loops.

Worse, the sight of all that lush, tawny skin and the feel of his strong hands on her body made her mouth water for a taste of him.

Her heart hammered at the sight of all the lean power and strength. At the smell of his warm, clean skin. His wet hair was slicked back from a face so well sculpted that she doubted any man could ever be more handsome.

He fixed those dark eyes with sinfully long eyelashes on

her. The raw hunger in them made her hot and shivery. He looked as if he could devour her, and in truth, she wanted to be devoured by him. Completely. Utterly.

And with relish.

"Now, this is interesting," Hunter said with a hint of amusement in his voice.

Amanda didn't know what to do as she stood there with her wrist dangerously close to the sudden bulge under the towel. Why was it they kept getting attached?

Her gaze slid over the multitude of scars covering his body and she couldn't help wondering how many of them were from the torture he'd mentioned to Julian.

"Most of them," he whispered as he moved one hand over to cup her neck in his hand. She felt his fingers stroking her hair. His grip on her shoulder tightened ever so slightly.

"What?" she asked, looking up.

"Most of them are from the Romans."

She frowned. "How did you know what I was thinking?"

"I'm cavesdropping on your thoughts much the same way you listened to me and Julian."

A chill went down her spine as she considered his psychic powers. "You can do that?"

He nodded, but he wasn't looking at her, he was staring at his hand in her hair as if he were committing the texture and feel of it to memory.

His gaze returned to hers so fast it actually made her gasp. "And in answer to the question you're too afraid to think, all you have to do is move your arm and you'll know."

"Know what?"

"If I look as *yummy* without the towel as I do with it."

Her face flamed at the way he used her own words to describe exactly what she was too terrified to think.

Before she could move, he released her and dropped the towel to hang from her bracelet.

Amanda gaped at the sight of him completely naked before her. His hard, well-toned body was perfectly sculpted. And she quickly learned that his skin was golden all over. It wasn't a tan, it was his natural skin color.

She wanted him with a desperate need.

All she could think of was taking him into the bedroom and pulling him on top of, over, and then under her for the rest of the night.

Oh, the things she wanted to do to this man.

A half-smile hovered on the edges of his lips, and by the light in his eyes, she knew he was reading her thoughts. Again.

He leaned forward, his face just to the side of hers. His hot breath fell against her neck, scorching her. "Ancient Greeks never had a problem with public nudity," he whispered in her ear.

Her breasts tightened.

Slowly, he lifted his hand so that he could tilt her chin up. His gaze held hers enthralled as he appeared to search her mind for something.

Before she could move, he lowered his lips to hers.

Amanda moaned at the contact. This kiss was different from his last one. This one was gentle. Tender.

And it made her burn.

He left her lips and trailed a blazing path down her jaw to her neck, his tongue laving her skin ever so lightly. She wrapped her arms around his bare shoulders and surrendered her weight to him.

"You are so very tempting," he whispered, then traced the curve of her ear with his tongue. "But I have a job to do and you hate all things not human. And *everything* paranormal." He pulled back and gave her a wistful look. "Pity."

He freed his towel from her bracelet, tossed it over his shoulder, then headed to the bedroom. Amanda clenched her teeth at the sight of that luscious, gorgeous backside.

Her body on fire, she watched until he closed the door behind him.

Suddenly, she remembered the diaper.

No sooner had the thought crossed her mind than Hunter opened the door, tossed her one, then closed it again.

Kyrian leaned against the closed door as he fought the raging need inside him. It was raw and vicious, and it made him ache for things he knew he could never have.

Things that could only hurt him more. And he had been hurt enough to last ten thousand lifetimes.

He had to put her out of his thoughts.

But even as he stood there, the loneliness of his life settled down on him with a vengeance.

"You let your heart lead you far too often, boy. One day, it's going to lead you to ruin." He winced at his father's warning in his head. Neither of them had any idea at that time just how true those words would one day prove.

I am a Dark-Hunter.

That was what he needed to focus on. He was the only thing standing between Amanda and annihilation.

Desiderius was out there and he must stop him.

But what he really wanted to do was go downstairs, scoop Amanda up in his arms, and carry her back to his house where he could spend the entire night exploring every inch of her body with his lips, his hands. His tongue.

"I am such a fool," he snarled, forcing himself to dress in the clothes Julian had left for him.

He would think no more of her or of his past. He had a higher calling. One that couldn't be ignored.

He was a protector. And he would live and die as a protector, which meant that physical comforts such as a woman like Amanda were strictly off limits to him.

A few minutes later, dressed in Julian's jeans and a black V-neck sweater, he left the room with his leather coat over his arm, and went downstairs where Julian, Grace, Amanda, and the children were waiting.

Julian handed him a small paper sack.

"Gee," Kyrian said as he took it, "thanks, Dad. I promise to be a good boy and play nice with the other kids."

Julian laughed. "Smart-ass."

"Better than a dumb-ass." Kyrian sobered as he looked at Amanda and a burning wave of desire scorched him. What was it about her that made him unable to look at her without wanting to taste that mouth? Feel her warm body in his arms?

Kyrian cleared his throat. "Make sure she stays here until morning. The Daimons can't enter without an invitation."

"What about tomorrow night?" Grace asked.

"Desiderius should be dead by then."

Julian nodded.

Kyrian turned to leave, but before he could reach the door, Amanda stopped him with a gentle hand on his arm.

"Thank you," she said.

He inclined his head to her.

Leave. Because if he didn't, he just might yield to that demanding need inside him.

He looked past Amanda to Julian's wife. "It was nice meeting you, Grace."

"You too, Commander."

As he started out the door, Amanda caught him again and turned him about. Before he knew what she was doing, she kissed him on the cheek.

"You be careful," she whispered as she pulled away.

Stunned, he could do nothing more than blink. But what touched him most was the concern he saw in her crystal-blue eyes, the concern he felt in her heart. She really didn't want him hurt.

Desiderius is waiting.

The thought tore through his mind. He *had* to leave.

Yet walking away from her was the hardest thing he'd ever had to do.

"Have a nice life, Cupcake," he said to her.

"Cupcake?" Amanda asked in an offended tone.

He smiled. "After the 'buff stud in black leather' remark, I figured I owed you one." He patted her hand, then reluctantly removed it from his arm. "It's almost eight, you better go call your sister."

Kyrian let go of her hand and instantly felt the vacancy.

He exchanged a knowing look with Julian. This would be the last time they saw each other and they both knew it. "Good-bye, *adelfos.*"

"Good-bye, little brother," Julian said.

Kyrian turned around, opened the door, and made his solitary way to his car.

Once inside, he couldn't resist looking back. Though he

couldn't see Amanda, he could feel her on the other side of the door, staring after him.

He couldn't remember the last time anyone had been sorry to see him go. Nor could he recall ever feeling this insane need to keep a woman with him at any cost.

CHAPTER 5

After Kyrian left, Amanda called Tabitha and reassured her she was safe, then took a quick shower and borrowed a pair of leggings and a sweatshirt from Grace. She sat on the couch with a plate of spaghetti while Grace and the babies retired for the night.

Julian came from the kitchen and handed her a Coke, then took a seat in the armchair. "All right," he said. "Where shall I begin?"

She didn't even have to think about it. "The beginning. I want to know exactly what Dark-Hunters and Daimons are. Where did the Apollites come from? And exactly how are the three of them related?"

Julian laughed. "You cut right to the chase, don't you?" He turned his glass of iced tea around in his hands as he appeared to think about how best to answer her question. "At times like this, I wish Homer's *Kynigostaia* had survived."

"Cog-no-whatever that word is, is what?"

He laughed again, then took a drink of tea. "It was the record of the birth of the *Kynigstosi,* the Dark-Hunters, and could have answered most questions you have about them. It detailed the rise of the two races that once held dominion over the earth. The humans and Apollites."

Amanda nodded. "Okay, I know where humans come from, what about the Apollites?"

"Aeons ago, Apollo and Zeus were walking through Thebes

when all of a sudden Zeus declared the greatness of the human race. He called humans the 'earthly pinnacle of perfection.' Apollo scoffed and said there was a lot of improving to be done. He boasted that he could easily create a superior race. Zeus told him to prove it. So Apollo found a nymph who agreed to bear his children.

"In three days the first four Apollites were born. Three days after that, those children grew into adulthood, and three days later, they were ready to be rulers of the earth."

Amanda wiped her lips with her napkin. "So the Apollites are the children of Apollo. Gotcha. Now what makes some of them Daimons?"

"Would you wait? I'm the one telling this story," Julian said patiently in the voice she was sure he reserved for his college students. "Because the Apollites were so superior to humans in intellect, beauty, and strength, Zeus banished them to the island of Atlantis where he hoped they would stay peacefully. I don't know if you've ever read Plato's *Dialogues*—"

"No offense, but I spent my entire college career avoiding liberal arts courses."

Julian smiled. "Anyway, most of what Plato wrote about Atlantis is true. They were an aggressive race who wanted to dominate the earth, and ultimately Olympus, as well. Apollo didn't mind since he would become the supreme god should they win."

Amanda knew where this was headed. "I'll bet that made old Zeus happy."

"He was delighted," Julian said sarcastically. "But not half so much as the poor Greeks who were being hammered by the Apollites. Fed up with it, they realized they were fighting a lost cause. So they devised a scheme to seduce Apollo to their side. They chose the most beautiful woman ever born to them, Ryssa, to be his divine mistress."

"More beautiful than Helen of Troy?"

"This was a *long* time before Helen, and yes, accounts claimed she was by far the most beautiful woman ever born. Anyway, Apollo, being Apollo, couldn't resist her. He fell in love with her and she ultimately bore him a son. When the Apollite queen heard of this, she became enraged and sent out a team of assassins to kill mother and child. The queen told her men to make it appear as if a wild animal had killed them so that Apollo wouldn't retaliate against the Apollites."

Amanda whistled low as she guessed what happened after that. "Apollo found out."

"Yes, he did, and it got ugly. You see, Apollo is also the god of plagues. He destroyed Atlantis and would have destroyed every single Apollite as well had Artemis not stopped him."

"Why did she do that?"

"Because the Apollites are part of his flesh and blood. To destroy them would be to destroy him and the world as we know it."

"Oh," Amanda said, her eyes wide. "That's a big, bad thing. Glad she stopped him."

"So were the rest of the pantheon. But still, Apollo wanted vengeance. He banished the Apollites from the sun so that he would never again have to see one of them and be reminded of their treachery. Since they had made it appear as if a wild beast had killed Ryssa, he gave them animal characteristics. Fangs, honed senses—"

"What about their strength and speed?"

"They already had that, along with psychic abilities that Apollo couldn't take from them."

Amanda frowned at that. "I thought gods could do anything they wanted to. Isn't that the point of being a god?"

"Not always. They have laws and such they abide by, same as us. But in the case of psychic powers, once that channel is opened, it can never be closed. That's why Apollo didn't take his gift of foresight from Cassandra when she spurned him, but rather made it so that no one would believe her prophecies."

"Ah, that makes sense." Amanda took a drink of her Coke. "Okay, so the Apollites are psychic and strong, and can't come into contact with sunlight. What about drinking blood? Do they do that or not?"

"Yes, they drink blood, but only if it comes from another Apollite. In fact, because of Apollo's curse, they have to feed from each other every few days or they die."

"Ew," she said, wrinkling her nose. "That's nasty." She shivered at the thought of having to live that way. "Some of them do drink from humans, right?"

Julian hedged a bit. "Not exactly. If they turn Daimon, they will drain the blood from humans, but it's not the blood they're after so much as the human soul."

She arched a brow as a tingle went down her spine. Kyrian hadn't been joking about that aspect of them. Great. "Why do they need to steal our souls?"

"Apollites only live thrice nine years. On their twenty-seventh birthday, they die a very slow and painful death in which their bodies literally disintegrate into dust over a twenty-four-hour period."

This time she cringed visibly at the thought. "How horrible. I guess the moral of this story is not to tick off the god of plagues."

"Yeah," Julian said grimly. "To avoid their fate, most Apollites kill themselves the day before their birthday. Others decide to go Daimon. As Daimons they cheat their sentence by taking human souls into their bodies. So long as they maintain the soul, they can live. But the problem is the human soul can't live in an Apollite body and it starts to die almost as soon as they take it. As a result, the Daimons are forced to continue preying on humans every few weeks to sustain themselves."

Amanda couldn't imagine how horrible it must be for the people killed by the Apollites—to lose both their life and their soul. "What happens to the souls that die?"

"They're lost forever. That's why we have Dark-Hunters. Their job is to try and find the Daimons and free the souls before they expire."

"And they volunteer for this?"

"No, rather they're drafted."

Her frown deepened. "Drafted how?"

Julian took another drink of tea. His gaze fell to the floor and she saw a strange light in his eyes as if he were remembering something out of his own past. Something painful.

"When someone suffers a horrible injustice," he said, his tone low, "their soul makes a scream so loud that it resonates through the halls of Olympus. When Artemis hears it, she goes to the one who cried out and offers them a bargain. For a single Act of Vengeance against those who wronged them, they will swear allegiance to her and fight in her army against the Daimon predators."

Amanda breathed deeply as all the information swam in her head. "How do you know all this?"

Julian looked up and his gaze scorched her with its vivid intensity. "Because my soul made that sound the day my children died."

She swallowed at the hatred and pain she saw in his eyes. It was so raw, she hurt for him. "Did Artemis come to you and offer you the bargain?"

"Yes, and I refused her."

"Why?"

He looked away. "I needed vengeance against another god and I knew she couldn't allow that."

Amanda knew the story of Julian's entrapment inside the book all too well. But what interested her more was Kyrian. "Kyrian traded his soul for vengeance against his wife, didn't he?"

He nodded. "But don't judge him too harshly."

"I'm not," she said honestly. She didn't know what Kyrian had been through, but until she did, there was no way she would hold his decision over his head.

"Tell me, Julian, is there any way for Dark-Hunters to get their souls back?"

"Yes, but almost no one succeeds, and each test is unique to every Dark-Hunter."

"Which means you can't tell me how Kyrian might be freed."

"Which means *I* have no idea how he might be freed."

Amanda nodded until her thoughts went to another matter. "Do Dark-Hunters have to drink blood, too?"

"No. Since they began as humans, they don't *have* to. Plus, if they had to worry about finding blood, it would interfere with their ability to track the Daimons."

"Then why do they have fangs?"

"In order to effectively track and kill the Daimons, they were given the same animal characteristics. The fangs are part and parcel of what goes with it."

That made sense to her. "Is that why the sunlight is deadly to Dark-Hunters too?"

"Sort of, but in the case of the Dark-Hunters it's more a matter that they serve Artemis, the goddess of the moon, and are an anathema to Apollo."

"That doesn't seem fair."

"The gods seldom are."

Hours later, Kyrian sat in his car, damning his treacherous thoughts.

He could still see Amanda. Hear the sound of her soft, gentle voice. Feel her body against his and her soft breast in his hand.

It had been so long since he'd wanted a woman like this. He thought he'd banished that part of himself the night he'd become a Dark-Hunter.

As the centuries passed, he'd felt only an occasional stirring for a woman, but he'd learned to control it. Learned to bury it.

Now those long-forgotten needs had been awakened by the touch of a temptress who was lethal to his well-being. Thoughts of her distracted him. Tormented him.

He wanted her in a way that bordered on desperate.

Why? What was it about her that he craved so much? He knew nothing about her except that she had a great sense of humor and held incredible grace under fire.

And yet he yearned for her as he had for no other woman. Not even his wife.

It made no sense.

Turning his car off, he got out and entered his house. He tossed the keys on the kitchen counter and paused. The house was completely silent except for a light, clicking noise coming from upstairs.

Kyrian walked through the dark rooms and up the ornate, mahogany staircase until he was upstairs, outside his office. Light spilled out from the closed door, across the Persian runner.

Silently, he turned the knob and opened the door.

"Nick, what the hell are you doing here?"

Cursing loudly, his Squire jumped out of his swivel desk chair.

Kyrian had to stifle a laugh at the sight of a six-foot-four human ready to kill him. Nick's blue eyes snapped fire as his jaw, which was badly in need of a shave, twitched. Nick brushed his hand through his shoulder-length dark brown hair. "Jeez, Kyrian, would you learn to make some sound when you move? You scared the hell out of me."

Kyrian shrugged nonchalantly. "I thought you were going home early."

Nick righted the chair and returned to sit in it, then scooted it back under the desk. "I was, but I wanted to finish up the research into Desiderius for you."

Kyrian smiled. Nick Gautier might be a hotheaded, smart-mouthed pain in the ass most of the time, but he was always reliable. It was why Kyrian had chosen him to be a Squire and had initiated him into the realm of the Dark-Hunters. "Learn anything new?"

"You might say that. I've learned he's about two hundred and fifty years old."

Amazed, Kyrian arched a brow. To his knowledge, no Daimon had ever lived so long. "How is that possible?"

"I don't know. Dark-Hunters keep going after him and he keeps killing them. It seems your little Daimon friend likes to make you guys suffer." Nick returned to the computer. "There's nothing in Acheron's database about his exact modus operandi and when I talked to Ash earlier, he said he had no idea where Desiderius came from or who all of his targets have been. But we're looking into it."

Kyrian nodded.

"Oh, by the way," Nick said, glancing over his shoulder, "you look like hell."

"Obviously so, since everyone I've seen tonight has said that to me."

Nick smiled until he saw what Kyrian was wearing. "Why aren't you in your bad-ass, Daimon-killing clothes?"

Kyrian didn't feel like going there. "Speaking of, I need you to buy me a new leather coat today."

Suspicion clouded Nick's blue eyes. "Why?"

"The old one has a hole in the shoulder."

"Why?"

"I got attacked. Why else?"

Nick looked less than pleased by the news. "You okay?"

"Don't I look okay?"

"No, you look like hell."

There was no hiding from Nick. "I'm fine. Now, why don't you go on and sleep in one of the guest rooms? It's four o'clock in the morning."

"I will in a little bit. I want to finish this up first. Besides, I'm in the middle of finding out what Sundown did to piss off Ash."

Kyrian heard the "uh-oh" sound that alerted Nick he had a new instant message on the computer. "Tell Jess to lay off taunting Ash before he gets toasted."

Nick frowned. "Jess?"

"Sundown's real name is William Jessup Brady. I thought you knew that."

Nick laughed. "Hell no. But I know a few Squires who would pay me lots of money to learn that." His blue eyes turned speculative. "Rogue isn't Rogue's real name either, is it?"

"No. It's Christopher 'Kit' Baughy."

Nick made a delighted noise. "Now that one is really worth some serious cash."

"No," Kyrian corrected. "It's worth some serious ass-kicking if Rogue finds out you know it."

"Good point. I'll tuck that in my blackmail folder for when I need a Dark-Hunter favor."

Kyrian shook his head. The boy was incorrigible. "I'll see you tonight."

"Yeah, night."

Kyrian shut the door and headed down the long hallway to his bedroom. The large, lush room welcomed him with dark, peaceful colors that didn't hurt his light-sensitive eyes. Nick had lit the three candles in the small wall sconce and the dull glow flickered against the burgundy wallpaper.

This room was Kyrian's haven from the daylight.

He'd had the windows sealed and covered as soon as he bought the old neoclassical antebellum house. No Dark-Hunter ever willingly slept where daylight might accidentally find him.

Kyrian stripped off his clothes and lay down on the large bed he'd had since the fourteenth century, but his troubled thoughts spiraled through his mind.

Desiderius had eluded him and for the next few days, he would be out of Kyrian's reach.

Damn. But there was nothing to be done about it. Nothing, except to wait and be ready when Desiderius emerged. At least he had the comfort of knowing Desiderius would come after him first.

It would give him time to keep Amanda and Tabitha safe.

Amanda.

Her name hovered in his mind, along with a mental picture of her bright blue eyes. His groin tightened instantly against the cool silk sheets. He growled at the deep-seated ache that burned through him.

"She is not mine," he whispered.

And by all the gods on Olympus, she never would be, no matter how much the corner of his heart that remained might wish otherwise.

CHAPTER 6

Amanda moaned as she felt a warm, strong hand sliding over her bare stomach to her hip. Instinctively, she turned into the caress, her body instantly on fire with need.

Kyrian rolled her over, onto her back, and captured her lips with his. Her head swam at the contact. At the feel of all his strength and power. Never in her life had she felt anything better than his tongue on hers. Or his exquisitely hard body sinuously sliding against her.

She burned even more.

His kiss was fierce and hot, yet strangely tender. Closing her eyes, she breathed in the spicy scent of his skin and tasted the heat of his mouth.

She ran her hands through the silk of his golden hair, delighting in the way the waves curled around her fingers.

He pulled back and stared down at her with a powerful hunger that made her burn as those gorgeous muscles of his shoulders bunched and flexed under her hands. "I will have you," he said fiercely, his voice possessive.

"And I will have you," she said, smiling as she wrapped her legs around his narrow hips.

His devilish, fanged smile took her breath. With her cradled in his arms, he rolled onto his back and pulled her on top of him. Amanda bit her lip as she stared down at his handsome face while she felt his hard, masculine body between her thighs.

Needfully, she rubbed herself against his long, hard shaft. He growled in response to her caress.

He swept a famished look over her, then reached up and cupped her breasts in his warm hands. She covered his hands with her own as he squeezed them gently.

"I could stare at you all night," he whispered.

She could definitely relate because nothing would please her more than watching him move around naked for the rest of eternity.

That walk . . . that body . . .

It was more than a mere mortal woman could handle.

He lifted his hips, sending her forward.

Amanda caught herself with her arms. She leaned over him, her hair falling around her face to form a dark canopy over them.

"Now that's what I want." Kyrian reached up to cup her face and pulled her lips to his. His mouth teased hers as he gently sucked her bottom lip between his teeth.

Amanda moaned at the contact as he trailed his hand from her breast down her side and to the center of her body. "And this is what I want most." He plunged two fingers inside her.

Amanda hissed in pleasure as his fingers teased her relentlessly. In and out and around they swirled, making a hot fire to consume her.

He pulled back from her lips. "Now tell me what you want."

"You," she breathed.

"Then you shall have me." Kyrian moved his hands to her hips and pressed her body toward his erection.

Biting her lip expectantly, she longed to feel him inside her. To have his fullness stretch her body while they shared the most intimate of experiences.

She felt the tip of his shaft pressing against her core.

Just as she was sure he'd slide inside, the alarm clock went off.

Amanda came awake with a start.

Dazed, she glanced around the unfamiliar room and it took

a full minute before she remembered she was asleep in the nursery at Grace's house.

It had all been a dream?

But it had seemed so real. She swore she could still feel Kyrian's hands on her body, his breath against her neck.

"Oh, it's so not fair," she groused as she got out of bed and turned off the alarm clock. It had just been getting *really* good.

How could it have been just a dream? Just a dream of a mysterious stranger who hid pain behind sarcastic quips and of eyes so dark and deadly they captivated her?

Trying her best to forget the intensity of her subconscious, Amanda wrapped Grace's thick robe around her, then headed for the bathroom.

"Where did it come from?" Grace asked.

Amanda paused in the hallway as she heard Grace and Julian talking below.

"I assume Kyrian left it," Julian said.

Yawning, Amanda went downstairs and found the two of them in the living room surrounded by shopping bags and boxes. Julian was already dressed for work in a pair of khakis and a sweater. Grace wore a blue maternity nightgown while Niklos pulled and shredded paper from a sack beside her.

"What's all this?" Amanda asked.

Julian shrugged.

"You're right," Grace said as she found a note in one bag. "They're from Kyrian." She read the note and laughed. "All it says is, 'Thanks for the Band-Aid.' " She handed the note to Julian.

Julian let out an exaggerated breath as he read the note. "It was customary in our time to bring gifts whenever you visited a friend. But I mean, damn, we didn't leave this many." He ran a hand through his hair as he surveyed the mountain of gifts. "Kyrian was always generous, but . . . damn," he repeated. "I guess he came back last night and dropped them off while we were sleeping."

Amanda was amazed. It looked like Christmas . . . at the Rockefellers'. She watched as Grace pulled out dozens of toys for the twins. Dolls for Vanessa, building blocks for Niklos. A train and a toy horse.

Grace pulled a small box out of one bag. "This one's for you," she said, handing it to Julian.

Julian opened the box, then paled.

Grace looked over and gasped. "It's your general's ring." They exchanged a stunned look.

"How did he get it?" Grace asked.

Amanda edged closer to take a look at the ring. Like Kyrian's, it had a sword of diamonds and emerald laurel leaves against a deep ruby background. "It looks like the one Kyrian wears. Except his has a crown on it."

Julian nodded. "His is marked with a royal seal while mine is strictly military."

Confused, Amanda looked up at him. "Royal?"

"Kyrian was a prince," he said simply. "Sole heir to the throne of Thrace."

Amanda's mouth dropped. "The Romans crucified an heir? I didn't think they could do that."

Julian's jaw ticced. "Technically, they couldn't, but Kyrian's father disowned him the day he married Theone."

"Why?" Amanda asked.

"She was a *hetaira*." He saw the bemused scowl on her face and added, "They were lower-class women who were trained to be entertainers and companions for wealthy men."

"Ah," she said, easily seeing how that could make his family angry. "Was he looking for a companion when he met her?"

Julian shook his head. "Kyrian met her at a friend's party and was enchanted by her. He swore it was love at first sight. All of us tried to tell him she was only after his wealth, but he refused to listen."

Julian laughed bitterly. "He did that a lot back then. His father adored him, but when Alkis found out Kyrian had broken his engagement to the Macedonian princess so that he could marry Theone, he was incensed. Alkis told him that a king couldn't rule with a whore by his side. They argued, and finally, Kyrian rode out of his father's palace, straight to

Theone and married her within the hour. When Alkis found out, he told Kyrian he was dead to him."

Her chest tightened at his words as sympathetic pain sliced through her heart. "So, he gave up everything for her?"

Julian nodded grimly. "The worst part is, Kyrian was never unfaithful to her. Neither one of you really appreciates what an accomplishment that was. In our day, there was no such thing as monogamy. It was completely unheard of for a man to be faithful to his wife, especially one of Kyrian's heritage and wealth. But once Kyrian married Theone, he never wanted anyone else. Never even looked at another woman."

Julian's eyes flashed angrily. "He really did live and die for her."

Amanda's heart ached for Kyrian. The pain he must still have over it.

Grace handed Amanda three bags that held gift-wrapped boxes. "These are for you."

Amanda opened the largest box to find a thickly woven designer coatdress. She ran her hand over the soft, navy blue silk. She'd never felt anything like it. Looking in the bags, she found shoes, and other boxes marked with the Victoria's Secret logo. Blushing, she didn't dare open those around Julian and Grace. Not unless she wanted to die of embarrassment.

"How did he know my size?" she asked as she checked the tags on the dress.

Julian shrugged.

Amanda paused as she found a note addressed to her. The handwriting was elegant and crisp.

Sorry about your sweater. Thanks for being such a good sport.

—Hunter

Amanda smiled, even though a tiny part of her was hurt by the fact he still refused to use his real name with her. No doubt it was his way of keeping a distance between them.

So be it. He had a right to his privacy. A right to live his dangerous immortal life without any kind of close entangle-ments with humans. If he wanted to remain Hunter to her, she would respect that.

Still, after all they had gone through last night . . .

In her heart, it didn't matter what name he used. She knew the truth of him.

Gathering her gifts, she headed back up the stairs to get ready for work, but what she really wanted to do was thank Hunter for his kindness.

After her shower, Amanda opened all her gifts to find a trea-sure of naughty lingerie. Hunter had bought her blue silk stockings with a matching garter belt. She'd never before owned or worn one, and it took her several minutes to figure out how to operate it. A matching silk bra and thong com-pleted the outfit.

"Hmm . . ." For a man wanting to keep his distance, he certainly made some very personal choices for her. But then, he was nothing if not an enigma.

Amanda bit her lip as she reached for her dress. She felt so incredibly feminine and soft wearing her new lingerie, and a tiny shiver went up her spine as she thought about the fact that Hunter's hands had touched them.

It was incredibly erotic knowing his hand had probably traced the delicate lace of the thong that now rested intimately between her thighs. That his hand had touched inside the cup that cradled her breast.

How she wished to have him there to undress her. To touch her as intimately as the garments did.

She drew her breath in sharply between her teeth as she imagined the dark, hooded look on his face he would have as he took her into his arms and made love to her. Her breasts tingled and swelled at the very thought of it.

She picked up the dress from the bed and held it against her. For the merest instant, she thought she caught a whiff of Hunter's exotic scent. It sent stabs of desire through her.

As she dressed, the silk of the dress slid against her skin, reminding her of her dream. The feel of Hunter's hands on her body.

Oh, how she wished he were here. How she wished she could watch him unbutton her dress to discover the woman beneath it. But it would never happen. Kyrian was gone forever back to his dangerous life.

Her stabs of desire ended instantly, and were replaced by a profound pain in her heart. A pain that made no sense to her and yet it was there. Aching. Wanting. Needing.

Sighing, Amanda slid the shoes on and made her way downstairs where Julian was waiting to take her to work.

"I am so sorry about you and Cliff."

Amanda looked up from her desk and counted to ten. Slowly. If one more person said that to her, she was going to go berserk, head down to Cliff's office, and carve him into little, bloody Cliff-kabob pieces.

He had told everyone in the office about their breakup and had arrogantly said she was too torn up by it to come in yesterday.

She could kill him!

"I'm fine, Tammy," she said to their office manager with a forced smile.

"That's it," Tammy said. "You keep your spirits up."

Amanda curled her lip as Tammy left. At least the day was over. Now she could go home and . . .

And dream of the tall, handsome man she'd never see again.

Why did that hurt more than the fact Cliff had broken up with her?

What was it about Hunter that made her miss him so . . . ?

But she knew. He was gorgeous and smart and heroic. He was mysterious and lethal. Better yet, he made her heart pound every time he flashed that dazzling smile at her.

And he was gone forever.

Depressed, she prepared to leave.

After putting her files in her briefcase, Amanda headed out of her office, to the elevator, and pushed the button to the lobby. She didn't want to keep Grace waiting outside with the twins. Besides, she was tired of the office.

This had been the longest day of her life.

Why had she ever wanted to be an accountant, anyway? Selena was right, her life was mind-shatteringly boring.

When the doors to the elevator opened to the glass-enclosed lobby, she stepped out and looked around. Even though it was dark outside, the parking-lot lights were so bright, she could tell Grace wasn't there yet. Damn! She was more than ready to go home.

Irritated, Amanda went to stand by the door.

As she shifted her briefcase, Cliff came out of the next elevator, surrounded by his friends.

Great, just great. Her day kept getting better and better.

Spotting her alone, Cliff preened like a peacock as he approached her. "Is something wrong?" he asked as he stopped by her side.

"No. My ride isn't here yet," she said curtly.

"Well, if you need a ride home . . ."

"I don't need anything from you, okay?" She headed out the doors to wait in the dark cold. Better to freeze in the winter chill than spend another minute around the last man on earth she wanted to see.

Cliff pulled her to a stop outside the building. The streetlights glinted dimly against his dark blond hair. "Look, Mandy, there's no reason why we can't be friends."

"Don't you dare be magnanimous about this after the stunt you pulled today. Who do you think you are, telling everyone about my family?"

"Oh, c'mon, Mandy—"

"Stop calling me Mandy when you know how much I hate it."

He looked over his shoulder and she realized half the office was standing there, listening. "Look, I'm not the one who had to stay home yesterday because I was so emotionally distraught over Saturday night."

Her anger ignited. Emotionally distraught? Her?

Over *him*?

Amanda took a good look at him. And for the first time, she realized just what a weasel he was.

"Excuse me, but I wasn't home yesterday, either. In fact, you know where I was? I spent the entire day in the arms of a gorgeous blond god. I am so over you."

He snorted. "See, I knew it was just a matter of time before your family rubbed off on you. You're crazy like the rest of them. I bet you show up tomorrow decked out in black leather and talking about staking vampires."

Never in her life had she wanted to slap anyone as much as she did him right then.

Why had she ever thought they were compatible? He was vile and rude. Worse, he was judgmental! Tabitha might be a nutcase, but she was her sister and no one not related to them had better insult her!

Suddenly, every flaw she had dismissed about Cliff came to the forefront. And to think she had spent a year of her life trying to please this jerk.

She was an idiot! And stupid, dumb . . .

Amanda felt the hairs on the back of her neck rise an instant before she heard the revving noise of a finely tuned engine in the distance.

Cliff turned his head toward the street and gaped.

She looked to see what had captured his attention and froze at the sight of a sleek black Lamborghini heading up the drive and stopping at the curb in front of them.

A smile broke across her face.

Surely not . . .

Her heart pounded as the door lifted and Hunter got out. Dressed in faded jeans, a gray and black V-neck sweater, and a black leather jacket, the man was drop-dead stunning.

And that deadly swagger of his made her weak in the knees.

"Oh baby," she heard Tammy whisper as he came around the car.

Hunter stopped in front of Amanda and raked a hungry look over her body. "Hi, luscious," he said in that deep, evocative voice. "Sorry I'm late."

Before Amanda knew what he was doing, he pulled her

into his arms and gave her a sizzling hot kiss. Her body burned in response to his tongue tasting hers as he fisted his hands against her back. Then, he dipped down and picked her up in his arms.

"Hunter!" she gasped as he carried her effortlessly toward the car.

He gave her that devilish tight-lipped smile. His midnight eyes were warm and alive with humor and hunger.

With the toe of his boot, he opened the passenger-side door and set her inside. He retrieved her briefcase and purse from the sidewalk where she had dropped them and handed them to her. Then, he turned and gave a knowing smile to Cliff. "You really have to love a woman who lives to see you naked."

The look on Cliff's face was priceless as Hunter closed the door, then gracefully walked over to the driver's side of the Lamborghini. In one fluid movement, he got inside the car and they were headed out of the lot.

A thousand emotions tore through Amanda. Gratitude, laughter, but most of all, happiness at seeing him again, especially after both Julian and her mind had convinced her that she never would.

She couldn't believe what he'd just done for her.

"What are you doing here?" she asked as he headed out of the parking lot.

"You have made me insane all day long," he breathed. "I could sense you in turmoil and pain, but I didn't know why. So, I called Grace and found out she was supposed to pick you up after work."

"You still haven't told me why you're here."

"I had to make sure you were okay."

"Why?"

"I don't know. I just did."

Warmed by his words, she toyed with her seat belt. "Thank you for the clothes. And for what you did back there with Cliff."

"My pleasure."

Right now, it was all she could do not to reach out and touch him. To kiss her scrumptious champion.

Hunter shifted gears and headed away from the business district. "I just have one question, why would a woman like you ever want to marry something like him?"

Amanda arched a brow. "How did you—"

"I'm psychic, remember? Your true feelings for the 'imbecilic jerk' are all over your mind at the moment."

She cringed and wished she could shield her thoughts.

"I heard that, too," Hunter teased, making her really wonder if he had.

"Is there anything I can do about your peeping into my head all the time? It really makes me uncomfortable."

"If you like, I could relinquish that power over you."

"Really? You can just drop a power anytime you want to?"

He snorted. "Not exactly. The only power I can relinquish is the ability to see into someone's thoughts."

"Once relinquished, can you get it back?"

"Yes, but it's not easy."

"Then banish it, buster."

Kyrian laughed and tried to focus on the road, but all he really noticed was the slit in her dress that bared a goodly portion of her silk-clad thigh. Worse, he knew what she wore beneath that dress. It was another image that had haunted him all day as he had tried to sleep.

The thought of her lush curves cupped by the garter belt and thong . . . It made his mouth water. And all he wanted to do was slide his hand underneath that well-crafted hem until he felt the tiny strip of silk that shielded her most private place. Oh yeah, he could imagine moving it aside with his fingers until he had full access to her.

Or ripping that tiny, frail piece of silk away from her hips and burying himself deep inside her while her silk-clad legs wrapped around his.

Hunter shifted in his seat and remembered too late he should have bought himself a pair of baggy pants.

Touching her would be paradise.

If only paradise were a possibility for a creature like him.

He tightened his grip on the gear shift as the thought tore through him.

"No woman will ever love you for anything other than your money. Mark my words, boy. Men like us will never have that one basic need. The best you can hope for is a child to love you."

His breath caught as the repressed memory flooded back to him with total clarity. And hard on its heels came the final words he'd spoken to his father.

"How could I ever love a heartless man like you? You mean nothing to me, old man. And you never will."

The pain of it stole his breath. Words he'd spoken in anger that could never be retracted.

How could he have said them to the one person he had loved and respected most?

"So," Amanda asked, distracting him, "what happened with Desiderius last night? Did you get him?"

He shook his head to clear his thoughts and focus on the here and now. "He went into a bolt-hole after our confrontation."

"A what?"

"A bolt-hole. Sanctuary for the Daimons," he explained. "They're astral openings between dimensions. The Daimons can go in for a few days, but when the door opens, they have to leave again."

Amanda was aghast at what he was describing. How could that be possible? "I can't believe the powers that be would give the Daimons such a haven to escape justice."

"They didn't. The Daimons discovered bolt-holes on their own." He flashed a wicked smile at her. "But I'm not complaining. It makes my job infinitely more interesting."

"Well, just so long as you're not bored," she said sarcastically. "I would really hate for your job to *ever* get dull."

He cast a glance at her that set her on fire. "Chère, I have a feeling being bored around you would be an impossibility."

His words struck a painful nerve in her. "You're the only one who feels that way," she said as she remembered her conversation with Selena. "I've been told I tip the scales way into Boredom City."

He stopped at a light and gave her a penetrating stare. "I don't understand that comment since I've been nothing but amazed by you ever since the moment I woke up to you calling me 'Mr. yummy leather guy.' "

Her face on fire, she laughed at the memory.

"Besides," Hunter continued, "you can't blame people for saying that when you're the one who puts up the shield."

"Excuse me?"

He shifted into first and headed down the street. "It's true. You bury the part of you that craves excitement underneath a career guaranteed to one day replace tranquilizers. You wear drab colors and turtlenecks that hide the passion you keep harnessed."

"I do not," she said, bristling with indignation. "You hardly know me well enough to say that. And you've only seen me in one outfit of *my* choosing."

"True, but I know your type."

"Yeah, right." She mumbled her denial.

"And I've sampled your passion firsthand."

Amanda's face flamed even more at that one. She couldn't deny the truth. However, it didn't mean she had to like the way he seemed to see straight into her heart.

"I think you're afraid of that other half of yourself," he continued. "You remind me of the ancient Greek nymph Lyta. She was two halves of one person. The two pieces warred with each other, making her—and anyone who knew her—miserable until one day a Greek soldier came upon the two halves and joined them. From that day forward she lived in harmony with herself and others."

"What, are you saying I make you miserable?"

He laughed. "No. I find you amusing, but I think you'd be much happier if you would accept your true nature and not try so hard to fight it."

"This coming from a vampire who doesn't drink human blood? Tell me, aren't you fighting your nature, too?"

He smiled at that. "Perhaps you're right. Perhaps I too

would be happier if I turned the wild beast inside me loose."
He glanced askance at her. "I wonder if you could handle that
part of me."

"Meaning?"

He didn't answer. "Where do I need to take you? Julian's,
your mother's, or your place?"

"Well, since you're headed toward my house, I suppose
there. I live a few blocks over from Tulane."

Kyrian did his best to stay focused on traffic, but over and
over he kept seeing flashes of his dream in his mind. Damn,
he couldn't remember the last time he'd had such a vivid
dream. He'd awakened early in the morning, hard and aching
for her. And he could have sworn her scent was on his pillows.
His skin.

He'd spent the rest of the day trying his best to sleep, but
it had been fitful at best. He wanted this woman with a need
so profound that it made him shake just to be near her.

Never in his life had he wanted anything more than to do
what she suggested: to turn himself loose on her and devour
her.

If only he dared.

As soon as it had turned dark, he had gone hunting for *her*.

It was the first time in his Dark-Hunter life that he'd pur-
sued a human.

"You know," she said, that soft, lilting drawl sending an
electric charge down his spine straight to his groin. "You
didn't have to pick me up. You could have just called the
office and checked on me."

Kyrian cleared his throat as he felt heat creep over his face.
Dammit! She had him blushing? He hadn't blushed since he
was a callow youth over two thousand one hundred and sixty
years ago. "I didn't have your number."

"You could have gotten it from any phonebook or information. And of course, Grace has it."

He felt her smiling at him.

"Heck, you could have probably picked it right out of my
brain." Her look turned devilish, suspicious. "I bet you just
wanted to see me again, didn't you?"

"No," he said a little too quickly.

"Umm-hmmm." Disbelief echoed in her tone. "Why don't I believe that?"

"Probably because I never could lie worth a damn."

They both laughed.

Amanda watched him while he drove. He had his small round sunglasses back on and looked more dashing than any man had a right to.

"Tell me something?" she asked.

He arched a brow expectantly, but didn't say anything as he kept looking straight ahead.

"Do you really like being a Dark-Hunter?"

He glanced at her and smiled a smile that actually showed his fangs. "Tell me how many jobs are out there where you get to play hero every night. My pay is astronomical and I live forever. What is there *not* to love about this job?"

"But don't you ever get lonely?" she asked.

"You can be in a crowd and be lonely."

"I guess so. Still . . ."

He looked sideways at her. "Why don't you ask me what you want to know?"

"Since you can read my thoughts why don't you answer it?"

His smile widened hungrily like a wolf that had just found its next meal. "Yes, sweeting, I think you're incredibly sexy. And I would love nothing more than to take you back to my place and make your toes curl."

Heat consumed her face. "I hate the way you do that. You're worse than Tabitha. Good Lord, do all Dark-Hunters have that kind of power?"

"No, baby, just me." Then he added, "Each one of us has our own set of abilities."

"I have to say, I really wish you had a different one."

"All right, love. For you, it's gone. No more mind reading."

As Amanda watched him, she realized that even though he was blustery and macho, there was still a decent heart underneath it all. "You're a good man, Hunter."

"I'm a good vampire, you mean."

"Yes, but you don't suck blood."

One corner of his mouth quirked at that. "So Julian told you that, did he?"

"Yes, he did. He said Dark-Hunters, unlike Apollites, were spared that part of Apollo's curse."

"For the record," he said ominously, "we don't need blood to live, but there are some Dark-Hunters, called Feeders, who do drink it." He shifted gears. "I think you and Julian spent entirely too much time talking last night."

"Perhaps." But then Hunter had become her favorite topic. She'd kept poor Julian awake half the night asking things about Kyrian and the Dark-Hunters.

"Is it true Daimons only live twenty-seven years?"

He nodded. "That's why they're so dangerous. Most Apollites will do *anything* to buy themselves another day."

Which was why the Dark-Hunters, according to Julian, were soulless. It kept the Daimons from taking the most powerful souls of all. And the more powerful the soul the Daimons took, the longer they lived on borrowed time.

"Someone like you," Kyrian said, "is prime Daimon bait. When they take your soul, they take all your psychic powers with it."

Amanda scoffed. "I have no powers."

"Whatever lie makes you happy."

"It's not a lie," she said defensively. "I have no abilities whatsoever. At least not unless it involves crunching numbers."

"All right, number-cruncher, I believe you."

His words might say that, but his voice didn't. Narrowing her eyes on the stubborn man, she directed him toward her house.

As they drew near, she saw clouds of gray billowing smoke against the night sky. "Is that a house fire?"

"Yeah, it looks like a big one, too."

"Oh no," she gasped as they got closer and she saw her house on fire.

But Hunter didn't stop there, he went down the street to Tabitha's where another blaze was roaring.

Tears filled her eyes as she fumbled for the door latch. "Tabitha!" she screamed, terrified her sister might be inside the house.

Faster than she could blink, Hunter got out of the car and ran into the burning house.

Her heart hammering, Amanda scrambled from the car.

After kicking off her high heels, she ran to the porch, but didn't dare try to run inside with her bare feet.

"Hunter?" she called, trying to see through the flames. "Tabitha!"

Please be okay, Tabby. Please still be at work!

As she waited for sight or sound of Kyrian, a motorcycle flew through Tabitha's yard and slid to a screeching halt next to the walkway.

Moving like lightning, a man pulled his black helmet off, tossed it to the ground, then ran toward the house so fast she couldn't even make out his features. He went around back at the same time Hunter came out the door, carrying Tabitha's roommate.

Amanda followed Hunter to the lawn where he laid Allison down on the grass.

"Tabitha isn't in there," he said. He inclined his head to Allison's unconscious body. "She inhaled a lot of smoke." He scanned the street around them; several neighbors stood nearby, but none of them came forward. "Where's the damned ambulance?" he snarled.

Terminator came running up to them. He licked Allison's face, then Amanda.

Patting the white and black dog, Amanda looked up to see the man who had arrived on the motorcycle. He was every bit as handsome as Hunter, yet there was something ethereal about him. Mystical.

His blond hair was cut short except for two long braids that fell from his left temple down to the middle of his chest. He wore a zipped-up black motorcycle jacket that had red and gold Celtic scrollwork painted all over it and a thick gold torc around his neck.

He knelt beside Hunter and passed his gloved hand over Allison's body about an inch above it.

"Her lungs are singed," he said quietly.

"Can you help her, Talon?" Hunter asked.

Talon nodded. He removed his gloves, then placed his hands against Allison's ribs.

After a few seconds, Allison's breathing became slow and steady.

Talon met Amanda's gaze. She shivered as she saw that he had the exact same eyes as Kyrian.

There was something very unsettling and strange about this new Dark-Hunter.

He was stillness, she realized. Like some bottomless pond. There was a calm serenity to him that was both beguiling and frightening.

And it dawned on her that something really bad must be going on. Why else would another Dark-Hunter be here at the same time?

"Desiderius set the fires, didn't he?" she asked.

Both of the men shook their heads no.

Hunter looked to Talon. "Your target?"

"My guess would be they've teamed up. Mine is trying to flush you out while yours is in hiding."

At last the fire crews arrived. An EMT team took over with Allison while the three of them moved to stand to the side.

"Well, damn, Talon, this is new," Hunter said as he raked a hand through his hair. "It leaves us completely vulnerable."

Talon inclined his head toward Tabitha's burning house. "Yeah, I know. It sucks that they can combine their strengths while we can't."

"Why can't you?" Amanda asked.

Talon turned to Hunter. "How much does she know?"

"A lot more than she should."

"Can we trust her?"

Hunter looked askance at her; the uncertainty in his eyes hurt her. She would never do anything to harm the man who had saved her life.

"I had a voice mail from Acheron this evening that said to give her whatever information she wanted."

Talon frowned. "That doesn't sound like T-Rex to me."

"You know, Acheron really hates when you call him that."

"Which is exactly why I use it. And I find it hard to believe T-Rex would give her carte blanche."

"Yeah, but you know Acheron. There must be a purpose to it, and in his own, decrepit time, I'm sure he'll get around to enlightening us."

"So tell me, then," she prompted. "Why can't you guys combine your strengths?"

"It's to keep us from cockfighting or using our powers against the humans or gods," Hunter explained. "As a result, as soon as we get together, we start draining each other's powers and dampening them. The longer we stay together, the weaker we become."

Amanda gaped. "That's not fair."

"Life seldom is," Talon said.

Hunter turned to Talon. "Any idea where your target is?"

"I lost the tracking signal here. So I'm guessing there must be a bolt-hole close by."

"Great," Hunter said, "just friggin' great."

Talon concurred. "I'm thinking we should call in Kattalakis to flush both of them out."

"No," Hunter said quickly. "This isn't the typical Daimon we're dealing with and something tells me siccing a Were-Hunter on Desiderius would be like tossing a grenade on a keg of dynamite. The last thing we need is for him to grab one of their souls. Can you imagine the damage he could wreak with that?"

"Were-Hunter?" Amanda asked. "Is that like a werewolf?"

Talon cleared his throat. "Not exactly."

"We protect the night," Hunter said. "Hence Dark-Hunter. And they . . ." He gave Talon a searching gaze.

Talon took up the explanation. "Were-Hunters are . . ." He looked to Hunter as if seeking the right word, too.

Hunter shrugged. "Sorcerers?"

"Works for me," Talon said.

Well, it didn't work for Amanda, who had no idea what they were talking about. "Sorcerers? Like Merlin?"

"Oh hell," Talon muttered. He locked gazes with Hunter. "You sure about what T-Rex said?"

Hunter unclipped his cell phone from his belt, scrolled through his saved messages, then handed it to Talon. "Listen for yourself."

Talon did. After a brief wait, he handed the phone back to Hunter and faced Amanda. "All right, then, let's explain it this way. There are four basic kinds of Daimons or vampires: bloodsuckers, soulsuckers, energy/dreamsuckers, and slayers."

Amanda nodded. That made sense to her. "You guys are the slayers."

Hunter snorted. "What? Were you born with a remote in your hand?"

"No," Talon corrected her while ignoring Hunter's sarcasm. "Slayers are the nastiest of all the vampires because they don't want anything from their victims. They merely destroy for the sake of destruction. Not to mention, they are the strongest of the vampires."

A shiver went down her spine. "Is Desiderius one of them?"

Hunter shook his head negatively while Talon continued to explain it to her. "To protect the world as we know it, there were three races of hunters created to police and destroy the Daimons. We are called 'the Pyramid of Protection.' Dark-Hunters pursue those who feed on human blood and souls. Dream-Hunters go after the energy- and dreamsuckers, and Were-Hunters stalk the slayers."

Amanda frowned. "I guess what I don't understand is why you don't have one group that does it all."

"Because we can't," Hunter said. "If one person or group was strong enough to walk all four realms of existence, they would be able to enslave the world. Nothing and no one could stop them. And the gods would be greatly pissed."

"What four realms?"

"Time, space, earth, and dreams," Talon said.

Amanda let out a deep breath. "Okay, now that is scary. Some of you guys walk through time?"

"And space and dreams."

"Ah." Amanda nodded. "So Rod Serling was a Were-Hunter?"

They didn't look particularly amused.

"Okay," she said. "Bad attempt at humor. I'm just trying to figure all this out."

Talon laughed. "Don't. I've been trying to understand it all for over fifteen-hundred years and I'm still learning things."

Hunter grimaced. "You? Every time I think I have it pegged someone like Desiderius comes along and completely alters the rules."

"True," Talon said with a short laugh. He rolled his shoulders. "And speaking of scary things, I need to leave. My guides are fading even as we speak."

Hunter faked a shiver. "I hate when you commune with the dead in front of me."

Talon gave him a droll, unamused stare. "Are you the asshole who sent the 'I See Dead People' T-shirt to me?"

Hunter laughed. "That would be Wulf. I thought he was joking about it."

"He wasn't. I got it three days ago. I am going to get him back for that." Talon looked at Amanda. "Keep her close."

Hunter nodded.

Talon glanced over his shoulder at one of the fire crews. "Is it just me or is the Apollite fireman behind me paying a little too much attention to us?"

"Yeah, I caught that, too. I think I should question him."

"Not tonight. Secure her first. I'll interrogate the Apollite."

Hunter cocked a brow in amusement. "Don't you trust me?"

"Hell, no, Greek. I know you too well." Talon headed back to his black Harley-Davidson and retrieved his helmet from the ground. "I'll e-mail you later with the results."

"E-mail?" Amanda asked. "Should I ask?"

Hunter shrugged. "We've come a long way. We used to pay runners to carry information between us."

"Ah," she said, then she noticed a solitary man standing across the street in the shadows. Instead of watching the fire, he seemed more concerned with Hunter and Talon.

Talon rejoined them.

"Question," Amanda whispered as she studied the gorgeous blond shadow across the street. "Are all Daimons blond?"

"Yes," Hunter said. "As are all Apollites."

"Then how can you tell an Apollite from a Daimon?"

"Unless they have us blocked, we can sense them," Talon said. "But the only way for a human to tell is that when an Apollite crosses over, a black tattoo-looking symbol appears in the center of their chest where the human souls gather."

"Ah," she said again, still watching the man who was watching them. "Tell me, do you think your targets are purposely putting the two of you together to drain your powers before they strike?"

The men gave her a puzzled look.

"Why do you say that?" Talon asked.

"Well, I'm no expert, but that guy behind you looks like a Daimon to me."

The words barely left her lips before a flash of light hit Talon straight in his back and sent him to the ground.

Hunter cursed as he shoved her toward the car. He leapt over it, and ran straight at the Daimon who had attacked Talon. The two of them locked arms and fell to the ground in a fierce struggle.

Amanda made her way to Talon. He was covered in blood. Her heart pounding, she tried to help him up, but before she could another Daimon attacked them.

Reacting on instinct, she grabbed the Celtic dagger from Talon's belt and caught the Daimon across the chest. The man hissed, then shrank back.

Talon came to his feet. Grabbing his dagger from her hand, he sent it flying into the back of the Daimon as he fled. The Daimon vanished in a flash of light.

Hunter came out of the darkness, his breathing labored as he retrieved Talon's dagger from the ground, then returned it to the Celt. "You all right?" he asked.

Talon grimaced as he flexed his arm. "I've bled worse. You?"

"I've bled worse."

Talon gave a curt nod to Amanda. "Thanks for the assist." He rubbed the back of his shoulder with his hand. "Secure your woman. We'll talk later."

"All right."

Amanda grimaced as she watched Talon sling his long leg over his motorcycle. His movements were slow and steady, and that alone was proof of the pain he must be in. "Is he really okay?"

"We heal fast. Most wounds vanish in less than twenty-four hours."

A siren sounded in the distance. Kyrian looked down the street where the lights were flashing. "The police are coming. We need to head out before they arrive."

"What about Allison?"

"She'll be all right once she wakes. Talon's touch can heal anything except death."

"And Terminator?"

Hunter gave a whistle and opened the door to his car. He put Terminator in her scat. "It'll be a tight squeeze, but I think we can manage."

Amanda got in the car and adjusted Terminator in her lap as best she could. It wasn't until Hunter sat next to her that she saw the blood on his hand and arm. "You're hurt?"

"Flesh wound on my forearm. It'll heal."

"Jeez, Hunter. How can you stand doing what you do?"

He laughed. "I've done it for so long, I honestly don't remember what life was like before I died."

His words sent a chill over her. "You're not really dead, are you? I'm kind of fuzzy on all this. You have a heartbeat and you bleed, not to mention that your skin is warm to the touch. That implies life, right?"

He started the car and headed down the street away from the police. "Yes and no. Once a human dies, Artemis uses her powers to trap our souls. After the soul is contained, we are brought back to life."

"How?"

"Since I was dead at the time, I have no idea. All I know

is that I felt everything go black, then I woke up with powers and strengths I never knew before."

Amanda thought about that as she stroked Terminator's ears and held the dog's head against her stomach to keep him quiet. "Does that mean you can die again?"

"Yes."

"Then what happens?"

Hunter took a deep breath. "If we die before we reclaim our souls, we walk the earth eternally without powers. We are trapped as Shades in our corporeal bodies, but we have no real substance, which means we can't touch anything or be heard by anyone other than the Oracles. We crave food and water, but have no way to appease the hunger or thirst. It's a short trip from partial damnation to a total damnation."

Amanda gaped at the horror of such a fate. She couldn't stand the thought of something like that happening to him. "Does that happen even if a Daimon kills you?"

He nodded.

"That's not fair."

He glanced over at her. "What kind of life have you lived, little one, that everything seems to be a question of fair and unfair? Life and death just are. Fair has nothing to do with it."

There was something very telling about that statement.

Just how many times had he suffered injustice to feel that way?

That thought was quickly followed by another. "Julian said you can get your soul back."

"In theory, yes."

"In theory?" she asked as Terminator lifted his head to look at Hunter.

Hunter reached over and patted the dog's head until Terminator settled down again.

"We are given an out clause, but in the last two thousand years, only a handful have succeeded. Most of the ones who tried ended up as Shades."

Amanda frowned. How horrible. By his tone she could tell

Hunter had resigned himself to the fact he would never even attempt it. Why?

"What would you have to do to get your soul back?"

He shrugged. "I don't know. None of us do since the path to redemption is different for each Dark-Hunter. All I know is that when the moment of truth comes, the Dark-Hunter is either set free or damned for eternity."

What Kyrian didn't tell her was that in order to be free, the Dark-Hunter must place his or her soul into the hands of someone who loved them. Having been burned so severely by his wife, he would never again trust anyone with his body or heart, never mind his immortal soul.

He had seen too many of his brethren trapped as Shades because the person they trusted had failed the test.

And in the back of his mind was the knowledge that no woman could ever love him. Not even a tiny bit. Let alone love him enough to set him free.

"Why did you agree to this life?" she asked.

He arched a brow. "I told you, I have unlimited income and immortality. What's not to like?"

Still, Amanda didn't buy that. It was too easy and he didn't seem so superficial. "You just don't seem the greedy sort to me."

"No?"

"No. You're more grounded than that. More generous. Greedy people don't leave the kind of thoughtful gifts you left for Julian and his family." She saw his jaw flex and she knew she'd pegged him perfectly. "How did you get his ring back, anyway? Julian said he had sold it a few years ago."

Hunter remained so quiet that she didn't think he would answer. Finally he spoke. "I saved a man who was wearing it about a year ago from a Daimon attack. I couldn't believe my eyes when I saw it. I offered to buy it from him, but he let me have it for saving him."

Amanda narrowed her eyes on him, wishing she could see into him the way he was able to see into her. "Why did you want it?"

A veil fell over his face and she could tell just how much the topic bothered him.

"Well?" she prompted when it became evident he wouldn't answer.

"What do you want me to say?" he asked, his voice sharp and moody. "That I had a moment of weakness when I saw it? That for an instant I felt the pang of being homesick? Yeah, I did. There, you now know the Dark-Hunter who has no soul has a heart. Are you happy?"

"I already knew you had a heart."

He stopped at a red light and looked at her. A fierce frown creased his brow as if he were trying to figure her out.

"Believe it or not," she continued, "it shows in everything you do."

He shook his head as if he couldn't believe her, then he looked back at the light. "You know nothing about me."

It was true and yet . . .

She was intrigued by him. Captivated. This man who wasn't a man called out to her and seduced her. All she had ever wanted in life was to be normal. To have a warm, loving home with children. A quiet life.

He could offer her none of that.

Yet when she looked at Kyrian, when she thought about him, the strangest things happened to her. It wasn't just lust.

There was something more.

Something undefinable that made her heart just a little happier, a little more tender. Something about being around him that made her soar.

She wondered if he felt that, too.

If he did, he kept it well hidden behind that tough exterior of his.

"Can I ask you something else?"

He sighed irritably. "What the hell? You've asked me everything else."

She disregarded his caustic words. "Why did you become a Dark-Hunter?"

"I wanted vengeance at any cost."

"Against Theone?"

This time there was no mistaking the pain on his face, the slight flaring of his nostrils. His hand was so tight on the steering wheel that she could see his knuckles protruding sharply against his skin.

Amanda took a deep breath as she stroked Terminator's ears. She couldn't fault him for wanting revenge against a woman who had been so cold-blooded as to turn him over to his enemies. "Julian told me the gods give you twenty-four hours to exact revenge. What did you do to her?"

A tic started in his jaw and when he spoke, his tone was rife with anger. "For her, I turned my back on my family. I gave up a kingdom and hurt the people who truly loved me. Because of Theone, the last words I spoke to my parents were hurtful and cruel. And when they delivered the news to my father that I had died, the grief of it drove him insane.

"He flung himself from the window of my childhood room onto the courtyard stones below, where he died a broken man, calling my name. My mother never spoke another word again until the day she died, and my youngest sister sheared her hair off to let the world know just how much she grieved.

"Without me to lead our forces, the Romans invaded and took over my homeland. My people lost their dignity, their nationality, and suffered for centuries under Roman occupation."

Hunter glanced at her. "Tell me, what would you have done to my wife?"

Tears welled in her eyes as she listened to the pain in his voice. How she ached for him. Dear Lord, no one deserved such punishment because they had mistakenly thought someone loved them.

But what struck her most was that there was no mention of what Theone had done to *him.* He was only sorry for what it had cost his family and country.

She wanted to touch him so badly that she wasn't sure how she refrained. Instead, she kept her attention on Terminator. Holding the dog the way she wanted to hold Hunter.

"I don't know," she whispered past the stinging lump in her throat. "I guess I would have killed her, too."

"One would think that, anyway."

A chill went up her spine. "You didn't, did you?"

"No, I didn't. I had my hands wrapped around her neck and was about to end her life when she looked up at me with those weepy, fearful eyes. One minute I wanted to kill her and the next thing I knew, I wiped her tears away, kissed her trembling lips, and left her there in peace."

He clenched his teeth. "So, you see, you sit beside the greatest fool ever born. A man who traded his soul for a vengeance he never took."

The *full* horror of his past hit her. After all he had suffered because of his wife, after all he had lost, he had still loved her. Greatly.

No matter what Theone had done to him, in the end he had forgiven her.

How could anyone have betrayed someone capable of so much love and loyalty?

Amanda couldn't fathom it. "I'm sorry."

"Don't be. As they say, I made my bed and I was crucified in it. I was the one who was blind and foolish. I realized too late that she had never, once, told me she loved me."

The regret and sorrow in his voice tore at her. "It wasn't your fault," she said as they headed into the Garden District. "She had no right to betray you."

"Theone never betrayed me. I betrayed myself."

Good Lord, he was strong. She'd never known anyone who was so willing to shoulder such responsibility on his own shoulders. How she wished for a way to reach through that iron wall he kept around himself.

Her heart heavy, Amanda watched as they passed by the antebellum mansions where large oaks and pines were draped with tons of hanging Spanish moss.

Hunter pulled into a drive at the end of the street. Trees obscured her view to the house, and two large stone pedestals secured a heavy wrought-iron, twelve-foot-high gate. A tall redbrick wall surrounded the grounds and seemed to go on forever.

The place looked like a fortress.

He grabbed a remote out of the glove compartment, pressed the button, and the heavy gates swung wide.

Amanda's breath caught in her throat as he drove up the long, curving driveway and she could finally see where he lived.

Her jaw dropped. His house was huge! The neoclassical architecture was some of the best she'd seen. Tall columns ran all the way around the house and the upper balconies had ornate white iron scrollwork.

Hunter drove around to the back of the house and into a six-car garage where she saw he also owned a Mercedes, a Porsche, a vintage Jaguar, and a new Buick that looked strangely out of place.

Okay, the Lamborghini had clued her in that Hunter had a lot of money, but she'd never dreamed he lived like this.

Like royalty.

She winced at the thought. Of course he did, since that was what he was. A prince. A real-life prince of ancient Greece.

As the garage door closed behind them, Hunter helped her out of the car. He turned Terminator loose in his backyard, then led her inside the huge house. Her gaze tried to take in everything at once as they walked down a small hallway into a kitchen where a thin, elderly Hispanic woman was pulling something delectable out of the oven.

His kitchen was mammoth, with stainless-steel appliances and antiques lining the dark green walls and marble countertops.

"Rosa," Hunter said in a chastising tone as he laid his keys down on the counter by the door. "What are you doing here?"

Rosa jumped and patted her chest. "Lord, *m'ijo,* you scared me out of ten years."

"I'm going to scare you out of more than that if you don't do what the doctor said. You and I had an agreement. Do I have to call Miguel again?"

She narrowed her large brown eyes on him as she set her pan of chicken on the stove. "Now, don't you go threatening me. I gave birth to that boy and I'm not about to let him go lecturing me on what I need to do. And that goes for you, too.

I was minding my own home long before you were born. You hear me?"

"Yes, ma'am."

Rosa paused as she caught sight of Amanda. A wide smile spread across her face. "It's good to see you with a woman, *m'ijo.*"

Hunter passed a sheepish look to Amanda. He stepped over to the stove to inspect the food. "This smells delicious, Rosa, *gracias.*"

Rosa smiled proudly as she watched him savor her work. "I know; that's why I made it. I'm tired of seeing TV dinners and fast food bags in the garbage. You need to eat real food once in a while. That processed stuff will kill you."

Hunter gave her a gentle, tight-lipped smile. "I think I can handle it."

Rosa snorted. "We all think we can, and that's why I have to take heart medicine now."

"And speaking of," Hunter said, turning to her with a chiding stare, "you are supposed to be home by now. You promised me."

"I'm going. I put a salad for you in the refrigerator. There should be enough for both of you."

Hunter took Rosa's coat from the back of the chair and helped her into it. "You are taking tomorrow off."

"But the gardener man, he comes."

"Nick can let him in."

"But—"

"Nick can handle it, Rosa."

She patted his hand affectionately. "You're a good boy, *m'ijo.* I'll see you Wednesday."

"But not before noon."

She smiled. "Not before noon. Good night."

"*Adiós.*"

"So," Amanda teased as soon as they were alone. "You actually do know how to be nice to someone."

She saw the corners of his mouth twitch as he fought down the urge to smile at her. "Only when the mood strikes me."

He pulled a fork and knife out of a drawer and cut a small bite of chicken.

"Oh, this is good," he said. He cut another piece. "Here, you have to taste this."

Before she realized what she was doing, Amanda allowed him to feed it to her. The spices filled her mouth at the same moment it dawned on her just how intimate a moment they were sharing.

By the look in his eyes, she would say it occurred to Hunter about two seconds after her.

"It's very good," she said, stepping back from him.

Without another word, Hunter set about putting out plates for them. As she watched him, the full horror of the night came crashing down on her.

"My house is gone," she breathed. "Completely gone."

Kyrian set the plates aside as he felt her pain reaching out to him. It was a staggering wave of loss.

She looked up at him, her eyes swimming in grief. "Why did he burn my house? Why?"

"At least you weren't in it."

"But I could have been. Oh God, Hunter, Tabitha is normally home at that time! What if you hadn't been there? Allison would be dead. Tabitha could have been killed." She sobbed as she looked about, panic-stricken. "He's not going to stop until we're dead, is he?"

Without thinking, he pulled her into his arms and held her close. "It's all right, Amanda, I've got you." Kyrian froze as he realized what he'd done.

He'd used her name. And with it, he felt some inner barrier shatter.

Tears rolled down Amanda's cheeks. "I know it's just a house, but all my things were in there. My favorite books, the blanket my grandmother crocheted for me before she died. Everything that was me was in there."

"Not everything. You're still here."

She wept against his chest. Kyrian closed his eyes and leaned his cheek against the top of her head as she clutched at him. It had been centuries since he'd comforted a woman.

Centuries since he felt this way. And it shook him deeply.

"Can Desiderius get to Tabitha?"

"No," he whispered against her hair, trying not to inhale the sweet rose scent. He failed and his body reacted instantly as his groin tightened and burned for her. "As long as she stays in a private, human dwelling he can't get to her. It's one of the limitations Apollo put on them when he cursed them so that humans would have some protection."

Amanda took a ragged breath and stepped away from him. "I'm sorry," she said, wiping the tears from her face.

He clenched his teeth as he noted the way her hand shook. He could kill Desiderius for hurting her like this.

"I don't normally cry in front of people."

"Don't apologize," he whispered, cupping her face in his hands. "You're actually holding up a lot better than anyone should under the circumstances."

She looked up at him from under those long, dark, wet eyelashes. His heart hammered at the vulnerability he saw. A vulnerability that touched him on a level he didn't want to think about.

He wanted her. Desperately.

He hadn't felt this in so long, no, he corrected himself, he had never felt this way about another woman, not even Theone. This wasn't just lust or love, he felt a bond with her. They were like two parts of a single heart.

But it was a lie. It had to be. He didn't believe in love anymore. Didn't believe in much of anything.

And yet . . .

She made him want to believe again. Made him long for things he had forgotten. Things like a tender hand in his hair when he woke up. The feel of a warm body lying next to him while he slept.

He was almost powerless before it.

His cell phone rang. Kyrian pulled it off his belt and answered it.

It was Talon.

"Is the woman with you?" Talon asked.

"Yes, why?"

"Because you have one big problem. The Apollite told me the fires were set from an electronic timer that was hidden inside the houses."

Kyrian frowned, then went cold as he remembered something else Amanda had said to him yesterday. "Amanda?" he asked, drawing her attention to him. "Didn't you say Desiderius had captured you while you were inside Tabitha's house?"

She nodded. "In her living room."

His stomach settled into a cold knot of dread. "Did you hear that?" he asked Talon.

Talon cursed. "How is that possible?"

"Someone must have invited Desiderius in, which means there's a human running around working with or for him. My money says Tabitha wouldn't be so stupid."

"Neither would Allison," Amanda inserted. "She knows to watch out for anyone suspicious."

Kyrian thought it over. "Any ideas?" he asked Talon.

"I don't know."

"What does your guide say?"

"Ceara knows nothing. And the next tiny problem, my back isn't healing."

If his stomach drew any tighter, it would make a diamond. "Not healing how?"

"I was hit with an astral blast. The same kind a god wields."

Kyrian went cold. "I didn't kill a god, I killed a Daimon."

"I know."

Kyrian cursed under his breath. "What have we gotten into?"

"Beats me, but until we know more, I suggest you sit tight on her. With the untapped powers she has, Desiderius will be after her full force. I'm sure by now he'd rather have her than her sister."

Kyrian shifted the phone as he watched Amanda take a seat at his table. Gods, he couldn't stand the thought of her being hurt. The pain of the idea racked him. "Do you need me to do anything for your back?"

"No. It just hurts like hell."

Kyrian knew the feeling. His shoulder was still stinging from Aphrodite. "I'm beginning to understand how Desiderius killed the last eight Dark-Hunters who went up against him."

"Yeah," Talon agreed. "And I don't want us to be nine and ten."

"Me, neither. Okay, I'll keep Amanda safe with me, but we still have the problem of her sister out there."

"I can have Eric put a leash on Tabitha for the time being. You just make sure Amanda stays in touch with her or she's likely to make our lives even more difficult."

"Will do." Kyrian hung up and tossed his phone onto his counter.

"Is something wrong?" Amanda asked.

He laughed in spite of himself. "I think a better question would be, is anything *not* wrong?"

"And that means?"

"It means your boring life has just ended. And for the next few days, it looks as if you're going to find out exactly how dangerous mine is."

CHAPTER 7

"Oh no," Amanda said, rising on her tiptoes to stand nose to nose with Kyrian. She arched a brow and dared him with her eyes to deny her words. As she spoke, each word was short and clipped. "You are so wrong. I want my life back. I want it boring and I want it *long*."

Her spirit amused him as she emphasized the last word. She was spectacular when riled and he wondered just how long he could keep that color high in her cheeks. The fire in those lush blue eyes.

Better still, as her breasts rose and fell with the weight of her conviction, images of other things that would make her breathless flashed though his mind.

He wanted to keep her breathless. Wanted to taste her passion fully.

Kyrian's lips itched to kiss hers, his hands ached to touch her body until she cried out with pleasure.

Gods, but this woman tempted him as he'd never been tempted before. And he had once loved temptation in a way that defied explanation. Over the centuries, he'd forgotten that small personality flaw, but ever since he had awakened with her next to him, he had been painfully reminded of the mortal man he used to be.

Slowly, bit by bit, he could feel her breaking down the barriers he had built around himself, the numbness. He had distanced himself from his feelings for centuries. And though he'd had mortals he cared about during that time, none of them had ever touched him as she did.

It was so strange to him.

Why her?

Why now? Now when he needed clarity of thought to deal with Desiderius.

The Fates were once again toying with him and he didn't like it in the least.

He could feel his blood pounding through his veins as he stared at those moist, full lips. Already he could taste them. Feel her. Dear gods, how he craved her.

She, alone, awoke the hungry beast in him. The part of him that wanted to growl and devour her body inch by slow, studied inch, all night long.

But Amanda was human and he could offer her nothing of himself. His soul and loyalty belonged to Artemis.

Besides, Amanda had a right to her dream of normality. Her dreams of a home and family with an average man.

After having his own dreams so cruelly, vengefully stripped from him, he refused to do that to her now.

She deserved to have her long, full, and boring life. Everyone deserved a chance to obtain their heart's wishes.

He swallowed the lump in his throat that ached with desire for her and knew, in that moment, he had to banish her from his thoughts.

She could never be his.

Her destiny was to return to a family who loved her and to find a mortal man who could . . .

He didn't finish that thought. It was too painful to even contemplate.

"For your sake," he whispered, resisting the urge to touch her hair, "I hope that's true, but I'm afraid with the raw, untapped powers you have and with the vampire-hunting Tabitha does, it's not going to be possible to live your boring life for the next few days."

She broke eye contact with him. "I have no powers." Her voice was sharp, yet it lacked her earlier conviction.

He reached out and fingered her chin, seeking to comfort

the trouble he saw on her face, the fears he didn't understand. Why wouldn't she acknowledge the gifts she had been given?

"You might not claim them, Amanda, but they're there. You have premonitions and telepathy. Projection and empathy. They're similar in many ways to Tabitha's, but your powers are a lot stronger than hers."

The vivid sapphire returned to her eyes. "You're lying to me."

Her accusation surprised him. "Why would I do that?"

She swallowed. "I don't know. I just know that I have no powers."

"Why are you so afraid of them?"

"Because . . ."

He cocked his head as her voice trailed off and she didn't finish her sentence.

"Because?" he prompted.

She looked up at him and the grief in her eyes took his breath. "When I was fifteen," she said in a hushed tone, "I had a dream." She blinked back tears as she gripped the counter beside her. "I used to have a lot of them back then. They always came true. In this one, my best friend was killed in a car wreck. I saw her. I felt her panic and I heard the last thoughts that went through her mind before she died."

Kyrian clenched his teeth at the pain he heard in her voice. Reaching out, he took her hand in his. Her icy fingers were shaking.

"When I saw her at school, I did everything I could to keep her from going home that day with Bobby Thibideaux. I even told her about my dream." Tears fell again. "She didn't listen. She told me I was stupid and mean and jealous because he liked her and not me."

She shook her head as she relived that day. "I wasn't jealous, Hunter, I just didn't want her to die."

He stroked her fingers, trying to warm her hand. "I know, Amanda."

"She got in the car with me screaming at her to get out. Everyone at school was staring at me, but I didn't care. Tabitha pulled me away so they could leave and everyone was laughing."

She licked her dry lips. "They weren't laughing the next morning when they found out the two of them had died on the way home. They called me a freak. For the next three years, no one wanted to be near me. I was that weirdo girl who saw things."

Anger flashed in her eyes as she looked up at him. "Tell me, what good are these so-called powers when they make people afraid of me? *Why can I see things I can't change? What good is that?*"

Kyrian had no answer for her. All he could do was feel her inner pain and turmoil.

"Don't you understand?" she continued. "I don't want to know the future when I can't stop it. I want to be normal," she insisted, her voice cracking on the last word. "I don't want to be like Talon or my grandmother and have dead people talking to me. I don't want to know what you're feeling. I just want to live my life like other people. Don't you ever want that?"

Closing his eyes against the unfounded agony that clenched his heart, Kyrian let go of the softness of her skin and stepped back from her. "It wouldn't matter if I did."

Amanda started at the look on his face. She'd wounded him somehow. "I'm sorry, Hunter, I didn't mean—"

"It's okay," he said slowly. He moved to stand by a chair and she watched the way he gripped the edge of it. Though he was trying hard to hide it, she could sense his pain.

"You're right," he said at last. "There are times when I do miss being able to feel the sunshine on my face. I miss so many things that I can't even begin to count them all. I have learned the best thing to do is to not torture myself with the memory of it." He looked up at her and the heat in his eyes scorched her. "But people like us have special gifts. We can't be normal."

Amanda didn't want to hear that. Her heart couldn't take that news. "Maybe you can't. But I can. I don't let myself feel those powers anymore. They are dead to me."

He laughed bitterly. "And you think I'm stubborn."

"Hunter, please," she said, hating the agony she heard in her tone. "I just wish it were the day before yesterday. I wish I could wake up and have all this be a nightmare."

In that moment, she felt something that scared her. It was just a quick twinge of the powers he referred to. And the sensation of it sliced through her as she heard his thoughts.

Wish you had never met me, you mean.

She moved toward him. "Hunter . . ."

He dodged her touch and went to the counter where the phone was. He picked the phone up and handed it to her. "Call Tabitha and tell her to stay at your mother's until Friday. She can come and go in the daytime, but after dark it is imperative that she stay indoors."

"She won't like that."

Aggravated fury smoldered in his midnight eyes. "Then have your mother tie her down. We're not dealing with regular vampires here. These Daimons have unlocked some exceedingly dangerous powers, and until Talon and I figure out what we're dealing with, she needs to lie low."

"Okay. I'll do my best."

He nodded. "While you talk to her, I'm going to change clothes."

Amanda watched as he walked out of the kitchen, her heart heavy. She didn't want him to leave her even long enough to change. She felt a peculiar urge to follow after him and help him shed those clothes . . .

Instead, she dialed Tabitha's cell phone.

"Oh, thank God you're all right," Tabitha said, her voice filled with tears. "The police just told me about the houses and I knew it was past time for you to be home."

Amanda's own eyes teared up, but she forced them back. Crying wouldn't accomplish anything. The houses were gone and all the tears in the world wouldn't bring them back. What she needed to focus on now was for all of them to survive Desiderius's wrath.

"How's Allison?" she asked, trying to distract herself from the fear.

"She's fine. Her mother's already at the hospital. I'm in the car on my way to see her even as we speak. No one knows what happened to Terminator."

"I have him."

Tabitha breathed a sigh of relief. "Thank you, sis. I owe you big time. So, where are you now?"

It was the question Amanda dreaded answering. Tabitha was bound to go ballistic when she found out. "I'd rather not say," she hedged.

Silence.

It stretched for several minutes and all Amanda heard from the other end was the noise of traffic.

Tabitha was trying to read her.

Damn!

Tabitha said the word at the same moment Amanda thought it. "You're with that vampire again, aren't you?"

Amanda cringed. How did someone tell her sister, the vampire hunter, that she had a crush on a vampire and planned on spending the night in his home?

There was no easy way around that one.

Sighing, she tried to think of some way to explain it. "He's not a vampire . . . Exactly. He's more like you."

"Uh-huh," Tabitha said. "Like me how? He has breasts? He has a boyfriend? Or he just likes to kill things?"

Amanda ground her teeth. "Tabitha Lane Devereaux, don't be such a bitch. I know you don't like to kill things, either, and I don't want to play Twenty Questions with you. The guy who attacked me in your place is really scary, and not like the other scary things you play with. This is different. Hunter wants you to lie low and I agree."

"Hunter? Is that the same bloodsucking ghoul who threatened your life to me earlier?"

"He didn't mean that."

"Oh no? So you're willing to bet your life on it?"

"I'm willing to bet both our lives on it."

"You're friggin' crazy, you know that?"

"Watch your mouth, little girl. Unlike you, I know what

I'm doing. I trust Hunter. And this guy Desiderius is seriously evil. Like Hannibal Lecter evil."

Amanda could just imagine Tabitha rolling her eyes as she made a disgusted snort. "I'm not afraid of either one of them."

"Maybe you need to learn a little fear. I for one am terrified."

"Then why don't you come home where we can protect you?"

Because I want to stay with Hunter. Amanda didn't know where the thought came from. But there was no denying it. She felt safe and protected with him.

He had yet to offer to take her anywhere else. She had no doubt that if she asked, he would let her leave, and yet . . .

She didn't want to.

But she didn't dare tell Tabitha *that*. Things were bad enough between them, so she offered her sister the only excuse she could think of. "I can't do that. Not while this thing is after me."

Tabitha cursed again. "How do I know this Hunter guy doesn't have you under some kind of mind spell?"

Amanda laughed at that as she recalled Hunter's words to her in the factory. "Because, much like you, I'm too stubborn for it to work. Besides, he's a friend of Julian Alexander. You trust Julian and Grace, don't you?"

"Well, yeah. Of course."

"Then trust their friend."

"Okay," Tabitha said reluctantly. "But my trust is wearing thin. I want you safe."

"And I want the same for you. Hunter said you're safe so long as it's daylight, but make sure you're in Mom's house once the sun sets and stay there. In fact, I don't think you should go to the hospital. You should probably go to Mom's right now."

"Allison is my best friend, I need to see her."

"What if you lead them to her? For all you know they're watching you already."

Tabitha growled low in her throat. "I don't like this. Not at all, but okay. You're right. I don't want to draw them to

Allison. Mom can handle anything. I'll turn around at the next street and head to Mom's for the night. You call if you need me."

"Will do."

Amanda set the phone down and picked up her plate from the counter where Hunter had left it. She carried it to the small breakfast table that was set next to a large picture window. It looked out onto a beautiful, old-fashioned courtyard behind the house, complete with a rose trellis, Greek statuary, and sculpted shrubs. The area was lit by antique oil lamps that cast an eerie glow against the white stucco walls.

Amanda sat alone for several minutes until Hunter returned. He'd changed into a long-sleeved, black T-shirt that hugged his broad shoulders. He had the sleeves pulled up on his forearms and she saw the vicious cut that ran along his arm.

"Did the Daimon bite you or is that a knife wound?"

Hunter glanced at it as he sat down across from her. "Bite wound."

She went cold. "You need that tended, don't you?"

"No, the entire wound will be gone by tomorrow."

"Yeah, but don't such things turn you into a vampire?"

He laughed and gave her a droll stare. "Technically, I already am a vampire. As for turning, it's impossible unless you're an Apollite."

"So they can't bite humans and make them into vampires?"

"Bedtime story."

She thought about that a minute. "So where do all these misconceptions about vampires come from?"

He swallowed a bite of his food and took a drink. "Scared villagers mostly. Since the day Atlantis was sucked into the ocean, Apollites and Daimons have been persecuted. At one time, all the Greek city-states knew about the Dark-Hunters and we were revered. But as time went on and the Dark-Hunters became more solitary, we were mostly forgotten except in myths and legends. Acheron and the others liked it that way. Ash even went so far as to collect and hide the ancient writings that referred to us."

"Acheron?" she asked, cutting a piece of her chicken. "You keep mentioning him. Who is he?"

"He was the first Dark-Hunter chosen by Artemis."

"And he's still alive?"

"Oh yeah. I think he's in California this week."

She arched a brow at him.

Hunter smiled. "He travels to a new location every few days."

"How? Why?"

He shrugged. "I guess when you're eleven thousand years old, things get rather boring. As for how, he has a custom-built helicopter that can break the sound barrier."

Amanda digested the news and tried to imagine what this oldest Dark-Hunter must look like. For some reason, Yoda came to mind. Some small, gray-green–skinned ancient who walked around stooped over, spouting broken words of wisdom to the others.

"Have you ever met Acheron?" she asked.

Kyrian nodded. "We all have. He trains all the new Dark-Hunters and in a way he is our unofficial leader. There's also the theory that he's the hit man the gods call in to execute us when we step over the line of propriety."

She didn't like the sound of that at all. "Step over how?"

"Preying on humans, for one. We have a Code of Conduct that has to be followed. No revealing of our powers before the masses, no association with Apollites or Daimons, et cetera."

It was strangely comforting to know that they had such a thing, but also scary to think of one of these guys turning bad with the powers they possessed. "If Dark-Hunters are forbidden to hurt each other and you drain one another's powers, how can Acheron be an executioner?"

"He doesn't drain our powers." He took a drink of wine. "Ash was the guinea pig Dark-Hunter. Since he was the first, the gods hadn't quite got the kinks out of the system. So he has some . . . peculiar, shall we say, side effects."

Now she definitely pictured some mutant life-form. A little hunchback Dark-Hunter with a lisp.

"And just how many Dark-Hunters are there?" she asked.

"Thousands."

Amanda's jaw went slack. "Seriously?"

By the light in his eyes, she could see the answer.

"How often are new ones created?"

"Not often," he said quietly. "Most of us have been around for quite some time."

"Wow," she breathed. "So if Acheron is the oldest, who is the youngest?"

Kyrian frowned as he thought about the answer. "Offhand, I would say Tristan, Diana, or Sundown, but I would have to check with Acheron on it."

"Sundown? Nickname, or did his mother not like him very much?"

He laughed. "He was a gunslinger and that was the name they used on his wanted posters. The authorities claimed he did his best work after dark."

"Okay," Amanda said slowly. Now she pictured some Wild Bill Hickok character. Complete with bowlegs and shaggy beard and a wad of tobacco in his cheek. "I take it you Dark-Hunters weren't merchants or um . . ."

"Decent law-abiding folks?"

She smiled. "I wasn't implying you were indecent, but you have the gist of what I was going for."

Kyrian returned her smile. "Indecent" would certainly describe the thoughts in his mind that concerned his guest. "It takes a certain demeanor and passion to become a Dark-Hunter. Artemis doesn't want to waste her time or ours by picking someone incapable of hunting. I guess you could say we are all mad, bad, and immortal."

Her smile widened, showing just a very tiny hint of a dimple in her right cheek. How odd he'd never noticed that before. "Bad and immortal I will give you, but are you truly mad?"

"If by mad you mean insane, what then would you say?"

Her eyes flashed wickedly. "That you are definitely mad. But you know, I think I like that about you. There's something to be said for unpredictability."

Kyrian wasn't sure which of them was most surprised by

her confession. She looked away quickly, her cheeks turning bright red.

She liked him . . . The words evoked a truly juvenile response inside him. He felt a peculiar urge to run tell someone, *"She likes me, she likes me."*

Ye gods, what was that?

He was two thousand years old. *Long* past the age for such behavior.

Yet there was no denying the satisfaction and happiness he felt.

Awkward silence fell between them while they ate.

As she finished, Amanda did her best not to think about her house. All she'd lost. She would deal with that tomorrow. At the moment, she just wanted to get through the night.

"Tabitha is staying put," she said as she watched Kyrian take his plate to the sink and rinse it off.

"Good."

"You know," she said quietly, "you still haven't told me how you knew so much about my sister the night we met."

He put the plate and silverware in the dishwasher. "Talon and Tabitha have a mutual friend."

Amanda's eyes widened at that. A mole . . . who would have thought. "One of Tabitha's Zoo Crew?"

He nodded.

"Who?"

"Since this person spies for us, I'm not about to tell you who it is."

She laughed at that, then narrowed her eyes, trying to divine who it was. "I'll bet it's Gary."

"I'm giving away nothing."

It was intriguing, but not nearly as much as the Dark-Hunter before her. Sighing, Amanda continued to eat and glance around the richly appointed kitchen while Kyrian put the food away. There was a marble breakfast counter that vaguely resembled a Greek temple. It separated the table where she sat from the rest of the kitchen. Three tall bar stools were set before it.

Everything was crisp and clean and enormous.

"This is a big house for one person. How long have you lived here?"

"A little over a hundred years."

She choked. "Are you serious?"

"There's no need for me to move. I like New Orleans."

She got up and took her plate to him. "You put down some serious roots, don't you? Where did you live before here?"

"Paris for a while," he said, putting the plate aside. "Geneva. London, Barcelona, Hamburg, Athens. Before that I wandered around."

She watched his face while he spoke. There was no telltale sign of his mood. He was hiding his feelings from her and she wondered if there was any way to draw him out. "It sounds really lonely."

"It was okay." Still no facial clues.

"Did you ever have friends in any of those places?"

"No, not really. I've had a few Squires over the centuries, but for the most part, I prefer solitude."

"Squires?" she asked. How strange. "Like in the Middle Ages?"

"Something like that." He looked at her, but didn't elaborate. "What about you? Have you lived here all your life?"

"Born and raised. My mother's parents immigrated from Romania during the Depression and my father's people were backwoods Cajuns."

He laughed at that. "I've known a lot of those."

"Living here for a hundred years, I'll bet you have."

Amanda considered the life Hunter must have lived. All the centuries of solitude, of watching people he cared about die of old age while he never changed. It must have been hard for him.

But along with that, his life must have had a few really neat perks.

"What's it like knowing you're going to live forever?"

He shrugged. "Honestly, I no longer think about it. Much like the rest of the world, I just get up, do my job, and go to bed."

How simple he made it sound. Yet she sensed something

else from him. A deep-rooted sadness. Living without dreams must be excruciating. The human spirit needed goals to strive for, and killing Daimons just didn't seem like much of a goal to her.

She dropped her gaze to the counter and tried to imagine what Hunter had been like as a man. Julian had told her how they would drink after battle and how much Hunter had wanted children.

Worse, she remembered the way Hunter had looked holding Vanessa.

"Have you ever had any children?"

Intense pain flashed through his eyes for only an instant until he recovered his stoicism. "No, Dark-Hunters are sterile."

"So you *are* impotent."

He gasped indignantly and looked at her. "Hardly. I can have sex, I just can't procreate."

"Oh." She wrinkled her nose devilishly at him and tried to lighten the mood. "That was really a nosy question. I'm sorry."

"It's all right."

Hunter started the dishwasher. "Would you like a tour of the house?"

"House?" she asked, cocking a disbelieving brow. "If this is a house, then I live in a two-room shanty." Her breath caught as she remembered that she didn't live anywhere any more. Clearing her throat, she pushed the thought aside. "Yes," she said quietly. "I'd like to see it."

Hunter led her through the doorway on her left, into a massively large living room. The walls, crown moldings, and medallions were absolutely gorgeous in their old-fashioned grace and elegance, but the furniture in the house was as modern as it could be.

The room was decorated for comfort, not to impress visitors. But then she imagined vampires didn't entertain guests too often.

A huge entertainment center lined one wall with a JVC component system, big-screen TV, double-decker VCR and DVD player.

Though there were lamps all around, the room was lit only by candles from three ornate sconces.

"You don't like modern light bulbs, do you?" she asked as Hunter moved to light a candelabrum.

"No," he said. "They're too bright for my eyes."

"Light hurts you?"

He nodded. "Dark-Hunters have eyes made for darkness. Our pupils are larger than yours and they don't dilate the same way. As a result, our eyes let in a lot more light than human eyes."

While he spoke, she noticed the floor-to-ceiling windows were covered with black shutters that would shield the house from daylight.

As she stepped around a black leather sofa, Amanda stopped dead in her tracks.

There was a coffin sitting in front of it.

"Is that . . ." She couldn't finish the sentence. Not while she held a gruesome image of Hunter lying asleep inside it every day.

Hunter glanced at it, then met her shocked gaze unblinkingly. "Yes," he said in a deadpan voice. "Yes, it is. It's my . . . coffee table."

He walked over to it, lifted the lid and pulled a remote out of it. "For the TV if you want to watch it tomorrow."

Amanda shook her head. Now that she noticed it, she saw there were all kinds of weird little vampire trinkets lying around. Miniature statues, small crossbows, even a vampire tarot deck on the mantel.

"Nick thinks it's funny," Hunter said as she picked up the deck of tarot cards. "Any time he finds something with a vampire in it or on it, he brings it here and leaves it for me to find."

"Does it bother you?"

"No, he's a good kid most of the time."

As he led her room by room through the old mansion, she began to get lost. "Just how big is this place?" she asked as they entered a game room.

"There are twelve bedrooms and it's a little over seven thousand square feet."

"Jeez, I've been inside smaller malls."

He laughed.

An elaborate pool table was set in the middle of the game room, along with a collection of arcade games and a big-screen TV with an entire array of game consoles lined up on a low coffee table in front of it. But what she found most peculiar was a pair of baseball gloves and a baseball on a drop-leaf table in one corner of the room. Amanda went over to them.

"I toss the ball around with Nick some nights," Hunter explained.

"Why?"

He shrugged. "It clears my head when I'm trying to sort through things."

"Nick doesn't mind?"

He laughed at that. "Nick minds everything. I don't think I've ever asked him to do something he didn't complain about it."

"Then why do you keep him around?"

"I'm a glutton for punishment."

Now it was her turn to laugh. "I would really like to meet this Nick."

"No doubt you will tomorrow."

"Really?"

He nodded. "Anything you need, you tell him and he'll get it for you. If he offends you in any way, let me know and I'll kill him when I get up."

There was a note in his voice that told her it might not be an empty threat.

Hunter opened the large French doors and led her into a glass-enclosed atrium. The ceiling was clear and showed a million stars flickering overhead and their shoes clicked idly on the tile floor.

"It's beautiful in here."

"Thanks."

She walked up to a large statue of three women in the center of the room. The piece was absolutely breathtaking. The youngest of them was lying on her side with a scroll while the other two were sitting with their backs to each other. One held a lyre while the other appeared to sing. But what amazed her most was the way they were painted. Each one looked real, and they bore a striking resemblance to Hunter.

"Is this from Greece?" she asked.

A painful look crossed his face as he nodded. "They were my sisters."

Her heart heavy, she studied them closely.

Hunter gently touched the arm of the one with a scroll. His brow furrowed ever so slightly while he gazed up at the life-sized statue of a girl in her late teens. The blue togalike dress matched her eyes perfectly.

"Althea was the youngest of us," he said, his voice a full octave deeper. "She was quiet and bashful, and she had a quaint stutter when she got nervous. Gods, how she hated it, but I thought it was sweet. Diana"—he indicated the one with a lyre who was dressed in red—"was two years older than me and had the temperament of a shrew. My father said we were too much alike and that is why we could never get along. And Phaedra was a year younger than me and had the voice of an angel."

Amanda looked up at the young woman dressed in yellow.

There was such delicate grace to his sisters. The sculptor had captured them as if they were in mid-movement. Even the folds of their clothes were realistic and dainty. She'd never seen such craftsmanship. They looked so real she half expected them to talk to her.

No wonder it hurt him so.

"You loved them a lot."

He nodded.

"What happened to them?"

He moved away. "They married and had long, happy lives. Diana named her first son after me."

A tenuous smile curved her lips that the one who had fought most with him had done such a thing. It spoke a lot for their relationship. While she looked at the women, she remembered what he had said about Althea in the car. She had shorn off all her long, wavy blond hair when she learned her brother was gone. They must have loved him as much as he loved them.

"What did they think of your transition into a Dark-Hunter?"

He cleared his throat. "They never knew. To them, I was dead."

"Then how do you know so much about—"

"I could hear them while they lived. Feel them, the same way you can open your heart to Tabitha and tell when she's troubled."

She stiffened at his words. "How did you know about that?"

"I told you, I can feel your powers."

A shiver went down her spine and she wondered if she could hide anything from him. "You are one scary man."

A strange light darkened his eyes. "I'm not a man. I gave up my humanity when I crossed over."

He said that, but she knew better. He might not have a soul, but the man had a good heart and was nothing if not humane. "Why did you agree to be a Dark-Hunter even though you never took your revenge against Theone?"

"It seemed like a good idea at the time."

With those few words something inside her melted. Perhaps it was the loneliness in his voice, the calm acceptance of his fate in his eyes. She didn't know exactly what it was, but she knew she couldn't just walk back into her old life and forget this man.

She'd seen too much of his goodness. Too much of his pain. And God help her, the more she learned about him the more she wanted him.

Wanted him in a way that defied explanation. They'd barely met and yet there was something that bound them together.

Amanda looked up at those tormented eyes that studied her with hunger and heat. He was what her mother had called the "missing half." It was the term her mother used to describe her father. The term Selena used when she spoke of Bill.

For the first time in her life, Amanda understood. And having found it with him, she knew she couldn't just let it go.

Not without a fight.

Unaware of her thoughts, Hunter turned and led her back into the house. He showed her to a bedroom suite on the bottom floor. "You can sleep in here. I'll bring you something more comfortable to wear."

Amanda wandered around the lush bedroom. The king-sized plantation bed looked like something out of an old movie. The dark green paint would have made a small room look tiny, but in this massive space, it gave it a quaint, homey feel.

Hunter returned a few minutes later with a black T-shirt and a pair of sweatpants that would swallow her whole. "Thanks," she said, taking them from him.

He stood before her, his eyes searching hers.

To her surprise, he lifted his hand and ran his finger down her jaw. His short fingernail gently scraped her flesh, sending chills through her. She knew he wanted to kiss her, and she was amazed at how much she wanted his kiss.

But he didn't kiss her. He just stared at her with those dark hungry eyes.

Then he ran the pad of his thumb over her lips and she barely bit back a moan at how good he felt. How good he smelled. The air between them was rife with tension. With mutual desire and need. The force of it took her breath and made her both weak and strong at the same time.

Just when she was sure he'd kiss her, he pulled away. "Good night, Amanda."

Her heart pounding, she watched him go.

Kyrian cursed himself with every step he took toward his office. He should have kissed her. He should have . . .

No, he'd done the right thing. There would never be anything between them. Dark-Hunters could take women for a few nights, but they were forbidden to become seriously involved with them. The danger was just too great.

It made the women vulnerable to the Daimons, and it made the Dark-Hunter weak. Made him cautious, and in this line of work, caution got you killed.

It had never bothered him before.

Tonight, the pain was almost enough to break him.

He hated these feelings inside him. Hated needing her. He'd long ago banished his emotions and he preferred to live that way; in a safe cocoon free of turmoil.

"I have to get her out of my mind." He entered his office and went to log on to the Dark-Hunter.com Web site.

His instant messenger program was blinking with incoming messages and as always, his e-mail was filled with notes from other Dark-Hunters. Technology was a wonderful thing. Being able to communicate with each other was a true godsend. It made dealing with the long nights more bearable and it allowed them to exchange important information.

Kyrian sat in his black leather chair and double-clicked the flashing icon. It was a note from Acheron.

Nick called, said Desiderius had kicked your butt. You okay?

Kyrian clenched his teeth, then typed in a response. "I'm going to kill him for that. I'm fine. Desiderius is down a bolthole. What do you know of him?"

He's the one who took out Cromley a few years back, so you're dealing with a major power. I talked with Cromley's Squire and he said Desiderius took a tremendous amount of pleasure from messing with Cromley's head. D. ended up killing Cromley in a manner best not mentioned. Personally, I wish D. would come after me, I need a good dance partner. My Daimons have lame legs.

Kyrian laughed at Ash's dry wit. The man truly had no patience for lame Daimons. "Talon said they're using astral blasts. Have you ever come across that?"

In eleven thousand years, I can honestly say ... hell, no. This is a first. I've called in the Oracles and they are communing with the Fates. But you know how they are. I'm sure it'll come back as "When the sky is green, and the earth turns black, the Daimons will give you lots of fluck. To kill the great awful one you seek, you'll have to find something unique." Or some bullshit like that. I really hate Oracles. If I wanted to play mind games, I'd buy a Rubik's Cube.

"I don't know, Ash, you're pretty good at that. Sure you don't want to take up an Oracle position?"

Picture this, General, my middle finger is extended all the way up, and aimed right at you. Now let me work. I have Daimons to track, Dark-Hunters to antagonize, and women to seduce. Talk to you later.

No longer in the mood to talk, Kyrian logged off the Dark-Hunter site. He opened his e-mail, but he didn't really want to read it, either.

What he wanted was beyond his ability to claim.

Against his will, he wandered down the hallway, then down the stairs.

Before he realized what he was doing, he found himself outside Amanda's room. He pressed his hand against the dark wood door and splayed his fingers. Closing his eyes, he could see her sitting in bed, her long legs bare beneath his T-shirt.

Fire pounded through his blood. He could feel her pain at the loss of her house. Feel her fear as she thought of Desiderius hurting her sister, and her worry over Tabitha's roommate.

Worse, he could sense the tears she was holding back. She was so strong. So capable. He'd never known a woman like her before.

His dream from the morning tore through him. He could still feel her in his arms.

"I want you."

He'd give anything to hear her say those words for real. To see her look at him as if she could devour him.

Right now, the only thing he wanted to do was to kick open the door and make love to her. To have her touch him. Hold him.

Welcome him.

But it wasn't meant to be.

His heart heavy, he forced himself to leave her.

He had work to do.

Amanda glanced at the clock. Twelve-thirty. Normally she would be fast asleep by now. But to Hunter the night would still be young.

She wondered what he did during the wee hours. Surely he didn't kill Daimons every night. There weren't that many of them, were there?

Before she realized what she was doing, she got out of bed and wandered through the enormous house. She didn't know where Hunter was. He hadn't bothered to show her his room while he had given her the tour.

But her instinct told her his room would be upstairs. Probably as far away from hers as possible.

She was halfway up the stairs when she heard something odd outside. It was a strange whooshing noise.

Backtracking, she found her way to the dark game room. There was no light, but the moon and stars were so bright outside that she could see a shadowy figure in the atrium. Her first impulse was to call for Hunter; she paused.

There was something very familiar about that figure. Walking closer to the French doors, she recognized Terminator and Hunter. Hunter was dressed in a T-shirt and sweatpants. He was tossing a baseball into a net-covered frame that bounced it back to him.

As soon as he threw the ball, Terminator would give chase, then the dog would bound back to Hunter.

She smiled at the sight. Hunter patted Terminator, then returned to tossing the ball.

She started to leave, but couldn't. Instead, she cracked open the door.

Hunter turned instantly. The forgotten ball rebounded and caught him on the head. He hissed as he rubbed his head and Terminator chased after the baseball.

"Did you need something?" he asked, his voice sharp.

I need you to kiss me.

She swallowed. "I just didn't know where you were."

"Now you do."

The ice was back in his voice. This wasn't the Hunter who had been with her a short time ago, this was the Dark-Hunter who had awakened in the factory with her. Guarded. Distant.

And it cut through to her heart. It wasn't just the lump on his head from the baseball making him snappish; his old barriers were back in place. He was pushing her away.

Taking the hint, she nodded. "Yeah, well, good night."

Kyrian watched her leave. He'd wounded her. He could sense it and he hated himself for it.

Call her back.

But to what purpose?

There could never be anything between them. Not even friendship.

Grinding his teeth, he went back to his pitching. As he worked out, he tried to focus on Desiderius. Tried to will the Daimon into his grasp.

It was useless.

Amanda was still with him. It was her face he saw when he closed his eyes. Her scent that permeated his senses.

If he didn't banish her from his thoughts, he would get himself killed. And if he died, Desiderius would go after her.

Growling, he threw the ball against the net. He twirled around to catch it on the rebound, but before his hand made contact, a fierce pain slashed through his skull.

Kyrian cursed. He put the heel of his hand over his right eye, and as he struggled with the pain, an image tore through him.

It was Desiderius.

As the image sharpened, he froze. With amazing clarity, he saw Desiderius kill him.

And he heard Amanda weeping.

CHAPTER 8

After Amanda fell asleep, her dreams drifted for a time like a bizarre, twisting kaleidoscope coalescing without shape or form. Foreign images, people, and places twirled and tumbled in her mind until her head swam from them.

After a while, they became more focused and she could see them clearly. Unknown people greeted her as she walked past them.

It seemed so incredibly real; like a forgotten memory more than a dream. Even though she'd never seen these people before, she knew them by name. Knew things about them only a friend would know.

She heard the sound of men laughing and celebrating. Felt a strange mixture of joy and sadness as she became aware of a faded red tent filled with soldiers wearing ancient armor.

"You were brilliant," an older soldier said, clapping her on the back. She recognized him as her second in command. A man she relied on and one who worshiped her. Dimitri had always looked to her for guidance and strength.

He had a fresh, open wound down the left side of his face, but his old gray eyes sparkled. Though his armor was covered in blood, he appeared remarkably unhurt. "It's a pity Julian wasn't here to see this victory. He would have been proud of you today, Commander. I can guarantee all of Rome is weeping this night."

At that moment, she realized the dream wasn't about her.

She was Kyrian . . .

Kyrian's face was smudged with sweat, dirt, and blood, his long, leather-bound hair tousled. He had three long, thin braids that fell from his left temple down to the middle of his chest. The man was simply gorgeous and completely human.

His dark green eyes shimmered from victory and he had the carriage of a man who had no equal. Of a man destined for greatness.

Kyrian raised the goblet of wine in his hand and addressed the men in his tent. "I declare this victory for Julian of Macedon. Wherever he is, I know he's laughing at Scipio's defeat."

A loud cheer roared from the men.

Kyrian took a drink, then looked to the older soldier beside him. "It's a pity Valerius wasn't there with Scipio. I was looking forward to facing him, too. But no matter." He lifted his voice so that all the men gathered inside could hear him. "Tomorrow, we march on Rome herself and we'll bring that bitch to her knees."

The men shouted their agreement.

"On the battlefield, with a sword in your hand, you are invincible," the old man said in an awed tone. "By this time tomorrow, you will be ruler of the known world."

Kyrian shook his head. "Andriscus will be ruler of Rome tomorrow. Not I."

The old man looked aghast, then he leaned close to Kyrian's neck and lowered his tone so that only Kyrian could hear him. "There are those who think he is weak. Those who would support you if you decided—"

"No, Dimitri," Kyrian said, cutting him off gently. "I appreciate the thought, but I swore to lead his army for Andriscus and that I shall do until the day I die. I will never betray him."

The look on Dimitri's face showed his confusion. He wasn't sure if he should applaud Kyrian's loyalty or curse it. "You're the only man I know who would turn down the opportunity to rule the world."

Kyrian laughed. "Kingdoms and empires don't bring happiness, Dimitri. Only the love of a good woman and children do that."

"And conquest," Dimitri added.

Kyrian smiled even wider. "Tonight, at least, that appears to be true."

"Commander?"

Kyrian turned toward the voice behind him to see a man cutting a swath through the men in the tent.

The soldier held out a sealed letter. "A courier brought this. It was discovered on a Roman messenger earlier today."

Taking it from him, Kyrian saw the seal of Valerius the Younger on the outside. Curious, he opened the vellum and read it, and with every word, his panic swelled. His heart beat faster. "My horse!" he shouted, running out of the crowded tent. "Saddle my horse."

"Commander?"

He turned to his second in command who had followed him outside. A worried frown creased his tired old brow. "Dimitri, you're in charge until I return. Pull the army back into the hills, away from the Romans until you hear from me. If I'm not back in a week, then lead the men to Punjara and combine forces with Jason."

"Are you sure?"

"Yes."

A youth came forward with his black stallion. His heart hammering, Kyrian swung himself up into the saddle.

"Where are you off to?" Dimitri asked.

"Valerius is riding to my villa. I'm going to head him off."

Dimitri grabbed the horse's bridle, horrified. "You can't go alone to meet him."

"I have no time to wait for you. My wife is in danger. I will not hesitate." Kyrian wheeled his horse about and spurred it through the camp.

Amanda twisted in bed as she felt Kyrian's rising panic. His need to protect his wife at any cost. The days ran together as he rode furiously, changing horses every time he happened upon a village. He never stopped to rest or eat. He was like a

demon possessed, with only one thought on his mind. *Theone.*
Theone. Theone.

He reached his home in the middle of the night. Weary and
terrified, he leapt from his horse and pounded on the door for
admittance.

An old man pulled open the heavy wooden door. "Your
Highness?" he asked in disbelief.

Kyrian pushed past the man, his gaze sweeping his grand
foyer looking for signs of hostility. Nothing out of the ordinary
met his fearful gaze. Still, he wasn't comforted. Not yet. He
would not be calm until he saw her with his own eyes.
"Where's my wife?"

The old servant looked confused by the question. His
mouth opened and closed like a fish. Finally, he spoke. "In
her bed, Highness."

Starving, exhausted, and weak, Kyrian ran down the long,
columned corridor toward the back of the house.

"Theone?" he called as he ran, desperate to see her.

A door at the end of the hallway opened. An incredibly
beautiful and petite blond woman came to stand in the hallway. She closed the door behind her and swept a chiding
glance over Kyrian's dishevelment.

She was alive and unharmed. And she was the most beautiful vision his adoring eyes had ever beheld.

Her long, golden hair was tousled, her cheeks bright pink.
She clutched a very thin white sheet over her nude body. "Kyrian?" she asked sharply.

Relief rushed through him and tears filled his eyes. She was
alive! Thank the gods. Blinking the tears away, he swept her
up into his arms and held her close. Never had he been more
grateful to the Fates for their mercy.

"Kyrian," she snapped, bristling under his touch. "Put me
down. You smell so bad I can barely breathe. Have you any
idea how late it is?"

"Aye," he said through the tight knot in his throat as joy
pounded through him. He set her down and cupped her face
in his hands. He was so tired he could hardly stand or think,

but he wouldn't sleep. Not until she was safe. "And I must get you away from here. Get dressed."

She frowned. "Take me where?"

"To Thrace."

"Thrace?" she asked incredulously. "Are you mad?"

"No. I've received word that the Romans are headed this way. I'm taking you to my father for safekeeping. Now hurry!"

She didn't. Instead, her face darkened dangerously as fury snapped in her gray eyes. "Your father? You've not spoken to him in *seven* years. What makes you think he'd shelter me?"

"My father will forgive me if I ask it."

"Your father will throw us both out. He made his proclamation quite public. I've been embarrassed enough in my lifetime, I don't need to hear him call me a whore to my face. Besides, I don't want to leave my villa. I like it here."

Kyrian disregarded her words. "My father loves me and will do as I ask. You'll see. Now dress."

She looked past his shoulder. "Polydus?" she said to the old servant who had been waiting all that time behind Kyrian. "Have a bath prepared for your master and bring him food and wine."

"Theone—"

She stopped Kyrian's words by placing a hand on his lips. "Hush, my lord. It's the middle of the night. You look dreadful and you smell even worse. Let us clean you, feed you, and put you to sleep, and then in the morning, we can discuss what needs be done to see me safe."

"But the Romans—"

"Did you see any on your way here?"

"Well . . . no."

"Then there can't be any danger at the moment, now can there?"

Too weary to argue, he conceded. "I suppose not."

"Then come." She took him by the hand and led him to a small room off the main corridor.

The next thing Amanda saw was a room lit by a small fire

and candles. Kyrian was leaning back in a gilded tub while Theone bathed him.

He captured her hand in his and held it to his whiskered cheek. "You've no idea how much I've missed you. Your touch soothes me like nothing else."

She smiled a smile that didn't quite reach her eyes and handed him a cup of wine. "I heard you took Thessaly from the Romans."

"Aye. Valerius was incensed. I can't wait until I march on Rome. I will have her yet, mark my words."

Kyrian drained the cup, then set it aside. His body burning, he reached for his wife and pulled her into the tub with him.

"Kyrian!" she gasped.

"Shh," he breathed against her lips. "I would have a kiss from you."

She acquiesced, but there was a coldness to her. He could feel it.

"What is wrong, my love?" he asked, pulling back. "You seem so distant tonight. As though your thoughts are somewhere else."

Her face softened as she straddled his waist and took him into her body. "I am not distant. I am tired."

He smiled, then groaned as she moved against him. "Forgive me for waking you. I just wanted to know you were safe. I couldn't live if anything ever happened to you." He cupped her face in his hands and stroked her cheeks with his thumbs. "I will always love you, Theone. You are the very air I breathe."

Kissing her lips, he savored her taste.

She seemed to relax some in his arms as she slowly rode him. All the while her gaze watched him as if she were waiting for something . . .

As soon as he climaxed, Kyrian leaned back in the tub to watch her. He was as weak as a newborn whelp. But he was home, and his wife was his strength. His haven.

No sooner had that thought crossed his mind than a strange buzzing started in his head. A wave of dizziness swept through him.

And in an instant, he knew what she'd done. "Poison?" he gasped.

Theone scrambled off him and left the tub. Hurriedly, she wrapped a towel around herself. "No."

Kyrian tried to get out of the tub, but another wave of dizziness gripped him. He fell back into the water. He couldn't breathe as thoughts wandered randomly through his drugged mind.

But foremost in his mind was the very treachery of the woman he loved. A woman he had given the world to.

"Theone, what have you done to me?"

She lifted her chin as she watched him coldly. "I'm doing what you can't. I'm protecting myself. Rome is the future, Kyrian. Not Andriscus. He will never live to ascend to the Macedonian throne."

Darkness fell.

Amanda groaned as she felt a severe pain lance through her skull. When the light returned, she found Kyrian lying naked against a cold stone slab that was tilted at a forty-five-degree angle. His arms and legs had been secured with ropes to winches.

He glanced around the medium-sized room to an old table set in one corner, the top of which was covered with all manner of torture instruments. A tall, black-haired man stood looking over the table's offerings, his back to Kyrian.

Kyrian felt so alone and betrayed. So completely defenseless.

It was a terrifying sensation for someone who had never known vulnerability.

The room was stifling hot from the fire in the hearth. Somehow, Amanda knew it was early summer outside. The windows were open and a gentle Mediterranean breeze blew across the room, carrying the scent of sea, flowers, and olives. Kyrian heard laughter from outside and his stomach knotted.

It was too beautiful a day to die . . .

The man at the table cocked his head. Suddenly, he turned and pinned a menacing glare on Kyrian. Though the man was incredibly handsome, there was a cold sneer on his face that robbed him of his appeal. The man had the cruel, glittering eyes of a viper. They were soulless, calculating, and completely lacking in compassion.

"Kyrian of Thrace." He smiled evilly. "At last we meet. Though I'm sure this isn't quite what you had planned, is it?"

"Valerius," he snarled as soon as he saw the banner on the wall over the man's shoulder. He would know that eagle emblem anywhere.

The Roman's smile widened as he crossed the room. There was no respect on Valerius's face. Only smug satisfaction.

Without another word, Valerius turned the winch that held the ropes to Kyrian's limbs. The ropes tightened, pulling at Kyrian's muscles, tearing ligaments and popping his bones from their joints.

Kyrian clenched his eyes tight and ground his teeth at the agony that whipped through his body.

Tightening the winch even more, Valerius laughed. "Good, you're strong. I hate to torture little boys who whimper and cry right away. It takes all the fun out of it."

Kyrian said nothing.

After locking the winch into place to keep Kyrian's body painfully stretched, Valerius walked over to the table where a number of weapons and tools rested. He hefted a heavy iron mallet in his hands. "Since you are new to my company, allow me to educate you on how Rome deals with her enemies . . ."

He sauntered back to Kyrian, offering Kyrian a goading smirk. "First, we crush your knees. This way, I know you won't be tempted to leave my hospitality until I'm ready for you to."

Valerius brought the mallet down over Kyrian's left knee, shattering the joint instantly. Unimaginable pain ripped through him. Biting his lip to keep from crying out, Kyrian gripped the ropes binding his hands. He could feel the warm blood from his cut wrists trail down his forearms.

Once he'd shattered Kyrian's other knee, Valerius picked up a hot iron from the hearth and brought it over to him. "I only have one question. Where is your army?"

Kyrian narrowed his eyes, but said nothing.

Valerius laid the hot iron against his inner thigh.

Amanda lost track of the wounds as Valerius tortured Kyrian. Hour after hour, day after day with resolute vigor.

She'd never known a person could suffer so much and continue to live.

She gasped as water was thrown into Kyrian's face.

"Don't think you can pass out to escape me. Nor starve until I will it."

Valerius grabbed Kyrian's hair and pulled his head viciously, then poured broth down his throat. Kyrian hissed as the salty liquid stung the cuts on his face, his lips. He choked on the broth, but still Valerius poured it into his mouth.

"Drink, damn you," Valerius snarled. "Drink!"

Kyrian passed out again, and again the cold water brought him back awake.

Days and nights blended together as time went by while Valerius assaulted him, again and again. Always asking the same question. "Where is your army?"

Kyrian never uttered a single word. Never once cried out. He kept his jaw so tightly locked that Valerius had to pry it open to force-feed him.

"Commander Valerius," a soldier said as he came into the room while Valerius again turned the winches against Kyrian's arms and legs. "Forgive my interruption, my lord, but there's an emissary from Thrace wanting an audience with you."

Kyrian's heart stopped beating. For the first time in weeks, a sliver of hope swept through him, overwhelming him with joy.

His father . . .

Valerius arched a curious brow at his underling. "This should be quite entertaining. By all means, show him in."

The soldier vanished.

A few minutes later, an older, well-dressed man entered the room with two Roman soldiers trailing him. The man looked so much like Kyrian that for a moment, Amanda thought it was his father.

As soon as the man was close enough to recognize Kyrian's bloody, misshapen form, he gasped.

His dignity forgotten, his uncle ran to his side. "Kyrian?" he breathed in disbelief, gingerly touching Kyrian's broken arm. His blue eyes were filled with pain and concern. "Dear Zeus, what have they done to you?"

She felt Kyrian's tremendous shame and grief at seeing his uncle's sorrow. She felt the need inside Kyrian to relieve the guilt that swam in Zetes's eyes and to beg him to ask his father to forgive him.

When Kyrian opened his mouth to speak, all that came out was a hoarse croak. He hurt so badly that his unclenched teeth chattered from the weight of his physical suffering.

Kyrian's throat was so sore and parched that he choked, but by sheer force of will, he finally spoke through trembling lips. "Uncle."

"Can it be, he can actually speak?" Valerius asked, joining them. "He's said nothing in four weeks. Nothing other than this . . ."

Again he laid a hot brand to Kyrian's thigh.

Clenching his teeth, Kyrian jerked and hissed.

"Cease!" Zetes cried, pushing Valerius away from his nephew.

He tenderly cupped Kyrian's bruised face in his hands. Tears fell down Zetes's cheeks as he tried to clean the blood away from Kyrian's swollen lips.

He looked up at Valerius. "I have ten wagons of gold and jewels. His father promises even more if you release him. I have been authorized to surrender Thrace to you. And his sister, the Princess Althea, has offered herself to you as a slave. All you have to do is let me take him home."

No! She heard Kyrian's inner scream, but the word was lodged in his burning throat.

"Perhaps. I'll let you take him home . . . After he's executed."

"No!" Zetes said. "He is a prince, and you—"

"He is no prince. Everyone knows he was disowned. His father was quite public with his decree."

"And he has recanted it," Zetes insisted. He looked back at Kyrian, his eyes kind and soothing. "He wanted me to tell you

he didn't mean what he said to you. He was foolish and blind
when he should have trusted and listened to you. Your father
loves you, Kyrian. All he wants is for you to come home
where he can welcome you and Theone with open arms. He
begs you to forgive him."

Those last words burned through Kyrian more painfully
than Valerius's iron brands. It wasn't his father who should
apologize. His father wasn't the one who had been a fool.

It was Kyrian who had been cruel to a man who had never
done anything other than love him. The agony of it swept
through him anew.

Gods have mercy on them both, for his father had been
right all along.

Zetes glanced to Valerius. "He will give you anything for
his son's life. *Anything!*"

"Anything," Valerius repeated. "How very tempting, but
how stupid would I have to be to release the one man who
has come close to defeating us?" He glared at Zetes. "Never."

Valerius took the dagger from his belt. Roughly, he grabbed
the three long, thin commander's braids at Kyrian's temple
and sawed them off.

"Here," he said, handing them to Zetes. "Take those to his
father and tell him that is all of his son he'll ever get from
me."

"No!"

"Guards, see to it *His Highness* is taken away."

Kyrian watched as his uncle was seized and dragged from
the room.

"Kyrian!"

Kyrian struggled against his restraints, but his body was so
sore and broken that all he succeeded in doing was hurting
himself more.

He wanted to call Zetes back. He wanted to tell him how
sorry he was for all he'd said to his parents.

Don't let me die without their knowing.

"You can't do this!" Zetes screamed an instant before the
doors slammed shut, cutting him off.

Valerius turned to his servant. "Fetch my mistress."

As soon as the servant was gone, he returned to Kyrian. He sighed as if greatly disappointed. "It appears our time together has ended. If your father is so desperate for your return, then it is only a matter of time before he marches against me. I certainly can't take a chance on him actually rescuing you, now can I?"

Kyrian closed his eyes and turned his head away from Valerius's triumphant sneer. In his mind, he saw his father on that last, fateful day as the two of them stood, toe to toe, in the center of the throne room. Julian had dubbed that day the Clash of the Titans. For neither he nor his father had been willing to listen or to yield.

He heard the words he'd said to his father. Words no son should ever utter to a parent.

The agony of it was a hundred times more severe than anything Valerius had dealt him.

While he grieved over his actions, the doors of his torture chamber opened to admit Theone. She walked into the room with her head held high, like a queen holding court. She stopped next to Valerius and gave him a warm, inviting smile.

Kyrian stared at her as the weight of her betrayal coursed through him. *Let this be a nightmare.*

Dear Zeus, please don't let this be real. It was more than his broken body and soul could take.

"You know, Kyrian," Valerius said as he wrapped his arms around Theone and nuzzled her neck. "I will commend you on your choice of wife. She is exceptional in bed, isn't she?"

It was the cruelest blow yet dealt him.

Theone met Kyrian's eyes without shame while Valerius circled behind her, cupped her breasts in his hands and kneaded them. There was no love on her face. No remorse. Nothing. She stared at him as if he were a stranger.

It cut him all the way to his battered soul.

"Come, Theone, let us show your husband what he interrupted the night he came home."

Valerius removed the clip from her himation and let it fall to the floor. He pulled her naked body into his arms and kissed her.

Kyrian's heart splintered at the sight of Theone removing Valerius's armor. The sight of her eagerly welcoming his touch.

Unable to bear it, he closed his eyes and turned away. But still he heard them. He heard his wife begging for Valerius to fill her. Heard her moaning in pleasure. And when she climaxed in the arms of his enemy, he felt his heart wither and die.

At last Valerius had broken him.

He let the pain take him then. Let it wash over him until he felt nothing at all. Nothing but utter and complete desolation.

When they were finished, Valerius sauntered over to him. He wiped his wet hand across Kyrian's face and Kyrian cursed the scent he knew so well.

"Have you any idea how much I love the smell of your wife on my body?"

Kyrian spat in his face.

Enraged, Valerius pulled a dagger from the table and embedded it savagely in Kyrian's stomach. Kyrian gasped as the cold metal invaded his body. Maliciously, Valerius rotated his wrist and twisted the knife, pushing it in deeper.

"Tell me, Theone," Valerius said, his eyes never leaving Kyrian's as he pulled the dagger out and left him weak and panting. "How should I kill your husband? Should I behead him as befitting a prince?"

"No," she said as she wrapped her himation around her and secured it with the brooch Kyrian had given her on their wedding day. "He is the spirit and backbone of the Macedonian rebels. You can't afford to make him a martyr. Were I you, I'd crucify him like a common thief. Let him stand as an example to Rome's enemies to know that there is no honor or glory in assaulting Rome."

Valerius smiled cruelly, then turned to face her. "I like the way your mind works." He kissed her lightly on the cheek, then dressed himself.

"Say good-bye to your husband while I make arrangements." He left them alone.

Kyrian struggled to breathe through his pain as Theone fi-, nally approached him. His body trembled from rage and agony. Still, her gaze was blank. Cold.

"Why?" he asked.

"Why?" she repeated. "Why do you think? I was the nameless daughter of a prostitute. I grew up hungry and poor with no choice except to let any man use me as he saw fit."

"I sheltered you," he rasped through his split, bloody lips. "Loved you. I kept you safe from anyone who would have hurt you."

She narrowed her eyes at him. "I am not about to let you war against Rome while I sit at home in fear of them tearing down my walls to get to you. I don't want to end up like Julian's wife, executed in my own bed, or sold into slavery. I've come too far to go back to scrounging for scraps, selling my body. I want my security and I will do anything to protect it."

She couldn't have hurt him any worse. She had never seen him as *anything* other than a rich pocket.

No, he couldn't believe that. He refused to believe it. There had to have been a moment, just one, when she had cared for him. Surely, he couldn't have been *that* blind?

"Did you *ever* love me?"

She shrugged. "If it's any consolation, you were the best lover I've ever known. I will certainly miss you in my bed."

Kyrian let out an agonized bellow of rage.

"Damn, Theone," Valerius said as he returned. "I should have let you torture him. I never once got that much pain out of him."

The soldiers came in with a large cross. They laid it on the floor next to the table, then cut Kyrian down.

His limbs broken, he sank to the floor.

Roughly, they picked him up and dropped him over the wood.

Kyrian continued to watch Theone. Not even pity graced her brow. She merely looked on in morbid fascination.

Again, he saw his parents' stricken faces when he had left

his home the day of the wedding. Heard Zetes's offer to Valerius.

Kyrian had betrayed them all for *her*. And now she couldn't even pretend to be sorry for what she'd done to him. What she had cost his family and his country.

He was Greece's last hope to stave off Roman tyranny. He was the only thing that stood between their people and slavery.

With one act of treachery, she had laid waste to all their dreams of freedom.

And all because *he* was a stupid fool . . .

His father's final, parting words rang in his ears. *She doesn't love you, Kyrian. No woman will ever be able to love you and you're a damned fool if you ever believe otherwise!*

A soldier placed a metal spike over his wrist and held it there as another drew back a heavy iron hammer.

The Roman guard brought it down on the spike . . .

Amanda came awake screaming as she felt the nail piercing her arm. Sitting up, she grabbed her wrist to make sure it had just been a dream.

She rubbed her arm, staring at it. She was just as she had always been and yet . . .

The dream had been real. She knew it.

Driven by a force she didn't understand, she left her room to find Kyrian. She ran through the dark house, just after dawn, up the mahogany staircase and down a long hallway. She followed her instincts to a set of doors on the west side of the house.

Without hesitating, she threw open the double doors to a bedroom twice the size of her own. A single candle burned next to an old-fashioned, curtained bed, casting shadows against the far wall. The gold and brown curtains were pulled back and fastened to the posts while cream-colored sheers shielded the bed. Even so, she could see her Hunter writhing on the rust-colored sheets as if caught in the midst of the same nightmare she had seen.

Her heart hammering, she ran to the bed.

Kyrian woke up from his nightmare the very instant he felt Amanda's cool, gentle hand on his chest. He opened his eyes to find her sitting by his side, her gaze dark with horror, her brows knitted as she examined him.

He frowned while her hands roamed all over his chest. It was as if she didn't really see him at all, as if she were in some kind of strange trance.

He lay in complete silence, stunned by her presence.

She pulled back the silk sheet and touched the scar on his stomach, just to the left of his navel.

"He drove the knife in here," she whispered, stroking the narrow scar.

Then she grabbed his wrist and tenderly traced the scars there. "They hammered the spikes in here and here."

Next she went to his hand and rubbed the pad of her thumb over his fingertips. "They pulled your fingernails off."

She reached up and cupped his stubbled cheek in her palm. Her eyes held a thousand emotions and the sight of those crystal-blue depths stole the breath from him.

No woman had ever given him such a look.

"My poor Hunter," she whispered. Tears streamed down her face and before he knew what she was doing, she pulled the sheet away from him, baring his entire body to her questing gaze. He hardened instantly, his body throbbing at the sight of her concern for him.

She touched his scarred thigh where Valerius had once placed a hot brand to it.

"Oh God," she gasped, her fingers brushing his puckered skin. "It was real. They really did that to you . . ."

She looked up at him, her eyes swimming in tears. "I saw you. I *felt* you."

Kyrian frowned even more. Was that possible?

He'd been dreaming of his execution when she woke him. Could their powers have combined to allow him to reach out to her even while he slept?

It was a terrifying thought. If it were true, then it meant they were bonded together on a much higher level than the physical.

It meant . . .

He didn't finish that thought. There was no such thing as

a soul mate, especially when one of them no longer had a
soul. It just wasn't possible.

As Amanda stared at him, she ached all the way to her
heart for the man before her. How had he borne such torture
and betrayal?

He had carried it with him through the centuries. Alone.
Always alone. Always hurting and wanting, with no relief.

No hope.

"So much pain," she whispered.

How she wanted Theone's head for what she'd done to him.
But most of all, she wanted to soothe Hunter. Wanted to ease
the torment in his heart. Erase the pain of his past.

She wanted to give him something to hope for.

She wanted to give him his dream of children and of a
woman who could love him.

God have mercy on her, but she wanted to be that woman.

Before she could stop herself, she leaned down and captured his lips with her own. He moaned at the contact and
cupped her face in his hands while he returned her kiss.

Amanda tasted him in a way she'd never tasted any man
before. As their tongues danced, she could feel him all the
way to her soul. She'd never in her life been bold in bed. But
then she'd never wanted a man like this.

With the whole of her.

Tears welled in Amanda's eyes as she buried her lips
against his collarbone, over the scar where Valerius had
dragged his ring and left it bloody.

Such strength. Such love. She would give anything to have
a man love her the way he had loved his wife.

More to the point, she wanted Hunter to love *her*. She
wanted his heart. She wanted this man who knew what love
was, who understood commitment and compassion.

Whether he would admit it or not, he needed her.

No man should walk eternity alone. No one should ever be
hurt the way he'd been hurt. Not when his only crime was
loving someone more than he had loved himself.

Her breath mixed with his as she climbed up his body and
straddled his waist.

Kyrian groaned as he realized she wore nothing beneath his T-shirt. Her thighs were hot and moist as she slid herself against his bare stomach, igniting a fire deep inside him that needed her so much it terrified him.

Push her away.

But he couldn't. Not tonight. Not after the nightmare that was still fresh in his mind.

Right or wrong, he needed comfort. He wanted to feel loved again. He wanted to know the softness of a woman's hands on his body. The scent of Amanda on his skin.

Kyrian shook as she reached down and wrapped her hand around him. "Oh gods," he breathed against her lips. No one had touched him like this in over two thousand years.

His entire body throbbed and ached as she stroked his hot, rigid shaft.

Today, he would have her. There was no way he could push her away now.

His breathing ragged, he trembled from the feel of her fingers gripping him, her palm brushing up, along his shaft, then down to the base where she cupped him gently. Her fingers skimmed the underside of him, making him even harder, hotter, until he thought he would burst from it.

He trailed his hands slowly over her body, savoring every dip and curve. Savoring the feel of her soft skin and the T-shirt against his palms and fingers. He nuzzled her neck and for the first time since his Dark-Hunter incarnation, he felt an overwhelming urge to feed off a human.

The sound of her blood coursing through her veins filled his ears. Her raw energy beckoned him, making the Dark-Hunter in him long to sample her life force.

It was forbidden. No Dark-Hunter was supposed to puncture a human neck. And yet as he stroked the hollow of her throat with his tongue, the deep-seated need burned in him.

He grazed her neck with his fangs and it took every piece of control he had not to taste the blood he could feel rushing under his lips. He felt the chills spread over her body, making the nipple under his hand even tighter.

Pulling back with a growl, he latched onto her mouth and

kissed her deeply as he slid his hand under the T-shirt, to the dark triangle between her legs.

He groaned at the feel of those tiny hairs teasing his fingers as he carefully separated them and touched her for the very first time.

She jumped in surprise, then moaned a welcoming murmur as she quickened her fairy strokes on his shaft.

Kyrian couldn't believe how wet she was already. Gods, how he wanted her. Wanted to taste every inch of her flesh. To drive himself deep into her fiery heat.

But he resisted because he wanted to savor the moment. Wanted to explore her tenderly, slowly.

He wanted this morning to last forever.

"You taste so good," he whispered as he ripped the T-shirt from neck to hem, pulled it from her, and threw it to the floor. He nibbled a path from her neck to her breasts.

Amanda arched her back as he gently teased her nipple with his tongue and fangs. The feel of those sharp teeth on her skin made her burn like lava.

Once more he dipped his hand back down between their bodies and touched her where she ached most. His fingers swirled around her, teasing and soothing, delving and stroking, making her burn even more for him as he slid them deep inside her and made hot, sweet love to her with his hand.

"I want you, Hunter," she breathed against his lips. "I've never wanted anyone like this."

He smiled, showing her his fangs as he rolled her over to lie beneath him with an ease of strength that awed her.

Amanda moaned at the feel of his hard, lean body on top of hers. His weight stole her breath and she wrapped her legs around his hips.

He was all sinewy power. It rippled from his body into hers.

Those sleek, honed muscles flexed around her with every graceful move he made. But even more captivating was the restrained power he showed. Like a fierce lion ready to strike.

She wanted more of him. She ached to feel him inside her. Ached to claim him in a way she knew no woman had claimed him in over two thousand years. She wanted this man's heart.

Even more, she wanted to claim him in a way no woman had *ever* claimed him before. She wanted to be everything he needed. His breath, his heart, but most of all his missing soul.

She wanted to give that back to him. To release him from his suffering. To free him from his past.

Arching her back, she kissed him deeply before she accidentally confessed her thoughts. Should he ever learn, she had no doubt he would pull away from her.

That was the last thing she wanted. So she summoned her repressed powers for the first time in over a decade and shielded her thoughts to hide her mind and her heart from him just in case he was still able to see inside her.

Today, she would be his comfort.

Kyrian growled at the sensation of Amanda's body beneath his. It had been so incredibly long since he had allowed himself to trust a woman like this.

Sweat broke out over his body as he left her breasts and nibbled her ribs, her hips, then he moved back up her body.

He wanted her with an inhuman need. Wanted things from her he dared not name. These thoughts of claiming her, of keeping her, should not be on his mind.

And yet they were.

Amanda ran her hand through his hair. She held him close as he nibbled his way from her lips to her throat, then down to her breasts where he took his time tasting her. His tongue circled her hardened nipple, teasing and stroking. He seemed insatiable as he devoured her like a starving man at a banquet.

Then slowly, carefully, he worked his way down her body. His long canine teeth scraped her skin with such tenderness that it amazed her. His hands burned her as he ran them beneath her hips. He slid his tongue down her hipbone, to her thigh.

He spread her legs wider and slowly laved his way up her inner thigh. She held her breath, writhing in anticipation of his touch.

When he hesitated, she looked down to find him staring up at her. The raw, possessive look on his face stole her breath.

His gaze held hers enthralled as he gently, slowly, ran his finger down her cleft, then back up. She shivered in response to his touch. He separated her tender folds, and took her into his mouth, all the while watching her.

Amanda cried out at the fierce ecstasy that ripped through her. No man had done that to her before.

He closed his eyes and moaned in a way that reverberated through her. His tongue slid in and around, making her entire body jerk and quiver with every sensuous lick he delivered.

Running her hand through his tousled curls, she arched her back, opening her legs wider to give him complete access to her.

Kyrian shook at the taste of her. He'd never wanted anything as much as he wanted this woman. There was something about her that drove him wild.

But he could feel his Dark-Hunter powers straining. Feel the animal in him awakening.

These were the powers he used when he fought or tracked. Powers that enabled him to sense his surroundings on a greater level. They made him aware of her heart pounding in her chest. Of the little tremors in her body that responded to his lips and tongue.

He felt the pleasure he was giving her and it made his body throb in time with the blood rushing through her thighs, which cradled his face. He closed his eyes as he fought the urge once again to sink his teeth into her thigh and taste her blood on his tongue.

Amanda clutched him to her as he continued to pleasure her. His fangs gently scraped her, sending a shudder through her. She opened her eyes and saw him intent upon his actions. It was as if he had zenned completely on her and nothing else.

He *was* sex, she realized. His very being was focused on her and her pleasure with the same intensity she was sure he only used to stalk the Daimons.

And when her release came, it was so fierce, so overwhelming, that she threw her head back and screamed out.

Still, he wasn't through with her. He growled as she released herself, but his licks never stopped. They became faster, stronger as he continued to feast on her body.

She hissed in pleasure.

It wasn't until she came twice more that he finally slowed. And even then he waited until the very last tremor had shaken her before he pulled away.

He rose up from between her legs and prowled up her body, slowly, methodically, like some hungry, powerful beast about to prey on its dinner.

His eyes flashed like jet, and his fangs were visible as he breathed raggedly.

"Look at me, Amanda," he commanded as he ran his hand down to her thigh. "I want to see your eyes when I take you."

Swallowing, she did as he asked.

He cupped her face in his hand and kissed her deeply, then he took her hand into his and guided it to his swollen shaft.

Without being told, she knew what he wanted. Arching her hips, she led him inside her, slowly, inch by long, full inch until he filled her deeply. She moaned at the sensation of his power inside her. At the hungry, needful look in his eyes.

As she started to pull her hand away, he covered it with his and held it against him.

The hunger in his eyes intensified. "I want you to feel us joined," he said raggedly.

Amanda swallowed as he slid himself between her fingers and went even deeper inside her. In and out. It was the most erotic, incredible thing she'd ever known.

They moaned simultaneously.

Amanda saw the pleasure on his face as he rocked himself forcefully against her hips. "Oh, Hunter," she breathed.

He paused and looked down at her. "It's not the Dark-Hunter inside you right now, Amanda. It's *me,* Kyrian."

Joy exploded through her as she realized what he was offering her. He had let her inside him the same way she had allowed him to enter her.

Reaching up, she cupped his face in her hands. "Kyrian," she breathed.

He smiled. "You feel even better than I thought you

would," he said as she felt a shiver run over his body.

He dipped his head down and took her lips in a tender kiss as he delivered fierce, fast strokes to her. Hard, long, and deep. They tore through her, spiking pure bliss through her body.

"Oh, Kyrian," she moaned against his lips as she felt her pleasure building again.

No sooner had his name left her lips than something strange started happening to her. Something shifted inside her and she felt an erotic surge.

"Oh my," she breathed.

Suddenly, she could feel him *feel* her.

It was as if they were really one person. She felt him inside her and she could feel herself around him.

Kyrian struggled to breathe as he felt it, too. They stared into each other's eyes.

Amanda ran her hand down his back. She felt the caress down her own spine. It was the most incredible thing she'd ever experienced.

He quickened his strokes, and she clung to him, both of them out of their minds with volcanic need.

They came together in one fierce moment of sublime plea-sure. Kyrian threw his head back and roared as he buried him-self deep inside her. Amanda cried out as he shook in her arms.

She held him close as he collapsed on top of her. She cra-dled him with her body while she floated back to herself.

Then, to her deepest regret, she could feel him receding from her.

"What happened?" he breathed.

"I don't know, but it was wonderful. Incredible. The ab-solute best."

Laughing softly, he lifted his head and she frowned at the sight of his eyes in the dull candlelight. They were no longer black, but a strange hazel-green. "Kyrian?"

He looked around the room, then grimaced. "My powers are gone," he whispered. And it was then she felt weakness overwhelm him.

He could barely move.

Worse, she felt intense agony invade his skull as he placed the heel of his hand over his right eye and hissed.

"Oh, my God," she breathed as he lay beside her in complete misery. "What can I do?"

"Call Talon," he said between clenched teeth. "Dial two and a pound sign on the phone."

She rolled over to reach the nightstand and pulled the phone to her, then quickly dialed.

Talon answered on the second ring.

By the sound of Talon's voice, she could tell he'd been fast asleep. "What's wrong?" he asked calmly after she told him who she was.

"I don't know. I've done something to Kyrian."

"What do you mean?" he asked in a tone that told her he found it hard to believe she could do anything to his friend.

"I'm not sure. His eyes are a different color and he's doubled over in pain."

"What color are his eyes?"

"Green."

Talon fell silent for several rapid heartbeats before he spoke again. "Let me talk to him."

She handed the phone to Kyrian.

Kyrian gripped the phone as another wave of pain racked him. He'd never felt anything like this before. It was as if his Dark-Hunter and human halves were at war with one another.

"Talon," he breathed.

"Hey, buddy," Talon said. "You okay?"

"Hell, no. What's going on?"

"Offhand, I'd say you just found the way to drain out your Dark-Hunter powers. Congratulations, bud, you found your out-clause."

"Yeah, and I feel peachy keen about it, too."

"Don't be a smart-ass. The thing to remember is it's temporary. I think."

Not comforted by the doubt in Talon's voice, he asked, "How long?"

"I have no idea. I've never had my powers drained."

Kyrian hissed against another wave of pain.

"Stop fighting it," Talon snapped. "You're only making it worse. Just relax."

"Oh yeah, like you know."

Talon snorted. "Trust me, there are times to fight and this isn't one of them. Just go with it."

"Go with it, my ass. It's not that easy. It happens to feel like I'm being cleaved in two."

"I know," Talon said, his voice thick with sympathy. "What were you doing when you lost your powers?"

Kyrian cleared his throat as he cast a sheepish look to Amanda. "I . . . um . . ." He hesitated with the explanation. The last thing he wanted to do was embarrass her.

But then, he didn't have to.

"Great *Diarmuid Ua Duibhne*," Talon roared, "you slept with her and it drained you, didn't it?"

Kyrian cleared his throat louder, then realized the futility of trying to hide something from a Dark-Hunter who could find out most *anything* he wanted to. "Nothing happened until the end."

"Ahhhh, I see," Talon said, dragging the words out as if something had become clear to him. When next he spoke, he sounded strangely like Dr. Ruth. "You know that moment you have after you come? When you're completely spent, sated, and helpless? Want to bet that's what sucked your powers out?"

Still, none of it made any sense to Kyrian. "The rest of you sleep with women all the time without this."

"Yeah, but every one of us has a different pressure point, you know that. In your mind you must equate that pinnacle moment with what made you a Dark-Hunter. Either that or maybe it was her powers. Maybe they fluxed with yours and sucked them out."

"That's insane." •

"About as insane as the headache you have which is making my head hurt for you, by the way. Now hand me back to Amanda."

Kyrian did. "He wants to talk to you."

Amanda took the phone.

"Listen," Talon said, his voice stern and sharp. "We have a serious problem here. Kyrian is down until his powers return."

"How long?"

"I have no idea. But it'll probably be a while, and until then, he's human, and since he hasn't been human in over two thousand years, he's weak from it. Vulnerable."

Panic gripped her as she looked back at Kyrian. He still had one hand over his eyes and she could tell by the tautness of his body how much pain he felt.

"Will he be back to normal by sundown?"

"I hope so. Because if he's not, the Daimons will have him."

Her throat constricted as fear gripped her. The last thing she wanted was for him to be hurt because of her. "Can't you help him?"

"No. It's against our Code. We hunt alone. I can't go after Desiderius until Kyrian is dead."

"What kind of Code is that?" she shrieked.

"The kind that doesn't usually pierce my eardrum," Talon hissed. "Damn, girl, with that set of lungs, you have a bright future as an opera soprano."

"You're not funny."

"I know. None of this is. Now listen to me for a second. It's going to be embarrassing, can you handle it?"

His dire tone gave her pause. What was he going to say to her? "I think so."

"Good. Now, I think our problem stems from when Kyrian came. It's imperative that you not let him do that anymore. Because there's a real good chance it will drain his powers out of him again. You need to stay away from him."

Amanda's heart ached at his words. She reached out and touched Kyrian. "Okay," she breathed.

"All right. It's a little after seven right now. Do us both a favor and watch over him until Nick gets there."

"I will."

Talon said good-bye and she hung up the phone, then returned it to the nightstand.

Kyrian looked up at her and the pain she saw in his green-ish eyes tore through her. "I only wanted to make it better. I never meant to hurt you."

He took her hand in his and held it gently. "I know."

He pulled her into his arms and held her close, but still she could feel the rigidness of his body.

"You made it better, Amanda," he breathed in her ear. "Don't take away what you gave me by feeling guilty."

"Is there anything I can do?"

"Just let me hold you for a little while."

His words tugged at her heart. She lay cradled in his arms and felt his warm breath fall on her throat.

Kyrian buried his face in her hair and breathed the sweet scent of her. He'd never felt as weak as he did just then and yet something about her presence gave him strength.

"You have your out-clause." Talon's words rang in his head. Once a Dark-Hunter found something to drain their im-mortal powers, they could regain their soul. It was something he'd never thought about before. Something he'd never dared dream about.

He could be human again.

Permanently.

But to what purpose? He was what he was. An eternal warrior. He loved his life. Loved the freedom and the power it gave him.

Yet as he lay there with Amanda nestled in his arms, bare skin to bare skin, he began to think of other forgotten things. Things he had banished to the deepest crevices of his heart.

Closing his eyes, he saw her holding Niklos. She would make a good mother.

And as he drifted back to sleep, a part of him knew she'd make a wonderful wife.

Amanda came awake to someone tracing slow, scorching cir-cles around her breasts. She opened her eyes and looked down to see Kyrian's hand gently kneading her. He had his thigh buried between her legs.

Her heart pounded as he slid his hand down, over her stomach, while he nibbled her neck with his long, pointed teeth.

"Are you going to bite me?" she asked.

His laughter vibrated down the column of her throat. "No, love, I'm going to *devour* you."

Rolling onto her back, she looked up and saw his eyes were even greener than before. They were a light, gorgeous, vibrant green. She reached up and ran her finger just below his right eye. "Why did they change color?"

"When I lost my Dark-Hunter powers, my eyes went back to their human color."

She frowned at him as she vaguely recalled the color from her dream. "This was the color of your eyes before you lost your soul?"

He nodded, then dropped his head and suckled the hollow of her throat.

"Should you be doing this?" she asked as she ran her hand down his spine. "Talon said you needed to rest."

"I am resting."

She sucked her breath in sharply as he separated the tender flesh between her legs and stroked her with his long, strong fingers. "You're not resting, you're playing."

His eyes searched hers. "I *want* to play with you."

"But won't this make you weaker?"

"I don't see how."

"But what if—"

He stopped her words with a hot, scorching kiss. Amanda's thoughts scattered.

He nibbled her lips with his teeth and pulled back. His green eyes tugged at her heart. "I can't feel what's inside you anymore, Amanda. Tell me you don't want me and I'll let you go."

"I want you, Kyrian." What an understatement that was.

He smiled at her, then drove himself deep inside her.

Amanda moaned at the strength of him filling her.

Kyrian's head swam at the warmth of her beneath him. If it were possible, she felt even better to him now than she had the hour before.

He stared at her face and took delight in her passion-drunk

eyes. The flush in her cheeks. She was truly beautiful.

A wave of fierce possession tore through him. A feeling so intense that he had all but forgotten it.

He couldn't fathom where it came from, but it rocked his very being.

And it made a mockery of what he'd once felt for Theone.

He didn't understand it, and in truth, he didn't dare investigate it. Knowledge of his feelings could only hurt him more.

Amanda wrapped her legs around his as she savored each of his long, lush strokes inside her. She'd never dreamed lovemaking could be like this. Never dreamed of such intense pleasure.

And when her release came, she cried out.

Kyrian captured her open lips with his and with three more forceful strokes, he joined her.

His breathing ragged, he stared down at her. "I think I'm addicted to you."

She smiled a smile that made his heart skip a beat.

"Hey, Kyrian!"

Kyrian barely had time to pull the sheets over them before his bedroom door burst open to show a tall, handsome man in his mid-twenties.

Amanda froze as she met Nick's hazel-blue, wide-eyed stare. His dark-brown hair was long, and combed back from his face, and when he smiled, he displayed a deep set of dimples. "I'll be damned, you got laid."

"Nick," he growled. "Get out."

"Yeah, but I have some news on Desiderius that you really want to know. Why don't you throw some clothes on and meet me in the office in a few minutes?" Unabashed, Nick swept another taunting look over them and sauntered out of the room.

"Remind me later, I really need to kill him."

Amanda laughed, until she met his gaze. "You look so different with green eyes," she whispered, placing her hand against his whiskered cheek.

He responded by capturing her lips for another scorching kiss. His tongue taunted and teased hers in a possessive way that made her breathless and weak. "What is it about you that I can't resist?"

"My charming personality?" she quipped.

Laughing, he kissed her lightly on the nose. Amanda watched him get out of bed. Her gaze feasted on his bare backside as he crossed the room to his bathroom.

She curled up in bed while he took a shower and just remembered the way he'd felt in her arms. His scent clung to her, and she reveled in it. It made her feel as if she belonged to him and yet she knew she never could.

He was a Dark-Hunter and she was an accountant. There had never been two more mismatched people born. Still her heart didn't listen. There was a part of her that wanted him on a level she'd never known existed.

And somewhere in the back of her mind, she couldn't help but wonder what it would take to free him of his Dark-Hunter oath.

CHAPTER 9

Kyrian walked down the hallway and opened the door to his office. Nick sat at the antique mahogany desk with his back to him. The black leather reclining office chair squeaked as Nick shifted in the seat while his fingers flew over the keys of the computer keyboard.

It was a familiar sight.

On the Internet, Nick was a demigod, which in hacker terminology meant he could pretty much infiltrate anything, no matter how secure the server. Because of that, Nick, Chris Eriksson, and Daphne Addams had been relegated to designing, maintaining, and securing the Dark-Hunter.com Web site where the Dark-Hunters and Squires kept all their records and communicated with each other.

It was nice to know Nick was picking up something other than women of questionable morals at school.

"So what had you barging into my room?"

Nick glanced over his shoulder with a devilish grin. "Man, you got laid. It's about time."

"Knock it off."

Snorting, Nick turned his attention back to his instant message. "You're the only man I know who can have sex with a woman who looks that good and be in this bad a mood ten minutes later. Damn, didn't you know sex is supposed to make you feel better?"

Kyrian rolled his eyes at his impudent Squire. Rules and

regulations had never applied to Nick Gautier. Nor had the boy ever been intimidated by him. Not even on the night he had learned what Kyrian was.

"Nick . . ." he warned.

Nick opened a small window on the computer and read the message. "Okay, okay. Here's the deal from the Oracles:

"Of Apollite birth and of Daimon born, he is the one who will make you mourn.

"Through the wine god's blood and bath, he exists as pure wrath.

"To bring him under final control, you must find the Dark-Hunter with a soul."

Kyrian frowned at the riddle, which was the typical garbage given to them by the Oracles. Gods, how he *hated* them. Just once, couldn't they actually come out and say it in plain, simple language?

Oh no. Zeus forbid, the Oracles should actually *help* them protect the humans.

"What the hell does that mean?" he asked Nick.

Nick swung around in the chair to face him. "Acheron interpreted it to say that only a Dark-Hunter with a soul can kill Desiderius. That's why no one has ever succeeded against him. It's simple prophecy, and you know how that works."

"There's no such thing as a Dark-Hunter with a soul. Not a full soul, anyway."

"Then according to the Oracles and Ash, Desiderius can never be killed."

Kyrian let out a slow breath. "That is *not* what I wanted to hear this morning."

"Yeah, and all I have to say is I'm damned glad I'm not in your boots on this one." Nick frowned. "Your eyes are green. What happened?"

"Nothing."

Nick tilted his head and gave him a suspicious stare. "Something's up." He reached for his cell phone. "Do I need to call Ash again?"

Kyrian took the phone from his hand and glared murderously at him. "Leave Acheron out of this. I can handle it."

"Yeah, you'd better. You get on my last nerve, but I'd hate to break in another Dark-Hunter."

Kyrian snorted at him. "What is that? A declaration of love?"

"It's one of loyalty. I don't want to see you go down like Streigar did."

The thought sobered Kyrian. Streigar had been a fierce Dark-Hunter who had been trapped by vampire-hunting humans who exposed him to daylight. His death had upset all of them, Dark-Hunter and Squire alike.

"Don't worry," he assured Nick, "I'm not going to be a dawn-surfer. I can handle myself."

"Want to bet that's what Streigar said, too?"

Kyrian growled. "Don't you have class today?"

Nick laughed at that. "Boy, I'm a backwoods Cajun, I ain't never got no class, cher." He cleared his throat and dropped the thick Cajun accent. "And no, today's registration. I've got to figure out what I'm taking next semester."

"Fine, but I have a few things I need you to do today."

"And that is different from any other day how?"

Sarcasm, thy name is Nick Gautier.

"I need you to take Amanda shopping for clothes. The Daimons burned her house down and she has nothing except the clothes on her back."

Nick arched a brow. "From what I saw, she had no clothes whatsoever on her back. Her front neither."

Kyrian narrowed his eyes on his Squire.

"Don't have a hissy." Nick held his hands up in mock surrender. "I know she's yours and I would never encroach, but man, I'm not blind, either."

"One day, Gator bait . . ."

"Yeah, right. That threat might actually carry weight if I didn't know how much you live to order me around. You'd go insane if you couldn't page me at all hours of the night."

Kyrian couldn't deny that. The nights did have a way of getting long and boring when there were no Daimons to pursue. And bugging Nick at three A.M. did provide *some* entertainment.

Nick pulled out his Palm Pilot and made notes on it. "All right, secret mission, take woman shopping." He looked up at Kyrian. "By the way, I want hazard pay for this. I seriously hate the mall."

Kyrian laughed. "*That* I can tell by the way you dress."

Nick gave him a fake wounded look. "Excuse me, Mr. Armani. I happen to like the grunge look."

"Sorry. I keep forgetting it's fashionable to look like you just rolled out from under a Dumpster."

Stuttering in indignation, Nick pretended offense. "Why don't you take your butt back to bed and save your oozing charm for your woman? 'Cause if you keep this up, *I'm* going to stake you . . ." then under his breath, he added, "while you sleep."

Kyrian crossed his arms over his chest. "All right, you'll get your bonus, but play nice with her. Keep your sarcasm to a minimum."

"Yes, O great Lord and Master." Nick added another note— "Be nice to woman, keep mouth shut"—then he looked up. "By the way, is there a limit on what I'm to spend for her clothes?"

"No. Whatever she wants to spend."

"Visit Needless-Markup and Lord and Taylor. All right, next?"

"Have her back here before dusk or I'm going to feed your Cajun hide to Talon's gators."

A glimmer of fear flashed in his eyes. Nick *hated* alligators, but Kyrian had no idea why. "All right, that scares me."

"I also want you to go by Talon's and pick up a *srad*. Let's give Desiderius a surprise he won't see coming."

Nick visibly cringed at the mention of Talon's circular daggers. It was an ancient weapon that made a Ginsu look like a butter knife. "Do you even know how to use that thing?"

"Yes, I do." Kyrian took a deep breath. "Now, I need some sleep. Your primary job today is to take care of Amanda."

Nick turned off his Palm Pilot and clipped it to his belt. "You like her, don't you?"

Kyrian didn't answer. He didn't dare. Neither one of them needed to know that one.

Instead, he left Nick sitting at the computer and went back to his room.

After a quick shower, Amanda quietly stepped into the bedroom to dress while Kyrian slept in his large four-poster bed.

The room was completely dark with the only light coming from the bathroom. No one would ever be able to tell if it was day or night from in here, and yet Kyrian always seemed to know when the sun was up.

She stepped over to the bed to watch him lying there with the sheet draped over his middle to shield his nudity. Oh, that man had a body . . .

She could stare at him all day long and not grow tired of all that lush, tawny skin that she longed to explore some more with her lips and hands. What was it about him that was so addictive?

She ached to kiss those poetic lips and run her hands through the golden waves on his head, but she didn't want to disturb his sleep. He needed his strength.

Tiptoeing from the room, she headed downstairs to the kitchen.

Daylight sparkled against the white marble of the room, bright and cheerful. Rosa was frying bacon while Nick sat on a barstool looking through a college course catalogue.

Probably no older than twenty-four, Nick was lean and handsome. His shoulder-length dark brown hair could have used a trim, but somehow it suited his sculpted features. He was wearing a baggy sweater that had seen better days, and faded jeans with a hole in the knee.

"Hey, Rosa," he said without looking up from his catalogue, "if I take Spanish next semester, will you help me study for it?"

"*Sí.* I imagine Kyrian will, as well."

"Great," he said sarcastically. "Between that and Ancient Greek Civilization, I'll have the friggin' time of my life."

"Nick!" Rosa chastised. "Such language you use. It is not becoming of a gentleman."

"Sorry."

Rosa set a plate of toast, bacon, and eggs down beside Nick, then turned and caught sight of Amanda in the doorway. "There you are, señorita. Are you hungry?"

"A little."

"Come," she said, indicating the stool beside Nick. "Sit and I'll make you breakfast."

"Thank you, Rosa."

Rosa smiled.

Amanda took a seat beside Nick. He brushed his hand off on his jeans and held it out to her. "Nick Gautier," he said with a charming, dimpled smile. "Better known as 'Nick, get your butt in here, I need you to . . .' Fill in the blank."

She laughed. "Bossy, isn't he?"

"You've no idea." Nick pulled his cell phone off his belt and handed it to her. "Speaking of, boss man said you'd need to call work."

"Thanks."

While Rosa made her breakfast, she called her boss and explained about her house. Luckily, her director was understanding and gave her a two-week leave of absence to take care of it.

As soon as she hung up, Amanda felt ill as she remembered her loss. "I can't believe they burned down my house."

"Your house?" Rosa asked. "Who burned it down?"

"The authorities are looking into it," Kyrian said from the direction of the living room.

Amanda turned around to see him standing in the doorway. He looked pale and uneasy.

Rosa smiled. "*M'ijo*, you are here today. Nick said you would be gone."

"I'm not feeling well." Even though his face was tender, he narrowed his gaze on Rosa. "You came in on time this morning, didn't you?"

Rosa ignored his question. "Come and sit. I'll make you something to eat."

Kyrian cast a wary look to the sunlight spilling into the kitchen from the open windows. He took a step back into the dark living room. "Thank you, Rosa, but I'm not hungry. Nick, I need to see you for a minute."

Nick gave her a knowing smile. "At least he didn't tell me to move my butt."

"Nick," Kyrian said. "Move your butt, boy."

While Nick went over to Kyrian, Rosa set a plate in front of her. "Poor little one. What are you to do without a house?"

"I don't know. I guess I need to call my insurance company. Find a place to live . . ." Amanda's voice trailed off as she thought over all the things that needed to be done.

She'd have to replace her entire life. Everything. Toothbrush, shoes, books, furniture, phones. She didn't even have a pair of underwear.

Overwhelmed, she lost her appetite.

Whatever was she going to do?

Nick came back to the counter and picked up his catalogue, then went back to Kyrian in the doorway. "I need a favor. I have to register at one o'clock, so if we're not back, can you sign up on-line for my classes? I know you need to sleep, but I really want to take Greek Civ next semester."

"Why?"

"Dr. Alexander is teaching it and he's supposed to be really good."

"Julian Alexander?" Amanda asked.

"Yeah," Nick said, looking back at her. "You know him?"

She exchanged a knowing look with Kyrian. "Not half as well as Kyrian does."

Nick shuddered. "Ah, man, not another one of *you*. Great. Shoot me now and put me out of my misery."

"Don't tempt me." Kyrian took the catalogue. "One o'clock. Anything else?"

"Yeah, do something about those eyes, they're creeping me out."

Kyrian arched a warning brow at Nick's commanding tone. "You two have fun."

"Fun?" Amanda asked as Kyrian left them.

Nick returned to sit on his stool. "We're going *shopping*." He curled his lips and shuddered at the word.

"For what?"

He took a drink of orange juice. "Whatever you need, my lady. Furs, diamonds, whatever."

"Diamonds?" she asked, laughing at the outrageous thought.

"It's on Kyrian, so I say go for broke. Literally."

She smiled. "I can't do that. I have my own money."

"Yeah, but why spend it? You have no idea how rich the man is. I promise you, buy the mall and he won't even notice."

Amanda had no intention of doing that. Still, she did need something else to wear. "All right, can we also stop by my mother's?"

"Sure. My assignment for the day is to serve you any way you want me to."

She shook her head at his devilish smile.

After she called her insurance company about the fire, Amanda let Nick take her shopping. But what frustrated her was Nick's inability to let her pay for *anything*.

"I'm under orders," Nick said for the fifth time. "You shop, I pay."

She growled good-naturedly at him. "Do you always follow orders?"

"I do so complainingly always."

She laughed yet again as they left the store and headed back out into the mall with Nick carrying her bags. "How long have you worked for Kyrian?" she asked as they got on the escalator.

"Eight years now."

She gaped. "Really, you don't look that old."

"Yeah, well, I was barely sixteen when I started."

"You can be a Squire at that age?"

Nick turned his head to ogle an attractive young woman in a tight, short skirt going up the escalator beside them, then he turned to flash a dimpled smile at her before he answered the question. "I didn't know what he was for a long time. I just thought he was some whacked-out rich guy with a 'pity the poor kid' complex."

She frowned as they left the escalator and walked through the downstairs level. "Why would you think that?"

Nick adjusted the bags he carried. "You see beside you, my lady, the son of a career felon. My father died in Angola eleven years ago during a prison riot."

Amanda winced at the thought of losing a father like that. "And your mother?"

"She was an exotic dancer down on Bourbon Street. I grew up in the back room of the club where she worked, helping the bouncers hustle clients."

Amanda cringed at the life he was describing. "I'm sorry."

He shrugged nonchalantly. "Don't be. My mother might have her faults, but she's a good mom, and a terrific lady. She did her best with what little we had. My father knocked her up when she was fifteen and her father threw her out. So it was just the two of us while my dad hit the revolving door in and out of the penal system. We never had much, but she's always loved me."

Amanda smiled at the love she heard in his voice. It was obvious he worshiped his mother. "So how did you meet Kyrian?"

He paused for a second as if gathering his thoughts. "When I hit my teens, I was sick to death of watching my mom hang her head in shame. Of her doing without food so I could eat a little bit more. I can remember walking to work with her and watching the way her gaze would stare longingly into store windows." He sighed. "She had such hungry eyes."

His stare was hard, penetrating. "My mother is the best-hearted woman God ever put on this planet. And I couldn't stand watching her degrade herself to feed me. Men groping her all the time. Or seeing the look on her face whenever she saw something she wanted and she couldn't afford it. At thirteen, I couldn't take it anymore, so I started stealing."

Amanda's throat tightened. She didn't condone it, but she wouldn't judge him for it, either.

"One night, the gang I was in decided to mug a couple of

tourists and I drew the line. It was one thing to shoplift and break into rich people's houses, but I wasn't about to hurt someone."

So, even as a thief, Nick had honor.

"What happened?" she asked.

"The guys were furious at me and decided to get a little practice in by beating the crap out of me. One minute, I was under their feet, getting bludgeoned to death, and the next thing I knew there was this guy holding his hand out to me, asking me if I was okay."

"Kyrian?"

Nick nodded. "He took me to the hospital and paid for them to stitch up my head and knife wounds. He stayed with me until my mom got there. While we were waiting, he asked me if I wanted to go to work for him, running errands after school."

She could just imagine Nick as a smart-mouthed teen. It said a lot about Kyrian's character that he had seen through Nick's caustic personality to find the goodness beneath it all. "You agreed?"

"Not at first. I wasn't sure I wanted to be anywhere near some guy who had all the money in the world. Plus, my mom was very suspicious of Kyrian. She still is. She can't imagine why on earth he pays me so much money to do practically nothing." He laughed. "She's still half convinced I deal drugs for him."

Amanda scoffed at the thought. His poor mother. "What do you tell her?"

"That he's Howard Hughes with a God complex." He sobered and gave her a harsh stare. "I owe Kyrian my life. There's no telling where I'd be if he hadn't found me that night. One thing's for sure, I wouldn't be a pre-law student at Loyola, driving around in a Jag. I know he's a major asshole, but he's really a good guy underneath it all."

Amanda thought about his words as they left the mall and stowed her purchases in the trunk of Nick's silvery-black Jag.

They got in the car and she buckled up. "When did Kyrian tell you what he was?"

Nick started the car, then backed out of the parking space. "When I graduated high school. He offered me a permanent job as his Squire."

"And what exactly is a Squire?"

He pulled out into traffic, and as he shifted gears, she noticed a strange spiderweblike tattoo on his right hand. It held some kind of odd Greek design and she wondered if all Squires held such a mark.

"We were set up to protect the Dark-Hunters during the daylight hours and to procure whatever they need. Food, clothes, cars, maintain their homes, whatever. At one time, we literally stood guard over the special crypts they slept in, which is what started the whole vampires-sleep-in-coffins myth. Since sunlight is deadly to them, they used to sleep in caves or isolated chambers where there was no possibility of sun exposure. In return for our service, they provide financial support to us."

"So each Dark-Hunter has a Squire?"

"No. Some Dark-Hunters prefer to go it alone. I'm the first Squire Kyrian has had in over three hundred years."

She flinched at the thought of Kyrian being alone all that time. She could just imagine him walking the floors of his mansion like some restless spirit in search of comfort and finding none.

"And if you want to quit?" she asked Nick.

He sucked his breath in between his teeth. "It's not really that easy. The Squires have a whole detailed organization that's kind of like the Hotel California—you can check out anytime you want, but you can never leave. Once you get out, they will monitor you until the day you die. If you ever betray them or the Dark-Hunters, you won't live to regret it."

His ominous voice sent a chill down her spine. "Really?"

"Oh yeah. Some of these guys come from a long family history of Squirehood that goes back thousands of years."

"Is it like slavery?" she asked.

"No. I can leave at any time I choose, I just can't breach my Squire's oath. Once taken, the oath is unbreakable and eternal. When I get married, my wife won't ever know what

Kyrian is, or what I do for him, not unless she's a Squire, too. After my children reach adulthood, I can decide to let them in on it or not. If I choose to let them in, they have to go before Acheron and Artemis, who will review and hopefully approve their application."

Now that was truly scary, because as he spoke those words, a horrible thought occurred to her. "What about me? Wouldn't they think I pose a threat?"

His face turned deadly serious as he paused at a red light and turned to face her. "If you do, one of the Squires *will* kill you."

She swallowed. "That's not comforting."

"It's not meant to be. We take our duties very seriously. The Dark-Hunters are all that stand between the human race and slavery or extinction. Without them, the Apollites and Daimons would own us all."

Kyrian lay in bed, trying his best to sleep, but over and over he felt Amanda inside him. She was at the remains of her house. He knew it. He felt her tears, her rage. Her despair.

And he ached for her.

How he wished he could be there with her right now. Comforting her. Never before had the loss of daylight freedom bothered him, but now it did. If he weren't a Dark-Hunter, he would be able to stand by her side and offer her his strength. His support.

Closing his eyes, he breathed deeply, trying to stave off the pain. In a fit of anguished rage, he had chosen this course. Now, there was no way out. Artemis guarded her army zealously and had set the bar so high that in all this time, Kyrian had only known three Dark-Hunters to ever regain their souls.

All the others had died trying.

"What do I need with a soul, anyway?" he breathed as he opened his eyes to stare up at the brown and gold canopy over his bed. "All it does is make a man weak."

His life had meaning. It had purpose.

Then why did something within him actually hurt in desperate need for Amanda?

It was a feeling he hadn't experienced in centuries and it was a feeling that had once caused him to betray everyone who had loved him.

"I won't be weak again," he whispered. It wasn't that he thought Amanda would hurt him intentionally. It was himself that he feared, for once he gave his heart or his loyalty, he never revoked it.

It came down to one basic fact. He was scared of himself and the lengths he would go to keep her safe.

After they visited the remains of Amanda's house and her mother's home, Nick drove into the heart of the French Quarter and parked on a side street so that they could walk over to Chartres. He led Amanda down the semicrowded retail area until they reached a small boutique called Dream Dolls and Accessories.

Amanda frowned. They were going to a doll store? How weird was that?

"What are we doing?" she asked as he opened the door for her.

"We're going to see the dollmaker."

Okay, ask a stupid question . . .

She looked skeptically at Nick. "You know, I don't think they make life-sized Barbies."

He snorted at her as she walked into the shop with Nick one step behind her. "I'm not looking for a Barbie and this trip isn't for me. I'm here for Kyrian."

Now she really was worried. "Why?"

Before he could answer, an elderly lady looked up from her workbench beside the door and caught Amanda's full attention. She held a Barbie doll whose face she was repainting.

The woman wore a strange orange headpiece with a light and a bifocal eye shield. It covered her stark white hair, which was pulled back into a tight bun. Her old, brown eyes were bright and friendly.

"Little Nicky," she said in a motherly tone. "What brings you here this afternoon and with such a beautiful guest? Why, I do believe this is the first time I've ever seen you with a woman." She gestured at him with the tiny paintbrush in her hand. "One worth being seen with, anyway. Why, she's plum nice-looking and I'm not talking about her looks, if you know what I mean."

Nick raked a hand through his hair and shot Amanda an embarrassed glance.

"Liza, my love," he said in a loud tone, flashing her a devilish, charming grin. "Do I really need a reason to come see your shining face?"

She laughed at that. "I may be old, Nicholas Gautier, but I ain't stupid yet." She tapped her head, making her headgear shake. "My old noodle is still up to snuff and it's been more years than I care to remember since a man like you came by to see me for a social call. Now come whisper in my ear and tell me what you be needing."

Nick went to whisper and it was then she realized Liza was a touch deaf. In fact, Nick ended up speaking so loudly, Amanda heard every word clearly.

Even when he ordered plastic explosives.

"Now, remember," he said. "Kyrian wants one just like Talon's."

"I heard you, Nicky," Liza said good-naturedly. "What, you think I'm deaf?" She winked at Amanda.

"When should I come back?" Nick asked.

Liza pursed her lips. "Give me a day or two. Can you?" She held up the doll in her hands. "Barbie waits for no Dark-Hunter."

Nick laughed. "Sure, Liza, thanks."

As they headed for the door, Liza stopped them. "You know," she said to Amanda as she tottered up to her. The old woman barely cleared five feet. She patted Amanda on the arm. "You have a graceful look to you. Like a pretty little angel."

Amanda smiled in gratitude. "Thank you."

Liza tilted the lenses up on her headgear and walked to a shelf by the door. She stood up on her tiptoes and took a custom-crafted Barbie off the shelf. It was all white, with long, curly black hair, and it had faint, wispy angel wings and a beautiful white beadwork gown.

Never had Amanda seen anything more beautiful or delicate.

Liza handed it to her. "Her name is Starla. I painted her face like a lady I know who comes in here all the time." She held the doll to her ear as if the doll were talking to her. She nodded, then handed the Barbie to Amanda. "She says she wants to go home with you."

Amanda's jaw dropped. Especially when she saw the four-hundred-dollar price tag on the doll. "Thank you, Liza, but I can't take this," she said, trying to give it back.

Liza waved her hand, refusing. "It's yours, hon. You need an angel to watch over you."

"But—"

"It's all right," Nick said, inclining his head to the door. Then in a low tone, he said, "Don't hurt her feelings by refusing it. She loves to give them away."

Amanda hugged the old woman. "Thank you, Liza. I will treasure her always."

They were almost out the door when Liza stopped them again. She took the doll back. "I forgot something," she said. "Starla is very special." Liza put the doll's legs together, then pressed her head down.

Two pencil-thin, three-inch blades shot out of her feet.

"It's for Daimons," Liza announced, pulling the head up until the blades retracted. "Beauty is sometimes best when it's lethal."

Okay, Amanda thought slowly. She wasn't quite sure what to make of all this.

Liza handed her the doll and patted her arm again. "You two take care."

"We will," Nick said and this time they made it all the way to the street.

Amanda stared at the doll in her hands, not sure what to think.

Nick laughed at her the whole way to the car.

"Liza's a Squire, isn't she?" Amanda asked as she got into

the Jag and placed Starla *very* carefully in her lap.

"She's retired, but yes. She was a Squire and an Oracle for about thirty-five years until she turned Xander's care over to Brynna."

"Is Liza the one who makes the boots for Kyrian?"

He shook his head as he started the engine. "Another Dark-Hunter makes the big weapons. The swords, boots, and such. Liza makes the small weapons like the pendulums that carry plastique. She's an accomplished artist who likes to make jewelry and other innocuous items lethal."

Amanda let out a deep breath. "You guys are scary."

He laughed at that, then checked his watch. "It's almost three. We still have to go to Talon's and I have to get you back before dark, so we need to rush."

"Okay."

They drove for a good forty minutes, out of the city and into the deep bayou.

Down at the end of a long, winding dirt road, they came to a large, old shed/houselike structure. If not for the new locks on it, she wouldn't have believed anyone had used it in a hundred years. Well, that and the peculiar mailbox in front of it. It was black with what appeared to be giant silver spikes going through the box both diagonally and horizontally.

"Talon is weird," Nick said as he caught her staring at it. "He thinks it's funny that he staked his mailbox."

Nick opened the garage door with the remote in his car. She gasped as they pulled inside and Nick parked the Jag.

Inside, the shed was tile and steel and housed a Viper, a collection of five Harley-Davidsons, and a small catamaran docked in the rear, over the swamp.

"Wow," she breathed as she spotted one Harley that stood apart from the others. Sleek and black, it gleamed in the dim light. It was obviously a prized possession and she remembered Talon riding it last night.

Nick paid no attention to the car or motorcycles as he headed for the docked catamaran.

"Talon lives all the way out here?" she asked as she joined him on the crisp, clean dock and noticed that they had left enough room for another boat beside the first one.

He helped her into the catamaran, then moved to open the garage door that led out to the swamp. "Yeah, being an ancient Celt, he loves nature. Even when it's gruesome."

Amanda arched a brow. "Is he really an ancient Celt?"

"Oh yeah. From the fifth or sixth century. He was a chieftain. His father was a druid high priest and his mother the leader before him."

"Really?"

He nodded as he untied the boat, then jumped inside it. Once she was seated, he started the whirring engine.

"How did he become a Dark-Hunter?" she shouted over the roar.

"His clan betrayed him," Nick said, steering the boat out into the swamp. "They told him they needed to sacrifice someone of his blood. It was either him or his sister. He agreed, but as soon as they had him tied down, they killed his sister in front of him. He went nuts, but since he was tied down, there was nothing he could do. As they turned to kill him, he swore vengeance on all of them."

Jeez, did *none* of them have a happy life?

"He killed his clan members?" she asked.

"I would imagine so."

Amanda sat in silence while she thought about that. Poor Talon. She couldn't imagine what it would be like to watch one of her beloved sisters die before her eyes. They might annoy her a large portion of the time, but they meant the world to her and she would kill anyone who hurt one of them.

The horror that man must have felt that day. It must still haunt him.

Nick navigated deep into the swamp until they came upon an incredibly small cabin. She doubted it was even eight hundred square feet. It looked even more rundown on the outside than the shed where they had left Nick's car. The rough wood was a light, sun-faded gray and it looked as if it would crumble under the slightest breeze.

As they approached it, she saw a dock behind the cabin with two large generators and another catamaran.

"What does he do during hurricane season?" she asked as Nick turned off the boat.

"Nothing really. One of Talon's powers is that he can control the weather so it's not that big a danger. But there's always the possibility the place could blow apart in the daylight while he's sleeping and not aware of weather conditions. In which case, he's toast."

"They like to live dangerously, don't they?"

He laughed. "It takes a certain breed to do what they do. Flirting with disaster is pretty much a basic requirement."

Nick got out of the boat first with a warning for her to stay put. He carefully walked along a narrow, old walkway that led from the makeshift dock to the cabin door, then motioned for her to join him.

"Back off, Beth," he snapped as an alligator approached her.

Amanda jumped back onto the boat.

"It's okay," Nick assured her. "They protect Talon in the daylight. As long as you're with me, they're harmless."

"I don't know about this," she said, reluctantly leaving the boat again.

Four massively huge alligators kept a vicious eye on her and followed her all the way to the door. Amanda's throat constricted in fear as the largest alligator climbed up on the porch behind them and swished its tail.

It hissed at them.

"Shut up, Beth," Nick snapped. "Or I swear I'll make luggage out of you." Nick knocked on the faded old door.

"It's not dark yet, Nick," Talon's thickly accented voice snapped from inside, making her wonder how he knew it was them. "What do you want?"

"I need your *srad* for Kyrian before it gets dark."

Amanda heard rustling on the other side of the door. A few seconds later, the lock clicked and the door opened the tiniest of cracks. Nick opened it wider and let them in.

She tried to see in the darkness, but had no luck until Nick turned on a small desk lamp.

Amanda froze as soon as she saw the interior. The walls were painted black and the place looked like a military control room. There were computers and electronic equipment everywhere. Though the location and-outside of the cabin would deny it, the man was a techno-junkie.

When her gaze touched on Talon, her jaw dropped wide open. The man was *completely* naked.

And he looked really good.

She stared at his perfect body, which was covered with strange red and black Celtic tattoos over the left side of his torso, front and back, and all the way down his left arm. His large, dragon-headed torc gleamed in the dim light. And though the man was sinfully handsome, she was strangely unmoved by him.

She appreciated him for the incredible picture he cut, but he didn't make her heart race like Kyrian did. Nor did she feel even a hint of sexual desire toward him.

And Talon was totally unabashed by his state of undress.

Nick gave her an amused grin. "I should have warned you, ancient warriors tend not to think much about nudity. Clothing is a modern hang-up none of them seem to have." He looked at Talon. "Celt, put some clothes on before you shock her."

Talon growled at him. "Why? I'm going back to bed. Take what you need and lock the door behind you." He paused at his futon in the back corner and raked a hungry look over Amanda. "Of course, if you want to leave Amanda, I might be persuaded to stay up for a bit and be sociable."

Nick scoffed. "Damn, Talon, can't you go an hour without a woman?"

"One is no problem. It's when I get to two or three that I get antsy." Talon returned to lie down on the black futon. He rolled over on his side and closed his eyes.

At least until his phone rang. Talon cursed, rolled over, and answered it while Nick went to the huge weapon cabinet and picked up two nasty-looking round dagger things.

"Wulf, I'm not even awake yet," Talon growled. "And I don't really care, and why would you ask me something about ancient Greece anyway? Did I live there? The answer is *hell* no . . . Don't know, don't care . . . Hang on." He turned over and looked at Nick. "Nick, ever heard of Cult of Pollux?"

Nick looked over at him. "You'd have to call Kyrian or one of the other Greeks."

"Did you hear that?" Talon listened a sec, then turned back to Nick. "Ash is walkabout, Brax, Jayce, and Kyros are MIA, and Kyrian isn't answering his phone. Wulf says it's *really* important."

The significance of that sentence seemed to hit both men at once.

Talon spoke into the phone. "When did you last try to reach Kyrian?"

Nick pulled his cell phone out and dialed.

"He might be in the shower," Amanda suggested.

Nick shook his head. "Even if he was, Rosa would answer."

After a minute, Nick turned off the cell phone. "Something's seriously wrong."

CHAPTER 10

Kyrian woke up the instant his bedroom door opened.

Not fully conscious, he sensed Rosa entering his room and wondered why she would disturb him. She'd never done so before.

He rolled onto his back. "Is something . . ."

The sentence died when a light, shimmering web covered him, pinning him to the bed. Kyrian froze as fury welled up inside him. He couldn't stand being trapped, especially flat on his back. Blood lust surged through him with a murderous frenzy.

Until he saw Rosa.

She stood by his bed, her brow covered in sweat as she stared at him with lost, dazed eyes. Over and over, she whispered the Spanish words, *"Debe matarle, debe matarle."*

Must kill him, must kill him . . .

She raised the cleaver in her hand.

"Rosa," Kyrian said as calmly as possible. "Put the cleaver down."

"Debe matarle . . ." She stepped closer to the bed.

"Rosa, no haga esto. Don't do this. Let me up. *Déjeme para arriba, por favor."*

She was shaking so badly, Kyrian feared she'd have a stroke or coronary at any moment. Her frail body couldn't sustain this amount of stress.

"Desiderius say you are bad, *m'ijo.* You must die."

Kyrian tried to think of some way to reach through her hazy madness and bring her back to reality. "Rosa, you know me better than that."

She lifted the cleaver higher.

Helpless beneath the net, Kyrian stared at the shining steel, waiting for it to slice into him. He wanted to implore her, to shout at her until she listened, but he didn't dare for fear of what it might do to the older woman. She was under enough stress without his adding to it. He would die before he harmed her.

His cell phone rang.

"I know, Desiderius," she whispered in Spanish. "I know. He must die." She placed a hand on Kyrian's chest as if to keep him still. Not that he could move. The net held him completely immobile. "Must be cut into pieces."

Kyrian tensed as she brought the cleaver down.

It missed him by a hairsbreadth.

"M'ijo," she whispered. Life returned to her eyes a second before they rolled back into her head.

She fell to the floor.

Terrified she was hurt, and panicking over his own vulnerability, Kyrian fought against the net with all his strength. It was no use. It was one of Artemis's nets, and once captured beneath it, any prey was completely trapped.

How in the gods' names could Rosa have gotten hold of it? Not even Desiderius should have had access to it. Only a god or demigod could claim an immortal weapon from its sacred resting place, and Artemis in particular guarded her weapons well.

And how could the Daimon reach out and control Rosa from a bolt-hole? No Daimon was that powerful.

Just what the hell was going on here?

Even though he knew it was futile, Kyrian fought against his confinement. As every minute passed, memories surged through him.

"How does it feel, Commander?" Valerius's voice taunted him from the past. "You are completely under my control. Totally powerless. Defenseless." He could still see the evil smile on the Roman's face, feel the agony of his torture. "I'm going to enjoy watching you squirm for me. Hearing you beg for my mercy."

Kyrian's sight dimmed as he relived every moment. He struggled to breathe. He would not be trapped again. Not like this.

Like a man possessed, he fought the net with every shred of strength he had.

An hour after dark, Nick entered the house first with Amanda and Talon only one step behind.

"Rosa?" Nick shouted, rushing through the kitchen and living room, toward the stairs. "Kyrian?"

No one answered. The eerie silence rang in Amanda's ears as they ran up the stairs toward Kyrian's bedroom. Nick threw open the doors so forcefully that the breeze stirred the bed's sheers.

The room was empty.

Amanda hesitated in the doorway as she surveyed everything. Nothing was out of place, except for the bed's covers. Yet . . .

She *felt* something wrong. Something deep within her stirred her dormant powers and allowed her to connect with Kyrian. She sensed his concern. His fury.

Talon moved to the bed and cursed as he lifted a shimmery, silver web. "This is unbelievable," he snarled, balling it up into his fist.

"What is it?" Amanda asked.

"A *diktyon*. One of Artemis's nets."

Amanda had absolutely no idea what that was, but she could tell by Talon's face it wasn't good. Nor should it be in Kyrian's bed while Kyrian was nowhere to be found. Panic sliced through her even more ferociously than before. "Why is it here?"

"I have no idea, but if Kyrian was under it, I would say he's been taken by whoever tossed it on top of him." Talon leaned over and picked a cleaver up from the floor.

Amanda's panic increased, and against her will, her powers

surged, searching for Kyrian. She hated the thought of letting her psychic abilities have control of her, but she needed to know he was all right. She had to know *something*.

Closing her eyes, she saw him in a sterile environment. He was worried, but she didn't sense any danger from him. "Try calling his cell phone," she said to Talon.

He gave her a "duh" stare. "I've tried a dozen times."

"Try a dozen and one."

His expression told her he didn't appreciate her commanding tone one iota. "All right," he reluctantly agreed: "What the hell? Futility has its purposes in life." Talon pulled his cell phone out of his jacket pocket and dialed.

"There's no sign of a struggle," Nick said, looking around.

"Kyrian," Talon snapped, giving Amanda an odd look. "Where the hell are you?"

Amanda took a step closer, her heart hammering as she realized that she had been right.

"You stay put until we get there." Talon hung up and looked at Nick. "He's at the hospital. Rosa had a heart attack."

"Oh, my God," Nick gasped. "Is she all right?"

"He didn't go into it since he's not supposed to be on the cell phone in the hospital. Said he'd fill us in when we get there."

Kyrian paced the waiting room anxiously. Anger and fear warred inside him. He wanted Desiderius's head for this. One way or another, he would make the Daimon pay.

"Just let Rosa be okay," he breathed for the millionth time.

"Kyrian?"

He turned at the sound of Amanda's soothing voice. An inexplicable joy and relief tore through him at the sight of her approaching him.

Before he realized what he was doing, he pulled her into his arms and held her so tightly that she protested. But he couldn't help himself. His relief at seeing her alive and unhurt was too great. Now that he knew just how easily Desiderius could enter someone's home, nowhere was safe for her.

Desiderius could reach her anywhere. Use anyone to kill her.

That thought terrified him, and somewhere in the back of his mind was a little voice that warned him Desiderius might use her against him.

If they gave him the chance.

Kyrian cupped her face in his hands and kissed her deeply. He was going to kill the Daimon. As soon as Desiderius emerged from his bolt-hole, the Daimon would live no more. And for the first time in his existence, he would relish taking a life.

He looked up and caught Talon's censuring gaze and knew what thoughts were on the Celt's mind. Dark-Hunters weren't supposed to become romantically tied to anyone. It was the first, and most necessary rule of the Code. No one could ever think clearly when their heart was involved. Of all men, Kyrian knew that for fact.

Still, it didn't change what he felt for her.

"I need you to keep Amanda safe," Kyrian told Talon.

Talon narrowed his eyes. "Tell me what happened."

"Desiderius used Rosa to trap me. He had complete control of her. If he can do that to Rosa, he can do it to *anyone*."

Talon let out a slow breath. "And you wonder why I live alone."

Kyrian ignored his warning tone and the meaningful look Talon gave Amanda.

Kyrian met Amanda's gaze and gently stroked her cheek with his thumb. "Amanda, I need you to call your sister. Tell her to guard her back and to not be alone. Have one of your sisters raise a cone of protection or whatever it is they do to protect her from Desiderius. We've no idea what other powers he might have."

He sensed her worry and fear. Her heart was pounding in her chest.

"I take it these aren't normal Daimon powers?" she asked.

"No. We've never encountered anything like it." He looked back at Talon. "I spoke to D'Alerian and he said Desiderius is messing with the human subconscious in order to weaken their resistance to his power. D'Alerian should be able to provide some help, but he can't guarantee absolute protection. Call Acheron and tell him I think we have a rogue god on the loose. One of them has to be helping Desiderius. There's no other explanation. And it would help if we knew who and why."

Talon nodded. "What are you going to do?"

"I'm going to do my damnedest to finish this tonight. If I can find his bolt-hole, I'm going into it."

Talon's eyes were harsh. "Kyrian, you're not a Were-Hunter. If you go in, you won't be able to come back out. You'll kill yourself trying, or worse, you'll be stuck between dimensions forever. Let me call Kattalakis—"

"I told you, we don't dare let a Were-Hunter near this guy. I'm more convinced of that now than ever. God help us all if Desiderius claims one of *their* souls. It's a risk we can't take." He glanced to Amanda and the concern on her face. He would protect her, no matter what. "Second rule of the Code, you've got to do what you've got to do. If I die, you're up next. And if you are, *don't fail.*"

Talon nodded even while Amanda grabbed Kyrian's arm. "Kyrian," she whispered, "I don't want you out there alone."

"I know, Amanda. But he's too powerful and dangerous to go unchallenged. He almost killed Rosa." Kyrian left out the part about how she'd almost killed him. They didn't need to know that.

Thank the gods D'Alerian had sensed Rosa's subconscious turmoil and come when he had. If not for the Dream-Hunter's intervention, Kyrian would still be trapped in his bed.

And trapped in his bed without Amanda was not something he wanted.

"Nick," he said, looking past her to his Squire. "Call me the instant you hear from the doctor." He started to leave, but Amanda stopped him.

Before he realized what she intended, she pulled him to her lips and kissed him blind. Her lips tugged at his while her tongue stroked his. He felt her hands clutching the lapels of his coat. Felt her fear for him, and it scorched his wounded heart with pure bliss. "You be careful," she said in a stern voice.

He touched her lightly on the chin. "I will."

Amanda watched him walk off with a sick feeling in her stomach. "Talon, are you sure you can't help him?"

"Believe me, I hate the 'no help' rule as much as you do. But if I tried to help, I'd only weaken him."

Nick handed her his phone. "Call Tabitha and warn her."

As Amanda dialed the first number another thought struck. "Who is D'Alerian and how can he guard our subconscious?"

"He's one of the Dream-Hunters we told you about," Talon said.

She frowned. "So do you guys get to pick which one you are?"

Talon shook his head. "Dream-Hunters are a whole other species. They're born of the gods and not made from humans."

"And the Were-Hunters? Where do they come from?"

"They are half human, half Apollites who got a hold of some seriously bad mojo."

She swallowed the fear that rose up to choke her. That didn't sound good at all. "I thought they were good guys."

"Some of them are, but some of them are slayers."

"With the powers of a sorcerer who can walk through time and space," she said, her stomach knotting.

"And occasionally dreams," Nick supplied.

Amanda laughed nervously. "You know, I was a whole lot happier when I didn't know about any of this."

"Which is why we do our best to keep this silent," Talon said. "Believe me, humans would never be able to sleep at night if they knew what was out there waiting for them."

Amanda nodded, wondering if she'd ever be able to sleep again.

Terrified, she finished dialing her sister's number. Now that she knew more about what they were dealing with, she needed to get her sister to watch out for Lord King Badass, and the Dark-Hunter who was their only hope.

*   *   *

Kyrian spent the entire night hunting the streets of New Orleans to no avail. Desiderius was still in his bolt-hole and there was no sign of him or any other Daimon anywhere. It may have been that his powers still weren't up to their full capacity or that the Daimon had some way of shielding his location. Whatever it was, Kyrian couldn't find a trace of him. Not even his electronic tracker helped.

He cursed his luck.

Never in his Dark-Hunter existence had he been so uncertain.

He didn't like the feeling one bit. Especially not when Amanda's life balanced on whether or not he could find the fiend and stop him.

Disgusted and weary, he made his way into his house. Everything was dark and silent. Amanda was upstairs in the house. He could feel her presence like a touch and it soothed him in a way he didn't want to contemplate.

Just knowing she was here . . .

Happiness surged through him.

But he didn't seek her out. He had too many things on his mind. Things he needed to sort out. Think through.

He entered the billiard room and grabbed his glove and baseball, then went to pitch it. Focusing on the ball, he let his mind wander. Wander through his painful past, and to the doubts that still lingered.

Why couldn't his wife have loved him?

Since the day Theone had betrayed him, he had been suspicious of anyone who came near him. He had given his wife everything he had, and still it hadn't been enough. If he couldn't win her love, then he could win no one else's. He knew it.

Over the centuries, Kyrian had convinced himself that it didn't matter. That he needed no one at all.

Until Amanda. She had breached his defenses and now he felt naked before her.

She, alone, had opened his heart and touched him deep inside it. He wanted her. Mind. Body. Soul. There was no part of her he didn't want to claim.

A movement to his left caught his attention.

Turning his head, he saw Amanda coming through the doorway, dressed in sweats. He couldn't believe how sexy he found them on her. She had her hair in two braids down the side of her face. There was something innocent and almost childlike in the way she was dressed, but there was nothing girlish about the woman approaching him.

She shook the man in him all the way to his foundations.

"How long have you been home?" she asked.

Kyrian would have answered, but she chose that moment to walk up to him and kiss his cheek. A strange sensation ran through him. Her actions were those of true affection.

"What are you doing up?" he asked. "It's after four."

"I couldn't sleep."

She left his side to walk to the other end of the atrium room. When she turned to face him, he saw Nick's baseball glove on her hand. Like a pro, she held the glove up to catch the ball.

He smiled and tossed the ball gently to her.

She caught it, then fired back a fast ball that hit his glove with a resounding smack and burned his palm beneath the leather. "Ow!" he teased at the sting on his hand. She threw better than Nick did. "I'm impressed."

She winked at him. "I was the closest thing to a son my poor father had. He taught me to play."

Kyrian tossed the ball back to her. "He taught you well."

Her smile widened. They tossed the ball for several minutes in silence. Gods, he had never thought to find a woman willing to do this with him at such an unholy hour. Even Nick complained, but Amanda seemed content just to be with him.

"How did it go?" she asked. "Did you find him?"

"No." He sighed. "I just can't figure it out."

"You will."

He hesitated as he heard the utter confidence in her voice. "You have no doubts?"

"None. I know you won't let him hurt us."

"I couldn't help Rosa."

"I'm sorry," she said as she caught the ball and returned it.

"It must be hard for you to accept that fact, but it wasn't your fault. You did your best to protect her."

Kyrian clenched his teeth. "It hurts. More than I thought possible. I can't believe he got to her."

Her eyes were sympathetic and warm as she smiled sadly at him. "I guess it explains how he got into our houses to start the fires."

He nodded. "He probably used Allison. I found her passed out in her room, much like Rosa. I think the human mind can't handle the stress of it."

"If it helps, Tabitha said Allison is fine and back home now, so Rosa should heal and be back to normal without any lasting damage."

"That's good to know." Kyrian watched her as she played ball with him. And with every toss of the baseball, he felt himself slipping more and more.

He knew he was falling for her and he was powerless against it.

In fact, the longer they played, the more he wanted her. He watched her shirt pull tight when she drew back to toss the ball. And he loved the way tendrils of her hair swept onto her face and she had to brush them back. Her lips were parted and her breathing heavy.

He found himself purposely throwing the ball over her head to watch her reach up to catch it. Every time she did, the sweatshirt rode up, baring a portion of her stomach to his hungry gaze. Then she would run after the ball, her breasts bobbing, her hips swaying. But the best part was seeing her well-proportioned backside when she bent over to retrieve the ball. Gods, but that woman had the best derriere . . .

Unable to stand it anymore, he tossed the glove to the ground.

Amanda froze as Kyrian took long, determined strides toward her. Before she could figure out his intent, he picked her up in his arms and kissed her fiercely.

Those wonderful, hard muscles flexed around her while he held her feet off the ground. Due to her size, no man had ever been able to pick her up, and yet Kyrian did it with such ease that it made her heart pound. She loved the way he made her feel. So feminine. So petite.

She wrapped her legs around his waist as his tongue ravished her mouth. Oh, the heaven of those hard, developed abs flexing between her thighs . . . The man was perfection.

Growling, he nipped her lips with his fangs while his hand cupped her bottom.

He left her lips and nuzzled her neck, nibbling his way under her chin. Her entire body melted at the feel of his hot breath on her skin. Oh yes, this was what she had wanted all day. Just to feel his arms holding her. To have him in her arms where she could give him all the love she felt for him.

She throbbed, needing him to fill her again.

Kyrian shook from the force of his want. Over and over, he remembered the way she had felt as he slid himself into her. The look on her face as she came in his arms.

He burned for her, and yet he dared not take her.

Not now. Not when he needed his strength to fight Desiderius.

Still, his body didn't listen. He had to touch her. Had to feel her skin.

Before he could stop himself, he sank to his knees and laid her down against the cold tile floor.

Amanda swallowed at the raw hunger on his face. He removed her clothes so fast that she barely felt his hands on her at all. But once he had her naked, it was another story entirely.

Only then did he slow down.

Fully clothed, he stared at her naked body in the moonlight as he ran his hands over her breasts, tracing them, teasing her hard nipples with his palms. "You are the most beautiful woman I've ever seen," he said, his voice low.

Amanda knew better than that. She'd seen the beauty of his wife, but the knowledge that he felt that way about her sent a shiver through her. He was definitely the best-looking man she had *ever* seen. Period.

As he leaned down to kiss her passionately, she reached to unbutton his shirt.

Kyrian caught her hands in his and shook his head no. If

he let those graceful, soft hands touch his skin, he knew he would be lost.

Instead, he kissed each palm in turn, then returned to her throat, her breasts. He sampled her body with his lips, his tongue, his fangs.

As Kyrian tasted her, he felt his honed powers surging. Desperate and hot, he trailed his mouth from her breasts down to her satiny stomach, then to her thighs. He heard her gasps of pleasure as she opened her legs to him.

Right then, he wanted to possess her with a ferocity that overwhelmed him. It was primitive and all-consuming. And all he could think of was Amanda.

Her blood pounded in his ears.

Shaking from the force of it, he closed his eyes and took her into his mouth to taste the sweetness of her body that he craved most.

Amanda moaned at the feel of his tongue inside her. Burying her hands in his hair, she lifted her hips to him. He was so wild as he tasted her. So ferocious and thorough that she hissed at the incredible feel of him making love to her with his mouth.

He was absolutely relentless with his hot caresses, and when she came, it tore through her, making her scream and writhe with the most blissful orgasm she'd ever experienced.

Still he tasted her. Again and again. His tongue and mouth swirled and teased, stroking her, coaxing her until she was lost in the throes of another orgasm even more intense than the first one. Her head spun from it and every single nerve ending in her body tingled.

Kyrian pulled away from her then, and crawled up her body like a hot, panting predator. His eyes were even blacker than they'd been before as he parted his lips and stared at her neck with a hunger so intense it startled her.

"Kyrian?" she asked.

Kyrian could barely hear her through the haze in his mind. All he could smell was her scent. Her body pressed against his as he throbbed and ached for more.

Take her. Taste her. Claim her.

Make her yours . . .

He ground his teeth as he watched the vein in her neck pulse. *Just one taste . . .*

One taste . . .

But it would be against her will.

"Is something wrong?" she asked.

He struggled against his hunger that demanded he take her regardless. His groin was on fire for her. His needs out of control.

Her scent was all over him. She was all he could focus on. All he could think of.

And it made him dangerous. Lethal.

Growling, he summoned up the last of his willpower and forced himself away from her. "Run, Amanda," he snarled.

Amanda didn't hesitate. Something was wrong with him. Grabbing her clothes, she ran to her room.

Kyrian heard her footsteps recede as he lay on the cold floor. He buried his hand against his burning erection as he writhed in pain.

This was unlike anything he'd ever experienced. Dear Zeus, another minute and he would have sunk his fangs into her.

Closing his eyes, he shook as he fought down the beast inside him. The beast that demanded he take her over and over, no matter the consequences.

Amanda didn't stop shaking until she reached her bedroom. She would never forget the feral look on Kyrian's face when he had told her to run.

She'd never feared him before, but right then she had seen the Dark-Hunter in him that she was sure made the Daimons wet themselves in terror.

Breathing deeply, she tried to calm herself. All she'd ever wanted was a normal relationship.

But then normality with a vampire was asking a lot.

Her heart pounding, she paused as she saw herself in the mirror. Her lips were swollen from his kisses, her neck red from where his whiskers had rubbed against her.

"Amanda?"

She paused at the sound of Kyrian's voice through the door. "Yes?" she asked hesitantly.

He nudged the door open, but didn't come inside. "Did I scare you?"

"Honestly?"

He nodded.

"Yes."

His heated gaze bored into her. "I'm sorry."

She knew he meant it. Could see the guilt in his eyes.

"Why haven't you asked to go home?" Kyrian asked, his low tone cutting across the quiet stillness of the room.

She tensed at his question. "You want me to leave?"

He was silent so long she didn't think he would answer. Finally he whispered, "No, I don't."

There was so much heartfelt emotion in those three words that she couldn't have been more stunned had he declared his love.

She started for him and he took a step back. She realized he still wasn't in full control of himself. Even so, she wanted him.

"Then I won't leave until I wear out my welcome."

Kyrian froze at her words. In the back of his mind was the thought that the earth would surely cease to exist before Amanda wore out her welcome in his house. And it was quickly followed by the knowledge that when the earth ceased to exist, he would still be alive and Amanda . . .

He winced at the truth of immortality and the knowledge that for the two of them there could never be a happily-ever-after.

CHAPTER 11

The next night, Kyrian was haunted by what had happened with Amanda.

He'd come so close to losing it with her. So close to . . .

He forced it from his mind as he walked the rooftops of the French Quarter at midnight. The frigid winds whipped at his leather coat while he walked along the roof's edge, looking down into the alleys below.

Like a cat, he often prowled high above where no one could see him coming. At least not until it was too late.

He paused as he heard something.

"Don't hurt me." The frightened voice was faint on the wind and came from several blocks over.

Twice as fast and as surefooted as a cheetah, he glided over the rooftops until he found the one who had spoken. To most, it would look like a poor man being mugged in a dark alley-way, but the four blond Daimons were highlighted by Kyrian's Dark-Hunter vision.

He arched a brow at the ordinariness of the scene. For some reason, Daimons liked to travel in fours or sixes.

They had the poor human man cornered against an old, rundown building.

Something about the human seemed strangely familiar to him.

The stench of the garbage was pungent as the man tried to

hand the Daimons his wallet. "Take it," he said, his voice wavering. "Just don't hurt me."

The tallest Daimon laughed. "Oh, we're not going to hurt you, little human. We're going to *kill* you."

Kyrian stepped off the roof with his arms spread for balance. His black coat fluttered in the wind as he fell three stories down to the alley below.

He landed in a silent crouch behind them.

"Did you hear something?" one of the Daimons asked, looking around.

"Just the sound of a human heart pounding." The tallest Daimon grabbed the man.

"Or," Kyrian said, rising slowly to his full height. He pulled his coat back and placed his hand over the hilt of Talon's *srad.* "The sound of four Daimons about to die."

As they stepped away from their victim, he recognized the human. It was Cliff.

Cliff recognized him at the same instant.

"You!" he roared. "What are you doing here?"

Damn you, Fates, Kyrian thought. The last thing he wanted to do was help the man who had hurt Amanda. She had told him the whole story of her ex-fiancé. Right down to Cliff's harsh criticisms of her family. The man didn't deserve his help.

Damn you, Code.

Out loud Kyrian said, "It would appear I'm saving your life."

"I don't need your help."

The four Daimons turned to look at Cliff, then burst out laughing.

"You heard him, Dark-Hunter," the Daimon leader said. "He doesn't need your help. So, go on. Go away."

More tempted to leave than he ought to be, Kyrian let out a slow breath. "Yes, but you know, sometimes you just have to save them even when they don't want to be saved."

The tallest Daimon attacked. Kyrian tossed the *srad,* but before it could make contact with the Daimon, Cliff grabbed the Daimon and whirled him away. "Now, I'll show you who's bad." He punched the Daimon who just stood there, laughing at him.

The *srad* bounced off the wall, breaking into two pieces. *Moron!* If not for Cliff's bullshit heroics, the Daimon would be dead.

Forcing himself, Kyrian ran to get between Cliff and the Daimon before the Daimon struck. He barely made it. As it was, he ended up being kicked into Cliff's flabby body.

The two of them fell to the ground. Rolling with the fall, Kyrian got to his feet in one swift move while Cliff struggled on the ground.

Kyrian fought the urge to roll his eyes at the weakling. "Would you run already?"

Cliff blustered as he gained his feet. "I'm just as capable of fighting them as you are."

Kyrian growled low in his throat at the imbecile. For one thing, Cliff was barely six feet tall while the Daimons were Kyrian's height and over. Cliff had the body of a couch-warrior and the Daimons were well-honed and ready to kill.

Oh yeah, Cliff was a big threat.

Before he could move, two Daimons rushed him. Kyrian caught the first one with his boot and obliterated the Daimon into dust. The other slashed out at him with a sword.

Kyrian flipped up and backward, coming to rest on the fire escape above them.

"Hey!" Cliff said. "How did you do that?"

He didn't have a chance to answer before the other three Daimons started up the ladder after him. Kyrian jumped back to the alley.

The Daimons followed.

Kyrian braced himself for them. As soon as the leader drew near, Cliff came running up beside him with a long two-by-four. He swung to hit the Daimons at the same time the Daimons moved for Kyrian.

Caught between the two, Kyrian couldn't maneuver. As a result, Cliff's board caught him across the back of his head.

Pain shot through his skull as he staggered back.

With a shake of his head, Kyrian recovered his senses a

second before two Daimons grabbed his waist and knocked him to the ground. They grabbed his arms and spread him out. Panic set in the instant they held him there as his old memories surged through him.

"We found his vulnerability," one of the Daimons said. "Tell Desiderius that with his arms spread out, he goes nuts."

They might have found it, but none of them would live long enough to reveal it.

Roaring with rage, Kyrian brought his legs up over his head and flipped himself up between them. His fangs bared, he stabbed one Daimon and then the other.

The remaining Daimon took off toward the street. Kyrian tossed the other *srad* straight into the Daimon's back. He evaporated.

Kyrian turned to see Cliff gaping at him.

His face ashen, Cliff's eyes rolled back in his head an instant before he passed out.

Disgusted, Kyrian went to check on him. His pulse was fast, but stable. "What did she *ever* see in you?" he asked as he pulled out his cell phone and called an ambulance.

Hours later—once he was sure Cliff would live—Kyrian made his way into his house.

Still no Desiderius to be found. Anywhere.

Damn.

He stopped at the kitchen door to watch Amanda curiously. It was almost five A.M. and she appeared to be making soup and sandwiches.

How very odd is this?

She moved around the kitchen like a graceful nymph, completely unaware of his presence. She hummed a gentle tune, "In the Hall of the Mountain King" by Grieg if he wasn't mistaken. What a strange choice.

He'd never seen a more beguiling woman in his life. She wore a silk dorm shirt that gave a hint of transparency, yet completely concealed her body from his view. The light blue color was a perfect complement for her pale skin and auburn hair.

His body reacted instantly to the sight of her, growing hard and hot.

The more he watched her, the more he wanted her.

She poured the soup into mugs, then dipped her finger into the soup to test the warmth.

It was more than an immortal man could take.

Moving like a shadow, he came up beside her and caught her hand.

She looked up with a gasp until she registered his identity. Smiling at her, he guided her finger into his mouth where he swirled his tongue around it, tasting the soup and the woman.

"Delicious," he breathed.

A blush covered her cheeks. "Hi, honey, how was work?"

He laughed out loud at her Donna Reed impersonation. "Been watching *Nick at Nite* again?"

She shrugged coyly. "I thought you might like to come home to a hot meal for once. It must get lonely to have nothing but an empty, dark house to greet you."

More so than she would ever know. He stared down at her, at those parted lips that beckoned him. It had been centuries since anyone greeted him when he returned. Centuries of untold loneliness and solitude.

Loneliness and solitude that had vanished the instant he woke up in that abandoned factory and had looked into those wide, intelligent blue eyes that scared him.

Amanda was completely unprepared for Kyrian's next actions. He kissed her like a man possessed. His tongue stroking and delving as his hands roamed her back, then cupped her derriere.

It still amazed her that she allowed him to handle her like this, and yet she didn't mind it in the least. She'd never thought of herself as a particularly sexy person. Not until she met him.

When it came to Kyrian, she couldn't get enough.

She wanted him around her all the time. Wanted to hold him, touch him, be with him.

If she could, she would handcuff herself to him forever.

Without breaking from the kiss, he slid his hand beneath the bottom of her shirt, seeking her wet heat that throbbed for him. She moaned as he touched her, as his fingers slid and teased her mercilessly. Heaven, how this man made her yearn for him.

"Kyrian, your soup," she said breathlessly.

He pulled back, his breathing ragged, his lips swollen from tasting her. "It'll wait."

There was something more untamed than usual about him tonight. Something wild and wicked. He carried her to the table and laid her across the top of it.

His eyes hot and hungry, he stood between her legs and looked down at her. "Now here's a banquet fit for a king."

And then he fell on her. Amanda gasped at the fury in his questing hands that seemed to be all over her at once. His touch electrified her. Satisfied her and left her craving more.

As he kissed her insane, she reached down between their bodies and unzipped his pants so that she could touch him. He was already rock-hard and throbbing and when she cupped him in her hands, he moaned against her lips.

He amazed her. This immortal warrior who needed no one and yet he was so tender in her arms. This man who trembled as she stroked his shaft and cupped him gently in her palm.

Kyrian couldn't think with her hands on him. All he could do was smell her, taste her.

He wanted her completely.

Wild with desire and unable to think past the moment, he pulled her hands away from him and drove himself into her.

Amanda groaned at the incredible feel of him deep inside her. He was so thick and hard. She felt so wonderfully full. She wrapped her legs around his waist as he rocked his hips hard and slow against hers.

"Oh yes, Kyrian," she moaned, arching her back.

He ran his hand over her gauze-covered body, and cupped her breasts in his hands as he continued to thrust into her.

They made love without any hurry. Amanda writhed at the power of his thrusts as he nibbled her throat, scraping her skin with his fangs. Closing her eyes, she again felt that incredible bonding with him. They were one.

He trembled in her arms and whispered her name against her lips, making her quiver with desire.

And when the world shattered, she swore she could see colors everywhere.

Kyrian watched her climax, felt her body clutching his. Gods, how he yearned to satisfy himself, but he didn't dare. Already he felt his powers waning. Powers he needed to keep her safe.

Grinding his teeth, he reluctantly withdrew from her.

He straightened his clothes in silence, but his entire being ached. Pressing the heel of his hand against his jeans, he tried to loosen the fabric that bit into his erection.

It was useless.

Amanda felt sympathy for him as she watched his stiff, awkward movements. How could he satisfy her and not take pleasure himself? It had to be sheer torture for him.

Yet he said nothing about it.

As he ate in silence, her heart wept for him. Her poor warrior.

And in the back of her mind came the little voice warning her that no matter how much she might want him, they could never have a relationship.

Amanda woke up a little after three in the afternoon. She got up, showered, and dressed while Kyrian continued to sleep.

Goodness, the man was handsome. He had one arm raised up around his head and looked more like a little boy as he slept than an immortal dark warrior.

Impulsively, she leaned over and kissed his parted lips. He reached for her, catching her about the neck. He held her so tightly that she could barely breathe.

"Kyrian?" she whispered, trying to get loose. "Honey, you're making me turn blue."

He paid no attention. It took her a full three minutes before she was finally able to extricate her head from his arms.

"Okay," she breathed as he turned onto his side. "Remind me not to do that again."

Amanda pulled the covers over him and tiptoed from the room.

She found Nick in the living room downstairs wearing a pair of Rollerblades as he zipped from one end to the other, sorting papers.

"What are you doing?" she asked.

He paused and shrugged. "Kyrian gets pissed when I use my skateboard in the house."

Amanda laughed. "Okay. But I imagine he's not fond of the skates, either."

"Probably not, but damn, this place is huge and I need to get from point A to point B without wearing my legs out."

She laughed again. Nick was infectious once you got used to him.

He turned a tight circle and skated to the kitchen. Before she could get halfway through the living room, he returned with a glass of orange juice for her.

"Thanks," she said, taking it from him. "What's the word on Rosa?"

"Miguel said she's better. She was up watching *Wheel of Fortune* when I called."

"Good."

"Yeah, Kyrian will be happy."

Suddenly, a loud crash sounded behind her. Terrified it was Desiderius bursting in, she whirled around to see a huge pile of gold and diamonds on the floor where a twelfth-century hand-carved table used to be.

"Oh man," Nick said with a disgusted look. "Kyrian really liked that table, too. Boy, is he ever going to be pissed."

"What is *that*?" Amanda asked, getting up to go look at the king's ransom in gold bars and diamonds.

Nick sighed. "It's payday."

"Excuse me?"

He shrugged. "Artemis hasn't caught on to the fact that she could just wire the money into her Dark-Hunters' accounts. So, once a month we end up with a wad of gold and diamonds somewhere weird. It was a real bitch the time it landed in the pool."

"No kidding," Amanda said, awed by the amount. "Someone could get hurt."

"That ain't no lie. It's what killed Kyrian's third Squire."

She turned to look at him and quickly learned he wasn't joking.

"So, what do you do with all that?" she asked.

He smiled. "I get to play Saint Nick. There's a Squire in town who will convert it into currency. From there most of it goes to charities. Two percent of it is funneled into a Squire's fund that takes care of the families of Squires who die in the line of duty or Squires who retire, and another two percent goes to a research facility that makes nifty toys for the Dark-Hunters."

"How much does Kyrian keep for himself?"

"None. He just lives off the interest of the money he had from when he was human."

"Really?"

He nodded.

Wow. The man had been seriously loaded as a mortal. "Okay, can I ask a really nosy question?"

Nick smiled. "You want to know how much I make?"

"Yeah."

"Enough to make me a very happy man."

The phone rang.

Nick skated off while Amanda took her juice to the couch and sat down to read the paper. She set her juice on the black coffin coffee table.

A few minutes later, Nick came rushing back in, his brow furrowed. He didn't speak to her as he moved to the armoire against the far wall. He opened the locked door to display an entire arsenal of weapons.

Dread consumed her. "What's going on? Who was on the phone?"

"That was Acheron calling with a full-alert warning."

She frowned. By his frenzied movements, she knew it wasn't good. "What does that mean?"

The look on his face chilled her. "You know the phrase 'All hell's breaking loose'?"

"Yes."

"It was invented for full-alert. For some reason, there is a high concentration of Daimons leaving bolt-holes in this area, and when that happens, the Daimons reach their full power and they feed whether they need it or not. The only thing worse than a full-alert is a solar eclipse. Tonight, things will get ugly."

At seven o'clock, Amanda learned firsthand what he had meant by that.

She was cleaning up Kyrian's "breakfast" while Nick briefed him on what Acheron had said.

Kyrian had chosen twice the weapons he normally went out with and he was on his way out the door when the phone rang. Amanda answered it.

"Mom?" she asked as she recognized the crying voice. Her heart stopped. "What is it?"

Kyrian went rigid at the door, then rushed to her side.

"Mandy," her mother said through her sobs. "It's Tabby . . ."

Amanda didn't want to hear anything more. She choked on her sob and dropped the phone. The next thing she knew, Kyrian held her in his arms while Nick talked to her mother.

Kyrian's sight dulled as he listened to her hysterical mother talking to Nick while Amanda trembled in his arms. Her tears soaked him, and as they fell, he vowed to kill Desiderius.

"It's all right," he whispered against Amanda. "She's just hurt."

She pulled back and looked at him. "What?"

Kyrian wiped the tears from her cheeks. "He didn't kill her, sweeting." Though she was in bad shape, from what he could gather from her mother, Tabitha would survive.

Desiderius, however, would not.

"Tabitha is in the hospital," Nick said, hanging up the phone. "Luckily, there were only two Daimons and her group was able to fight them off." He looked to Kyrian. "You know, it sounds to me like Desi was just toying with her to make you mad enough to lose your head in a fight. There's no other reason why he would send only two Daimons and not more."

"Nick, shut up!" Kyrian snapped. The last thing he wanted was for Amanda to be any more upset. He kissed her lightly on the lips. "Nick will take you to the hospital."

He pulled out his cell phone and called Talon, who was already on his way into the city. He told the Celt to get over to his house and escort Amanda just in case Desiderius was waiting for them.

"Kyrian," Amanda said as he hung up. "I don't want you to go out tonight. I have a really bad feeling."

So did he. "I have to go."

"Please, listen to me—"

"Shh," he said, placing a finger over her lips. "This is what I do, Amanda. It's what I am."

As soon as he could, Kyrian had her in Nick's car with Talon tailing them while he headed downtown to find that bloodsucking, soul-stealing pig and do what he should have done the night they met.

Hours went by as Kyrian scoped out the French Quarter, looking for Desiderius. The Daimons would replenish their strength tonight, and sooner or later, he knew they would make an appearance in their prime feeding ground.

Desiderius, much like the rest of his brethren, preferred to haunt the French Quarter where unwary and often drunk tourists could be found.

So far, there was nothing.

"Hey, baby," a prostitute called as he passed her. "You want some company?"

Kyrian turned to face her, then pulled out all the money, about five hundred dollars, he had in his wallet and handed it to her. "Why don't you take the night off and go get a good meal?"

Her face stunned, she grabbed the money and ran.

Kyrian sighed as he watched her dodge through the crowd. Poor woman. He hoped she put it to good use. Even if she didn't, she could certainly use the money a lot more than he could.

Out of the corner of his eye, he saw a flash of silver. Turning his head, he found two young men in the crowd. They were definitely human.

At first, they appeared to be the typical kind of street-gang youths Nick had once been, tough as nails and wearing black jackets, until he noticed the way they watched him.

As if they knew what he was.

His instincts alert, Kyrian returned their stares. The tallest, who appeared to be in his early twenties, crushed out his cigarette and crossed the street, his eyes never leaving Kyrian.

He raked a cold look over Kyrian's body. "You the Dark-Hunter?"

Kyrian arched a brow. "You the flunky?"

"I don't like your tone."

"And I don't like you. Now that we've dispensed with the introductions and have declared our mutual distaste for one another, why don't you take me to the one who holds your leash?"

The man narrowed his eyes on him. "Yeah, why don't I do that?"

It was a trap. Kyrian knew it. So be it. He wanted this confrontation. Was more than prepared for it.

Willingly, he followed after them.

They led him down the back alleys into a small, enclosed courtyard. Shrubs obscured most of the walls and tall plants blocked the streetlights from the area.

Kyrian didn't recognize any of it. But it didn't matter.

As they rounded a large hedge, he caught sight of Desiderius waiting. His smile evil, the Daimon held a panic-stricken pregnant woman in his arms with a knife at her throat.

"Welcome, Dark-Hunter," he said, his free hand stroking the woman's distended belly. "Can you believe what I was lucky enough to find? Two life forces for the price of one." He bent his head and rubbed his nose against the woman's neck. "Mmm, just smell the strength."

"Please," the woman begged, her voice hysterical. "Please help me. Don't let him hurt my baby."

Kyrian took a deep breath as he fought the fury inside him

that demanded Desiderius's blood on his hands. "Let me guess, you'll trade her life for mine?"

"Exactly."

Trying to rattle his opponent, Kyrian let out a tired breath as he surveyed the six Daimons and two human criminals around him. If not for the woman, he could have taken them easily. But one move against any of them and he had no doubt Desiderius would cut her throat. Indeed, Daimons valued very little more than taking the soul of a pregnant woman.

"Couldn't you think up something a little more original than this?" Kyrian taunted him, knowing Desiderius was pompous enough to take insult. "I mean, push your limits. You're supposed to be a crazed mastermind and this is all you have to offer?"

"Well, since you're unimpressed, let me kill her." He pressed the knife against her throat.

The woman screamed.

"Wait!" Kyrian snapped before the Daimon could draw blood. "You know I'm not going to let you hurt her."

Desiderius smiled. "Then drop your *srads* and move to stand against the fence."

How did he know about those?

"Okay," Kyrian said slowly. "And why?"

"Because I said so!"

Trying to figure out his reasoning, Kyrian pulled Talon's weapons out from under his coat and moved slowly toward the fence. Once he stood in front of it, the two human men grabbed his wrists and placed ropes around them.

Suddenly, he was pulled backward, his arms spread out against the fence. Kyrian fought wildly. His heart pounding, he jerked at the ropes holding him pinned. All his calm, cool Dark-Hunter rationale evaporated, leaving him in the throes of panic. He fought his restraints like a wild animal caught in a trap.

He had to get out of this. He would not be tied helpless. Not like this. Not ever again.

He fought against the ropes, tearing the flesh around his wrists. He didn't care. All he wanted was his freedom.

"I told you I knew your weaknesses," Desiderius said. "Right down to the fact you would never let me hurt a pregnant human." He leaned down and kissed the girl on her cheek. "Melissa, be a good girl and thank the Dark-Hunter for his sacrifice."

Kyrian froze as she left Desiderius's embrace and moved to stand by the oldest human male.

She'd been in on it all along.

Son of a bitch, when would he learn?

"Are you ready to die?" Desiderius asked.

Kyrian bared his fangs at him. "I wouldn't be so cocky. You haven't killed me yet."

"True, but the night is still young, isn't it? I have plenty of time to play with Artemis's errand boy."

Kyrian gripped the ropes and pulled with all his strength as another wave of panic threatened to consume him. He had to calm down. He knew it, and yet those old, haunting memories of his torture in Rome tormented him.

"What's the matter?" Desiderius asked, stepping forward. "You look a bit pale, Commander. Are you remembering the humiliation of your defeat? The touch of the Roman executioners as they prepared you?"

"Go to hell!" Kyrian toed the release for his boot and kicked out at Desiderius.

Desiderius jumped back out of range. "Oh yes, I forgot about those boots. After you, I shall have to go find good old Kell as my next Dark-Hunter target. With him out of the way, what would all of you do without your weapons expert?" He inclined his head to the girl. "Melissa, be a dear and rid the commander of his boots."

Kyrian ground his teeth as the girl came forward. Dark-Hunter law allowed him to protect himself against humans who sought to do him harm, but he couldn't bring himself to hurt her, especially while she was pregnant. Though she didn't know it, she was still a little girl. "Why would you mess up your life with him?" he asked her as she pulled his boots off.

"Once my baby comes, he's going to make me immortal."

"He doesn't have that power."

"You're lying. Everyone knows vampires can take or give life. I want to be one of you."

So that was how Desiderius was enlisting his human helpers. "You could never be one of us. He'll kill you once he's finished."

She laughed at him.

Desiderius clucked his tongue. "Still trying to protect her even while she prepares you for your slaughter. How sweet. Tell me, were you so considerate of your Roman brothers?"

Kyrian threw his body toward Desiderius.

A Daimon came out of the shadows with a large hammer. Kyrian froze the instant he recognized it. He hadn't seen one in over two thousand years.

"Yes," Desiderius said as he moved closer to Kyrian. "You know what this is, don't you? Tell me, do you remember the way it felt when Valerius used it to break your legs?" Desiderius cocked his head. "No? Then let me refresh your memory."

Kyrian clenched his teeth as Desiderius brought the hammer down across his left knee, instantly splintering the bones. Once he had delivered a like blow to his right leg, the Daimon dared to stand before him.

Kyrian held himself up with his hands. He tried to put weight on his legs, but the pain made it impossible.

Desiderius smiled at him as he handed the hammer back to the Daimon. Then he pulled something out of his pocket.

Rage filled Kyrian as he recognized the ancient Roman spikes they had used for crucifixion.

"Tell me, Dark-Hunter," Desiderius said with a smile, "would you like me to put you up for the night?"

CHAPTER 12

Amanda came awake with a start. It took a full minute to realize she had fallen asleep in Tabitha's hospital room, lying against Nick. Her mother was asleep on the cot they had rolled in a short time ago, and she and Nick had taken the two uncomfortable chairs by the door.

Tabitha was still asleep on the bed where the doctors wanted to monitor her until morning. A Daimon had viciously cut a line down her sister's cheek that would leave an ugly scar. Bruises and cuts lined her body, but the doctor had assured them that Tabitha would heal.

Their sisters had gone home at their mother's urging, but Amanda had stayed just in case either of them needed anything. Her heart pounding, she looked up as her father returned to the room with two cups of coffee in his hands. He handed one to Nick. "You want mine, kitten?" he asked Amanda, holding his cup out to her.

Amanda smiled at her father's kindness until she remembered her vision.

"You okay?" her father asked.

She looked at Nick, her heart pounding. "Kyrian's in trouble."

Nick laughed before taking a drink of coffee. "You were dreaming."

"No, Nick. He's in trouble. I saw him."

"Just relax, Amanda, you've had a really bad day and

you're worried about Tabitha. It's understandable, but Kyrian never gets in over his head. He's fine. Trust me."

"No," she insisted, "listen to me. I'm the first to admit I hate my powers, but I know they're not lying to me. I can feel his panic and pain. We have to find him."

"You can't go out there," her father said. "What if this Desiderius is waiting for you? What if he sends someone to hurt you like he did Tabby?"

She met her father's pale blue eyes and offered him a small smile. "Daddy, I have to go. I can't let him die."

Nick sighed. "Amanda, come on. He's not going to die."

She dug at his coat pocket. "Then give me the keys to your car and I'll go myself."

Nick playfully captured his keys from her hand. "Kyrian would have my head."

"He can't have your head if they kill him."

She saw the indecision on his face. Nick set his coffee on the floor, then picked up his cell phone and dialed it.

"See," she said. "He's not answering."

"That doesn't mean anything this time of night. He could be in the middle of a fight."

"Or he could be seriously hurt."

Nick pulled his PDA out of its cradle on his belt and turned it on. After a few seconds, his face paled.

"What is it?"

"His tracer's off."

"Meaning?"

"I can't track him. No Dark-Hunter turns their tracer off. It's their lifeline if they get into trouble." Nick shot to his feet and shrugged his coat on. "Okay, let's go."

Her father stepped between them and the door. He stood even in height to Nick and had his entire body braced for a fight. "You're not taking my baby out there to get hurt. I'll kill you first."

Amanda stepped around Nick and kissed her father on his cheek. "It's okay, Daddy. I know what I'm doing."

By the light in his eyes, she knew he doubted her.

"Let her go, Tom," her mother said from her cot. "There's no danger to her tonight. Her aura is pure."

"Are you sure?" he asked her mother.

She nodded.

Her father sighed, but still he looked doubtful. He glared at Nick. "Don't you let her get hurt."

"Believe me," Nick said, "I won't. I answer to a much scarier person than you for her welfare."

Reluctantly her father let them leave.

Amanda rushed through the hospital, to the parking lot, then ran over to Nick's Jag.

Once they were in Nick's car, Amanda did her best to remember where she had seen Kyrian in her vision. "It was a small, dark courtyard."

Nick snorted. "This is New Orleans, chère. That doesn't tell me anything."

"I know. I think it was in the Quarter. But I don't know. Dammit, I just don't know." She scanned the dark streets as they passed them. "Is there a Dark-Hunter we could call who might be able to help find him? Maybe we should get Talon back?"

"No, Talon is hunting his own target." He handed her his cell phone. "Push redial and keep trying to call Kyrian."

She did, repeatedly, but there was still no answer.

As dawn approached, Amanda became desperate. If they didn't find him soon, he'd be dead.

Terrified, she did what she had never dared before. She leaned her head back on the seat and purposefully reached down deep inside herself to touch the full strength of her untested powers. A terrifying surge went through her, making her warm and throbbing.

Images swam in her head, some old, some undefinable.

Just as she was sure her powers would tell her nothing, a clear image came to her. "St. Philip Street," she whispered. "We'll find him there."

They parked on St. Philip and got out of the car.

Amanda didn't know how, but she guided Nick down the

alleys, straight to a dark courtyard. They rounded the buildings and saw nothing.

"Dammit, Amanda, he's not here."

She barely heard him. Following her instincts, she rounded a tall hedge, then stopped dead in her tracks.

Kyrian hung against a fence, his entire body slumped.

"Oh, my God," she breathed as she ran to him.

Gently, she lifted his head and gasped as she saw his bloodied face. They had beaten him so severely that he could barely open his eyes.

"Amanda?" he whispered. "Is it really you, or am I dreaming?"

Tears filled her eyes. "Yes, Kyrian. It's me."

Nick cursed as he stopped beside her and reached to touch one of the nails in Kyrian's arm. He drew his hand back sharply before it made contact and hurt Kyrian more. She saw the rage in Nick's eyes as he cursed again. "My God, they nailed him to a board."

Amanda wanted to throw up at the thought. She could tell by the wounds exactly what Desiderius had done. He had re-enacted Kyrian's execution.

"We've got to get you out of here," she said.

Kyrian choked, then coughed up blood. "There's not enough time."

"He's right," Nick concurred. "It'll be dawn in five, maybe ten minutes. We'll never get him home before the sun rises."

"Then call Tate."

"He couldn't get here in time." A tic appeared in Nick's jaw as he touched Kyrian's hand where someone had embedded a nail into the center of it. "I'm not sure how we could get him loose even if Tate did make it in time."

"It's all right," Kyrian said, his voice strained. He swallowed and met Nick's tormented gaze. "Take Amanda to Talon and have him protect her and Tabitha."

Nick took off running.

Ignoring Nick, Amanda focused on Kyrian. "I'm not going to let you die," she insisted, her tone high-pitched and sharp.

"Damn it, Kyrian, you can't die like this and become a Shade. I won't let you."

The tender look in his eyes stole her breath. "I'm only sorry I failed you. I wish I could have been the hero you deserved."

Amanda took his face in her hands and made him look at her. Her hands shook as she wiped the blood away from his lips and nose. "Don't you dare give up. Do you hear me? If you die, who's to say Desiderius won't get Talon, too? Fight for me, Kyrian. Please!"

Kyrian grimaced. "It's all right, Amanda. I'm just glad you found me. I didn't want to die alone . . . again."

Her heart lurched at the words as tears fell down her face. No! The scream reverberated through her soul.

She couldn't let him die. Not like this. Not after he had protected and cared for her. Not after he had come to mean so much to her.

Over and over in her mind, she pictured her precious Dark-Hunter roaming the earth trapped between worlds. Forever hungry. Forever alone.

She couldn't allow that to happen.

Nick returned with a crowbar in his hands.

"What are you doing?"

Nick gave her a hard stare. "I'm not going to let him die like this. I'm going to get him free." He tried to pry the nail out of Kyrian's hand.

Kyrian drew rigid from the pain.

"No!" Amanda shouted.

Nick went flying. "What the hell?"

Before she knew what she was doing, she felt her powers well up inside her. They surged forward like a waterfall, out of her control.

In that instant, the nails came free of Kyrian's body and he fell into her arms. "Help me, Nick," she breathed, trying to stay on her feet and hold him up.

Nick was aghast.

Shaking off his stupor, Nick picked Kyrian up in his arms. He staggered from the weight of him, but made his way to the car as fast as he could. "We still don't have enough time to get him home before sunrise," he panted out in broken syllables.

"We can take him to my sister's. She only lives a block over."

"Which sister?"

"Esmeralda. You met her earlier, the one with the long black hair."

"The voodoo high priestess?"

"No, the midwife."

Without another word, Nick drove them to Essie's house in record time. It took some doing, but they managed to get Kyrian to the porch just as the sun started to rise over the roof opposite them.

Amanda pounded on the door to her sister's narrow Victorian home. "Esmeralda? Hurry! Open the door."

She saw her sister's shadow through the Victorian lace curtain an instant before the doorknob turned. Amanda shoved the door open and Nick carried Kyrian into the foyer without a second to spare.

"Pull the shades down," Nick ordered Esmeralda as he laid Kyrian on the dark green contemporary sofa.

"Excuse me?" Esmeralda asked. "What is this?"

"Just do it, Essie, I'll explain in a minute."

Reluctantly, Essie followed Nick's orders.

Amanda touched Kyrian's face. "They made a terrible mess of you."

"How's Tabitha?" Kyrian asked weakly. Amanda was touched by his concern for her sister when he was so hurt himself.

"I'm calling an ambulance," Esmeralda said, picking up the phone from the end table.

Nick grabbed the phone from her hands. "No."

The look on Esmeralda's face would have quelled most men. Nick just glared back at her without flinching.

"It's all right, Essie," Amanda assured her. "We can't take him to a hospital."

"He's going to die if you don't."

"No," Nick said, "he won't."

Esmeralda cocked a disbelieving brow.

"He's not human," Amanda explained.

Esmeralda narrowed her eyes suspiciously. "What is he, then?"

"He's a vampire."

Rage suffused her face as she railed against them all. "You brought a vampire into my house? After what happened to Tabitha? My God, Amanda, where was your brain?"

"He's not going to hurt you," Amanda insisted.

"You're damned straight. I'm going to call—"

Nick stepped between Esmeralda and the phone. "You call anyone and I'll rip the phone out of the wall."

"Boy," Essie said in a warning tone, "don't think for two seconds you—"

"Stop it!" Amanda shouted. "Kyrian needs your help, Esmeralda, and as your little sister, I'm begging you for it."

"Do you—"

"Essie, please."

She saw the indecision warring in Essie's eyes and knew the thoughts in her mind. On the one hand Esmeralda didn't want to help the evil undead; on the other, she couldn't really say no to her sister.

"Please, Es, I've never before asked a favor of you."

"Not true. You borrowed my favorite sweater in high school to wear to that game where Bobby Daniels was playing."

"Es!"

"All right," she relented, "but if he bites anyone in this house, I'm staking him."

Kyrian lay still while Esmeralda and Amanda peeled his bloodied clothes from him. He hurt so badly he could barely breathe. Over and over, he saw the Daimons attacking him and he wanted blood.

"Let the sun have him." Desiderius's mocking voice rang in his ears.

That bastard would pay. Kyrian planned to make sure of it.

Amanda's heart wrenched at the wounds on Kyrian's body.

His forearms and hands were covered with nail holes.

Never in her life had she hated anyone, but right then she hated Desiderius with so much passion that if he were here, she'd rip him apart with her bare hands.

She left Kyrian only long enough to call her parents and check on Tabitha.

While Essie bandaged Kyrian, Nick paced the floor.

"What do you want me to do about Desiderius?" Nick asked Kyrian.

"Stay away from him."

"But look at you."

"I'm immortal. I will survive this. You wouldn't."

"Yeah, well, had we taken another three minutes to get there, you wouldn't have survived it, either."

"Nick," Amanda warned. "You're not helping. He needs to rest."

"I'm sorry," he said, raking a nervous hand through his tousled dark brown hair. "I attack when I'm worried. It's a defense mechanism."

"It's all right, Nick," Kyrian said. "Go home and get some sleep."

His jaw rigid, Nick nodded. He looked at Amanda. "Call me if you need *anything*."

"I will."

As soon as he was gone, Esmeralda finished tending Kyrian. "That really must hurt. What happened?"

"I was stupid."

"Okay, Stupid," Esmeralda said pointedly, "we're going to have to set those legs and I don't have a splint."

"Can I borrow the phone?" Kyrian asked.

Frowning, Esmeralda handed it to him.

Amanda carefully bathed the blood from his face as he dialed. "How can you be so lucid?" she asked him. "This has to be excruciating for you."

"I was tortured by the Romans for over a month, Amanda. Believe me, this is nothing."

Still, it made her ache for him. How could he stand it?

She listened while he talked to whomever he'd called.

"Yeah, I know. I'll see you shortly."

Amanda took the phone from him.

Kyrian closed his eyes and rested while Esmeralda motioned her into the kitchen.

"Now I want an explanation. Why is there a wounded vampire on my couch?"

"He saved my life; I'm just returning the favor."

Esmeralda glared at her. "Have you any idea what Tabitha would do if she *ever* found out?"

"I know, but I couldn't let him die. He's a good man, Es."

Her cheeks paling, Esmeralda's jaw dropped. "No, not *that* face."

"What face?"

"That weepy, Brendan-Fraser-is-on-the-screen face."

"Excuse me?" Amanda asked, offended.

"You're infatuated with him."

Amanda felt her face turn red.

"Mandy! Where's your brain?"

She avoided her sister's probing stare by looking back to the couch where Kyrian lay. "Look, Essie, I'm not stupid and I'm not a child. I know there can never be anything between us."

"But?"

"What but?"

"You look like there should be a 'but' on the end of that sentence."

"Well, there isn't." Amanda pushed her gently toward the stairs. "Now go on back to bed and get some sleep."

"Yeah, right. Are you going to make sure Mr. Vampire doesn't snack on one of us while I sleep?"

"He doesn't suck blood."

"How do you know?"

"He said so."

Essie folded her arms over her chest and gave her a piqued stare. "Oh well, that makes it official, then, doesn't it?"

"Would you stop?"

"C'mon, Mandy," she said, gesturing toward the couch. "The man is a killer."

"You don't know him."

"I don't know any alligators, either, but I sure as hell wouldn't leave one in my house. You can't change the nature of a beast."

"He's not a beast."

"Are you sure?"

"Yes."

Still she saw the skepticism in her sister's eyes. "You damn well better be, little girl, or we'll all pay a foul price."

While Esmeralda dressed for work several hours later, Amanda made a small breakfast for Kyrian.

"I appreciate the thought, but I'm really not hungry," he said gently.

She set the plate on the coffee table. Tenderly, she traced her hand down the bandage on his arm where blood had already seeped into it. "I wish you had listened to me and stayed home."

"I can't do that, Amanda. I have an oath and a duty to fulfill."

The job. It was all that mattered to him and she wondered if he protected her because he cared, or if she were just part and parcel of what his duty entailed. "Still, you tell me you believe in my powers and then when I tell you—"

"Amanda, please. I had no choice."

She nodded. "I hope you kill him."

"I will."

Amanda squeezed his hand. "You don't sound quite as sure as you did before."

"That's because I spent the night nailed to a board and I don't feel very well this morning."

"You're not funny."

"I know," he said. "It just bothers me that he really did know where to strike to do the most damage. Right down to—"

She waited several minutes, but he didn't elaborate. "To?" she prompted.

"Nothing."

"Kyrian, talk to me. I want to know how he got you into this condition."

"I don't want to talk about it."

Before she could press him, someone knocked on the door.

"Please," he said quietly, "go let D'Alerian in."

"The Dream-Hunter?"

He nodded.

Curious, she got up and opened the front door, then stepped back. The man on the porch was nothing like she'd expected. Towering over her, the Dream-Hunter had hair as black as night and eyes so colorless and pale, they seemed to glow. Dressed all in black like a Dark-Hunter, the man before her would command attention if not for the strange tendency of her eyes to want to look away from him. It was weird. Really weird. She had to force herself to look at a man who should make any woman gape in lustful awe.

Without a word, he stepped past her and went to Kyrian. The door jerked itself out of her hands and slammed shut to keep the daylight out of the room.

D'Alerian had a sleek, graceful walk as he moved toward the couch where Kyrian lay. He shrugged his leather jacket off and pulled the sleeves of his black shirt back on his arms.

"Since when do you knock?" Kyrian asked.

"Since I didn't want to scare the human." D'Alerian swept a gaze over Kyrian's body. "You're a mess."

"That's what people keep telling me."

There was no humor in D'Alerian's face. Nothing. He was even more serene and calm than Talon. It was as if he had no emotions whatsoever.

D'Alerian held his hand out and one of the armchairs moved to rest beside the couch.

Without paying her any heed, he touched Kyrian on the shoulder. "Sleep, Dark-Hunter." And before he finished the words, Kyrian fell soundly asleep.

Amanda watched as the Dream-Hunter kept his hand on Kyrian's shoulder and closed his eyes. Only then did she see emotions cross D'Alerian's face. He gasped and tensed as if he were the one being tortured. In fact, he showed all the pain she would have expected from Kyrian.

After a few minutes, D'Alerian pulled his hand away and leaned forward in the chair, his breathing labored. He covered his face with his hands as if trying to banish a nightmare.

When he looked up at her, the intensity of his stare made her jump.

"I've never, in all eternity, seen anything like that," he whispered hoarsely.

"Like what?"

He let out a deep, ragged breath. "You want to know how Desiderius got to him?"

She nodded.

"His memories. I've never felt such agonized pain in anyone. When they come upon him, they weaken him. And so long as they do, he will always lose his battle calm."

"Is there anything I can do?"

"Not unless you can think of some way to erase those memories. If they continue to plague him like this, he's doomed." D'Alerian looked at Kyrian. "He will sleep until tonight. Don't disturb him. When he wakes, he'll be able to walk, but he will still be weak. Try not to let him go after Desiderius for a few days. I will speak to Artemis and see what can be done."

"Thank you."

He nodded and was gone in a golden flash of light. Two seconds later, his jacket evaporated, too.

Taking his vacated seat, Amanda looked up at the ceiling and laughed nervously. All she'd ever wanted in her life was normality. Now she had a vampire lover and a Dream-Hunter, whatever that was, poofing in and out of her sister's house while yet another vampire was trying to kill her.

Life was nothing if not ironic.

She turned her head to watch Kyrian. His breathing was easier than it had been before and the stern frown had faded from his features. The marks on his body were horrendous, but even they appeared to have faded out some.

Just what had Desiderius done to him?

*   *   *

Kyrian came awake to the moonlight streaming through the open windows. At first, he couldn't remember where he was, until he tried to move and pain sliced through him.

Clenching his teeth, he sat up slowly and found Esmeralda standing with a huge cross in front of her and a garlic necklace around her neck.

"You stay right there, buster. And don't try any of that mind-meld stuff."

In spite of himself, Kyrian laughed. "You know, crosses don't work on us and neither does garlic."

"Yeah, right," she said, inching closer to him. "Would you still say it if I touched you with it?"

When she came close enough, Kyrian grabbed the cross out of her hand. "Ow, ow, ow!" he feigned, then he held it to his chest. "Really," he said seriously, handing it back to her. "It has no effect. As for the garlic, well, it's garlic and it stinks, but if it doesn't bother you, I can live with it."

Esmeralda pulled the necklace off. "So what is your vulnerability?"

"Like I'm going to tell you."

She cocked her head. "Mandy was right, you are infuriating."

"You should have talked to my father before I ate him."

Esmeralda paled and took two steps back.

"He's teasing you, Es. He never ate his father."

Kyrian turned to see Amanda standing in the doorway behind him. "Are you sure about that?"

She smiled. "Very much so, and you must be feeling better to taunt us." Amanda came forward and checked the bandages on his arms. "Good Lord, they're practically healed."

He nodded as he reached for one of the shirts Nick had dropped off that afternoon while he slept, and put it on. "Thanks to D'Alerian. After another few hours, they'll be gone completely."

Amanda watched as he slid off the couch. Only the slowness of his movements betrayed the fact he was still recovering. "Should you be up?"

"I need to move, it'll help with the stiffness." As he walked past her, he mumbled under his breath, "Some of it anyway."

She helped him into the kitchen. "Essie, is there any spaghetti left?"

"He eats spaghetti?"

Amanda looked up at him. "Do you?"

He cast a menacing glare at Esmeralda. "It's not as good as sucking the necks of Italians, but it's not bad."

Amanda laughed at the horrified look on her sister's face. "You better leave her alone or she might stake you while you sleep."

He took a seat at the kitchen table and cast a hot, longing stare at her body. "Personally, I'd rather *stake* you while we're awake."

She smiled at his double entendre as she fixed a plate of spaghetti. "I'm so glad to have you teasing me again. I was terrified I'd lost you this morning when we found you."

"How's Tabitha?"

"She's fine. They're sending her home even as we speak."

"Good." By his expression she could tell he was deeply troubled.

"What is it?" she asked as she set the microwave timer.

"Desiderius is out there and he will kill again. I can't just lie down and—"

Amanda stopped his words by placing her hand over his lips. "If you get yourself killed, what good would it do anyone?"

"It would help Nick since he would inherit all my property."

"You're not funny."

"You say that to me a lot."

She smiled tenuously. "Before you go after Desiderius again, we need to think this through. Right now, he believes you're dead, so we have one shot at surprising him."

"We?"

"I'm not going to let you fight him alone again. He threatens me and mine and I'm through sitting on the sidelines waiting for him to strike."

Kyrian reached up and cupped her face. "I don't want you hurt."

"Then teach me what I need to know to help you kick his butt."

He smiled at that. "I haven't fought with anyone else in over two thousand years."

"Well, you're never too old to learn."

He snorted. "You can't teach an old dog new tricks."

"There's no time like the present."

"Time is of the essence."

"God helps those who help themselves."

He laughed. "You're not going to let me win this, are you?"

"Nope. Now let me get you fed, then I'll show you the research I did while you were sleeping."

Kyrian watched as she dribbled cheese over his spaghetti. He'd never in his life come across a woman like her.

After Desiderius had left and he'd been waiting to die, he had spent the last moments with his eyes closed, remembering the way she looked in his bed. The way she felt in his arms.

It had given him more comfort than he had a right to ask for.

What if you fail again to kill Desiderius?

The idea horrified him. Amanda would be alone. He closed his eyes and thought of her lying in the hospital like Tabitha. Or worse.

No, Amanda was right, he needed to teach her to protect herself.

Desiderius was too dangerous. Too crafty. Worse, the bastard had delivered on his promise. He knew exactly where to hit.

"Kyrian?"

He looked up at Amanda.

She brought the plate of spaghetti and salad over to him and set it on the table, then placed her hand against his brow. "Don't think about it."

"Think about what?"

"Desiderius. You were thinking so hard, I swear I could hear your thoughts."

Esmeralda stuck her head in the kitchen. "I'm headed out to deliver Cara's baby. Are you sure you're all right alone with him?"

"I'm fine, Essie. Go, shoo, begone."

"All right, but I'll call later."

Amanda growled at her sister and looked at Kyrian. "Have you ever tried to live with nine mothers?"

"No, I can't say that I have."

After he had finished eating and called Nick, Amanda took him upstairs to bathe.

Kyrian stood completely still as she unbuttoned his shirt and removed it, then she undid his pants. He hardened as her fingers brushed against him. "You know, I haven't had an actual bath in decades. I always shower."

"Well, this will be more fun—I promise." Rising up on her toes, she kissed him lightly on the lips.

Kyrian followed her lead as she placed him in the tub. The hot water felt wonderful against his skin as she lathered a washcloth. He traced the line of her jaw with his fingers.

Amanda removed her clothes, then joined him in the tub.

Kyrian wrapped her in his arms, but as she moved against him, old memories assailed him.

All of a sudden, he was in his old home and he could feel Theone against him. See her cold face.

Amanda felt him stiffen. "Did I hurt you?"

"Let me up," he said, pushing her away.

Something was wrong with him. Something bad. "Kyrian?"

He wouldn't meet her eyes and suddenly she understood what D'Alerian had meant earlier.

Determined to rid Kyrian of his demons, she grabbed his face in her hands and forced him to look at her. "Kyrian, I am not Theone and I will never betray you."

"Let me—"

"Look at me!" she insisted. "Look into *my* eyes."

He did.

"I fed you, I didn't drug you. I would never hurt you. Never."

Kyrian frowned.

She moved higher up on his stomach, her body sliding against his. "Love me, Kyrian," she said, placing his hand on her breast. "Let me erase those memories."

He didn't know if it were possible, but as he felt her bare, wet skin against his, her hot breath on his neck, he realized he didn't want to push her away. He had been so long without a woman's comfort. So long without a caring touch.

She slid herself against him, banishing his thoughts. "Trust me, Kyrian," she whispered in his ear an instant before she swirled her tongue around the sensitive flesh of his earlobe.

Fire shot through him. "Amanda," he breathed, her name a prayer for salvation on his bruised lips.

He had tried so hard to let go of his past, tried so hard to banish it, and yet it was always there just under the surface waiting to stab him when he least expected it.

But not now. Not with her in his arms.

Amanda saw the veil in his eyes fall. For the first time, she saw the soul of the man who had no soul. Better still, she saw the heat and the yearning. The need he had for her.

Smiling, she gently kissed his lips, careful not to hurt him any more.

To her surprise, he deepened the kiss and slid his arms around her. He buried his hand in her hair and held her so tight against him that it stole her breath. His tongue stroked hers with a hunger that fired her own.

Amanda reached down between them and took him into her hand, then led him slowly, inch by wonderful inch, into her.

She rode him slow and easy, careful of his injuries.

Kyrian leaned his head back and watched the satisfied look on her face as she stroked his body with hers. Reaching out, he cupped her chin in his hand. "You are so much more than I deserve."

Amanda took his lips with hers and kissed him hard, tugging at his lips with her teeth. Goodness, but the man could kiss. Her tongue grazed his fangs as she quickened her strokes. His moan reverberated through her.

He cradled her head with his hands as he deepened his kiss. Overwhelmed by her emotions, she came fiercely in his arms. He kissed her even harder.

"That's it, Amanda," he whispered, taking her breast into his hand and gently squeezing it. "Come for both of us."

Amanda opened her eyes and saw the raw hunger in the midnight depths. "This is so unfair to you."

He smiled. "I truly don't mind. Just being inside you is enough."

Not believing it for a minute, Amanda helped him from the tub and toweled him off. She tucked him into the bed in the guest room, then carefully sealed the windows to make sure no daylight would leak through in the morning.

She watched as Kyrian slept, his ravaged body healing so fast she could almost see it.

If only she could heal his damaged heart as easily.

Damn his wife for her cruelty.

She heard a knock on the door downstairs.

With one last look at her guest, she crept to the hallway and went downstairs to open the door and found Nick standing on the porch with a small suitcase.

"I thought he'd need some more clothes and a few other things."

Amanda smiled at his thoughtfulness and let him into the house. "Thanks. I'm sure Kyrian will appreciate it."

Nick set the suitcase by the couch. "Where is he?"

"Upstairs, sleeping, I hope."

"Listen," Nick said sternly. "Talon's dogging Tabitha on the way back to your mother's to make sure she's okay and I have a couple more Squires looking after Esmeralda and the rest of your family. Now that Desiderius thinks Kyrian is dead, there's no telling what he might do, or which one of you he might go after. Tell everyone in your family to watch their backs."

Kyrian listened to them as he lay in bed. He could hear the fear in Amanda's voice. The anxiety. And he knew one way to dispel it.

If Desiderius knew he was still alive, he would wait to go after Amanda's sisters. Kyrian was the prime target to the Daimon; they were merely bonuses.

Slowly, painfully, he rolled out of bed and dressed.

CHAPTER 13

"Kyrian, I hate to disturb you—" Amanda broke off as she opened the bedroom door and found the bed empty.

"Where is he?" Nick asked, moving into the room behind her.

"I don't know, he was here a second ago."

Cursing, Nick pulled his phone out, then stopped. "Dammit, he doesn't have a phone with him."

"Surely he wouldn't leave."

She started to go check the bathroom, but he stopped her with a "duh" stare.

"Surely he would." He went to the window and they watched as Kyrian pulled Nick's Jag out of the driveway.

Kyrian's first stop was the doll shop. His intention was to find one of Desiderius's flunkies and the last thing he needed was to be unarmed when he met him.

It was just after eight when he swung open the door and heard the little bell tinkle above his head. Liza came immediately from the back, her wrinkled face warm and friendly until she caught a look at the healing bruises on his face.

"General," she said, her voice chiding. "Are you all right?"

"I'm fine, Liza, thank you. I just came to pick up my order."

She frowned. "I gave it to Nicky yesterday, didn't he tell you?"

Kyrian cursed silently. It figured. The *one* time Nick had remembered to pick up something would be the one time Kyrian wanted him to wait.

Then, Kyrian heard a faint rustling sound in the back of the shop, behind the burgundy curtains. Kyrian felt a strange stirring. One he hadn't felt in a long time.

No sooner had the chill gone down his spine than the curtains parted of their own accord. Cast in shadows, the figure emerging dominated the small shop. At six feet eight inches, and dressed all in black, he was a man who made all life-forms either quiver in fear or straighten in respect.

Or in Kyrian's case, it made him glare.

A wide smile broke across Acheron's roguish face. Though his black Ray-Ban Predator sunglasses obscured his eyes, he was still able to make women swoon when they saw him. Arrogant and tough, he took no prisoners and showed little mercy on anyone.

Acheron was a creature of many idiosyncrasies, the most peculiar one being his ever-changing hair color. He changed it so often, many of the Dark-Hunters made bets on what color he was going to dye it for the week. Tonight, he wore his long, dark green hair pulled back in an old-fashioned queue with one thin braid falling loose from the nape of his neck, over his chest.

"Acheron," Kyrian greeted him irritably. "Come to check up on me?"

"Never, little brother. I'm here to sightsee. Can't you tell?"

"Yeah. You look like a tourist. That dark green hair passes every time."

Ash laughed at the sarcasm. "Well, I figured since Talon is protecting what's her name . . . Tabitha? And you're after Desi-do-wrong, the two of you could use a hand."

"The last time I asked for a hand, Artemis sent me a dis-embodied one."

Ash grinned. "You know that when dealing with the gods, you have to be specific. Besides, I have information."

"You could have e-mailed it."

Ash shrugged. "My presence here means nothing. You

know I won't interfere with you and Desiderius."

Now, why didn't he believe that?

Oh yeah, because Acheron Parthenopaeus had never minded his own business when it came to badass Daimons. "Seems I've heard that one before."

"Fine," he said, shrugging nonchalantly, "I'll take my unwanted information and—"

"I've already heard what the Oracles said."

"But you don't know the rest of the story," Liza interjected.

Acheron frowned at her.

"What story?" Kyrian asked.

Acheron took a piece of gum out of his coat pocket and unwrapped it. Meticulously. "You said you didn't want to know."

"Fine, I'll go after him without it."

As Kyrian reached the door, Ash's voice stopped him. "Don't you find it odd that Desiderius has powers beyond anything you've seen from a Daimon?"

"Oh," Kyrian said, turning back to face him. "Let me think. Yeah."

Liza sniggered until Acheron gave her a sideways glare. She straightened up, then burst out laughing. Excusing herself, she ran to the back of the store, and cackled.

Acheron watched her leave, then turned to face Kyrian. He sobered. "All right, here are the facts. It seems old Bacchus got horny one night and made out with an Apollite babe. Nine months later, she had Desiderius."

"Shit."

"Yeah," Acheron concurred as he picked up one of Liza's dolls she had fashioned to look like Artemis. He frowned at the startling likeness, then set her back on her shelf. "The good news is old Daddy Bacchus couldn't care less since he has bastards strung out all over history. The bad news is Desiderius was just a little ticked off that Daddykins doesn't care about the twenty-seven-year time limit on his life. Since he's half-god, he thought he should have a little longer life span than that. One, say, that reaches immortality."

"So, he turned Daimon."

Acheron nodded. "And with those added demigod powers, he is equal to us in speed, strength, and skills. And unlike us, he has no Code."

"That explains a whole lot, doesn't it? If you can't get back at the gods themselves, then go after those who serve them."

"Exactly. And we are prime Desi bait."

"One question."

"Answer."

Kyrian ignored his sarcasm. "Why does it have to be a Dark-Hunter with a soul who defeats him?"

"Because that is the prophecy, and you know how prophecy works."

"How do you know all this?"

Acheron looked back at the doll he'd picked up. "I talked to Artemis last night. It took a while, but I wormed it out of her."

Kyrian considered that for a minute. Acheron had always been the goddess's favorite Dark-Hunter. Her preference for Acheron had been a long-standing grudge in the hearts of many Dark-Hunters. But Kyrian didn't mind. He was grateful for the Atlantean's ability to find out information from Artemis and give it to them.

"You know," he said to Acheron, "one day you're going to have to explain to me this relationship the two of you have and why you're the only Dark-Hunter who can be in a god's presence and not get fried."

"One day, I might. But it won't be tonight." Acheron handed him a retractable sword and a throwing dagger. "Now get your ass back to bed. You have a job to finish and you need your strength."

Kyrian started away from him.

"Oh and Kyrian?"

He turned to face him.

"Don't go home alone."

"Excuse me?"

"Desiderius has your number. It's no longer safe there."

"I don't give a damn if—"

"Listen to me, General," Acheron said, his voice menacing.

"No one here doubts your ability to make Desi the next menu item at the Road Kill Diner; however, you have other people to protect, including a headstrong Cajun who listens about as well as you do, and a sorceress with virtually untapped powers. So, for once, could you just do as I ask and not argue?"

Kyrian smiled tightly. "Just this once, so don't get used to it."

Acheron watched as Kyrian left the shop. No sooner had he gone than Liza came from the back.

"Why didn't you tell him that you got his soul from Artemis?" she asked.

Ash slid his hand into his pocket where the medallion rested. "It's not time yet, Liza."

"How will you know when it's time?"

"Trust me, I will."

She nodded, and held the curtains open for him. "Now, speaking of people who should tend their wounds, you need to come back here and let me help you. Goodness, but I've never seen anyone with their back in worse shape than you. Why on earth you let anyone beat you like that is beyond me. And I know you had to let them. A Dark-Hunter with your powers would never take something like that unless he wanted to."

Ash didn't answer, but he knew the reason. Artemis never willingly let go of one of her Dark-Hunters. The price of their freedom was a high one.

He had agreed to sacrifice some of his flesh in order to gain Kyrian a chance to kill Desiderius.

Most of all, his torn and bruised back had bought the General a chance for happiness. It was a bloody ritual he willingly underwent every time a Dark-Hunter wanted his or her soul back.

A ritual none of them knew about.

What went on between him and Artemis was private. And he would always keep it that way.

Kyrian eased his way over to Bourbon Street where he'd found the punks before. The pain in his side was lessening, but still excruciating. It took him a full half hour before he found what he was looking for.

And the look on the punk's face was priceless.

"Holy shit!"

Kyrian grabbed him before he could run. "Tell Desiderius we're not finished."

The kid nodded.

Kyrian released him and watched as he tore down the street at a dead run.

He knew the first rule of war was that a surprise attack virtually guaranteed a victory, and he had just blown his best surprise. Still, he refused to keep his advantage at the risk of Amanda or one of her family members being hurt. Desiderius wouldn't go after them so long as he had a Dark-Hunter to contend with.

Limping, he returned to Nick's car and finally headed back to the one thing that gave him peace.

"Where have you been?" Amanda asked as soon as Kyrian returned.

"I had something to do."

Nick cursed. "You went to find Desiderius, didn't you?" He cursed again. "You sent word to him that you were alive."

Kyrian ignored him as he headed to the couch and sat down.

"Are you okay?" Amanda asked.

He nodded as he stretched out.

Nick glared at him. Rounding the sofa, he clenched and unclenched his fists at his sides. "Dammit, Kyrian, why would you—"

"Nick, lay off me. I'm not in the mood."

Nick's nostrils flared. "Fine, go and get yourself killed. What do I care anyway? I get the house, the cars, everything. So you go right ahead and tell him you're wounded and half-dead. Tell you what, why don't I just leave the door unlocked and invite him on in here?"

"Nick, you're not helping," Amanda said gently.

She saw the agony in Nick's eyes. The filial affection he

had for his Dark-Hunter. "You know what?" he said through gritted teeth. "I don't give a damn. 'Cause I don't need anyone." He pointed at Kyrian. "I don't need you, your money, or a damn thing. I've never needed anyone but myself. So you go right on and die, 'cause I don't care."

Nick turned to leave.

Faster than she could blink, Kyrian was on his feet in front of Nick.

Nick glared at him. "Get out of my way."

Kyrian's face showed the patience of a father with a rebellious teen. "Nick, I'm not going to die on you."

"Yeah, right. How many times do you think Streigar said that to Sharon before he was turned into an extra crispy fried Dark-Hunter?" Nick shrugged Kyrian's hold off his arm and stormed out of the house.

A tic started in Kyrian's jaw as he pulled his cell phone off his belt and dialed it.

"Acheron," he said after a brief pause, "I have a renegade Squire who is no doubt headed out to the Quarter in a new anthracite Jag XKR convertible. Can you catch him before he does something stupid?"

His brow creased with worry, Kyrian met her eyes as he listened. "Yeah, thanks."

He looked extremely peeved at something Acheron was saying. "Yes, O great lord and master, I'm resting."

A shocked look came over his face. "How do you know I'm standing?"

After a brief pause, he snorted. "Bite me, Ash. Good luck with Nick." He hung up the phone.

Even though she didn't know exactly what Acheron had said, she caught the gist of it. "He's right, you need to lie down."

Kyrian's black eyes flashed. "I don't need to be coddled."

"Fine, *Nick*. Want to tell me how you need nothing and no one too and then storm out of the house?"

Kyrian offered her a sheepish smile. "Now you know why I tolerate him. Two peas in a pod."

Amanda laughed, even though her heart felt for both of

them. "Let me guess, you were just like him at his age?"

"Actually, he's a lot more tolerable than I was. Not quite as stubborn, either."

Amanda stepped into his embrace and wrapped an arm around his waist. "Come on, let's go upstairs."

To her amazement, he allowed her to take him back to the guest room and put him back to bed.

As she undressed him, she saw his pink, healing wounds. Taking his arm in her hand, she touched the small nail holes. "I can't believe you're up so soon after what happened."

He sighed. "You can't keep a Dark-Hunter down for long."

Amanda barely heard his words. As she touched the wounds, images flashed through her mind. She felt Kyrian's rage, his pain. Then she saw a flash of the future. Of Kyrian spread out against a wall and at Desiderius's mercy.

Of Kyrian dying.

Gasping, she let go and stepped back.

Kyrian frowned at her. "What is it?"

Amanda patted her chest as panic swirled through her. She fought her anxiety attack as hard as she could, but inside she was screaming over what she'd seen.

She couldn't let him die. Not like that.

Forcing herself to calm down, she stared at Kyrian. "You have to let go of your past. So long as you hold on to it, Desiderius will be able to destroy you."

He looked away. "I know."

"What are you going to do? If you don't stop remembering it, he'll have you again."

"I can handle it, Amanda."

"Can you?" she asked, her throat tight as she saw him dying again. Oh, dear Lord, please not that. She couldn't bear to lose him. The thought of going a single day without feeling his arms around her, hearing his voice . . .

His laughter.

It was unimaginable. The pain unbearable.

"I can control myself," he insisted.

But she knew the truth. She had experienced his execution

firsthand. Worse, she knew he had never dealt with it. Not really. He had only pushed it out of his mind.

All of a sudden, she had an idea how to purge it from him. At least she hoped it would work.

"I'll be right back."

Kyrian watched her leave, his emotions churning. Better than anyone, he knew his weaknesses. All Desiderius had to do was spread his arms out and he was lost to panic. Lost to memories so painful that he was powerless against them.

He ran his hands over his eyes. There had to be some way to push it all out of his mind. Some way to face the Daimon with a clear head.

The minutes ticked by as he considered possible solutions.

Kyrian became aware of someone watching him.

He rolled over in the bed to see Amanda in the doorway holding a tray and dressed in a long, flowing white satin robe. A warm smile on her face, she entered the room and set the tray on the dresser.

Kyrian frowned.

She approached the bed gracefully, then bent one knee. It peeked out from the slit in the robe. Bracing her leg against the bed, she rolled him over, onto his back. Still he stared at her stockinged leg and the hint of a garter belt underneath the robe.

Her smile grew wider as she reached into her pocket and pulled out a long silk scarf.

Kyrian's frown deepened as she wrapped it around his wrist. "What are you doing?"

"I'm going to make it better."

"Make what better?"

"The past."

"Amanda," he growled as she pulled his arm toward the bedpost. As soon as he realized she intended to tie it there, he jerked away from her. "No!"

She grabbed his arm and held it between her breasts. "Yes."

Amanda watched the panic in his eyes. "No," he reiterated firmly.

Licking her lips, she lifted his hand to her lips. Opening

her mouth, she gently suckled the pad of his forefinger. "Please, Kyrian? I promise you won't regret it."

Desire coiled through his stomach as he watched her. Her tongue flicked across his skin, down between his fingers. Then, she scraped the inside of his wrist and forearm with her fingernails, raising chills the length of his body.

She led his hand from her lips, to the parting of the robe, then inside to her bare breast. "Pretty please?"

His breathing ragged, he closed his hand over her. It was all he could do to remember what she was asking him.

She was asking for his complete trust. Something he hadn't been able to give to anyone in more than two thousand years.

Terrified of what had happened to him the last time he'd made that mistake, he met her gaze and felt his will crumble. Would she one day betray him?

Dare he take the chance?

This time when she guided his arm to the post, he ground his teeth, but didn't move as she secured it to the carved wood. Still, his heart pounded.

Amanda knew she had just won a small victory. Smiling, she tied the scarf loosely. "You can get loose at any time," she told him. "Just say the word and I will release you, but if you do, it will stop immediately."

"What will stop?"

"You'll see."

Amanda took his other arm and tied a scarf to that wrist. Kyrian watched her, his breathing sharp and unsteady. To her amazement, he said nothing as she tied him down. Sweat beaded on his forehead.

He pulled against the scarves, his muscles rippling and bunching. "I don't like this." He moved to free himself.

Climbing up on his body, Amanda caught his wrists in her hands and held him there. She dipped her head down and touched his lips with hers.

Kyrian tensed as he felt her tongue darting along the seam of his lips, begging for entrance. Opening his mouth, he welcomed her inside. He moaned at the way she stroked his tongue with hers, at the taste of her.

Her mouth was as close to heaven as a soulless man was likely to ever come. Her rose scent invaded his head, making him dizzy and hot. Breathless. Time stood still as her hands stroked his chest and he felt her breasts pressing against him.

It wasn't until he reached to hold her that he remembered she had him tied down.

Growling in frustration, he yanked at the silk.

At the sound of tearing fabric, Amanda pulled back from her scorching kiss. "Remember," she said huskily, "if you get free, you'll get nothing but a cold shower."

He stopped moving instantly.

To his chagrin, Amanda pulled back from him.

She ran her hands slowly down her robe, over her breasts, until she reached the belt. Taking her time, she unknotted the belt and parted the robe to show him her bare breasts.

His body burned as she let the robe flutter to the ground at her feet.

To his delight, she wasn't naked. She wore the dark blue garter belt he'd bought for her.

His mouth watered at the sight.

Slowly, seductively, she walked to the bed and climbed up his body again like a sensuous cat as her breasts trailed from his stomach to his chest. Kyrian hissed at the feel of her stretched out over him, of her breasts caressing him.

"How are we doing, General?"

He swallowed. "Fine."

Smiling, she traced the line of his jaw with her lips and tongue.

"I'm better when you do that," he whispered, his body on fire from her touch.

She pulled back with a laugh. "How about I make you blind with ecstasy, then?"

He strained against the ties. "It would appear I'm all yours, sweeting."

How she wished that were true. Amanda left the bed and moved to the tray. As she picked up the warm honey, she remembered the boiling oil the Romans had used on Kyrian.

Remembered the look on his face as they poured it over his skin, scalding him.

Her heart constricting, she moved back to where he lay at her mercy. She held the bottle over his chest and saw the shadow pass across his eyes as he too remembered.

Kyrian involuntarily cringed as the warm honey first touched his bare skin. But there was no scalding pain. No blisters forming or skin burning. It actually felt good.

Relaxing, he watched as Amanda drew small circles in the honey, smearing it around his nipples where she dragged her nails, sending chills over him, and then down to his stomach.

She set the honey aside, then slowly licked every bit of it from his skin. He writhed in blissful pleasure as she laved him. Her tongue delved into his navel, making him even harder for her.

She laughed low in her throat as she looked up at him from his lower abdomen. Then she moved up his chest with one long lick that culminated at his Adam's apple. Hissing, he leaned his head back to give her greater access to his neck, and when she lightly bit his skin, chills shot through him.

"Amanda," he breathed.

Smiling at him, she left the bed and grabbed a small bowl.

Amanda didn't know where her boldness came from. Never had she behaved this way, but she wanted to save Kyrian at any cost. Besides, something strange was happening to her as she did this for him. It was as if some part of her were gaining its freedom.

Shaking the thought off, she dipped her fingers into the bowl of whipped cream, then brought them to his lips. She traced the outline of that poetic mouth with her thumb.

Kyrian licked the whipped cream from his lips as Amanda straddled his waist. Oh, the feel of her wetness on him. It drove him wild. And when she moved, grinding herself against his swollen shaft, he thought he would die from the pleasure of it.

"Let me feed you, Commander," she whispered, then slowly she used her finger to feed him the whipped cream.

Kyrian swallowed as his emotions swirled. She was reenacting Valerius's cruelty. But there was no pain from her. Only an ecstasy he'd never known before.

Locking gazes with her, he offered her a tentative smile.

"Why are you doing this?" he asked.

"Because I care for you."

"Why?"

"Because you are the most wonderful man I have ever known. Granted, you're stubborn and infuriating, but you're also kind, strong, and giving. And you make me feel so . . ."

He arched a brow.

Amanda sat back and eyed him. "Now what's that supposed to mean?"

"What?" he asked innocently.

"That look."

Kyrian frowned. "What look?" He tried to reach for her, then remembered his restraints. How odd that he could have forgotten them.

Amanda dipped her head down to kiss him.

Kyrian moaned at the feel of her lips on his, of her tongue darting in and out of his mouth, carrying with it the taste of whipped cream.

She pulled back. "Do you like that?"

"Yes, I do."

"Then you're going to love this."

He watched as she scooted down his body, then took the whipped cream and made him a loincloth with it. Her fingers grazed his erection as the cool cream coated him.

Kyrian moaned at the sensation that sent heat all over his body.

Amanda nudged his legs apart and stared down at her handiwork.

She locked gazes with him, then laid her body down at his feet and took his sac gently into her mouth.

He growled at the feel of her tongue licking the tenderest part of his body. Her mouth closed around him as her tongue swirled, licking and delving as she worked her way to the other side, where she sucked him in tenderly and rolled her tongue around him.

Kyrian clenched the ties on his hands as waves of pleasure racked him. Nothing had ever felt better than her mouth on him or her tongue darting over his skin.

When she was through licking the cream from his sac, she started on his shaft. Kyrian strained against the ties as she closed her mouth around him, all the while watching him watch her.

She dropped her head down to tease the tip of his shaft with her tongue. His breath caught as she swirled her tongue around the tip, then took his entire length into her mouth. His head swam from pleasure while her hand stroked him from underneath.

He hissed and jerked at how incredibly good she felt. Instinctively, he arched his back, sending himself deeper into her mouth. She didn't protest.

Kyrian moaned as he felt the animal in him awaken. He craved her with blind obsession. "Amanda," he said, his voice hoarse and ragged. "I want to taste you."

She lapped at him, then raised her head to look at him. "Taste me how?"

His breathing intensified as she scaled his body.

She straddled his waist, braced her hands on his ribs, and looked down at him. "Tell me what you want to do to me," she said, her cheeks blushing at her words.

As he looked at her, he felt her emotions. She was scared and unsure, but wanted to help him at any cost. Touched more deeply than he should be, Kyrian licked his lips. "I want to feel your breasts," he said raggedly.

"Like this?" she asked as she cupped them for him.

The sight of her hands on herself, clutching her breasts, made him moan. "Yes," he gasped. "And I want to taste them."

Smiling at him, she held her breast to his parted lips.

Kyrian strained against the ties as he took her swollen nipple into his mouth and tasted her. Her blissful murmurs of pleasure filled his ears, spurring him on.

He pulled at the ties, shredding the fabric more.

She laughed evilly. "If you free yourself, Kyrian, then I get dressed and we stop. Is that what you want?"

He shook his head and relaxed his arms.

"Then what else do you want?"

"You." The heartfelt word poured out of his lips before he could stop it.

"Me?" she asked, her face hopeful.

Unable to lead her on when he knew there was no future for them, he added, "I want to be inside you."

He felt her pang of disappointment and it cut him deeply. "Amanda—"

"Shh," she said, placing her hand over his lips. "I am all yours," she whispered as she impaled herself on his swollen shaft.

Kyrian closed his eyes at the incredible feel of her wetness sliding down the length of him.

Amanda leaned forward and captured his lips with hers as she rode him hard and slow. She nuzzled his neck with her lips and felt his moan against her tongue as she quickened her strokes.

She could feel him writhing as she rotated her hips against him.

He leaned his head back and growled like a caged beast. He braced his feet against the mattress and pressed his hips up, driving himself even deeper into her.

When Amanda came, she screamed from the force of it.

She felt Kyrian go ramrod stiff.

"Don't move," he hissed.

She obeyed without question as he clenched his eyes shut and ground his teeth. His body trembled beneath hers and she saw more sweat beading on his forehead.

After a minute, he let out an elongated breath. He opened his eyes and stared at her. "Now can I get free?"

She nodded as she realized he still hadn't come. He had fought it with all his strength.

Even though she understood why, a part of her was hurt to realize he didn't trust her enough.

SHERRILYN KENYON

Stop that! she snapped at herself. *What kind of selfish stupidity is that? He needs his powers.*

Now more than ever.

Startling her, Kyrian easily ripped the fabric of the ties and freed his hands. Immediately, he gathered her into his arms and held her close. "Thank you, sweeting," he said, kissing her softly.

She smiled at him. "My pleasure."

He laughed at that and settled her down to lie by his side. He spooned up behind her and held her as if he were afraid to let go.

It wasn't long before he fell asleep. His hot breath fell against her bare shoulder.

Amanda reveled in it and hoped that because of what she'd done tonight, he would survive his next confrontation with Desiderius.

Amanda came awake to the sound of the phone ringing. Pulling back from Kyrian, she realized they were lying entwined. Her face flamed as she recalled what she had done with him. Never had she been so unabashed and yet with him she didn't mind.

Sliding out of his arms, she grabbed the phone in Esmeralda's room. "Hello?"

It was Esmeralda. "Mandy, thank goodness you're still there. My car broke down. I'm on the side of the road. Any chance you can come pick me up?"

"Sure."

She jotted down the location, then took a quick shower and went back to the guest room to dress.

She leaned over Kyrian and kissed his cheek. As she pulled away, he grabbed her. "Where are you going?"

"To pick up Essie."

"It's not safe."

"It's broad daylight. I'm fine."

She saw the reluctance in his eyes. "How long to sundown?"

"Hours still."

"All right, but come right back."

"Yes, sir, Commander, sir."

"You're not funny."

She kissed him on the lips and left.

Kyrian woke up a short time later. Getting up, he saw his wounds were almost all gone.

He unwrapped the bloody bandages and tossed them into the small wastebasket by the door.

"Amanda?" he called at the door.

No one answered. He listened for sounds in the house and only silence greeted him.

She must not be back yet.

Grabbing his clothes, he went to the bathroom.

It didn't take long to shower, shave, and change. Once clean, he made his way slowly back to the room. He paused at the door as he caught sight of Amanda. She was dressed in a pair of tight jeans and a black sweater that hugged those curves he loved to feast on.

Her hair down, she looked luscious.

He walked up behind her silently while she was examining the trash can.

Without speaking, he dipped his head down to nibble her neck. No sooner had he brushed her skin with his lips than he caught her scent.

This wasn't Amanda.

It was Tabitha.

CHAPTER 14

Kyrian took a step back as Tabitha whirled to face him. Her battered face was still bruised from the beating she had taken from Desiderius's minions and she wore a bandage over one cheek to cover the sutures. She dropped into a wobbly, tough fighting stance.

Anguish swept through him that he had failed to protect one of the people Amanda loved best in the world.

He swore it wouldn't happen again.

"Who are you?" she demanded. "Where's Esmeralda?"

Kyrian glanced to the mirror to see his missing reflection and quickly took a another step back before Tabitha noticed it, as well. "Her car broke down on her way home. Amanda went to pick her up."

He realized too late that he should have kept his mouth closed because recognition flared in her eyes as she registered his unique accent.

"You!" she screamed. "What have you done to my sisters?"

"They're safe."

"Like hell!" She rushed him.

Unwilling to hurt her, Kyrian pivoted on his feet and ran down the hallway.

"Vampire!" she screamed.

He heard rustling downstairs and realized she wasn't alone in the house.

"Pull open the curtains." As she screamed out the order,

Tabitha grabbed the curtain cord in the upstairs hallway that shielded the line of windows there, and gave a yank.

Kyrian hissed as the daylight touched him. Leaping over the banister, he landed in the living room below.

Two pairs of eyes widened as they took in his size. The dark-haired man turned pale, but the blond woman reacted quickly, running to the window to open more shades.

Before Kyrian could move, Tabitha was on him. She kicked out' and caught him right in his sore side. "Die, vampire scum!"

Kyrian hissed, baring his fangs at her, then back-flipped away from her, and started for the kitchen. He slid to a halt in the doorway as he saw the sunlight streaming through the room. There was no place to go in there that wouldn't kill him.

Something hard and sharp bit into his shoulder. Growling, he turned to see Tabitha with a long dagger. She drew back to stab him again.

Kyrian caught her wrist at the same time her two friends rushed him. The four of them stumbled back. Kyrian slung one of them off and broke free. He tried to run back to the living room, but Tabitha somehow managed to get in front of him.

Hatred burned in Tabitha's eyes as she swung the dagger in a way meant to slice open his stomach.

Kyrian jumped back into a ray of light. Pain lacerated his back. Hissing again, he dodged her and ran for the living room, trying to stay in the shadows.

They rushed him at the door, slamming him against it. Desiderius's words rang in his ears as they tackled him to the floor.

"They'll take you down like a pack of wild dogs."

Tabitha sat on his chest, her hand on his throat as her two friends grabbed his arms and held them down. Had they attacked him like this yesterday, he would have gone mad with panic. But today he felt a strange lucidity as he remembered Amanda restraining him last night.

"What did you do to my sister?" Tabitha demanded.

"Nothing."

"Don't you lie to me! I saw the blood in the trash can."

Trying his best not to hurt her, Kyrian brought his legs up and wrapped them around Tabitha's upper body and pulled her away as the dagger slashed, barely missing his throat.

He caught the man on his right in the stomach with his fist, then sent the woman flying over them, onto the couch. He cursed as Tabitha sank her teeth into his thigh.

Kyrian pulled the knife from Tabitha's hand and embedded it deep into the hardwood floor. "Listen to me."

"No!" she shrieked, squirming and punching.

Kyrian rolled over with her, pinning her to the floor. Instinct demanded he knock her unconscious, but as he caught sight of the face so close to Amanda's he realized he could never hit her.

That moment of hesitation cost him as her friends grabbed him again. Kyrian rolled with them, rising to his feet at the same time the door opened, spilling more light into the room.

Cursing, he barely made it into a corner.

Amanda's shrill tone rang out. "Stop!"

The humans froze when they heard Amanda's voice, while Kyrian tried to catch his breath. His new wounds throbbed as blood oozed down his back. Amanda rushed to his side and slid her hands over him to inspect the damage.

Tabitha pulled the dagger from the floor. She approached him with a determined stride, her angry eyes never leaving him. "Out of my way, Mandy. I'm going to kill a vampire."

"Wrong," Esmeralda inserted, closing the door and moving to stand between him and Tabitha. "You're about to kill your twin sister's *boyfriend*."

Tabitha gaped and paused mid-stride. She looked from Kyrian to Amanda. "Excuse me?"

Amanda ignored her. "Are you all right?"

He rubbed his hand over his bleeding arm. "Never better."

"Him?" Tabitha asked in disbelief. "What about me and the guys? I don't see you asking about us. He almost tore our heads off."

Amanda glared at her sister. "I don't see any of you *bleed-*

ing. Believe me, if he had really wanted you hurt, none of you would be standing."

Tabitha raked them with a disgusted sneer. "You're defending a vampire?"

"I'm defending Kyrian," she said emphatically.

Curling her lip even more, Tabitha looked back and forth at them. "What are you? Insane? You want a boyfriend who drinks blood, lives forever, kills for fun, and can't go outside in the daylight? Why, Mandy, I do believe you've finally found the King of the Losers. Congrats. I didn't think anyone could top Cliff's loserness."

That set off a whole deluge of insults and shrillness.

"Loser? I don't want to hear it from a woman who dates a man who hasn't worked more than two weeks in the last three years."

"At least Eric has a soul."

"Kyrian has a heart."

"Oh, please. You think that makes up for it? Tell me, Mandy, are you willing to give up everything for him? Your life, your future? What can a *vampire* offer an accountant? You want kids. Can he give you those?"

Kyrian's heart sank as he listened to them fight. With every word out of Tabitha's mouth, he became more and more aware of just how right she was.

He looked at the daylight streaming into the house.

Daylight that was lethal to him and vital to Amanda. Humans needed sunlight as much as they needed to breathe. As long as she was with him, Amanda would never have peace. She would have to sacrifice all her dreams for him.

It was something he could never allow her to do.

Heartsick, he crept along the shadows, toward the stairs.

"Would you two stop fighting!" Esmeralda shouted.

Kyrian paid them no more heed as he went up the stairs.

Several minutes and a truckload of insults passed before Amanda realized Kyrian was gone. "Kyrian?"

"He went upstairs," Esmeralda told her.

Amanda started for the stairs, but Tabitha stopped her. "You can't do this to yourself."

"You know nothing about him, Tabby. He's a Dark-Hunter, not a vampire."

"Yeah, and Julian Alexander said there's no real difference between them. They both have animal qualities and are *killers*."

"I don't believe Julian said that."

"I don't care if you believe it or not, it's true. And while you're mulling that one over, let me tell you another thing Julian said. Artemis will kill your *boyfriend* before she ever lets him walk free."

Her heart screaming a denial, Amanda pulled away and went upstairs. She found Kyrian in the bedroom gathering up his things.

"What are you doing?"

"Leaving."

"You can't go outside. It's just after noon."

His face was blank, cold. "I called Tate."

"Kyrian . . ." She reached out to touch him.

"Don't touch me," he snarled, baring his fangs to her. "You heard what Tabitha said. I'm an animal, I'm not human."

"It wasn't an animal I slept with last night."

"Wasn't it?"

"No." She laid her hand on his cheek.

She saw him savor her touch for only an instant before his face went rigid. He removed her hand from his cheek. "You say that, Amanda, and yet do you know how many times I've had to pull back from sinking my teeth into your neck? How many times I have felt your blood under my tongue and have craved a taste of it?"

She swallowed in fear. But she refused to give in to it. He was only trying to scare her off. "You have never hurt me and I know you would die before you did."

He said nothing as he grabbed his suitcase and left her.

She followed him down the hall, to the top of the stairs. "You can't leave like this."

"Yes I can."

She pulled him to a stop before he could descend down to the foyer. "I don't want you to leave me."

Kyrian paused at her words. Words that tore him apart. He didn't want to leave her, either. He wanted to toss her over his shoulder, carry her back to the room, and make love to her for the rest of eternity.

He wanted the right to claim her. The right to have her.

But it wasn't meant to be. He was a servant to the goddess. His life wasn't his own.

"Go back to your world, Amanda. It's safe there."

She cupped his face in her hands. Her bright blue eyes searched his with such an aching need that it made him hurt all the more. "I don't want safe, Kyrian. I want you."

He pulled away from her tender touch and headed down the stairs. "Don't say that."

"Why not?" she asked, following him. "It's the truth."

"You can't have me," he said between clenched teeth as he whirled on the stairs to face her. "I'm already owned."

"Then let me love you." The plea in her voice ate at his will. Gods, how easy it would be to open himself to her. To take her into his arms and . . .

Watch her grow old while he stayed the same. Hold her in his arms when she died of old age and left him to live out eternity. Alone.

The pain of the thought was enough to cripple him. Life without her was not something he wanted to contemplate. And if it hurt this much to let her go after only a couple of days, how much worse would it be in a few decades?

It was more than his wounded heart could bear.

"You can't."

"Why?" she asked.

"Some things are not meant to be."

She touched his arm, her eyes begging him to see her side of things. But he couldn't. He didn't dare.

"Maybe this *is* meant to be."

"You're wrong."

A knock sounded on the door.

Amanda watched as Esmeralda opened the door. Tate wheeled his stretcher in.

The resigned, pained look on Kyrian's face as he saw the body bag would be forever etched in her heart.

"Don't leave, Kyrian," she begged one last time, praying this time he would listen.

"I have no choice."

"Yes you do. Damn you, you stubborn man. You do have a choice. Don't leave me."

He rubbed his hand over his eyes as if he had a throbbing headache. "Why do you want me to stay?"

"Because I love you."

Tabitha's angry curse rang from the kitchen and was followed by silence so loud, it was deafening.

Kyrian closed his eyes as agony assailed him. He'd waited an eternity to hear a woman say that to him and mean it.

But now it was too late.

"The last time I believed a woman loved me I gave up an empire for her and watched her laugh while I was crucified. Don't be a fool, Amanda. Love isn't real. It's an illusion. You don't love me. You can't."

Before she could argue, he flipped gracefully into the body bag and zipped it closed.

"Don't you leave me!" she shouted, grabbing his arm through the thick plastic.

"Get me home, Tate."

Tate gave her a sad smile as he pushed the stretcher through the door.

Amanda growled her frustration. "Damn you, Kyrian Hunter. Damn you."

Kyrian heard her muffled words. They tore through him. He was such a godless fool.

Don't leave her, his heart begged.

But he had no choice.

This was the path he had chosen. His decision had been made with full knowledge of the consequences and sacrifices.

Amanda belonged to the light and he belonged to the darkness. Somehow, he would find a way to reclaim his soul without her, and once he did, he would kill Desiderius.

Amanda and Tabitha would be free and he would return to the life he knew. The life he had sworn himself to.

But deep in his heart, he knew the truth. He loved her, too. More than he had ever loved anything else in his life.

And he had to let her go.

CHAPTER 15

It was just after five o'clock and nearing dusk when Amanda reached Kyrian's. She parked her dark blue Taurus in front of the house and walked up to the grand front door, then knocked.

She expected Nick to answer; instead, the door swung open slowly to show her no one at all.

Frowning, she walked inside.

The door instantly slammed shut behind her, making her gasp in startled alarm. Now that she thought about it, the front gates had done the same thing. Only then she had assumed Kyrian had seen her car on the video monitors and had opened the gates before she had a chance to buzz the house.

Now she wasn't so sure.

Her heart hammering, she still didn't see anyone about. The silent house appeared completely empty. "Hello?" she asked, entering the foyer slowly. "Nick? Kyrian?"

"So you're Amanda Devereaux."

She froze when she heard the voice coming from the living room. It was deep and provocative, with an accent unlike anything she'd ever heard before. The rich sound reminded her of quiet thunder.

For an instant, she feared it might be a Daimon, until her eyes adjusted enough to where she could see the stunningly gorgeous man on the sofa. He was lying on his back with his legs dangling way over the arm of the sofa and his hands behind his head as he watched her from the darkness.

Shirtless and barefoot, he wore a pair of tight leather pants. He had long, dark green hair and a stylized small birdlike tattoo on his left shoulder, the tail of which curled down and around his biceps. His skin was the same golden tone as Kyrian's and it set off to perfection the small gold necklace he wore around his neck.

"And you are?" she asked.

"Acheron Parthenopaeus," he said in that steady, deep voice. "Pleased to meet you." His words were devoid of any warmth or emotion.

Okay, this was no Yoda. Well, except they both had green heads.

The man on the sofa looked to be no more than in his early twenties and yet there was a hardness to him that belied his youthful appearance. It was as if he had seen hell firsthand and had returned from the journey forever wiser.

Even while lying down, he commanded awe, and a shiver of fear went down her spine. Something about Acheron was truly frightening, but she couldn't put her finger on what it was.

He just made her greatly uneasy.

"So you're the infamous Acheron."

A smile played across his devastatingly handsome face. "Lord and master of the great barbarian horde that roams the night."

"Are you truly?"

He shrugged nonchalantly. "Not really. I would have better luck harnessing the winds."

She laughed nervously.

He rose slowly to his feet and approached her like a great, stalking beast. As he drew near, the force of his presence and the sheer size of him overwhelmed her.

At least six-foot-eight, he towered over her with an indescribably powerful essence.

"My God," she breathed as she craned her neck to look up at him. "Is there some unwritten law that you guys have to be giants?"

He laughed, showing her a glimpse of his fangs. "What can I say? Artemis likes her Dark-Hunters tall. Short men need not apply."

As he stopped before her, she saw his eyes.

Her jaw went slack. Unlike Kyrian's, they shimmered. There was no other word for it. As she watched him, his eyes shifted through an entire blue and silver spectrum. Like quicksilver, the colors changed and blended. It reminded her of a turgid sea with shifting waves.

"Off-putting, aren't they?" he asked as he watched her watch him.

"Are they supposed to do that?"

He smiled a tight-lipped smile, but didn't respond as he pulled a pair of black opaque sunglasses from his back pocket and put them on. Now that his eyes were covered, she noticed the strange scar on his neck. It looked as if someone's hand print had been burned into his throat while he was being throttled. Very, very strange.

"What brings you here, little human?" Acheron asked.

"I've come to see Kyrian."

"He doesn't want to be seen."

"Well," she said, stiffening her spine to stand strong against this Dark-Hunter she was sure could splinter her in a nanosecond. "We don't always know what's best for us."

He laughed at that. "Very true. So you think you can save him?"

"You doubt me?"

He cocked his head as if assessing her mettle and walked a small circle around her. As he passed, she saw the healing wounds on his back. They overlapped and crisscrossed like some twisted river map. But the most peculiar part was that they seemed to form an intricate pattern that was as beautiful as it was horrifying.

Her heart lurched at the sight. He must have endured untold hours of agony for each visible welt.

Dropping her gaze from his lean, muscular back, she found the bow mark of Artemis that was identical to the one Kyrian had on his shoulder. Only Acheron's was located over his right hipbone.

"You know," he said in a low, ominous tone. "I've walked this earth for over eleven thousand years, my lady." He paused and leaned to whisper in her ear. "I have seen things in my life that are unimaginable to you, and you ask if I doubt you?"

He took a step back so that he could watch her face before he finished his sentence. "Lady, I doubt the very air you breathe."

"I don't understand you."

He ignored her confusion. "You want his soul."

"Excuse me?" she asked as a nervous tremor went through her.

"I feel you, lady. I hear you. Your mind is a whirlpool of feelings and fears: Can you have him? Does he love you? Could he *ever* love you? Do you honestly love him? Is there even the tiniest chance that the two of you can find a way to be together? Or are you just fooling yourself?"

She shivered as he laid bare the very thoughts and doubts in her heart.

He stopped in front of her and tilted her chin until she looked up at him. She could sense him probing her soul through her eyes, but she could see nothing of his liquid silver gaze. All she saw was herself reflected in the black lenses of his sunglasses.

When he spoke, his voice seemed to be coming from inside her head. "The one question that bothers you most is how to save him without killing your sister in the process."

"How do you know all that?"

He gave an odd half-smile. "My powers are unfathomable to you."

"Then why don't you kill Desiderius before he hurts Kyrian again?"

He dropped his hand from her chin. "I can't."

"Why not?"

"For the same reason Kyrian can't. I have no soul with which to fight him. He would kill me, and given the sins of my past, I shudder to think of the means he would use."

She thought about that for a moment. Desiderius had tried to kill Kyrian the same way Kyrian had died as a mortal, which meant Acheron must have suffered something even worse than crucifixion.

Just what had killed this fearsome Dark-Hunter?

And hard on the heels of that thought was another. "How does a Dark-Hunter get his soul back?"

He backed her against the wall like a lion cornering its prey. The very air around him seemed to sizzle with mystical energy and power. "Souls are strange things, lady. They can only be passed by free will. The one who owns it must willingly let it go."

"So I need to summon Artemis since she holds Kyrian's soul?"

He laughed evilly at that. "She would eat you alive, little girl."

His tone set her anger off. He might be Mr. Badass, but she wasn't a child. "Don't patronize me."

"Oh, I'm not patronizing you. I am only warning you. You are incapable of taking on the goddess. She is the wind. The mistress of our destinies and you, little girl, are nothing more than a tiny morsel she would gobble up and spit out for fun."

"Thank you for that vivid imagery," she said, her stomach turning at the thought.

He smirked at that. Then his harsh features softened. "You do want to save him, don't you?"

Again she had the feeling he was eavesdropping on her thoughts. "Of course I do. He means everything to me."

He nodded. "You are pure of heart. This might actually work."

Now that scared her more than anything else he'd said or done. Something in his tone told her his idea was the worst kind of risky. "What might work?"

Acheron moved to a black backpack that rested on the coffin coffee table. He reached inside and pulled out a black carved wooden box. Silver symbols and classical Greek writing covered it. "What you seek is in here."

He opened the box to show her rich black velvet lining that

cradled a red medallion. Like Acheron's eyes, it shimmered. But its colors turned from red to yellow to orange. Colors that seemed to lick the center carving that looked like a swirling wind.

"How beautiful," she breathed as she reached to touch it.

Acheron pulled it from her reach. "Touch it and it will burn you like the very fires of hell."

She dropped her hand instantly. "What is it?"

"Kyrian's soul."

Her heart stopped beating when she heard his blasé tone. Swallowing, she stared at the medallion. Could it really be his soul?

No, it wasn't possible. "You're lying to me."

"I never lie," Acheron said simply. "I have no need to."

Still, she wasn't ready to believe he had possession of what she wanted more than anything. "What are you doing with it?"

"I was hoping you might help me return it to him so that he could kill Desiderius."

"Return it how?"

Acheron picked the medallion up, cradled it in his palm, and closed the box.

"It doesn't burn you?" she asked.

He gave her a sly smile. "I told you, my powers are beyond your imagination."

"Then why don't you return it to Kyrian?"

"Because he doesn't trust me and, unlike you, I have no heart, pure or otherwise." He turned the medallion over as if studying it. "You see, there is only one way for a Dark-Hunter to regain his soul. A pure, loving heart must take the medallion into his or her palm and hold it while the Dark-Hunter is drained of his supernatural powers. Only when the human part of him remains can a Dark-Hunter die a normal death."

"I beg your pardon?"

He looked at her, and even though she couldn't see his eyes, she knew he was staring at her. "The only way to give his soul back is to stop his human heart from beating. When it beats for the last time, the medallion must be placed against the mark where the soul was captured. It will leave the medallion and reenter his body."

Her head throbbed as she tried to come to terms with what he was saying. "I don't understand. How do you stop his heart from beating?"

"You drain his Dark-Hunter powers, then you stake him through the heart."

She stepped back, her mind whirling. "No! He'll vaporize like a Daimon. You're trying to get me to kill him, aren't you?"

"No," he said earnestly. "The Dark-Hunters are my children and I would sooner damn myself to a Shade before I ever let one be hurt. You asked how to return his soul to him and I've answered you. If you want to free him, you have to drain him and kill him."

Before she could say another word, Acheron took her hand and brought it over the medallion in his. The heat from it was excruciating. It was like holding her hand over a propane torch.

"Now imagine touching it," he whispered. "Then think of holding it. You will have to keep the medallion in your hand from the moment he is staked until his heart stops beating and you release it back into his body."

His grip tightened on her wrist and she could feel his hidden gaze boring into her. "Do you love him enough?"

"I . . ." Amanda hesitated. "How long do I have to hold it?"

"As long as it takes. I can't tell you that. It is different for every Dark-Hunter."

"And if I let go of it before the soul is free?"

"Then Kyrian is doomed for eternity to walk as neither Dark-Hunter nor Human. He will be trapped between this world and the next as a Shade. He will yearn for food and never be able to eat. He will thirst and never drink. He will suffer eternally."

Amanda stared at the medallion in horror. "I can't chance it."

Acheron released her hand, then returned the medallion to the box. "Then he will die anyway when he faces Desiderius."

"There has to be another way," she whispered.

"There isn't."

Her chest tight, she tried to imagine draining Kyrian's powers and leaving him vulnerable. Could she do that to him?

Acheron moved to return the box to his backpack.

"Wait," she said, stopping him. "You said the medallion must be placed exactly where the soul was captured."

"Yes."

"How would I find that?"

He gestured to the bow mark on his hip. "The brand will always show you where Artemis was touching us when she captured our souls."

Amanda opened her mouth to speak, but a booming voice silenced her.

"What are you doing here?"

Amanda whirled to find Kyrian behind her.

He looked to Acheron. "Why did you let her in?"

Acheron passed a warning look to her. *Say nothing,* his voice whispered through her mind. "It suited me to," he said aloud.

Kyrian's face hardened. "I told you not to."

Acheron smiled, his fangs flashing for an instant. "And I listen to you since when?"

Kyrian glared.

Amanda's gaze drifted down Kyrian's body and she noted he was dressed again in his black jeans, shirt, and boots. "You're not going after him *tonight,* are you?"

"I have no choice."

She looked over her shoulder at his boss. "Acheron . . ."

Acheron shrugged nonchalantly. "It's his decision."

"He's wounded," she insisted.

"He's a Dark-Hunter. He knows his strength and weaknesses. It's for him to decide."

Frustration welled up inside her and she wanted to kill them both. "You would let him die?"

"This has nothing to do with Acheron," Kyrian said, cutting her off. "As he said, it's for me to judge."

"Yeah, well, your judgment sucks."

"Yeah, well, Tabitha says the same about yours."

She glared at him.

He glared back until she broke eye contact with him. Then he glanced to Acheron. "Watch over her for me."

"Is that an order?" Acheron asked in disbelief.

"Don't be an ass."

He cocked a taunting brow. "I'm an Ash, not an ass."

A tic appeared in Kyrian's jaw. "And I have an appointment to keep. Later." He turned around and stalked out of the room.

Amanda stood frozen in the living room.

And her heart shattered at the sound of the garage door opening and Kyrian's car starting. The man was so damned stubborn!

"He was wrong, Acheron. You're not the ass, he is."

Acheron laughed.

Amanda rubbed her hands over her eyes as she tried to think of what she should do. But in her heart she knew. Kyrian was going to die one way or another.

At least if she killed him, he stood a chance. "Give me the medallion."

Acheron handed her the box. "Are you sure?"

"Absolutely not."

She tried to take the box, but he held on to it. "Whatever you do, *don't* change your mind after you take this into your hand. It would be the cruelest thing you could do to him. I would rather he die fighting Desiderius than die by the hand of the woman he loves. Again."

Her hand trembled under his. "I would never hurt him."

"No offense, but the last time I heard that, the woman dropped the medallion ten seconds after she picked it up. Don't make me wrong again."

"I won't."

He nodded grimly and released the medallion to her. "Remember, you have to take it into your hand the moment he's staked. Hold it until he's dead, then place the medallion over the bow mark."

"How will I know when it's done?"

"Trust me, you'll know."

Amanda placed the medallion in her backpack purse next to the box with the Barbie doll Liza had given her. She'd started carrying the doll the night Tabitha had been attacked. It was probably stupid, but knowing the doll was there just in case comforted her. Besides, it was better than carrying a gun, and even with the spikes in the legs, she was sure it was safer.

As she closed her purse, her cell phone started ringing. Digging it out of the side pouch, she answered it.

"Mandy, is that you?"

She wrinkled her nose when she heard Cliff's nasal voice. "I thought—"

"Listen," he said, interrupting her. "Something terrible has happened . . ."

He sounded as if he'd been crying. Even though they were over romantically, she couldn't help feeling concern for him. He might be a jerk, but up until a couple of weeks ago, she had intended to marry him. "What?"

"It's my mother," he said, choking on a sob. "Look, I know we're not on the best of terms, but I have no one else to call. Could you please come over here? I don't want to be alone."

She hesitated. A strange, sick feeling clenched her stomach. Attributing it to the fact she couldn't stand the thought of seeing Cliff again, she realized just how selfish denying him would be. He needed her. She would go for a few minutes, then return here to wait for Kyrian. "All right, I'm on my way."

"Thank you."

Acheron cocked a brow at her. "Something wrong?"

"A friend in need."

He nodded. "You go and I'll find your sister and watch over her." Acheron pulled on a black T-shirt. "By the way, be careful."

"Of?"

"It's nighttime and evil things are roaming out there."

Another ripple of fear went through her. "Should I be afraid?"

"Follow your gut, little girl. Do what you have to do."

She hated the way he referred to her as "little girl" all the time, and yet she couldn't seem to get ticked off about it. "You like being vague, don't you?"

"It was a choice of being a Dark-Hunter or a prophet. Personally I like the slash-and-kill stuff much more than prayers and the lotus position."

Acheron Parthenopaeus was a very odd individual.

Amanda fished her keys out and made her way back to her car. As she drove out of the driveway, toward the expressway, it dawned on her how strange that Acheron would send her out alone . . .

Why would he do that when Kyrian had asked him to watch over her?

Because Tabitha is far more likely to get into trouble walking the streets than you are going to Cliff's.

Oh yeah. That explained it. The only danger at Cliff's would be him boring her to death.

It didn't take her long to get there.

Amanda walked up to Cliff's first-floor apartment, then knocked on the door and waited for him to answer.

He opened the door. He was wearing a pair of Levi's and a yellow button-down shirt. "What?" he asked, looking over her shoulder. "No friend driving you this time?"

She glared at the jealousy she heard in his voice. How dare he! "What's that supposed to mean?"

He shrugged and opened the door wider. "Nothing. I'm just upset tonight. Thanks for coming on such short notice."

Again she heard that voice in her head telling her to leave. Like a fool, she ignored it and stepped inside.

He shut and locked the door behind her.

"Well, well," a familiar voice said from the kitchen. "What have we here?"

Amanda froze as Desiderius stepped out of the shadows.

CHAPTER 16

"You!" Amanda screamed and started for the door.

Cliff caught her. "Not so fast."

"How could you?" she asked Cliff. Then she turned to glare at Desiderius. "I don't understand why you're here. How?"

Desiderius sighed. "Please don't make this any more cliché than it has to be. It's bad enough that I had to stoop to such a primitive ploy to trap Kyrian. Now you expect me to dump my entire plan on you so you can escape and kill me?" He shook his head. "You know, I watch bad movies, too."

Suddenly, she felt Desiderius in her thoughts. Felt him goading and prying into her memories. Her head ached and swam as bizarre images played through her mind. Images of Desiderius embracing and caressing her. Of his breath on her neck.

Worse, Amanda felt the barriers of her mind collapsing under the pressure of his fierce mental onslaught.

"She is as you promised, Cliff." His voice came at such a faint distance. Like a vague whisper on the wind. "Her powers are pure, virtually untouched."

"I know. It's what drew me to her the first time I met her." Cliff smiled. "And with the information we gathered on how Kyrian fights from that night in the alley, we should have no trouble defeating him."

Desiderius paused as he looked upon the lesser beast. He

considered humans to be the lowest of low. They were, after all, only food for the gods.

The only thing below them were mongrels such as Cliff. Half Apollite, half human, the sniveling coward had served his uses.

All in all, he should be grateful that Cliff's Apollite father had died before he could impart the real truth of the boy's heritage to him.

As for Cliff's human mother . . .

Well, she had been a tasty morsel.

Desiderius had always known having a mongrel for a pet would one day pay off. All the years of having to rear the vile creature didn't seem so repulsive now.

· And when Cliff had found this little sorceress in his own office, Desiderius had bided his time waiting for Cliff to expose and develop her psychic powers before Desiderius took her soul and her powers along with it.

But she had been resistant.

Who could have guessed the outcome of all this? After Cliff had panicked and broken up with Amanda over her sister's behavior, Desiderius had known he would have to act quickly to claim the sorceress before she escaped their clutches.

As soon as Cliff told him how close the twins were and how often Cliff had been inside Tabitha's home, Desiderius's plan had formed.

When he had handcuffed Amanda to the Dark-Hunter, he had pretended to confuse her with her sister, hoping Amanda would panic and use her powers to kill the Dark-Hunter to protect Tabitha. He'd never dreamed she would reach into her powers to protect the Dark-Hunter.

Not that it mattered.

Now with the channel open, she was ripe for the plucking.

"You will bring me over now?" Cliff asked. "Make me immortal, too?"

"Absolutely."

Amanda barely registered the sight of Desiderius walking over to Cliff and taking him into his arms. She saw his fangs

flash an instant before Desiderius sank them into Cliff's willing neck.

Her head swimming even more, she felt herself floating
toward the floor. Too late, she realized her thoughts were no
longer her own.

Kyrian paused in the heart of the French Quarter looking
around as his long black leather coat billowed around his legs.
Tourists lined Bourbon Street, walking around, oblivious to
the danger. Some of them paused as they caught sight of him
dressed in black, wearing his sunglasses because the garish
lights hurt his eyes.

He could hear the cacophony of jazz, rock, and laughter
mixing in the cool winter winds.

Numbing his mind to the distractions, he reached out with
both his powers and his technology and still he had no sign
of Desiderius.

"Dammit," he snarled.

He rubbed his aching shoulder where Tabitha had attacked
him.

As he massaged the pain, the image of Amanda replaced
her sister's. He saw her laughing face the way she'd been last
night draped over him as she made the tenderest of love to
him. No one had ever touched him so deeply.

"Because I love you."

Those words seared his heart. More so because he had
heard her feelings in her voice. She meant them in a way no
woman had ever meant them before.

She loved him.

And he loved her. Loved her so much that inside he wanted
to die knowing he couldn't have her. The Fates were cruel
bitches. He'd learned that centuries ago. And yet on this cold
night, that one basic fact burned inside him.

Come to me, Amanda, I need you.

He flinched at the thought.

"Don't think about it," he whispered, knowing it was futile.

If he could have one single wish . . .

He forced the thought away. He had a mission to accomplish. He must stop Desiderius.

His phone rang. He pulled his cell phone off his belt and answered it.

It was Talon. "Ash wanted me to tell you something weird is going down. The Daimons are attacking in droves tonight. I've nailed ten so far and he's on the tail of four more. He wants you on your toes."

"Tell Gramps not to worry. Everything is quiet in the Quarter."

"All right, just don't get jacked out there."

"Don't worry. I can handle myself."

"By the way," Talon said. "Eric is with Tabitha. He said she's loose in the Quarter, hunting Desiderius, too."

"You've got to be kidding me."

"I wish. Ash was tailing her in the Garden District, but had to let her go when he spotted a group of Daimons after tourists."

Kyrian hung up at the same time his tracker hummed. It signaled that there were Daimons nearby. Grabbing his tracker from his coat pocket, he trailed their neural activity to a side alley a block away.

He entered the darkened area to find six Daimons attacking four humans.

"Hey!" Kyrian called, distracting them from their victims. He smoothed back the edge of his coat and pulled out his retractable sword. Pressing the stone on the hilt, he extended it out to its full five-foot length.

"Tell me," Kyrian said to the Daimons as he twirled it around himself, "have you ever seen a pissed-off ancient Greek general?"

The Daimons passed a wary look among themselves.

Kyrian fell into his crouch with his sword held in both hands as he sized them up. "It's not a pretty sight. Really."

"Get him!" the leader called and at once they rushed him.

Kyrian caught the first one with a parry that caused him to explode into powder. He twisted around like a graceful cat and caught a second one with an upper cut to the middle. The Daimon gasped and vaporized.

Before Kyrian could rebound from that attack, one of the Daimons caught his sore arm and clawed the sword from his grasp. Kyrian twisted and caught him with the toe of his boot. He too evaporated.

Another one caught him about the waist and rammed him back against the wall.

The other two closed in.

He kicked at the one on his waist at the same time the two approaching him vaporized.

He saw Tabitha standing on unsteady legs. "Eat steel, you vampire dogs," she said as she tossed a throwing star at Kyrian.

Stunned by the fact she had tossed it to him as protection and not to harm him, he caught it in his hand and used it to kill the last Daimon.

By the time he reached Tabitha, she was kneeling on the ground. Her neck was bleeding steadily, her face pale. Kyrian tore part of his shirt to make a compress, then dialed for an ambulance.

"Eric?" she asked, her voice strained as she tried to see into the darkness where the other victims lay. "Is he dead?"

"I'm right here, baby."

Eric staggered over to where they were. He fell down beside Tabitha and gathered her into his arms.

"She's not going to die," Kyrian assured him.

Eric nodded. "I tried to tell her not to come out tonight. That it was going to be bad. She doesn't listen."

"It runs in the family."

Tabitha touched Kyrian's arm while he gave directions to 911. After he finished, she stared at him, her brow dark with disbelief. "Why did you save me?"

"It's what Kyrian does, Tabby," Eric whispered.

While Eric held her, Kyrian checked on the other two people on the ground. They were the same ones who had attacked him in Esmeralda's house. Unfortunately, they weren't as lucky as Eric and Tabitha.

"Eric," he said, returning to them, "what happened?"

Eric shrugged. "One minute we had them and the next, they turned on us."

"Did they say anything?"

Erik looked sick as he held Tabitha close. " 'I'll swallow your soul.' "

Kyrian stared at him for a heartbeat, then clenched his teeth at their warped sense of humor. "Daimons watch way too many B movies."

Tabitha reached out and touched Kyrian's hand. "Thank you."

He nodded. "I return the gratitude."

"Man, Kyrian," Eric breathed. "You were right about them. I've never seen Daimons move like that before. I should have listened to your warning."

Frowning, Tabitha looked between them. "You two know each other?"

"My father used to work for Kyrian's friend Talon." Eric met Kyrian's gaze. "I've known Kyrian all my life, Tabby. Believe me, he's one of the good guys."

Before she could say anything else, the ambulance arrived.

Kyrian waited until they were both inside and under medical care before he called Amanda to tell her the news.

She didn't answer her cell phone.

He called her mother, her sister, and his house. No one answered.

His stomach knotting with fear, he headed for his car. Maybe Amanda was still at his house waiting for him.

Or maybe Desiderius has her . . .

He imagined her being attacked like Tabitha. Saw her bloody and dead like Tabitha's friends. The terror and pain of the thought wracked him.

Amanda had to be all right. He couldn't live if anything happened to her.

Like a demon possessed, he drove home as fast as his Lamborghini would go.

His body shaking in fear for her welfare, he rushed through the garage and into the dark house, listening.

Please, gods, anything. Just don't let her be harmed.

He heard Amanda upstairs, humming her Grieg tune in his bedroom. Relief and gratitude rocked him so hard, he almost staggered. He had to see her to make sure she was fine and healthy. Taking a deep breath in relief, Kyrian sprinted up the stairs and opened the door.

He froze.

Amanda had lit the candles on his wall sconces. She wore the skimpiest, sheerest white nightgown he had ever seen in his life. Her long legs were encased in stockings and a lacy white garter belt. With her back to him, she was leaning over the bed, scenting his sheets with the rose oil she rubbed onto her skin after her bath.

The candlelight displayed the outline of her creamy body to perfection.

His entire body burned at the sight of her. Overwhelmed by his emotions, he went to the bed and pressed himself against her back. He held her tight in his arms, leaning his head against hers as he shook with relief.

Amanda was alive and unharmed.

She moaned in pleasure. The sound reverberated through him, heightening his desire even more.

"Touch me, Kyrian," she breathed, taking his hands from her waist and leading them to her breasts. "I need to feel you tonight."

He needed it, too. After being so terrified that she was lost to him, he needed to feel her in a way that made his mind whirl.

Growling at the feel of her hardened, gauze-covered nipples in his palm, he dropped his head to taste the scented flesh of her neck.

She turned in his arms, reached up and removed his sunglasses from his face, then she claimed his lips with hers.

"Amanda," he breathed as her rose scent encircled his head, beguiling him. "What is it you do to me?"

She answered him by tracing her tongue along his jaw, then down under his chin to his neck. A thousand chills shot through him as she slid his coat over his shoulders and dropped it to the floor.

She untucked his shirt and ran her hands underneath it, branding his skin.

The voice in his head wanted to push her away, but he couldn't. In truth, he never could.

He loved this woman. There was nothing more to be said about it than that. She truly was his soul mate. He would deny it no more.

For this one tiny moment, he would revel in the love he felt for her. Revel in the way he craved her.

Her eyes hungry, she undid his pants and slid her hands over his swollen shaft. "I love how you feel in my hands," she whispered, stroking him. "Tell me, Kyrian, can you read my thoughts?"

Kyrian closed his eyes as he savored her touch. When she cupped him, he shivered. "No," he breathed. "I relinquished that power when you asked me to."

Picking her up, he set her on the edge of the bed and stood between her knees. She smiled a smile that lightened his heart as she unlaced the front of her gown and bared her breasts to him.

His body burning, Kyrian nudged her legs farther apart so that he could look at her. Gods, how he loved looking at her. Dropping to his knees, he took her into his mouth.

She let out a strangled cry as he tasted her completely. Kyrian closed his eyes as he ran his tongue over her. Her thighs trembled around his face as he brought her to climax.

Her hand clutched at his hair and all the while she rocked her hips against his face.

"Oh yes," she moaned.

Kyrian waited until she was completely finished. Only then did he stand up.

Her eyes were liquid and hot as she stared up at him. She rose up on the bed and finished undressing him, then she slid off the bed in front of him and offered him her back.

Without being told, he knew what she wanted. Growling low in his throat, he drove himself inside her with one forceful thrust.

She moaned in pleasure, rising up on her tiptoes and then dropping herself down to take him into her body all the way to his hilt.

Kyrian's entire body shook.

Kissing her shoulder, he slid his hand over her soft belly, then down through her nether curls so that he could touch her swollen nub. He stroked her tenderly with his hand while he kept his hips completely still. He let her take control of their pleasure.

Amanda milked him with her body until she came again, screaming his name.

Just as he felt their pleasure combining and his powers slipping from him, he pulled out of her. His breathing ragged, it was all he could do not to double over from the pain of his unspent lust.

For once, Amanda didn't take pity on him. Instead, she turned around and kissed him avidly.

"Amanda," he said, trying to get away from her.

"Shh, Kyrian," she whispered against his lips. "Trust me."

Against his instincts, he did. She laid him down on the bed, then climbed on top of him. Kyrian shook as she guided him back into her body.

She felt so incredibly good as he felt her inside him. Felt her pleasure as his as she rode him.

His ecstasy mounting, he let her roll him over until he was on top, cradled between her thighs. Feeling a little better, he rode her hard and fast.

This time when he went to pull out, she wrapped herself around him and held him tight.

Kyrian frowned as she rocked herself against him, drawing his shaft deeper into her body. She moaned as her body clutched at his.

"Amanda, stop," he breathed raggedly. If she continued, he would be lost.

Again he tried to pull away and again she held tight, sliding herself against him. Kyrian ground his teeth, trying to stave off his orgasm.

It worked until he felt her climax again. The sound of her

cry combined with her clutching him was more than he could take. Against his will, his body released.

Kyrian leaned his head back and shouted from the ferocity of his pleasure. There was truly nothing better than being in Amanda's arms. Her body.

For the first time in two thousand years, he felt at home.

And as those tender feelings swept through him, he felt his Dark-Hunter powers recede again.

No!

Amanda kissed him lightly on the lips and rolled over with him. He was too weak to protest. All he could do was stare up at her.

She left the bed and pulled on a robe.

"Amanda?" he called.

She returned a moment later with a glass of wine. "Everything is all right. I'm here, my love," she said.

She held the glass of wine to his lips. Trusting her completely, he drank it.

After a few minutes, the room began to swim. "What are you doing?" he asked as a feeling of dread consumed him.

But he already knew.

Like Theone all those centuries ago, she had drugged him.

The last sight he had was of her opening the door to admit Desiderius into his bedroom.

CHAPTER 17

Kyrian came awake with his hands tied above his head. He was positioned against a dark, dank wall inside an unfamiliar house. The old-fashioned room was lit by candles that cast dancing shadows around him and he heard whispers surrounding him. By the looks of the place, he would surmise it was an older home probably not all that far from his own house down in the Garden District.

Scanning the room, he found Amanda and Desiderius standing a few feet away from him with Desiderius's arm draped around her shoulders.

Disbelief overwhelmed him.

Not again. Dear gods, not again.

How could he have been so damned stupid?

His mind had tried to tell him something had been wrong. He'd even known Desiderius would be able to get to Amanda. But he hadn't listened. He'd let his love for her, his need for her, blind him.

Kyrian clenched his eyes shut.

What hurt most was knowing what Desiderius would do to her once he killed him. Without him to protect her, Amanda was at Desiderius's utter mercy.

It really would be like Theone all over again. Once Valerius had executed him, the Roman had thrown Theone out, saying he didn't want a whore in his bed who might ruthlessly hand him over to his enemies someday.

Since Theone had betrayed the military leader of the Macedonians and caused their defeat, she'd been unable to return home. The villa she had loved so much had been burned to the ground. Everything she'd held dear had been confiscated.

Persecuted by his countrymen, she had fled Greece to Rome where she ended up a prostitute in a rundown stew.

She'd died of disease less than two years after him.

In the end, she had caused the very fate she had tried so hard to avert.

Opening his eyes, Kyrian saw Amanda a few feet away from him. She was dressed in a pair of jeans and a black turtleneck. With her hair pulled back, he could see her profile perfectly as she clutched a doll to her.

How could she do this to him?

But then, he knew. Desiderius's powers had been more than she could take. Somehow, in spite of D'Alerian's efforts, the Daimon had invaded her dreams and turned her mind.

Rage darkened his vision. He wouldn't let her die. Not like this. In spite of his weakness, he grabbed the ropes and pulled as hard as he could.

"So, you're awake."

Desiderius and Amanda moved to stand before him. His eyes taunting, Desiderius placed one hand on Amanda's shoulder. "It's painful, isn't it? Knowing I'm going to bed her before I kill her and there's nothing you can do to stop me."

"Go to hell."

Desiderius laughed. "You first, Commander. You first." He trailed one long, evil finger down the line of Amanda's jaw. She didn't react at all. It was as if she were in some kind of trance. "I would take her in front of you, but I never could stand an audience. I was never *that* twisted." He laughed at his own joke.

Kyrian felt the rope slacken a degree. Working it, he put all his attention into gaining his freedom.

The ropes drew tight again.

Desiderius laughed. "Do you honestly think I'm so stupid as to let you get free?" He took a step forward and stood practically nose to nose with Kyrian. "This time, I won't chance your survival."

Kyrian smirked as if the Daimon were a little gnat buzzing by his head. "Ooo, if I were wearing boots, I'd be shaking in them."

Desiderius eyed him in disbelief. "Don't you *ever* get scared?"

Kyrian gave him a dry look. "I faced down an entire Roman legion with only a sword to protect me. Now, why would I be afraid of some two-bit, half-god Daimon with an inferiority complex?"

The Daimon hissed at him, baring his fangs. He grabbed the crossbow off the table and loaded a steel bolt into it. "You will learn not to taunt me. I am not one you mess with."

"Why not? What makes you special?"

"My father is Bacchus. I am a god!"

Kyrian snorted. The first rule of war: make your opponent lose his temper. Emotions clouded judgment and made one do stupid things, and it would give him the opening he needed to get free and save both of them.

Besides, he liked the way the throbbing vein stood out in Desiderius's temple. It let him know he hadn't lost his touch when it came to taunting his enemies. "What you are is pathetic. You're a bully and a psycho. No wonder Daddy has no use for you."

Desiderius screamed in fury. He brought the crossbow down hard against Kyrian's face.

Kyrian's entire head ached from the blow. He tasted blood on his lips. Running his tongue over the cut, he tsked the Daimon.

"You know nothing of my life, Dark-Hunter. You don't know what it's like being born to die."

"We are all born to die."

"Oh yes, the humans and their finite lives that are three times the length of ours. How I pity them."

He grabbed Kyrian by the throat and pressed his head back against the wall. "Do you know what it feels like to watch the woman you love decay before your eyes? Eleanor was only twenty-seven. Twenty-seven! I did everything I could to save her. I even brought a human to her and still she refused to take the soul that would save her. She was pure unto the end."

Desiderius's eyes turned dull at the memory. "She was so beautiful and gentle. I had begged my father for help and he turned his back on me. So I watched my beautiful wife turn old in a handful of hours. I watched her body age until it decayed in my arms."

"I'm sorry for you," Kyrian said quietly. "But it doesn't excuse what you've done."

Desiderius screamed his outrage. "What I've done? I've done nothing except be born to a cursed race while I watch the humans squander the gift of life they have. I do them a favor by killing them. I alleviate their boring, insipid lives."

His blue eyes darkening dangerously, Desiderius curled his lip. "You know, I obtained a copy of your Dark-Hunter handbook when I killed one of your brethren ninety years ago. The entry that struck me most was the one where it said to always go for a Daimon's heart. To strike at his most vulnerable spot."

He aimed the crossbow at Amanda. "Your heart would be her, wouldn't it?"

Kyrian masked his terror. His fear. Even though he was weak, he tightened his grip on the ropes holding him and lifted his feet up to kick Desiderius with all his remaining strength before the Daimon had a chance to hurt Amanda. Desiderius staggered back, the crossbow dropping away from her to point toward the floor.

"Run, Amanda!" he shouted.

She didn't move.

Kyrian fell back against the wall. "Damn it, Amanda, please run for me."

She didn't appear to hear him at all. She merely stood staring into space as she hummed and gripped her doll.

Desiderius laughed as he righted himself. He licked the blood from his lips while he eyed Kyrian with malice. "She's mine, Dark-Hunter. You can die with the knowledge that I will use her well before I take her soul and her powers."

Desiderius smiled an evil smile a second before he shot the crossbow straight into Kyrian's heart.

The force of the bolt embedding itself into his body drove him into the wall. Kyrian gasped at the pain of the steel biting into his body.

Desiderius came forward to stand before him. His eyes amused, he ran his finger around the small amount of blood that seeped from the wound. "What a pity Dark-Hunter blood is poisonous to drink. I'm sure it's richer and thicker than what I normally have to live on."

Kyrian barely heard the words as his heart struggled to beat. His ears buzzed. It was the most painful thing he'd ever felt. His sight dulling, he turned to look one last time at Amanda.

Her features were pinched as she watched him and for a moment he could pretend that she remembered him. That she knew he was dying and that she cared.

Had she been herself, he knew she would run to him.

Unlike his wife, she would cry when she heard of his death. And in a strange way, that comforted him.

Desiderius left him and went to pat her on the shoulder. "Go on, Amanda, kiss your lover farewell."

Kyrian struggled to breathe as she approached him. He had so many things he wanted to tell her. So many things he wished he'd said to her while she'd been able to really hear his words.

At least he wouldn't die alone.

"I love you, Amanda," he whispered, hoping that somehow she would later recall his words to her and know that he meant them.

Her eyes blank, she leaned forward and covered his lips with her own and pressed her hand to his shoulder.

He felt the blackness of death descend over him and as he died, he heard her last whispered words. "I will love you for eternity, my dark warrior."

Then everything vanished.

Amanda held her breath as she felt the heat seeping out of the medallion she clutched underneath the doll's dress, into Kyrian's lifeless body. Her hand shook as she waited for him to reawaken, and with every second that passed, she shook more.

It wasn't working . . .

Oh God, no! Acheron had lied to her after all!

Tears stung her eyes as the medallion turned icy cold and fell from her grasp.

Still, Kyrian didn't move.

He lay limp against the wall, his face pale. His body cold.

No!

It was over and Kyrian was dead.

No!

Desiderius's evil laughter rang out through the dark room and made her entire soul weep in anguish.

Right then, she wanted to die, too. This was all her fault. She had stood by and let Kyrian die and had done nothing to save him. Her grief welled up and lodged as an unreleased scream in her throat.

"I love you, Amanda." His words would haunt her forever.

Sobbing, she wrapped her arms around Kyrian's body and held him close, willing him to wake up and speak. *Please, God, take anything from me, but please let him live.*

"Amanda?" Desiderius's voice was sharp as he commanded her back to his side.

She held tighter to Kyrian, laying her head on his chest, beside the bolt, and willing her life force into him.

Amanda froze as she heard something. It was a faint sound, but it made her soar.

She heard Kyrian's heart beating.

Pulling back, she watched as his eyes fluttered open.

Kyrian gazed into Amanda's dark blue eyes that sparkled from her tears. No longer blank, her eyes stared into his with a purpose. And with love.

Her face softening, she passed her hand over his chest and the bolt shot free.

In that moment, he knew she hadn't betrayed him. She had set him free.

"You have your soul back, Kyrian of Thrace," she whispered as the ropes around his wrists unknotted. "Now let's make this bastard pay."

Desiderius screamed in fury as he realized what was happening. Kyrian didn't have his Dark-Hunter powers, but it didn't matter.

For the first time in over two thousand years he had his soul, and the feel of it and the knowledge that Amanda hadn't betrayed him invigorated him.

The Daimoh was a dead man.

Desiderius ran for the door.

It slammed shut. "I wouldn't want you to leave the party so soon," Amanda said. "Not after everything you've done to make us so welcome."

"Amanda?" Kyrian said uncertainly.

She looked at him, her eyes shimmering ever so slightly in a way that reminded him of Acheron's. "Desiderius unlocked my powers for me," she said quietly. "He thought to use the telekinesis and telepathy for himself." She looked at Desiderius and smiled. "Surprise. When you unleashed them, you lost all control over me."

Desiderius struggled to open the door.

Kyrian stalked him like a hungry panther after its prey. "What's the matter, Desiderius, afraid of a mere human?"

He turned with a snarl. "I can beat you. I'm a god."

"Then do it."

Cursing, Desiderius charged him. He grabbed Kyrian around the waist and drove him against the wall. Desiderius opened his mouth to bite him.

"Oh, like hell," Kyrian snarled. "I didn't just get my soul back to lose it to you." He kneed the Daimon in the groin.

Desiderius stumbled away from him.

"Kyrian."

He turned to see Amanda with his sword. She tossed it to him.

Extending the blade, he went for Desiderius. The Daimon dodged his swing and lifted his hand to astral-blast him. Kyrian cursed as the blast hit him in the chest right where the crossbow bolt had been. He staggered back.

Oh, it hurt.

Dazed, he couldn't defend himself as Desiderius rushed him. He braced himself in expectation of Desiderius's blow.

It never came.

Instead, Amanda popped the Daimon with a blast of her own.

Kyrian frowned at her. "Baby, can I handle this, please?"

She poked her lip out at him. "I was only trying to help. Besides, haven't you been battered enough?"

Before he could answer, Desiderius ran at him again.

Amanda held her breath as she watched them fight. Even weak, Kyrian was amazing. He flipped over Desiderius and retrieved his sword. Desiderius grabbed a sword from the table and charged him.

The sound of clashing steel echoed as the two of them engaged.

"Go, baby," she whispered, clutching her doll in her hands.

Kyrian would win. He had to. She'd gone through too much to see him die now.

As she watched them fight, she realized the sun was rising. She could see it just peeping through the closed windows.

Desiderius saw it and cursed, then he landed an upper blow to Kyrian that knocked the sword free from his grasp.

She held her breath.

Desiderius smiled as he stalked Kyrian away from where his sword had fallen. "Tell you what," he said evilly. "Why don't you give Hades my best?"

"Kyrian!"

Kyrian turned to see Amanda lob her doll at him. Instinctively, he caught it. He cursed as the blades in the doll's feet bit into his hand.

A smile broke across his face.

Laughing, he ducked Desiderius's blow, and caught the Daimon right in the heart with the doll's feet. "Tell Hades yourself," he said as Desiderius gaped.

Time stood still as Desiderius met Kyrian's eyes. The Daimon's face went through an entire array of emotions, disbelief, fear, anger, and pain.

Then, in the blink of an eye, Desiderius disintegrated.

Kyrian and Amanda stood frozen as the full impact of the moment hit them.

It was over. Desiderius was dead. Amanda and Tabitha were safe.

Kyrian had his soul.

And the woman he loved had saved his life.

His heart pounding, Kyrian dropped the doll to the floor and walked toward Amanda. "You are a very accomplished actress."

"No. I was terrified." She reached a shaking hand out to his chest. "I almost screamed when he did that. You have no idea how hard it was. Acheron told me that you had to die in order to be free and I knew I couldn't kill you. I knew the only chance we had was to let Desiderius do it for me."

Kyrian took her hand in his, and as his fingers brushed her palm, he felt the blisters. He turned her hand over to see the medallion symbols branded into her flesh. "It must have been excruciating."

"I'm all right."

He swallowed at her nonchalant tone. How could she dismiss what she had done for him? He arched a brow in disbelief. For him, she had ruined her hand. "You're scarred for life."

"No," she said, smiling. "I think it's the most beautiful thing I've ever seen." She leaned forward and whispered in his ear. "Second to you, that is."

Kyrian cupped her face in his hands and kissed her. "Thank you, Amanda."

As she watched him, the joy faded from her face and she gave him a scared look. "Julian and Acheron said you could summon Artemis now and return your soul to her, if you chose to."

"Now, why would I choose such a thing?"

She shrugged. "You're a Dark-Hunter."

He kissed her lightly on the lips. "What I am is a man in love with a woman. I want *you*, Amanda. For the rest of my blessedly short mortal life. I want to wake at dawn with you in my arms and watch our children play and fight. Hell, I even want to hear them back-talk me."

She smiled at him. "Are you sure?"

"I have never been more sure of anything in my life."

She took his hand and led him from the room.

Kyrian stopped dead in his tracks as he saw the early morning light in the living room. From habit, he stepped back as he stared at it.

The bright sunlight didn't hurt his eyes. There was no burning of his skin.

Tightening his hand on Amanda's, he forced himself to walk forward, through the door.

And for the first time in over two thousand years, he walked out into daylight. The feel of the sunshine on his skin was incredible. The warmth, the tingly early breeze. His heart pounding, he looked up into the light blue sky and saw the white clouds.

It was a glorious day.

One he owed to Amanda.

Scooping her up in his arms, he held her close. "All hail Apollo," he whispered.

Amanda smiled as she hugged him dearly. "No. All hail Aphrodite."

CHAPTER 18

Kyrian stared in amazement at the wedding band on his left hand. He still couldn't believe the good fortune that had brought Amanda into his life.

Seven months had passed since the day Amanda had returned him to the light. Seven wonderful months of being with her night and day. Of helping her to accept, develop, and harness her powers, which were now stronger than his own.

Not that it mattered to him. He still had more than enough of his Dark-Hunter powers left to keep her safe. And her safety was the most important thing to him.

That and waking every morning to see the smile on her beautiful face.

And now they were married.

Amanda grabbed him from behind and squeezed him tight. "What are you doing out here alone?" she asked.

He turned to see her in her wedding dress. The milky-white color set off her skin to perfection. Her cheeks were flushed with excitement, and the moonlight glowed in her eyes.

"I was getting some fresh air."

She smiled a smile that made him weak and strong at the same time. "Want to ditch the party and run for it?"

He laughed. "Only eight out of that gargantuan crowd are mine, the rest are *your* guests."

"Oh," she said, wrinkling her nose. "Never mind. It could get really ugly. Besides, my Aunt Xenobia might curse us."

He draped his arm over her shoulders as she led him back into the ballroom of his house.

The orchestra played while a hundred and fifty members of the Devereaux-Flora clan danced, ate, and talked. Miguel, Rosa, and Liza sat with Amanda's sister Selena at a table where they were laughing with Grace and her infant son.

Amanda left him to visit with her mother and father.

Talon, Nick, Julian, and Acheron closed in around him.

Julian congratulated him. "This one's a keeper," he said.

Kyrian nodded. "Yes, she is."

"Man," Talon said wistfully. "I'm going to miss our three A.M. bullshit sessions. Wulf's already climbing the walls because he's lost his Doom opponent."

Kyrian smiled as he recalled the lonely nights he had spent with his Dark-Hunter brothers and sisters on-line. "Tell the Viking not to worry. I'll sneak up every now and again and challenge him."

Acheron took a drink of his champagne. "So, what are you going to do with your short life?"

Kyrian watched Amanda grab three-year-old Niklos up and dance with him. She was going to make a wonderful mother someday. "I'm going to live it. Happily."

Nick had his hands in his pants pockets. "Guess I have to start looking for another Dark-Hunter to serve . . ." He looked meaningfully at Talon.

"Like hell, Gator bait, don't cast those eyes at me. I don't have Kyrian's patience. Besides, there's only enough room in my cabin for me and my computer."

"Don't worry," Ash assured Nick. "I'll find you someone to serve."

Nick looked horrified. "Please don't do me any favors. I have visions of you sending me up to Alaska to serve Zarek's psycho ass."

Kyrian laughed until Amanda rejoined them with a severe frown on her face.

"What is it, baby?" he asked.

"There's, um . . . a, um . . ."

The men looked at her expectantly.

"Yes?" Kyrian prompted.

"There's a fleet of UPS trucks in the driveway."

The men exchanged puzzled looks before they all headed out to the front of the house where seven UPS trucks were lined up.

One of the drivers approached Kyrian. "Hi," he said in greeting. "I'm looking for a Mr. K. Hunter."

"That would be me," Kyrian said.

"Good. Any idea where you want this stuff?"

"What is all this stuff?"

The driver handed him a clipboard with the names of the people who had sent the items. "Wulf Tryggvason, Zoe, Blade Fitzwalter, Diana Porter, Cael, Brax, Samia, Arien, Kyros, Rogue, Kell, Dragon, Simon, Xander St. James, Alexei Nikolov, Badon Fitzgilbert..." On and on the Dark-Hunter names went.

"You know, Kyrian," Acheron said with a laugh, "you're going to have to buy a bigger house."

"Yeah," Talon said, "but just wait until you have kids. I'll bet you get twice as much as this."

They all burst out laughing.

Amanda stepped into Kyrian's embrace and looked up at him. "I think your Dark-Hunter cohorts are going to miss you. You sure you have no regrets?"

Kyrian kissed her lightly on the cheek. "None whatsoever. You?"

"Never."

Acheron watched as the two newlyweds headed into the house arm in arm.

"Wanna bet where they're going?" Talon asked.

Ash laughed. "No bet. I already know." He turned to the driver and told him to leave the gifts in the living room. "I think my wedding gift will be to hire an unpacking crew in the morning."

Nick laughed. "Let me go show them where to stack it so Kyrian doesn't get ticked."

"I'll help," Talon said.

Ash watched Nick run ahead of the drivers with Talon following at a much more conservative pace. He listened to the darkness and to the sounds of the night that he knew so well. He felt a slight stirring behind him.

It was a presence he knew even more intimately than the night.

He drained the last of his champagne. "What are you doing here, Artie? I wasn't aware you had an invitation."

A long, gracefully tapered hand touched his shoulder. Even through the tuxedo, he could feel the warmth of her as she caressed him. Unearthly tall and statuesque, she moved like a sleek, sensuous wind. Soft. Elegant.

And capable of total destruction when stirred too vigorously.

"I'm a goddess," she spoke, her Greek accent smooth and cultured. "I don't need an invitation."

Acheron turned his head to see Artemis standing to his left. Her rich light auburn hair glowed in the moonlight and her iridescent green eyes sparkled.

"I hope you've come to wish them well," he said.

She glanced askance at him as she toyed idly with his newly dyed black hair. A sly smile curved her perfect lips. "I do. But the real question is, do you?"

Ash stiffened at the implication. "What kind of question is that? You know I do."

"Just checking to make sure that little green-eyed monster wasn't making you have second thoughts."

He narrowed his gaze at her. "The only green-eyed monster I know is you."

She sucked her breath in sharply at his words, but her smile never wavered. "Oooo," she crooned in a sexually charged tone. "Acheron is getting nasty in his old age." She leaned her chin to rest on his shoulder as she stroked his jaw with a well-manicured fingernail. "It's a good thing I like you, otherwise you'd be baked bread."

He sighed. "Yeah, lucky me. By the way, the correct term is 'toast.' "

Artemis could never keep track of colloquial slang, yet she seemed to enjoy using it. Or misusing it, anyway. There were times he suspected she did it on purpose just to see if he would dare to correct her.

"Mmmm," she said, playfully wrapping her arms around his waist. "I like it when you get all feisty."

Acheron stepped away from her. "So who are you transferring to New Orleans to take over Kyrian's spot?"

She licked her lips impishly and mischief glowed in her eyes. But before she could answer, Julian approached them.

"Little Cousin Artemis," he said in greeting.

"Julian of Macedon," she said coldly. "Didn't know you were here."

"Same."

"Well," Acheron said. "Nice to know no introductions are needed."

Artemis passed a threatening glare to Julian. "Yes, well, I wish I could stay, but I can't."

Before she vanished, she leaned forward and whispered the answer in Acheron's ear.

He went cold with the news as she twinkled into mist.

There were times when Artemis could be the biggest bitch on the planet.

Julian cocked a brow at him. "What did she say?"

"Nothing." The last thing Acheron wanted was to drop that bomb on Julian and Kyrian. And he certainly wasn't going to do it in the middle of a wedding.

He turned to Julian. "So, General, you have your best friend back. I'll wager the two of you are going to get into some serious trouble."

Julian laughed. "Not likely."

Somehow Acheron had a hard time believing that. Just as he had a hard time believing that Artemis would leave well enough alone.

EPILOGUE

Amanda brushed Kyrian's hair back from his face as she kissed his lips. Her wedding dress and his tuxedo were piled in a heap on the floor while they were tangled in the silk bedsheets.

"We're being awfully rude, aren't we?" she asked.

Kyrian smiled. "Yeah, but I like rudeness."

She laughed. Then he kissed her and she forgot everything else in the world.

"So, tell me," he asked as he nibbled below her ear with his human teeth. "Do you miss being an accountant?"

"Not at all. You?"

"I never was an accountant."

She nipped his nose. "You know what I mean. Do you miss being a Dark-Hunter?"

He licked her ear, sending chills over her. "At times, yes. But I'd rather have you."

"Do you really mean that?"

He pulled back to look into her eyes. "With every piece of my heart and soul."

"Good," she whispered, kissing him. "Because now that you're mortal again, the baby and I need you to be careful."

Kyrian froze. "What?"

She smiled down at him. "We're pregnant, Mr. Hunter. About six weeks along."

Kyrian kissed her deeply and held her close in his arms.

"That, Mrs. Hunter, is the best news I've ever heard."

Amanda cupped his face in her hands. "I love you, Kyrian of Thrace. And I never want to lose you."

"I love you, Amanda Devereaux-Hunter, and I swear to you, you never will."

Amanda kissed him again, knowing for the first time in her life that there really was such a thing as happily ever after. Even if it did mean marrying a vampire.

NIGHT
Embrace

For my fans who support me and who have given me untold smiles at conferences and booksignings and when I read my e-mails and letters.

To the RBL Romantica and DH posters whose presence is always a source of warmth.

For my family and friends who make my life worthwhile. And for my Kim and Nancy who believe in me and who are willing to give me the opportunity to introduce the world to the people who live in my heart and mind.

Thank you all! I hope each of you has all the blessings and riches you deserve. Hugs!

Prologue

The roaring village fires burned high into the night, licking at the dark sky like serpents twining through black velvet. Smoke wafted through the misty darkness, pungent with the scent of death and vengeance.

The sight and smell should bring joy to Talon.

It didn't.

Nothing would ever bring joy to him again.

Nothing.

The bitter agony that welled inside him was crippling. Debilitating. It was more than even he could bear and that thought was almost enough to make him laugh . . .

Or curse.

Ayc, he cursed from the excruciating weight of his pain.

One by one, he had lost every human being on earth who had ever meant anything to him.

All of them.

At age seven, he'd been orphaned and left the heavy responsibility of caring for his baby sister. With nowhere to go and unable to provide for the infant himself, he had returned to the clan that had once been led by his mother.

A clan that had banished both his parents before his birth.

His uncle had been in his first year as king when Talon

had forced his way into his hall. The king had grudgingly accepted him and Ceara, but his clan never had.

Not until Talon had forced them to.

They might not have respected his parentage, but Talon had made them respect his sword arm and temper. Respect his willingness to maim or slay any and all who insulted him.

By the time he'd entered manhood, no one dared to mock his birth or impugn his mother's memory or honor.

He had risen through the ranks of warriors and learned all he could about weapons, fighting, and leadership.

In the end, he had been unanimously voted his uncle's successor by the very people who had once mocked him.

As the heir, Talon had stood by his uncle's right side, protecting him relentlessly until an enemy ambush had caught them off guard.

Wounded and in physical agony, Talon had held his uncle in his arms while Idiag died from his injuries.

"Guard my wife and Ceara, boy," his uncle had whispered before his death. "Don't make me regret taking you in."

Talon had promised. But only a few months after that, he'd found his aunt raped and murdered by their enemies. Her body desecrated and left for the animals to prey upon.

Less than a full year later, he'd cradled his precious wife, Nynia, to his chest as she, too, drew her last breath and left him all alone, forever bereft of her gentle, soothing touch.

She had been his world.

His heart.

His soul.

Without her, he had no longer wished to live.

His spirit as broken as his heart, he had placed their stillborn son into her lifeless arms and buried the two of them together by the loch where he and Nynia had played as children.

Then, he'd done as he had been taught by his mother and uncle.

He had survived to lead his clan.

Laying aside his grief as best he could, he had lived only for the clan's welfare.

As a chieftain, he had spilled enough blood to fill the raging sea and had taken countless wounds on his own flesh for his people. He had led his clan to glory against all the mainlanders and northern clans who had sought to conquer them. With most of his family dead, he had given his clan everything he had. His loyalty. His love.

He had even offered them his own life to protect them from the gods.

And in one heartbeat, his clansmen had taken the last thing on this earth he had loved.

Ceara.

His cherished little sister whom he had sworn to his mother, father, and uncle he would protect at any cost. Ceara with her golden hair and laughing amber eyes. So young. So kind and giving.

To satisfy one man's selfish ambition, his clan had slain her before his eyes while he lay tied down, unable to stop them.

She'd died calling out for him to help her.

Her horrified screams still rang in his ears.

After her execution, the clan had turned on him and ended his life as well. But Talon's death had brought no relief to him. He had felt only guilt. Guilt and a need to right the wrongs done to his family.

That vengeful need had transcended everything, even death itself.

"May the gods damn you all!" Talon roared at the burning village.

"The gods don't damn us, we damn ourselves by our words and deeds."

Talon turned sharply at the voice behind him to see a man clothed all in black. Cresting the small rise, this man was unlike any he'd seen before.

The night wind swirled around the figure, billowing out his finely woven cloak as he walked with a large, twisted

warrior's staff held in his left hand. The dark, ancient oak
wood was carved with symbols, the top decorated with
feathers fastened by a leather cord.

Moonlight danced upon hair that was an unearthly jet-
black which the man wore in three long braids.

His silvery, shimmering eyes seemed to swirl like phan-
tom mists.

Those glowing eyes were eerie and haunting.

Standing to the height of a giant, Talon had never before
had to look up at anyone and yet this stranger seemed the
size of a mountain. It wasn't until the man drew nearer that
Talon realized he was only a few inches taller and not as
ancient as he'd first seemed. Indeed, his face was that of a
perfect youth who stood on the precious threshold between
adolescence and maturity.

Until one looked closer. There in the stranger's eyes lay
the wisdom of the ages. This was no lad, but a warrior who
had battled hard and seen much.

"Who are you?" Talon asked.

"I am Acheron Parthenopaeus," he said in a strange accent that spoke Talon's native Celtic tongue flawlessly. "I
was sent by Artemis to train you for your new life."

Talon had been told by the Greek goddess to expect this
man who had roamed the earth since time immemorial.
"And what will you teach me, Sorcerer?"

"I will teach you to slay the Daimons who prey upon
hapless humans. I will teach you how to hide during the
day so that the rays of the sun don't kill you. I will show
you how to speak without revealing your fangs to the humans, and all else you need to know to survive."

Talon laughed bitterly as blinding pain swept through
him once more. He ached and he hurt so much that he could
scarcely breathe. All he wanted was peace.

His family.

And they were gone.

Without them, he no longer wished to survive at all.
Nay, he couldn't live with this weight in his heart.

He looked to Acheron. "Tell me, Sorcerer, is there any

spell you have that can take this agony from me?"

Acheron gave him a hard stare. "Aye, Celt. I can show you how to bury that pain so deep inside you that it will prick you no more. But be warned that nothing is ever given freely and nothing lasts forever. One day something will come along to make you feel again, and with it, it will bring the pain of the ages upon you. All you have hidden will come out and it could destroy not only you, but anyone near you."

Talon ignored that last part. All he wanted for now was one day when his heart wasn't broken. One moment free of his torment. He was willing to pay any cost for it.

"Are you sure I will feel nothing?"

Acheron nodded. "I can teach it to you only if you listen."

"Then teach me well, Sorcerer. Teach me well."

Chapter 1

"You know, Talon, killing a soul-sucking Daimon without a good fight is like sex without foreplay. A total waste of time and completely un . . . satisfying."

Talon grunted at Wulf's words while he sat at a corner table at the Café Du Monde, waiting for his waitress to return with his black chicory coffee and beignets. He had an ancient Saxon coin in his left hand that he rolled between his fingers as he scanned the dark street in front of him and watched the tourists and locals drift by.

Having banished most of his emotions fifteen hundred years ago, there were only three things Talon allowed himself to enjoy anymore: loose women, hot chicory coffee, and phone calls with Wulf.

In that order.

Though to be fair, there were times when Wulf's friendship did mean more to him than a cup of coffee.

Tonight, however, wasn't one of them.

He'd awakened just after dusk to find himself pathetically low on caffeine, and though the theory went that immortals couldn't have addictions, he wouldn't wager on it.

He'd barely taken time to pull on a pair of pants and his leather jacket before he came seeking the goddess Caffeina.

The cold New Orleans night was uncommonly calm.

There weren't even many tourists on the street, which was unusual this close to Mardi Gras.

Still, it was prime Daimon season in New Orleans. Soon the vampires would be stalking the tourists and preying on them like an open banquet.

For the moment, though, Talon was glad it was quiet, since it allowed him to deal with Wulf's crisis and feed the one craving that wouldn't wait.

"Spoken like a true Norseman," Talon said into his cell phone. "What you need, my brother, is a mead hall filled with serving wenches and Vikings ready to battle their way into Valhalla."

"Tell me about it," Wulf agreed. "I miss the good old days when Daimons were warriors and combat trained. The ones I found tonight knew nothing about fighting, and I'm sick of the whole 'my gun will solve all' mentality."

"You get shot again?"

"Four times. I swear . . . I wish I could get a Daimon up here like Desiderius. I'd love a good down-and-dirty fight for once."

"Careful what you wish for, you just might get it."

"Yeah, I know. But damn. Just once, can't they stop running from us and learn to fight like their ancestors did? I miss the way things used to be."

Talon adjusted his black Ray-Ban Predator sunglasses as he watched a group of women walk past on the street nearby.

Now there was one challenge he could sink his fangs into . . .

Under his closed lips, he ran his tongue over his long left canine tooth while he watched a beautiful blond woman dressed in blue. She had a slow, seductive walk that could make even a fifteen-hundred-year-old man feel underage.

He *so* wanted a piece of that.

Damn Mardi Gras.

If not for the season, he'd be hanging up on Wulf and running after her to fulfill his first comfort.

Duty. How it reeked.

Sighing, he turned his thoughts back to their conversation. "I tell you, what I miss most are the Talpinas."

"What are those?"

Talon cast a wistful look at the women who were quickly drifting out of his line of sight. "That's right, they were before your time. Back in the better part of the Dark Ages, we used to have a clan of Squires whose sole purpose was to take care of our carnal needs."

Talon sucked his breath in appreciatively as he remembered the Talpinas and the comfort they had once provided to him and his Dark-Hunter brethren. "Man, they were great. They knew what we were and they were more than happy to bed us. Hell, the Squires even trained them how to pleasure you."

"What happened to them?"

"About a hundred or so years before you were born, a Dark-Hunter made the mistake of falling in love with his Talpina. Unfortunately for the rest of us, she didn't pass Artemis's test. Artemis was so angry, she stepped in and banished the Talpinas from us, and implemented the oh so wonderful   you're-only-supposed-to-sleep-with-them-once rule. As further backlash, Acheron came up with the never-touch-your-Squire law. I tell you, you haven't lived until you've tried to find a decent one-night stand in seventh-century Britain."

Wulf snorted. "That's *never* been my problem."

"Yeah, I know. I envy you that. While the rest of us have to pull ourselves back from our lovers lest we betray our existence, you get to cut loose without fear."

"Believe me, Talon, it's not all it's cracked up to be. You live alone by choice. Do you have any idea how frustrating it is to have no one remember you five minutes after you leave them?"

Wulf expelled a long, tired breath. "Christopher's mother has come over here three times in the last week alone just so she can meet the person he works for. I've known her for what? Thirty years? And let's not forget that time sixteen years ago when I came home and she called the cops on me because she thought I had broken into my own house."

Talon grimaced at the pain in Wulf's voice. It reminded him why he no longer allowed himself to feel anything except physical pleasure.

Emotions served no purpose in life and he was much better off without them.

"I'm sorry, little brother," he said to Wulf. "At least you have us, and your Squire, who can remember you."

"Yeah, I know. Thank the gods for modern technology. Otherwise I'd go insane."

Talon shifted in his fold-up chair. "Not to change the subject, but did you see who Artemis relocated to New Orleans to take Kyrian's place?"

"I heard it was Valerius," Wulf said in disbelief. "What was Artemis thinking?"

"I have no idea."

"Does Kyrian know?" Wulf asked.

"For an obvious reason, Acheron and I decided not to tell him that the grandson and spitting image of the man who crucified him and destroyed his family was being moved into the city just down the street from his house. Unfortunately, though, I'm sure he'll find out sooner or later."

"Man, human or not, Kyrian will kill him if they ever cross paths—not something you need to cope with this time of year."

"Tell me about it."

"So, who got Mardi Gras duty this year?" Wulf asked.

Talon dropped the coin in his hand as he thought about the ancient Greco-Roman slave who would be temporarily moved into the city tomorrow to help combat the Daimon explosion that occurred every year at this time. Zarek was a known Feeder who preyed on human blood. He was unstable at best, psychotic at worst. No one trusted him.

And it was just Talon's luck to have Zarek here, especially since he'd been hoping for a Dark-Huntress to come visit. It might drain his powers to be in the presence of another Dark-Hunter, but he would still rather have an attractive woman to look at than deal with Zarek's psychosis.

Besides, for what he had in mind, he and a Huntress didn't need their Dark-Hunter powers anyway . . .

"They're importing Zarek."

Wulf cursed. "I didn't think Acheron would ever let him leave Alaska."

"Yeah, I know, but word came from Artemis herself that she wanted him here. Looks like we're having a psycho reunion this week . . . Oh wait, it's Mardi Gras. Duh."

Wulf laughed again.

At last the waitress brought his coffee and a small plate of three beignets that were heavily covered with powdered sugar. Talon sighed appreciatively.

"Coffee arrived?" Wulf asked.

"Oh, yeah."

Talon took a whiff of his coffee, set it aside, and reached for a beignet. He'd barely touched the pastry when he saw something across the street, on the right side of Jackson Square down the Pedestrian Mall. "Ah, man."

"What?"

"Friggin' Fabio alert."

"Hey, you're not too far from the mark either, *blondie.*"

"Bite me, Viking."

Peeved by the timing, Talon watched the group of four Daimons stalking the night. Tall and golden blonde Daimons who possessed the godlike beauty of their race. They strutted around like punkish peacocks, drunk on their own power as they scoped out tourists to kill.

By nature, Daimons were cowards. They only stood their ground and fought against Dark-Hunters when they were in groups and only then as a last resort. Because they were so much stronger than humans, they preyed openly on them, but let a Dark-Hunter near them and they ran for cover.

There had been a time once when it wasn't like that. But the younger generations were more careful than their ancestors. They weren't as well trained or as resourceful.

However, they were ten times cockier.

Talon narrowed his eyes. "You know, if I were a negative person, I would be seriously annoyed right now."

"You sound annoyed to me."

"No, this isn't annoyed. This is mild perturbance. Besides, you should see these guys." Talon dropped his Celtic accent as he invented a conversation for the Daimons. He raised his voice to an unnaturally high level. "Hey, Gorgeous George, I think I smell a Dark-Hunter."

"Oh no, Dick," he said, dropping his voice two octaves, "don't be a dick. There's no Dark-Hunter here."

Talon returned to his falsetto. "I dunno . . ."

"Wait," Talon said, again in the deep voice. "I smell tourist. Tourist with big . . . strong soul."

"Would you stop?"

"Talk about inkblots," Talon said, using the derogatory term Dark-Hunters had for Daimons. It stemmed from the strange black mark that all Daimons developed on their chests when they crossed over from being simple Apollites to human slayers. "Damn, all I wanted was a drink of coffee and one little beignet."

Talon glanced wistfully at his drink as he debated what should take priority. "Coffee . . . Daimons . . . Coffee . . . Daimons . . ."

"I think in this case the Daimons better win."

"Yeah, but it's *chicory* coffee."

Wulf clucked his tongue. "Talon wanting to be toasted by Acheron for failure to protect humans."

"I know," he said with a disgusted sigh. "Let me go expire them. Talk to you later."

Talon stood up, zipped his phone into the pocket of his motorcycle jacket, and stared longingly at his beignets.

Oh, the Daimons would pay for this.

Taking a quick drink of coffee that scalded his tongue, he skirted through the tables and made his way toward the vampires, who were stalking toward the Presbytere building.

His Dark-Hunter senses alert, Talon headed to the opposite side of the square. He would head them off and make sure they paid for their soul-stealing ways.

And for his uneaten beignets.

Chapter 2

It was one of *those* nights. The kind that made Sunshine Runningwolf wonder why she bothered leaving her loft.

"How many times can a person get lost in a city where she's lived the whole of her life?"

The number seemed to be infinite.

Of course, it would help if she could stay focused, but she had the attention span of a sick flea.

No, actually she had the attention span of an artist who seldom stayed focused on the here and now. Like an out-of-control slingshot, her thoughts drifted from one topic to the next and then back again. Her mind was constantly wandering and sifting through new ideas and techniques—the novelty of the world around her and how best to capture it.

To her there was beauty everywhere and in every little thing. It was her job to show that beauty to others.

And that neat building they were constructing, two or three, maybe four streets over, had distracted her and got her thinking up new designs for her pottery as she wandered through the French Quarter toward her favorite coffeehouse on St. Anne.

Not that she drank that noxious stuff. She hated it. But the retro-beatnik Coffee Stain had nice artwork on the walls and her friends seemed partial to drinking gallons of the tar-liquid.

Tonight she and Trina were going to go over . . .

Her mind flashed back to the building.

Pulling out her sketchbook, she made a few more notes and turned to her right, down a small alley.

She took two steps, and ran into a wall.

Only it wasn't a wall, she realized, as two arms wrapped around her to keep her from stumbling.

Looking up, she froze.

Ay, Caramba! She stared into a face so well formed that she doubted even a Greek sculptor could do justice to it.

His wheat-colored hair seemed to glow in the night and the planes of his face . . .

Perfect. Simply perfect. Totally symmetrical. Wow.

Without thinking, she reached up, grabbed his chin and turned his face to see it from different angles.

No, not an optical illusion. No matter the angle, his features were perfection incarnate.

Wow, again. Absolutely flawless.

She needed to sketch this.

No. Oils. Oils would be better.

Pastels!

"Are you all right?" he asked.

"I'm fine," she said. "I'm sorry. I didn't see you standing there. But do you know your face is pure eurythmy?"

He gave her a tight-lipped smile as he patted the shoulder of her red cape. "Yes, I do. And do you know, Little Red Riding Hood, the Big Bad Wolf is out tonight and he's hungry?"

What was that?

She was talking about art and he . . .

The thought faded as she realized the man wasn't alone.

There were four more men and one woman. All insanely beautiful. And all six eyed her as if she were a tasty morsel.

Uh-oh.

Her throat went dry.

Sunshine took a step back as every sense in her body told her to run.

They moved in even closer, penning her between them.

"Now, now, Little Red Riding Hood," the first one said. "You don't want to be leaving so soon, do you?"

"Um, yes," she said, preparing to fight. Little did they know, a woman who made it her habit to date mean biker types was more than able to deliver a swift kick when she needed it. "I think it would be a really *good* idea."

He reached for her.

Out of nowhere a circular something whizzed past her face, grazing his outstretched arm. The man cursed as he pulled his bleeding arm to his chest. The thing ricocheted like Xena's chakram, and returned to the opening of the alley where a shadow caught it.

Sunshine gaped at the outline of a man. Dressed all in black, he stood with his legs apart in a warrior's stance while his weapon gleamed wickedly in the dim light.

Even though she could see nothing of his face, his ever-changing aura was mammoth, giving him a presence that was as startling as it was powerful.

This new stranger was dangerous.

Deadly.

A lethal shadow just waiting to strike.

He stood in silence, looking at her attackers, the weapon held nonchalantly, yet somehow threateningly, in his left hand.

Then, total chaos broke out as the men who surrounded her rushed the newcomer . . .

Talon fingered the release for his srad and folded its three blades into a single dagger. He tried to get to the woman, but the Daimons attacked him en masse. Normally, he'd have no trouble whatsoever obliterating them, but Dark-Hunter Code forbade him to reveal his powers to an uninitiated human.

Damn.

For a second, he considered summoning a fog to conceal them, but that would make fighting the Daimons more difficult.

No, he couldn't give them any advantage. So long as the woman was here, he was fighting with his hands tied behind his back, and given the superhuman strength and power of the Daimons, that wasn't a good thing at all. No doubt that was why they'd attacked.

For once they actually stood a chance against him.

"Run," he ordered the human woman.

She started to obey him when one of the Daimons grabbed her. With a kick to the groin and a whack across his back after he doubled over, she dropped the Daimon and ran.

Talon arched a brow at her move. Smooth, very smooth. He'd always appreciated a woman who could watch out for herself.

Using his Dark-Hunter powers, he summoned a fog wall behind her to help shield her from the Daimons, who were now more focused on him.

"Finally," he said to the group. "We're all alone."

The one who appeared to be the leader rushed him. Talon used his telekinesis to lift the Daimon up, spin him head over heels, and slam him into a wall.

Two more came at him.

Talon caught one with his srad dagger, the other he kneed.

He tore through the two of them easily enough and was reaching for another one when he noticed the tallest of them running after the woman.

That momentary distraction cost him as another Daimon attacked and caught him in the solar plexus. The force of the blow knocked him back, off his feet.

Talon rolled with the punch, and shot upright.

"Now!" the female Daimon shouted.

Before Talon could catch his balance completely, another Daimon grabbed him by the waist and shoved him backward, into the street.

Straight into the path of a mammoth vehicle that was going so fast he couldn't even identify it.

Something he assumed was the grill of it hit his right leg, shattering it instantly.

It pitched him forward, onto the pavement.

Talon rolled for about fifty yards, then came to rest under a streetlight on his stomach while the dark vehicle went careening down the street, out of sight. He lay with his left cheek against the pungent asphalt, his hands spread out beside him.

His entire body ached and throbbed and he could barely move from the pain. Worse, his head pulsed as he struggled to stay conscious.

But it was hard.

An unconscious Dark-Hunter is a dead one. The fifth rule of Acheron's handbook came to mind. He had to stay awake.

With his powers waning from the pain of his injuries, the fog shield began to dissipate.

Talon cursed. Any time he felt any sort of negative emotion, his powers diminished. It was yet another reason he kept such a stranglehold on them.

Emotions were deadly to him in more ways than one.

Slowly, carefully, Talon pushed himself to his feet at the same time he saw the Daimons fleeing down another alley. There was nothing to be done about it. He'd never catch them in his current condition, and even if he did, the worst thing he could do to them was bleed on them.

Of course, Dark-Hunter blood was poisonous to Daimons . . .

Shit. He'd never failed before.

Grinding his teeth, Talon fought the wave of dizziness that consumed him.

The woman he'd saved ran to him. By the confused look on her face, he could tell she wasn't sure how to help him.

Now that he could see her up close, he was taken by her pixielike face. Fire and intelligence burned deep in her large, dark brown eyes. She reminded him of the Morrigán, the raven goddess he had sworn his sword and loyalty to all those centuries before when he had been human.

Her long, straight black hair fell in braids of all sizes around her head. And she had a smear of charcoal across one cheek. Impulsively, he brushed his hand over it and wiped it from her face.

Her skin was so soft, so warm, and it smelled strangely like patchouli and turpentine.

What an odd combination . . .

"Oh my God, are you okay?" the woman asked.

"Yeah," Talon said quietly.

"I'll call an ambulance," she said.

"Nae!" Talon said in his own language, his body protesting the gesture. "No ambulance," he added in English.

The woman frowned. "But you're hurt . . ."

He met her gaze sternly. "No ambulance."

She scowled at him until a light appeared in her intelligent eyes, as if she had had an epiphany. "Are you an illegal alien?" she whispered.

Talon seized on the only excuse he could give her. With his heavy, ancient Celt accent it would be a natural assumption. He nodded.

"Okay," she whispered to him as she patted him gently on the arm. "I'll take care of you without an ambulance."

Talon forced himself to move away from the glaring lamplight that hurt his light-sensitive eyes. His broken leg protested, but he ignored it.

He limped over to lean against a brick building where he could take the pressure off his damaged leg. Again the world tilted.

Damn. He needed to get to safety. It was still early evening, but the last thing he needed was to be trapped in the city after sunup. Whenever a Dark-Hunter was injured, he or she felt an unnatural urge to sleep. It was a need that would make him dangerously vulnerable if he didn't get home soon.

He pulled his cell phone out to notify Nick Gautier he was hurt, and quickly learned that his phone, unlike him, wasn't immortal. It was in pieces.

"Here," the woman said, moving to stand beside him. "Let me help you."

Talon stared at her. No stranger had ever helped him

like this. He was used to fighting his own battles and then cleaning up after them alone.

"I'm all right," he said. "You go do—"

"I'm not going to leave you," she said. "You got hurt because of me."

He wanted to argue, but his body throbbed too badly to bother.

Talon tried to move away from the woman. He took two steps and the world started to shift again.

The next thing he knew, everything went black.

Sunshine barely caught the man before he hit the ground. She staggered from the sheer size and weight of him but somehow kept him from falling over.

As gently as she could, she lowered him to the sidewalk.

Note, she said *as gently as* she could.

As it was, he slammed into the pavement rather forcefully, making her hurt for him all over again as his head practically made a dent in the sidewalk.

"I'm sorry," she said, straightening up to look down at him. "Please tell me that didn't just give you a concussion."

She hoped she hadn't hurt him even worse by trying to help.

Whatever was she going to do now?

The illegal biker-looking alien dressed all in black was huge. She didn't dare leave him on the street unattended. What if their attackers came back? Or some street punk rolled him?

This was New Orleans where most anything could happen to a person while conscious.

Unconscious . . .

Well, there was no telling what the unsavory ones might do to him, so leaving him alone was not an option.

Just as her panic was getting the better of her, she heard someone call her name.

She looked around until she saw Wayne Santana's beat-up blue Dodge Ram pulling up to the curb. At thirty-three, Wayne had a ruggedly handsome face that looked a lot older. His black hair was laced liberally with gray.

She breathed a sigh of relief at seeing him there.

He rolled his window the rest of the way down and leaned out. "Hey, Sunshine, what's going on?"

"Wayne, could you help me get this guy into your truck?"

He looked really skeptical about that. "Is he drunk?"

"No, he's hurt."

"Then you should call an ambulance."

"I can't." She gave him a pleading look. "Please, Wayne? I need to get him back to my place."

"Is he a friend of yours?" he asked even more skeptically.

"Well, no. We just kind of collided out here."

"Then leave him. The last thing you need is to get involved with another biker. It's none of our business what happens to him."

"Wayne!"

"He could be a criminal, Sunshine."

"How could you say such a thing?"

Wayne had been convicted of involuntary manslaughter seventeen years ago. After he'd served his time, he'd spent several months trying to find a job. With no money, no place to live, and no one willing to hire an ex-con to do anything, he was on the brink of committing another crime to return to jail when he'd applied for a job at her father's club.

Against her father's protests, Sunshine had hired him.

Five years later, Wayne had never missed a day of work or been late. He was her father's best employee.

"Please, Wayne?" she asked, giving him the puppy-dog look that never failed to bend the men in her life to her will.

As he left the truck to help her, Wayne made a series of irritated noises. "One day, that big heart of yours is going to get you into trouble. Do you know *anything* about this man?"

"No." All she knew was that he had saved her life when

no one else would have bothered. Surely such a man wouldn't hurt her.

She and Wayne struggled to get the unknown man upright, but it wasn't easy.

"Jeez," Wayne muttered as they staggered with him between them. "He's huge and he weighs a friggin' ton."

Sunshine concurred. The man was at least six feet five inches of lean, solid muscle. Even with the thick leather motorcycle jacket concealing his upper torso, there was no doubt just how well toned and muscular he was.

She'd never felt such a hard, steely body in her life.

After some doing, they finally got him into the truck.

As they headed toward her father's club, Sunshine held the stranger's head on her shoulder and brushed his wavy blond hair back from the chiseled features of his face.

There was a wild, untamed look about him that reminded her of some ancient warrior. His golden hair brushed against his shoulders in a loose style that said he was attentive to his appearance, but not obsessive about it.

Dark brown eyebrows arched over his closed eyes. His face was ruggedly scrumptious with a full day's growth of beard. Even unconscious, he was compelling and drop-dead gorgeous, and his nearness stirred something needful deep inside her.

But what she liked most about this stranger was the warm masculine and leather scent of him. It made her want to nuzzle his neck and inhale the heady mixture until she was drunk with it.

"So," Wayne said as he drove. "What happened to him? Do you know?"

"He got hit by a Mardi Gras float."

Even in the dim light of the truck's cab, she could tell Wayne was giving her the are-you-nuts? stare. "There's no parade tonight. Where did it come from?"

"I don't know. I guess he must have ticked off the gods or something."

"Huh?"

She brushed her hand through the man's tousled blond

hair and toyed with the two thin braids that hung from his left temple as she answered Wayne's question. "It was a big Bacchus float. I was just thinking this poor guy must have offended our patron god of excess to have been run over by him."

Wayne muttered under his breath. "Must be another frat-boy prank. Seems like every year one of them is stealing a float and taking a joy ride in it. I wonder where they'll leave it parked this time?"

"Well, they tried to park it on my friend here. I'm just glad they didn't kill him."

"I'm sure he will be too, when he wakes up."

No doubt. Sunshine leaned her cheek against the stranger's head and listened to his slow, deep breaths.

What was it about him that she found so irresistible?

"Man," Wayne said after a brief silence. "Your father is going to be pissed about this. He'll have my balls for dinner when he finds out I took an unknown guy up to your place."

"Then don't tell him."

Wayne gave her a mean and nasty glare. "I cannot not tell him. If something happened to you, it would be my fault."

She sighed irritably as she traced the sharp line of the stranger's arched brows. Why did he seem so familiar to her? She'd never seen him before and yet she had a strange sense of déjà vu. As if she knew him somehow.

Weird. Very, very weird.

But then she was used to weirdness. Her mother had written the book on the subject, and Sunshine had redefined it.

"I'm a big girl, Wayne, I can take care of myself."

"Yeah and I lived for twelve years with a bunch of big hairy men who made meals off little girls like you who thought they could take care of themselves."

"Fine," she said. "We'll put him in my bed and I'll sleep at my parents'. Then in the morning, I'll check on him with my mother or one of my brothers."

"What if he wakes up before you get home and steals you blind?"

"Steals what?" she asked. "My clothes won't fit him and I have nothing of any value. Not unless he likes my Peter, Paul and Mary collection anyway."

Wayne rolled his eyes. "All right, but you better swear to me you won't give him a chance to hurt you."

"I promise."

Wayne looked less than pleased, but he remained technically quiet as he drove them toward her loft on Canal Street. However, he cursed underneath his breath the entire way.

Luckily Sunshine was used to ignoring men who did that around her.

Once they reached her loft, which was located directly over her father's bar, it took them a good fifteen minutes to get the stranger out of the truck and inside her home.

Sunshine led Wayne through her loft to the area where she'd strung tie-dyed pink cotton fabric along a wire to seal her bedroom area off from the rest of the large room.

Carefully, they placed her unknown guest on her bed.

"Well, let's go," Wayne said, taking her by the arm.

Sunshine gently shrugged his touch away. "We can't leave him like that."

"Why not?"

"He's covered in blood."

Wayne's face showed his exasperation. It was a look everyone had around her sooner or later—okay, it was most often sooner. "Go sit on the couch and let me undress him."

"Sunshine . . ."

"Wayne, I'm twenty-nine years old, a divorced artist who took nude drawing in college, and I was raised with two older brothers. I know what men look like naked. Okay?"

Growling low in his throat, he stepped out of her bedroom and went to sit on her sofa.

Sunshine took a deep breath as she turned back to her hero dressed all in black. He looked humongous on her bed.

He was also a total mess.

Tentatively, so as not to hurt him, she reached to unzip his motorcycle jacket, which was the neatest thing she'd ever seen. Someone had painted gold and red Celtic scrollwork all over it. It was simply beautiful. A true study in ancient artistry, and she should know. All her life, she had been drawn to Celtic things. She'd cut her teeth on their art and culture.

As soon as she unzipped the jacket, she paused in shock as she saw he wore nothing underneath it. Nothing except lush, tawny skin that made her mouth water and her body instantly throb. Never in real life had she beheld a man with a body so hard and so well toned. Every muscle was defined, and even while relaxed, his strength was evident.

The man was a god!

She ached to draw those perfect proportions and immortalize them. A body this fine definitely needed preserving. She pulled the jacket off and carefully laid it on the bed.

Turning on the lamp that rested on her scarf-covered nightstand, she took a good look at him and was floored by what she saw.

Ca-ram-ba!

He was even more gorgeous than the people who had attacked her. His wavy blond hair curled becomingly around the nape of his neck, and two long, thin braids hung down to his bare chest. His eyes were closed, but his dark eyelashes were sinfully long. His face was perfectly sculpted with high, arching brows and he had a very dignified, yet untamed look to him.

Again, she had a strange sense of déjà vu as her mind flashed on an image of him awake and poised above her. Of him smiling down at her while he slid himself slowly in and out of her body . . .

Sunshine licked her lips at the thought as she throbbed in painful need.

It had been a long time since she had been this attracted

to a stranger. But something about this man really made her ache for a taste of him.

Girl, you have been too long without a man.

Unfortunately, she really had.

Sunshine frowned as she moved closer and got a better look at the torc he wore around his neck. Thick and gold, it had Celtic dragon heads facing each other.

What was so odd was that she'd sketched that very same design years ago in art school and had even tried to cast it into a torc for herself, but the piece had ended up a big mess. It took a lot of metalworking talent to make something that intricate.

Even more impressive was the tribal body tattoo that covered the entire left side of his torso, including his left arm. It was a glorious maze of Celtic artwork that reminded her of the Book of Kells. And unless she missed her guess, it was designed as a tribute to the Celtic war goddess, the Morrigán.

Without thought, she ran her hand over his tattoo, tracing the intricate design.

His right arm had a matching three-inch band of scrollwork around the biceps.

Incredible. Whoever had drawn his tattoos certainly knew their Celtic history.

And as her finger brushed against his nipple, she was jarred from her artist's appreciation of the design.

The woman in her snapped to the forefront as her gaze darted over his lean muscular ribs and abs so tight and well formed they should be part of a body-builder show.

Oh yeah, this was one fine-looking man.

Even though there was a lot of blood on his pants, there didn't appear to be any injury to have caused it. Come to think of it, there weren't even many bruises. Not even where the Bacchus truck had slammed into him.

How weird was that?

Her throat dry, Sunshine reached for his fly.

Part of her couldn't wait to see what was underneath those black pants.

Boxers or briefs?

If he was this studly fine so far, it could only get better . . .

Sunshine!

It was just an artist's appreciation for his body, she told herself.

Yeah, right.

Ignoring that thought, she unzipped his pants and discovered that he wore *nothing* underneath them.

Commando!

Her face flamed at the sight of his extremely endowed maleness nestled against dark blond curls.

Oh come on, Sunshine, it's not the first time you've seen a guy naked. Jeez! Six years of art school, you saw naked men galore. And you've had plenty of them to date, not to mention that Jerry the ex-ogre wasn't exactly small.

Yeah, but none of them had looked *this* good.

Biting her lip, she pulled his heavy, black Harley boots off, then slid his pants down his long, muscular legs. She hissed as her hands came in contact with his skin, which was liberally laced with short blond hairs.

Oh yeah, he was definitely hot and fine.

As she folded the pants, she paused and ran her hand over the fabric. They were made of the softest material she'd ever touched. Almost like chamois, only different. It was a strange texture. They couldn't possibly be real leather. They were so thin and—

Her thoughts stopped as she caught sight of him on her bed.

Oh yeah, baby. Now that was every woman's fantasy. A gorgeous naked guy at her mercy.

He lay across the pink comforter with one tanned arm draped over his stomach and his legs slightly apart, as if waiting for her to join him there and run her hands up and down that lean, hard body.

He was a luscious one to stare at.

She sucked her breath between her teeth as she ached to climb up that strong, magnificent body and lay herself over him like a blanket. To feel his large, strong hands on her skin as she took him into her body and made wild monkey love to him for the rest of the night.

Umm-hmmm!

Her lips burned for a taste of that marvelous golden skin. And he was *all* golden skin. There wasn't a tan line on him.

Gimme!

Sunshine shook her head to clear it. Goodness, she was acting like a total goober over him.

And yet . . .

There was something very special about this man. Something that called out to her like a siren's song.

"Sunshine?"

She jumped at Wayne's impatient call. She'd completely forgotten his presence. "Just a minute," she said.

I just want one more peek. A woman needed a good ogle every now and again, and how often did a woman get a chance to ogle an unconscious handsome god?

Resisting the urge to fondle her guest, she covered him with a blanket, picked his jacket up from the bed, then left the room.

As she walked to the sofa, she studied his bloodied pants. Where had the blood come from?

Before she could investigate the pants, Wayne pulled them from her hands and grabbed the wallet out of the back pocket.

"What are you doing?" she asked.

"Checking him out. I want to see who this guy is." Wayne opened the wallet and scowled.

"What?"

"Let's see, seven hundred and thirty-three dollars in cash and not a bit of ID. Not even a license or credit or debit card." Wayne pulled a huge dagger out of the other pocket and flicked a release that spread the dagger out into a circle of three lethal-looking blades. Wayne cursed even louder. "Shit, Sunshine, I think you found yourself a drug dealer."

"He's not a drug dealer."

"Oh yeah, how do you know?"

Because drug dealers don't rescue women from rapists. But she didn't dare tell Wayne that. It would only get her lectured and give him indigestion.

"I just do, now put that back."

"Well?" Camulus asked Dionysus as Dionysus entered the hotel room.

Styxx looked up from his magazine at the sound of his voice. The Celtic god, Camulus, had been sitting on the couch across from him in the hotel suite while they had waited for news.

Dressed in black leather jeans and a gray sweater, the ancient deity had been flipping channels incessantly since Dionysus left, making Styxx want to snatch the remote from his hand and slam it down on the iron-and-glass coffee table.

But only a fool took a remote from a god.

Styxx might have a death wish, but he had no desire to be ruthlessly tortured before he died.

So Styxx had gnashed his teeth and done his best to ignore Camulus and wait for Dionysus's return.

Camulus wore his long black hair pulled back in a ponytail. There was something devilish and evil about him, but then, given the fact he was a god of war, that was understandable.

Dionysus paused just inside the door. He shrugged out of his long cashmere coat, then pulled his brown leather gloves from his hands.

At six ten, the god of wine and excess would be an intimidating sight to most people. But then, Styxx was only two inches shorter, and being the son of a king and a man who longed for death, he found very little intimidating.

What was Dionysus going to do? Send him back to his hellish isolation?

He'd been there, done that, and had the Ozzy T-shirt to prove it.

Dionysus was dressed in a tweed jacket, navy turtleneck, and pleated brown slacks. His short dark brown hair was perfectly streaked with blond highlights and he had an immaculate goatee. He looked like a successful billionaire magnate, and did, in fact, run a major international corporation where the god got his jollies by crippling his competitors and taking over other businesses.

Forced against his will into retirement centuries ago, Dionysus spent his time between Olympus and the mortal world, which he hated almost as much as Styxx did.

"Answer my question, Bacchus," Camulus said. "I'm not one of your dickless Greeks to be kept waiting for an answer."

Rage flared in Dionysus's eyes. "You better take a more civil tone with me, Cam. I'm not one of your flaccid Celts to shake in terror of your wrath. You want to fight, boy, bring it on."

Camulus shot to his feet.

"Whoa, hang on a second," Styxx said, trying to calm them down. "Let's save the fighting for when you two take over the world, okay?"

They both looked at him as if he were insane to come between them.

No doubt, he was. But if they killed each other, he'd never die.

Cam glared at Dionysus. "Your pet is right," he said. "But when I have my godhood back, you and I are going to talk."

The gleam in Dionysus's eyes said he was looking forward to it.

Styxx took a deep breath. "So, is the woman with Talon?" he asked Dionysus.

Dionysus smiled coldly. "Just like clockwork." He looked at Camulus. "Are you sure this will immobilize him?"

"I never said it would immobilize him. I said it would neutralize him."

"What's the difference?" Styxx asked.

"The difference is he's about to become an even bigger distraction and concern for Acheron. Yet another way to weaken the Atlantean in the end."

Styxx liked the sound of that.

Now they would just have to ensure that the Dark-Hunter and the woman remained together. At least until Mardi Gras, when the threshold between this world and Kolasis would be thin enough to breach so that they could release the Atlantean Destroyer from captivity.

It had been six hundred years since the last time this had occurred and it would be over eight hundred years more before it occurred again.

Styxx cringed at the thought of living another eight hundred years. Another eight centuries of lonely, never-ending monotony and pain. Of watching his keepers come and go, grow old and die, as they lived out their mortal lives surrounded by family and friends.

They didn't know how lucky they were.

As a human, he had once feared death. But that was ancient aeons ago.

Now the only thing Styxx feared was that he would never escape the horror of his existence. That he would keep on living, century after century, until the universe itself exploded.

He wanted out, and up until thirty years ago he hadn't had a hope of it.

Now he did.

Dionysus and Camulus wanted to reclaim their godhoods and they needed the Destroyer and Acheron's blood to do it. It was a pity Styxx didn't have Atlantean blood in him or he would gladly offer himself up as sacrifice.

As it was, Acheron alone held the key to the Destroyer's release.

Styxx was the only creature alive who could deliver Acheron to them.

Just a few days more and everything would be set right. The old powers would return to dominate the earth and he . . .

He would finally be free.

Styxx sighed in sweet expectation. All he had to do was keep the Dark-Hunters at each other's throats and keep them distracted while he prevented the gods from killing each other.

If either Talon or Acheron ever realized what was happening, they would stop it. They alone had the power to do so.

It was him against them and this time, this time, he would finish what he had started eleven thousand years ago.

When he was through here, the Dark-Hunters would be without leadership.

He would be free and the carth as all knew it would be a whole new place entirely.

Styxx smiled.

Just a few days more . . .

Chapter 3

Talon woke up to find his arm on fire.

Hissing, he jerked his hand away from the sunlight that was streaming in through the window, across an extremely pink bed. He pushed himself back against the white wicker headboard to avoid any more of his body from coming into contact with the deadly rays.

He blew cool air across his hand, but still it burned and ached.

Where the hell was he?

For the first time in centuries, he felt a wave of uncertainty run through him.

Talon was never out of his element. Never out of control. His entire life was one of extreme balance and moderation.

Never in his Dark-Hunter existence had he found himself unsure or confounded.

But right now, he had no idea where he was, the time of day, or who the women were he heard on the other side of the pink drapes.

Squinting against the bright sunlight that painfully pierced his eyes, he looked around the odd room and realized he was trapped between two open windows. His heart hammered. There was no safe way off the bed. The only direction he could go was to his left and into the corner that was occupied by a frothy pink nightstand.

Damn.

Through the pounding pain in his head, the night before came flooding back to him with stunning clarity. The attack.

The woman . . .

The great big whatever slamming into him.

Though his body ached and was sore, his Dark-Hunter powers had allowed him to heal while he slept. In a few hours, even the soreness would be gone.

Until then, he needed out of this death trap of sunlight. Closing his eyes, Talon willed a dark cloud to cover the sun so that the bright daylight would no longer play havoc with his eyesight.

If he wanted to, he could summon enough clouds to turn the day sky as dark as night. But it wouldn't do him any good.

Daylight was still daylight.

His unique Dark-Hunter powers gave him a great deal of control over the elements, weather and healing, but not control over Apollo's domain. Light or dark, the daytime still belonged to Apollo, and even though Apollo was technically retired, the Greek god would never tolerate a Dark-Hunter walking about on his shift.

If Apollo caught sight of him outside or near a window during the light of day, Talon would be nothing more than a strip of fried bacon on the sidewalk.

Extra-crispy Celt didn't appeal to him in the least.

His eyes no longer burning, Talon started to leave the bed, then paused. There was nothing between him and the patchouli- and turpentine-scented sheets.

What's happened to my clothes? He was quite sure he hadn't undressed himself last night.

Had they . . . ?

He frowned as he searched his memory. No, it wasn't possible. If he'd been awake enough to have sex with her, he would have been awake enough to leave this place long before sunup.

"Where is it?"

He looked up at hearing the unfamiliar voice on the other side of the pink tie-dyed fabric, which was hung to form a wall around the bed.

Two seconds later, the fabric slid open to reveal an attractive woman who appeared to be in her late thirties. Her long black hair was pulled into a thick braid and she wore a long flowing black skirt and tunic.

She looked remarkably similar to the woman he'd met last night. And at first glance, she would be easy to mistake for her younger counterpart.

"Hey, Sunshine, your friend's awake. What's his name?"

"I don't know, Starla. I didn't ask."

Oh, but this is getting stranger and stranger.

Unperturbed by his presence, the woman walked into the room to the side of the bed where the nightstand stood. "You look like a Steve," she said as she bent down, lifted up the pink scarves, and started digging through a stack of magazines that was hidden beneath it. "Are you hungry, Steve?"

Before he could answer, she raised her voice. "It's not here."

"It's under the old copies of *Art Papers.*"

"It's not here."

Sunshine entered the room. Walking with the grace of a fairy princess, she wore a long-sleeved purple dress so bright, he had to squint from the hue. As she crossed in front of the window, he realized the material was rather sheer, gifting him with a pleasant view of her lush, ample curves and the fact that she wore nothing beneath that dress.

Nothing except her tanned skin.

His throat went dry.

She was wiping paint from her hands with a towel as she moved to the nightstand without even glancing his way.

"It's right here," she said, pulling out a magazine and handing it to the older woman.

Finally, Sunshine looked to the bed and met his gaze. "Are you hungry?"

"Where are my clothes?"

She cast a sheepish look at Starla. "Did you ask his name?"

"It's Steve."

"It's not Steve."

Sunshine paid him no attention as she turned Starla to face him. Both women stared at him lying there on the bed as if he were some inanimate curiosity.

Talon moved the pink sheet up higher over his waist. Then, suddenly self-conscious, he moved his bare leg under the cover as well, and bent his knee so that the center part of his body wasn't quite so obvious underneath the thin cotton.

Still the two women stared at him.

"You see what I was telling you?" Sunshine asked. "Does he not have the most incredible aura you've ever seen?"

"He's definitely an old soul. With Druid blood. I'm sure of it."

"You think?" Sunshine asked.

"Oh, yeah. We need to talk him into letting us do a past-life regression and see what we come up with."

Okay, they were both nuts.

"Women," he said sharply. "I need my clothes, and I need them *now*."

"See," Sunshine said. "See the way his aura changes. It's absolutely living."

"You know, I've never seen that before. It's really different." Then Starla drifted out of the room as she flipped through the magazine.

Sunshine was still wiping paint off her hands. "Hungry?"

How did she do that? How could she shift from one topic to the other and then back again?

"No," he said, trying to keep her on the main point. "I want my clothes."

She actually cringed. "What happened to the tags in your pants?"

Talon frowned at the odd question. He was keeping a

rein on his irritation and temper, but something about being around this woman made it difficult. "I beg your pardon?"

"Well, you know they were covered in blood . . ."

A bad feeling settled into his stomach. "And?"

"I was going to clean them, and—"

"Oh shit, you washed them?"

"It wasn't the washing that damaged them so much as the drying."

"You dried my *leather* pants?"

"Well, I didn't know they were leather," she said softly. "They felt really soft and strange so I thought they were pleather or something. I wash my pleather dress all the time without it disintegrating and shrinking like your pants did."

Talon rubbed his forehead with his hand. This was so not good. How on earth could he get out of her apartment in the middle of the day with no clothes on?

"You know," she continued, "you really shouldn't cut the tags out of your clothes."

It had been a long time since he had felt real, deep aggravation, but he was starting to feel it now. "Those were *custom,* handmade leather pants. They never have tags."

"Oh," she said, looking even more sheepish. "I would have bought you some more, but since they didn't have tags in them, I didn't know what size to buy."

"Great. I live to be stuck in strange places, naked."

She started to smile at him, then pressed her lips together as if thinking better of it. "I have some pink sweatpants that really wouldn't fit you, and even if they did, I'm sure you wouldn't want to wear them anyway, would you?"

"No. Did you wash my wallet too?"

"Oh, no. I took it out of your pants."

"Good. Where is it?"

She became quiet again and a feeling of doomed dread consumed him.

"Do I want to know?" he asked.

"Well . . ." He was beginning to hate that word since it seemed to portend doom for him and his belongings. "I put it on the washing machine at the Laundromat with your keys, and then I realized that I didn't have change for the washer, so I went to the change machine. I was only gone a second, but when I got back your wallet was gone."

Talon grimaced. "And my keys?"

"Well, you know when you wash just one thing it unbalances the machine? Your keys ended up getting jarred off the top of it and they went down a small drain."

"Didn't you get them back?"

"I tried, but I couldn't reach them. I had three other people try, but they're gone too."

Talon sat in stunned disbelief. Worse, he couldn't even get mad at her since she'd only been trying to help him. But he really, really wanted to be mad.

"I have no money, no pants, no keys. Do I still have my jacket?"

"Yes, it's safe. And I saved your Snoopy Pez dispenser from the washer too. And your boots and knife thing are right here," she said, holding them up from the floor by the bed.

Talon nodded, feeling strangely relieved by the knowledge that she hadn't destroyed everything he'd had on him last night. Thank the gods his motorcycle had been left by the Brewery. He shuddered to think what she might have done to it. "Is there a phone I can use?"

"In the kitchen."

"Could you please bring it to me?"

"It's not cordless. I always lose those things or I drop them someplace and break them. The last one I had ended up drowning in the toilet."

Talon looked uneasily at the woman and the faint sunlight in the room. He wondered which one of them was the most lethal to him.

"Would you mind pulling down the shades?" he asked.

She frowned. "Does the sunlight bother you?"

"I'm allergic to it," he said, falling into the lie Dark-Hunters used when caught in similar situations.

Although he doubted if *any* Dark-Hunter had ever found himself in a situation similar to this one.

"Really? I've never known anyone allergic to sunlight before."

"Well, I am."

"So you're like a vampire?"

The word hit just a little too close to home. "Not exactly."

She moved to the window, but when she pulled the shade down, it fell.

Gray sunlight spilled across the bed.

With a curse, Talon shot into the corner, narrowly missing the pale sunbeams.

"Sunshine, I . . ." Starla's voice broke off as she entered the room and caught sight of him standing naked in the corner. She eyed him in an odd, detached way, as if he were an interesting piece of furniture.

Talon and modesty were strangers, but the way she stared at him made him damned uncomfortable.

In spite of the sunlight, Talon grabbed the pink blanket off the bed and clutched it to his middle.

"You know, Sunshine, you need to find a man like that to marry. Someone so well hung that even after three or four kids, he'd still be wall to wall."

Talon gaped.

Sunshine laughed. "Starla, you're embarrassing him."

"Oh, believe me, that's nothing to be embarrassed over. You ought to be proud. Strut it. Trust me, young man, women your age would love to have some of that."

Talon snapped his gaping jaw shut. These were the strangest women he'd ever had the misfortune of being near.

Gods, get him out of here.

Starla looked up at Sunshine in the window. "What are you doing?"

"He's allergic to the sun."

"It's so cloudy outside, it's almost dark."

"I know, but he says he can't be in it."

"Really? So you brought home a vampire? Cool."

"I'm not a vampire," he reiterated.

" 'Not exactly,' he said earlier," Sunshine said. "What's not exactly a vampire?"

"A werewolf," Starla said. "With his aura, it makes sense. Wow, Sunny, you found yourself a werewolf."

"I'm not a werewolf."

Starla looked really disappointed by the news. "What a pity. You know, when you live in New Orleans, you expect to meet the undead or damned at least once in a while." She looked back to Sunshine. "You think we should move? Maybe if we lived over by Anne Rice we might catch sight of a vampire or werewolf."

Sunshine replaced the shade. "I'd be happy to see a zombie."

"Oh, yeah," the older woman concurred. "You know, your dad said he saw one out on the bayou right before we got married."

"That was probably the peyote, Mom."

"Oh. Good point."

Talon's jaw went slack again as he looked back and forth between them. Mother and daughter? They certainly didn't act that way, and Starla didn't look that much older than Sunshine, but there was no denying the similarities of their features. Or the oddity of them both.

Oh yeah, insanity ran deep in the roots of that family tree.

Sunshine lowered the shade for the other window.

Wrapping the blanket around him, Talon carefully stepped through the room and was relieved to find a rather bare, open loft on the other side of the drapes.

There was another row of windows on his left where Sunshine had sectioned off a small drawing studio. But the rest of the loft was blissfully dark and devoid of sunlight. Keeping the blanket wrapped around his hips, he made his way toward the phone in the kitchen.

"Well, Sunshine, now that he's awake and I agree he's not threatening—"

Talon arched a brow at that comment. There had never been a time in his life he hadn't been threatening! He was a Dark-Hunter. That term alone inspired terror in the things that gave evil a bad name.

"—I'm going to go down to the club and pay some bills, make some orders, and do real work."

"Okay, Starla, I'll see you later."

He had to get out of this place. These women not only lacked sense, but they were too weird for words.

Starla kissed Sunshine's cheek and left.

After several minutes of looking, Talon found the phone cord in the wall and trailed it to the old-fashioned dial phone, which was hiding in a kitchen drawer that also contained a wide assortment of dry paintbrushes and tubes of acrylics.

He pulled the phone, painted with wild fluorescent colors, out of the drawer and placed it on the counter next to a pink pig-shaped cookie jar that held small cinnamon-scented rice cakes.

Picking up the receiver, he dialed Nick Gautier, who had once been the Squire, or human helper, for Kyrian of Thrace. Since Kyrian had married Amanda Devereaux a few months ago and had left behind his official Dark-Hunter status, Nick had become Talon's unofficial, part-time Squire. Not that Talon wanted a Squire. Humans had a nasty way of dying around him, and Nick had a mouth on him that was guaranteed to get the boy killed one day.

Still, there were times when a Squire came in handy. Now was definitely one of them.

The phone rang until the message came on that the cellular customer was unavailable.

Damn. That meant making the one call he'd rather be killed again than make. If the other Dark-Hunters ever found out about this, he'd never hear the end of it. Squires were sworn to an oath of secrecy. They were forbidden to ever reveal anything that was embarrassing about a Dark-Hunter or anything that could endanger them.

Unfortunately, other non-Squired human helpers didn't make such an oath.

Oh yeah, Nick Gautier was a dead man when he got his hands on him.

Preparing himself mentally for what was to come, he called Kyrian of Thrace who answered on the first ring.

"Talon?" Kyrian said as soon as he recognized his voice. "It's noon, what's wrong?"

Talon slid a glance to Sunshine, who was singing "Puff the Magic Dragon" as she passed him to enter the kitchen. "I . . . uh . . . I need a favor."

"Anything."

"I need you to go to my place and get my spare keys, another cell phone and some money."

"Yeah, okay. Did you have to ditch your bike?"

"Yeah, she's in the Brewery parking lot so I need you to bring her to me for tonight."

"Okay, where do I bring her?"

"Hang on." Talon pulled the phone away from his ear. "Sunshine?"

She turned to look at him.

"Where the hell am I?" Even with the phone on his shoulder, he heard Kyrian's mocking laughter.

"You know the nightclub Runningwolf's that's on Canal Street?"

He nodded.

"We're directly over it."

"Thanks." He relayed the information to Kyrian.

"Talon, I swear, your hormones are going to get you killed someday."

He didn't bother to correct Kyrian. They'd known each other for over a thousand years and Talon had never before been caught out like this. Kyrian wouldn't believe the truth of how he came to be in this loft. Hell, he barely believed it himself. "I also need you to bring me some clothes."

The silence in his ear was deafening.

Oh yeah, Nick was such a dead man when Talon got his hands on him.

"What?" Kyrian asked hesitantly.

"I lost my clothes."

Kyrian laughed. Hard.

"Shut up, Kyrian, it's not funny."

"Hey, from where I'm standing it's funny as hell."

Yeah, well, from where Talon was standing, with a pink blanket wrapped around his hips, it wasn't.

"Okay," Kyrian said, sobering. "We'll be over there as soon as we can."

"We?"

"Me and Julian."

Talon cringed again. An ex-Dark-Hunter and an Oracle. Great. Just great. They would never let him live this down and by nightfall one of them would be guaranteed to post this on the Dark-Hunter.com Web site for everyone to laugh about.

"All right," Talon said, tamping down his ire. "See you in a little while."

"You know," Sunshine said as soon as he hung up. "I could just go buy you some clothes. I do owe you."

Talon glanced around the loft. It looked as if a bottle of Pepto-Bismol had exploded, or the Cat in the Hat had come for a visit. There was pink everywhere. But what struck him most was the dilapidated condition of her furniture and her piecemeal decorations. Definitely a starving artist, the last thing this woman could afford was a pair of two-thousand-dollar pants, and the earth would stand still and shatter before Talon ever put denim on his body.

"It's all right," he told her. "My friends will take care of it."

She brought him a plate of muffins and what appeared to be grass. "What's this?"

"Breakfast . . . or lunch." When he didn't take it, she added, "You need to eat. It's good for you. It's a cranberry bran muffin with flaxseed and alfalfa sprouts."

There was nothing on that plate that came close to resembling food. Especially to a man who was born and bred to be a Celtic chieftain.

Okay, Talon, you can cope with this. "Do you have any coffee?"

"Ew! No, that stuff will kill you. I have herbal teas, though."

"Herbal teas? That's mulch, not a beverage."

"Oooo, Mr. Picky woke up on the wrong side of the bed."

No human had ever been so flippant with him. Even Nick knew better. Feeling totally out of his element, Talon gave up.

"Fine. Where's your bathroom?"

Then right behind that came the thought, *Please tell me you have one inside this loft and not out back in a parking lot.*

She pointed to a dark corner of the loft. "Right there."

It was another area sectioned off by a hanging curtain. How wonderful was this?

And he'd mistakenly thought the Middle Ages were over.

Oh, what fond memories . . . not.

Talon walked over to it and had just pulled the curtain closed and dropped the blanket to the floor when Sunshine joined him. She held a pink towel and washcloth in her hands and stopped dead in her tracks when she caught sight of him standing there naked.

She put the towel on the sink and moved around him, looking him up and down. "You are just simply male perfection, you know that?"

He would have felt flattered had she not looked like someone sizing up a car. It wasn't desire for him that made her say that. Her tone was detached, the way her mother's had been.

She ran her warm, smooth hand down his back, over his tattoo. "Whoever gave you this tattoo was a very talented artist."

Chills spread over him as her hand glided down his spine to his hip. "My uncle did it," he said before he could stop himself. He hadn't spoken of his uncle with anyone in centuries.

"Really? Wow." She slid her hand up across his shoul-

ders to the Dark-Hunter bow-and-arrow brand on his right
shoulder blade. "Where did this come from?"

Talon shrugged her touch away. That was one mark he
would never talk about to an uninitiated human. "It's nothing."

It was then her gaze fell to his erection. Her face turned
as pink as the towel. "Sorry," she said quickly. "I tend to
not think before I act."

"I noticed." But what made it so bad was that she continued to stare at his erection. She had yet to look anywhere
else.

"You really are a *big* man."

For the first time in over a thousand years, he felt his
cheeks warm. Grabbing the towel, Talon covered himself.

Only then did she look away. "Here, let me get you a
razor." She dropped to her knees, giving him a nice view
of her bottom as she rummaged around in a makeshift pink
wicker cabinet next to the pedestal sink. Her hips moved
provocatively as she searched, only adding to his desire.

He clenched his teeth. That woman had the sexiest bottom he'd ever seen. One that made his groin burn even
more as he thought about lifting that gauzy skirt and burying himself deep inside her. Of sliding himself in and out
of her moist heat until they were both sweaty and spent.

Oh yeah, she was definitely a woman who could satisfy
a man. He'd always been partial to women with lush curves
and . . .

She emerged with a pink razor and toothbrush.

Talon curled his lip at the thought of using such girly
items. "Do you own anything not pink?"

"I have a purple razor if you'd rather."

"Please."

She pulled out a darker pink one.

"That's not purple," Talon said. "It's pink too."

She rolled her eyes at him. "Well, that's all I have unless
you want my X-Acto blade."

Extremely tempted, he took the razor from her.

Sunshine didn't move until he got into the claw-footed

tub and pulled the shower curtain closed. Only then did she allow herself to bite her knuckles at the luscious view of his naked backside. She was definitely going to have to sketch him.

That man was *hot*. Burning. And every time he spoke with that wildly exotic accent of his, she melted. It sounded like some unique combination of English and Scottish.

Fanning her face, she forced herself to leave the bathroom and head back to her kitchen. But what she really wanted to do was peel her clothes off, climb into the shower behind him, and lather that lush, tall, lean body of his until he begged her for mercy.

The feel of all that supple, hard skin under her hands . . . Heaven. Pure heaven.

And he hadn't even gotten mad about his pants! She still couldn't believe how well he took it all. Normally, guys would be shouting at her by now and she'd be giving them the heave-ho out the door.

But he had merely shrugged it off. Oooo, she liked that.

Now that she thought about it, he really didn't have a whole range of emotions that he showed. He was patience incarnate, which was a very nice change of pace.

"Hey, Steve?" she called.

"My name isn't Steve," he said from the shower. "It's Talon."

"Talon what?"

"Just Talon."

She smiled. Talon. It suited him.

"What did you want?" he called.

"What?" she asked.

"You called me like you had a question. What do you need?"

Sunshine bit her lip as she tried to remember. Oops. "I forgot."

She actually heard him laugh. Wow. That was a first. By now most guys would be flaming mad at her.

Sunshine spent the next five minutes trying to find her sketchbook, which she had somehow placed in the refrigerator. Again. She took a seat at her breakfast counter and started sketching her newest find.

Talon.

She took her time drawing the well-sculpted planes of his face, the intricate tattoo on his body. She'd never seen any man with proportions more perfect. And before she knew it, she was lost in those lines. Lost in her mind as she let her creativity flow and reproduce the things she found so incredibly fascinating about the man in her shower.

Before she realized how much time had passed, he turned the shower off and came out from behind the curtain with a damp towel draped around his lean hips.

Oh, mama.

Sunshine once again felt the urge to bite her hand in appreciation. With the exception of the two thin braids that swung with his movements, his golden-blond hair was slicked back and his jet-black eyes flashed with intelligence and arcane power. She'd never seen eyes so dark, especially on a blond man.

He had such a powerful presence that it made her breathless just to look at him. It was as if the very air around him were rife with energy and strength, and she wished most of all that she could capture that with her art.

But no one would ever be able to duplicate or create an aura so intense. It was something that could only be experienced in the flesh.

With every step he took closer to her, her heart pounded harder. The man was so overwhelmingly masculine. So very choice.

His intensity, his raw animal magnetism . . . set fire to her blood.

He'd been handsome last night in her bed, but upright and conscious, he was totally devastating.

"You know, Talon," she said, tracing the lines of his perfect muscles with her gaze. "Towels look really good on you. You go outside like that and you'll start a whole new fashion craze."

An amused smile hovered at the edges of his lips. "Do you always say everything that comes to your mind?"

"Mostly. I do have some thoughts I keep to myself. I used to not care and would say anything at all, but then one time my college roommate called the psycho unit on me. You know, they really do have white coats."

Talon arched a brow at the sincerity he sensed from her. That was a true story. The woman was eccentric, no doubt, but far from a crackpot.

Well, maybe not *that* far.

She reached over to his untouched "breakfast" and picked up the so-called muffin that had shiny little particles in it he couldn't even begin to identify. "You still haven't eaten your muffin."

Yeah, right. He still hadn't eaten his boots either, and he'd rather feast on one of them than that thing in her hand.

"I'm not hungry."

At least not for food.

She dropped the muffin to the counter and he swore it thunked. Her brow furrowing, she reached out and touched his torc. Her fingers brushed against the skin of his neck, raising chills and other things on his body.

"This is so beautiful. I've always wanted a torc, but never could find one that seemed like me." She ran her thumb over the right dragon head. "Are you from Scotland?"

"Not exactly," he said, watching the way she studied the piece, which had been a gift from his aunt on his wedding day. Both he and Nynia had received matching torcs from her. He didn't know why he still wore it, other than the fact that taking it off would cause him more pain than he was willing to deal with. In some odd way, removing the torc would be like losing Nynia all over again.

Against his will, his mind drifted back to the moment when Nynia had placed the torc around his neck. Her smile had been blinding and her face filled with love as she kissed him on his lips.

Gods, how he missed her. Even after all these centuries.

There were times when he swore he could still smell the warmth of her hair. Feel her touch. It was like the ghost itch of a missing limb that, even years later, you swore you could still feel.

There was something about Sunshine that reminded him of his wife. And it wasn't just the fact that both women possessed the ability to drive him crazy.

Sunshine was strangely fascinating. Much like him, she saw things on another level, things that were hidden from this plane of existence.

Her mind flashed from one thing to another like bursts of lightning, which was as intriguing as it was confusing. Nynia was the only other person he'd ever met with that trait.

As a mortal man, he had often been confounded by Nynia's unique logic.

"You know," Sunshine said, "you say 'not exactly' a lot. You're not exactly a vampire. You're not exactly from Scotland, and you're allergic to daylight. What else?"

"I hate bran muffins and grass."

She laughed at that, a rich, throaty sound that warmed him. He watched in fascination as she used a stained rag to clean the charcoal from her long, elegant fingers. "So how long until your friends get here?"

"A couple of hours, no doubt. I live way outside of town."

Sunshine looked down at the towel around his hips. If she kept him here like that, there was no telling what might happen.

Actually there was, which meant she really needed to get some clothes on him . . . fast.

He took a deep breath, the gesture accentuating the muscled indentations of his hard, defined abs.

Oh yeah, she needed to cover up that temptation.

"I tell you what, Mr. Talon No-Last-Name. Why don't I go out and get you something to put on until your friends get here?"

Because I don't want you to leave. Talon blinked at the bizarre, uncharacteristic thought.

Where had that come from?

There was something compelling about this woman. Something strong and at the same time vulnerable. He felt in her a need to make amends for what she'd done to him. Why, he couldn't imagine. Especially since she had saved his life.

Had she left him out on the street, he would be dead now. A fried stain on the sidewalk.

"You don't have to, you know."

"I know. But I insist. It's the least I could do since I destroyed your pants."

As he looked at her kind, compelling face, which was framed by straight, jet-black hair, he became fascinated by the way her lips curved. The way they held a hint of a smile even while she was relaxed. Sunshine was more than just her name, it was also her attitude. Happy, warm.

She was totally irresistible and he wanted a taste of her so badly that he wasn't sure why he hadn't already sampled her.

He needed to taste her. To *feel* her.

Sunshine watched while Talon studied her lips. There was enough heat in his obsidian gaze to set fire to a glacier. He had yet to touch her and still she swore she could feel him surrounding her with heat, with need.

The air around her seemed sexually charged. It practically sizzled with eroticism and longing. She'd never felt anything like this in her life.

Talon oozed an inhuman sexual attraction. She was drawn to him in a way she'd never been drawn to any man.

His eyes narrowing, he dipped his head and took possession of her lips with a masterful kiss that made her head literally spin. Her body melted.

She moaned at the taste of his lips against hers as his tongue swept passionately into her mouth. He pulled her up from her bar stool, into his strong arms, and ran his hands over her back, clenching the fabric of her dress in his fists.

The raw, manly scent of him invaded her as she felt his muscles flex around her. His virile potency was almost more than she could take.

This was an earthy man who knew his way around a woman's body. She could feel it in his masterful kiss, in the way he knew just where and how to caress her.

Her body burning with desire, she clutched at his bare shoulders as she felt him harden even more against her stomach.

She'd never experienced anything like this. It was as if he were starving for her.

Only her.

When he finally pulled back, she realized she had surrendered her weight to him and he had supported all of her without even tightening his muscles. Jeez, the man was strong.

He brushed his thumb over her swollen lips, his eyes so warm and tender that it made her even more breathless than his kiss. "I'm a thirty-three waist and a thirty-eight inseam."

"Um-hmm," she breathed without hearing him. She swayed toward him for another kiss.

Talon felt a strange stirring inside him at the dazed and adoring look on her face.

"Kiss me again," she whispered an instant before she claimed his lips with hers.

He cupped her head in his hands as he explored her mouth, being careful not to let her accidentally brush her tongue against his fangs and learn the truth about him.

But it was hard to pull back when the taste of her drove him so close to madness. Her patchouli-and-turpentine scent intoxicated him and he ached to pull the hem of her dress up and slide his hand over her lush thighs to her . . .

Her tongue came dangerously close to his fangs.

Pulling back, he released her.

That had been just a bit too close for comfort, but not nearly as close as he wanted to get to her. He dropped his gaze to her body, outlined by her dress. She was a full-bodied woman, not tiny or petite. And she had large, lush breasts—something he'd always been partial to.

Clenching his teeth, he fought the vicious need to take her into his arms and sample those breasts with his mouth. His hands.

His tongue.

Better still, his fangs . . .

"Okay," she said in an odd, high-pitched voice. "That was nice." She clapped her hands together and took a step back. It wasn't until her gaze fell to the towel that the light came back into her dark brown eyes. "Clothes. You need clothes before I do something I might *not* regret. What was your size again, Steve?"

"Talon."

"Talon. Size. Clothes. Cover him up."

Talon smiled as he watched her trying to keep her mind focused while her eyes continued to drift over him with desire.

He liked this woman. In spite of her peculiarities, there was something very refreshing and pure about her.

"I'm going to go get *Talon* clothes." She left, then came back a few seconds later. "Keys," she said, heading to a pink canister on the kitchen counter. "Need keys for car." She left only to return again. "Purse. Money for clothes."

Talon raked his hand through his wet hair as she left one more time and wondered if she'd forgotten anything else.

She had.

"Shoes," she said the next time. "Must have shoes to shop and keep feet warm." She slid her feet into a pair of mules by the door.

"What about a coat?" Talon asked as he noticed she was heading out again. "It is wintertime."

"Coats are good in the winter," she said, going to a rack by the door he assumed was her closet. She pulled on an old brown overcoat that seemed completely not her style. "Be back shortly."

"Wait."

She paused to look at him.

Talon quirked his lips as he crossed the room and undid her misbuttoned coat. Straightening it, he buttoned it correctly.

"Thank you," she said, smiling a smile that did the oddest things to his groin and stomach.

All Talon could do was nod, especially since what he really wanted to do was pick her up in his arms and carry her to the bed and make love to her for the rest of the afternoon.

"I'll be back," she said, heading out.

After she was gone, he finally allowed himself to smile broadly. She was definitely something else.

Something that reminded him of a warm spring day after a harsh winter. It had been a long time since anyone had touched him the way she did. A long time since someone had stayed in his thoughts.

"You like her."

He turned his head to look over his shoulder at the spirit that flickered there. "She's interesting," he said to Ceara.

Ceara moved forward to stand by his side. Her pale cheeks held an ethereal blush as she shimmered between this plane of existence and the next.

She should have crossed completely over to her eternal rest or rebirth centuries before, but she had refused to leave him alone.

And though it was terribly selfish, Talon had been grateful for her company. Especially back in the days when he'd been unable to stay in touch with his Dark-Hunter brethren via modern technology.

Back then, his isolation had been hellish. He'd spent days alone, never daring to let any human near him for fear of his curse. Never daring to reach out to anyone for anything.

The only relief he'd known was his sister's infrequent visits.

But every time he looked at Ceara, he was painfully reminded of how badly he had failed her. He should have been able to help her the day she died. Had he not been a fool, she would have lived out the life she deserved. A life filled with a husband and children.

Instead, she'd been sacrificed because he had been a stupid, arrogant ass.

The first time she'd come to him after their deaths had shattered him. There had been no accusations from her, no hatred, even though he deserved it.

She had shown him only compassion and love.

"I promised you I would never leave you alone, my bràthair. *And I won't. I will always be here for you."*

Over the centuries, her presence had been the only thing that kept him grounded and allowed him to function. Her friendship and love had always meant everything in the world to him.

Ceara brushed a sisterly hand over the bruise on his right thigh. He couldn't feel it like a real touch, but the gesture caused his skin to tingle. "It no longer bothers you?"

"No. I'm fine."

"Speirr," she said, speaking his name in their native Celt. "You know to be honest with me, *bràthair.*"

He reached to brush a tendril of blond hair from her cheek, only to remember he couldn't touch her.

He closed his eyes as he remembered the past.

Their clan had slain her just days before her sixteenth birthday.

"She will be our sacrifice to the gods and they shall forgive us for the transgressions of our leader . . ."

Talon clenched his teeth against the grief and guilt that swelled inside him. Her death had been his fault. He had killed her as surely as if he'd been the one holding the knife.

But he pushed those thoughts away and found the numbness he needed to function.

I'm no longer human and there is no past. Acheron's litany ran through his mind, allowing him to suppress everything.

There was only now and the future. His human life far

behind him, he was a Dark-Hunter whose entire existence was to seek out and destroy the evil that preyed on the humans who had no knowledge of what lay in the darkness waiting for them.

"My leg"—unlike his heart—"only hurts a little."

She shook her head at him. "This is not a safe place for you, Speirr. There is too much light. I don't like for you to be here."

"I know. I'm leaving as soon as I can."

"Very well, then I shall leave until you need me."

She faded away and left him alone. Again.

Talon's gaze fell to the counter where Sunshine had been sitting when he joined her. He frowned as he caught sight of the sketch she'd been working on.

Picking it up, he was impressed by how well she had captured his likeness.

The woman was a brilliant artist. She was able to put emotions and meaning into even the simplest of lines. He'd never seen anything like it.

Unfortunately, he couldn't leave it here.

He tore the page out and used his powers to burn it. Dark-Hunters were forbidden to allow their likenesses to be captured in any medium or form. No one needed proof of their immortality. Such evidence would only lead to questions and complications none of them wanted.

He just hoped she didn't reproduce it after he left.

Talon glanced around the loft and noted that the entire area was littered with framed and unframed art. The floor, a long drawing table, and three easels were scattered with half-finished projects.

Crossing the room, he went to examine them closer. He lost track of time as he looked them over, then found more paintings leaning against the wall by the bedroom. Sunshine liked vivid colors in her work, and her brushstrokes on canvas were as light and gentle as the lady herself.

But it was her pottery that fascinated him most. The pieces were a fiery mixture of color, and the designs of them were far from modern. She must have studied Greek and Celtic cultures extensively to reproduce such authentic copies. It was remarkable how true to the past they were. If he didn't know better, he would swear a Were-Hunter had brought them forward in time.

A knock sounded on the door.

Talon set the bowl he was looking at back with the others on the shelf by the door. He stepped to the door and opened it to see Kyrian and Julian standing on the other side.

They both gaped as they caught sight of him standing virtually naked in the loft.

Talon quickly slammed the door shut.

Kyrian roared with laughter. Talon cringed.

"C'mon, Tally," Kyrian teased from the other side. "Don't you want your clothes, your keys? Oh wait, how about some dignity?"

Talon opened the door, grabbed Kyrian by the shirt and hauled him inside. "You are such an asshole."

Kyrian laughed even harder as Julian Alexander walked in.

By his expression, Talon could tell that Julian wanted to laugh too, but he was trying hard not to. Talon appreciated it.

Kyrian, on the other hand, wasn't so kind. "Nice knees, bud, but the hairy legs could use a Bush Hog."

"Shut up." Talon grabbed the bag of clothes from Kyrian's hand and pulled his leather pants out. "Julian, I just want to thank you for being a grown-up and not laughing at my expense."

His hands in his pants pockets, Julian nodded. "Well, having been in your shoes, I can relate. Of course, in my defense, my towel was at least dark green and not pink."

The two of them roared with laughter while Talon groaned.

Kyrian flicked at the edge of the towel. "What is this? Lace?"

"No," Julian said, "I think it's called crochet."

Talon bared his fangs at the two of them. "Better be

careful, *humans,* or I might decide to feed off you."

"Uh, half-human," Julian reminded him. "Feed off me and I'll give you a bellyache from hell."

Growling at them, Talon quickly exchanged his towel for his pants.

"So," Kyrian said. "Have you become Ravyn now? Do I need to forewarn Nick you'll be shedding your clothes on a daily basis or what?"

Talon rolled his eyes at the mention of the Katagari Dark-Hunter. Ravyn was a shapeshifter who often got caught naked after sunup. "No, it's a one-time thing." *I hope.* "Speaking of Nick, where is he? I tried to call him for this chore."

"He's in class."

"Yeah, well, he's still on Dark-Hunter payroll, so tell him to keep his phone turned on."

"Ooo," Kyrian said. "Getting testy in your fierce naked-ness."

Talon ignored him as he pulled his black T-shirt on.

Sunshine paused beside Selena Laurens's tarot-card stand in Jackson Square. Selena's brown frizzy hair was tied back with a leopard-print scarf, and her thin body was covered with a black-and-white houndstooth coat.

"Hey, Sunny," Selena greeted her. "I was wondering if you were sick or something since you're not out here with your art."

"Oh no, someone came up."

Selena arched a brow at her. "Someone old or someone new?"

"New."

Selena looked a bit skeptical. "I hope this one is nicer than that last bozo you dated."

Sunshine wrinkled her nose as she remembered Greg. A rough biker, he'd been less than desirable and he'd kept confusing her with his ex-girlfriend Sara—nothing like being called the wrong name while having sex with someone.

Not to mention, he'd borrowed three hundred dollars from her the day before she'd kicked him out. Although, all things considered, it was worth the three hundred dollars to be rid of him.

"He seems to be." She patted her bag with Talon's clothes. "Well, I need to be getting back to him—"

"Sunshine!" Selena snapped. "Tell me you didn't."

"Didn't what?"

"Leave him in your loft unattended."

"It's okay. He's safe."

Selena groaned. "Woman, that generous heart of yours gets you into more trouble. Do you know this guy at all?"

Sunshine took a deep breath. She was so tired of everyone lecturing her. "I'll see you later, Madame Selene." She rushed back down the street toward her car with Selena fussing at her the whole way.

Ugh! Why couldn't anyone ever trust her? She wasn't a two-year-old. And being absentminded didn't equate to stupidity. If her kindness killed her, then she was better off dead than living a cold, unfeeling life where she misered up all her feelings and possessions.

Besides, Talon wasn't like other men. She knew it. He seemed to have a lot more heart than most men she'd known.

He was electrifying. Dangerous. Mysterious.

Best of all, he was waiting naked in her loft.

Getting into her car, she headed home.

It didn't take long to reach her father's club and pull around to the back where she always parked. Sunshine frowned as she saw a huge black Harley motorcycle parked beside a black Lamborghini.

Talon's friends?

Hmm, maybe Wayne was right. Maybe Talon *was* a drug dealer.

Not quite so sure of him, she got out of her car and used the back door that opened into the empty club.

She rushed up the steel-and-concrete stairs to her loft.

Pushing open the door, she froze as she caught sight of

three men, all of whose testosterone levels were off the Richter scale. They were absolutely devastating.

Whoa, she needed a sketchbook. Pronto.

Talon was dressed in black leather pants and a tight T-shirt that hugged every crevice of his deadly male perfection.

He stood talking to the two men in her kitchen—two incredibly handsome men. Men who were dressed like professionals and not out-of-work bikers.

How wonderfully refreshing.

"Hi, Sunshine," Talon greeted her. "These are my friends."

The one who was Talon's height held his hand out to her. "Kyrian Hunter," he said in an enchanting accent that was nothing like Talon's.

Sunshine shook his strong, callused hand as she recognized the name. "So you're Selena's brother-in-law. She talks about you and Amanda all the time."

Kyrian was slightly leaner than Talon, with laughing green eyes and an easy smile. His blond hair was a shade darker than Talon's and cut in a very hip style. "I think I should be afraid of what she says about me. Knowing her, there's no telling."

Sunshine smiled. "It's all good, I promise you."

"This is Dr. Julian Alexander," Talon said, introducing the other man, who wore a navy sweater and khakis.

"Nice meeting you," Julian said, extending his hand.

Sunshine responded in kind. Julian was about two inches shorter than the other two and yet his aura was every bit as strong and powerful. His eyes were a gorgeous blue and his hair the same shade as Kyrian's. He was also the most subdued of the three of them, but his eyes were no less friendly.

"Doctor?" she asked.

"I teach Classics at Loyola."

"Oh. Do you know Selena Laurens too?"

Julian nodded. "Very well. She's best friends with my wife."

"Grace?" Sunshine said. "You're married to Gracie?"

Recognition hit them at the same time.

"That was you?" she asked, stepping around to view him from behind. Oh yeah, now *that* she remembered. "You're Mr. Hot Bottom!"

His face went flush with embarrassment.

"Hot Bottom?" Talon asked. "This I've got to hear."

"Oh yeah," Kyrian added.

"We need to be going," Julian said, pushing Kyrian toward the door.

"Oh, like hell," Kyrian said. "Not until I hear this."

"Nice seeing you again, Sunshine," Julian said, shoving Kyrian out the door.

"Don't worry, Kyrian," Talon called. "I'll be sure to give you the *full* details."

Sunshine set the bag of clothes on her counter as the door slammed shut. "I guess you won't be needing these after all."

"Sorry." He leaned against the counter and watched her. "So, tell me how you met Julian."

She shrugged. "I sell my artwork at Jackson Square and I have a booth space next to Selena. A couple of years ago, she brought this bodacious guy to work with her wearing a tight tank top and shorts. Julian had really long hair back then. Anyway, there was this huge crowd of women who had gathered around to watch him. Selena thought it was a disaster, but I made so much money selling sketches of him that I didn't care."

Talon frowned as a very peculiar wave of jealousy went through him. And before he could stop himself, he asked, "Did you keep any of the sketches?"

"I only had one left, and I gave it to Grace about a year ago."

More relieved than he cared to admit, Talon watched her watch him. Her gaze traced the curve of his lips, the line of his jaw, and it made him ache to possess her, to kiss her lips one more time.

"You know, you are really handsome when you smile."

"Am I?" he asked, taking a strange amount of satisfaction from that.

"Yes, you are."

Sunshine swallowed as she realized there was no more reason for him to stay. Not that she should care; she needed to get back to her work. And yet at the same time she didn't want him to leave. "I guess you'll be going now that you're all dressed."

He looked askance at the sunlight. "I'm afraid I can't leave until the sun goes down."

"Oh." Sunshine tried to stifle the giddiness inside her.

He cleared his throat. "If you have things you need to do . . ."

"Oh no," she said quickly, then paused. "I mean, I . . . um . . . it would be rude, *very* rude, to leave you here alone. Especially since I don't have a TV or anything else for you to do." She licked her lips. "Well, since you can't leave, what would you like to do for the rest of the afternoon?"

"Honestly?"

"Yes."

"I'd like nothing better than to make love to you."

Chapter 4

Sunshine pulled back, startled by Talon's frankness. But more than that, she was stunned by how much she she wanted the same thing from him, a man she barely knew at all. And yet there was no denying how much she wanted to make love to him.

How much she ached to caress every inch of that divinely powerful masculine body.

Her lust didn't seem wrong to her. It seemed oddly right and only natural. In a strange way it felt as if she did know him. As if they were supposed to be much more intimate than just strangers who had collided by happenstance out on a dark street.

She wanted him on a level she didn't comprehend.

"You don't beat around the bush, do you?" she asked flippantly.

"No," he said, his jet-black eyes burning her with their heated potency. "I don't."

The power of his desire rolled over her, captivating her. He was so intense, so mesmerizing. And she found herself inexplicably drawn to him.

He reached out and touched a lock of her hair. Desire coiled through her veins, making her throb.

Nowhere else did their bodies touch and yet she swore she could feel him with every single cell of her body.

She quivered with need.

With heat.

With desire.

He bent down and whispered in her ear, his breath tickling her skin. "I've always been a firm believer in seizing the moment. In taking what I want when I want it. And right now, Sunshine, I want *you*. I want to taste every inch of your body. To feel your breath on my neck while I make love to you. To take my tongue and explore every part of you until you beg me to stop."

She shivered at the way he said that. "Life is short, I suppose."

He gave a short laugh at that as he nuzzled her cheek with his lips. His whiskered skin teased hers and she shivered at the manly feel of him. "More so for some than for others."

Sunshine drew in a deep breath as seriousness settled back over them both. The mood of the room wasn't just serious, the air between them was rife with salacity.

With sexual electricity.

Talon moved his mouth dangerously close to hers.

Slowly.

Seductively.

Time was suspended as she waited for his lips to claim hers. As she waited to taste his passion again.

Then, he took her into his arms and kissed her so possessively that it made her breathless.

Sunshine moaned as she tasted him with her lips and with her heart. He invaded every sense she possessed. His muscles bunched and flexed under her hands as his tongue swept against hers. She heard him growl low and deep in his throat like some uncaged beast.

She shivered again.

She brushed her fingertips against the warm nape of his neck, playing with the soft, tender skin there before she ran her fingers upward, through the golden strands of his hair, letting them wrap around her flesh.

How she liked the way this man felt in her arms. The scent of leather and Talon invaded her head and made it reel. He surrounded her with the strong hardness of his body.

She felt his desire for her as his erection pressed against her stomach, and it ignited her own, making her ache for his body, his touch. She wanted him inside her so desperately it stunned her. Never in her life had she wanted a man like this.

He lifted her up in his arms, supporting her weight as he deepened his kiss. Effortlessly, his strong hands held her bottom against his hips so that his bulge pressed against her core. She moaned at the intimate contact with leather and man.

Kissing him back as hard as she could, she wrapped her legs around his waist.

She felt his satisfied laugh rumble out of his body. It made his stomach caress her between her legs, his chest brush against hers, enflaming her even more.

Oh, hon, what are you doing?

Sunshine heard her reasonable voice in her head. She hadn't had a one-night, or in this case one-day, stand since college. The one time she'd done it, she'd felt so sleazy afterward that she had sworn she'd never do it again.

And here she was on the verge of repeating that fiasco.

Good grief, she knew nothing about this man.

Not even his last name.

But for some reason, none of that mattered. The only thing she could focus on was how good he felt as she held him. How wonderful he'd looked in her bed, and the fact that she really liked him. More than she should. More than what made sense.

Right or wrong, she wanted to share her body with him.

No, she *needed* this. It was what she wanted deep down in her heart. And she'd always followed her heart—wherever it led her.

There would be no regrets about this. No second-guessing.

He slid the hem of her dress back, over her thighs. She shivered at the feel of the cool material crawling up her

skin, followed by the heat of his hands. He glided his palms
up the backs of her thighs until he cupped her bare bottom.
He growled in pleasure, the sound deep and primal.

Needful.

"I like the way you feel, little Sunshine," he breathed
against her lips.

Sunshine couldn't think straight with his large, strong
hands on her naked skin. He dipped his head to her neck
where his lips burned her. His teeth scraped her skin as he
nipped it tenderly.

She was about to comment on how sharp his teeth were
when he delivered a hot, shivery lick to her skin.

Her thoughts scattered.

The man was simply too delectable; she couldn't let him
leave without sampling that lean, hard body. She pulled his
T-shirt over his head and ran her hands over his chest and
tattoo. Oh yeah, she wanted this!

She wanted *him*.

Talon gave her a tight-lipped smile as he saw the raw
hunger in her dark brown eyes. He was going to savor this
woman.

Every last tiny inch of her.

What with her passion and zest for living, he could only
imagine how good a lover she would prove.

It had been a long time since he had found a woman
who fascinated him. As a Dark-Hunter, he had chosen his
lovers randomly, knowing he'd never see them again.

For centuries, he'd contented himself with one-night
stands. With wanton women who wanted nothing more
from him than the few hours of pleasure he could give
them.

He had met them all in the dark of night.

Never in the light of day.

After minimal conversation to placate them, he had
screwed them wildly, and in the end, they had gone their
separate ways. Most of the time, he hadn't even bothered
asking their names.

But in the back of his mind, he knew something was different today.

Something was different about Sunshine.

He couldn't count how many centuries had passed since he had last shared a real laugh with a lover.

And this woman made him laugh. She made him crazy. Best of all, she made him burn.

Sunshine had stumbled into his world and turned it upside down. She'd touched the emotions he'd buried long ago. Made him feel strangely alive again, which for a man who had died fifteen hundred years ago was quite a feat.

She gave him feelings he didn't understand. He felt like a kid on Christmas morning, overloaded with sights and smells. His senses were overwhelming him with need.

With desire for her.

Licking his lips in anticipation, he ran his hand over her silken thigh, up to her hips. This woman had the finest ass he'd ever caressed. He pushed her dress up to her waist while she locked her ankles behind his back.

His head spun at the feel of her wrapped around him like this. The heat of her inner thighs burned his waist as he felt her wetness against his stomach.

Returning to her lips, he carried her to the bed and laid her down on the mattress. Without breaking his hold, he lay down on top of her and kissed her fully, deeply, as he ground his swollen groin against the part of her he couldn't wait to bury himself into. He sampled the warmth of her mouth and listened to her moans of pleasure.

Closing his eyes, he inhaled her unique scent and let it wash over him.

Sunshine wanted to weep at how good he felt on top of her. The leather of his pants caressed her intimately as his lips tormented hers. His braids tickled her neck with every movement he made. And his hands felt wickedly wonderful as he ran them over her body, seeking out every part of her.

She almost whimpered in protest when he moved away.

He pulled her dress from her and tossed it to the floor.

She felt more than just physically naked in front of him. For some reason she felt spiritually bare as well. It was as if he could see deep inside her somehow, as if he knew things about her no one else knew.

As if they were connected on a level that transcended their physical bonding.

At least she thought so until he returned to lie on top of her. Then her thoughts scattered again and she became one with the moment. It was strange, really, this sensation of him.

Sunshine hissed at how wonderful he tasted. All that lush, tawny skin made prickly by his masculine whiskers. She so loved the taste of a man's jaw.

No man had ever tasted more perfect.

She brought her hands around his waist, to his fly. His bulge was huge. Pulling back slightly, she watched his face as she opened his pants and touched him for the first time.

He closed his eyes and growled deep in his throat as he rocked himself gently against her hands. Oh, she liked the feel of him there. He was so hard and ready for her.

She laced her fingers through his short curls, moving her hand lower until she could cup the soft heat of him in her palm.

Talon moaned in pleasure. It felt so incredibly good to have her holding him like that. He'd had sex more times than he could count and yet there was something new about this experience.

Something fresh.

She pulled his pants down lower so that she could tuck her toes into them and pull them off. It wasn't until she frowned that they both remembered he still wore his boots.

"Oops," she said with a smile.

Talon chuckled, kissed her deeply, then rolled over to remove his boots. She rose up on her knees and leaned her naked body against his bare back, making him tremble from the feel of her breasts against his spine.

"I just love this tattoo," she said as she slowly traced it down his back with her tongue.

"I love when you do that," he said, tossing his boots and pants into the corner. He gripped the edge of the bed as she explored his back with her mouth.

"Does it have any special meaning?"

He closed his eyes as she returned to tracing the marks with her tongue. "They're Celtic symbols for protection, power, and longevity." Talon clenched his teeth at the irony. His uncle had had no idea what was awaiting his nephew when he had placed those markings on his skin. Just how long his life would be.

She gave one long, warm lick, then pulled back. "I can't believe your uncle did this. My father had a cow when he saw mine."

Talon looked at her over his shoulder. "You have a tattoo?"

She wrapped her left leg around his waist and showed him her inner ankle. It was a very small, stylized Celtic sun with the jagged symbol for creativity.

Smiling, he ran his hand over it. "Very nice."

"Yes, but it hurt for days. I can't imagine how much worse yours must have been."

She had no idea. Especially since his had been performed long before the days of sterilized needles and machinery. His uncle had meticulously tapped the design into his body over a three-month period. Some of it had gotten infected and only Nynia's herbal abilities had spared his life.

"It wasn't so bad."

"Ooo," she said teasingly, wrinkling her nose. "Mr. Tough Guy."

"Would you rather I say it hurt?"

"It never hurts to admit that you feel pain."

"Baby," he said gently. "I don't feel pain. Ever."

She looked at him in surprise. "Really? Not even a little?"

He shook his head as he clamped his emotions down. He didn't dare allow himself to feel the pain of all he'd lost. Even after all these centuries, it would destroy him.

"It's a waste of time and energy. It also drains the mind and makes it weary."

"But without pain, you can't have joy. It's the balance that makes us appreciate the extremes."

Now that was a deep concept. Very deep, considering they were sitting bare-assed on her bed. "Do you always philosophize while you're naked with a man?"

She nipped his shoulder impishly with her teeth. "It's rather hard to find a man who's willing to do that."

He dropped his gaze down to her breasts. "I imagine it would be a lot easier if you didn't look so damned good without your clothes on."

She moaned as he dipped his head and took one of her breasts into his mouth. She lay back on the bed, drawing him with her.

Talon sighed at the feel of her puckered areola under his tongue. He brushed his hand down the curve of her hip, over her soft thigh, and through the moist tangle of curls until he could touch the part of her he craved the most.

She groaned and shivered as he carefully separated the tender folds until he could tease her cleft.

Oh yeah, he wanted this part of her. Wanted to see her head thrown back against the pillows and hear her scream out loud while she came for him.

Sunshine clutched his head to her breast as she opened her legs wider, giving him access to her body. She ached and throbbed at the feel of his hand stroking her. And when he plunged his fingers inside, she cried out.

Her body burned for his in a most unbelievable way. It was hot and fierce and made her tremble with need. She'd never wanted a man as much as she wanted this one. She wanted to pull him close to her. Closer and closer until they truly melted into one being.

Unable to wait any longer, she reached down between their bodies so that she could guide him deep inside her.

They groaned in unison.

Sunshine arched her back, drawing him in even deeper.

He was so hard and hot, so full. She'd never felt anything better than him filling her.

He sat back on his legs and pulled her hips so that he could slide into her, slowly, deeply. It was a rolling rhythm that made her writhe from the intense pleasure of his intimate strokes.

She stared at him as he watched her with a tender look on his face.

"You are beautiful," he breathed, rolling his hips against hers and thrusting himself even deeper and harder inside her.

"You too," she said as she clutched at his knees.

His eyes darkened as he watched her and he gave himself over to their union. She'd never had a man make love to her like this. It was as if he were nothing but sex. As if he could feel nothing but her body.

He had such a way with his hips as he slid himself in and out, hard and deep. He teased her with his hands, his fingers stroking her in time to his thrusts. The pleasure of his touch permeated every fiber of her being.

And when she came, the orgasm was so intense that she screamed.

Talon growled at the sound of her ecstasy as her body clutched his. Crying out, she reached up and pulled him down on top of her.

Then, she did the strangest thing of all . . . she nuzzled his neck and face, raining kisses all over his cheek and shoulder.

Talon froze.

Her arms held him tight against her as she wrapped her entire body around his. The tenderness of her touch and actions pricked him, breaking through the chokehold he kept on his emotions.

It was as if she really cared for him. As if he meant something to her. As if she were making love *with* him.

Only one woman had ever held him like this . . .

He could barely breathe. For the first time in fifteen hundred years he actually felt as if he were making love to a woman, not just satisfying a primitive urge.

No, this wasn't meaningless sex.

He *felt* her. Felt connected to her. Felt as if they were something more than strangers with no ties to each other.

Her lips scorched his skin as she continued to nuzzle his neck and thrust herself against him. He held her tight and closed his eyes. His senses and emotions reeled from the pleasure of the moment.

When he came in her arms, he shivered to the core of his battered and weary heart.

He lay there, vulnerable and panicked.

No, he couldn't have felt that. He couldn't have felt *her*. It wasn't possible.

He was mistaken. What they had was sex. Incredibly great sex, but nothing more than that.

Sex.

Simple.

Basic.

Uncomplicated.

And he was going to prove it to himself one way or another . . .

Sunshine lay in complete satisfied bliss, breathing raggedly, drifting slowly back into herself. That was the most incredible orgasm she'd ever experienced. She couldn't believe the way he'd felt, the way he'd touched her.

She held his head close to her heart and felt his ragged breath falling against her breast. She cradled him with her entire body and just soaked up the warm masculine weight of him.

Used to men who quickly dosed off after they came, she was completely unprepared when he rolled over onto his back and pulled her to lie across his chest.

"You didn't think I was through with you, did you?" he asked in her ear.

"Well, yeah."

He laughed. "Lady Sunshine, I've only just started."

To her delight and awe, he proved those words well over the course of the next few hours.

They made love on her bed, on the floor, on her sofa. He took her in so many different positions that she felt as if he were reenacting the entire *Kama Sutra.*

Finally, they ended up in the kitchen where he set her up on the counter and then made slow, tender love to her.

Oh heaven, the man felt incredible! He had more stamina than an entire team of athletes and was completely shameless when it came to making love to her. She'd never been with a man and felt so at ease with her body and his expectations.

A man like this was all too hard to come by.

After they had finished with the counter, which she would never be able to look at again without blushing, Talon stood naked, looking into her refrigerator with his two braids tucked behind his ear as he searched for food.

He was still breathing heavily from their last go-round and Sunshine wondered idly if she'd gone bow-legged at some point from this afternoon's marathon.

Still, he looked scrumptious as he moved containers around in his quest for nourishment. His bare backside was a feast for the eyes and when he bent over to look into her bottom drawer, she couldn't resist running her hand up his muscular thigh, between his legs, to cup and fondle him.

He sucked his breath in sharply between his teeth and straightened.

Sunshine gave him a mischievous grin that garnered her a quick kiss before he returned to searching her fridge.

"My lady, do you own anything made of meat?"

Sunshine ran her hand across his back, smoothing down the red marks where she'd sunk her nails in during her last orgasm. "I have soy burgers, and I did pick up some granola bars, wheat germ, and oatmeal while I was out."

He actually whimpered.

"Sorry. I'm a strict vegetarian."

He sighed. "And I'm a strict carnivore."

She licked her lips and smiled as she remembered his

playful nips and bites on her flesh. "I noticed."

He turned toward her and gathered her naked body against his. He kissed her lips as if he were still able to savor her even after all they had done this afternoon. Then, he pulled back. "As much as I want you again, I have got to have something more to nourish me than your hot, lush body."

He grabbed her soy cheese from the top shelf and the whole wheat crackers she had on the counter.

Sunshine started to warn him about the cheese, but thought better of it. He did need something other than her to nibble on, though to be honest, she liked being his chew toy.

The man was insatiable, and best of all, he was the champion at what he did.

She watched curiously as he grabbed his Snoopy Pez dispenser from her counter, then went back to the living room.

Sunshine picked up their glasses of water and followed him to the Art Deco coffee table.

Talon sat down before it and sliced the cheese, then placed it on the crackers. He fed her one. "So tell me, if I wasn't here, what would you be doing today?"

She laughed. "I'm sure I would probably be sitting more comfortably, for one thing."

His face amused, he dipped his head to nuzzle at her neck. "Can I rub anything to make it feel better?"

She hissed at his deep, sensuous voice. "Your rubbing it is what got me into trouble."

He ran his tongue over her collarbone, then he pulled back and ate a cracker.

He choked.

Sunshine handed him the water.

Talon drank it down fast and scowled at her. "How old is this stuff?" He checked the expiration date on the cheese and his scowl deepened. "Soy?" he said as he finally recognized the package. "You let me eat *soy* cheese?"

"It's good for you."

"It's nasty."

"Oh," she said, as if she were talking to a child. "You poor baby. I'm so sorry."

"No you're not."

"Not true. I *am* sorry I don't have anything a big he-man like you can stand."

Talon sat back and shook his head at her. He should have had Kyrian bring him a burger along with his clothes. Even so, he had thoroughly enjoyed the day with her.

Even if it did mean eating things that should be classified as toxic waste products.

Cringing, he reached for another cracker, more prepared this time for the disgusting taste of it. By sheer force of will, he downed six crackers with cheese, though they barely took the edge off his hunger.

Thank the gods he had his Pez. Grabbing Snoopy, he quickly popped three Pez cubes into his mouth to kill the taste.

"How can you eat that?" she asked. "It's nothing but flavored sugar."

"Yes, but it's *good* sugar."

She wrinkled her nose at him.

Talon gave her a wicked grin. "You know the best way to eat these, don't you?"

She shook her head.

He pulled Snoopy's head back and took the small square out with his fingers. He held it up to her lips. "Bite down gently on it and hold it between your teeth."

She hesitated, then obeyed.

For a full second, Talon watched her sitting there naked with the cube between her teeth. Then, he leaned forward and used his tongue to pry it loose.

Sunshine moaned at the taste of him combined with the sugar. Opening her mouth, she gave him a long, hot kiss. "Now, that was nice."

"Worth polluting your system for?"

"Umm-hmm," she breathed, running her fingertip along his jaw.

Once all the Pez were gone, she picked up the Snoopy dispenser and looked at it. "This seems so out of character for you, Mr. Tough Man. I find it hard to believe a guy who can fight off six criminals single-handedly would haul around a Peanuts Pez."

He brushed her black hair back from her shoulder and let his hand linger in the strands. "Actually, I collect the dispensers. This one is a vintage 1969 one."

"Really?"

He nodded.

She looked at it again. "Is it worth much?"

"A couple hundred dollars."

"No kidding?"

"No kidding."

"Wow. And I almost fed it to the washing machine."

He laughed at that. "I'm glad you didn't. Me and Snoopy go way back."

He took Snoopy from her hands and set it on the coffee table. When he turned back to face her, the gleam in his eye was one she'd become quite familiar with.

"Are you really sore?" he asked.

All things considered, she should be, but his touch was so gentle that she wasn't. "I'm not. You?"

"Never better."

. He leaned back on the floor and pulled her across him. Sunshine straddled him and moaned at how good his steely abs felt against her.

To her amazement, he was already hard again. "You don't ever wear out, do you?"

He cupped her face in his hands and gave her a dark, serious stare. "It's you, love. Definitely you. With anyone else, I would have been curled up and sleeping hours ago."

"You mean that?"

He led her hand to his swollen shaft. "What do you think?"

"I think I should have taken more vitamins this morning."

"And I'm thinking there are still several positions we haven't tried."

Talon woke up in Sunshine's bed just as the sun set. He smiled in sleepy pleasure as he smelled the scent of turpentine and patchouli on his skin.

Sunshine.

She was still nestled in his arms, sound asleep. To his amazement, he felt his body starting to harden again.

After this afternoon, he should be sated for at least a day or two, if not for a full week.

For that matter, he shouldn't be able to move.

Yet he wanted to take her again. Right now. He wanted to feel her arms and legs wrapped around him, holding him close as he lost himself to the sensation of her flesh sliding against his.

Only Nynia had ever made him feel like this. He had been completely insatiable with her. To look at her was to burn for her.

He'd never thought to find another woman so appealing. And yet all he wanted to do was spend the rest of the night inside Sunshine. To feel her breath against his neck as he buried himself in her moist heat over and over again.

But he couldn't. He was supposed to meet Acheron at Jackson Square.

Not to mention that there were Daimons on the street ready to kill, and he had innocent people to protect.

"Talon?"

Inwardly, he cringed at the sound of her sleepy voice. He'd hoped to make a quiet exit while she slept.

How he hated messy exits.

"Evening, love," he murmured, kissing her brow.

She smiled a smile that dazzled him. "Are you leaving?"

"Yeah, I have to go meet someone."

"Okay," she said.

She got up from the bed, and wrapped a sheet around

herself. "It was really great meeting you, Talon. Thanks for a wonderful day."

She left him alone then.

Talon frowned. This was normally the part where his lovers begged him to stay, at least for a little while longer. Where they told him he was the best lover they had ever known and then cried at the thought of never having him again.

But Sunshine seemed completely fine with his leaving. She didn't seem to be the tiniest bit sad.

What was this?

He scooted out of bed and left the room to find her in the kitchen, holding a rice cake between her teeth while she poured herself a cup of pink juice.

"Sunshine, are you okay?"

She took the rice cake out of her mouth and looked at him. "I'm fine."

Her face paled a degree. "Oh Lord, you're not going to get possessive or weird on me now, are you? Please tell me you're not one of those guys Trina told me about who gets a little sex from a woman and then thinks he owns her."

A *little* sex?

A little sex!

Talon was dumbstruck. He was used to leaving his lovers, but this had to be the easiest time he'd ever experienced, and he found it strangely disconcerting.

Unsettling.

Humbling.

Especially given the way the two of them had carried on. This had been the best marathon of sex he'd ever had. She had met his passion and stamina in a way that was unbelievable.

Now she was fine with him just walking out the door?

"Are you sure you're okay?" he asked again.

"Look, it's cool, okay? I knew when I agreed to this that you wouldn't be hanging around afterward. I'm not stupid, you know. I'm a big girl. You're a really big guy and I'm sure you have a life to get back to." Panic drifted through her eyes. "Oh God, you're not married, are you?"

"No, I'm not married."

She let out a relieved breath. "Then, no harm, no foul."

She crossed the short distance to her fridge to return the juice jug.

"Sunshine?"

She paused to give him a peeved stare. "What, Talon? You're not having separation anxiety, are you? Today was fun and it was worth it, but I've got to get back to work. I have a ton of stuff that I need to do tonight."

"Yeah, but . . ." He didn't finish the sentence. He refused to.

"But?"

He clamped his jaw shut. Fine, if she wanted him gone, he was gone.

He shouldn't have spent the day with her anyway.

This close to Mardi Gras, he couldn't afford *any* distractions. Never mind one that came in the form of a dark-haired temptress.

"Nothing," he said.

She looked relieved. "Since you have to meet someone, you go ahead and shower and I'll make us some dinner."

Talon took her up on the shower, but when he was finished, he declined eating her tofu salad and soy steaks.

"Thanks again, Sunshine," he said as he shrugged his leather jacket on over his T-shirt. "I had a really good day."

"Me too," she said with a smile while she nibbled her salad and flipped through an art magazine.

He still couldn't believe how well she was taking his leaving her. Damn.

A part of him continued to expect her to at least beg him to call her.

Ask for his e-mail.

Something.

But she didn't.

Man, how he hated the twenty-first century.

She looked up as he headed for the door. "You take care of yourself, Talon. And in the future, please try and stay out of the way of runaway Mardi Gras floats, okay?"

Talon lifted both brows in stunned shock. "Excuse me?"

"Don't you remember last night when you got mowed down?"

Talon nodded hesitantly, unable to believe that that was what had slammed into him. "I was hit by a Mardi Gras float?"

"Yeah, it was Bacchus."

Now that was adding insult to injury. Jeez. He only hoped Nick didn't find out about it. Ever.

Nicholas Ambrosius Gautier had come into this world with not a lot of prospects. Born the bastard son of a career felon and a teenage Bourbon Street stripper, he wasn't exactly the most law-abiding of folks. In fact, his junior high guidance counselor had once voted him Most Likely to Get the Death Penalty.

But one night when Nick had made a stand against the gang he ran with, fate had changed his life and sent in a Dark-Hunter guardian angel who had taken a smart-mouthed kid, cleaned him up, and given him a real future.

Now, nine years later, he was a pre-law student, and instead of playing penal roulette like his father, he was almost a respectable citizen. *Almost* being the operative word.

All thanks to Kyrian of Thrace and Acheron Partheno-paeus.

There was nothing he wouldn't do for them and that was why he was sitting in his car, parked in a vacant field just after sunset, instead of being off with his latest girlfriend, putting a really big smile on her face.

Even with the car running, it was cold out here. That damp, frigid cold that could go deep into the bones and make them ache. His thermos of coffee all gone, Nick just wanted to get back home and thaw out.

Instead, he was waiting for Talon's Mardi Gras reinforcement to be delivered, because Zarek, having spent the last nine hundred years in Alaska, had no idea how to drive a car. Apparently, cars weren't the transportation of choice for snowbound Dark-Hunters.

Yee-freakin'-haw. This was one event he could have waited his lifetime for.

"Nick, you there?"

"Yeah," he said into the portable radio he had in the passenger seat of his Jaguar that kept him in touch with the incoming helicopter. "What's your ETA?"

"About two minutes," Mike said.

Nick started scanning the dark sky for the black H-53E Sea Dragon Sikorsky helicopter. It was a long-range, custom-built military-class chopper that the Squires often used to transport Dark-Hunters. The helicopter was fast and versatile, and could be refueled while in flight.

Its back section was equipped with a steel passenger area that kept sunlight from touching the Dark-Hunters. The windows in the passenger compartment could be lightened with a flip of the switch to allow a Dark-Hunter to see outside after dark should he desire it.

A few Dark-Hunters such as Acheron owned their own helicopters and flew them when needed.

Tonight, though, Mike Callahan, who was a Dorean Squire (meaning he didn't have a particular Dark-Hunter he served) was bringing in Zarek from Alaska.

Nick had heard a lot of rumors through the on-line Squire bulletin boards about Zarek of Moesia being psychotic. He wasn't sure how accurate that information was, but in a few minutes he'd find out firsthand.

"Hey, Mike," he said, radioing the pilot. "How bad is he?"

Mike snorted. "Let me put it to you this way. If you have a gun, unload it."

"Why?"

"Because if you don't, you're going to shoot this asshole which will only piss him off more. For once, I actually pity the Daimons."

That didn't sound encouraging.

"What? He's worse than Acheron?"

"Nick, take my word for it. You ain't never seen anything like this one. I now know why Artemis and Ash locked him in Alaska. What I can't figure out is why on earth Artemis wanted him moved into a large population. My opinion, it's like tossing a grenade on a gas station."

Oh yeah, his gut was knotted now.

Nick waited as the helicopter landed on the private airstrip Acheron used when he visited. At one end of the field stood a building that appeared to be a dilapidated barn. In actuality, it was a modified modern hangar equipped with an alarm system and doors so thick it could double as a bomb shelter. That barn currently housed the twenty-eight-million-dollar MH-60K Sikorsky helicopter that Acheron used to transport himself and his custom-built Buell motorcycle.

Ash had arrived in style the day before.

Now Zarek.

Yup, Mardi Gras was starting to look scary.

Nick got out of the car and locked his radio in the trunk, then stood to the side of the field until Mike cut the motor and the blades stopped spinning.

When everything quit moving, the lean, middle-aged Squire got out of the helicopter and removed his helmet. Mike had never been overly friendly, but tonight he looked thoroughly disgusted and extremely irritable.

"I don't envy you this," Mike said as he tossed his helmet back into his seat.

"C'mon, stop messing with me, Mike. He can't be that bad."

Nick changed his mind as soon as Mike slid open the passenger door and he caught his first look at Zarek of Moesia.

Zarek emerged from the opening like Lucifer from his deepest pit, with a chip on his shoulder so large, Nick was amazed they had managed to get the helicopter off the ground.

Dressed all in black, Zarek wore jeans, Harley biker

boots, and a long-sleeved T-shirt. He seemed completely oblivious to the cold damp air that made up a New Orleans winter night. He had a long silver sword earring in his left ear, with a hilt made of a skull and crossbones.

Zarek stepped out with a sneer that was made more sinister by his black goatee. His straight black hair brushed his shoulders and his jet-black eyes were filled with contempt and hatred. Nick was used to bad attitude; hell, he'd been weaned on it. But he'd never met a man who had one worse than Zarek.

He reminded Nick of the murderers his father had brought home. Cold. Unfeeling. Lethal. Whenever Zarek looked at you, you got the feeling he was measuring you for your coffin size.

Zarek braced his left hand against the side of the chopper, and leaned back in long enough to grab a large black duffel bag. Nick stared at Zarek's huge hand in awe. Each finger, including his thumb, was covered with a long, articulated silver claw and tipped with a point so sharp that Nick knew it must be Zarek's weapon of choice.

This man liked to get down and dirty with his kills.

Shit, for Zarek, being called psychotic would be a step up.

As he walked away from the chopper, Zarek hissed at Mike, baring his fangs.

For once, Mike didn't comment. That told Nick more than anything else just how vicious Zarek was. He'd never known Mike to take something like that and not make a smart-mouth comment.

"Well, if you're through taunting poor Mike, are you ready to go?"

Nick regretted those words as soon as Zarek looked at him. The glacial, hostile glare chilled him even more than the frigid winds. "You give me any lip, little boy, and there won't be enough left of you to run through a sieve."

Nick didn't scare easily, but those words were said with such growling sincerity that he actually took a step back, and for once kept his big mouth shut.

Without another word, Zarek walked with a predator's deadly grace toward the car, with his lips curled into a permanent snarl. He pitched his duffel bag onto the floorboard, then got in and slammed the car door shut.

In that moment, Nick seriously regretted buying a car with no backseat.

Then again, given Zarek's vicious, unpredictable nature, Nick would much rather have him beside him than *behind* him.

Mike let out a relieved breath and clapped him on the back. "May God take a liking to you, kid. I damn sure wouldn't want to be in your shoes tonight."

Nick had never been overly religious. But as he walked to his anthracite Jag, he found his religion all over again.

He got in and started the car, then headed toward the city. They were supposed to meet up with Talon, Valerius, and Acheron in about half an hour at Jackson Square. Damn, this was going to be the longest drive of his life.

He pushed the accelerator down even more—warp speed would suit him just fine.

As he drove, Nick couldn't keep his gaze from repeatedly wandering over to Zarek's left hand, covered with the silver claws, which was splayed out over his left knee.

The silence was deafening and stagnant, and was relieved only by Zarek flexing his claws against the black denim. After a time, the metallic scratching sound started to get on Nick's nerves. He turned on the radio.

"You like rock?" he asked.

The radio shut off immediately.

Nick swallowed as he realized one of Zarek's Dark-Hunter powers was telekinesis.

"Little boy, I'm not your friend. I'm not your Dark-Hunter and I'm not your friggin' date. You only speak to me when I ask you a question. Otherwise you keep your mouth shut, your eyes off me, and you might live long enough to get me to the French Quarter."

Nick gripped the wheel. Okay, now that pissed him off,

but not to the point it made him suicidal. Only an absolute fool would tangle with a man this lethal.

Zarek flipped open his duffel bag and pulled out a credit-card-sized MP3 player and a pair of dark sunglasses. He put on his headphones and sunglasses, then leaned his head back against the seat. Nick heard Nazareth's *Hair of the Dog* playing in a whisper from the headphones. The true antisocial anthem. How incredibly apropos.

When the car radio unexpectedly flipped back on, Nick actually jumped.

Oh yeah, Zarek was one psychotic SOB and the sooner he got him out of his car and to Acheron, the happier Nick would be.

Talon was still thinking of Sunshine when he crossed the Pedestrian Mall to meet with Acheron. He glanced down the street to where he had met Sunshine the night before, and his gut wrenched.

How he missed her. And that was the craziest part of all. He barely knew her. She had swept into his life like a hurricane, wreaking total destruction and chaos, and still . . .

He sighed. She'd been a nice diversion. But he had business to attend to.

His excursion with her was over. He would never see her again.

That was that.

As of this moment, she no longer existed.

Yeah, right.

Talon ignored the derisive voice in his head. He had no choice but to forget her. He'd made a pact centuries ago and it was a pact he would honor for the rest of eternity. For him there would never be a home, a family, and most definitely not a girlfriend or a wife. Even if he hadn't taken Artemis's oath, those things would be forbidden to him.

Besides, he liked his life as it was. He had a lot of

freedom. Time to do what he wanted and enough money to purchase anything that appealed to him.

Life as a Dark-Hunter was good.

Very good.

Entering the square, he caught sight of Acheron Parthenopaeus standing against the wall of a building with his arms folded over his chest. The tall Atlantean warrior stood apart from a crowd that was listening to a street performer sing his rendition of the Scooby-Doo theme.

Standing six feet eight with long metallic purple hair and wearing black wraparound sunglasses long after sundown, Acheron was a hard man to miss.

Talon usually referred to Acheron as T-Rex. The nickname stemmed more from the man's intimidating, carnivorous presence than from his ancient age.

There was something truly eerie about Acheron's lethal aura. It flowed out of him like a dangerous tsunami. The very air around the man seemed charged with mystical energy so powerful that it could make the skin on your arms or back of your neck crawl if you stood too close to him.

And judging by the berth the crowd had given T-Rex, Talon would say he wasn't the only one to feel it.

Then again, Talon amended, as he noted Acheron's black motorcycle jacket with silver chain mail draped over one sleeve and his leather pants that had laces instead of seams, maybe it was Acheron's eccentric, unorthodox looks that made people leave him alone.

Whatever it was, no one wanted to get in that man's way.

Acheron turned his head.

Even with the black wraparound sunglasses covering his eyes, Talon knew T-Rex was staring straight at him. Talon gave a short laugh as he noticed Acheron's new facial addition. A silver nose stud.

T-Rex had two very strange penchants: he was always finding new places to pierce his body, and his hair color changed faster than the unpredictable Louisiana weather.

T-Rex also had a strange scar of a hand print that came

and went on his neck. No one was sure if the scar was real or if it was some weird trick to throw them off guard that Acheron used. His accent was the same way. There were times when Acheron's voice was heavy with an odd melodic accent Talon assumed to be his native one from Atlantis, and other times T-Rex sounded just like any other television-programmed American.

The ancient warrior seemed to take a great deal of pleasure in keeping people guessing about him. He was even more private than Talon and that was saying something.

Acheron retrieved his black suede backpack, which was decorated with an anarchy logo from the street. He slung it over his shoulder, then tossed a few bills into the musician's guitar case and headed over.

Several members of the crowd visibly tensed and recoiled as Acheron moved through them with the fluid long-legged gait of a dangerous predator. Those who dared to look at him quickly averted their gazes.

It was ironic, really, since Acheron was the last person on earth who would ever harm a mortal. He was the oldest protector mankind had.

For centuries he had fought the Daimons single-handedly.

Alone.

Without friend or Squire.

Talon had heard rumors that Acheron had been trained to fight by Ares himself. Other rumors claimed Acheron was the son of a god and a legendary Atlantean hero.

But basically no one knew anything about Acheron other than he was tall, private, intimidating, and very, very strange.

As Acheron drew near, Talon inclined his head toward Acheron's purple hair with its four small braids that framed his face. "You know, I think I need to drop the T-Rex and start calling you Barney."

One corner of Acheron's mouth quirked up. "Don't start on me, Celt." He raked an amused look over Talon's leather pants, T-shirt, and jacket. "Nice to see you *fully* dressed for the occasion."

Talon winced at the underlying meaning of that comment. "Kyrian told on me, huh?"

"Oh, yeah. The pink towel bit was my favorite part."

Kyrian would pay for this. Even if Talon had to hunt him down. "I swear . . . Does Nick know?"

Acheron smiled a real smile that flashed a tiny bit of fang.

Damn, he was screwed now.

Oh, what the hell, it'd been worth it. Spending the afternoon with Sunshine had more than made up for any embarrassment.

T-Rex looked over his shoulder as if sensing something, and a corner of his leather jacket fell away from his throat to show the hand print was gone again.

Talon followed his line of vision to see Valerius approaching them. He'd only met the Roman general one other time when Valerius had first arrived to assume Kyrian's Dark-Hunter duties.

Valerius had taken one look at Talon's jacket and torc, and sneered the word *Celt*, thus letting Talon know friendship with this Dark-Hunter was about as likely as finding a parking space for a tank on Bourbon Street during Mardi Gras.

And just think, he was doomed to spend eternity in New Orleans with this prick. As Nick would say, yee-freakin'-haw.

The Roman's black hair was pulled back into an impeccable queue. He wore black pleated pants, loafers, turtleneck, and a long cashmere coat. If one didn't know better, he would appear to be an affluent attorney, not a Daimon executioner.

And it was all Talon could do not to laugh at how out of place Valerius looked standing next to him, and most especially Acheron, who was a poster boy for the goth movement. Right down to the silver stud in Acheron's nose and the silver buckles that decorated the side of his pointy-toed boots.

"How very punctual you are," Acheron said to Valerius as he looked at the cracked pocket watch he'd pulled out of his jacket pocket. The watch had suffered a mishap about a hundred years ago during a major Daimon uprising. The watch had survived, the Daimons hadn't.

Valerius's black eyes smoldered with resentment as he looked up at Acheron. "I might not like the fact that you are my commander, Greek, but as a soldier I will obey you regardless of my personal distaste for your company."

Talon smirked. "Gee, T-Rex, doesn't it make you all warm and fuzzy just to be near him?"

"Show respect to your betters, Celt," Valerius snarled, curling his upper lip. "Or I'll show you how we Romans dealt with your barbaric kind."

The words didn't elicit any emotion other than bored amusement, but Talon had never been the kind of man to let an insult pass without comment.

He was certainly too old now to change his ways.

"Ah, respect this," he said, flipping Valerius off.

Acheron barely caught Valerius as he lunged for Talon. He placed himself physically between them; not that Talon needed it, but judging by the fury in Valerius's eyes, the Roman certainly did.

"Children, don't make me separate you again." Acheron glared at Valerius and forced the Roman to take a step back. "Believe me, Val, I don't need you to fight my battles and I take no offense to Talon."

"My name is Valerius." Valerius straightened his coat with a regal, arrogant jerk. "And I do take offense to him."

Yeah, well, what was new? The man seemed to take offense at everything.

As usual, whenever two or more Dark-Hunters came together, Talon felt his powers weakening. It was a safeguard Artemis used to ensure her Dark-Hunters couldn't combine strengths and go after the gods or prey on mankind. The only exception to that was Acheron. As the designated trainer and the eldest of their breed, his presence didn't drain their powers, but everyone else's did.

They wouldn't be able to stay together much longer or they would be depleted for the night.

Talon glanced past Valerius's shoulder to see Nick and Zarek walking past the bakery on the corner and heading toward them. "Look unalive, men," he said to Acheron and Valerius, "here comes our reinforcement."

Valerius turned around and let out a vulgar curse that seemed at odds with his regal Roman air of refinement and good breeding.

"Back at you," Zarek snarled as he paused beside Acheron.

Disgust was evident on Valerius's face. "Not another friggin' Greek."

"What's the matter, Roman?" Talon asked. "Greeks bother you?"

His nostrils flared, Valerius raked a sneer over Zarek. "Trust me, had I been at Troy when they left the horse behind, there would have been roasted Greek on the beach that day."

Talon hissed in mock sympathy. "Damn, T-Rex, he really hates your ancestors."

Acheron gave him a droll stare. "No offense, Talon, I was around before they were."

"Oh yeah, sorry." Talon exchanged glances with Nick, who was much quieter than normal. The Squire looked a bit strained.

Hmm, that was interesting. He'd have to keep Zarek around if the man had that kind of suppression power. It was nice to know Nick had an off switch.

"Any problems with your flight?" Acheron asked Zarek.

"I didn't eat my pilot if that's what you mean. And little Nicky here is still breathing and not bleeding."

"Well," Acheron said, his tone flat. "I suppose that's an improvement over last time."

Talon wasn't sure if Acheron was joking or not, but knowing Zarek's reputation, he didn't really doubt it was true. Rumor had it that Zarek had cut up and eaten the last Squire Acheron had sent for him.

Talon swept a glance around the five of them.

Were they a motley bunch or what? The only thing they had in common was height. Collectively, they must look like refugees from the NBA since they ranged in height from Nick's six feet four to Acheron's six feet eight.

Nick was dressed in jeans, a dark green sweater, and bomber jacket—the perfect image of a rich college student. Talon looked like a biker who had just left Sanctuary, New Orleans's premier biker bar. Acheron looked like a refugee from the Dungeon—the local underground goth hangout. Valerius was the professional contingent, and Zarek . . .

Zarek just looked like he was ready to kill something.

"So why are we congregating?" Zarek asked.

The repugnant hatred in Valerius's eyes was searing. "Did anyone speak to you, *slave*?"

Acheron barely caught Zarek's hand before his claw sliced Valerius's vulnerable throat. Never before had Talon seen Acheron struggle so hard to hold someone back. It spoke a lot for Zarek's power.

And his temper.

"Cease!" Acheron ordered Zarek. "I know it's been a long time since you were around another Dark-Hunter, Z, but remember, whatever you do to him, *you* will feel it tenfold."

Zarek's face hardened. "Pain I can take, it's him I can't."

Valerius still had his lips curled. "I don't see why we need a whipping boy for the Daimons to play with. You know, he was so worthless in his lifetime that my father had to pay a slaver to take him off our hands."

Zarek let out the snarl of a wild beast. An instant later, Acheron was thrown clear of him and Zarek bolted at Valerius. He caught the Roman around the waist and the two of them hit the street. Hard.

Before Talon could pull him off Valerius, Zarek got in a number of solid punches and one last kick to the Roman's ribs as Talon hauled him up.

Just as Acheron had said, Zarek's face showed every
blow he had given to Valerius. His nose and lips were
bleeding profusely. Zarek didn't seem to notice and if he
did, the satisfied gleam in his black eyes said the ex-Roman
slave thought it well worth the cost.

Valerius was only slightly more subdued as he regained
his feet. "You should be beaten for that."

Talon tightened his hold on Zarek.

Angrily, Zarek shoved him away. "Get your fucking
hands off me, Celt." Then he turned back to Valerius. "Try
beating me, you sorry piece of shit, and I'll force-feed you
that black heart of yours."

"Enough!" Acheron roared. "Another word from either
one of you, and I swear I'll rip both your hearts out."

Valerius wiped the blood from his lips.

Zarek raked his hand across his face, removing the
blood, while he glared murderously at Valerius.

Acheron was a man of infinite patience and Talon had
never seen Acheron exasperated before. But he saw it now.

Acheron glared at the Dark-Hunters. "Next time I'll just
send the three of you e-mails. What was I thinking when I
decided to have this meeting?"

Nick spoke up. "Oh, I know. That men who are a couple
of thousand years old could actually behave like grown-
ups?"

Zarek elbowed Nick in the stomach.

"Oops," Zarek said to Acheron. "Involuntary arm spasm."

Acheron cursed under his breath. "I swear, Daimons or
not, if you don't behave, Z, I'm going to send you to Ant-
arctica and leave you there to rot."

"Ooo," Zarek breathed in a bored tone. "I'm terrified.
Those killer penguins and hairy seals are *really* scary."

Acheron growled a low warning at Zarek.

Talon felt for his frustrated leader. He knew why Acheron had set up this meeting. The Atlantean had wanted to
know what would happen when the three of them crossed
paths. Better to see how much hostility there was up front

and be here to control it than to chance a random meeting where Zarek could beat the snot out of Valerius without someone there to break them up.

Now Acheron knew exactly what he was dealing with and how much space to put between them. Talon had to salute the Atlantean's wisdom. Acheron might be young in appearance, but he was truly ancient in his powers, knowledge, and ability to handle the rogue Dark-Hunters who answered to him.

Acheron passed a look to each of them. "If you can control yourselves for five minutes, we need to divide up the city. Since I'm the only one able to take the cemeteries, I'll grab those. Valerius, I want you in the garden and business districts, Zarek and Talon can take the Quarter. On Mardi Gras itself, we all need to be in the Vieux Carré no later than nine."

He turned to Nick. "You are on standby. In the event one of us goes down, I need you to mobilize quickly."

"Just one little problem."

"And that is?"

Nick indicated Valerius with his head. "If he goes down, he's on his own."

Zarek smiled. "I knew I liked this kid for a reason."

Nick shot him a disbelieving stare.

"Nick," Acheron said, his voice laced with warning, "your duty is to all of us. Valerius is a Dark-Hunter same as me, Talon, and Zarek."

"I know I swore my oath, but I swore it to protect Kyrian of Thrace and hell will freeze colder than Santa's iceberg before I ever lift even an eyebrow to help the man who tortured and crucified him."

Valerius's eyes blazed.

"That was his grandfather, not him."

Nick pointed a finger at Valerius. "He was there, too, watching it happen, and he did nothing to stop it. I refuse to render aid to someone who could do that." He looked back at Ash. "You, psycho-ass, and Talon, I'll cover, but not him."

"Psycho-ass?" Zarek repeated. "Hmm, I like that."

Acheron ignored Zarek. "Nick—"

"It's all right, Greek," Valerius interrupted. "I would rather die than have his plebeian help anyway."

"Make that three votes, then," Zarek said. "I would rather he died too. Now all together, let's vote this asshole off the island."

Talon hid his amusement and wondered how much longer it would be before Acheron splintered Zarek and Valerius into itty-bitty Dark-Hunter pieces.

Maybe he should tell Nick to get a dustpan ready. The look on Acheron's face said the wait wouldn't be much longer.

"Fine, then," Acheron said to Nick. "Call Eric St. James and have him resume Barnacle Squire status for Valerius should Valerius need anything."

Nick nodded. "Can I have him cover Zarek too? I still have school to worry about."

Before Acheron could answer, Valerius sneered, "I will not work with a slave as an equal nor will I share a servant with him."

Zarek's nostrils flared. "Trust me, boy, we're not equal. You're so far beneath me that I would sooner sit in shit than let you wipe my ass."

Talon caught Valerius before he reached Zarek.

He exchanged looks with Acheron. "This is going to be fun, isn't it? Constantly separating the two of them while fighting off the Daimons. Should we just forget the whole thing and hole up in our homes until it's over?"

But even more discouraging was the knowledge that if Kyrian found out Valerius was in the city, he would make Zarek's attack look like a loving embrace. And since Kyrian was no longer a Dark-Hunter, his powers wouldn't be dampened by Artemis's restriction. He would have free rein to kill the Roman.

Acheron sighed irritably. "I'm almost ready to agree with you." He turned to Valerius. "Go patrol your districts."

Valerius gave him a rather sarcastic Roman salute, then turned on his heel and left them.

The air between them warmed up considerably. Hell, Zarek even looked almost . . . tolerable. A noticeable amount of tension left the man's body.

"Am I staying with you and Kyrian or Nick?" Zarek asked.

Acheron fell quiet while he fished a key out of his jacket pocket. "We thought it best that you have your own place. I had Nick rent a townhouse for you over on Dauphin Street. He painted the windows black and made sure they were all blocked from daylight."

Zarek's face returned to stone and his black eyes blazed. For some reason, the man was furious as he snatched the key from Acheron's hand and turned to leave.

"I'll have Nick show you where it is," Acheron said.

"I don't need anyone to show me a damn thing," Zarek snarled. "I'll find it on my own."

After Zarek stalked off, Nick grimaced. "I know," he said to Acheron. " 'Nick, go after psycho-ass and show him where he lives.' But might I point out that in doing this, I should qualify for hazard pay?"

Acheron arched a brow. "Might I point out that staying here with me is far more hazardous to your health?"

Nick feigned surprise. "What? Am I still here? Oh no, sorry, thought I'd left ten minutes ago."

He sprinted off after Zarek.

Once they were alone, Talon raked a hand through his hair. "Some nights it's not worth getting up, is it?"

"You've no idea." Acheron let out a long, deep breath as if he were expelling all the tension in his body.

"So tell me, T-Rex, what did you do to Artemis to make her dump this on you?"

As expected, Acheron said nothing. To Talon's knowledge, he had never divulged anything personal about himself or the exact nature of his relationship with the goddess.

"Walk with me, Talon."

That didn't sound good, but Talon followed him.

Acheron remained silent as they left the Pedestrian Mall and headed down Pirate's Alley in the direction of Royal Street.

Just beside the St. Louis Cathedral, near the small garden behind it, Acheron stopped. Talon glanced about uneasily. Dark-Hunters didn't do well around holy places. Since they were men who had lost their souls, souls that had lost their bodies tended to want to take up residence with them. A strong Dark-Hunter could fight the souls off, but only Acheron was completely immune to possession.

It was the main reason Dark-Hunters lived only in new houses and why Nick had taken a psychic into Zarek's townhouse to ensure no ghosts were hanging out. A possessed Dark-Hunter was a scary thing.

"Tell me about the woman you spent the day with."

He started at Acheron's words. The man's powers had never ceased to amaze him. "Nothing to tell, really."

"Don't lie to me, Talon. Sunshine is still within you. I can feel her there. She's in your thoughts and your blood."

The man was truly eerie. "Look, I know where my duties lie. I made an oath to Artemis and I'm not trying to find a way to break it."

"That's not what concerns me."

"Then what is?" Talon asked.

"Do you remember what I told you the night you took vengeance against your clan?"

"Nothing comes without a price."

"Exactly. This woman is inside you, little brother. If you don't get her out, she will unlock those emotions I taught you to bury."

"Would that be so bad?"

Acheron removed his sunglasses and gave him a hard, serious stare with those ageless, timeless glowing eyes. "Yes, it would. You are the one Dark-Hunter I can depend on to have a clear, level head. I need you to stay focused, especially since we have Daimon Fest coming up and two Dark-Hunters in town who hate each other.

"Your emotions are the key to your powers, Talon.

When you lose your control, you lose your Dark-Hunter immortality with it, and I don't want to see you dead because you can't control your libido."

"Don't worry. I'm under control."

"Good. Just make sure you stay that way because if you don't, you *will* get yourself killed."

Chapter 5

"Oh, thank God you're there," Selena said in Sunshine's ear as soon as Sunshine answered the phone. "Where have you been? I've been ringing the phone off the hook all day long trying to reach you. I know you can never find the damn thing, but dang, girl . . . I've been so worried that I was about to head over there and see if you were okay or if this unknown guy had murdered you in your loft." Selena finally took a breath in the midst of her tirade. "Please tell me he's not still there."

Wiping off her paint-stained hands while she cradled the phone between her ear and shoulder, Sunshine smiled at Selena's concerned voice and her motherlike lecture. "No, Selena, Mr. Bodacious is gone. He had to go meet some friends."

"Well, what time did he leave?"

"A few minutes ago."

"Sunshine!"

"What?" she asked in feigned innocence.

"Oh, honey," Selena gasped, "don't tell me you spent the whole day with him playing Parcheesi or something."

Sunshine bit her lip as she remembered exactly what they had spent the day doing. It made her warm and tingly all over again. "We didn't get to the Parcheesi, but we did it on the backgammon table a couple of times. And on the couch, the kitchen counter, the floor, the coffee table, and—"

"Oh, my God, TMI—way too much information. Tell me you're joking about this."

"Nope, not a bit. I'm telling you, Selena, forget the Energizer Bunny, this guy had it all."

Selena groaned. "What were you thinking? You just met him."

"I know," Sunshine said, agreeing completely with her friend that she was a lunatic for doing something so stupid. "It's so not like me, but I couldn't help myself. It was just like that weird magnetic force that grabs me when I'm walking past the Frostbyte Cafe and makes me swerve in to get a triple scoop of Ben and Jerry's Chunky Monkey."

That was her one major vice. Sunshine had never been able pass up Chunky Monkey.

"The power of temptation was just too much, Selena. I couldn't resist it. He was a Chunky Monkey container and all I could think was, 'Someone give me a spoon.' "

"Oh, good grief," Selena said.

"Yeah. It was weird. I was here, he was here, and then he said, 'Let's do it,' and the next thing I knew, the spoon was in my hand and I was going for it."

Selena made a disgusted noise. "Please tell me no one was using a spoon."

Sunshine smiled devilishly. "No, no spoon, but there was a whole lot of licking going on."

"Oh, oh, oh! You're killing me. Don't go there."

Sunshine laughed. "I can't stop myself. He was so hot that I feel this deep need to share his spectacular hotness with you."

Selena snorted at her. "Are you at least going to see him again?"

"No, unfortunately not. I didn't even get his last name."

"Sunshine! Girl, you are nuts."

"Yeah, I know. It was just a once-in-a-lifetime kind of thing."

"Sheez, are you okay, though? He didn't hurt you or anything?"

"Oh no, not at all. It was the best day of my life. Freaky, ain't it?"

"Ah jeez, Sunny. I can't believe you did this. You've been hanging around all those weird friends of yours so much that you're picking up their bad habits. Bringing home stray men you don't even know. Next thing you know, you'll be dancing naked on tabletops . . . Oh wait, that was me."

Sunshine laughed. "Don't worry. It'll never happen again. You know me, I do date occasionally, but I usually spend at least a few normal, boring days with a guy before we rock the house down. Of course, no one ever rocked my house down the way this guy did. He leveled the mother to its foundations."

Selena shrieked. "I can't believe you keep telling me this."

Sunshine laughed at the tortured angst in Selena's voice as she continued to tease her. "I can't believe I spent the day in bed with this guy, but I'd do it again in a heartbeat. I'm telling you, these were the best eighteen hours of my life."

"Jeez, you didn't even know him a whole day?"

"Well, I know him now. Every last yummy inch of him. By the way, he had a lot of inches."

"Stop it, Sunny," Selena begged, her voice cracking with laughter. "I can't take any more. I don't need to know the sexual athlete of all time is running around New Orleans and I'm married to the lawyer. This is so cruel."

Sunshine laughed again. "Well, Bill is nice, in a very Bill sort of way."

"Oh gee, thanks, now you're ripping on my Bill."

"I'm sorry. You know I love Bill, but this guy was really, really great." Sunshine, dragging the heavy, psyche-delic phone in her wake, crossed the kitchen toward her fridge to get some guava juice. Teasing Selena was fun, but oddly enough there was a part of her that was extremely sad Talon had left.

He really had been a lot of fun and not just in the bed, or on the floor, or on the other five thousand places where they'd had sex. He'd been fun to talk to too.

Best of all, he hadn't lost his patience with her.

She opened the fridge, then laughed again.

"What?" Selena asked.

Sunshine saw Talon's prized Snoopy Pez dispenser standing up, looking straight at her. She couldn't believe it.

So that was what he'd been doing in the fridge while she was in the shower. No wonder he had looked uncomfortable when she caught him.

How adorable.

"Awww, he left me his Snoopy Pez dispenser on top of the soy cheese."

"What?" Selena asked.

"Nothing," Sunshine said, taking the cold plastic toy into her hand. "It's an inside joke."

"Oh, don't tell me you did something with the cheese."

"No, we just ate it. Jeez, Selena, get your mind out of the gutter. Not everything has to do with sex."

"Well, with the two of you it does. The basis of your whole entire relationship seems to be nothing but sex . . . Oh wait, it's only been eighteen hours since you met him. Does that qualify as a relationship?"

"Believe me, the way he does sex, it counts. Besides, he did leave me his Pez dispenser."

"Ooo," Selena teased, "he's bodacious and generous. What a guy."

"Hey now, be fair to my bodacious biker. It's a valuable Pez dispenser. A 1960-something collector's item."

"Yeah, but did he leave you his phone number?"

"Well no, but he did put Snoopy on the top shelf so I would find it."

"Enough said. Case closed. You're still riding the loser train when Snoopy becomes something valuable."

"Okay, fine, Selena, you're bringing me down from my love fest and I'm losing my afterglow. It's been ten months since I last slept with a guy and it'll probably be forever and a day before another one who's not gay darkens my doorstep, so let me go back to work where I can bask in the after-greatness of my afternoon."

"Okay, sweetie. I'll call you later. I was just concerned. You go back to work and I'll see you tomorrow."

"Okay, thanks. Bye."

Sunshine hung up the phone and looked down at the Snoopy in her hand. She laughed.

Talon might not be perfect, he might even occasionally screw up and get run down by a Mardi Gras float, but he had been a great guy, and great guys were hard to come by in this day and age.

It was a pity she'd never see him again. But then, she wasn't the kind of woman to mope over what could have been. She was an artist with a good career that she had worked very hard for.

A serious relationship with someone wasn't something she was looking for right now.

She liked living alone. Loved having the freedom to just pick up and go whenever and wherever she wanted to. Her brief marriage in her early twenties had schooled her well on what a man expected from a wife.

She had no intention of *ever* revisiting that fiasco.

Talon had been a fun afternoon diversion, but that was all he was. Her life would now go on just as it always had.

Her heart lighter at the thought of him, she took Snoopy into her bedroom and set him on the nightstand by the bed.

Sunshine smiled. She'd never had a memento before. But that's what Snoopy was to her. A token reminder of a wonderful day.

"Have a nice life, Talon," she said, turning off the light by the bed before she headed back to her work. "Maybe someday we might meet again."

It was just after one A.M. when Talon found himself outside the club Runningwolf's on Canal Street. He'd tried to tell himself that he was here because Daimons were often found hanging in and around clubs where drunken humans made easy pickings.

He'd tried to tell himself that he was just doing his job.

But as he looked up at the dark windows above the club and wondered if Sunshine was up there in her bed or if she was at her easel painting, he knew better.

He was here because of her.

Talon cursed under his breath. Acheron was right. She was inside him in a way no one had been inside of him in centuries.

No matter what he tried, he couldn't get her out of his mind.

Over and over, he could feel her. Feel her body under his, her breath on his skin. Hear the sound of her soft Southern drawl whispering in his ear.

And when she had touched him . . .

It was like a song from heaven.

The physical comfort and companionship she'd given him this afternoon had touched him profoundly.

He'd felt welcomed in a way that wasn't sexual.

What had she done to him? Why after all these centuries had a woman crept inside his feelings?

His thoughts?

Even more frustrating, he knew if he were human, he'd be with her now.

You're not human.

He didn't need the reminder. All too well, he knew what he was. He liked what he was. There was a special kind of satisfaction that came with his job.

And yet . . .

"Speirr? What are you doing?"

He tensed at Ceara's voice coming out of the darkness and at the fact that someone had caught him doing something he shouldn't be doing.

"Nothing."

She appeared beside him. Her shimmering face smiled knowingly.

He let out a disgusted breath. Why did he bother trying to hide anything from the ones who could see straight into his thoughts?

"Yeah, okay," he admitted reluctantly, "so I wanted to check up on her and see how she's doing."

"She's fine."

"And that *really* irritates me." The words were out before he realized it.

Ceara laughed at that. "You were expecting her to be sad?"

"Of course. She should at least have had a moment or two of regret or something."

Ceara clucked her tongue. "Poor Speirr. You found the only woman alive who doesn't think you hung the moon and the stars."

He rolled his eyes at her. "So maybe I'm being a little arrogant . . ." She arched a brow and he corrected himself. "So I'm being a lot arrogant, but damn, I can't get her out of my thoughts. How can she feel nothing?"

"I didn't say she felt nothing, I only said she's not sad."

"So she did feel something for me?"

"If you like, I could do more investigating."

"*Nae,*" Talon said quickly. The last thing he wanted was for Ceara to find out what he and Sunshine had been doing all afternoon.

Ceara was naive and he wanted to keep her that way.

His sister walked a small circle around his body. For some reason she'd always liked to do that. As a little girl, she'd made him dizzy as she raced around him at a dead run, giggling as she went.

Even though she was a young woman before him now, in his heart he always saw her as that chubby little toddler who used to sit on his lap for hours, playing with his braids as she gibbered her baby speech at him.

Just like Dere . . .

His stomach clenched at the memory.

Ceara hadn't been his only sister. Three more had been born between them. Fia had died her first year of life. Tress had lived to age five when she perished of the same illness that had claimed their mother.

And Dere . . .

She had died at age four.

She'd gone out at sunrise, wanting to see the fey folk Talon had teased her with. He'd told her how he often saw them out the window at daybreak while she slept.

Only five years old himself, he had heard someone leave their hut. At first he had thought it was his father. But as he snuggled back down to sleep, he'd realized Dere wasn't in their bed.

He'd gotten up immediately and rushed out to find her.

She had slipped on the rocks along the edge of the cliff that looked out onto the sea where he'd told her the fey frolicked in the early dawn's light.

He heard her scream and had run as fast as he could.

By the time he reached her, it was too late. Her young arms had been unable to hold on until he got there.

She lay below on the rocks with the waves rushing over her.

Even now, he could see her lying there. Could see the looks on his parents' faces when he had awakened them with the news.

Worst of all, he could see the accusation in his father's eyes.

Neither of his parents had ever uttered the words aloud, but in his heart he knew they had blamed him for it.

Not that it mattered. He blamed himself. He always had.

It was why he had been so protective of Ceara and Tress. Why he had been so determined that nothing bad would ever happen to his youngest sister.

Tonight, he saw a hesitancy in Ceara's steps.

"So, what's the news from the Daimon world?" he asked her.

Ceara paused. "How did you know?"

"You've been strangely quiet tonight. It's not like you

to stay hidden while I hunt unless you're conferring with the others."

Her eyes glowed warmly. "I never could hide from you." She wrapped her arms around herself. "There was talk. There is a force here. One not Daimon born."

"Goblin, ghoul, demonic? What?"

"No one seems to be sure. There are Daimons surrounding the source of it, but it is not one of them. It's something else."

"A god?"

She looked up, exasperated. "I'm trying to find someone who knows, but as yet . . ." She paused and wrung her hands. "I want you to be careful, Speirr. Whatever this thing is, it holds a great deal of malice. Hatred."

"Can you locate it?"

"I have tried, but it moves whenever I draw near. It is as if the source knows to avoid me."

This wasn't good, especially with Mardi Gras right around the corner. When Bacchus came to town, even the most moderate of things went wild. To Talon it sounded like something or someone was counting on the excesses of the celebration to propel whatever plan it had.

Talon's thoughts were distracted as a car drove down the street in front of him. It was an old VW Beetle. Someone had painted the top of it dark blue with glow-in-the-dark stars and the lower half was bright sunshine yellow with red peace symbols.

He smiled at the sight. It had been parked outside the club earlier when he had left. Instinct told him it had to belong to Sunshine. No one else would be caught dead in such a monstrosity.

True to his suspicions, the car turned into the alley behind Runningwolf's.

With his honed Dark-Hunter sight, he watched her leave her car and pause to pull a sealed box out of the backseat. His body hardened instantly.

Tonight, she wore her black hair in two braids down the side of her face. She was dressed in a long fuchsia sweater coat that displayed her lush curves to perfection.

In his mind, he could imagine walking up to her, pulling her back against his front, and just inhaling her warm patchouli scent. Letting his hand trail down the front of her, to her tight black sweater held closed by small buttons. Of working those buttons through the cloth until she was exposed to him.

His body burned with aching want.

"Speirr?"

Ceara's voice jarred him from his reverie. "I'm sorry, I was distracted."

"I said I will go and investigate further. Or do you need me to stay here and keep you grounded?"

"No, thanks. I'm grounded."

"I'm sensing conflict inside you. Are you sure you want me to leave?"

About as sure that the world would end in fifteen minutes. No, he wasn't sure. Because every time he looked at Sunshine, he had a nasty tendency to forget everything else.

To want nothing more than to stare at her. To touch her.

"I'm sure."

"Very well, then. I shall listen out for you. If you need me, call."

"I will."

Ceara vanished and left him alone in the darkness.

Sunshine slammed her car door closed and entered the rear door of the club.

He took a step toward her before he even realized what he'd done.

Talon ran his hands over his face. He had to get her out of his thoughts. There was no point in this. Dark-Hunters didn't date and they damn sure didn't have girlfriends. Well, no one except Kell, but he was weird anyway and Kell's girlfriend was a constant source of irritation for Acheron.

Not that Talon minded being an irritation to Acheron. It

was actually enjoyable to nettle the Atlantean, but he couldn't screw up Sunshine's life that way.

Dark-Hunters didn't date and most especially not this one. He'd already learned his lesson and he'd learned it hard.

Unlike the others, he was cursed by his own gods. It was why he refused to have a Squire. Why he refused to have *anyone* near him.

"For what you have taken from me, Speirr of the Morrigantes, you will never again know the peace or happiness of a loved one. I curse you to walk eternity alone. Curse you to lose everyone you care for.

"One by one, they will suffer and die, and you will be powerless to stop it. Your agony will be knowing they are doomed because of your actions and wondering when, where, and how I will strike them down. I will claim them all and live only to watch you suffer."

Even after all these centuries the angry god's words rang in his ears.

Talon groaned at the pain of the memory of his wife dying in his arms. *"I'm afraid to die, Speirr . . ."*

It had been all his fault.

Every death.

Every tragedy.

How could so many lives have been shattered by one stupid mistake? He had let his emotions lead him and, in the end, he had destroyed not only his own life but those of the ones he loved.

He winced at the truth of it.

Agony seared him so deeply that he cursed aloud from the force of it.

"You were born cursed," Gara's gnarled old voice whispered in his head. *"Born bastard to a union that should never have been. Now get out and take the babe with you before the wrath of the gods falls to my head."*

At age seven, he had stared in helpless disbelief at the old crone his mother had worked for. When his mother and

Tress had taken sick, Gara had allowed him to do his mother's tasks.

After his mother's death, the old woman had turned on him.

"But Ceara will die if I leave. I don't know how to care for an infant."

"We all die, boy. It's no concern of mine what becomes of the child of a whore. Now get out and remember how quickly our fates change. Your mother was a queen. The most beloved of the Morrigantes. Now she is a dead peasant, like the rest of us. Not even worth the dirt that covers her."

The cruel words had torn through his child's heart. His mother had never been a whore. Her only mistake had been to love his father.

Feara of the Morrigantes had been worth all the treasures of the earth to him. Her value was beyond measure . . .

"Push it away," he said, taking deep breaths to calm himself.

Acheron was right, he had to keep his emotions buried. They were what had led him astray to begin with. The only way he could function was to not remember. Not feel.

And yet he couldn't help feeling. He couldn't seem to repress the memories that he had buried fifteen hundred years ago . . .

"So the son of the whore has returned to beg you, my king, for his shelter. Tell me, King Idiag, should I cut off his head, or just slit his nostrils and then turn this pitiful wretch out into the storm to die like the worthless dung he is?"

Talon could still hear the laughter of his mother's people. Feel the fear in his young heart that his uncle, like everyone else, would forsake him and Ceara. He had clutched his sister close to his chest while she squalled, wanting the food and warmth he had been unable to provide her.

Barely two months in age, Ceara had refused to suckle the bladder he had tried to feed her with.

For three days as they traveled without stopping, she'd done nothing but scream and cry.

No matter what he tried, Ceara would not be placated.

Idiag had stared at him for so long that he was sure his uncle would send them to their deaths. The fire in the hall had crackled while the people held their collective breath, waiting for their king to pronounce judgment.

Talon had hated his mother then. Hated her for making him beg for his sister's life. Making him suffer like this when he was just an untried lad who wanted only to run away and hide from his humiliation.

Hide from the screaming baby who never took pity on him.

But he had made a promise and he never broke his word. Without his uncle's help, another sister would die.

When Idiag finally spoke, his eyes were blank. Unfeeling. *"No, Parth,"* he'd said to his guard. *"He has suffered much to travail the winter's harshness to reach us, especially with nothing more than rags on his feet. We will give them shelter. Summon a wet nurse for the babe."*

Talon had wanted to collapse in relief.

"And the boy?"

"If he survives the punishment his mother ran away from, then he will be allowed to stay here as well."

Grinding his teeth, Talon remembered the grueling torture they had meted out. The days of beatings and starvation.

The only thing that kept him alive was the fear that should he die, Ceara would be turned out after all.

He had lived solely for her.

Now he lived for nothing at all.

Talon forced his feet to carry him down the street away from Sunshine's club and her comfort. Away from these memories that had somehow been set loose.

He had to find his peace.

He had to forget the past. To bury it.

But as he walked, repressed thoughts and memories tumbled through his mind.

Against his will, he remembered the day he had discovered his wife . . .

Nynia.

Even now, the mere mention of her name was enough to bring him to his knees. She had been everything to him. His best friend. His heart. His soul.

She, alone, had given him solace.

In her arms, he hadn't cared what the others thought of him. Only the two of them had existed in the world.

As a mortal man, he had taken her as his first and only lover.

"How could I ever lay hands to another woman, Nyn, when I have you?"

Those words haunted him now along with the memory of how many women he'd slept with since his death. Women who had never meant anything to him. They had merely been passing flings designed to ease a physical craving.

He had never wanted to know anything about them.

Never really wanted to know any woman except his wife.

Nynia and the perfect love she had given him had touched something inside him and given it wings. She'd shown him things in the world that he'd never seen before.

Kindness.

Comfort.

Acceptance.

She had confused him, aggravated him, and made him deliriously happy.

When she had died, she had taken him with her. He had survived physically, but not his heart.

It had died that day too.

And he'd never thought to desire a woman that way again. Not until he had felt the warmth of a graceful artist's hand on his skin.

The mere thought of Sunshine was enough to make him feel sucker-punched.

"Get her out of my head," he said between clenched

teeth. He would never again let himself be open to so much excruciating pain. He would never again hold someone he cared for in his arms and watch her die.

Never.

He had been hurt enough in his life. He couldn't stand any more.

Sunshine was a stranger to him and she would remain that way. He didn't need anyone.

He never had.

Talon froze as an odd noise on the wind intruded on his thoughts. It sounded vaguely like a Daimon feeding . . .

He pulled his Palm Pilot out of his jacket pocket and opened up his tracking program. Designed to pick up traces of the Daimons' elevated neuron activity that came from their psychic abilities, the tracking program allowed Dark-Hunters to pinpoint any concentration of Daimons after dark. During the daylight hours while the Daimons rested, their brain activity was too human for the trackers to be of any use.

But once the sun set . . .

Those little brains of theirs started snapping and humming.

Talon frowned at his findings.

It showed nothing and his Dark-Hunter senses didn't pick up a Daimon either, but his gut instinct was off the radar.

He headed toward a dark alley. A woman stumbled out, falling against him. Her eyes were glazed as she glanced up at him. There was a small bite wound on her neck that was healing even as he looked at it and the collar of her blouse held traces of blood.

"Are you okay?" he asked as he righted her.

She smiled a smile that was delirious and vague. "I'm fine. Never better." She stumbled away from him and headed into the building to his right.

In that instant, he knew what had happened.

Unmitigated rage descended on him as he stalked farther

into the alley where she'd been. He saw the dark shadow and knew it in a heartbeat.

"Damn you, Zarek. You better lay off the feeding crap while you're in this city."

Zarek wiped the blood away from his lips with his hand. "Or what, Celt? You going to hit me?"

"I'll rip your throat out."

He laughed at that. "And kill yourself in the process? You don't have it in you."

"You have no idea what I'm capable of. And you better pray to whatever god you worship that you never find out."

His expression pure evil, Zarek smacked his lips in a way Talon knew was designed to piss him off thoroughly.

It worked.

"I didn't hurt her. She won't even remember it in three minutes. They never do."

Talon moved to grab him, but Zarek caught his hand. "I warned you not to touch me, Celt. No one touches me. *Ever.*"

Talon shrugged off his hold. "You swore an oath, just like the rest of us. I won't have you preying on innocents in my town."

"Oooo," Zarek breathed. "How cliché, little partner. Wanna tell me to be out by sunup, or better yet, this town ain't big enough for the two of us?"

"What is your problem?"

Zarek started past him.

Unwilling to let him prey on someone else, Talon shoved him against the wall. His own back throbbed viciously as if he'd been slammed against the wall too, but he didn't care.

He wasn't about to let Zarek have free rein over the lives of innocent people.

Zarek's eyes flared with hatred. "Let go of me, Celt, or I'll rip your arm off. And you know what? I don't care if I lose both of mine in the process. That's the difference between us. Pain is my friend and ally. You fear it."

"Like hell I do."

He shoved Talon away from him. "Then where is it? Hmmm? You buried your pain the night you left your village in flames."

Talon paused at the words, wondering how Zarek knew that, but his anger overrode it as he thought about Zarek judging him. "At least I don't wallow in it."

Zarek laughed at that. "Do I look like I'm wallowing? I was having fun with her until you showed up." He licked his lips again as if resavoring the feeding.

"You should try it sometime, Celt. There's nothing like tasting human blood. Haven't you ever wondered why the Daimons feed before they take human souls? Why they don't just kill the human quick? It's because it's better than sex. Did you know you can see straight into their minds when you do it? Feel their emotions? For one instant, you actually bond with their life force. It's one hell of a high."

Talon glared at him. "Nick's right, you are psychotic."

"The correct term is *sociopathic* and yes, I am. But at least I have no delusions about myself."

"Meaning?"

He shrugged. "Take your meaning wherever you can find it."

The man was disgusting. Insufferable. "Why do you have to make everyone hate you?"

Zarek snorted at that. "What? You want to be my friend now, Celt? If I clean up my act, will you be my buddy?"

"You're such an asshole."

"Yeah, but at least I know what I am. I have no pretensions. You don't know if you're a Druid, a Dark-Hunter, or a playboy. You lost yourself a long time ago in the dark hole where you buried the parts of you that once made you human."

Talon was aghast at such a low, self-serving life-form trying to play sage with him. "*You* are lecturing *me* on humanity?"

"Ironic as hell, isn't it?"

Talon's jaw ticced. "You don't know anything about me."

With his silver claws flashing, Zarek slowly pulled a cigarette out of his jacket pocket and lit it with an old-fashioned gold lighter.

Putting the lighter back in his pocket, he took a long drag on the cigarette, exhaled the smoke, then cast Talon a sardonic, lopsided sneer. "Ditto."

With one last, parting grimace, Zarek walked slowly away from him, out of the alley and back toward the street.

"Lay off the feeding, Zarek, or I will kill you myself. I swear it."

Zarek raised his clawed hand and flipped him off without breaking stride or looking back.

Talon growled low in his throat as Zarek vanished into the night. How could Acheron stand dealing with him? That man could try the patience of a tree.

One day, Artemis was going to have to put Zarek down. In truth, Talon was astounded the order for Zarek's execution hadn't already been handed out. But then maybe that was why Artemis had sent him here. In Alaska, Zarek was on his home turf where he knew the terrain better than anyone and he would be able to avoid an executioner.

Down here, Zarek was at the mercy of Acheron, who knew these streets like the back of his hand. If the order came down, Zarek would have nowhere to hide.

It was definitely a thought.

Talon shook his head to clear it of Zarek. The ex-slave was the last person he wanted on his mind tonight.

His cell phone rang. Talon answered it to find Acheron's thick Atlantean accent.

"Hey, I'm down on Commerce Street in the Warehouse District. There's a murder scene here that I would like to confer with you about."

"I'm on my way." Talon hung up and headed to where he'd left his motorcycle.

It didn't take long to grab his bike and make his way over to the scene. Cops were everywhere, questioning witnesses, marking off the area, and taking notes and pictures.

A large crowd of locals and tourists had gathered to watch the spectacle.

His eyes aching from all the bright police lights, Talon parked his bike and made his way over to Acheron, whose hair was now blond.

Jeez, the man changed hair colors more often than most people changed socks.

"What's up, T-Rex?"

Acheron grimaced at the nickname, but didn't comment. He inclined his head toward the body that had been draped with a body bag, but not yet sealed up. "That woman died barely an hour ago. Tell me what you feel."

"Nothing." As soon as the word left his lips, Talon understood. Whenever someone died, their soul lingered for a brief time before it moved on. There was only one exception to that—when the soul was captured and trapped by someone else. "It was a Daimon kill?"

Acheron shook his head no.

"Is she a new Dark-Hunter?"

Again the *no* shake. "Someone fed on her until they drained the life out of her and could steal her departing soul. Then they ripped her apart with something like a claw. The police are trying to convince themselves that it's an animal, but the depth and precision of her wounds are too precise."

Talon went cold. "Claws like the ones Zarek wears?"

Acheron turned his head to stare straight at him. All Talon could see was himself in the dark lenses. "What do you think?"

Talon ran his hand along the edge of his jaw as he watched the police work over the area. This was disturbing.

"Look, T-Rex, I know you have a soft spot for Zarek, but I have to tell you that I found him having lunch a few minutes ago outside of a club. It looked like he was enjoying himself a little too much, if you know what I mean."

"So you think he killed this woman?"

Talon hesitated as he remembered what Zarek had said when he had caught him with the woman in the alley. *I didn't hurt her.* Was that an admission he had hurt someone else or was it a statement that he never hurt the women he fed on?

"I don't know," Talon answered honestly. "If you're asking me if he's capable, I'd definitely say yes. But I sure would hate to consign a man to Shadedom without more evidence."

Shadedom was the hellish existence that came to any Dark-Hunter who died without a soul. Since they no longer had a real body or a soul, their essence suffered eternity trapped between this plane of existence and the next. It was said to be the most grueling torture imaginable.

"So what do you think?" Talon asked. "Do you believe he did it?"

A slow smile slid across Acheron's face, but he didn't answer the question. The hair on the back of Talon's neck rose. Something about all this just didn't seem right.

For that matter, something about Acheron didn't seem quite right either.

Acheron took a step away from him. "I'll go talk to my good buddy Zarek, and see what he says."

Talon frowned. This definitely wasn't right. Acheron never referred to anyone as his "buddy."

"By the way," Acheron said. "How are you doing? You seem tense. Uneasy."

He was. It was like someone had opened a floodgate on his hormones and emotions, and he wasn't sure how to close it again.

But he didn't intend to burden Acheron with that. He could control himself.

"I'm fine."

Talon glanced away from Acheron for a second to watch the arrival of the coroner. "By the way, T-Rex, what happened to your nose stud and . . ." His voice trailed off as he turned back and saw nothing but empty space.

Talon looked about.

Acheron was gone. The only trace of his presence was

two bloody shoe prints that marked the concrete where he'd stood a second ago.

What the hell?

Acheron had never done that before. Man, this night was getting stranger by the hour.

". . . there's a disturbance on Canal Street. At Club Runningwolf's . . ."

Talon's heart stopped at the words he overheard from a police scanner.

Sunshine.

Every instinct he possessed told him it involved her. He ran for his bike and quickly headed back toward the club.

Chapter 6

By the time Talon reached Sunshine's club again, it was complete chaos on the street outside the club's entrance and in the alley behind it.

A large crowd of people stood around outside where two ambulances were parked while medics tended three wounded officers. Someone had beaten them to a pulp.

He paused near one ambulance as he heard the officer giving his report to a detective.

"He was at least six feet six. Lean, muscular build. Caucasian male dressed in black, with long black hair and a goatee. Mid- to late twenties with this huge silver claw thing on his hand. He looked like the devil himself when we came up on him. Man, he tore through us like we was nothing. I got at least two bullets into him and he didn't even flinch when I shot him. He just kept on coming at us. He must be on PCP or something."

Talon froze.

Zarek. There was no one else who could fit that description.

Damn. He shouldn't have left the area while Zarek was here. Zarek must have attacked them just a few minutes after he left.

"So what happened?" the detective asked.

"Me and Gabe had a disturbance call about a fight in the alley. We got here in time to see the claw guy fighting two men. We yelled for them to stop, but the guy ignored us. He ripped their hearts right out of them. Right in front of us."

Talon groaned. They had seen Zarek take out a pair of Daimons. Great. Just great. He closed his eyes and cursed. This night was starting to rate right up there with abscessed teeth.

"Johnny got here right as I pulled my weapon and ordered the claw guy to stop. He turned on us like a wild beast. Next thing I know, I'm on the ground bleeding, you guys are here, and he's gone."

"And the bodies?"

"He must have taken them with him while we were trying to get to the cars for safety. I'm telling you, Bob, the man was insane."

Talon raked his hands through his hair. Not even in town one night and now Zarek had the entire police force looking for him.

How had the man managed to last so long?

His phone rang again, but the caller ID didn't display the caller's identity. Expecting it to be Acheron since Acheron's phone almost never registered a number, he was surprised to hear Zarek's thick Greek accent on the other end. "The Daimons wanted to party with your girlfriend, Celt. Don't leave her unprotected."

The phone went dead.

An eerie chill went up Talon's spine. How could Zarek have known about him and Sunshine?

The man's powers were rating right up there with Acheron's.

His instincts on alert, Talon looked up to the roof above his head—to the old abandoned drugstore next door to the club. Silhouetted against the dark sky was a figure. To a human's eyes, the man standing on the rooftop would be invisible, but Talon's honed Dark-Hunter vision saw him clearly.

It was Zarek.

Zarek inclined his head to him, put the phone in his

pocket, then stepped back and vanished into the darkness.

Talon frowned. Psycho Zarek had been watching over Sunshine all this time? Even while the cops were looking for him?

How unlike Zarek was that?

Talon immediately hit the automatic call-back feature on his phone.

"What?" Zarek asked, his voice surly. "Can't you see I'm trying to get out of here before the cops find me?"

"What were you doing at Runningwolf's?"

"Picking my nose, Celt. What do you think? I saw the Daimons on the street and I tracked them inside."

That explained that, but Talon had a bigger concern. "How did you know about me and Sunshine?"

"I overheard the Daimons talking about the two of you. You should be more careful, Celt. A mistake like that one could be costly."

"Costly how, Zarek? I've just seen the body of a woman who'd been drained of her blood and her soul."

"Ooo," Zarek breathed. "Here's a news flash. It was a Daimon attack. Ever notice that tends to be their MO?"

"Yeah, but I've never known a Daimon to *claw* a woman up while killing her. Have you?"

There was a brief pause. "What are you saying?"

"I think you know, Zarek."

"Yeah, and you can kiss my ass, Celt. Maybe I should have left your bitch to them after all."

The phone went dead again.

Talon ground his teeth, torn between the deep need to find Zarek, beat the crap out of him, and wash his mouth out, and a deeper need to make sure Sunshine was okay.

Putting his phone in his pocket, he decided to leave Zarek to Acheron, who'd already said he was going to talk to him. Acheron was much better at handling Zarek anyway.

At least Ash could kill the bastard and not die in the process.

Talon expelled a long breath as he thought over Zarek's

warning that the Daimons were after Sunshine. It didn't make a bit of sense.

Why would the Daimons be after her? And how could the Daimons know about the two of them?

This made the second attack on her in as many nights. Daimons took their victims where they found them. They didn't stalk someone who got away. They just moved on to the next handy meal.

He didn't know what they wanted with her, but until he found out, he wasn't going to leave her in danger.

Scanning the crowd, Talon found Sunshine standing just under a light outside the club, next to a large, muscular man with black hair who was speaking to a uniformed police officer. She wore only her thin black sweater without the fuchsia one she'd had on earlier. Her arms were crossed over her chest as if she were cold.

Talon made his way through the crowd to her side.

Her face lit up the moment she saw him. "Talon? What are you doing here?"

He was more relieved than he would have thought possible. Just seeing her here, unharmed, and hearing his name on her lips . . .

He shouldn't feel anything for her and yet there was no denying the raw emotions he felt every time she met his gaze.

"Are you okay?" he asked, shrugging off his jacket and holding it up for her.

She nodded as she allowed him to help her into his jacket. "Did you hear what happened? Some guy went nuts in the alley where I park my car and killed two men. Then, he attacked the police. It's terrible!"

Before he could think, Talon pulled her into his arms and held her close. She was shaking and cold, but she still felt so wonderful that he didn't want to let go of her. "I'm glad you weren't hurt."

The man who'd been talking to the police officer looked at them with a stern scowl. "You know, bud, I don't know you from Adam, but that's my baby sister you're hanging on to. So I'm thinking the wisest course of action for you is to let her go and introduce yourself. Pronto."

Talon bit back a smile. He knew exactly what the man meant. Some things were very sacred and little sisters were one of them.

Reluctantly, he withdrew from her.

Sunshine punched her brother gently on his arm. "Talon, this is my brother Rain. Rain, meet Talon."

Her brother snorted. "God, with a name like Talon your parents must have been holdover hippies too."

"Something like that."

"That's his pet phrase," Sunshine told her brother. "That and *not exactly*."

Rain sized him up, then offered him his hand. "Nice meeting you, Talon. I better get back to work. Sunny, yell if you need one of us."

The implied threat wasn't lost on Talon, who bit back a smile. If the man only knew how much power a Dark-Hunter wielded . . .

"Us?" Talon repeated.

Her brother indicated two men over Talon's shoulder who were also talking to the police. The older man was a Native American whose shamanic powers were easily discernible, and her other brother was almost a facial clone of Sunshine. "Our father and older brother, Storm, work in the club too."

Talon gave a tight-lipped smile as he turned back to face Rain. "Storm, Rain, and Sunshine, huh?"

She grimaced. "My mother's doing. I'm just glad she stopped at three. I was told the next one would have been named Cloudy Day."

He laughed at that. Gods, how he'd missed her. All he wanted to do right now was take her into his arms and run her up to her bed and inspect every inch of her to make sure she was unhurt.

Yeah, okay, so he had another, less pure, motive for that thought too. But still he felt an insane need to prove to himself that no one had touched her.

That she was completely whole and safe.

He darted his gaze all over her body, assuring himself that she was fine. His concern for her was so unlike anything he'd experienced in such a long time that he wasn't really sure how to cope with it.

Rain excused himself and drifted back into the club, leaving them alone.

An awkwardness fell between them as he tried to think of something to say to her.

Finally, she cleared her throat. "I didn't think I'd see you again."

He didn't know what to respond to that, especially since that had been his intention. "I . . . um . . ."

"Oh, you want Snoopy back."

"No," he said quickly. "I came back for you."

A slow, seductive smile spread over her face. "Really?" she asked.

"Yeah. I heard about the attack and was worried," he said before he could stop himself.

"Really?" she repeated.

He nodded.

Smiling wider, she walked herself into his arms. "That was very sweet of you."

Not really, Talon thought as he held her and inhaled her warm patchouli scent. But he had to admit she felt good in his arms. Her breasts were flattened against him and all he could think about was how delicious they had tasted, how soft and good they had felt in his hands.

He groaned inwardly at the thought.

Walk away from her . . .

I have to protect her.

He was sworn to protect humans. Especially those the Daimons would prey upon. It was his duty to keep her with him. To watch over her.

Hey, how stupid do you think I am, Talon? This is yourself you're talking to and all the lies in the world aren't going to convince me that you have a moral or noble reason for this. You want in her bed again. Admit it.

Oh, come on, I can control myself for a few days. She

has to be protected and who else could do it?

Zarek was out of the question. He'd end up feeding off her and Talon would kill him if the psycho dared to touch her. Valerius would sooner die than watch over a "plebeian." Nick would make a move on her, and he'd have to kill the horny toad. Kyrian had a new baby and was too exhausted to think, and Acheron . . .

He had too many responsibilities pulling at him to worry about baby-sitting.

That left him and him alone.

"You know, Sunshine, I don't think you should stay in your loft alone."

She stepped away from him. "Believe me, I'm not. I'm going home with Storm tonight."

Talon paused. That wasn't an option either. Her brother was a big man, but no match for a Daimon.

"I don't know, Sunshine. I'm thinking . . ." Well, he couldn't really say what he was thinking, especially the part that bordered on salaciousness.

But then he didn't have to. She smiled a wicked smile. "You know, if you want me to go home with *you,* all you have to do is ask."

"I didn't think it would be that easy."

She rose up on her tiptoes and gave him a devilish look. "For anyone other than you, it wouldn't be."

Those words made his heart soar. He really liked this woman. She was bold, quirky, and sassy.

Sunshine took his hand and led him into, and through, the club to a door in the far right rear corner. It opened into the back hallway that Talon recognized from earlier in the evening. On the right was the door to the outside where her car was parked and on the left was the steel staircase that led up to her loft. She headed for the stairs.

Sunshine held tight to Talon's hand as she mentally castigated herself. She probably shouldn't be doing this, especially since two murders had been committed tonight. But instinctively she knew Talon would never hurt her.

He'd saved her life and he'd done nothing even remotely harmful to her.

Besides, she liked being with him. She could take her art supplies with her and get back on schedule tomorrow.

Tonight, she just wanted a few more minutes with him. One more evening to bask in his warmth before she went back to the rigors of her life.

It had been so considerate of him to offer her his jacket. His warmth and scent clung to it, making her want to snuggle in deep.

She entered her loft, gave him back his jacket, and left him by her white and pink striped couch while she went to pack an overnight bag. In all honesty, she'd rather stay with him than Storm anyway.

Storm snored.

Loudly.

Not to mention that the last time she had gone to her brother's place, she'd had to spend two hours cleaning it before she was able to touch anything in the apartment without cringing. He was an absolute pig and he didn't care about making her feel welcome. Rather, he treated her as a live-in servant who should be happy to do for ole big brother.

And ole big brother stunk. Not literally, but in the figurative sense.

She grabbed a change of clothes, shoes, and hair ties and shoved them into her wicker tote bag along with her toothbrush and moisturizer—a woman always needed her moisturizer—then she rejoined Talon.

He stood at the rear of the loft, near the windows, looking through the landscape paintings she'd done of Jackson Square. Her breath caught in her throat.

What was it about this man that was so powerful? His wavy blond hair fell around his face while his two thin braids hung down to his shoulder. His black leather pants cupped a butt so fine that it should be stamped with *Grade A Prime* on each cheek. And his back . . . Even with his jacket on, she knew how perfect and well sculpted it was.

She stared at his large, tawny hands that held her work. They were so strong and at the same time tender. She loved the way they had felt on her body, the way his fingers had tasted when she nibbled them.

The man was simply scrumptious from the top of his blond head to the bottom of his black biker boots.

He turned slightly as she joined him. "I like the way you painted the sun coming in over the cathedral. I can almost feel the sun when I look at it."

His compliment warmed her. An artist never heard enough compliments on her work. "Thank you. My favorite is the sunset over it. I love to watch the light fading around the buildings. When it hits some of the signs and glass, it makes them glow and sparkle like fire."

He reached out and cupped her face in his warm palm. "You have such an incredible way of capturing things."

She bit her lip and gave him an impish smile. "Yes, I do." And little did he know it, but she fully intended to capture him as well. At least for a little while.

He was like some wild, untamed creature that you could keep and feed for a time, but in the end you knew you'd have to let it go for its own sake as well as yours.

"So, tell me, where do you live?" she asked.

He cleared his throat and dropped his hand from her cheek.

The uncomfortable look on his face made her stomach sink. "Oh Lord, you do have your own place, don't you? You don't happen to live with your mom or some creepy old aunt?"

He looked offended by that. "Of course I have my own place. It's just . . ." His voice trailed off and he looked away.

Oh sheez, here it comes . . . "You have a live-in girl-friend?"

"No."

Ugh! It was even worse than she thought. "Live-in boy-friend?"

He gaped at her while his midnight eyes flashed with

indignation. "Jeez, Sunshine, what do you think I am?"

"I don't know, Talon. I asked a simple question and you got all weird on me. What am I supposed to think?" She swept her gaze down the expensive biker's outfit he wore. The man had a body to beat the band and was too bodacious to be real. That tended to make a woman go, hmmm . . .

"And you do wear a lot of leather."

"What's that supposed to mean?"

She gave him a *duh* stare. "I am an artist, you know. I tend to hang out with an awful lot of homosexual and bisexual guys."

If he had looked offended before, it was nothing compared to the look on his face now. "Now there's a stereotype I hadn't even considered. Thank you very much. For your information, I happen to like leather since it tends to protect *my* hide on the occasions when I wreck my motorcycle and go skidding down asphalt."

"Well, that's true too. So why did you get all weird on me when I asked you where you live?"

"Because I figured if I told you where I lived, you'd get *all weird* on me."

She hesitated as a million scary locations came to her mind. He lived in a cemetery or crypt. A run-down shack. A cardboard box. A dock house. A broken-down camper or bus. Good Lord, in this city there was no telling where he might make his home. "Okay, you live somewhere freaky, don't you?"

"I live out in the bayou."

Relieved, she scoffed at his evasiveness over something so silly. "Oh please, I know several people who live out by the bayou."

"Not *by* the bayou, Sunshine. I live *in* the bayou."

Was he serious? Who in their right mind lived in the bayou with the snakes and gators and other things she didn't want to even think about? Things that carried guns and did lots of illegal activities like feeding murdered bodies to gators.

"You live *in* the bayou?"

He nodded. "It's really peaceful out there. No modern sounds to intrude on you. No neighbors. No traffic. You can almost feel like you're living centuries ago."

There was a wistful look to him as he said that. "That means a lot to you, doesn't it?"

"Yes. It does."

She smiled. Yeah, she could see Talon out in the bayou all alone. He reminded her a lot of her father, who loved to spend hours outside just soaking up nature. They both shared that quiet kind of peace-with-the-universe attitude.

"How long have you lived there?"

He avoided looking at her. "A really *long* time."

Sunshine nodded.

As they started for the door, she dropped her wicker tote and retrieved her Studiopack French Easel Backpack from the corner. She always kept it well stocked in case she decided on a whim to go some place else and paint.

"What is that?" he asked.

She winked at him. "An artist on the go, that's me. I never go anywhere without supplies."

He smiled as he took the backpack from her. "So, you're still feeling adventurous, huh?"

"Always. Just bring the gator-be-gone spray and I'm all yours."

Talon stared at her as he felt another stupid urge to grin. His face was starting to ache from the effort it took to not expose his fangs to her. She was extremely funny and amusing.

If not, to an extent, insulting.

He was still chafing over her assumptions about his clothes. The things this woman got into her head . . .

But he liked that about her. She didn't play games with him, but spoke whatever thought, no matter how outrageous, was on her mind.

Sunshine locked the door, got halfway down the stairs, then stopped. "Oh man, I forgot my overnight bag." She made a disgusted sound before sprinting up the stairs and rushing back inside her loft.

She came out a few minutes later with her wicker bag, reached the top of the stairs, then remembered she had no coat.

One more time, she went back inside before she rejoined him. "I swear I'd be wearing a pumpkin on my shoulders."

It took a second for her words to sink in—she'd lose her head if it ever came off her body.

Laughing, he paused on the stairs as she walked past him. "By the way, I don't look gay in leather."

Sunshine turned to look up at him. She passed a hot, lustful glance over his body that made him harden instantly. "No, baby, you don't. I honestly have to say you wear that outfit like nobody's business."

A slow smile spread across his face as he followed her the rest of the way out of the club.

Oh yeah, the two of them had some unfinished business to take care of once he got her home.

Business he shouldn't even be contemplating, but he had his reputation to uphold. Besides which, he owed her a payback. When she left his cabin, she'd never again doubt his sexual orientation or his attraction to her.

As they reached the outside doors, Sunshine led Talon away from the club.

"Are you going to tell your brother where you're going?"

She shook her head. "I'll call him in a little bit and tell him. Believe me, it's not something I want to do face to face."

"Stern, is he?"

"You've no idea."

Talon led her to his bike and pulled out a spare helmet from the saddlebags. "You want to put your backpack in here?"

She shook her head as she took the backpack from him and shrugged it on. "It's designed for motorcycles and hiking. I'm fine wearing it. It's really not that heavy."

"Ride many bikes, do you?"

"Yup, I do."

Talon watched her pull her helmet on and fasten it. Man, the woman was beautiful to him. Her long, graceful fingers tucked her braids in easily and her dark brown eyes glowed.

He removed the small sunglasses that he wore at night and pulled his own helmet on, then got on the bike and kick-started it. Sunshine joined him on the bike. Her arms came around his waist as she slid her body closer to his.

Talon almost moaned. He could feel every inch of her pressed intimately, erotically against him. Her breasts on his back, her inner thighs against his hips.

And the way her arms held him . . .

He could just imagine her sliding her hand down from his waist to the hard bulge in his pants where she could cup and stroke him through the leather. Of her unzipping his pants and kneading him gently with her hand as he hardened and strained to possess her.

Better yet, he could see her down on her knees in front of him, taking him into her mouth . . .

Unknown feelings swirled inside him, turning him inside out. All he wanted was to keep her here like this for eternity. To stop the bike and sample every inch of her lush, full figure with his mouth and fangs.

He wanted to devour her.

To taste and tease her until she called out his name while her body shook from ultimate pleasure.

Unbidden, he mentally felt her body arch against his as she clutched at his back in the midst of an orgasm.

He'd learned today that she always tensed her body until the last orgasmic shudder had subsided, and then she relaxed and rained kisses on his skin.

It was a sweet sensation that had no equal.

Talon clenched his teeth in an effort to control himself from yielding to the craving he felt for her body. He drove them through town, out toward the bayou where he lived.

As they rode, Sunshine leaned her head to rest between his shoulder blades and tightened her hold around Talon's lean, muscular abs. She remembered how he'd looked standing naked in her loft. The way he'd looked leaning over her as they made love. Slow. Easy. Then fast and furious.

This man had an indefinable way with his body. He knew every way and then some to give a woman pleasure.

Sunshine could feel his chest rise and fall under her arms as they rode through the dark night. What she was doing with him was insane and yet she couldn't seem to stop herself.

Talon was compelling. Dangerous. Dark and mysterious. Something about him made her just want to crawl inside him and stay there forever.

Crazy, huh?

Yet there was no denying what he did to her. What she felt every time she thought about him. The way she wanted to yell at him to stop the bike so that she could tear off his jacket and lick every inch of his tattoo.

Every inch of his powerful, masculine body.

Oh, how she wanted this man.

"Are you okay?"

She tensed at the sound of Talon's deeply accented voice in her ears. "Hey, your helmets are microphoned."

"Yeah, I know. But are you okay?"

She smiled at his concern. "I'm fine."

"You sure? You kind of jumped a second ago like something startled you."

"No, really. I'm fine."

Talon wasn't so sure and at the moment he wished one of his Dark-Hunter powers included mind-reading. Unfortunately, his powers ran more along the lines of commanding the elements, healing, projection, and telekinesis. He was better able to shield himself and others, which was why, unlike Zarek, he never had to worry about cops or anyone else seeing him slay a Daimon.

He could summon the elements to shield him from people's sight or to confuse them. If need be, he could even project new thoughts to someone to alter their perceptions of reality.

But he preferred not to do that. The human mind was frail and such tactics had been known to leave lasting damage.

With his arcane powers came a great deal of responsibility. Acheron had taught him that.

Having been abused as a child by those who had more strength and power than he did, Talon had no wish to victimize anyone else. There was nothing he wanted or needed so badly that he would violate someone else to get it.

They didn't speak again until he reached his garage at the end of a long, winding dirt road. There were no lights out here, no pavement. Nothing but Louisiana wildlife.

Sunshine frowned as their headlight illuminated a strange mailbox out in the middle of nowhere. It was a black box that appeared to be pierced by two long silver nails. One was going horizontally through the box, the other diagonally.

She cringed at the sight of the dilapidated shack they neared and she hoped this wasn't his house. It looked like it was ready to cave in.

If not for the clean, crisp mailbox, she wouldn't have believed anyone had been out here in a hundred or more years.

Talon stopped the bike and held it upright between his muscular thighs. He pulled a small remote from his pocket and used it to open the dilapidated shack door. It lifted up slowly.

Sunshine gaped as the lights came on and she saw inside the "shack."

There was nothing run-down about the inside of the building. It was high tech and sparkling, and filled with a fortune in motorcycles and one sleek black Viper.

Oh God, he *was* a drug dealer!

Her stomach knotted in fear of what she had let herself in for. She should never have come out here with him!

He parked the motorcycle next to the car, then helped her off the seat.

"Um . . . Talon?" she asked, looking around his collection of vintage Harleys. "What do you do for a living? You said you were an illegal alien, right?"

He gave that familiar tight-lipped smile as he placed his helmet on a rack that contained twelve helmets she was sure cost a minimum of a thousand dollars each. "Yes, and to answer your first question, I'm independently wealthy."

"And you got that way how?"

"I was born into it."

Sunshine felt a little better, but she still had to ask the one question that was nagging her most. "So you don't do anything illegal like run drugs, right?"

Once again, he looked offended. "Good Lord no, woman. Why would you think that?"

Her eyes wide, she looked around the expensive garage and high-tech male toys. "I have *no* idea."

He pressed a button and closed the main door, sealing them in.

She followed after him while he led her to the back of the garage where he had two very nice, expensive catamarans docked. Everything in this building was truly state-of-the-art. "If you have all this money, why are you an illegal alien?"

Talon snorted. He could tell her that he was in this bayou before America was even a country, and that he didn't need any stinking piece of paper to make him legal, but as a Dark-Hunter he was forbidden to tell her anything about their lifestyle or existence. So he opted for an easy and true excuse. "You have go to the courthouse during daylight hours to fill out the paperwork. Since I can't go out into sunlight . . ."

She looked at him skeptically. "Are you sure you're not a vampire?"

"I wasn't until the moment I saw you."

"Meaning?"

He moved to stand next to her so that she had to crane

her neck to look up at him. His jaw flexed as he stared down at her while his body craved hers in a way most desperate. "Meaning I would love nothing more than to sink my teeth into your skin and devour you."

She bit her lower lip and gave him an impish, heated once-over. "Mmm, I like it when you talk like that."

She stepped into his arms.

Talon's body burned as he dipped his head down to kiss her.

Sunshine moaned at the taste of him. What was it about this man that attracted her so and made her want to gobble him up?

He pulled back suddenly and she pouted in protest.

"We'd best hurry," he said. "It'll be dawn before much longer and it's still a ride to my cabin."

"Your cabin? Is it anything like this shack?"

"You'll see." He moved away from her to start the catamaran.

Sunshine took a seat and strapped herself in. Once she was secured, they left the comfort of the garage and headed out into the eerie darkness of the swamp. The engine's motor was so loud, it made her ears ache as they sped toward his cabin.

It was so dark out here that she couldn't focus her eyes on anything at all.

How could Talon see to drive the boat? Any minute, she half expected them to plow into a tree or stump.

And yet Talon maneuvered them effortlessly without any hesitation or slowing of speed.

After a few minutes, her eyes adjusted to the blackness and she was able to see outlines and swamp gas. Mostly, she just saw fog and a few things that looked vaguely like animals falling into the water.

Maybe she was better off blind after all.

At long last, they reached a small isolated cabin set deep in the swamp. Alone. Isolated. Spanish moss hung down from the top of the porch and the wood of the place had lightened to a faint gray that stood out even in the darkness of the night.

Talon parked the catamaran beside a small dock and got out. He helped her onto the dock and as she followed him up the narrow plank toward the dark porch, she realized there were two alligators in front of the door.

She screamed.

"Shh," Talon said with a laugh. "There's nothing to fear."

To her extreme astonishment, he bent down and patted the biggest gator on the head. "Hey Beth, how's it going tonight?"

The gator snapped its jaw and hissed at him as if it had understood his question.

"I know, girl. I'm sorry, I forgot."

"What are you? Dr. Dolittle?"

He laughed again. "No. I found these two when they were small hatchlings and raised them. We're family. I've known them so long that I can almost read their minds."

Well, she had reptiles in her family tree too. Only hers walked on two legs.

The big one came up to her and eyeballed her like she was the daily special at the Crocodile Cafe. "I don't think she likes me."

"Be nice, Beth," Talon said.

The gator swished its tail, then ambled off the porch, into the swamp water. The other one looked at her, snapped its jaws, then joined its friend.

Talon opened the door to his cabin and turned on a dim desk lamp. Sunshine stepped inside hesitantly, half afraid he'd have the housekeeping abilities of her brother.

Or that there would be something worse than gators inside. Something like a monster anaconda he intended to feed her to.

She hesitated in the doorway.

The place was bigger inside than it appeared from the outside, but it was still basically only one room. There was a small kitchen off to her left and a door to her right she assumed was the bathroom.

He had three big tables set up with computers and other electronic equipment. And there was a large black futon on the floor to the rear of the cabin.

She was thankful everything was clean and sanitary. How wonderfully refreshing to know that all men weren't the pigs her brothers were.

"Interesting place you have here, Talon. Have to say I love the blank, black walls."

He snorted at her tone. "This from a woman who lives inside a pink cloud?"

"True, but everything here is so dark. Don't you find it depressing?"

He shrugged. "Not really. I no longer think about it at all."

"Not to be rude, but it seems to me that you do that a lot."

"Do what?"

"Not think about things. You're one of those guys who just exists, aren't you? No thought about the past or tomorrow. Just what you plan on doing in the next hour or so."

Talon dropped his keys on the table next to his primary computer. She was very astute. One of the drawbacks of immortality was the fact that you weren't really goal-oriented. His world existed of getting up, tracking and slaying Daimons, and then returning home.

A Dark-Hunter never thought about the future. It just kept on coming regardless.

As for the past . . .

There was no need to go there. All that would do was dredge up memories he was much better off not remembering.

He looked at her and the passionate gleam in her dark brown eyes. She had a love of life that glowed and it captivated him. What would it be like to live that way again? To actually look forward to the future and plan for it?

"You probably think about the future all the time," he said quietly.

"Of course."

"And what do you see in your future?"

She shrugged her backpack off and placed it by his desk. "It depends. Sometimes I dream of having my art hung in the Guggenheim or the Met."

"Do you ever dream of having a family?"

"Everyone has those dreams."

"No, not everyone."

She frowned. "You really don't?"

Talon fell quiet as he recalled his wife's face and remembered the nights he'd lain awake while she slept by his side with his hand on her belly so that he could feel their son moving inside her.

The dreams he'd had then.

When he had looked into Nynia's eyes, he had seen into forever. Had imagined the two of them old and happy and surrounded by their children and grandchildren.

And with one overwrought emotional act, he had damned both of them and ruined every dream the two of them had shared.

Every hope they'd had.

He winced as pain lacerated his chest.

"No," he whispered past the sudden lump in his throat. "I don't think about having a family at all."

Sunshine frowned at the thickness she heard in his voice. He cleared his throat.

What about her question could have possibly hurt him?

As he showed her where to store her bag and backpack, the phone rang.

Talon moved to answer it while she set about unpacking a few essentials and laying them about the cabin.

"Hey Nick . . . yeah, I heard about Zarek." He gave her a sheepish look as he listened. "Nah, man. I . . . um. I'm not alone right now, okay?"

He moved away from her, but still she could hear him

plainly. He was acting kind of nervous and she wondered why.

"I spoke with Zarek earlier, and he had definitely been sucking on the red mojo juice right before that happened. I don't know what got into him, but he was in a foul mood." He paused for several minutes. "Yeah, and listen, I have a woman here, her name is Sunshine. If she calls you for anything, get it for her without shooting off your mouth . . . Yeah, back at you." He hung up the phone.

"Who's Nick?" she asked.

"He's my personal assistant. He's on payroll, so anything you need, you just push four and the pound sign and it'll ring his cell phone."

Ooo that was neat. "Really? You have a personal assistant?"

"Unbelievable, isn't it?"

"Well, I have to say you are the first biker I've ever met who has a stock portfolio and an assistant."

He laughed.

"So, what's 'red mojo juice'?" she asked. "Some kind of wine?"

He looked *very* uncomfortable. "Something like that."

There he went again with his secrets. Ugh! The man needed to loosen up a bit. Be more trusting.

She'd definitely have to work on him.

Talon headed for the small kitchen. "I don't know about you, but I'm kind of wired. I don't normally go to sleep until a couple of hours after dawn. You hungry?"

She watched him search through his cabinets and pull out a couple of pans. "Not really, but I can make you something if you like."

He looked up, his face startled by her offer. "Thanks. That'd be nice."

She took the pan from his hand and set it on the stove. "So what are you in the mood for?"

He licked his lips sinfully as his gaze roamed over her body, making her instantly hot. Needful.

"How about naked Sunshine al dente covered in

whipped cream and chocolate?" He brushed the hair back from her neck. "We could even put a cherry on top."

She laughed at that. "That could be arranged."

Sunshine moaned as he dipped his head down and nuzzled her neck while he cupped her breasts in his hands.

Her breasts tingled and swelled as desire swept through her, making her instantly wet and throbbing for him.

"Are you always this insatiable?" she asked.

"Only when I see something I want," he said, moving his hand to cup her between her legs. "And you I want most of all."

She hissed at how good his fingers felt stroking her through the denim.

Her heart pounding, she looked down to watch his hands as he unfastened her jeans. His long, finely shaped fingers opened her fly, pushing the flaps aside until her lacy white panties showed. He teased her ear with his tongue, his breath hot against her skin, as he dipped his hand under the elastic band and found the center of her body.

Sunshine reeled at the sight of his hand there, of his fingers gently caressing her nether lips. His tanned skin stood out darkly against the white as he slid his fingers inside her.

Groaning, she rubbed herself against him, needing to feel him deep inside her again.

He growled like a ferocious beast before he knelt down behind her and pulled her jeans and panties free.

At his bidding, Sunshine allowed him to remove her shoes and jeans.

He was on his knees and still completely dressed as he turned her to face him and stared at the dark triangle between her legs.

His obsidian gaze met hers and she saw the fire inside him. "Open yourself for me, Sunshine. I want you to invite me in."

She blushed at what he was asking. She'd never in her life done anything like this and yet she wanted to please him.

Swallowing her inhibitions, she parted her legs and

reached down to open her nether lips for him. "I'm all yours, baby."

He was like a wild, hungry beast as he buried his face between her legs and took her into his mouth.

Sunshine cried out in pleasure. She leaned back against the counter for support. His tongue swirled, then he gently sucked and nibbled. She buried her hands in his soft hair, her body burning at his touch.

Her nipples were so tight they hurt. "Oh yes, Talon, yes," she breathed, pressing him closer to her.

Talon growled deep and low in his throat as he tasted her. Her feminine scent invaded his head as her graceful hand tugged at his hair.

He ran his tongue over the hard edge of her cleft, sampling and tasting the woman before him. It had been so long since anyone or anything had given him this much pleasure.

But please him she did.

Her passion, her creativity, her quirkiness. All of it was a magnet that drew him against his will.

He licked and teased her. Tasted her. Let her murmurs of pleasure become his and when she came, calling out his name, he swore that he saw stars from it.

Sunshine's breath came in short, sharp gasps as she looked down to see Talon rising up from the floor. He towered over her, his eyes dark, his face still hungry.

"What is it about you that I can't resist?" he asked. "Every time I get near you, all I can think of is tasting you."

He led her hand to his groin where she felt him hard and throbbing for her.

"I don't know," she said, her voice ragged as she dipped her hand below his waistband and trailed her fingers through his short, crisp hairs until she could wrap her fingers around his swollen manhood.

He drew his breath in sharply.

"But I feel the same for you," she said, sinking her hand lower, seeking out his soft sac.

He closed his eyes, his jaw flexing, as she caressed him. She knew she gave him pleasure and yet he acted as if her touch pained him.

She felt strangely vulnerable as she stood there with her lower body exposed while she wore her sweater and bra. Talon was still fully clothed.

It was erotic and disconcerting.

As if sensing her thoughts, Talon removed the rest of her clothes. She was completely naked now.

He was not.

He ran his hands over her, masterfully, tenderly. "Tell me your fantasies, Sunshine. Tell me what you dream about late at night when you're lying in bed alone."

She'd never in her life shared such an intimacy and yet before she realized what she was doing, she found herself confiding in him. "I dream of a handsome stranger approaching me."

He circled behind her. "And?"

"It's dark and hot. I imagine him standing behind me and pulling me against him. Feeling him take me from behind while I can't see him at all, I can only feel him."

Talon moved away from her and turned out the light.

Sunshine shivered in the darkness. "Talon?"

"Shh." His deep, accented voice seemed to engulf her.

Then she felt his hands on her. Completely blind, she was all sensation as he pulled her back to his front and she realized he'd removed his jacket and shirt. He ran his hands over her breasts, cupping them while he nibbled the back of her neck.

She'd had this fantasy for years, but never before had it been real. Never had she seen her dream man's face. Tonight, she envisioned Talon. She imagined what his hand looked like as he resumed stroking her between her legs.

She heard him unzip his pants. The heat of his body warmed hers as he whispered to her in a language she didn't understand. It deepened his voice, made it even more enticing.

Erotic.

Then, he was inside her, hot and hard. She moaned, arching her back, as he sank himself deep into her over and over again.

He buried his hands in her hair while nibbling her shoulders. Her neck.

His touch was hot, scorching.

He bent her forward.

Sunshine gasped as he penetrated her even deeper than before. He thrust himself against her, pounding pleasure into her body with such intensity that she found herself moaning and gasping in time to his movements.

Talon clenched his teeth as he felt her body clutching his. She was so wet and hot, so silky. It was crazy but when he was inside her, he could almost feel his missing soul.

"Come for me, Sunshine," he whispered in Gaelic, then he remembered that she couldn't understand him so he offered her the translation.

"Talon." Her voice was a mixture of pain and pleasure. Of hot, demanding need. She was on the edge of climax.

Seeking to help her reach it, he reached his hand down to her cleft and stroked her in time to his thrusts.

She screamed out almost immediately as she came in his arms. Talon quickly joined her in that place of divine pleasure.

They were both sweaty and panting as he pulled her naked body back against his. He laughed in her ear, grateful that for once he didn't have to hide his fangs when he smiled.

In the dark, she couldn't see him.

But he could see her plainly. Her long, black braids were hanging down, trapped between her back and his chest. The scent of them hung thick in the air and she was wet and hot against him.

He carried her to a chair and sat down with her in his lap. They were both still panting and weak.

She leaned back against him, then reached her arm up

around his neck to hold him close. He ran his mouth and tongue over her cheek, nibbling her gently.

Sunshine had never before been like this with a man.

Sure, she'd had sex and her ex-husband had been a horny toad, but she'd never wanted anyone the way she wanted Talon.

His body was so warm and hard beneath her, so innately masculine, that she had no desire to ever move again from his lap.

She sighed contentedly.

"Talon, do you do this with every woman you meet?"

"No," he whispered in her ear. "I don't, and I've never brought a woman out to my cabin before. You're definitely a special case."

"You sure?"

"Positive. What about you? Do you go home with every guy you meet?"

She leaned back, wishing she could see his face. "No. I promise you, you're a special case too."

He kissed her gently.

They sat like that for a long time, just holding each other, lost in the quiet stillness of the dawn.

Sunshine wasn't sure what she felt for Talon. There was a part of her that wanted to hold on to him like this forever and another part of her that told her she was an idiot for thinking any such thing about a guy she had just met.

Yeah, he looked great in leather pants and could rock every piece of her body, but at the end of the day would he bother hanging around, or would he be just like every other guy she'd known? Selfish. Possessive.

Judgmental.

She didn't know for sure.

She wasn't sure if she wanted to wait around and find out.

Sunshine yawned. It had been a long night, emotionally and physically draining.

Now all she wanted to do was cuddle up to that warm masculine body and sleep.

Talon felt suddenly awkward. Bringing her here had seemed like a good idea at the time, but now that he thought about actually going to bed with her to sleep . . .

It was an intimacy that he hadn't experienced since the death of his wife. There were plenty of times he'd had sex with women and afterward they had both drifted off to sleep for a little while, but this was entirely different.

They would actually spend the day together. Sleeping. Their bodies touching . . .

She yawned again. "I'll be right back."

Turning on the light for her, Talon didn't say anything as she grabbed a T-shirt from her bag and headed to his bathroom.

While she was gone, he listened to her in the other room. He could hear the water running as she washed her face and brushed her teeth.

This felt so strange.

Memories drifted through his head. Memories of a life he'd purposely forgotten.

Memories of a man he'd buried.

He remembered countless nights when he had climbed into bed to wait for his wife as she readied herself for sleep. Nights when he had watched her brush her hair until it gleamed in the firelight and then braided it before she joined him.

Nights of listening to her hum while she sewed before the fire . . .

He gazed over to his dresser where Sunshine had placed a small cosmetics bag, a pink hairbrush, and a small bottle that probably contained her patchouli oil.

He stared at the dainty items that looked so out of place among his belongings. Items that were feminine and foreign, and that wrung his gut.

How he'd missed sharing his life with someone. Having someone to care for, someone who cared for him.

It was something he hadn't thought about in a long, long time. Something he hadn't dared think about.

Now that he thought about it, he had to admit life as a

Dark-Hunter did have moments of profound loneliness.

Sunshine came out with her black hair still braided and her legs peeking out from the hem of the shirt. The smile on her face tugged at his warrior's heart.

Centuries ago, he'd looked forward to battle, knowing that if he survived, he would return to the warm embrace of loving arms. The comfort of a friend.

As a Dark-Hunter the best he could hope for after battle was curling up to the computer or phone and sharing the fight with someone who lived hundreds, if not thousands, of miles away.

That had never bothered him before.

Tonight for some reason, it did.

"You okay?" she asked.

He nodded.

Sunshine wasn't so sure of his answer. There was a haunted look to his face. "Have you changed your mind about me staying over?"

"No," he said quickly. "It's just been a long night."

She nodded. "Tell me about it."

She climbed into his bed and pulled the black comforter over her body, then turned out the lamp by the bed.

Talon turned to look at her. She lay on her side, facing the wall. Her head looked small against his king-sized pillow and she looked so tiny and womanly against the blackness of his bed.

Most of all, she looked delectable.

He lay down beside her. Before he could stop himself, he pulled her into his arms, spooning up behind her.

"Mmm," she breathed sleepily. "I really like it when you do that."

Pain ripped through him as he closed his eyes and inhaled her unique scent. She felt so incredibly good in his arms.

Nae! his mind roared. He couldn't do it. He couldn't let himself care for her that way.

There could never be anything between them. Tomorrow

he would have to let her go back to her life while he returned to his.

That was the way of things.

Kissing her gently on the back of her head, he sighed and forced himself to sleep. He could never have her; she could never be more than a passing whim for him.

Never.

Sunshine lay there for quite some time listening to Talon breathe. There were no words to convey exactly what she felt lying beside this man. It was as if they fit. As if they were meant to be together.

Why was that?

She wasn't sure how long she lay there before sleep overtook her, but when she finally slept, she found herself having the strangest dream . . .

She saw Talon as a young man, probably no older than twenty. His long golden-blond hair was braided down his back while the two shorter, thinner braids dangled from his left temple. His youthful face was covered in a thick dark blond beard, but still she recognized him.

Recognized him as a young man who meant the entire world to her.

He held himself above her, his hard, masculine body naked and pressed against her own as he slid himself in and out of her with such tenderness that it made her heart soar and ache at the same time.

"Oh, precious Nyn," he breathed in her ear. He drove himself deep and hard into her, punctuating each word he spoke. "How can I leave you?"

She cupped his face in her hands and kissed him, then forced him back so that she could look into his amber eyes as he made love to her. "You've no choice, Speirr. You've fought too hard and suffered too much to be heir not to do this. This will ensure that the clan will take you as their king when your uncle dies."

She saw the anguish in his eyes and felt his body grow rigid around hers. "I know."

They loved each other so much. They always had. Ever

since the day when she was six and he eight, and he had nobly saved her from a flogging by a rooster.

He had been the hero of her heart.

They'd grown up apart and yet never parted.

Even as children, they had known their friendship would be stopped or ridiculed, and Speirr had suffered enough ridicule to last ten thousand lifetimes.

She would never hurt him more.

So they had never told anyone of the times when they would sneak away from their families and duties to be together.

For years their meetings had been innocent. Meeting to play a game or to fish. Sometimes to swim, or to share the heartbreaks they felt.

It had only been during this last year that they had dared touch each other's bodies.

She was the daughter of a fishmonger—the lowest of the low. Even so, Speirr had never treated her as the others did. He never mentioned that she smelled of fish oil or wore clothes that were threadbare and patched.

He'd respected her and treasured her friendship as much as she treasured his.

She had given him her virginity gladly, knowing there could never be anything between them. Knowing the day would come when he would have to marry another.

And though it broke her heart, she knew she had no choice except to let him go now. He needed to marry another to erase the taint his mother had left with him. To prove to everyone that he was noble in blood as well as in spirit.

"You will make a fine husband, Speirr. She is lucky to have you."

"Don't," he said, holding her tighter. "I don't want to think of anyone else while I'm with you. Just hold me, Nyn. Let me pretend for one moment that I'm not my mother's son. Let me pretend that there's only you and I in the world and no one and nothing to ever separate us."

She clenched her eyes shut as pain assailed her.

How she wished it were true.

He pulled back to look down at her. He cupped her face tenderly. "You are the only warmth in my heart. The only sunshine my winter has ever known."

Oh, how she loved him like this. When he, the fierce, bold warrior-prince, dared to be the bard who lived in his heart. Only she knew this side of him. Only she had ever known he had the talent of a poet.

To the rest of the world he must always be fierce and strong. A fighter of unquestionable prowess and skill.

But it was his poet's heart she loved best.

"And you are my fire," she breathed. "And if you don't go off and meet with your uncle now, he'll extinguish you."

He cursed as he pulled away from her.

She watched him dress and helped lace him back into his armor. He was a prince. Not just in title, but in bearing and form. There had never been a more noble man.

After she was dressed, he pulled her into his arms and gave her one last scorching kiss. "Meet me tonight?"

She looked away. "If you wish it, Speirr. I will do anything you ask, but I don't think it will be fair to your new wife to meet you on your wedding night."

He flinched as if she'd slapped him. "You're right, Nyn. Most of all, it wouldn't be fair to you."

Sunshine moaned as she felt herself leaving Nynia and moving toward Speirr. They were still by the loch, only now it was him she felt. His emotions.

It was through his eyes she saw them.

Speirr was heartbroken as he watched Nynia step out of his embrace. The pain inside him was so intense that he feared it would cripple him.

He reached his hand out for her, knowing she was gone. Lost.

Lost to him forever.

Just as his mother had been.

Just as his sisters and father were.

Gods, it was so unfair.

But then, life was never fair. Especially not to a man

who had duties and responsibilities. A man who had to force respect for himself and his sister at the point of his sword.

His life had never been his own.

Turning away from her, he mounted his horse and rode to meet his aunt and uncle so that they could finalize the marriage between their clan and the Gaulish-Celt tribe that bordered them to the north.

This marriage would finally silence the tongues of the gossips and doomsayers who wanted someone else to be named heir.

Sunshine thrashed in her sleep as her dream shifted. She saw Talon later that day, standing between a beautiful woman in her early thirties and a man only a few years older. The woman had the same blond hair and blue eyes as Talon while the man was black haired and black eyed.

They stood in the middle of an old wood hall. The room was crowded with people who were strangers to the three of them. Everyone was dressed in fine plaids and wore gold jewelry.

Speirr's uncle was dressed in black leather armor and his aunt in gold armor with a long, plaid skirt.

To the people gathered there, Talon looked strong and proud. Fierce and princely.

The Gauls' whispered voices echoed in the room as they retold stories of his prowess in battle, told each other that he was the Morrigán's favored warrior.

It was said the goddess herself walked beside him in battle and dared anyone to mar his beauty or dull his sword.

What no one knew was that Speirr was ready to bolt as he waited to meet his bride.

"I swear, lad, you're as skittish as a colt," his aunt whispered with a laugh.

"You were too, Ora," his uncle teased her. "I remember your father threatened to tie you to his side if you didn't stop fidgeting while our parents bound us together."

"Aye, but I was much younger than he is."

His aunt placed a comforting hand on his shoulder.

Speirr took a deep breath as a young woman was brought forward to stand before him.

"My daughter Deirdre," King Llewd said.

She was beautiful. That was Speirr's first thought. With hair as golden fair as any he'd ever seen and blue eyes that were kind and gentle.

But she was no match for his Nynia. No other woman could ever come close to her.

Speirr stepped back instinctively.

His uncle pushed him forward.

Deirdre smiled invitingly. Her eyes warm and accepting.

He stepped back again.

This time, his aunt nudged him toward his bride. "What have you to say to her, lad?"

"I . . ." Speirr knew the words that would bind them together. He'd rehearsed them incessantly.

But now they lodged in his throat.

He couldn't breathe.

He stepped back again, and again his aunt and uncle moved him forward, toward her and a destiny that seemed suddenly bleak. Cold.

"Speirr," his uncle said with a warning note in his voice. "Say the words."

Do it, or you will lose everything.

Do it, and I will lose the only thing.

In his mind, he saw the hurt in Nynia's eyes. Saw the tears she'd tried to hide.

Speirr clenched his teeth, flexing his jaw with determination. "I willna do this." He whirled around and left the hall, hearing the shocked gasps as he made his way to the door and out into the village.

A few seconds later, his aunt and uncle came rushing out behind him. He was halfway to his horse when his uncle grabbed his arm and pulled him roughly to a stop.

"What is wrong with you?" he demanded.

"Speirr?" his aunt said in a gentler tone. "What is it?"

He looked back and forth between them, searching for

the words to make them understand what was in his heart. "I willna marry her."

"Oh aye, you will," his uncle said sternly. His dark eyes snapped fire at him. "Now march yourself back in there and finish this."

"Nae," he said stubbornly. "I willna marry her while I love someone else."

"Who?" they asked in unison.

"Nynia."

They exchanged a deep frown.

"Who the blazes is Nynia?" his uncle asked.

"The fishmonger's daughter?" his aunt said.

The two questions came at him at once. Until his aunt's comment registered in his uncle's mind.

"The fishmonger's daughter?" he repeated.

His uncle moved to pop him on the back of his head, but Speirr caught his hand and glared at him. His days of being hit by his uncle were long over.

"Are you mad?" his uncle demanded, wrenching his arm free. "How do you even know her?"

Speirr tensed, expecting his uncle's condemnation. No doubt they would finally banish him from their clan just as they had done his mother.

None of that mattered.

Nynia was the only person who had ever really accepted him.

He would not fail her by marrying someone else while she had to go back to the misery of her life.

He refused to grow old without her.

"I know you don't understand and I know I should just go and marry the Gaul's daughter, but I can't." He looked at his aunt, hoping someone would understand his plight. "I love Nynia. I don't want to live without her."

"You are young and foolish," his uncle said. "Just like your mother, you let your heart rule you. If you fail to do this, you will never live down your mother's shame. You will be seen as nothing more than a ridiculed whoreson. Now get back in that hall and marry Deirdre. Now!"

"Nae," he said firmly.

"So help me, Speirr, fail to do this and I will see you banished for it."

"Then banish me."

"Nae," his aunt said, intruding on their argument.

She held that distant, faraway look that she got whenever she saw through the natural world into a higher level. "The gods are at work here, Idiag. Look into his eyes. Nynia is his soulmate. They are meant to be together."

His uncle cursed. "This would have been a great alliance for our clan," he muttered bitterly. "It would have ensured peace between our peoples and guaranteed that no one would have contested Speirr as my heir. But I won't argue with the will of the gods."

He patted Speirr on the arm. "Go, Speirr. Go claim your Nynia while I try and salvage what I can from this meeting and hopefully avert a war."

Speirr blinked in disbelief. It was the first time in his life that his uncle had ever been kind or merciful toward him. "Do you mean it?"

He narrowed his eyes at him. "Lad, you'd best be off before common sense returns to me."

Speirr shouted as he raced for his horse. Then he ran back and hugged his aunt, then his uncle. "Thank you. Thank you both."

As fast as he could, he ran to his horse and jumped up onto the back of it. He set his heels into its flanks and headed toward their own lands.

Speirr tore through the forest at a dead run. His black stallion flew through the tangled underbrush and weeds, kicking up dirt in their wake. The sunlight drifted through the trees, dappling his armor as he urged the horse faster.

He had to reach his Nynia . . .

Nynia sighed as her mother handed her the tattered old basket that held ten nasty-smelling fish. "Must I deliver this?" she asked her mother, her voice pleading for clemency.

"Your brother is off on an errand and they be wanting it. Now go, child. I'll brook no more arguments from you."

Nynia clenched her teeth as she took the basket. How she hated this. She would rather be beaten than travel to the smith's home where Eala would no doubt be waiting to take her delivery. Her own age, Eala was the smith's daughter but she acted as if she were descended from a line as noble as Speirr's.

The girl took great pleasure in humiliating her.

And today, Nynia was in no mood for it. Not while her heart was so sore from its loss.

By now her Speirr would be married to another. He would be lost to her forever.

Blinking back tears, she left the tiny hut she shared with her mother, father, and brother, and headed for the nicer side of the village where the rest of the people resided, upwind from the fishmonger, tanner, and butcher.

"Oh, Speirr," she whispered as she wiped away her tears. How could she make it through a single day without him? All her life she'd had him to see her through the misery of her work. She'd always looked forward to their meetings. Looked forward to sharing laughter and fun with him down by the loch.

Now those days were gone forever.

When he returned, it would be with a new wife.

One day, his queen would bear his children . . .

Pain assailed her even more. Nynia walked aimlessly through the village, her thoughts on the only man she would ever love and on the fact that she would never bear his children. Never be able to hold him again.

She drew near the smith's cottage and saw Eala wasn't alone today. She stood with a small group of friends, talking. She recognized three of the boys, and the girls would have been her friends, too, had she, as they so often reminded her, not smelled of fish.

"Oh bother," Eala said disgustedly. "It's the fish girl

with her fetid stench. Quick, everyone, hold your breath or you'll turn blue."

Nynia lifted her chin. They couldn't hurt her with their words. Not today. She was hurt enough.

She shoved the basket into Eala's hands.

Eala shrieked. "You're vile, Nynia!" she shouted, dropping the basket and dancing away from it. "No man will ever want so smelly a woman. Will he, Dearg?"

Dearg turned a speculative eye on Nynia. "I don't know. From what we saw her giving to Speirr the other day, I'd be willing to hold my nose."

Her face on fire, Nynia was horrified that someone had stumbled upon her and Speirr while they were making love in the woods.

"What say you, Aberth?" Dearg asked another handsome youth.

"Aye. She'd be good for a tup or two, especially since she's sheathed a strong sword, but you can marry her if you're like Speirr and common filth is to your taste. I'd rather not."

Their mean laughter rang in her ears.

Humiliated and embarrassed, Nynia had started away from them when she caught the sound of a horse approaching at a dead run.

Everyone in the village grew quiet at the sound. It was obvious the rider was in a dire hurry. His thick, deep voice could be heard urging the horse onward toward the village.

The instant Speirr came flying out of the woods, people scattered out of his way.

Nynia couldn't move as she watched him.

He had his head bent low, and both he and the horse were covered in sweat. United in power, beauty, and form, the two of them were a fierce and frightening sight to behold.

They flew as if the demons of Annwn were hot on their heels.

She expected him to keep riding past her, toward his home.

He didn't.

Instead, Speirr reined his horse in sharply before her, the fierce beast rearing and pawing at the air.

He jumped from his saddle and swept her up into his arms.

Her heart pounded with joy, but she was scared of this. Scared of what his disheveled appearance here meant.

"Fiù?" she asked hesitantly, using the proper term for *prince*, knowing that with so many witnesses, she could never call him by his given name. "What is it you would have of me?"

His amber eyes were shiny and bright and filled with his heart as he stared at her. "I would have you, my love," he breathed. "Every day for the rest of my life. I've come to marry you, Nyn. If you'll have me."

Tears filled her eyes. "Your uncle?"

"He wishes us well and will meet you when he returns."

Her hands shook as she held him tight.

"You are mine, precious Nyn," he whispered. "I want no other in my life."

"Even though I smell like a fish?"

He laughed at that. "And I smell like a sweaty horse. We're a perfect pair, you and I."

Only he would say such a thing.

Tears rolled down her face as she held him close and wept from happiness.

Her Speirr had come back to her and she would never let him go. They were meant to be together.

Forever . . .

Sunshine woke up with a feeling of warm serenity deep in her heart. She felt the weight of Talon behind her and smiled sleepily.

She didn't really remember her dream other than the fact that it had been about Talon.

And it had comforted her.

She checked her wristwatch and saw it was just after

noon. She should be at work by now, hawking her artwork in the square.

Yet she had no desire to get out of this futon.

Rolling over, she snuggled into Talon's body.

She laid her head on his shoulder and traced the tattoo on his chest. He was so warm and inviting.

"It's good to have you home, love." He whispered those words to her in a language she'd only heard once before when they had been making love last night, and yet she understood him.

She lifted herself up and realized he was still sound asleep. "Talon?"

He didn't budge.

"Speirr?" she asked, wondering why that name came to her mind, but somehow it seemed only right that she should call him that.

His eyes fluttered open. He frowned at her. "Do you need something?"

Sunshine shook her head.

He closed his eyes, rolled over and returned to sleep.

Oh, this was just too friggin' weird.

Why did she know that name and why did he respond to it?

Had it been part of her dream?

She tried to recall it, and for her life she couldn't.

As he lay there with his back to her, she saw something in her mind's eye. It was like a vague childhood memory.

She saw Talon as an adolescent youth, stretched out over a large stone table. There were other monolithic stones around them, forming something that vaguely reminded her of Stonehenge.

Talon was lying on his stomach, his arms under his head, as a tall, dark-haired man leaned over him. The man's black robes billowed as he beat Talon with a frayed whip.

Talon was looking straight at her, his eyes shining with unshed tears while he kept his jaw firmly locked.

Meet me later. He mouthed the words to her and she nodded.

Sunshine pulled back, alarmed.

Her dream rushing back to her, she scrambled from the bed and grabbed Talon's cell phone, then called her mother. She stepped outside the cabin's door so that Talon couldn't overhear her conversation.

"Sunshine?" her mother asked as soon as she recognized Sunshine's voice. "Where are you? Storm said you blew him off last night without calling."

"I'm sorry, Mom. You know me. I got distracted and forgot to call. Listen, I need to know something. Do you remember years ago when you and Grandma did that whole past-life regression thing on me?"

"Yes?"

"I remember you and Grandma telling me that I was an ancient Celt, right?"

"Yes."

"Do you remember anything more specific than that?"

"No, not really. I'd have to call Mom and see if she remembers. Knowing her, she might. Why? You sound panicked."

"I am panicked. I'm having some bizarre flashback kind of thing. I don't know what else to call it. It's just very, very weird."

"Are you with Steve?"

"Talon, Mom, his name is Talon. And yes, I am."

"You think you knew him in a previous life?"

Sunshine looked back at the door and swallowed. "Honestly, Mom, I'm thinking I was married to him."

Chapter 7

It was shortly after sunset when Acheron knocked on Zarek's door. He'd spent most of the day with Artemis, discussing what needed to be done since the human authorities were now looking for Zarek.

He could still see Artemis lying nonchalantly on her white-cushioned throne, her beautiful face completely disinterested. *"I already told you, Acheron, kill him. Only you are blind to the man's character. It's why I wanted him in New Orleans in the first place. I wanted you to see firsthand just how far gone he is."*

Ash refused to believe it. He, better than anyone, understood Zarek's nastiness. The need to strike the first blow before it struck you.

So he'd bargained with Artemis for more time for Zarek to prove to the goddess that he wasn't some rabid animal in need of a mercy killing.

But how Ash hated bargaining with her for anything. Still, he wasn't going to sign the order for Zarek's execution. Not yet. Not while there was still hope.

He knocked again. Harder. If Zarek was sleeping upstairs, he might not hear him.

The door swung open slowly.

Ash walked inside, his eyes instantly adjusting to the pitch-blackness. He closed the door with a mental push and reached out with his senses.

Zarek was in the sitting room on his left.

The ex-slave had neglected to turn on the heat so the house had a frigid chill to it. But then, Zarek was so used to the subzero temps in Alaska that he probably didn't even notice the more moderate cold of New Orleans in February.

Heading for the sitting room, Ash stopped as he caught sight of Zarek lying on the floor by the Victorian sofa. Dressed only in black sweatpants, Zarek appeared to be asleep, but Ash knew he wasn't.

Zarek's senses were as honed as his own and the ex-slave would never allow anyone to enter his sleeping area without being fully alert and ready to strike.

Ash let his gaze wander over Zarek's bare back. On the lower part of his spine was a highly stylized dragon. It was the only mark his back currently held, but Ash remembered a time when Zarek's flesh had been covered in scars so deep that Ash had actually flinched the first time he'd seen them.

A whipping boy for Valerius's family, Zarek had grown up paying the price every time Valerius or his brothers had crossed the line.

The scars hadn't been just on his back. They had been on his legs, chest, arms, and face. One facial scar over his blinded left eye had been so severe that Zarek had barely been able to open the eye. The scar on the cheek below that eye had given his face a twisted, misshapen look.

In his human lifetime, Zarek had walked with a pronounced limp and his right arm had barely functioned.

When he'd first crossed over and become a Dark-Hunter, Zarek hadn't even been able to meet Ash's gaze. He'd stared at the floor, cringing every time Ash moved.

Normally, Ash gave newly created Dark-Hunters a choice of keeping their physical scars or having them removed. In Zarek's case, he hadn't asked. Zarek's body had been so badly damaged that he had erased them immediately.

His second course of action had been to teach the man to fight back.

And fight back he'd done. By the time Ash had finished his training, Zarek had unleashed a fury so strong that it gave him incredible powers.

Unfortunately, it also made the man uncontrollable.

"You gonna keep staring at me, Great Acheron, or are you ready to chew me a new one?"

Ash sighed. Zarek still hadn't moved. He lay there with his back to him, his arm tucked under his head.

"What do you want me to say to you, Z? You knew better than to attack a cop. Never mind three of them."

"So what? I was supposed to let them handcuff me and take me to jail where I could wait for sunup in a cell?"

He ignored Zarek's rancor. "What happened?"

"They saw me kill the Daimons and tried to apprehend me. I merely protected myself."

"Protecting yourself doesn't require giving one a concussion, one a set of broken ribs, and another one a busted jaw."

Zarek rolled to his feet and glared at him. "What happened to them was their own fault. They should have backed off when I told them to."

Ash returned Zarek's glare even keel. Zarek possessed the ability to stir his anger even faster than Artemis did. "Dammit, Z, I'm tired of taking shit from Artemis because you can't behave."

"What's the matter, Highness? Can't take the criticism? I guess that's what happens when you grow up noble. You never have to worry about having your behavior censored. Everyone thinks you're perfect. Meanwhile you're free to frolic through your life. Tell me, what made you a Dark-Hunter? Someone scuff your boots and get away with it?"

Ash closed his eyes and counted to twenty. Slowly. He knew ten would never be enough to calm him.

Zarek raked him with that familiar sneer. The ex-slave had always hated him. But Ash didn't take it personally. Zarek hated everyone.

"I know what you think of me, O Great Acheron. I know how much you pity me and I don't need it. Do you honestly think I could ever forget the way you looked at me the first night we met? You stood there with horror in your eyes as you tried not to show it to me.

"Well, you achieved your good deed. You cleaned up your little foundling and made him all pretty and healthy. But don't even think that means I have to lick your boots or kiss your ass for it. My days of subjugation are over."

Ash growled low in his throat as he fought down the urge to splinter the man against the far wall. "Don't push me, Z. I'm the only thing standing between you and a deathly existence so bad it's beyond even your comprehension."

"Go ahead then. Kill me. Do you really think I give a damn?"

No, he didn't. Zarek had been born with a death wish. Both as a mortal man and as a Dark-Hunter. But Ash would never again kill a Dark-Hunter and send him into the agony of Shadedom. He knew firsthand the horrors of that existence.

"Shave your goatee, take the earring out, and keep your damn claws hidden. If you're smart, you'll stay away from the cops."

"Is that an order?"

Ash used his powers to lift Zarek from the floor and pin him roughly against the ceiling. "Stop pushing your luck, boy. I've had it with you."

Zarek actually laughed. "Have you ever thought of hiring yourself out to Disneyland? People would pay a fortune for this ride."

Ash growled louder, baring his fangs at the impudent ass.

It was seriously hard to intimidate a man who had nothing in life that meant anything to him. Dealing with Zarek made him feel like a parent with an out-of-control child.

Ash lowered him to the floor before he yielded to the temptation of strangling him.

Zarek narrowed his eyes as his feet connected with the floor. He walked nonchalantly to his duffel bag and pulled out a pack of cigarettes.

He knew better than to taunt the Atlantean. Acheron could extinguish him in a heartbeat if he chose to. But then, Acheron still held his humanity. He actually had compassion for other people, which was a weakness Zarek had never possessed. No one had ever given a damn about him so why should he care about anyone else?

He lit his cigarette as Acheron turned to leave.

"Talon will patrol around Canal, so I want you to take the area from Jackson Square to Esplanade."

Zarek exhaled the smoke. "Anything else?"

"Behave, Z. For the love of Zeus, behave."

Zarek took a long drag on his cigarette as Acheron opened the door without touching it and strode out of his house.

He held his cigarette between his teeth and raked his hands through his tousled black hair.

Behave.

He could almost laugh at the order.

It wasn't his fault that trouble always came looking for him. But he'd never been one to dodge anything either. He'd learned a long time ago to take his hits and his pain.

He clenched his teeth as he remembered last night. He'd seen the Daimons on the street as they headed to Sunshine's loft. Heard them talking about how they intended to damage her. So he'd followed them, until he had a chance to fight them without anyone seeing them.

The next thing he knew, he had four bullet wounds in his side and a cop screaming at him to freeze.

At first, he'd intended to let them arrest him and then call Nick to bail him out, but when one of the cops had hit him across the back with his nightstick, all good intentions had gone straight to hell.

His days as a whipping boy were over.

No one was ever going to touch him again.

Sunshine sat outside Talon's cabin, working on the paintings Cameron Scott had commissioned from her. While

Talon slept inside, she'd been out here for hours, trying to figure out why she was still here with him in his swamp.

Why she had come out here with him last night when she should have just gone over to her brother's.

Her revelation about their past life together had really freaked her out.

She had been his passive, June Cleaver wife . . .

Sunshine shivered. She didn't want to be anyone's wife. Not any more.

Marriage was a losing venture for a woman. Her ex-husband had taught her well that guys didn't want a wife so much as a maid who could provide them with sex on tap.

An artist like her, Jerry Gagne had seemed the perfect match. They had met in art school and she had fallen in love with the moody, mysterious goth chicness of him.

At that time in her life, she had loved him zealously and couldn't imagine a day without him in it.

She thought they were two comfortable peas who could carve out a pod that would last them for the rest of their lives. She'd assumed Jerry would understand her need to create and that he would respect her and give her the room she needed to grow as an artist.

What Jerry had wanted was for her to take care of him while *he* grew as an artist. Her needs and desires had always taken a backseat to his.

Their marriage had lasted two years, four months, and twenty-two days.

Not all of it had been bad. Part of her still loved him. She'd enjoyed having company and someone to share her life with, but she didn't want to go back to being the one who was responsible for where someone else put his socks—she could barely remember where she put her own socks. Dropping her projects and going to the store because someone forgot to get the eggs that he had to have for his homemade paints.

It was always her plans that changed. Her stuff that could wait.

Jerry had never made any kind of concession to her.

She didn't want to lose herself to a man again. She wanted her own life. Her own career.

Talon was a great guy, but he struck her as a creature like herself. A loner who valued his privacy. They had had a great time so far, but she was sure they weren't compatible.

She was someone who actually liked to get up and paint in the daylight. Talon stayed up all night long. She loved tofu and granola. He loved junk food and coffee.

She and Jerry had kept the same schedule, had all the same likes, and look what had happened. If they couldn't make a go of it, then it certainly didn't bode well for any kind of real relationship with Talon.

No, she needed to get back to her life.

As soon as he got up and they ate, she was going to tell him to take her home.

Talon sighed in his sleep. It had been a long time since he had last dreamt of his wife. He hadn't dared. Thoughts of Nynia had always had the ability to tear his heart out.

But today, she was there with him. There in his dreams where they could be together.

His throat tight, he watched her sitting before his hearth, her belly distended with his child while she sewed clothes for the baby. Even after five years of marriage and a lifetime of friendship, she was able to stir his blood and make his heart swell with love.

Growing up under his uncle's scornful eye and the disdain of the clan, he had only found her to give him comfort. She alone had made him feel loved.

He listened to her hum the same lullaby his mother had once sung to him when he was a very small child.

Gods, how he needed her. Now more than ever before. He was weary of fighting, weary of the demands his people had placed upon him since the death of his uncle.

Weary of hearing the whispers about his mother and father.

He was a young man, but tonight he felt ancient. And cold.

Until he looked at Nynia. She warmed him deep inside and made everything better.

How he loved her for it.

Moving forward, he sank down in front of her chair and placed his head in her lap. He wrapped his arms around her as he was wont to do and felt the baby kick his arm in protest.

"You've returned," she said gently, brushing her hand through his hair.

He didn't speak. He couldn't. Normally he would have bathed the blood from his armor and body before he sought her out, but the grief of the day was still too raw in his heart.

He needed to feel her gentle, soothing touch on his body, needed to know that for the moment she was safe and still with him.

Only she could ease the aching pain inside his heart.

His aunt was dead. Mutilated. He'd found the body when he'd gone to look for her after she didn't show up for the midday meal.

If he lived an eternity, he would never forget the grisly sight. It would live inside him along with the memory of his mother dying in his arms.

"It's the gods' curse," Parth had whispered earlier that evening, not knowing Talon was close enough to hear him speak to his brother. *"He is the whore's son. She lay with a Druid to beget a cursed lineage and now we'll all pay for it. The gods will punish us all."*

"Do you wish to challenge Speirr's sword for leadership?"

"Only a fool would challenge one such as he. Not even Cuchulainn could equal him."

"Then you'd best pray to the gods that he never hears you."

Talon clenched his eyes shut, trying to dampen the whispers that had haunted him all the days of his life.

"Speirr?" Nynia stroked his face. "Are they all slain?"

He nodded. After he had brought his aunt home, he had gathered his men and ridden after the Northern Gaul tribe. He'd found one of their daggers near her body and had known instantly they were responsible.

"I really am cursed, Nyn." The words stuck in his throat. After a lifetime of trying to prove to others that he wasn't cursed for his parents' actions, he was now cursed because of his own. "I should have listened to you when my uncle died. I should never have taken vengeance against the Northern clan. Now all I can do is fear what their gods will take from me next."

But in his heart, he already knew. There was nothing on earth more precious than the woman he held.

She was going to die.

Because of him.

It was *all* his fault. All of it.

He alone had brought the wrath of the Northern clan's gods down upon their heads.

There was no way to stop it. No way to keep her by his side.

The pain of it was more than he could bear. "I have offered up sacrifices to the Morrigan, but the Druids tell me it isn't enough. What more can I do?"

"Maybe this is the last. Maybe it will end now."

He hoped so. The alternative . . .

Nae, he couldn't lose his Nynia. Their gods could have anything but her . . .

Talon groaned as his dream shifted forward, into the future. He held his wife as she labored to bring their baby into the world.

They were both covered in sweat from the fire and hours of exertion. The midwife had opened a window and let in a cool breeze from the snow that was falling outside.

Nynia had always loved the snow, and the weather had

given them both hope that maybe everything would work out. Maybe the baby would be a new chance for all of them.

"Push!" the woman ordered.

Nynia's fingernails bit into his arms as she gripped him and screamed. Talon placed his cheek to hers, holding her close and whispering into her ear. "I've got you, my love. I'll never let you go."

She groaned deep and then relaxed as their son rushed out from inside her, into the hands of the midwife.

Nynia laughed as he kissed her cheek and hugged her tight.

But their joy was cut short as the child refused to respond to the old woman's attempts to wake him.

"The babe is dead." The woman's words rang in his head.

"Nae!" he snarled. "He sleeps. Rouse him."

"Nae, my *triath.* The child is stillborn. I'm truly sorry."

Nynia wept in his arms. "I am so sorry, Speirr, that I couldn't give you your son. I didn't mean to fail you."

"You didn't fail me, Nyn. You could never fail me."

Horrified and heartbroken, Talon held Nynia close as the midwife washed and dressed their son's small body.

He couldn't take his gaze from the babe.

His son had ten tiny fingers, ten perfect toes. A mop of thick, black hair. His face was beautiful and serene. Perfect.

Why did the child not live?

Why did he not breathe?

Grinding his teeth to stave off the pain, Talon willed the child to wake. Silently demanded his son to cry out and live.

How could something so perfect not breathe? Why couldn't the baby move and squall?

He was their son.

Their precious babe.

There was no reason why the child should not be alive and well. No reason other than the fact that Talon was a fool.

He had killed his own son.

Tears welled in his eyes. How many times had he held his hand over Nynia's stomach and felt the strength of his son's movements? Felt the loving pride of a father?

They had marked the days to the baby's birth. Had shared their hopes and dreams for him.

And now he would never know the boy who had already won his heart. Never see the child smile or grow.

"I am so sorry, Speirr," Nynia murmured over and over again, weeping.

He tightened his arms around her and whispered words of comfort. He had to be strong for her. She needed him now.

Kissing her cheek, Talon forced his tears away and offered her solace. "It's all right, my love. We'll have more children." But in his heart, he knew the truth. The god Camulus would never permit a child of his to live, and Talon would never again put Nynia through this. He loved her too much.

He was still holding her an hour later when all the color had faded from her face. When the last of his hopes had shattered and left him bereft of anything except resounding agony.

Nynia was dying from blood loss.

The midwife had done all she could, but in the end she had left them alone to say their goodbyes.

Nynia was leaving him.

He couldn't breathe.

He couldn't function.

She was dying.

Talon had picked Nynia up and cradled her against him. He was covered in her blood, but he didn't even notice. All he could think of was keeping her with him, making her well.

Live for me!

He willed his own life force into her body, but it wasn't enough.

Silently, he bargained with the gods to take anything

else—his life, his lands, his people. Anything. Just leave him his heart. He needed it too much to lose it like this.

"I love you, Speirr," she whispered softly.

He choked.

"You can't leave me, Nyn," he whispered as she shivered in his arms. "I don't know what to do without you."

"You will take care of Ceara as you promised your mother." She swallowed as she traced his lips with her cold hand. "My brave Speirr. Always strong and giving. I shall wait for you on the other side until Bran brings us together again."

He closed his eyes as tears seeped past his control. "I can't live without you, Nyn. I can't."

"You must, Speirr. Our people need you. Ceara needs you."

"And I need *you*."

She swallowed and looked up at him, her eyes full of fear. "I'm scared, Speirr. I don't want to die. I feel so cold. I've never gone anywhere without you before."

"I'll keep you warm." He pulled more furs over her and rubbed her arms. If he could just keep her warm, she would stay with him. He knew she would . . .

If he could just keep her warm.

"Why is it getting dark?" she asked, her voice trembling. "I don't want it to be dark yet. I just want to hold you for a little while longer."

"I'll hold you, Nyn. Don't worry, love. I have you."

She placed her hand against his cheek as a single tear fell. "I wish I had been the wife you deserved, Speirr. I wish I could have given you all the children you wanted."

Before he could speak, he felt it. The last expulsion of breath from her body before she went limp in his arms.

Enraged and heartsick, Talon threw his head back and gave his battle cry as pain tore through him. Tears fell down his face.

"Why!" he roared at the gods. "Damn you, Camulus. Why! Why couldn't you just kill *me* and have left her in peace?"

As expected, no one answered. The Morrigán had abandoned him, left him alone to face this pain.

"Why would the gods ever help a whoreson like you, boy? You're not fit for anything except licking the boots of your betters."

"Look at him, Idiag, he's pitiful and weak like his father before him. He'll never be anything. You might as well let us kill him now and spare the food to nurture a better child."

The voices of the past whipped through him, lacerating his aching heart.

"Are you a prince?" He heard Nynia's childhood voice from the day he had saved her from the rooster.

"I am nothing," he had answered.

"Nae, my lord, you are a prince. Only one so noble would brave the fearsome rooster to save a peasant."

She alone had ever made him feel noble or good.

She alone had made him want to live.

How could his precious Nynia be gone?

Sobbing, he held her and the baby for hours. Held them until the sun was shining bright outside on the snow and her family begged him to let them make preparations for the burials. But he didn't want to prepare them.

He didn't want to let them go.

Since the day they'd met, they'd never been apart for more than a few hours.

Her love and friendship had seen him through so much. Over the years, she had been his strength.

She was the best part of him.

"What am I to do, Nyn?" he whispered against her cold cheek as he rocked her. "What am I to do . . ."

Alone, he had sat there with her, lost. Cold. Aching.

The next day, he'd buried her out by the loch where the two of them had first started their childhood meetings. He could still see her waiting for him, her face bright with expectation. He could imagine her running across the snow, gathering up a handful to make a ball so that she could sneak up on him and drop it down his tunic.

He would have chased her then, and she would have run away, laughing.

She had adored the snow so much. Had always loved to tilt her head back and let the white, pure flakes fall onto her beautiful face and into her golden fair hair.

It seemed somehow wrong that she would have died on a day like this. A day that would have filled her with such happiness.

Wincing in pain, he wished that he lived somewhere where it never snowed. Someplace warm so that he would never again have to see this and be reminded of all he'd lost.

Oh gods, how could she be gone?

Talon growled from grief. He was on his hands and knees in the freezing snow, his heart bereft of anything except painful misery.

All he could focus on was Nynia lying in the ground, holding their baby to her breast. Of the fact that he wasn't there to protect her, to warm her. To take her by the hand and lead her wherever she was headed.

He felt a tiny hand on his shoulder.

Looking up, he saw the small face of his sister. Ceara had seen more than her fair share of tragedy.

"I'm still with you, Speirr. I won't leave you alone."

Talon wrapped his arms around her waist and drew her close. He held her as he wept. She was all he had left. And he would defy the gods themselves to keep her safe.

He hadn't been able to protect Nynia, but he would protect Ceara.

No one would harm her without dealing with him . . .

Talon came awake just before sunset with a sick feeling in his stomach.

He felt so alone.

His emotions were raw and tattered. He hadn't felt like this in centuries. Hadn't hurt like this since the night Acheron had taught him to bury his emotions.

Tonight, he truly felt the solitude of his life. The aching burn of it sliced through his chest, and he had to struggle to breathe.

Until he caught a whiff of something strange on his skin and in his bed.

Patchouli and turpentine.

Sunshine.

His heart instantly lightened as he thought of her and the way she stumbled through her vibrant life.

Inhaling her precious scent, he rolled over and found his bed empty.

Talon frowned. "Sunshine?"

He looked around and didn't see her anywhere.

"Would you leave me alone, you walking pair of boots!"

He cocked a brow at Sunshine's voice on the other side of his door. Before he could get up, the door swung open to show Sunshine fussing at Beth and the alligator hissing back in protest.

The two of them struggled in the doorway.

"Let go of my easel, you refugee from a luggage factory. If you need some wood for a toothpick, there's a bunch of it on the porch."

The side of his mouth quirked up at the sight of them battling it out, Sunshine inside his cabin and Beth on the porch.

"Beth," he snapped. "What are you doing?"

Beth opened her mouth, releasing the easel. Sunshine stumbled backward, into the cabin, with her easel in her hands. The gator hissed and snapped at him, swishing its tail and eyeballing Sunshine irritably.

"She says she was forcing you inside before it got dark and something decided to eat you," he told Sunshine.

"Tell Swamp Breath I was headed this way. Why was she . . ." Sunshine stopped and looked at him. "Oh jeez, am I really having a conversation with a gator?"

He grinned. "It's all right. I do it all the time."

"Yes, but no offense, you're kind of weird."

If that wasn't the pot calling the kettle black . . .

She shooed Beth out, slammed the door, then put her art supplies in the corner.

Talon watched her with interest, especially since the denim of her jeans cupped her rear rather nicely as she leaned over.

"How long have you been up?" he asked.

"A few hours. What about you?"

"I just woke up."

"You always sleep this late?" she asked.

"Since I stay up all night, yeah."

She smiled at him. "I think you've taken being a night owl to a whole new level."

She moved to sit on the futon beside him and rubbed her paint-stained hands against her thighs, drawing his attention to just how perfectly shaped they were and how much he would love to run his hand up the insides of them to the center of her body . . .

He hardened at the thought.

"Would you like me to make you some breakfast?" she asked. "There's not much in the kitchen that's not guaranteed to kill or rot you, but I think I could scrounge up an egg-white omelette."

He grimaced at the thought of what an egg-white omelette would taste like. It would probably be worse than the soy cheese.

Jeez, someone needed to introduce this woman to chocolate Reddi-wip shots. And on the heel of that thought came the question of what Sunshine would taste like covered in chocolate—he'd never gotten the chance to do that with her last night.

Oblivious to his thoughts, she continued her tirade. "Haven't you ever heard of bran flakes? Whole wheat?"

"No, I haven't." He trailed his hand up her arm to her neck where he could tease the softness of her skin with his fingertips. Hmmm, how he loved to touch her flesh.

She continued to lecture him. "You know, eating the way you do, you'll be lucky to live another thirty years. I swear there's more nutrition in Willy Wonka's Chocolate

Factory than anything I found in your kitchen."

Talon just smiled.

Why was he so fascinated by her? He listened to her voice as she lectured him, and instead of being irritated, he actually enjoyed it.

It was nice to have someone concerned enough about him that they would bother telling him what to eat.

"How about I just snack on you for a bit?" he asked.

Sunshine paused mid-sentence. Before she could think to respond, he pulled her across him and claimed her lips.

She moaned at how good he felt. How wonderful he tasted. She could feel his erection under her hip.

Her body melted against his.

The next thing she knew, he had her flat on her back on the futon and was leaning down over her, unbuttoning her sweater as her breasts tightened in expectation of his touch.

"You're very talented at distracting me," she said.

"Am I?" he asked, kissing the valley between her breasts.

"Um-hmmm," she breathed.

Chills shot the length of her body as he nibbled the skin just below her jaw. His hot breath scorched her while he cupped her breast with his hand and kneaded her gently with his fingers.

She ran her hands through his tousled hair, holding him close to her while his braids brushed against her skin, tickling and teasing her. Her body throbbed and burned, craving his blistering touch.

Talon closed his eyes and inhaled the sweet scent of her skin. She was so warm and soft. So womanly. He ran his hand over the bounty of her tanned skin while he teased her neck with his tongue and teeth.

Her hands slid over him.

Oh, he liked how this woman tasted. Loved how she felt under him.

He ran his hand over the black lace of her bra, cupping her gently. She hissed in pleasure, her legs sliding against his. He'd never cared for the sensation of denim on his body before, but when Sunshine was wearing it, he didn't mind at all.

He opened the catch on the front of her bra and released her breasts to his questing hand. He ran his palm over the hard nubs, back and forth, delighting in the way they felt.

He kissed his way down to them.

Sunshine held his head to her and she arched her back. He teased one breast with his tongue, flicking and sucking it until she wanted to scream from pleasure. It was as if he knew some secret way of wringing every bit of sensual ecstasy from the lightest touch.

And as he held her, something strange happened. She flashed back to a time long ago . . .

She saw Talon holding her just as he was doing now.

Only it was late spring and they were lying out in the woods, beside a quiet lake. She was fearful of being caught and, at the same time, she ached with longing for him.

His eyes were a deep amber and dark with passion as he braced himself above her on one arm and unlaced the top of her gown with his free hand.

"I've wanted you forever, Nyn." His whispered words tore through her as he dipped his head and sampled her freed breasts. She moaned in pleasure at the foreign sensation of a man kissing her there. She'd never allowed a man to touch her before. Never had allowed one to see her body.

Somewhat embarrassed, she still couldn't deny him this. Not when it gave him so much pleasure.

Her mother had told her long ago about the needs and wants of men. About the way they planted themselves inside a woman and took possession of her.

From that moment, she'd known she would never want any man but Speirr to take her that way. For him, she would do anything.

He lifted the hem of her dress up to her hips, baring her lower body to his warm, hungry gaze. She shivered as he nudged her legs apart so that he could look at the most private place of her body.

Her instinct was to lock her ankles together, but she forced herself to comply. She opened herself for him and held her breath as he stared at her with so much longing that it made her ache.

He traced his hand down her stomach, and outer thigh. Then ever so slowly, he ran his hand up her inner thigh, making her burn and shiver at the same time. She closed her eyes and moaned as his questing fingers touched the throbbing virgin flesh between her legs.

Her head swam at the strange feeling of him stroking and teasing her. He spread her legs wider, then slid his fingers inside her where he delved deep, making her body quiver.

She moaned as he moved his hand and placed his body between her legs. She felt his rigid shaft throb against her inner thigh.

"Look at me, Nynia."

She opened her eyes and looked up at him.

The love in his eyes scorched her. "It's not too late yet. Tell me you don't want me and I will go away without any damage being done."

"I want you, Speirr," she whispered. "I only want you."

He leaned down and kissed her tenderly, then slid himself inside her.

She tensed at the pain he caused as he tore through her maidenhead and filled her to capacity. She bit her lip and held him close as he slowly rocked himself against her.

"You feel so good beneath me," he breathed, his voice a deep half-groan. "Even better than I thought you would."

"How many women have you had beneath you, Speirr?" She was horrified by her words, but wanted to know and was too young to realize just how foolish her question was.

He stopped moving inside her and pulled back to stare down into her eyes. "Only you, Nyn. I'm as virgin as you are. I've had other women offer themselves to me, but you're the only one I dream of holding."

Her heart soared. Smiling, she wrapped her legs around his lean, naked hips. She cupped his face in her hands and pulled him down to her until their noses touched.

"Oh, Speirr," Sunshine whispered, holding him close.

Talon went rigid in her arms.

In the last thousand years, no one other than Ceara had ever used his real name. And only one woman had ever said his name the way Sunshine did just now.

It wasn't just what she said, it was the cadence of her voice when she'd said it. The shiver it had sent down his spine.

"What did you call me?"

Sunshine bit her lip as she realized her slip. Oh jeez, he probably thought she was calling him by another man's name. He would have no memory of his former life. Nor should she. She didn't know where these flashbacks were coming from.

All she knew was that they were freaking her out.

Her grandmother was really into past-life regression and had raised her with a devout respect for reincarnation. One thing Grandma Morgan had tutored her well on was that when you're reborn, you always forget your former life.

Why, then, did she remember him?

"I was clearing my throat," she said, hoping he would buy it. "What did you think I called you?"

Talon relaxed. Maybe he was hearing things. Maybe it was what this woman made him feel that was dredging up his long-forgotten memories. Or maybe it was the guilt he felt for wanting her the way he did.

Only Nynia had ever made him really burn like this.

Sunshine was so different. She made him feel even when he didn't want to. Even when he fought against it.

She buried her hands in his hair and pulled him down so that she could nibble his jaw. The feel of her hands on him, the warmth of her body under his . . .

He lowered himself over her, and buried his lips against her shoulder where he could taste the salt of her skin.

Talon sighed deeply. Contentedly.

Then, to his deepest aggravation, his phone rang.

Cursing, Talon answered it and found Acheron on the other end.

"I need you to guard the woman tonight. Keep her at your place."

Talon frowned. He wondered briefly how Ash knew Sunshine was with him, but the man's powers were nothing if not scary. "I thought you told me to stay away from her."

"Things have changed."

Talon bit back a moan as Sunshine nuzzled his nipple with her teeth. Keeping her here was far from a hardship. "Are you sure I'm not needed tonight?"

"Yes." Acheron hung up.

Talon tossed the phone aside and looked at Sunshine with a devilish grin. This night just got a whole lot better.

Chapter 8

It was near midnight when Ash left Club Runningwolf's.

Where the hell was Talon? He should be out on the streets, patrolling.

Ash had been trying to reach him for hours.

He called Nick again only to find out that Nick had neither seen nor heard from Talon either.

This was so unlike the Celt. He could sense that Talon was all right and not hurt, and if he wanted to, he could track Talon down. But Ash had never been that intrusive with his powers. Having been hunted and stalked, he couldn't bear to do that to anyone else. Not unless it was a dire emergency.

Free will was not something he would tamper with lightly.

As Ash returned the phone to his jacket, the hair on the back of his neck stood up.

"Look how helpless she is . . ."

"Yes, but she's strong enough to feed us all."

The voices whispered through his mind much like Spider-Man's spidey-sense . . .

And the wall-crawler thought he had super powers.

Pah-lease.

Ash closed his eyes and located the source of the voices. Four male and two female Daimons were in an alley off Royal Street. He started for his motorcycle, then stopped himself. There was no way he'd reach them in time by conventional means.

Glancing around, he made sure no one could see him, then he gathered the ions in the air around him. He let his body disintegrate into nothingness and used his powers to bend the physics of time and matter.

Unseen, he whispered through the city, straight to the alley where they had a woman cornered. She stood cringing, surrounded by the Daimons, her arms wrapped about her.

"Please don't hurt me," she begged. "Just take my purse and leave me alone."

The tallest Daimon raked his hand through her hair and smiled evilly. "Oh, this won't hurt. Not for long anyway."

Acheron solidified. He summoned a shield for the woman, to protect and confuse her. In her mind, she would see and remember an unknown figure scaring her attackers away.

In reality, he whistled.

The Daimons turned toward him in unison.

"Hi," he said nonchalantly as he walked toward them. "You Daimons wouldn't happen to be planning on sucking the soul of an innocent human, now would you?"

They looked at each other, then started to run.

"Oh, I don't think so," Ash said, throwing another shield up behind them to keep them from fleeing the alley. "No Daimon gets out of here alive."

They hit the invisible wall and rebounded off it.

"Man," Ash said, feigning a cringe. "It really makes you feel for the bug on a windshield, doesn't it?"

They scrambled to their feet.

The tallest of them, who was almost even in height to Ash, narrowed his eyes. "We're not afraid of you, Dark-Hunter."

"Good. It makes the fight more fair that way." Ash spread his hands out, creating a staff with his thoughts.

The male Daimons rushed him at once while the women backed away.

Acheron flipped the first Daimon to reach him over with his staff, then rammed the tip of it into the second. He embedded one end of the staff into the concrete and used it to balance as he jumped up and kicked at a third. He released the blade from the toe of his boot and sent it straight into the Daimon's chest. The Daimon disintegrated.

Ash landed gracefully on the street while the first two pushed themselves up and the other two backed off.

"Oh, come on, girls," he taunted them. "Don't be bashful. At least I give you a fighting chance, which is more than you give *your* victims."

"Look," the leader said, his voice shaking. "Let us go and we'll give you some important information."

Ash scoffed. "What information could you possibly have that would be worth me letting you go so that you could kill more humans?"

"It's worth it," another one said. "It's about—" His words broke off into a strangled cry.

Before Ash could move, all the Daimons disintegrated.

For the first time in centuries, he was too stunned to move.

What the hell just happened?

The human woman came flying up from her crouch and launched herself into his arms. "You saved me!"

Ash frowned. He couldn't figure out how she could see him until she kissed him passionately.

"Dammit, Artemis," he snarled, pushing her away. "Get off me."

She made an irritated noise low in her throat. Releasing him, she flashed from her blond human disguise into her fiery goddessness. Her auburn hair curled around her shoulders as she stood, hands on hips, and pouted at him. "How did you know it was me?"

"After eleven thousand years, don't you think I know what you taste like?"

Sulkily, she folded her arms over her chest. "If I'd been a real human, I bet you would have slept with me tonight."

He sighed disgustedly and allowed his staff to fade into

vapor. "I don't have time for your petty jealousy. You know, I do have other things to take care of."

She licked her lips and stepped to his side, then trailed her hand over his shoulders. She leaned to whisper in his ear. "I'm one of those things you need to take care of, love. Come home with me, Acheron. I'll make it well worth your while." She ran her tongue around his ear, raising chills over his body.

Ash shrugged her away. "I have a headache."

"You've had a headache for two hundred years!"

He looked at her dryly. "And you've had PMS for eleven thousand."

She laughed at that. "One day, my love, one day . . ."

Ash put a little more room between them. Enough so that she couldn't casually run her hands over his body. "Why are you here?"

She shrugged. "I wanted to see you fight. I just love the way you get all serious and lethal. The way your muscles ripple when you move. It really turns me up."

For once he didn't bother to correct her misuse of American slang. Instead, his vision turned dark that she would manipulate him like this. He hated the games she played, especially when they involved the lives of other people. "So you created Daimons out of nothing and then killed them?"

She closed the distance between them. "Oh no, they were real. And I'm not the one who zapped them. Believe me, I love the way your body moves when you attack. I would never give them in while you fought."

"You mean 'take them out'?"

"Mmm . . . in . . . out . . ." Artemis nipped at his shoulder while she ran her hands down his chest. "You keep talking like that and I *will* take you home with me."

His head was starting to pound. He removed her hand from his crotch where she cupped him. "Artie, could you stay focused for a minute? If you didn't zap them, who did?"

"I don't know."

He moved away from her. Again.

She stamped her foot like a child who just had her favorite toy taken away and glared at him. "I hate it when you mess up your hair, and what is this thing you have in your nose?"

Ash felt the stud vanish and the hole close. He clenched his teeth. No doubt his hair was blond again too. "Dammit, Artemis, you don't own me."

Her eyes flashed dangerously. "You belong to me, Acheron Parthenopaeus," she said, her voice full of rage and possession. "All of you. Mind, body, and soul. Don't you ever forget it."

He narrowed his eyes. "You have no real hold over me, Artie. We both know that. When all is said and done, my powers make a mockery of yours."

"Oh no, love. So long as your Dark-Hunter army and the humans they protect mean more to you than you do, I will always have power over you." She smiled coldly at him, then flashed out of the human realm.

Ash cursed and felt a childish impulse to send a lightning bolt slashing through the alley. No doubt she was trying to lure him back to her temple.

Like an idiot, he was going to go. He had to. He still didn't know who had zapped the Daimons, and if it wasn't Artemis, then there was someone else toying with him.

And woe to any other fool who dared to cross him. He tolerated Artemis because he had to.

He didn't have to put up with anyone else. And by Archon's thorny hammer, he'd tear the head off the next person who annoyed him.

"So," Sunshine said to Talon as she sat on his bed wearing nothing but a borrowed T-shirt, her legs tucked up under her. "Are you planning on keeping me here forever, or what?"

Lying on his side, he picked through the platter she had made for them until he found the M&M's he had insisted she include. "Depends. Do you plan to keep making me eat this healthy crap or can I have the leftover steak out of the fridge?"

She wrinkled her nose at him as she munched another strawberry. It still amazed her that she had found his small, secret stash of fresh fruit in the bottom drawer of his refrigerator. The man seemed to have an aversion to eating anything nontoxic.

"I don't see how you stay healthy eating the garbage you have in your cabinets. Did you know I counted five different kinds of potato chips?"

"Really? There should be six. Did I eat all the barbecue?"

"You are not funny." But she laughed anyway.

"Relax," he said, reaching for the banana chips she'd made. "Have a banana."

She gave him an arch look, then trailed her gaze impishly down his gorgeous naked body. "I already had your banana."

He smiled at her. "I think it would be more correct to say my banana had you."

Sunshine laughed again as she leaned over to feed him a strawberry. He held her hand to his lips while he ran his tongue over her fingers and gently nipped her skin before he let her withdraw.

He was unlike anyone she'd ever met before.

But unfortunately, it couldn't last.

Her heart sank as the reality of it hit her. She needed to get out of here before leaving him became even more difficult than it already was. She didn't want to hurt him or herself.

"You know, Talon," she said, picking through the strawberries. "It's been fun the last couple of days, but I really do need to get back home."

Talon swallowed his food and took a drink of water. That was easier said than done. He couldn't take her home, not if the Daimons were still after her and not if Ash wanted her protected.

Dereliction of duty wasn't something the Atlantean was forgiving about.

Dark-Hunters were protectors. Anyone who failed to uphold their code quickly found themselves spending eternity in painful torment.

Not that he needed that threat. The truth was, he didn't want to see Sunshine hurt. He liked her a lot more than he should.

Worst of all, he liked spending time with her. It had been so long since he'd just shared an evening with someone. And she was so easy to talk to. So funny and warm.

"Would you stay the night if I asked you to?"

He saw the sadness in her eyes. "I would like to, but what about tomorrow? You can't exactly take me home then, and if I use your boat, you won't have a way to leave your cabin."

"I could take you home tomorrow night."

She reached out and toyed with his small braids. Her smile was gentle and filled with regret. "No, Talon. As much as I would like to, I need to get back home. I have a job to do and I'm not independently wealthy. Every day I'm not in the Square, it's a day I'm not making money. I have to eat, you know. Wheat germ isn't cheap."

"If it's just the money—"

"It's not, Talon. I have to get back to my life."

He knew she was right. Sooner or later they would have to part company.

He would take her back as she wanted and then he could still protect her after dark, hidden in the shadows.

"Be a part of the world, but never in it."

He remembered the long-ago night Acheron had said those words to him.

"Because of what we do, we have to interact with people. But we must be unseen shadows who move among them.

"Never let anyone know you. Never give them a chance to realize you don't age. Move through the darkness ever watchful, ever alert. We are all that stands between the

*humans and slavery. Without us, they all die and their souls
are lost forever.*

*"Our responsibilities are great. Our battles numerous
and legendary.*

*"But at the end of the night, you go home alone where
no one knows what it is you have done to save the world
that fears you. You can never bask in your glory. You can
never know love or family.*

"We are Dark-Hunters.

"We are forever powerful.

"We are forever *alone."*

Talon drew a deep breath. His time with her was over.
"All right," he said. "I'll take you back."

He cupped her face in his hands and kissed her deeply.
And as he tasted her, his thoughts drifted back into the past.

*"Speirr?" his uncle's irate voice called from the other
side of his door. "Can you please tear yourself away from
your wife's embrace for one afternoon to actually attend
business with me? My troth, the way you two carry on I
can't imagine why you don't have five dozen children by
now."*

*Nynia laughed from above him as she gently rode him.
"You're in trouble again."*

"Aye, but you're worth it, Nyn."

*As she so often did, Nynia leaned over and rubbed noses
with him before she kissed him passionately and slid off
him. "You'd best be going or your uncle will have both
our heads."*

Talon winced at the memory and the pain it awoke inside him.

Sunshine pulled back and rubbed her nose against his
just like Nynia had always done.

He went cold.

Something wasn't right. These memories, her actions . . .

The way she awoke his emotions.

He cupped Sunshine's cheek so that he could stare into
her dark brown eyes. There was nothing about her features
that reminded him of his wife, but her actions . . .

"Talon? What's wrong?"

He couldn't speak. He didn't dare tell her that she reminded him of a woman he had loved fifteen hundred years ago.

"Nothing," he said quietly. "You need to dress."

She got up.

"Speirr?"

Talon grabbed the blanket and covered himself as Ceara shimmered into his cabin.

"Is something wrong?" Sunshine asked as she noted his sudden discomfort.

He shook his head.

Ceara drew up short as she caught sight of Sunshine. Her eyes widened. "You have company?"

He didn't answer. He couldn't without clueing Sunshine into the fact that Ceara was with them.

"Is there a problem?" he asked.

"No," Sunshine said.

"Yes," Ceara responded. "Did you know Acheron is looking for you?"

Talon scowled. He grabbed his cell phone from the nightstand and dialed Acheron's number.

No one answered.

"Is his phone turned off?" he asked.

Sunshine's scowl matched his. "Whose phone?"

Ceara shook her head. "He's been trying to reach you all night."

His frown deepened. Looking down, he dialed Nick.

Again, no answer.

"This is weird," Talon said. "No one answers."

Sunshine shrugged the matter away. "Not really. It's almost two A.M. Maybe they're asleep."

"Trust me," he said, "these guys are wide awake right now." He turned back toward his sister. "Ceara, where's Acheron?"

"Ceara?" Sunshine asked. "Acheron? What are you talking about?"

Ceara ignored her interruption. "He's with Artemis at

the moment, but he's been worried about you."

"Why did you wait so long to come?" Talon asked.

"I couldn't get here any earlier. Something kept me blocked from you."

"Since when?"

"I don't know. Something has its power cocooned around you. Something dark and evil."

"Who are you talking to?" Sunshine asked.

"Sunshine, please, I'll explain in a minute. First, I need a few answers." He looked back at Ceara.

Ceara was staring at Sunshine curiously. She walked over to her and placed a hand on her shoulder.

Sunshine shivered. "What was that?"

Ceara jumped back as if the contact had shocked her. "Nynia," she breathed, looking up at him with a startled frown.

Something inside him screamed out a denial. This time when he spoke to Ceara, he spoke in their native Celt. "*Nae,* she's not. It's not possible."

"Possible or not, *bràthair,* it is her. She has Nynia's soul. Can you not feel it?"

Talon stared at Sunshine, his heart hammering.

Could it really be?

Wrapping the blanket around his hips, he moved over to where Sunshine stood and placed his hands on each side of her face. He tilted her head up so that he could look into her dark eyes.

In spite of his denials, he felt her. He had felt her the first moment he had looked at her under the lamplight.

From the deepest corner inside him, he'd known all along she was his Nynia. Known the first instant he had tasted her.

His hands shook from the truth of it.

"How can this be?" he asked.

But in his heart, he already knew. Camulus had sent her to him.

She was here to destroy him all over again.

His chest tightened to the point he couldn't breathe.

That was why he had been so attracted to her. Why he didn't want to leave her. Camulus wanted her to seduce him so that he would have to watch her die once again. In his arms.

Closing his eyes, Talon pulled Sunshine against him and held her tight, torn between wanting to fight heaven and earth to keep her and knowing in the end he would invariably lose.

No one ever defeated a god.

Sunshine struggled to breathe inside his crushing embrace. "Talon, you're scaring me. What's going on?"

"It's nothing. I just need to get you home."

Away from me before the gods realize that you're here and decide to punish you for it.

"Speirr?" Ceara asked, her voice sounding distant. "I can't stay here. I'm being pulled away again."

"Ceara?"

She was gone.

Talon clamped down hard on his emotions. He couldn't afford to have them right now. He had too many things to do and he needed all of his powers to face the challenge of keeping Sunshine safe.

Not to mention, he needed to find out what was interfering with Ceara's powers and Acheron's phone.

Sunshine's life was in his hands. This time, he wouldn't fail her.

Talon ground his teeth, wishing he could change history.

"Stay with me, Speirr, please don't ride out with vengeance in your heart."

Had he listened to Nynia the day his uncle was killed, his life would have taken an entirely different course.

But overwrought with grief and rage, he had denied Nynia's request and she hadn't argued the matter.

As always, Nynia had stepped aside and let him have his way. He'd gone straight to the northern Gaul tribe and had laid waste to them, never knowing that both he and the Gauls had been set up.

By the time he'd learned the truth, it had been too late to apologize.

The Gauls had been under the protection of the war god Camulus and under the leadership of Camulus's human son. The war god's wrath still resonated through Talon's life.

"I will exist only to see you suffer . . ."

It was a promise Camulus had delivered well on.

No, he couldn't fight Camulus and win. As a Dark-Hunter, he was strong and powerful, but not to the point he could kill a god.

Basically, he was screwed unless he got Sunshine back to her life and out of his, pronto.

Once they were dressed and Sunshine had her things, which she'd had to go back for three different times, Talon helped her into his boat and headed back toward New Orleans. The sooner he put distance between them, the safer she would be.

He would contact Acheron once they were in the city and see if maybe Acheron could call in another Dark-Hunter or Squire to watch over her until Mardi Gras. Someone whose presence wouldn't endanger her even more than the Daimons who were after her.

Once they reached his garage, Talon decided to leave his motorcycle behind and use the Viper tonight. He needed speed and had no desire to put Sunshine in any more jeopardy.

Breaking more speeding laws than he wanted to contemplate, Talon took her to her loft and then used her wall phone to call Acheron.

"What are you doing in the city?" Acheron demanded.

"I was told you were trying to reach me."

"Told by whom? I thought my directions were clear. You were to stay at your cabin with the woman."

Talon frowned. This was peculiar. Ceara had never been wrong before, nor had she ever lied to him. "You did, but then . . ." He paused as he tried to sort it out.

What was going on here?

"Yes?"

"Nothing, T-Rex. I guess I misunderstood."

"So why are you still on the phone with me?" Ash asked. "You need to get her back to the cabin. Now."

Talon didn't care for his haughty tone at all. Ash could be evasive and annoying, but he'd never before been an authoritative dick. "I can't, T-Rex. Something weird is going down. I have to leave her here."

"Why?"

Talon glanced around to make sure Sunshine couldn't overhear his conversation. She hadn't said a word to him the whole way back to her loft and now she was sitting on the sofa sketching and appeared completely oblivious to him.

He wanted to keep it that way.

Just to be safe, he lowered his voice. "She's my wife."

"Excuse me?"

Talon lowered his voice even more. "I think Sunshine is Nynia reincarnated."

"Well, isn't this interesting?"

"Yeah, and I can't protect her any more. I need someone else to watch her, okay?"

"Yes, I can see your dilemma."

Talon frowned. Dilemma? That wasn't an Acheron kind of word. "Is something wrong with you, T-Rex?"

"No. I'm just concerned about this situation. Are you leaving her now?"

"I need to."

"Perhaps you should wait until tomorrow night."

"What?"

"I can't get anyone there tonight. Why don't you continue to protect her until I can get someone else to take over? I don't really trust Zarek to watch her, do you?"

"Hell no. You're right. I definitely don't want to leave her here unprotected."

"Yes. It could be a problem. You spend the day there, and tomorrow I will take care of the matter."

The phone went dead.

Talon hung up with a weird feeling in his stomach. Something about that conversation just didn't seem right.

But as he looked across the room, his concerns were overshadowed by the vision of Sunshine.

She was still sitting on her sofa, sketching on her pad and humming a light tune.

It was Nynia's lullaby. The same song she used to sing while she worked.

Longing and pain tore through him so powerfully that he could barely move.

But it was the love he felt for her that overwhelmed him.

Against his will, he found himself approaching her. He knelt before her, laid his head in her lap and held her tight, grateful to have her with him, no matter how different she looked or acted.

His Nynia was back.

Sunshine was stunned by the familiarity of his actions. Instinctively, she ran her hand through the softness of his golden hair as she remembered even more about their past life together. He'd done this before. Many times.

"What is going on, Talon?"

"I wish I could tell you." He lifted his head up to look at her. The torment in those jet eyes reached out to her and made her heart pound for him.

Talon pulled back.

Now that he knew who she was, it made leaving her almost impossible.

But there was nothing else he could do. She would have to live out this life with someone else.

What choice did he have? He would never do anything to hurt her. Not again.

He'd killed her once, he wouldn't kill her again.

There was no way they could be together while the curse still bound him.

Styxx toyed with his cell phone as he thought over his conversation with Talon.

He smiled.

Oh, this was sweet. Talon already knew Sunshine was his dead wife reincarnated.

Perfect. Just perfect. He couldn't have hoped for better timing. Everything was going along according to their plans.

Zarek had swallowed the bait and allowed himself to be framed. Talon was now adequately distracted by his wife. Valerius was under the control of Dionysus.

And Acheron . . .

Well, he had something very special planned for that one.

As the Cajun French people of New Orleans would say, *Laissez les jeux commencer . . .* Let the games begin.

Chapter 9

"I guess you'll be leaving now," Sunshine said quietly even though part of her didn't want him to go. Her large loft suddenly seemed a bit desolate as she thought of him leaving.

They'd had a lot of fun at his cabin, creating their platter of food, making love to each other.

But now her sexcapade with him was over. It was time for them to go their separate ways.

Why, then, did it hurt so much to think of never seeing him again?

Talon nodded. "Yeah, I guess so."

He let go of her hand and started for the door. He could find someplace to sleep in the abandoned building next door to her. Find a floor that wasn't too far from this one so that he could keep watch over her until dawn. Then he could sleep in the building until tomorrow night.

It would be easier that way. Easier for both of them if he just broke off the relationship now.

There was no point in spending another day with her. Not when he knew he couldn't give her anything more of himself.

Not so long as he posed a danger to her

Sunshine ached as he reached for her doorknob.

He was going.

It was over.

She couldn't breathe. A vicious pain stabbed her in the stomach at the thought of not seeing him anymore.

She couldn't just sit here and let him leave like this. "Talon?"

He paused and looked back at her.

"Why don't you stay the night? I know you can't get back home before sunup."

"No, I better not."

"But where will you go?"

He shrugged.

Let him go . . .

She couldn't. Not like this. It just didn't seem right. "C'mon. I'll be out of the loft early tomorrow morning and you'll have the place all to yourself while I work. No one will disturb you. I promise."

Talon hesitated.

Leave.

The command echoed in his head. He needed to.

He couldn't.

"You sure you don't mind?" he asked.

"Not at all."

Talon took a deep breath and headed back toward her. His wife.

His ultimate salvation.

His ultimate destruction.

Nynia had been everything to him. He'd thought all these centuries that he was safe from his emotions. Safe from the pain that came with the memories of his wife.

Now it was all back. Even more painful than before.

"Is something wrong?" Sunshine asked.

"I'm just tired, I guess," he said, pulling his jacket off and setting it down.

Sunshine swallowed at the sight of his tight T-shirt that displayed his well-developed body. She was riveted by his impressive form. The man had the best butt leather had ever cupped. His legs were long, well shaped, and gorgeous, and all too well she remembered what they felt like when they were entangled with hers.

The feel of all his masculine power and beauty lying in her arms . . . thrusting between her legs . . .

She almost moaned aloud at imagining it.

But there was a wall between them now. As if he had closed part of himself off from her.

Gone was the tender man who had shared his body and laughter with her. Now she saw the powerful beast who had clobbered her attackers and sent them running in terror.

How she missed the gentler side of him.

"You've gone all stiff on me, haven't you?"

He arched a puzzled brow at her and looked baffled by her question. "Lady, I get stiff every time you come near me."

Heat rose in her cheeks and she scoffed. "I don't mean that kind of stiff. Though that kind of stiff is much better than the other one. At least with that one I know you like me."

Talon groaned as she glanced down at his pants where he was sure his erection was plainly visible. He felt his barriers crumbling. Felt a desire to be the man with her that he had always been with Nynia.

With Nynia he had been himself. She'd never expected that he be anything other than her friend.

Nyn had never seen the pathetic little boy who was spat upon and rejected. The one who had been made to clean up after his betters.

The one they had forced to grovel.

She had never seen the cold-hearted lad he had become because he was tired of being beaten and abused.

As a child, he had hardened his heart and learned to take their punches. He had learned to spit back and take down anyone who cast a jaundiced eye or who made a comment about either him, his mother, or his sister.

He'd told himself that he didn't need anyone's love or caring. And so he had learned to live like a feral animal, always ready to strike out when someone tried to touch him.

Until Nynia. She had tamed the beast in him. Had allowed him to be gentle with her. To be something other than hard and unyielding. Defensive and brutal.

With her he had just been Speirr. The boy/man who wanted someone to love him. Who wanted someone to love.

It had been so long since Talon had been himself with anyone.

His Dark-Hunter brethren turned to him for advice. Acheron depended on him for his strength, wisdom, and calm leadership.

None of them, not even Wulf, really knew him. He had never opened his heart up to anyone other than the woman who sat before him now.

A woman he didn't dare open himself up to in this life-time.

"You are insatiable, aren't you?" she asked.

"Only with you," he whispered, moving closer to her as he tried to reconcile the woman she had been with the woman she was now. "I never could resist touching you. Being inside you. Feeling your breath on my skin. Your beautiful hands on my body."

Sunshine shivered at his words.

He approached her like some great stalking beast. His body was a symphony of movement.

His masculine, leather scent invaded her senses and made her mouth water.

Her head swam at his kiss, but she pushed him back, perplexed by his comments. "You say that as if you've known me for a long time. Why is that?"

"I feel like I've known you forever. Like I've held you in my heart for centuries."

She trembled at the words. This was the man who haunted her dreams. The Celtic poet and chieftain. The man she remembered riding out to battle, then riding home to love her.

But that couldn't be *this* man, could it?

And yet as she thought about it, she realized just how

weird her dreams really were. In them, she was blond and blue-eyed, but Talon . . .

Talon looked the same.

Right down to the tattoo on his body. The braids at his temple. He even wore the same torc. The only thing different was his eye color.

This couldn't be right. There was something strange about all this. Something that scared her on a level she'd never known existed.

Could he be the same man?

Could he?

It didn't seem possible, and yet living with her father and mother, she'd seen a lot of impossible things in her life. There were otherworldly powers at work in this world.

She pulled back from Talon's kiss and tilted his head so that she could see the skin just below his right ear.

There was a small scar there. A small scar that she, as Nynia, had once given to Speirr when they were fishing as children. She'd drawn back her rod to cast it and the hook had caught his ear.

The star-shaped scar was still there.

Just as it had always been.

Just as it was now.

No, it wasn't possible.

Was it?

She trembled in uncertainty.

His eyes were hooded as he stared hungrily at her. His breath fell gently against her face. She could feel his heart pounding under her hands, feel his strength and heat reaching out to her.

"I've missed you so much, Nyn . . . Nyn . . . neighbor."

Sunshine froze as he pulled back instantly. By his face, she could tell he was as surprised at what he'd said as she was.

"What did you call me?"

"Neighbor," he said quickly.

"Before that."

"Nothing."

Okay, this was too friggin' weird. And she wanted, no she *needed,* an explanation.

"Talon," she said, leaving the chair to stand before him. "Tell me what's going on. You know who Nynia is, don't you?"

His obsidian eyes flashed. "Do you?"

Oh God, it was true! He knew her. Somehow he remembered the past too.

He hadn't changed a bit. He couldn't be in daylight. He wasn't an American citizen and yet . . .

Oh, it didn't take a rocket scientist to figure this one out. Somehow, Talon was Speirr.

He *was* a vampire or an immortal or something. She knew it.

"How do you remember me?" she asked him.

"How could I ever forget you?"

She ducked his lips and pushed him back again. "Smooth, but that doesn't answer my question. There's something really odd about you, Talon. And it doesn't make sense that you are now as you were in my dreams. Not even I look the same. But you do. Why?"

Talon wanted to tell her, but couldn't find the words. *After you died I sold my soul for vengeance to a Greek goddess who now owns me so that I can spend eternity hunting down and killing vampires for her.* Even he had a hard time believing the truth of that statement and he'd been living the reality of it for fifteen hundred years.

She growled at him. "You're stiff again."

"Can't you just live for the moment? Accept me as I am?"

"Okay. But answer me one thing."

"What?"

"When did you graduate high school?"

He looked uncomfortable with her question. "I didn't."

"What year did you drop out then?"

Talon backed away from her. These were things he couldn't answer. Things he refused to answer.

The hurt in her eyes tugged at his heart.

"What's the deal, Talon? I'm not stupid. No one is so allergic to sunlight that they can't even walk in front of a window. And don't think it has escaped my notice that you never show your teeth. If I get too close to them when we kiss, you immediately pull away."

Talon wished he dared use his powers to make her forget him. To change this subject to something less volatile. "What? You want me to admit that I'm a vampire? That I howl at the moon when it's full?"

"Are you? Do you?" She stepped up to him and placed her hand against his chin as if ready to pry his mouth open. "Show me your teeth, Talon."

He stepped back. "I can't."

She gave him a mean glare. "You're Speirr, aren't you? Somehow it is you, *you,* I see when I dream. Isn't it?"

He looked away.

"I won't tell anyone," she insisted, softening her voice. "I just need to know."

"What difference would it make?" he snapped, growing tired of this conversation. "Would you throw me out?"

"No," she said breathily, sounding reconciled. "I don't think I could ever throw you out."

"Then why do you have to know?"

The fire returned to her eyes as she narrowed them on him. "Because I want you to be open and honest with me, to share your life."

Her words tore through him. Bitter longing swelled inside his heart as he remembered how hopeless having her had seemed as a mortal man. Back then only social standing and gossips had stood between them. Now the entire universe was united to keep them apart. "What makes you think I want to share my life? Maybe I'm just using you for sex."

Her face stricken, she backed away from him. "Are you?"

The pain in her eyes ripped him apart. He didn't want to hurt her.

"Are *you?*" he asked, turning the question back on her.

"Tell me what it is you want from me, Sunshine."

"I honestly don't know. Part of me is drawn to you and part of me is scared of you. There's something very dark inside your eyes. If I wanted to get to know you better, would you let me?"

"No," he said between clenched teeth, "we can't."

"Then you owe me a reason why we can't. You know I'm not some child in need of a father to make my decisions for me. I thought you respected me."

"I do."

"Then treat me like an adult. Tell me why it is you refuse to answer even the most basic question about yourself."

What she asked for was impossible. He could never tell her about his current life, not unless Acheron or Artemis released him from his oath.

"If I tell you who I am, your life will be in danger."

"I live in New Orleans over one of the most popular clubs in town and park my car in an alley where two men were murdered last night. My life is always in danger."

"Those weren't men last night and they weren't murdered." Talon didn't know why he let that escape.

"Then what were they?"

Tell her . . .

The command was so strong. Never once had he broken his Code of Silence. Never.

"The Daimons wanted to party with your girlfriend, Celt. Don't leave her unprotected."

She had a right to know what was out there gunning for her.

"Talon." She stepped into his arms and placed her hands on his face. Her touch was soothing and warm.

It almost succeeded in breaking him.

"Trust me. Whatever it is, I won't ever tell a soul."

"I can't, Sunshine. I can't."

"You won't, Talon. You won't." She expelled an irritated breath and dropped her hands. "Fine. Keep your secrets. Go ahead and blow me off. Live a happy life and do whatever it is you do."

She moved away from him.

Talon reached for her, but she bypassed his hand. "Sunshine . . ."

"Don't touch me. I'm mad at you."

"Please don't be mad at me."

She shook her head. "Oh, you're good with those puppy-dog eyes. That deep note in your voice. But I'm too far gone now to care. Just leave."

He winced at the pain in her voice and her command. It cut him all the way to his heart.

In that moment, he realized something. Zarek and Acheron were right. He was scared. Scared of leaving and scared of staying.

The last thing he wanted was to lose Nynia again and yet as he looked at Sunshine, it dawned on him that though she might have his wife's soul, she wasn't his wife.

She was someone else. Someone new and exasperating. Nynia would never have gotten mad at him. Not even when he deserved her anger. She'd always been timid and shy. Not bold and demanding like Sunshine.

If he said to leave a matter alone, Nynia would nod and drop the subject. She would never have kneed a Daimon or fought an alligator.

But even more astounding, he had to admit that he liked the fire in Sunshine. Her ability to stand up to him and the world around her.

"What?" she asked, blinking her eyes as if she couldn't believe what she saw. "You're still here? I thought I gave you an order."

He smiled in spite of himself. "I don't want to leave you, Sunshine. Can't you just accept me as I am?"

Sunshine looked away. "I like what little I know about you, Talon, but the problem is just how little I do know about you. You live in the swamp, seem to have a lot of money and no last name, and you like big, creepy gators and have a guy named Nick who runs errands. That's it.

That's the extent of my Talon knowledge and it's a really short list."

She met his gaze. "I refuse to have a relationship with a man who won't even trust me with his basic bio. Now if all you want is to get laid, there's the door. If you really want to stay, then tell me something about yourself. Something meaningful."

"Like what?"

"Tell me the name of your best friend."

"Wulf Tryggvason."

Shocked, she dropped her jaw. "Oh my God, you just answered a question. I think the world may end over it."

"You're not funny. So do I get to stay?"

She pursed her lips as she thought about it for a minute. "Fine, but only because I know you can't get back home before the sun rises."

Determined to keep distance between them until he answered her questions, Sunshine turned around and went to her bedroom. She grabbed a pillow and blanket from her bed, then returned to the living room and handed them to him.

He looked completely dumbfounded as he held her pink quilt and pillow. "What's this?"

"Until you come clean with me, you can take the sofa."

"You're kidding."

"Oh no. Not even a little. I'm not going to let you back into my bed until you let me inside your head."

Talon was completely stupefied as she walked over to the far wall and lowered her blinds.

"I told you about Wulf," he said.

She turned toward him, her look unamused. "You gave me a single name. Oooo. That tells me so much about you, doesn't it? Well, my best friends are Trina Devereaux and Selena Laurens. Now what does that tell you about me? Nada. Zilch. Nothing. It just means I have someone I can call when I get ticked off, and believe me, if it wasn't so late, I'd be dialing one of them like a madwoman."

Talon growled, but it didn't faze her in the least. The woman had entirely too much chutzpah.

"So tell me about Wulf," she said slowly, taking a step toward him. "What does he do for a living? Does he live here in New Orleans? Is he married? How long have you known him?"

"He lives in Minnesota and he's not married."

She looked pleased and yet at the same time managed to pull off a piqued look too. "How did you meet him?"

At Mardi Gras one hundred and two years ago when Wulf had been moved into the city for temporary duty— which was something he could never tell Sunshine.

Talon let out an aggravated breath. "I've known him a long time."

"Ooo," she breathed again. "Answers like that will get you voted into office, but they won't get you back into my bed. And they definitely won't let you near my body."

"You're being unreasonable."

"Hah!"

This was so unfair. He was trying to protect her and here she was asking him for something he couldn't give. Denying him her body because he didn't want to see her hurt.

How could she do this to him?

Angered by her continued insistence, he snapped, "I'm your husband."

She snorted and raked him with a bemused stare. "Not in this lifetime, buddy." She held up her left hand for his inspection. "I don't see no wedding ring on my finger, and the last time I checked, you didn't come charging into town on the back of your black warhorse, sweeping me off my feet and asking me to be yours."

Talon went cold at her words. "You remember that?"

Some of her anger seemed to fade as she nodded. "And I want to know how *you* remember it."

He tossed the blanket and pillow on the couch and lay down stiffly. "I told you, I can't tell you that."

"Then good night, sweetheart. Have pleasant dreams."

She came forward to kiss him on his forehead and walked to her room.

Royally ticked off, Talon watched as she made a grand show of pulling the drapes closed. That woman had a way of making him burn and this time it wasn't in a good way.

He was furious.

Especially when she switched on the light on the nightstand and he could see her body plainly through the thin fabric.

His heart pounded. He couldn't tear his gaze away from her as she peeled her clothes from her lush body and then climbed naked into her bed.

He could just imagine her lying there, the pink cotton sheets nestled between her warm, wet thighs. Her breasts pressed together as she lay on her side with her arm grazing and partially concealing the dark tip of her left breast. Her back naked and bare to his eager gaze and her hair fanned out around her head, just waiting for him to lie down behind her and pull her close to his body.

Then he would slide his hand up her thigh where he would cup her soft flesh and lift her leg, opening up her body so that he could slide himself deep inside her from behind.

Oh yeah, he could already feel her soft rear against his groin as he slid himself in and out of her hot body. Feel her head tucked under his chin as he buried his hand between her legs and stroked her with his fingers while he made the sweetest, tenderest love to her.

Her woodsy patchouli scent would surround him as she writhed to his touch and moaned in ecstasy.

Every hormone in his body snapped awake and his groin tightened, demanding her.

Nynia would never have done this to him. She'd never denied him access to her. Not once. All he had to do was crook a finger or cock an eyebrow and his wife had gladly stepped into his arms.

Right now, he missed her more than he ever had before.

"Sunshine?"

"No, Talon," she said firmly, turning off her light. "The answer is still no."

"I didn't ask you anything."

"I know that note in your voice when you said my name and I know what you want, and you know what I want. Guess which one of us is going to have to give in?" She paused, then added, "And for the record, it's not me."

He cursed under his breath. She was so damn stubborn in this lifetime. What had happened to his mild-mannered Nynia who gave him whatever he wanted, whenever he wanted it?

Fine, then, let her lie in there all unmolested and naked.

His body leapt at the word.

Groaning, he rolled over and faced the back of the couch so that he couldn't see her anymore.

He was a grown man, he could handle this. He could control himself.

Oh, bloody hell! No woman had turned him down before. This was excruciating and infuriating.

He plowed his fist into the pillow as he hardened even more. He was much too large for the couch and it was damned uncomfortable, but he would sleep here or die.

Sunshine listened to Talon moving around on the sofa. She almost felt sorry for him. Almost.

But she was tired of his secrets. Tired of his cryptic games. She'd done enough snooping around his house to learn that he probably wasn't a drug dealer, especially since he didn't even have a bottle of Tylenol, but he'd had all kinds of interesting electronic gadgets. Lots of leather, imported beer, and enough DVDs to sink a battleship. Not to mention the weird weapons she'd found. Some of them quite ancient in design.

There was something very odd about his life and until she knew what it was she wasn't going to let herself get any closer to him. She owed it to herself to know more 'about him before she let her goo-goo eyes lead her astray again.

She rolled over and forced herself to go to sleep. She needed to work tomorrow. Unlike him, she didn't have an endless supply of income.

"Well, look who's back."

Sunshine put down the book she was reading and smiled at Selena as Selena wheeled her small cart over to her. Dressed in a loose purple dress and black cape, Selena parked her cart to the right of Sunshine's stand of pottery and sketches, and started setting up her card table and psychic stuff.

"I know," Sunshine said wistfully as she bookmarked the page of her romance novel *Born in Sin* and set it aside. "I've been preoccupied the last few days. Sorry."

Selena spread a purple cloth over her card table. "So do I get to learn anything about this guy? Want me to do a reading for you?"

Sunshine sighed as she scooted off her stool to help Selena set up her signs. "I don't know much about him except he's a giant blond biker sex god who eats nothing but junk food, has a ton of money, lives in the swamp, and knows your brother-in-law, Kyrian . . . Oh, and he knows Grace's husband too."

Selena's face went pale. She looked up, startled. "Talon? You've been seeing Talon? More than once?"

Sunshine froze, torn between excitement and trepidation. Selena didn't look right. She looked rather sick at the news.

"You know him?" she asked incredulously.

Uncomfortable, Selena glanced around. "Oh Lord, please, please tell me he's not the sexual athlete who got hit with the Mardi Gras float. Please tell me that the guy I've been fantasizing about isn't Talon. I've had dinner with him, for goodness' sake."

"Okay, I won't tell you it's him, but . . . it's him. Ain't he great?"

Selena groaned. "Oh jeez. I'd heard rumors about him, but who knew they were really true? I can't believe this."

Sunshine was relieved. Finally, someone who could give her some answers, provided she pried them out of Selena. But Selena looked like she was going to be less than forthcoming.

"Lainie, you better spill what you know about him."

Selena opened her mouth, but by the set of her jaw, Sunshine knew what she was about to say.

"Don't you dare tell me you can't tell me anything," she said before Selena could. "I've heard enough of that from him."

Selena closed her mouth. "Well, he's a good guy for once. He's not your usual out-of-work biker and he does have a future. A really *long* future."

"And what else?"

Selena hedged.

Sunshine opened up Selena's folding chair that Selena used for her clients, then sat down beside her. "C'mon, Lainie. I really, *really* like this guy, and it's driving me crazy that he won't tell me anything, not even his birthday. So what do you know?"

"I'm not supposed to say anything, Sunny. I was sworn to secrecy."

"Sworn by whom?"

Selena set her tarot card box on the table. "I'm not supposed to say," she repeated.

"What is he, Mafia?"

"Oh no," she said, her voice thick with warning. "They make the Mafia look like Boy Scouts. These are guys no one crosses with impunity."

Someone worse than the Mafia?

"Who are they?"

"Look," Selena said. "Let's just say he's in Tabitha's line of work, okay?"

Sunshine frowned. "Ladies' lingerie? He hardly looks the type to sell that."

"No, goof-ball. What she does at night."

Sunshine formed a small O with her mouth as she understood. "He's a vampire slayer?"

"Yes, and a really good one too."

That explained how they had met in the alley. Sort of, except the people who had attacked her hadn't looked like vampires. They'd actually looked like yuppies.

"There's a lot more to it than that, isn't there?" Sunshine asked.

Selena nodded.

She smiled devilishly. "And you, my *best* friend on earth, my soul sister who shares Chunky Monkey scoops and beefcake e-mails at the drop of a hat, the woman who made me wear a frothy, ruffled lime-colored bridesmaid dress that added fifteen pounds to my hips, are going to spill your guts to me, aren't you?"

Selena stiffened. "No fair and the dress wasn't lime, it was mint."

"It was lime-icky green and I looked like a sick pistachio. But that's beside the point. You're going to spill everything because all's fair in love."

Sunshine wasn't sure which of them was most startled by the last part of that statement.

Selena turned to face her. "What? You're telling me you love Talon?"

Sunshine sat back as she tried to sort through her feelings for Talon. There was so much about him that she adored, so much about him that she craved, and at the same time she knew nothing about who and what he was *now*.

All she knew was how he made her feel whenever she looked at him. The way she wanted to go home right now and be with him.

"Honestly, Selena, I don't know. Every time I'm around him I feel so alive. So warm and protected—like nothing in the world can touch me or blight my happiness. He just fits with me. I know this sounds crazy . . ."

She paused as she glanced at Selena's psychic stand, which was filled with trinkets, rune stones, and tarot symbols. On second thought, crazy to Selena was par for the course.

Sunshine stared at her, trying to make her understand. "Talon and I were married in another life."

A dark light appeared in Selena's eyes. When she spoke, her voice was scarcely more than a whisper. "Does Talon know this?"

She nodded. "He even called me his wife last night when I made him sleep on the couch."

"Sleep on the couch?"

"Long story."

Selena turned one of her cards over. She looked at the Death card, then looked at Sunshine. "Did he say it was in *his* former life?"

"No. In fact, when I dream about him I look different, but he doesn't. He even has the same tattoos and that is weird beyond weird. I even recalled him getting those tattoos done. Now I'm not sure if I'm insane or what."

Selena covered Sunshine's hand with hers and gave a light, sympathetic squeeze. "No, hon. You're not a loon, at least not about this."

"Then what is going on?"

Selena looked around, then leaned closer and lowered her voice again as if fearful someone would overhear them. "Sunny, tell me truthfully, what are your intentions toward Talon?"

Sunshine was irritated by the question. "What are you? His mom? I promise I'll respect him in the morning."

Selena rolled her eyes. "This is really serious, Sunshine. Your current interest plays with some seriously bad things that wouldn't hesitate to kill either one of you if they thought you or he would betray them."

Sunshine winced at the deadly earnest tone of Selena's voice. This wasn't good. "He's a vampire, isn't he? I knew it!"

"Not exactly."

"That's what he said. So I'll ask you what I asked him— what is 'not exactly a vampire'?"

"A Dark-Hunter."

Sunshine was stunned that she finally had an answer. Of course, the answer made no sense whatsoever, but still it was a long-awaited start. "And that would be . . . ?"

"An immortal vampire slayer who sold his soul for an Act of Vengeance."

A chill went up her spine. "Sold his soul to who, the devil?"

"The goddess Artemis."

Sunshine scowled. Now that was the last thing she'd expected to hear. But then, given how weird this whole conversation was, she shouldn't be surprised by anything. "You're kidding, right?"

Slowly, Selena shook her head no.

"But that doesn't even make sense. I mean, there aren't that many vampires in the world, are there? Just how many Dark-Hunters could there be? Is he the only one?"

By Selena's expression she knew the answer wouldn't be pleasant. "There are thousands of Dark-Hunters and countless vampires. More correctly, they're called Daimons since they've been around a whole lot longer than the word *vampire.*"

Sunshine sat there in a stupor as she tried to take it all in. "I don't get this. I mean, I always believed in vampires in theory, but not really in the flesh, and I'm having a hard time believing that there are so many out there that we have to have real slayers for them." She locked gazes with Selena. "No offense, but I always thought your sister Tabitha was a bit wacked."

Selena gave an odd half-laugh. "She is, but that's beside the point."

Sunshine tried to come to terms with what Selena was telling her. She still wasn't sure if she should believe it. Could Talon really be an immortal vampire slayer?

And yet, in a very odd sense, it explained a lot of things. A *lot* of things.

Oh Lord, he really was a vampire slayer!

She felt ill. "Where do the vampires come from?" she

asked Selena, "Are they demons or are they made from people, like in the movies?"

Selena paused, then spoke softly. "Okay, let me give you a short history lesson and see if that helps you make some sense of this. Aeons ago, two races were created—the human race and the Apollites. The Apollites were the children of the god Apollo. He wanted to create a super race that would outdo us in every shape, form, and fashion. They were beautiful, extremely tall, and they had massive psychic powers."

Sunshine swallowed as she recalled her attackers. That definitely sounded like them.

"But like many others who have such powers," Selena continued, "the Apollites abused them and started warring against humans, trying to subjugate mankind."

"The Apollites were vampires?"

"No," Selena said, "you're getting ahead of me. During the war between the Greeks and the Apollites, the Apollites killed Apollo's mistress and son. In anger over their murders, Apollo destroyed the Apollite homeland, Atlantis.

"For their betrayal, the Apollites were cursed so that they would have to drink each other's blood to survive, and they were forbidden to ever set foot under a single ray of daylight where Apollo could see them. Because his mistress was twenty-seven when they killed her, the Apollites were all condemned to die a horrible death on their twenty-seventh birthday."

"Die how?"

"They disintegrate and decay slowly over a twenty-four-hour period."

Sunshine gaped. "Oh, how horrible."

Selena agreed as she picked up her card and returned it to the deck. "They avoid that fate one of two ways. They either kill themselves the day before their birthday or they turn Daimon and start killing humans and gathering their souls into their own bodies to prolong their lives."

"How?"

Selena shrugged. "I'm not sure exactly. I just know that

they drain the blood out of us until we die, then they take our souls into their bodies. So long as the soul is alive, they can live longer. But the problem is, the human soul starts to die as soon as they capture it. So it's a constant quest to gather new souls to maintain their lives."

"And this gathering of souls is what makes them vampires?"

"Daimons, vampires, ghouls, whatever you want to call them. They suck your blood and your soul and leave you with nothing. Kind of like lawyers." Selena smiled. "Oh wait, I just insulted my husband."

Sunshine appreciated the attempt at humor, but she was still trying to digest all this. "And the Dark-Hunters? Where do they come from? Are they Apollites too?"

"No, they're ancient warriors. After Atlantis sank into the ocean, the Greek gods were angry that Apollo had created and then unleashed the Daimons on us, so his sister Artemis created an army to hunt and destroy them. The Dark-Hunters. Talon is one of her soldiers."

"She created them how?"

"I don't know. She does something to capture their souls and then returns the Hunter to life. Once they're brought back, the Hunters are given servants and money so they can concentrate on hunting and killing the Daimons. Their only job is to free the stolen souls before the souls die."

Sunshine breathed deeply as she absorbed all this information. It wasn't looking good for her or for Talon. "So Talon is sworn into Artemis's service forever, then." Sunshine let out a ragged breath. "Jeez, I can really pick them. Talk about a go-nowhere, hopeless relationship."

"Not necessarily."

Sunshine looked up and caught the sneaky look on Selena's face. "What?"

Selena shuffled her cards. "You know, Kyrian was once a Dark-Hunter . . ."

Sunshine's heart leapt at the words. "Really?"

Selena nodded. "They do come with an out clause. True

love can restore their souls to them and free them from Artemis's service."

"So there's hope?"

"Honey, there's always hope."

Chapter 10

After gleaning every juicy detail she could from Selena,
Sunshine packed up her stand early and decided to go back
to her loft. When she got there, Talon was still sleeping on
the sofa.

Her lips twitched as she watched him. He looked so
adorable and uncomfortable. He was really much too large
for the pink and white couch, and his arms and legs dangled
off into nothingness.

He'd pulled his shirt and jacket off and left them folded
neatly on her coffee table, and his large Harley boots were
on the floor underneath it.

His blond hair was tousled and his features relaxed while
his sinfully long lashes were nestled against his cheeks. His
two thin braids lay on the pillow as he breathed in blissful
slumber.

He had one large, tanned masculine hand up by his face.

Looking at him now, she found it hard to believe he was
an ancient immortal warrior whose very name was synon-
ymous with death. But one who made her heart soften and
her pulse race.

He was scrumptious.

Sunshine stared at the intricate tribal tattoo on his body.
So, he really was a Celt. A real live, breathing, run-naked-
through-the-heather-and-moors Celt.

Her grandmother would love it.

Closing her eyes, Sunshine let her memories as Nynia wash over her. But those memories weren't really· *hers.* They were like memories of a movie she had once watched.

They were real to her and, at the same time, they weren't. She was no longer Nynia, and Talon . . .

He wasn't the same man he'd been then either.

Speirr had been full of fury and volatile emotions. Talon had bursts of emotion, but for the most part, he was calm and detached from his feelings.

Neither one of them was the same and yet she couldn't shake the feeling that they were somehow meant to be together.

But if what Selena had said was true, then he had a much higher calling than being her lover.

Not to mention that she was no longer Nynia. Parts of Nynia lived inside her, but she was a whole new and other person.

Did she love Talon because she was Sunshine or was it something left over from her previous life?

Would she ever know for sure?

"I will never love anyone but you, Nyn." His Celtic words echoed in her head.

Bit by bit, all her memories of their former life together were coming back to her. It was as if someone had opened a sealed door and the memories came pouring out.

She knew about his sister, his mother, his father. Even his uncle and aunt and bastard cousin.

She remembered the way he had looked as a young boy the first time the two of them had sneaked off together to play by the lake.

She remembered the way the clan had treated him. The scandal of his queenly mother being seduced by his Druid father. How Talon's parents had run off in the middle of the night to keep the clan from killing his father and beating his mother for their forbidden affair.

Everyone had hated Talon because of it. They had blamed him for his mother's weakness, for the fact that she had seduced their High Priest and left them without leadership.

They had blamed him for the fact that his mother had put her needs and wants above those of her people.

To atone for her actions, Talon had put everyone's needs and wants above his own.

Sunshine's throat tightened as she remembered everything he had suffered.

Nynia had been there that cold, snowy night when Talon had stumbled, frozen, into the hall, holding a screaming baby in his arms. His cloak had been wrapped around his sister to keep her warm. His shoes had been sold to buy Ceara milk that she had refused to drink.

Talon had stood defiantly before them all. His young body braced to take whatever malice they offered. Even now she could see the raw determination that had made his young amber eyes blaze.

"Your mother?" King Idiag had asked. *"Where is she?"*

"She has been dead almost two weeks now."

"And your father?"

"Six months past he was killed during an attack, protecting us from the Saxons." Talon had looked down at the screaming baby he held, then back up at his uncle. His face had softened and betrayed his fear. It was the only chink in his brave façade. *"Please, Your Majesty, please have mercy on my baby sister. Don't let her die too."*

Idiag had eyed him curiously. *"And what of you, boy? Do you ask for mercy for yourself?"*

Talon had shaken his head. *"No, Majesty. I ask nothing for me."*

His uncle had adopted Ceara as his daughter, but he had never really acknowledged Talon. He had scorned him just as everyone else did.

Idiag had never protected him from the clan's malice or blows.

Instead, he had told Talon to take it like a man because he deserved it and to never snivel.

And so Talon had.

Sunshine couldn't count the times she had found Talon by the lake practicing with his sword.

"I will make them accept me, Nyn. I will be the best warrior ever born and they'll never dare to speak to me with anything less than respect."

She had watched the angry, hurt boy grow into an embittered, fierce man. He had walked with a deadly swagger and a scowl so stern that even the stoutest of heart shrank at his approach.

He had fought his way into his uncle's heart. Fought until even the clan that hated him knew he was the only one capable of leading them against their enemies.

No one had dared meet Talon's gaze and only in fearful whispers did they dare to disparage his mother or him.

His uncle had had no choice but to accept him. It was either acknowledge Talon or lose his throne to him in war.

Talon had been invincible. Strong. Unyielding.

A man of power.

Until she was alone with him. Only then did his features soften.

Only then did he dare to laugh and smile.

And what haunted her most was the memory of Talon whispering his love to her as she died in his arms . . .

Her throat tight, Sunshine set her bag and thermos of coffee on the table, then knelt on the floor by his head. Tenderness flooded her.

She really did love this man.

She had changed in many ways.

In many ways, Talon had not.

He was still the same fierce warrior who walked alone. The same man who put others before him.

She traced the line of his brows with her fingertip. Then she leaned forward and kissed his cheek.

Startled, he jerked awake so fast, he actually fell off the couch.

Sunshine stifled her laughter. "I'm sorry."

Talon looked around groggily as he slid back on the couch, upright. It took him a few seconds to remember where he was. Clearing his throat, he frowned at Sunshine who was sitting back on her legs and watching him with an odd, weepy kind of look on her face.

"What were you doing?" he asked.

"I was kissing Sleeping Beauty awake."

He frowned at her words until he smelled something almost as enticing as her patchouli scent. "Coffee?"

She handed him the thermos from the coffee table. "And beignets. I thought you'd rather have those than my guava juice and cranberry muffins."

Talon looked at her suspiciously and wondered if a pod person had kidnapped her and was using her body. This couldn't be the same woman who had scavenged his cabin for hours looking for something "nontoxic" to eat. Nor the angry temptress who had banished him to a miserable day spent alone on her couch. "You're not mad at me anymore?"

"I want you to trust me, Talon. That hasn't changed."

Talon glanced away, unable to stand the pain in her eyes. He didn't want to hurt her, didn't want to keep anything from her. But he had no choice.

In so many ways she was his wife and in so many more she wasn't. He was having to learn her all over again.

But what surprised him most was how much he enjoyed getting to know her.

Sunshine was an incredibly sexy, entertaining and fun woman to be around.

She pulled a sugar-coated beignet out of the sack. "Hungry?"

Yes, he was, and not just for food. He was hungry for her body, hungry for her company.

Most of all, he was hungry for her eyes to laugh at him again and not be shadowed by hurt.

She lifted her hand toward his lips, offering him the pastry. He didn't take it from her hand. Instead, he leaned forward and took a bite of it, all the while watching her watch him.

Sunshine shivered as he nibbled the pastry, then he

moved to kiss her lips. She moaned at the sugary taste of him.

Sighing in contentment, she forced him to sit back on the couch so that she could straddle his hips.

"Mmm," he breathed. "I like waking up like this."

She set the beignet aside and carefully poured him a cup of coffee from the thermos.

He looked a bit nervous as he watched her. "Please don't spill that on me."

She gave him an arch look. "I'm forgetful, Talon, not clumsy."

Still, he took the cup from her hand as soon as he could, and drank the chicory-flavored coffee. She screwed the top back on the thermos and set it aside.

Sunshine ran her hand through his tousled hair while he drank, letting the golden waves wrap around her fingers. His muscles rippled with his movements, making her burn with desire. He really was a gorgeous, irresistible man.

"Just think how much nicer I would be if you told me something personal about yourself."

He clenched his teeth. "You are relentless."

She ran her finger down the line of his whiskered jaw and watched his eyes darken as he hardened underneath her. "Only when I see something I want."

Talon pulled another beignet from the sack and held it up for her to eat.

She pulled back with a grimace. "That stuff is hazardous to your health."

"Baby, life is hazardous to your health. Now take a little bite and I'll answer a question."

Skeptical, but willing to try, she took a bite, then groaned at how decadent and good it tasted. It reminded her a lot of Talon.

Talon smiled as he watched her savor her beignet. Until he noticed the sugar that had fallen from the pastry to her breasts. His body hardened even more.

She took another bite and more sugar fell over the tops of her breasts.

His throat went dry.

Before he could stop himself, he dipped his head and licked the powdered sugar from the flesh in the deep V of her sweater.

She moaned in pleasure as she cupped his head to her. She laid her head on his and spoke. "So, how long have you known Wulf?"

Distracted by her taste and scent, he answered without thinking. "A hundred years."

He went rigid as soon as the words registered. "I mean, I um . . ."

"It's okay," she whispered before licking his ear and sending chills over him. "I know you're a Dark-Hunter."

He pulled back and frowned. "How do you know that?"

"A friend told me."

"Who?"

"Does it matter?" She slid herself against him and placed her hands on his shoulders so that she could stare at him. Her dark brown eyes scorched him with sincerity. "I told you I would never betray you. I meant that."

"You're not supposed to know that term."

"I know."

Talon glanced away as he feared what would happen to her if anyone found out she knew about the Dark-Hunters and their world. "What else did your friend tell you?"

"That you're immortal. She didn't know how old you were, but said that you sold your soul for vengeance against your clan."

He narrowed his eyes. "Did she tell you why?"

"She didn't know why."

"What else did she say?"

"That true love could restore your soul to you and free you from your oath to Artemis."

It was true and yet in his case it didn't matter. Free or not, he could never have her. "Provided I want my freedom, you mean."

"Don't you?"

He looked down at the floor.

She cupped his chin in her hand and forced him to look at her. "Talon?"

He took her hands in his and kissed each one, then held them. How he wanted a lifetime with this woman. It was all he had *ever* wanted.

It was the one thing he could never have.

"It's not an easy question to answer, Sunshine. I took an oath and I always stand by my oaths."

"Do I mean anything to you at all?"

Talon flinched at her question. He would gladly sell his soul all over again for them to spend the rest of eternity together. "Yes, you do, but you have to admit that we barely know each other."

"I know and yet when I look at you, Talon, I do know you. I can feel you so deep in my heart that it aches. Do you not feel that too?"

Yes, he did. But he couldn't tell her that. He didn't dare. There was more than just feelings standing between them. There was the wrath of two ancient gods who would be extremely unhappy if he chose to be with her.

"I live a dangerous life, Sunshine. There's no guarantee whatsoever that Artemis will ever hand over my soul. There have been numerous cases in the past where she's refused Dark-Hunters that request, and even if she does give it up, there's still no guarantee you will pass her test and free me.

"Not to mention the small fact that I pissed off a major Celtic god centuries ago and every time I allow myself to love a human, he kills them. Why do you think I live alone in the swamp? Do you think I enjoy being a hermit? I would love nothing more than having a Squire or a human friend, but I don't dare."

That familiar steely look came into her eyes as if she had a plan. "Who did you tick off?"

"Camulus."

"What did you . . ." Her voice trailed off and she had a faraway look, as if she were remembering something. "You killed his son."

Talon closed his eyes. How he wished he could go back

and undo his actions that day. Had he just stayed home with Nynia and grieved for his uncle, none of this would have happened.

"Yes," he breathed. "I thought his son had led the attacking party that killed Idiag."

"Because you chose to marry me and not his daughter."

He nodded. "I was blinded by grief and didn't take time to learn that his daughter had married someone else." He swallowed as he remembered that day and the agony that still lived inside his heart.

"Nynia tried to stop me and I wouldn't listen. After I had slain their warriors and king, Camulus came to me on the battlefield and cursed me. I didn't learn until afterward that my uncle's attack had been staged by his illegitimate son, who was trying to get me and Ceara out of the way so that he could be king. Then it was too late. The die had been cast and all our fates sealed. The truth of it all didn't come out until my death."

He cupped her face in his hands as the agony of that day washed through him anew. "I'm so sorry for what I did to you. What I did to us. There hasn't been a day in my life when I haven't wished that I could go back and right that wrong."

"You didn't do it, Talon. You did what you thought was right." Sunshine held him close to her, trying to soothe his guilt and pain. "Surely there is some way to beat Camulus's curse. Isn't there?"

"No," he said. "You have no idea how powerful he is."

She pulled back to look at him. "But have you ever tried to appease him or talk to him about it?"

Before he could respond, her door crashed open.

Sunshine gasped, then scooted off Talon's lap. Her heart pounded as she saw a man coming slowly through her doorway, walking as if he had all the time in the world.

He wasn't nearly as tall as Talon, probably no more than six feet. He had long black hair that fell freely around his face and he was dressed in a pair of black leather jeans, a gray henley, and a black V-neck sweater.

He was startlingly handsome, but at the same time there was a dark, sinister aura around him. One that said he delighted in making other people suffer.

Talon got up, ready for battle.

The stranger gave a cocky, arrogant smile. "Hope you don't mind the intrusion, but my ears were burning. Naturally, I just had to come and see what the two of you were talking about."

Without being told, she knew this was Camulus.

Talon let out a curse, then the next thing she knew, two daggers came out from under Talon's coat on her coffee table and flew into Talon's hands.

He sprung the release with his thumb, ejecting the blades into a circle of three blades, then crouched into a menacing stance that said he was ready to engage the god.

"Wait!" she said, hoping to avert a fight that could cost Talon his life. She looked at Camulus. "Why are you here?"

Camulus laughed evilly. Coldly. "I'm here strictly to torture Speirr by killing you. Why else would I bother coming?"

Horrified, she stepped back.

So much for negotiating with this man. He was evil incarnate.

Talon leapt across the couch, straight for the god's throat.

Camulus pulled a sword out of thin air. "Oh Speirr, how I have missed you. No one ever fought like you."

Sunshine's eyes widened as they engaged each other. She'd never seen anything like it in her life. Forget Hollywood. It had nothing on the two of them. They fought with malice and with consummate skill.

Talon deflected Camulus's sword with the srads, then ducked the next swing. While the god prepared his next attack, Talon swung about and caught him on the arm with one dagger.

The god hissed as his blood flowed from the wound.

"I won't let you take her," Talon said from between clenched teeth. "I'll kill you first."

Camulus attacked even harder than before. Faster.

Talon met him stroke for stroke. Lethal assault for lethal assault.

"You never could learn your place, Speirr. You never knew when you should just lay down the sword and play nice."

Talon caught his sword between two blades. "I don't play nice with enemies. I execute them." He head-butted Camulus, who staggered back.

The god shook his head. "You've improved."

"I've had fifteen hundred years to perfect my skills."

As Talon lunged, six more men came through the door. Two of them shone bright flashlights into his eyes.

Talon cursed and ducked, covering his eyes as if the lights were searing to his senses.

"I really wish I had more time for this," Camulus said. "But I fear I'm bored now."

Talon turned toward Sunshine who grabbed the lamp from her end table and brought it down on the head of the first man who reached her.

"Damn you, Camulus!" he snarled.

"Och now, Speirr. It's you who are damned."

Talon tried to reach Sunshine, but one of the men opened fire on him. The bullets weren't lethal, but they were extremely painful as they lacerated his chest, back, and arms. He staggered and then fell.

Sunshine screamed as she saw Talon hit the floor. Terrified, she started for him and then felt a bullet rip into the back of her shoulder. All she could think of was saving Talon and herself. She didn't have a gun in her house, but she did have a baseball bat in her bedroom.

She had to get to it.

It was little protection against a god. Still, a slim chance was better than none at all.

As she ran for her bedroom, she realized it wasn't a bullet that had hit her.

It was a potent tranquilizer.

The room swam in front of her eyes as she struggled to

walk. Her legs were heavy, hard to move, and felt as if she were trying to walk through murky concrete.

It was too much effort to move.

The next thing she knew, everything went black.

Bleeding and hurt, Talon fought as best he could. Every time he got up, someone shone another light straight into his eyes and shot more bullets into his body. His eyes burned like fire and he could barely open them.

He struggled to reach Sunshine.

Camulus hit him with a god-bolt and slammed him against the far wall.

Talon stared at him, his body throbbing and aching as he bled.

Nonchalantly, Camulus picked Sunshine up in his arms and stared at her. "She's a pretty little thing, isn't she? Even more lovely than she was the first time." He looked back at Talon with a sinister grin twisting his lips. "You have no idea what I intend to do with her." He kissed her on the cheek. "But I promise you, you will find out."

Talon roared with the weight of his rage. "So help me, Camulus, I'll kill you if you harm her."

Camulus threw his head back and laughed, then strode casually from the room.

Talon could barely breathe from the pain as Camulus lowered him and he fell to his knees. He was covered in blood, which made it even harder to move across the now slippery hardwood floor. But it didn't stop him from trying.

Keeping Sunshine safe was all that mattered.

Someone started ripping the blinds down from the windows, spilling sunlight into the room.

Talon growled as the daylight singed his skin and he lunged for the door where Camulus had vanished.

Three men rushed him, knocking him back.

He kicked and punched his way through them and followed Camulus.

He ran after them to the back door of the club where they vanished into the alley.

Thinking only about saving her, Talon didn't realize he

was in the sunlight until he felt his skin catching fire. Cursing, he fell back into the club and watched helplessly as Camulus paused at the car and held Sunshine's head up so that Talon could see her face.

"Say goodbye to your wife, Speirr. Don't worry. I'll take really *good* care of her."

Camulus put her in a car and drove away.

"No!" Talon shouted. He wouldn't be the death of Sunshine.

Not again.

Chapter 11

It was close to four in the afternoon when Nick rounded the corner of the Pedestrian Mall and caught sight of Ash standing outside of the Corner Cafe, waiting for him. The Atlantean was leaning back against the red-brick wall with his arms folded over his chest and one leg bent and braced on the wall in a way that looked nonchalant, and yet Nick knew Ash could launch himself into action at the slightest provocation.

Dressed in black leather pants, a black T-shirt, and a long, pirate/Colonial style coat, Ash was watching the tourist crowd cut a wide berth around him.

A lethal, dark aura surrounded him. An aura like the one around a wild predator that was both graceful and attractive to behold, but one that let a person know that at any minute they could wind up as lunch.

No one was ever sure how to approach the oldest Dark-Hunter and so most people treated Ash like a visit to the dentist.

In all honesty Nick felt sorry for him. It must be hard to wield so much power and not have anyone to confide in. Ash kept a big distance between him and anyone who would get close to him—both physically and mentally.

Nick tried to treat him just like he would any other guy he hung with and he suspected Ash liked that.

At least he seemed more relaxed around Nick than he did the other Hunters or Squires.

"Look, Mommy, a giant!"

Nick turned to see a little girl around the age of five pointing up at Ash.

Her mother took one look at Ash, gathered her daughter into her arms, and hurried across the street toward the cathedral as fast as her legs would carry her.

Ash waved at the little girl who was still telling her mom to look at him. Poor guy.

Nick closed the distance between them. "You know, if you dressed a little less scary, people might not do that to you."

Pulling his sunglasses low on the bridge of his nose with his forefinger, Ash gave him a wry smile. "Trust me, Nick, it's not the clothes."

He was probably right. Ash had a way about him that was unnaturally intimidating and lethal—kind of like you knew something about Ash wasn't quite human.

· Nick noticed Ash had changed hair color. Again. This morning when he'd been at Kyrian's, Ash's hair had been purple. "Back to being black-haired, eh?"

"Back to being annoying, eh?" he quipped.

Nick laughed.

Ash pushed himself away from the wall and picked his black backpack up from the ground. Nick had never known Ash to leave it behind and he'd always been curious about what it contained.

However, he wasn't suicidal enough to try to find out. Ash guarded that bag like a treasured jewel.

"So, how was your test?" Ash asked.

"It sucked. I could have used my microscopic two-way communicator with you. I'm taking Classical Greek civilization with Julian Alexander and he's kicking my ass. That man is one tough drill instructor."

"Yeah, he was never one for nepotism."

Nick inclined his head toward the restaurant, which was only about half full. "Do you mind if I eat while we have this meeting? I skipped lunch to study and now I'm starving."

"Sure," Ash said, then held the door open for him to enter first.

Now that Nick thought about it, Ash did that a lot. He never let anyone get behind him. He always stood with his back to something or kept the crowd in front of him.

His mother would call that a gunfighter's itch. That nervous twitch of someone who expected at any moment to face an unseen attack.

Nick sat at the far end of the bar counter while Ash straddled a stool and kept his back to the wall so that he could watch the diners and the door.

A burly, older bartender came over to them. "What can I get the two of you?" he asked in a deep, hoarse voice.

"Give me a Bud Light," Nick said.

The bartender nodded, then turned to Ash. "What about you?"

"Same."

The bartender narrowed his eyes and gave Ash a thorough once-over. Nick clenched his teeth to keep from smiling. He knew what was coming before the bartender spoke. "You got any ID on you, kid?" he asked Ash.

Nick laughed.

Ash kicked Nick's stool as he fished his mock ID out of his back pocket and handed it to the bartender who studied it very carefully.

"No offense," the bartender said at last, "but with those sunglasses on I can't tell if this is you or not. If you want a beer, kid, you'll have to take them off."

His jaw muscle ticcing, Ash removed his sunglasses.

The bartender cleared his throat as soon as he caught sight of the eerie silver color. "Man, I'm sorry. I didn't realize you were blind. Here's your ID."

Nick laughed even harder as the bartender took Ash's hand into his and put the state-issued ID card into it. Ash was the only Dark-Hunter who ever got carded.

As the bartender walked off, Nick couldn't resist teasing

Ash. "So, does this make you visibly challenged?"

"No," Ash said, putting his ID back into his pocket, "but if you don't lay off me, I'm going to make you breathing impaired."

Nick sobered. Slowly. "Sorry, it's just funny as hell to me. I love that ID Jamie made for you. Born 1980. Yeah, right. What year were you really born, anyway?"

Ash rubbed his forehead. "9548 B.C."

"Whoa," Nick breathed, impressed by the date. He'd known Ash was old, but this was the first time he'd been told the exact year. "You really are older than dirt."

The bartender returned with their beers. "Are you eating anything?" the bartender asked.

Nick ordered red beans and rice, then returned to their conversation as the bartender ambled off again. "How old does that make you?"

Ash took a drink of beer before answering. "Eleven thousand five hundred and fifty-one years old, and yes, I feel every day of it."

"Wow, I had no idea. Hell, I didn't even know we had people back then."

"Yeah, I was part of the original Bedrock crew who worked in the quarry on the back of dinosaurs and ran with the Flintstones. Barney Rubble was short, but he played a good game of stone-knuckle."

Nick snorted, then laughed. He really did like Ash even though the guy was extremely strange. "So, why am I here?"

"I wanted to talk to you in a place where I knew Kyrian couldn't overhear us."

"Okay, why?"

Before Ash could answer, a tall brunette knockout with long, shapely legs and wearing a very short black skirt walked up to the bar beside them. She glanced at Nick disinterestedly, then she placed an elegant, manicured hand against Ash's chest, stood on her tiptoes and whispered in Ash's ear.

He gave her a kind smile. "I appreciate it, love, but I'm involved with someone."

The brunette pouted and handed Ash a business card. "You change your mind, let me know. I promise, I don't bite."

"Yeah, but I do," Ash said under his breath as she walked off.

Nick wasn't sure he'd heard that so he chose to ignore Ash's hushed comment as the bartender brought his food.

"You know," he said to Ash, "that's so not fair. I don't understand how it is you dress like a freak and still women want to do you."

Ash turned his head and gave him an amused smirk. "When you got it, you got it."

"Yeah, but it's seriously annoying to those of us who want it. The least you could do is share." Nick took a bite of food. "Who are you involved with anyway?"

Ash didn't answer. He never did. "Back to our discussion. The reason you're here is that I need your help to break the news to Kyrian that Valerius is in New Orleans."

Nick choked on his bread. "Oh, like hell."

"Nick, this is serious. Sooner or later they will cross paths and I want both him and Julian prepared for it. If, Zeus forbid, one of them kills Val, Artemis will have free rein to go after them. I don't want to see either one of them suffer or die. They have wives and kids who need them."

Nick wiped his mouth and swallowed. "What do you want me to do?"

"I want you to back me up. Help me convince Kyrian that he doesn't need to extract revenge on Valerius."

Nick let out a tired breath as he raked his plastic fork through the beans. That was something that was much easier said than done. "You're asking a lot of me, Ash. Personally, I'd like to help him beat the crap out of that arrogant bastard."

"Nicholas Ambrosius Gautier, you watch your language!"

Nick jerked around at the sound of his mother's melodic

Cajun drawl. She stood behind him with the Nick-you're-in-trouble-buster scowl on her face. At forty, she looked a lot younger and had her long blond hair put up in a bun. Dressed in jeans and a blue sweater, she would have been very attractive if she weren't his mother.

Ash moved Nick's beer closer to him.

His mother clucked her tongue at Ash. "Now don't you be covering for him, Ash." She wagged her finger at Nick. "Are you driving?"

"No, Mom, I'm sitting."

"Don't get smart with me. You know what I mean."

He offered her his charming smile that usually worked to get his butt out of trouble. "It's my first, and I won't drive if I have any more."

She turned to Ash with the same motherly scowl that managed to be both peeved and loving. "What about you? Are you on that motorcycle of yours?"

"No, ma'am."

"Mom," Nick said, annoyed by her interruption, "what are you doing here?"

"I was walking to work and saw you two in here. I just wanted to stop in and say hi since I won't be home until late and you busted out of the house at dawn without so much as a goodbye to me." She gave him a hurt look. "Can't a mother spend five minutes a day with her son without it being a criminal offense?"

Now he felt like a total heel. "I'm sorry, Mom. I had to do a few things for work this morning and I wanted to get it done so I could have more study time."

She ruffled his hair. "It's okay, I understand."

Then she looked Ash up and down, opened his coat and sighed in concern. "I swear you're even thinner than you were the last time I saw you." She motioned the bartender over and ordered red beans and rice for Ash. "You want anything else?" she asked him.

"No, thank you."

She wagged her finger at Ash. "You're going to eat all of it, right?"

"Yes, ma'am."

Nick pressed his lips together to keep from laughing at Ash's Eddie Haskell impersonation and his mom trying to mother an eleven-thousand-year-old warrior. Only Cherise Gautier would have that kind of gall. "Mom, he doesn't need you to baby him."

She straightened the collar of Acheron's coat and smoothed it with her hand. "Trust me, Nick, he needs someone to watch out for him, just like you do. You boys just think you're all grown-up and ready to take on the world."

If she only knew . . .

"Now," she continued, "why don't you bring Ash over to Sanctuary tonight and let me make him some strawberry shortcake and Cajun hash browns to put some meat on those lean bones of his? You can study in the back room if you need to and keep me company while I work."

His mother would never accept the fact he was grown. To her, he would always be five years old and in need of her to watch out for him. Still, he loved his mother.

"Yeah, okay. If I don't have to work, I'll stop by."

"Good boy." She reached into her purse and pulled out two twenties, then handed them to Ash. "You can pay for the red beans and rice with that, and if you have another beer, you better take a cab home too. Got me?"

"Will do, Mrs. Gautier," Ash said as he took the money. "Thanks."

She smiled, then kissed Nick on the cheek and squeezed Ash's forearm. "You boys behave and try to stay out of trouble."

Nick nodded. "We will."

Once she was gone, Nick turned back to Ash. "Man, I'm sorry about that. Thanks for being so cool with her."

"Nick, never apologize for your mother. Just be damned grateful you have her." Ash handed him the forty dollars.

"Believe me, I am," Nick said as he pocketed it. He smiled at his mother's loving nature. She'd always had this insane need to mother the world, but then, she'd been thrown out of her father's house at age fifteen when they had learned she was pregnant with him. So, she tended to have an affinity for anyone she thought was another abandoned or neglected youth.

The bartender returned with Ash's red beans and rice. .

Ash took one look at it and slid it over to Nick. "I hope you're hungry."

Nick was, but two orders was more than even he could handle. Suddenly, it dawned on him that he had never once seen Ash eat food. "Do you ever eat?"

"Yeah, but what I need isn't on the menu."

Not wanting to pursue that one, Nick frowned. "Now that I think about it, why are we meeting in daylight? How can you be out in the sun and not go up in flames?"

"I'm special."

"Ahhh, so we're back to the visibly challenged thing, huh?"

Ash shook his head.

As Ash reached for his beer, he noticed the TV out of the corner of his eye. Turning his head, he felt his body go numb in disbelief as he saw Zarek's picture on the early news.

A waiter turned the sound up.

". . . believed to be the same man who murdered a woman in the Warehouse District earlier last night . . ."

Nick cursed. "Is that who I think it is?"

Ash could only nod as he watched the webcam pictures that had captured Zarek's fight with the Daimons and the arrival of the police.

". . . the police department is offering a reward for any information on the suspect."

Nick and Ash cursed in unison as they showed a perfect sketch of Zarek's face.

"We're screwed," Nick breathed.

"Screwed blue and tattooed," Ash snarled. He pulled his cell phone from his coat and left the bar to call Zarek. The last thing he needed was for anyone to overhear this particular conversation.

Nick followed him outside. "What are we going to do?"

Ash hit the cancel button. "His phone is off. He must still be asleep."

"Are you ignoring my question or did you not hear it?"

"I heard you, Nick. I don't know. We have to keep him hidden. With those pictures, he's as good as convicted."

"Can you monkey with them?"

"I don't know. My powers are iffy at best with modern electronics. The best I can do is blow them . . ." His voice trailed off as he saw something even more gut-wrenching than Zarek's face on the news.

Ash let out a disgusted sigh and looked up at the darkening sky. "Are you bored up there, Artie, or what?"

"Huh? What's up?"

Ash inclined his head down Chartres Street to the two figures who were headed straight for them. Almost equal to him in height, the brothers moved like two dangerous predators, slowly, rhythmically. They looked to the left and right, scoping out everyone they passed as if sizing them up as an opponent, a conquest, or a victim.

Dressed in black, both of them wore long leather coats that swirled around their biker boots. They each had one hand tucked into the folds of the coat as if concealing a weapon.

Oh yeah, these were two of the most dangerous creatures Ash had ever known. More so because they would kill anyone who threatened them without a moment's hesitation.

"Who let the dogs out?" Ash snarled.

Nick frowned. "What?"

"We have two members of the Katagaria moving in," he explained to Nick.

Katagaria were animals who could take human form and pass through society to procure victims or anything else they craved. Like any other wild animal, they were extremely lethal and unpredictable.

"Oh God," Nick breathed, "don't tell me they're Slayers."

"That depends on who you ask."

"What do you mean?"

"The Arcadians would call them Slayers. But to their Katagaria brethren, they're Strati."

Nick frowned. "*Strati* means what?"

"It's the correct term for Katagaria soldiers. Slayers kill indiscriminately anyone and anything that crosses their paths. Strati kill mostly to protect themselves, their pack, and their territory."

"So, they belong here?"

Ash shook his head as the two wolves drew closer. They slowed as they caught sight of him.

"Acheron Parthenopaeus," Vane said, stopping in front of him. "It's been a while."

Ash nodded. It'd been at least a couple of hundred years since he had last seen them. They had been on the run then from the human Arcadians who hunted their unique species through time. The two brothers had been trying to find someplace safe to hide their sister from their enemies.

Vane was the older of the two brothers; he had shoulder-length dark brown hair with reddish highlights. His feral green eyes never missed anything. Fang was about an inch taller than Vane and had short black hair and hazel eyes. Either one was dangerous when alone—together, they were damn near invincible.

"Vane. Fang," Ash said, inclining his head to each in turn. "What brings you two to New Orleans?"

Vane cast a suspicious look to Nick, then must have decided something about Nick wasn't too threatening. "We're denning."

Ash grimaced at the term, which meant the Katagaria wolves had a pack here, and were planning on settling in New Orleans for a while. "That's a real bad idea. It's Mardi Gras and we have a lot of Daimons who tend to party then. You need to take your pack—"

"We can't," Vane said, cutting him off. "We have six females in our group about to give birth."

"And another one who gave birth this morning," Fang

added. "You know our laws. We're stuck here until the pups are old enough to travel."

This was getting better and better. Pregnant Katagaria were Daimon magnets due to the strength of their souls and the psychic powers their breed carried. Not to mention the fact that New Orleans was home to three groups of Arcadians who would love nothing more than to claim the skins of Vane and Fang.

"You do know there are three groups of Arcadian Sentinels here?" Ash asked.

Vane's eyes darkened threateningly. "Then you'd best tell them to back off. We have young, and if I catch them anywhere near our den, I will rip them to pieces."

Ash took a deep breath and would have laughed at the absurdity of what he faced had he not felt ill. This just wasn't his day.

He had a horny, pissed-off goddess to contend with. A Celt who was MIA. A Roman general in a city with three men who wanted to disembowel him. An uncontrollable Dark-Hunter the police wanted for murder. And now a Katagaria wolf pack that was popping out seven litters of pups right in the heart of their enemies.

Yes, it was good to be in charge . . .

Nick sniffed the air and looked around. "What is that? Do I smell gumbo?"

Vane and Fang stiffened as Nick moved closer to them.

In spite of the fact that Vane was growling under his breath, Nick pulled back a corner of Vane's coat to display a bright pink box that he had hidden in his left hand.

"What is that?" Nick asked.

"Gumbo," Vane said, his voice low and gravelly.

"Since when do werewolves eat gumbo?"

Ash cringed at Nick's question.

Fang lunged at Nick, but Ash caught him and forced him back before he could reach Nick's throat.

"We're not *were*wolves, cattle-boy," Fang snarled. "We are wolves. Period."

Nick looked bemused by the insult. "Cattle-boy?"

"Slang term," Ash supplied. "Stemming from the fact that they view humans as food."

Nick took a step back.

"Pink boxes, huh?" Ash asked, amused at the thought. No wonder they were hiding them.

Vane passed a menacing glare from Nick to him. "Anya had a craving for gumbo and chocolate. And she wanted it from the Flamingo Room and nowhere else."

Ash felt the corners of his lips twitch. "I can't believe you would run this errand for your sister."

Fang snorted. "Yeah well, remember, the term *bitch* was invented for our females."

Vane growled at him. "She's our littermate, Fang. Show her respect."

Fang's eyes flared, but he tilted his head down in submission to his older brother.

Vane handed the pink box to Fang, then pulled a pen from his pocket and wrote down a number. He handed it to Ash. "That's my cell. You need help with the Daimons, let me know. We have a dozen Strati in our pack and the last thing we want are Daimons sniffing around our females and pups."

Ash took the number and put it in his pocket. He'd barely concealed it when he noticed the rest of the Strati moving in.

They moved stealthily around the street corner like a herd of wild dogs. Fanned out and dressed in black, they looked very much like the lethal killers they were. Everyone on the street rushed away from them, and eyed them nervously.

So much for being low-key. But then, the Were-Hunters had never cared who or what knew they existed. If anyone gave them trouble, they ended up as lunch.

The Strati surrounded him and Nick.

"Dark-Hunter," Stefan growled. Standing even in height with Ash, he was the Strati leader and Vane's mortal enemy. The two of them fought together when they had to, but otherwise couldn't stand each other. "What are you doing with our *filos*?"

Ash noted the way Stefan's lips curled as he used the affectionate term for a male pack member. There was no love lost between Vane and Fang and their packmates. Still, Ash was an outsider and the pack always presented itself as a unified whole to any outsider.

"I was sharing information," he said.

Stefan narrowed his eyes on Vane. "Did you acquire our supplies?"

Vane snorted as he glanced at Nick. "It's a sad day when cattle can smell it and you can't."

Stefan started to attack, but the steely look on Vane's face set the older man back. Stefan was leader because of his age and experience. Vane was subordinate only because he had yet to challenge him. Should Vane ever choose to challenge Stefan for supremacy, there was no doubt who would win.

"Later," Stefan said to Ash before he led the bulk of the Strati away.

Vane and Fang stayed behind.

"Use the number if you need us, Ash," Vane said.

Ash nodded.

They joined the rest of their pack and mounted the motorcycles they had parked on the street behind them.

Ash didn't move until they were gone from his sight.

"Now that's a scary bunch of folks, ain't it?"

"No, Nick," Ash said slowly. "They're not folks. They're animals. They might walk in human form for a short time, but at the end of the day, they are all wolves."

His cell phone rang.

Ash answered it. It was Talon, his voice filled with pain and rage.

"I need your help, T-Rex. I'm at Club Runningwolf's. They took Sunshine."

"Who took Sunshine?"

"The Celtic god, Camulus. As soon as the sun sets I'm going after him."

Chapter 12

Talon was furious. He'd been calling for Ceara and she had yet to respond. He'd tried to spirit-walk and couldn't.

His unleashed emotions were restricting his powers and he had to get hold of them so that he could think straight.

But it was impossible.

He had to find Sunshine.

She was out there alone with no one to protect her. And if anything happened to her, he was going to find some way to make Camulus pay—god or no god, no one was ever going to hurt her again.

He paced the area inside the back door of Runningwolf's like a caged lion. Anger boiled through his veins. It was pungent and tangible. He wanted to rip something apart with his hands. Shred something with his fangs.

The darkest part of the Dark-Hunter was unleashed and, for the first time, he understood some of what Zarek felt.

It was a rage so raw, so powerful, that it controlled him completely.

He slammed his hand against the brick wall beside the door.

"I will get her back!" he growled.

His ravaged body throbbing and bleeding, he had no intention of going back upstairs to Sunshine's loft even though his injuries hurt so much that he felt the overwhelming need to sleep.

He was not going to lie down and tend his wounds.

He would stay awake if it killed him again.

Over and over in his mind, he kept seeing Nynia die in his arms, only now it was Sunshine's face he saw. Her sweet, Southern voice he heard calling out to him.

As soon as the sun set, he was heading out to find Sunshine and bring her home. No matter what it cost him.

God help anyone who was dumb enough to get in his way.

It was fifteen minutes to sunset when Acheron and Nick arrived at the back door and entered the dark hallway of the club. Talon stepped back, away from the fading sunlight that streamed in through the opening.

"What happened?" Ash asked as Nick closed the door.

Talon struggled with the fury and worry inside him. The emotions were so strong that if his powers hadn't been dampened, he was sure he would have been able to use nothing more than his thoughts to level this building to its foundation. "Camulus broke in with about half a dozen humans. They came loaded for Dark-Hunter and carrying halogen flashlights."

"Are you bleeding?" Nick asked as his eyes adjusted to the darkness. Looking pale and horrified, he squinted at Talon's wounds. "Jeez, you're bleeding like crazy."

Talon disregarded Nick's nervous tone. "They shot me."

"No, bud," Nick said. "They turned you into Swiss cheese. Ash, look at his back."

Ash growled when he saw it. "Are you all right?"

"I'm sore, but well enough to hunt and plenty able to kill."

"Jeez," Nick breathed. "I thought your powers included healing."

Talon looked at him drolly. "They do, but I heal by absorbing pain and injuries into *my* body. It's kind of hard to do that when I'm the one who's hurt."

"Nick," Ash ordered. "Go get Talon more clothes. Now."

Nick left immediately to carry out the order.

Ash gave Talon a hard stare with those eerie silver eyes. "You can't go out there covered in blood, with dozens of bullet holes riddling your flesh. I think people might get a little suspicious and wonder how it is you can stand upright and not be, say, *dead*. The last thing I need is for another Dark-Hunter to make the evening news."

Talon stood firm against the order. "I told you, T-Rex. I'm heading out as soon as that sun sets. Thirteen minutes and counting."

Ash glared at him. "Dammit, Celt. You better get a hold of yourself and think through this."

"I'm fine, Acheron. There's nothing wrong with me that killing a few people won't cure."

Ash's eyes narrowed even more. "Turn around and face the wall."

Unsure of what Ash intended, but trusting him completely, Talon obeyed.

He felt Ash splay his hand against the center of his back. His touch was hot and electrifying, and it radiated heat all the way through his body. Talon hissed as his injuries began to throb even more. Then in the span of a few heartbeats, the bullets worked themselves out of his skin and the bullet holes began knitting themselves shut.

Son of a bitch, he'd never known Ash had this kind of power. He was seriously impressed.

While his wounds were healing, Talon's cell phone rang. Ash stepped away from him while he answered it.

"Missing her yet, Speirr?"

"Damn you, Camulus. Damn you!"

A laugh answered him. "Tell me, is it better to know love and have lost it or to have never known it at all?"

Talon saw red. "Where is she?"

"Talon?"

His stomach twisted violently at the sound of Sunshine's terrified voice. "Baby, are you okay?" he asked, his voice cracking.

"They haven't hurt me, but they want you to come to a warehouse on Commerce Street. I—"

"Sunshine!" Talon shouted, his heart pounding. "Sunshine, are you there?"

"Oh, she's here, Speirr. But she needs you. If you want her, be at 609 Commerce at seven o'clock sharp. Bring as many friends as you want and let's see who gets to take Sunshine home tonight and in how many pieces."

The phone went dead.

Blind, torrid rage pierced him. Oblivious to the threat of the sun, he headed for the door.

Ash caught him. "Talon, look at me."

He refused. All he could see was Sunshine dead.

"Talon!" Ash shouted. "Get a friggin' grip. If you go out there like this, you're dead."

"What the hell do you know about it?"

"Celt." Ash tightened his grip on him. "You're doing just what they want. You're about to run headlong into the last minutes of daylight. Think. Out of all the Dark-Hunters I have, you are the one I depend on to keep his head on straight. Don't let them do this to you."

Talon's breathing was ragged as he tried to tamp down his anger and fear. "I can't let her die."

"She won't if you control yourself. You have to leash your temper." Ash released him.

Talon clenched and unclenched his fists as he stared at the door.

"Think, Talon," Ash said, his voice strangely soothing. "Remember what I taught you. Remember that you became a Dark-Hunter because you couldn't control your rage. You have to find your peace. Your balance."

Talon took a deep breath and expelled his anger slowly. *Very* slowly. "All right. I'm mostly calm."

"Good. Because I don't want you to be mostly dead." Ash stepped away from him. "We'll wait on Nick to return with your clothes and then we'll go get her."

Talon nodded, his gut still knotted over having to wait. But Ash was right.

If he didn't do *exactly* what Camulus said, he would kill her just for spite.

Talon winced at the thought. "He's going to kill her now, isn't he?"

"I don't know, Talon. I hope not."

Talon paused for a moment as he remembered the address Camulus had given him. "Commerce Street. Isn't that almost right where that woman was murdered?"

Acheron looked puzzled. "What woman?"

"The one you called me over to see."

Ash stared at him blankly.

"You know," Talon insisted, "the woman you said you thought might have been murdered by Zarek."

Acheron scowled. "I didn't call you over to see a murdered woman and I damn sure never thought Zarek would kill a woman."

"Yes you did."

Acheron shook his head slowly. "No I didn't."

Talon duplicated his scowl. What the hell was wrong with the guy? Was Acheron finally going senile?

It wasn't like him to be so scattered.

That was Talon's job at the moment.

"T-Rex, I met you over there. Remember? You called me, and while I was with you, Zarek had his little party with the police. I know it was you. There's not another man on this earth your height who looks like you."

The color faded from Acheron's cheeks. If Talon didn't know better, he'd swear he saw real worry in Acheron's eyes.

Something was really wrong.

"What is it, Ash?"

Acheron stepped away from him. "There's something I need to do. Stay here and I'll be back in plenty of time to go after Sunshine."

Talon caught his arm as Acheron headed for the door. "You better fill me in on this. Now."

"I can't."

"Acheron, this is no time to play Oracle. If you know what's going on and what we're dealing with, you need to come clean."

To Talon's complete amazement, Acheron vanished.

Ash couldn't breathe as he flashed himself into Katoteros, a small nether region between dimensions. This was his private domain where no one but he was ever supposed to tread.

Centuries ago, Hades had relegated him to this nonplace. Or more correctly, Hades had incarcerated him here.

Since the day Artemis had freed him, Ash had used this place as a touchstone to remind him of what he was.

What he had been . . .

Now, Ash struggled for control. He had to have a few minutes to collect his thoughts. His emotions.

His stomach knotted, he felt ill as memories and pain took turns assailing him. The air around him sizzled and snapped in time to his volatile state.

He had to get a hold of himself. He couldn't afford to unleash his emotions.

No one would ever be able to stop him if he did.

Ash raked his hands through his long black hair and shouted his ancient battle cry. Lightning flashed and gray thunder clouds roiled across the eerie blue-black sky above him.

This couldn't be happening. Not now.

And yet there was no other explanation. Styxx was free. Somehow he had escaped from the Vanishing Isle and been turned loose in New Orleans.

How could it have happened?

Now Styxx was pretending to be him. He was mixing with Ash's men and talking to them . . .

Horror pierced his heart.

He had to stop him before Styxx revealed Ash's past to anyone. Ash couldn't bear the thought of anyone knowing about his human life. Knowing about what he'd been.

What he'd done . . .

"Acheron?"

He flinched at Artemis's voice. "This is my place, Artie. You promised me you would never come here."

She materialized before him. "I felt your pain."

"Like you care."

She reached out to touch his face, but he folded his arms over his chest, and moved away from her. She sighed and dropped her hand. "I do care, *akribos*. More than you know. But that isn't why I'm here. I have learned of Zarek."

Ash growled low in his throat. Of course, she would never come because he was hurt. She'd taught him long ago that his suffering meant nothing to her. "I'm handling it."

"Handling it how? He has been exposed and is now being sought by the human authorities. He jeopardizes everything. He must die."

"No." He snarled the word at her. "I will take care of it. I just need more time."

She had that familiar calculating look on her face. "And what will you give me for this time you request?"

"Dammit, Artemis, why must everything be a bargain with you? Can't you, just once, do something because I asked it of you?"

"Nothing is free," she said as she walked a circle around him. He cringed as she raked her hand over his back. "You of all people should know that. A favor requires a favor in turn."

He took a deep breath and prepared himself for what was to come. Like it or not, he would have to play supplicant to her to keep Zarek safe. "What do you want?"

She pulled his hair back from the nape of his neck and nuzzled him with her lips and nose. Against his will, his body broke out in chills and hardened.

When she spoke, her voice was low and husky. "You know what I want."

"Fine," he said resignedly. "You can have me, just don't send Thanatos in yet. Let me get Zarek back to Alaska."

"Mmm," she breathed against his neck. "See . . . it's so much better when you cooperate."

He stiffened as she licked his skin.

"Question?" he said coldly. "Did you free Styxx just so you could screw me?"

She pulled back sharply and stepped around him to give him a shocked stare. "What?"

Ash watched her carefully, wanting to know the truth. "Styxx is loose in New Orleans."

Artemis appeared flabbergasted. "I would never do that to you, Acheron. I had no idea he had escaped. Are you sure?"

In spite of himself, he was relieved to know she hadn't betrayed him. Again.

"Talon saw him and thought he was me."

Artemis pressed her hand to her lips. Her green eyes were terrified. "He'll be coming for you."

"He already is. I'm sure that little dance with Zarek outside of the club was a setup to get you to kill Zarek. No doubt, Styxx is trying to neutralize my men. Either to keep them from protecting me or to keep me distracted."

"I won't let him have you," she said emphatically.

"This is between me and my brother, Artie. I want you to stay out of it." Ash moved farther away from her. "I'll be back at dawn to fulfill our bargain. In the meantime, leave Zarek to me."

Vane was still in human form as he helped his sister eat her gumbo.

She was the only living creature he had ever allowed to see the tender side of him. To the rest of the world, he must always be ruthless and harsh lest their pack prey on Anya and Fang because of their mixed heritage.

Vane clenched his hand against Anya's thick, soft fur and fought down the pain inside him. She and Fang were all he really had in this world.

All that had ever meant anything to him.

On the day Anya had mated with the Strati warrior Orian, Vane had thrown a fit. He had always known her reckless and stupid mate would meet an early death.

A few weeks ago, the Fates had proven him right.

He could still hear the sound of her voice when she had learned of Orian's death and had told him that she was more than mated to Orian. She had allowed the wolfswain to bond her to him as well. With their life forces melded into one, Orian's death would normally have been hers, except for the fact that she carried Orian's young.

But as soon as the pups came into this world, she would join her mate on the other side of eternity.

His heart broken, Vane blinked back tears.

Anya looked up and licked his face.

"You like the gumbo, huh?" he asked, stroking her ears with both of his hands.

He heard her laughter in his head. *Thank you for getting it.*

He nodded. For her, he would walk through the fires of hell to claim a simple drink of water.

She sank down beside him and rested her head on his lap. *"You should take wolf form before the others grow suspicious."*

He watched the way her fur cradled his fingers. How he was going to miss her when she was gone. She was the most beautiful wolfswan he'd ever seen, and he didn't mean her looks. It was her gentle heart he would miss most of all. The way she always worried after him.

"I will, Anya. I just want a few more minutes."

He sensed Fang coming up behind him in wolf form. His brother butted him in the back with his head, then nipped playfully at his shoulder.

A flash of light appeared to the right of them. Vane looked up to find Acheron standing in the swamp. The Atlantean glanced around to make sure they were alone, then spoke quietly. "Can I have a minute?"

Fang growled.

"It's all right, *adelfos*," Vane said, pushing his brother back. "Watch over Anya."

Vane rose to his feet and walked Acheron into the woods, away from the den. If any of his pack learned he had brought a Dark-Hunter into it, his life was over.

"You should have called me, Ash."

"This couldn't wait. I have a problem and you're the only one I trust to help me."

Now that shocked him. Immensely. "*You* trust *me*?"

Ash gave him a wry look. "No, not really. But I have a renegade who is pretending to be me and threatening my Hunters."

"What's that got to do with me?"

"You owe me one, Vane, and I need you and Fang to act as backup. I need some muscle that they won't see coming."

"When?"

"Now."

Talon paced the floor of Sunshine's loft. He'd quickly showered the blood from his body and changed into the clothes Nick had brought. He was staying calm, but it was a real challenge.

"She is unharmed, Speirr," Ceara said. "I swear it."

He let out a long, weary breath in relief. He was grateful Ceara had managed to come to him this time, but it was a hard struggle for her to stay with him. The power that was blocking her was one they had never before encountered.

He only hoped Ceara could battle it a little longer and continue to help him protect and watch over Sunshine.

"Can you tell me where she is exactly?" he asked his sister.

"Oh jeez," Nick said from the breakfast counter where he sat, waiting for Ash to return. "You're not talking to the dead again, are you? I hate it when you do that."

"Shut up, Nick."

Nick curled his lip. " 'Shut up, Nick, heel, sit, fetch.' Love you too, Celt."

Talon glared at him. "Why don't you go scrounge up something to eat so that your mouth is occupied?"

"That I can do." Nick scooted off the bar stool and headed into the kitchen.

"*Nae,* I can't find her," Ceara said. "I can't pinpoint her exact location. I told you, something powerful protects her. Something that is beginning to feel like a god's power to me."

"Camulus?"

"I'm not sure. Part of it feels like it could be a Celtic god and yet there is something more."

"What?"

"It's more like powers are commingled. Like two gods are protecting themselves."

"Why?"

She shrugged.

Nick cursed. "There's no food in here. There's nothing but grass and tofu and shit. There's not even a Coke. Man, T, your girlfriend is whacked."

Nick pulled out the block of soy cheese and smelled it. "This looks kind of edible though. I mean, you can't really screw up cheese, right?"

"Yeah, Nick. Eat the cheese." He turned back to Ceara while Nick searched for a knife to slice it. "Will they free her?"

"I can't tell you the future, Speirr, you know the rules."

"I have to know she's going to live."

Ceara hesitated before she answered. "Today, she will."

"And tomorrow?"

Ceara looked away. "I can't tell you that."

Talon cursed.

Suddenly, a bright flash of light entered the room. Talon shielded his eyes from the glare and watched as Acheron and two men appeared just inside the doorway. He'd never seen the two men before, but one look told him they were Katagaria. The air around them was rife with animalistic, psychic power.

"Oh man," Nick snapped. "I hate that poofing shit. You scared me so bad, Ash, you made me eat this crappy cheese." He looked back at Talon. "What is this stuff any-way?"

"Soy cheese."

The Katagaria exchanged a disgusted look.

"So much for *my* dinner," the taller Katagaria said. "Now his whole system is polluted. Be at least a week before it leaves his cell tissue and he's edible again."

Nick paled considerably.

"You ready to go after Sunshine?" Acheron asked Talon.

Steeled with determination, Talon nodded. "Let's do it."

Acheron glanced to Nick in the kitchen. "Nick, I want you to head over to Zarek's and keep him out of sight for the time being. He's under house arrest, so if I catch him out and about, he's in deep shit and so are you."

Nick grimaced. "Okay, but for the record, I want you to know that if a woman's life wasn't on the line, I'd tell you to stuff that order."

Nick walked out the door, past the Katagaria, mumbling all the while. " 'Nick, fetch my car, fetch my clothes, sweep the chimney, make my bed, watch my psychopath, fetch my slippers.' Yeah, I'll fetch those slippers and stick them someplace real uncomfortable." Just when Talon thought he was through, he heard one last parting comment. "I swear, my mother should have named me Fido."

"Hey, I'll have you know my best friend is named Fido," the taller Katagaria said over his shoulder.

The other Katagaria shoved him lightly. "Would you stop?"

Acheron indicated the taller Katagaria with short black hair who had made the first comment. "Talon, meet Fang." He motioned to the one with longer hair and green eyes. "And his brother, Vane."

"Why are they here?" Talon asked Acheron.

"Let's just say that if the bad guys are armed with hal-ogen lights again, they won't have the same effect on the Katagaria that they had on you."

"Yeah," Vane said, smiling evilly. "Lights just make us attack more."

Good, they had at least one surprise in their corner.

Now if he could just get his hands on Camulus.

"So, what's the plan, girls?" Fang asked.

"For none of us to get killed," Acheron said.

Vane led them out of the loft, downstairs to Talon's car. Talon saw the two black and gray Ninja motorcycles that must belong to the Katagaria. Since the were-animals had to move quickly to avoid their enemies, they tended to prefer racing bikes to running or walking, which depleted the strength they needed for fighting.

Talon checked his watch. It was twenty minutes to rendezvous. Part of him wished Ash would just poof them over to the warehouse, but he knew better than to ask.

Ash was capricious with that one power and got rather testy when asked to use it.

Talon got into the Viper while the other three started their bikes. He pulled out of the alley first, with the guys right behind him, and headed for Commerce Street.

They reached the Warehouse District a few minutes later.

The streets were bustling with activity, both tourist and local. This popular area was New Orleans' premier art district and was often referred to as the SoHo of the South.

It didn't take long for Talon to find the old abandoned warehouse that had been a popular art gallery during the 1980s. It had closed down in the early 1990s and been vacant ever since. The large-paned windows were dark, some partially boarded up and broken. The once red doors were now cracked and peeling, and held together by a thick chain and padlock.

There wasn't a single sound coming from inside as the men left their vehicles and gathered into a group.

"Uh, guys," Fang said slowly as he removed his helmet, "you do realize this is most likely a trap?"

"No, you think so?" Talon asked sarcastically.

Fang rolled his eyes.

Talon summoned his powers, letting them surge and feeling just how fragmented they were. This wasn't good.

He didn't know what was waiting inside that building, but he would fight his way through hell itself to keep Sunshine safe. Powers or no powers.

They headed for the building with Ash pulling up the rear.

"Ooo," Fang said as Talon worked the padlock. "Breaking and entering. Brings back fond memories, eh, Vane?"

"Shut up, Scooby," Vane said, using the derogatory wolf Katagaria term for a brainless, cowardly pup. "And watch your back."

Talon snapped open the lock and opened the door. It creaked loudly as the door fell off its hinges.

Talon cursed, then irritably shoved the door aside.

Entering the building one by one, they fanned out, and then paused inside the dark, empty room that was covered with at least a decade's worth of dust, spiderwebs, and grime.

Every so often, a car would go by outside, the headlights illuminating some of the dilapidated interior.

The place was totally silent except for a strange, rhythmic thumping coming from upstairs and the sound of rodents scurrying around the floor.

"Ewwww-eee-wwww," Fang sang in a voice reminiscent of some B-movie soundtrack. "Hey Ash, you vant to suck my blud?"

Ash gave him a droll, blank stare. "No, thanks. The last thing I want is to catch parvo from you, or some other freaky dog disease that makes me lift my leg around hydrants."

Vane smacked his brother on the back of the head. "Next time I'm leaving you home."

"Hey, that hurt," Fang said, rubbing his head.

"Yes, but not as much as this will." The disembodied voice came out of nowhere.

Talon heard something whirling through the air. He moved his head sharply to the left to avoid its trajectory and caught it as it started past his shoulder.

Arching a brow at the huge medieval throwing ax he held, he passed it over to Vane.

Vane curled his lip. The Katagari looked less than amused. "Hey dickhead, you should know something." Vane tested the edge of the blade with his thumb. "You attack my brother, you really piss me off."

Vane tossed the ax back at the one who'd thrown it.

Talon heard a groan an instant before searchlights pierced the darkness.

Talon and Ash hissed in pain, ducked low, and shielded their eyes.

In the next second, something crackled and the lights went out.

Ash tossed a lightning bolt into a corner where it must have hit its mark, since Talon heard someone shriek. The odor of burning flesh wafted through the room.

Then, Daimons came out of the darkness, attacking. Talon caught the first one to reach him, and flipped him to the floor. He toed the release for the blade in his boot, but before he could use it to kill the Daimon, another one caught him about the waist and shoved him back.

"Hot damn, Daimon food," Fang said with a laugh. "Hey Vane, you want the white meat or dark?"

Vane caught one of the Daimons in the chest with a knife, right in the heart. The Daimon disintegrated. He laughed at his brother who was slugging it out with another Daimon. "How about I grab one leg, you grab the other and we make a wish and pull?"

Talon rolled his eyes at them, then he spun around and used the toe of his boot to finish off the Daimon who had grabbed him.

He went after the first Daimon, who was making his way toward Fang's back. Talon caught him just before he reached the Katagari.

The Daimon turned on him with a hiss, and tried to stab him. Talon turned his wrist under and snapped the knife out of his hand.

"Bad move, inkblot," Talon said, slugging the vampire.

The demon staggered back. Talon used the knife to finish him off. The Daimon disintegrated as the stolen souls ran free of his body and drifted up toward the ceiling.

Something out of the corner of his eye caught Talon's attention. He turned his head to see Ash being mobbed by a group of Daimons.

Ash was fighting them off with his staff, but there were so many of them attacking that it was like trying to brush ants off while standing in the middle of an anthill.

Talon went to help.

Where had all the Daimons come from?

They usually congregated in New Orleans this time of year, but damn . . . it looked like half their world population was here in this room.

Working together, Talon, the Katagaria, and Ash finished them off.

"Thanks," Ash said as the last one disintegrated.

Talon nodded and folded up his srad into a single dagger, then returned it to his boot.

"Well," Fang said, mimicking a thick Southern drawl. "I have to say it's mighty nice of them Daimons to clean up after themselves when you kill them. It's much better than slaying an Arcadian." He held his hands up to them. "Look, Ma, no mess."

"Does Fang have an off switch?" Talon asked Vane.

Looking a bit apologetic, Vane shook his head no.

But Talon was no longer paying attention to them.

He had far more important things to focus on. "We have to find Sunshine," he said, heading for the stairs.

"Wait," Ash called. "You have no idea what's up there."

Talon didn't slow at all. "And I won't know until I get there."

With no thought except to save her, Talon followed the thumping noise to a door at the far end of the upper hallway. By the time he reached it, Vane, Fang, and Ash had caught up to him.

Talon flung open the door, ready for battle.

Instead of another group of Daimons, what they found

was Sunshine tied on a bed in a room that was lit by a small lantern. Moaning, she was writhing and twisting as if she were on fire.

Terrified something was wrong with her, Talon rushed to her side while Vane and Fang searched the room for more Daimons.

What had they done to her?

If they had touched or harmed her, he would hunt them down and tear them to pieces.

As soon as Talon released her from the bed she latched onto him with a viselike grip.

"Hi, baby," she breathed throatily, rubbing herself against him as she ran her hands through his hair and over his body. "I've been thinking about you, wanting you to come to me."

Oblivious to the others in the room, she kissed him feverishly and started trying to pull his clothes off. For a full minute, Talon was too stunned to move.

Then his hormones surged, wanting her as much as she wanted him.

She pushed him back on the bed, climbing up his body as if she were ready to do him on the spot.

His body instantly on fire, Talon had never seen anything like it. He had to literally struggle to keep his clothes on. Not that he would have objected had they been alone. But there was no way he was going to perform before an audience.

Acheron watched her, his eyes haunted.

There was something about Acheron's expression that reminded Talon of someone reliving a bad nightmare.

"Sunshine?" Talon said, trying to inspect her for damage. "Are you okay?"

"Umm-hmm," Sunshine groaned as she nibbled her way down his chin to his neck. His body was instantly hot and hard for her.

"C'mon, baby," she breathed in his ear. "I need you. Right now."

"Hey, Vane," Fang said. "I didn't know human females could go into heat, did you?"

Vane gave his brother a droll look.

It didn't curb Fang in the least. "You think she'll need a stand-in after she wears out Talon, like a Katagari female would? I don't normally do humans, but for a piece of that I might be tempted."

Talon saw red.

Vane clapped his hand over his brother's mouth and pulled him back. "Fang, I think you better stop or Talon might turn you into a wolf kabob."

Ash shook his head as if forcing himself to wake up from a trance. He pulled Sunshine back, away from Talon. Sunshine fought and hissed like a wildcat as she struggled for her release. Ash whispered something in a language Talon couldn't understand and Sunshine immediately went limp in his arms.

"What did you do to her?" Talon asked angrily.

"Nothing dangerous." He carefully placed Sunshine back in Talon's lap. "It's a small sleeping spell to keep her calm and let you get her home safely."

Ash lifted Sunshine's hand and sniffed her skin.

Talon had already caught a whiff of the strange spicy orange scent that seemed to permeate Sunshine's body.

Ash turned to Vane and Fang. "Would you guys mind waiting for us downstairs?"

Vane inclined his head. "We'll do another sweep of the building to make sure there aren't any more Daimons hiding out."

He led his brother from the room.

Talon cradled Sunshine against his chest, grateful to have her again, but concerned over what had been done to her. He had also noticed how strangely Ash was behaving; the man was much weirder than normal. "What's wrong with her?"

Ash let out a long, tired breath. "She's on a drug called *Eycharistisi.*" At Talon's frown, he defined the unfamiliar word. "Pleasure."

"Come again?"

"It's a very potent aphrodisiac. It floods the body with endorphins and destroys any and all inhibitions. One hit and all the user can think about is finding someone to stimulate them to orgasm."

Rage descended as Talon thought about why someone would give her such a thing. "You think Camulus had sex with her?"

"No, I think someone else did it as a message to me and a warning to you."

"How so?"

Ash's cheeks were mottled with red—something that only happened when the man became truly angry. In fifteen hundred years, Talon had only seen Ash's skin mottled three times.

"Pleasure was the drug du jour in Atlantis and hasn't been produced since the entire continent sank to the bottom of the Aegean."

A bad feeling settled in Talon's gut. This wasn't just about Sunshine and him.

He narrowed his eyes on Acheron. "What's going on, T-Rex? First someone is messing with me who looks like you but isn't you. And now someone has access to a drug that vanished eleven thousand years ago along with your homeland, and he's fed it to Sunshine who was kidnapped by Camulus. What's the deal?"

"Offhand, I would say Camulus has teamed up with someone else."

"Who?"

As expected, Acheron didn't answer. "I need you to stay out of this."

"It's rather hard for me to stay out of it when this person keeps dragging me into it. And I won't stay out of it so long as Sunshine is threatened."

"You'll do as I tell you, Talon."

"I'm not your boy, Ash. You better take another tone with me. Quick."

Ash's cheeks turned even redder. "Are you questioning my authority?"

"No, I'm questioning your judgment. I want you to come clean with me about who and what we're dealing with and why this man gave Sunshine this drug."

"I don't owe you an explanation, Celt. All you need to know is that I have an old enemy pretending to be me."

"Why?"

"Well, it obviously isn't to be nice to me and win over my friends, now is it?"

Talon growled at Acheron's inability to tell anyone jack about his past. Why was the man so damn secretive?

"Is he a shapeshifter or a demigod?"

"Last I checked, he was human."

"Then why does he look like you? Is he a relative?"

"I'm not going to play Twenty Questions with you, Talon. He's not your concern. He's mine."

"Will you at least explain to me how in the future I can tell you two apart?"

Acheron removed his sunglasses. "Our eyes. I'm the only human ever born with eyes like these. He won't have them and he won't remove his sunglasses for fear of revealing himself."

"Why is this guy after you?"

"He wants me dead."

"Why?"

Acheron stepped away from him. "Your orders are simple. Take her back to the swamp. I don't know how much of the drug they gave her, but I'm sure she'll still be feeling it when she wakes up. Trust me, when she does, she's going to put a really big smile on your face."

"Trust you," Talon repeated. "Funny how you keep saying that when you never trust anyone with even the most basic facts about yourself. Why is that, Ash?"

As expected, Ash didn't answer. And in that instant, Talon realized how Sunshine must feel when dealing with him.

It was a wonder she tolerated him at all.

"Hey Ash," Vane called from downstairs. "There's something down here you need to see."

Talon picked Sunshine up and carried her downstairs. Ash followed behind them.

Vane and Fang were in a small room off the main one. On the far wall someone had painted an eerie Greek symbol of three women and a flock of doves. Three notes were taped to it—one above each woman's head.

Talon saw that one was for him, one for Sunshine, and one for Ash.

Crossing the room, Acheron pulled the letters down, opened the one addressed to Talon and read it out loud. " 'You didn't listen to me, Celt. I warned you to keep her in your swamp where she would be safe.

" 'I'll bet it's now tearing you up that you don't know when, where, and how I'm going to kill her. But rest assured, I *am* going to kill her.' "

He opened Sunshine's next and read it out loud as well. " 'Talon, are you reading Sunshine's letters? What? Don't you trust your girlfriend?

" 'Don't worry. She hasn't been unfaithful to you. At least not yet, though it was hard. We had to tie her down to keep her from screwing every one of us.' "

Talon bellowed with rage. "So help me, I'm going to find that son of a bitch and rip his heart out."

Furious, Ash opened the last one, but this time he didn't read it out loud.

The note was addressed to him. The handwriting was different.

I know you, little brother. I know all you've done. I know how you live.

Most of all, I know the lies you tell yourself so that you can sleep.

Tell me, what would your Dark-Hunters think of you if they ever learned the truth about you?

Keep them out of my way or I'll see them all dead.

And you I'll be seeing on Mardi Gras.

Ash balled the note up in his fist and disintegrated it with his thoughts. Impotent rage rushed through him, setting fire to his blood. If Styxx wanted a war, then he'd better gather a whole lot more Daimons.

Styxx had no idea what he was playing against.

"What did that one say?" Talon asked.

"Nothing. Take Sunshine to your place and keep her there until the drug wears off, then call me." Ash rubbed his eyes as the Katagaria led them from the building.

Once outside, Talon placed Sunshine in the car while the others stood nearby.

Vane had his arms folded over his chest as he looked at Ash. "So, Ash, where does all this leave you?"

"Basically screwed. In the next twenty-four hours I have to find a way to get Zarek out of here before the cops find him, and unless I miss my guess, the next act of my nemesis will be to tell Kyrian and Julian who their new neighbor is."

Talon caught Acheron's gaze. "He wants your attention scattered and unfocused."

Ash nodded. "Yeah, and he's doing a really good job at it."

An idea occurred to Talon. "You know, I think we've all been forgetting something."

"And that is?"

Talon indicated the Katagaria to remind ·Acheron that the wolf patria wasn't the only group of Were-Hunters in town. "That your pal doesn't know about Sanctuary. I think we need to go put the bear clan on standby. I'm sure Papa Peltier and the boys would be more than happy to lend us a hand on Mardi Gras. They owe me a few favors, and if the Daimons come out like they did tonight, we'll be needing all the help we can get."

"True."

"And if I were you," Talon continued, "I'd go ahead and break the news to Kyrian about Valerius just like you were planning on doing. And keep Zarek on standby here in the city."

"What about the police?"

"Trust me, T-Rex, I know my city. The police will be so distracted on Mardi Gras that Zarek could introduce himself to them and they wouldn't realize it's him. But if I were you, I'd pretend that I was getting Z out of here just in case your 'friend' is watching. Call Mike and have him fly in and ride Eric out under the cover of darkness so that they'll think it's Z. And keep Zarek in hiding and bury Valerius until that night."

Acheron set his jaw. "It's risky."

"So's living in a swamp."

Vane moved forward. "I can set up sentries around Talon's place. If they make a move on him again, Fang and I can be there in a heartbeat."

"Why are you willing to help us?" Talon asked. "I thought it was your policy to let Dark-Hunters rot."

"It is. But I still owe Acheron a debt." He turned to Acheron. "After this is over, consider it paid in full."

Acheron nodded. "Done."

Talon said his goodbyes to the group, then got in the car and headed home.

As he drove away from the district, he reached over and took Sunshine's hand into his and held on to it tight. Her bones felt so fragile in his palm and yet he knew the strength this lady possessed. The grace and determination.

He'd been so afraid when Camulus had taken her.

He didn't like living with this fear. He didn't like feeling anything. He'd been without emotions for so long that having them now hurt even more.

How he missed his calm serenity. He was used to having complete control and yet every time he looked at her he felt his emotions spin out of control.

Sunshine touched him so deep in his heart that he knew he'd never be the same again. And it wasn't just because she was Nynia. It was because she was her.

Sunshine held strength, courage, and fire. She was her own person and he loved the challenge of her.

She was precious to him.

Talon loved her more now than he ever had as a man.
And the pain of that thought was enough to cripple him.

Talon got her back to his place and laid her carefully on
his futon. He wasn't sure what Acheron had done to her,
but she slept peacefully.

His phone rang.

He answered it to find Ash on the other end.

"Did you make it back with her?"

"Yeah, she's still asleep."

"Good. I was worried about you two."

He frowned. It was Acheron's voice but that wasn't
something Acheron would normally admit to.

All his instincts went on full alert. This was definitely
not Acheron. The voice and tone were the same, but now
that he knew there were two of them, he could hear the
difference in their personalities.

This was the imposter.

"So how long do you think it'll be before the drug leaves
her system?" Talon asked.

"I don't know. One dose can keep you pumped anywhere from one to three days."

"Really? You seem to know a lot about it."

"Yeah, well, when I was mortal I was so addicted to it
that I was willing to sell my soul for it."

"And who might you be?" Talon asked.

"Excuse me?"

"I know you're not Acheron."

A dark laugh sounded in his ear. "Very good, Dark-
Hunter. Very good. For that, I shall let you and Sunshine
live another day."

Talon snorted. "Boy, you've got a lot to learn about me
if you think you could ever be a threat to me or mine. You
come near her again and I'll make boots out of your hide."

"Oh, I don't think so. But I am impressed that this time
you figured me out. I had begun to wonder if you would
ever be able to tell us apart."

Talon tightened his grip on the phone. "Yeah well, if you're going to impersonate Acheron, you might try learning a little more about him."

"Trust me, Dark-Hunter," he said, his voice confident and evil. "I know Acheron a lot better than you do. I know things about him that would stun you into silence and make you hate him forever. He's not what you and the others think."

"I've known him for fifteen centuries. I think by now I know a thing or two about his character."

"Do you?" he asked sarcastically. "Did you know that he had a sister he let die? That she was only a few feet down the hall, screaming for his help. And while he lay in a drugged and drunken stupor, she was torn to pieces?"

Talon was horrified by what the man described. But he knew Acheron better than that. Acheron would never, drugged or not, be so far gone that he wouldn't render aid to a stranger. When it came to those who fell under his protection, Acheron would move heaven itself to keep them safe.

"I don't believe you."

"You will. Before I am through here, all of you will learn the truth of him." The imposter hung up the phone.

Talon tossed his phone to the nightstand and ran his hands over his face. This was a nightmare.

He was torn between his need to protect a friend he had known a thousand lifetimes and a woman whose soul meant more to him than his own life.

And he'd never felt more helpless. Not even when he had watched his uncle slain. At least then he'd held a weapon in his hand and had seen his attackers.

This time, there was nothing solid to grasp onto. There were two enemies out there. One pretending to be Acheron and the other a cowardly god with a vicious vendetta.

What was he going to do?

He turned around and looked at Sunshine.

Her black hair was a dark cloud on his pillow. Her face was relaxed and peaceful, her tanned skin a soothing sight against his sheets. Even now he could feel her in his arms, feel the heat of her body under his, the warmth of her touch on his skin.

How could he protect her?

"Trust in the Morrigán, Speirr. Never doubt her loyalty to you. Never question her actions. Just know that when she can, she will always help you." Those were the last words his father had ever spoken to him.

Closing his eyes, Talon could still see his father's face in the firelight that night. See the older man's pride and love shining at him as his father embraced him and sent him to bed.

He had held tight to those words, and no one had ever defeated him in battle. Not by ambush or by trickery.

In the end, it had been the enemy at home who had destroyed him. The last person he had suspected.

His cousin had wanted to be king so badly that he had known the only way to power would be to kill off both Talon and Ceara.

Talon had never suspected his cousin of setting up the death of his aunt and uncle.

Talon had learned of the man's treachery only after the Druids had slain him and Ceara.

The night Talon had shown up to take vengeance on his clan, his cousin had confessed everything, trying to get Talon to spare him.

It hadn't mattered. Young, angry, and hurt, Talon had taken his revenge against all of them, and then cast off his emotions and hardened his heart.

Hardened it until a fey beauty had looked up at him on a quiet street with large brown eyes that seared him.

He loved her. Her laughter, her wit.

She had made him feel again. Made him complete.

Without her, he didn't want to live at all.

But he refused to see her killed because of him.

"I have to let her go."

He had no choice.

Chapter 13

Zarek stood outside on the upper crosswalk of Jackson Brewery, looking down Wilkinson Street. He had his hands braced on the iron banister as he stared at the people below who were walking along Decatur Street, drifting in and out of shops, restaurants, and clubs.

Word had come down from Acheron that he was supposed to stay inside his townhouse until Mardi Gras. He probably should have listened, but taking orders wasn't exactly something he excelled at anymore.

Besides, the harsh February climate in Alaska kept him housebound entirely too much. He hated feeling trapped.

When he'd left Fairbanks, it had been fourteen below zero. It was currently fifty-seven degrees in New Orleans and even with the chill wind coming off the river, it was nothing like what he was used to.

This was a balmy summer night in comparison.

Though late June and July days in Fairbanks could get as high as the low nineties, by the time the sun set and he could go outside into the eerie twilight that never turned completely dark, he'd be damned lucky to feel a night as warm as this one.

And of course, in the dead of summer in Fairbanks, he'd be really fortunate if he could go outside for more than a few minutes before the sun rose again and forced him back indoors.

For nine hundred years, he'd been banished to that harsh, extreme terrain.

Now at long last, he had a reprieve.

Closing his eyes, Zarek inhaled the air, which was thick with life. He smelled the mixture of foods and river. Heard the sound of laughter and revelry.

He really liked this city. No wonder Talon and Kyrian had claimed it.

He only wished that he could stay here for a little while longer. Stay where there were others of his kind. Where there were people who would talk to him.

But he was used to wanting things he couldn't have.

The door on his right opened and a small boy stepped out. The runt was cute enough for an ankle-biter. He had short brown hair and was sobbing. The kid pulled up sharply at the sight of Zarek standing there.

Zarek ignored him.

"Hey, mister?" the boy said, his voice trembling. "Can you help me? I'm lost."

Zarek took a deep breath and pushed himself away from the railing.

He tucked his clawed hand into his pants pocket and turned around. "Believe me, kid. I know the feeling."

He offered the child his bare hand and was stunned at how small and trusting the boy was. He couldn't remember a time in his life he would have ever reached out to someone and trusted them not to hurt him. "So, who are we looking for? Your mom or your dad?"

"My mommy. She's really pretty and big."

Zarek nodded. "What's her name?"

"Mommy."

Now that was really helpful . . . not. "How old are you, kid?"

"I'm this many." He sniffed back his tears and held up four little fingers. "How old are you?"

"A lot more than four fingers."

The boy held up all ten. "This many?"

Zarek smiled in spite of himself. "C'mon," he said,

opening the door. "I'm sure there's someone inside who can help you find your mommy."

The boy wiped his face with his sleeve as Zarek led him into the Brewery. They hadn't gone far when he heard a woman gasp.

"What are you doing with my son?"

"Mommy!" The boy bolted toward the woman.

She grabbed the child up and the feral, suspicious look she cast Zarek let him know a hasty exit would be wise.

Some nights it didn't pay to appear dark and sinister.

"Security!" she shrieked.

Zarek cursed and ran back out the door. He leapt over the banister, to the stairs a story below, and quickly lost himself in the crowd.

Or so he thought.

As soon as he was halfway down Wilkinson, he saw Acheron waiting in the shadows.

This was just what he friggin' needed—Acheron to chew him out for locking Nick in the closet and leaving the house while he was under orders to stay put.

Zarek snarled. "Don't start on me, Ash."

Acheron cocked a brow at that. "Start on you for what?"

The hair on the back of his neck rose. Acheron was too relaxed and there was no tensing of his shoulders like Acheron always got when they came into contact with each other.

They had declared their mutual dislike for each other over two thousand years ago.

The man in front of him was acting as if Zarek were one of the Dark-Hunters Acheron was friendly with.

It sent a chill up his spine.

Hatred and anger he could take, a friendly Acheron made him nervous.

"Aren't you here to chew me out?" Zarek asked.

"Now, why would I do that?" He clapped him on the shoulder.

Zarek hissed as he moved away from him. "Who the hell are you?"

"What's wrong, Zarek?"

There was no way this was Acheron.

Zarek used his telekinesis to pull the sunglasses off the man's face. Instead of swirling mercury eyes, this man had blue ones.

The stranger narrowed his human eyes on him. "That was unwise."

The next thing Zarek knew, he was hit with a god-bolt.

Talon was strapped to his exercise bar, doing inverted sit-ups when Sunshine finally came awake

Hissing, she sat up in bed, slowly. Languidly. "It's so hot in here," she said, her voice low and throaty.

Talon relaxed his body as he watched her, letting himself hang upside down while his fingertips brushed the floor. "How are you feeling?"

She pulled her shirt off, over her head, and he instantly tensed at the sight of the black lace bra cupping her breasts.

"Hungry," she breathed, releasing the front catch on her bra. "And not for food."

He arched a brow at that, and at the way she trailed her hands over her breasts, down to her pants.

Oh, this was cruel.

She pulled her pants off slowly, sensually. "I need you, Talon."

"I think you need a cold shower."

She moved toward him like a stalking lioness.

Mesmerized, Talon didn't move until she reached him and ran her hand down his thighs. She bent her head to nuzzle and lick the back of his knees.

Talon moaned at how good she felt. His body hardened and throbbed as he pulled himself up, intending to unhook his boots from the bar. But he never got the chance. Sunshine waylaid his lips and kissed him passionately.

Sunshine couldn't think straight as she pulled back and stared into his midnight-black eyes. Her body was alive. On fire. All she could focus on was her throbbing need to have him inside her. A burning itch to have his hands on her body.

She'd never felt such potent lust. Such a hunger to taste and feel every tiny morsel of a man's body.

Oh, how she wanted him.

She took his hands and led them to her breasts. "Make love to me, Talon. Please."

Talon hesitated. "I don't know if we should do this while you're under the infl—" He stopped mid-sentence as she pushed his shorts up to his knees.

Possessed with a powerful lust she'd never known, Sunshine gently nibbled his sensitive hipbone. He moaned deep in his throat, spurring her on while she raked her hand through his short curls, letting them wrap around her fingers until she cupped him in her hand.

Talon couldn't move as wave after wave of pleasure racked him.

She ran her hand down his shaft, making him harden even more. "Hmm," she breathed. "What have we here?"

She took the tip of his shaft into her mouth, circling him with her tongue, drawing him deep into her moist heat. Reaching for her bare legs, he growled in pleasure and pulled her closer to him.

She sucked more of him into her mouth while her fingers stroked his sac, sending spikes of pleasure through his entire body.

It was a damned good thing he was hanging here. As good as she felt, had he been standing he would no doubt have been on the floor right now.

Closing his eyes, Talon savored the feel of her tongue and mouth caressing him, licking him, sucking him, of her hand spurring his ecstasy on to a dangerous level.

Talon encircled her waist with his arm and nibbled the tender spot of her hipbone. She moaned deep in her throat. The vibration of it reverberated through his entire body.

Sunshine shivered as Talon nudged her legs apart. She wrapped her arms around his waist, feasting on him while he stroked her tenderly with his fingers. She could feel his stomach muscles flex with his every move. The steeliness of them made her delirious, and when he took her into his mouth, she moaned aloud.

Her head reeling, she continued to tease him with her tongue and lips while he worked magic on her body with his mouth. She'd never felt anything like this mutual giving. The mutual need to touch each other and give each other pleasure.

His tongue slid over her core, caressing her, stoking her to such a height that her knees felt weak. She ran her hands down his back, to his shoulders, pressing him closer to her.

She rocked herself shamelessly against him, all the while licking and teasing him in return, tasting the saltiness of his body.

Her body quivered in bliss an instant before waves of pleasure tore through her. Crying out, she let her release wash over her.

Still he nibbled and teased until he had wrung the very last tremor from her body.

Only then did Sunshine pull back. He looked up at her and smiled. "I love the way you taste," he said, his voice hoarse.

She returned his smile. "You know, your face is *very* red."

He laughed as he pulled himself up and unhooked his feet from the bar. "And I have a headache from it, but I don't really care if my head explodes. You are more than worth it."

He started to pull his shorts up, but she stopped him.

Trailing her hands and lips down his steely abs, to his legs, she removed the shoes and shorts. "I'm going to lick you from head to toe."

He arched a brow.

She ran her fingers between his toes, sending chills all over him. "I am going to make you scream for mercy before I'm through with you."

Now there was a promise he wanted fulfilled. Talon closed his eyes and groaned as she licked his toes, one by one. Her tongue slid sensually between them, electrifying him and making his body even harder. Stiffer.

Then, she moved up his body, her nails scraping against his flesh. "You are mine to toy with," she said in a bad Slavic-style accent.

Talon hissed as she nibbled her way back up his legs. Her tongue and teeth teased the flesh of his legs, his inner thighs.

With a throaty laugh, she pulled back and smiled up at him.

Talon watched her heatedly as she cupped her breasts in her hands and wrapped them around his shaft. He fisted his hands while she rubbed herself up and down him.

"You like that?" she asked in an evil tone.

"Yes," he said, his voice deep and ragged.

"Then let's see what else I can find that you like."

Sunshine moved him to the futon and pushed him back into a reclining position, then she crawled slowly up his body, and straddled his hips.

She gasped as he slid his fingers inside her. She was so wet for him, so hot. She needed his touch.

He laid her back against the mattress, then knelt between her legs.

Her heart pounding, she stared up at him.

"Put your feet on the wall behind me."

She did as he asked.

He lifted her hips, then drove himself inside.

Sunshine cried out as he filled her with pleasure. He was so thick and full, his strokes masterful, as he rocked himself between her legs. From this position, he was able to penetrate her completely while she was able to lift her hips more and meet him stroke for stroke, driving him in ever deeper and harder.

Talon growled at how good she felt. He placed his hands on her hips, moving faster.

He braced himself over her with one arm on the mattress, and kissed her lips while he trailed his free hand down so that he could slide his fingers through the moist triangle of dark hair and stroke her cleft.

Her entire body quivered as he used his fingers to stroke her in time to his thrusts. He drove himself deep into her and then paused, savoring the feel of her moist heat. Oh, how he needed this woman. Needed this connection to her.

This wasn't just physical between them. It was so much more.

She moaned, then slowly started rocking herself against him.

"That's it, baby," he whispered in her ear. "Ride me all you want to."

And she did.

Closing his eyes, he ground his teeth to stave off his orgasm so that he could just feel her taking pleasure from him. He loved her like this. Wild and demanding. She was completely shameless in his arms.

How he had missed her and how damned grateful he was to have her again.

He wanted to possess her. To chain her to him for the rest of eternity.

If only he knew how.

Desperate with need, he sat back on his knees and took control again.

Sunshine growled with ecstasy as Talon slammed himself into her, even deeper than before. She met his strokes with a frenzied need.

And when she came again, she moaned his name.

She heard him laugh deep in her ear before he joined her.

She smiled as he pulled away from her and then lay down on the futon. Kissing him, she placed herself over him like a blanket.

"Mmm," she breathed. "This is what I wanted to do to you the first night we met."

"What? Screw my brains out?"

She punched playfully at his stomach. "That too, but no, I wanted to be your blanket."

He ran his hands through her hair, cupping her head. "Baby, you can be my blanket any time you feel the urge."

She definitely felt the urge. Smiling wickedly, she rubbed herself against him, then gave him a deep, passionate kiss.

"You do know I'm not through with you?" she said, using his words.

"No?"

She shook her head. "I'm just getting started."

By dawn, Talon was sweaty and exhausted. And he was sore in places he hadn't known a man could get sore.

He wasn't sure if he ever wanted to have sex again . . .

Talon laughed at the thought. Yeah, right. But he at least wanted a few hours of rest before they had another marathon.

He was still breathing heavily as Sunshine finally drifted off to sleep, lying by his side with her hand tangled in his hair and her leg draped over his bare thighs.

Jeez, Ash hadn't been kidding about her appetite. She had contorted his body into positions he hadn't known he was capable of. Right now, he had no energy whatsoever. In fact, he never wanted to leave this bed again, and if she had rolled over one more time and grabbed him, he might even have whimpered.

Groaning at the thought, he reached over to his nightstand, grabbed his phone, and called Acheron to check in. He only hoped that this time the phone actually worked.

It did.

As always, Acheron answered on the first ring.

"Hey, is it the good Ash or the bad Ash?"

"Good, bad, I'm the one with the gun."

Talon snorted at the answer. It was a quote from the campy movie *Army of Darkness* that Acheron adored. "Only the real Ash would be weird enough to pull that quote."

"Gee, thanks, Celt. So what's up? Has Sunshine come awake yet?"

"Yes, she did."

"And you're still able to walk and move?"

"Let's not go there."

Ash gave a short half-laugh. "Yeah, okay. So what do you need?"

"I got a call from the imposter not long after I got back here with Sunshine."

Total silence answered him. He couldn't even hear static on the cell line.

"Hey, T-Rex, you there?"

"I'm here. What did he say?"

"Mostly that he hates you. At first I thought it was you, but he said a couple of things I knew didn't sound right."

"Such as?"

"He said he—meaning *you*—had been addicted to this drug he fed Sunshine. Getting anything that personal out of you is like removing a tooth from a lion without a tranquilizer."

Again Acheron was totally silent.

"Hey, bud, you still with me?" Talon asked.

"Did he say anything else?"

"Yeah, he said you had a sister you let die. I called him a liar and we passed a few insults, then he hung up on me."

Talon heard Nick in the background calling for Ash while Zarek growled for Nick to let go of him. "Something wrong?"

"Nick just brought Zarek in. He's hurt. Let me let you go."

"Okay, but call back and let me know what's going on."

"Will do." The phone went dead.

Now that was weird too. Frowning, Talon set his phone down and returned to Sunshine.

Sunshine came awake screaming.

Talon grabbed her as she thrashed about on the futon.

"Shh," he breathed against her hair. "It's me, Talon. You're safe."

She was trembling against him. "I thought I was still . . ." She tightened her arms around him. "Oh God, Talon, I was so scared."

Anger pierced his heart. "I'm sorry I couldn't protect you. Did they hurt you?"

She shook her head. "They just scared me. Especially the one they called Styxx."

"Styxx? Liké the Greek river?"

She nodded. "He had this crazy look to him. Spooky. His eyes were so full of hatred and he had a constant snarl. Camulus had to keep calming him down."

Talon ground his teeth. He fully intended to find both assholes and put a major hurt on them. "I'm sorry, baby. I promise you, they'll never get their hands on you again."

Sunshine tightened her arms around him. "I'm so glad you found me, but how did you know where I was?"

"Camulus called me."

The news stunned her. "Why?"

"I don't know. I think he just wants to play with my head. He's twisted that way."

She sat there, feeling sick to her stomach. "What did they give me?"

"Some kind of drug. An aphrodisiac. Did they use it with you?"

"No," she said. "They forced me to drink it, then left me alone. It was really nasty stuff. I still feel so light-headed and strange." She looked at him and smiled. "But I remember what I did with you."

"Yeah, so do I."

She laughed and her body protested the movement. "Are you as sore as I am?"

"Let's just say I'm in no hurry to get out of bed."

Sunshine traced his tattoo as she took comfort in being safe with him. It was so good to just feel him by her side again. To hear the sound of his voice. She remembered the gunshots they had fired into him and how terrified she had been that he would somehow die from the wounds.

Now there was no sign at all that he had ever been shot.

"I'm so glad they didn't kill you," she breathed.

"Believe me, I feel the same way about you."

She ran her hand over his nipple and then froze as she felt suddenly sick.

"Sunshine?"

She left the bed and rushed for the bathroom.

Talon followed after her and then held her while she unloaded the rest of the drug from her system.

Sunshine didn't know how long she was in there. It seemed like she would never stop heaving.

Talon stayed with her the entire time, holding her hair, washing her face with a cold, damp cloth.

"Are you okay?" he asked when she finally stopped.

"I don't know. I feel awful."

He kissed the top of her head. "I'll go get you a Coke and some crackers. It'll help you settle your stomach."

She thanked him, then went to the sink to brush her teeth while he went to get the Coke.

When she left the bathroom, she found Talon waiting in bed for her.

She sat down beside him and pulled the covers over her body. She was still shaky and queasy.

Talon handed her a cracker and a can of Coke.

"Hmm," she said, taking them from him. "You must like me a lot to let me eat crackers in your bed."

He brushed the hair back from her face. His eyes burned her with their intensity. "Yes, I do."

His words sent a chill over her. "Do you, Talon? Or is it Nynia you love? When you look at me, do you see Sunshine or your wife?"

"I see you both."

Sunshine cringed at his answer. That wasn't what she wanted to hear. All her life, she had struggled to be herself. Her parents accepted her, but the guys she'd dated had all wanted to change her.

Even Jerry.

The last guy she dated had only been interested in her because she reminded him of his ex-girlfriend.

Now she reminded Talon of his ex-wife.

She couldn't win for losing.

Why couldn't someone just love her for being Sunshine?

Would Talon be so tender and attentive now if she weren't his wife reincarnated?

"What do you like about me?" she asked, nibbling her cracker.

"I like your fire and I love your body."

"Gee, thanks. Does that mean if I were fat and hideous you'd run for the door?"

"Would you run for the door if I was?"

Touché. The man was quick with a comeback. "Probably so. No doubt, I'd break it down trying to escape you."

He laughed at that. "I'd run after you if you did."

"Would you?"

"Yes, I would."

But would he run after Sunshine or Nynia?

The question haunted her.

Sunshine leaned over and kissed his forehead. "You need to get some sleep. You look really tired." And he did.

It was almost noon and, unlike her, he wasn't used to staying up all day.

"Okay. Remember, Nick is four and a pound sign on the phone if you need anything. And don't go far. Camulus will be coming back, I just don't know when. At least here I know the gators will slow them down. So make sure you stay close enough that I can reach you if something happens."

She nodded. "If I'm not in the cabin, I'll be right outside the door painting. Promise."

"Okay." He nuzzled her cheek tenderly, then kissed her. "I'll see you in a few hours."

Sunshine tucked him into the bed, got dressed, turned out the lights, and quietly went outside to paint.

As the afternoon went by while she sat on the porch, she realized that Talon had lived out here for centuries and in all that time he had never once seen the beauty of the swamp during the light of day.

He'd never seen sunlight dappling the water. Never seen the vibrant green of the moss on the stump by his dock. At night the edge was taken off the colors.

It was such a shame that he had to live like that. Alone in a world without . . .

She cringed as the word *sunshine* popped into her head. "Jeez," she muttered. "How cheesy is that?"

Still, it didn't stop her heart from aching for him.

He was loneliness.

Because of Camulus, Talon didn't dare let anyone close to him. How terrible it must be.

At dusk, she packed up her art supplies and headed inside with Beth eyeballing her from the dock. Sunshine wrinkled her nose at the bossy gator and tossed her the remains of her crackers.

Physically, Sunshine felt a lot better, but mentally she ached.

She watched Talon as he slept. He was a creature of the night. Literally. She couldn't change him. Ever.

He was immortal.

She was human.

There was no hope for them.

The thought made her want to cry.

"They do have an out clause."

But Talon would have to agree to it, and then what? Would she have to be his wife? Would he expect her to be as Nynia was?

She shivered at the thought. No offense, but as Nynia she had been a ninny.

Not that it was wrong to live to please your husband, but as Nynia she'd taken that to a whole new level. Nynia had never questioned him, never said anything back to him.

He said jump, she'd jumped and not even bothered to ask how high. Whatever he'd wanted, she'd done, regardless of her own thoughts or wants.

She had been a Stepford wife. Ew!

Sunshine didn't think she could behave that way if she had to. She was outspoken and stubborn. At times, she was even a little selfish.

She wanted a mutual partnership with a man. Someone who could handle her needs as an artist. Someone who could appreciate her while she appreciated him, faults and all.

She liked herself. Liked her life.

With Talon, she would never be quite sure if he loved her for being Sunshine or if he tolerated her because of Nynia.

How would she ever know the truth?

Talon woke up to the softness of a hand brushing through his hair. He didn't have to open his eyes to know who it was who touched him. He could feel her all the way to his heart.

Sunshine.

He blinked open his eyes to see her sitting beside him.

"Good morning," she said.

"Evening."

She handed him a cup of coffee. Talon took a drink, expecting to cringe, but it was actually good. *Very* good.

At his surprised look, she laughed. "My parents sell coffee at the bar. I may not drink the stuff, but I do know how to make it."

"You do it very well."

She beamed.

Talon sat back in bed to watch her. "What did you do while I slept?"

"Worked. I have to meet a client and show him some pieces he commissioned. If he really likes them, he's going to give me a contract to supply artwork and murals for his restaurant chain."

"Really?" he asked, impressed by the news.

Her eyes glowed with excitement, her cheeks pinkened. He could tell it meant a lot to her. "If I get the contract, no more stand at the square. I'll finally have enough money to open my own studio."

"You know, I could give you the money for that."

A sadness came over her. "So could my parents, but this is something I want to do on my own. I don't want anyone to hand me anything."

He well understood that. He'd spent most of his mortal life proving himself to others. "It never hurts to have help."

"I know. But it wouldn't be the same. Besides, I think it would be really neat to walk into a restaurant and see my stuff hanging there."

"Yeah, it would be. I hope you get the contract."

She smiled again. "What about you? What do you hope for?"

"I hope my cabin never blows apart in a hurricane during the daylight hours."

She laughed. "Seriously."

"I am serious. It could get ugly if it did."

She sat back on her heels. "You really don't have any plans for the future, do you?"

"There's nothing to plan for, Sunshine. I'm a Dark-Hunter."

"Do you ever think about quitting?"

"Never."

"Not even now?"

He fell silent as he thought about that. "If I could get past Camulus maybe. But . . ."

Sunshine nodded, understanding that stumbling block all too well. Camulus had laughed at her when she'd asked if he would/could ever forgive Talon.

"The earth will perish before I leave him in peace. So long as I live, he will pay for taking my son's life."

But she didn't tell Talon about that. She didn't want to upset him.

Somehow, she would find another way around Camulus.

"All right," she said. "I won't mention it again. Let's just enjoy what time we have."

"Sounds like a plan."

They spent the night quietly, playing games and talking. Sunshine scrounged through his kitchen and even found enough supplies to make edible body paint.

Talon introduced her to chocolate Reddi-Whip shots and delighted in the ecstasy on her face while she ate the decadent whipped cream.

And Talon finally got to douse her in chocolate and to lick it off her.

Who knew having an artist could be so much fun?

Talon had never in his life enjoyed anything more than this night. He'd never laughed so much. Felt so at ease and comfortable. There was no more hiding from her. She knew what he was, both as a Dark-Hunter and as a man.

She fell asleep not long after midnight and left him alone to think about them.

Talon went outside to sit on the porch. It was peaceful and cold outside. The fog on the swamp was thick and he could hear the water ripple all around him.

For centuries this had been his solitary existence.

He couldn't count the times he had sat here alone, just listening to the darkness.

And on the other side of the closed door he had heaven itself waiting for him.

If only he could keep her.

How did a man beat back a god? Was it even possible?

As a mortal man, the thought had never occurred to him, but now . . .

Now he wondered . . .

Talon went to bed a few hours after sunup. He'd only been asleep about an hour when he heard Sunshine rummaging around his desk.

"What are you doing?" he asked groggily.

"I'm looking for the keys to the boat."

"Why?"

"I told you, I have to go meet a client."

Talon rubbed his blurry eyes as he tried to focus on what she was saying. "What?"

"I told you about it last night, remember? I'm supposed to meet him at my stand at eleven. I promise I'll meet with him and then be back as soon as I can."

"You can't do that."

She paused and looked at him. "I told you how important this is to me. To my career."

"Sunshine, don't be stupid. This is your life we're talking about."

"Yes, it is." She went back to searching the desk. "And I'm not going to let some sick psycho screw up my one shot at what I want. Believe me, if that weirdo comes near me today, I'll make sure it's the last mistake he ever makes. I didn't know they were after me before. Now I do and I can take care of myself."

Angered that she would dare disregard him, Talon got up. "I'm not about to let you leave here."

"Don't tell me what to do, Talon. My own father doesn't order me around. I'm a grown woman, with my own thoughts, and I will not have anyone dictate my life to me."

"Dammit, Sunshine, be reasonable. I don't want you hurt."

"Why? Because you love me?"

"Yes, I do."

They both froze as he snarled the angry words.

Her heart fluttered. She wanted to believe that. Desperately. But was it true?

"Do you really?" she asked, her voice thick and heavy.

Talon watched as she opened the velvet-lined silver chest on his desk that held the torc that was identical to his, only smaller.

A woman's torc.

Nynia's torc.

She handed him the open box. "Or is it Nynia you love?"

Talon closed his eyes, unable to bear the sight of his wife's torc. He should have destroyed it centuries ago.

But he couldn't.

He'd shut it away and kept it out of sight.

It had never been out of his thoughts.

Sunshine closed the box and returned it to his desk. "I have to do this. *For me.* I won't live my life afraid. Camulus knows we're together. He can take or kill me here as easily as he can in town. He's a god, Talon. It's not like we can hide from him."

Talon winced as her words tore through him. In his mind, he saw his uncle cut down as he struggled to his side. Saw the killing blow that had sent his uncle to the ground before Talon could reach him.

Pain ripped through his chest. He well understood Sunshine's need to prove herself, to have something of her own. But he couldn't send her out there alone, unprotected.

Besides, he needed his full strength to fight and protect her, which meant he needed more rest. If he went out tonight while he was exhausted, he could get them both killed.

If he returned to bed while she was here, he had little doubt that she would sneak out of the cabin the minute he closed his eyes.

And if she took his boat, he'd be stranded out here until he could get Nick to bring him the other boat in the shed.

Dammit.

"Fine," he said irritably, reaching for his cell phone. There was only one person besides Ash who had the strength and powers to fight a god and possibly escape him. "You can go, but you're taking someone with you."

"Who?"

He held his hand up to silence her as Vane answered.

The Katagari didn't sound particularly happy to hear his voice. "I didn't give you permission to call me, Celt."

"Bite me, Wolf-boy. I need a favor."

"You'll owe me a favor for it."

He looked at Sunshine.

For her, anything.

"And I'm willing to pay it," he said to Vane.

"All right then, what do you need?"

"Can you take human form in daylight?"

Vane scoffed. "Obviously so. Ever tried to answer a phone without opposable thumbs? Not to mention the fact that I am speaking to you in English and not wolf."

Talon growled low at the sarcasm. "Yes, but can you hold and fight in human form during daylight?"

He snorted at that. "Oh yeah. Daylight doesn't bother me."

"Good. Sunshine needs to go to Jackson Square for a little while this morning."

"Did you okay this with Ash?"

"No."

Vane laughed. "Living on the edge. I love it. Okay, so what do you need me to do?"

"I want you to guard her until I can take over after nightfall."

"One guard dog coming up. Give me about half an hour to get there."

"All right, thanks."

"I would say anytime, Celt, but this is a one-shot-only deal."

"Yeah, I know."

Sunshine frowned as he hung up the phone. "Who was that?"

"That was Vane."

"Is he a Dark-Hunter too?"

"No, love. You're about to meet your werewolf."

Chapter 14

Vane wasn't just any werewolf, Sunshine discovered. He was *the* werewolf, judging by the tough, hard-edged aura he projected.

He entered the cabin wearing a pair of faded jeans and a white T-shirt with a weathered motorcycle jacket, black cowboy boots, and a body that would cause a traffic jam.

And when he removed his sunglasses, her breath caught in her throat.

Even in height with Talon, he was stunningly gorgeous. His startlingly green eyes were a perfect contrast for his hair which at first glance appeared an extremely dark chestnut, but on closer view seemed to be made up of every color known. There were traces of ash and gold, red and black. She'd never seen hair like that in her life.

At least not on a human . . .

He wore it long, hanging just below his collar. She could tell he didn't spend any time with it, just brushed his hands through it and went.

But what captivated her most was the raw, overt male sexuality he oozed. One that ranked right up there with Talon's sexiness. Vane moved with the fluid grace of a predator, with his head held low as if ready to attack.

Grrrr, but the man was a fetching beast.

"You're early," Talon said.

Vane shrugged, his body a symphony of movement. "It

didn't take as long to leave the pack as I thought it would."

The werewolf looked to her and gave her a knee-melting smile. "You really going to trust me with your female, Celt?"

"Yes, I am, because in this swamp, *I* rule."

Vane arched a skeptical brow. "That a threat?"

"It's a promise, Vane. I have my army camped on your doorstep to protect your family. I ask the same of you."

"I'll respect your trust, Celt. But only because I know how rarely you give it."

A look of mutual understanding passed between them.

Vane put his sunglasses back on. "You ready, baby?"

Sunshine stiffened at his offhand endearment. He might be cute, but she had no intention of letting him get away with that one. "You're not my boyfriend or my brother, so lay off the 'baby' thing, okay?"

He flashed a set of killer dimples. "Yes, ma'am." He held the door open until she walked past him. "See you after dark, Celt."

"Yes, you will."

Sunshine paused on the porch and looked about for their ride out of here. "Where's your boat?"

"I don't do the boat thing. It's loud and it takes too long."

"Then how are we going to get out of here?"

Vane smiled devilishly and held his hand out to her. "Trust me?"

Was he joking? "No, I don't even know you."

He laughed, a warm, rich sound that was seductive and charming, although strangely enough, it had no real effect on her. She could appreciate how appealing he was, but her heart and loyalty belonged to Talon.

"All right, then, Dorothy," he said. "Close your eyes, click your heels three times, and say, 'There's no place like home.' "

"What?"

Before she could blink, he took her hand and they flashed from the porch to a wooded area where a small trail broke through the trees. She had no idea where they were, but Talon's cabin was nowhere in sight.

Sunshine gasped. "What did you do?"

"I beamed you over."

"What are you, Scotty?"

He gave her a taunting look as if he were enjoying her discomfort. "It's correctly called a lateral time jump. I just moved you through horizontal time from Talon's porch, across the swamp to where my motorcycle is hidden. Simple."

"Horizontal time? I don't understand."

"Time flows in three directions," he explained. "Forward, backward, and laterally. If you do nothing at all, time always flows forward, but if you catch the Rytis just right, you can choose one of the other directions."

Totally confused, she frowned at him as she tried to comprehend what he was telling her. "What's the Rytis?"

"For lack of a better term, it's warp space."

When she continued to scowl, he pulled his jacket off. "Let me explain it this way." He held the shoulder of his jacket in his right hand and the end of the sleeve in his left. "Time is like this . . . If you want to get from here"—he moved his right hand—"to here," he said, moving his left, "you see how far you have to travel?"

She nodded as she noted the long length of his sleeve. The man had really long arms.

"The Rytis is essentially invisible waves that move around us all the time. Through everything on the planet. They echo and flow and sometimes they buckle. In essence, they do this." He compacted the sleeve between his hands so that his left and right hand were next to each other. "Now to travel from hand to hand, it takes a few seconds instead of several hours."

"Wow," she breathed as she understood. "So you can travel in any time direction? You can even go back in time?"

He nodded.

"And how do you do that? How do you catch this Rytis?"

He shrugged his jacket back on. "Baby, in this world, I'm the all-powerful Oz and there's not much I can't do."

Oh, this guy was getting irritating. "Stop calling me baby."

He inclined his head to her and moved to a tree. Two seconds later, a sleek dark gray motorcycle appeared out of nowhere.

"Okay, how did you do that?"

"In short, I'm a sorcerer. I can bend every law of physics known to mankind and a few not yet discovered."

She was impressed. "That's some serious talent."

Again that dark, deep laugh. "Baby, if you weren't with Talon, I would show you where my true talents lie."

She just bet he would too.

He handed her a helmet.

"You're calling me baby strictly to irritate me, aren't you?"

"My father always said I was born to be the barnacle up his nether regions. I guess I can't help it."

"Do me a favor. Try."

Flashing his dimples, he removed his sunglasses, put them in the inside pocket of his motorcycle jacket, and placed a helmet on his head.

"So tell me," she said. "If you can do all this magic stuff, why are we riding a bike into town? Couldn't you just time-jump us over to the square?"

He fastened his chin strap as he answered her. "I could. But as Acheron so often says, just because you can do something, it doesn't mean you should. Personally, I don't want to be some guy's lab experiment, so I try not to pop in and out of populated areas if I can help it."

That made sense to her. "Since you can time-travel, do you ever think about changing the past?"

"Yes."

"Have you ever done it?"

He shook his head and a dark earnestness came over his

face. "There are some powers in this world that are best left alone. Altering someone's destiny is definitely one of them. Believe me, the Fates have a nasty way of putting a hurt on anyone dumb enough to mess with their domain."

His ominous words rang in her ears. He sounded as if he had once made that mistake, and she wanted to ask if he had, but something inside told her to let it be.

Sunshine put her helmet on, then climbed on the back of the motorcycle and did her best to keep some distance between them. Vane was a handsome man, but something about him made her extremely nervous, and it wasn't the fact he was a werewolf or time-walker.

There was something about him she didn't trust.

At her request, he took her to the small art gallery where she kept her cart of artwork locked up and helped her wheel it to Jackson Square.

By the time they got there, it was a little after ten, and there was a huge crowd already gathered.

"I don't get it," Vane said as he wheeled her cart toward Selena's card stand. "Why are you setting up shop if you just want to meet a client?"

"Cameron said he wanted to see everything I sell. If I have to drag it all out for him, I might as well sell it to other people too."

She showed him where to set it up.

Vane did, but he didn't look too pleased about it.

Selena did a double take as she caught sight of them. "Someone new, Sunny?"

"No, he's just a—"

"Guard dog," he said, extending his hand out to her. "You're Selena Laurens, right? Amanda's older sister?"

Selena nodded as she shook his hand. "You know Amanda?"

"I know Kyrian."

"Is it just me or does everyone know Kyrian?" Sunshine asked.

Selena laughed, then turned back to Vane who was opening up Sunshine's card table where she usually placed her cheaper pottery pieces. "It's daylight so I know you're not a DH. Are you a Squire?"

He stiffened. "Don't insult me. I fetch for no one."

"He's not real friendly," Sunshine explained as she set up her stand. "I think he has rabies or something."

Vane gave her a half amused, half perturbed smile. "You know, Sunshine, I like your spirit."

Sunshine started to respond, but she felt someone watching her.

Scared and anxious, she looked around the crowd until she saw a bright, smiling face that was as familiar to her as her own.

Sunshine beamed.

Even though she wasn't very tall, the elderly woman stood out in the crowd and it wasn't just the insanely bright red shirt she wore. The older woman had an essence and presence that was as powerful and strong as Talon's or Vane's.

Her steel-gray hair was worn up in braids that were wrapped around her head. Her face was lined by a lifetime of happiness and smiles, and her dark brown eyes were bright and kind. The kind of eyes that drew people to the extremely wise woman.

"Grammy!" Sunshine said, as the older woman drew near. "What are you doing here? I thought you swore to never step foot in New Orleans again during Mardi Gras."

Her grandmother squeezed her tight, then pulled back to look at her. It'd been almost a year since they had last seen each other.

Oh, it was great to see her grandmother again!

Her grandmother ran her hand up and down her arm as if reassuring herself that Sunshine was healthy. "Well, that was my intention, but your mother called and told me that you were having all kinds of questions about being a Celt. So I thought I'd just pop in and surprise you."

"You certainly did. But I'm glad you're here."

Her grandmother arched a censuring brow as she caught sight of Vane. "And you are?"

"Vane Kattalakis."

She looked back at Sunshine. "Where's this Talon your mother told me about?"

"He'll be here later, Grammy."

She nodded, then pulled a small medallion out from under her shirt and placed it around Sunshine's neck.

"What's this?"

Her grandmother adjusted it so that it would be obvious to anyone who glanced at her. "Keep that close to your heart, little one. If that man comes after you again, you let him know who protects you."

"What man?" she asked, hoping her grandmother didn't know about her kidnapping.

She did.

"I know what happened, Sunny. You know I do."

Drat. Her grandmother had some eerie psychic talents.

"I don't think your necklace will scare him, Grammy."

"You'd be surprised. And if it doesn't, then he deserves what he gets." Her grandmother patted her on the shoulder and turned to Selena. "Have you been practicing those exercises I showed you, Ms. Laurens?"

"Yes, ma'am. I can feel my powers growing every day."

"Good. Now I better get back to Starla's. If that rank bastard comes near my baby—"

"Grandma!" Sunshine gasped. She'd never in her life heard her grandmother use such a word.

"Well, he is. Messing with my granddaughter. I'll boil his warts in oil and feed his head to the wolves."

Vane choked on that one. "You know, wolves don't really like to eat heads. Meat, yes, but heads are really hard on the jaws. Not to mention, the cranium gets caught between your teeth."

Her grandmother gave him a withering stare. "Are you being smart with me, boy?"

"Yes."

"Young man," her grandmother said in a haughty tone, "didn't your mother teach you any manners?"

"My mother only taught me one thing and, I promise you, it wasn't manners."

Her grandmother nodded. "I can see that. But you still have a very important lesson to learn in life."

"And that is?"

"One day you're going to have to let someone other than your brother and sister get close to you."

His face turned to stone and the look in his eyes was feral and fierce. "What do you know about my siblings?"

"More than you would care for. You have a hard road ahead of you, Vane Kattalakis. I wish I could ease it for you, but it's yours alone to travel. Just remember, you're a lot stronger than you think you are."

"Believe me, lady, my strength is the one thing I never doubt."

Her grandmother smiled at that. "It's amazing the lies we tell other people, isn't it?"

Her grandmother turned her back on him. "Selena, Sunshine. You two take care. And Sunshine, when tonight comes, follow your heart. Do as it commands, and it won't fail you."

"Okay, Grandma, I will."

Her grandmother kissed her cheek, then headed off toward St. Anne.

After she was out of sight, Sunshine turned back to see Vane looking agitated. "I'm sorry. She does that a lot to people. She tends to just say whatever pops into her head."

Vane didn't speak. Instead, he folded his arms over his chest and leaned back against the black iron fence that surrounded the square.

Sunshine finished setting up her stand, then checked her watch.

It was still a little while before Cameron was due, so she pulled out her sketchbook and started doodling.

Before she realized it, she'd drawn a picture of the man who had kidnapped her.

Vane looked at the sketch. "Damn good likeness."

Sunshine went cold. "You know this guy?"

"Well, yeah. Of course I do. So does Talon. Selena probably knows him too."

"Selena," Sunshine said, heading to her friend. "Do you know who this is?"

"Sure, it's Acheron."

"Who's Acheron?" she asked. Everyone kept mentioning his name around her, but she had no idea who or what he was.

"For lack of a better explanation," Vane said, "Talon's boss."

"Why would Talon's boss kidnap me? Do you think it's to keep me away from Talon?"

Vane laughed at that. "Not his style. If Ash wanted to keep you away from Talon, he'd just show up at your door and scare the crap out of you. Besides, he was the one leading the rescue party to you."

Well, that was nice to know.

But why did he look just like the guy who'd kidnapped her?

Her frown deepened. "He was there when Talon got me away from Camulus?"

"Yeah and I was too. Don't you remember?"

She shook her head. All she could remember was Talon. "How well do you know Talon and Acheron?" she asked Vane.

He shrugged. "I just met Talon, but I've crossed paths with Acheron a time or two over the centuries."

"Are you immortal too?"

He shook his head no. "My kind just lives a lot longer than humans."

"How long?"

"About a thousand years, give or take a century or two."

Wow. That was quite a while.

Sunshine couldn't imagine what it would be like to have that long to plan her future. But something inside told her that it might be as big a curse as a blessing to live that long, especially if you had to live it alone.

Sunshine watched Vane as he scanned the crowd around

them. Those hazel-green eyes seemed to take in everything.

"Why are you so open to talk about this while Talon refuses to tell me anything?"

He shrugged. "I didn't swear an oath of secrecy, and I figure you've seen enough spooky shit the last few days that knowing about me is the least of your problems. Besides, I dare you to tell anyone I'm really a wolf pretending to be human."

He paused and grinned devilishly at her. "I double *dog* dare you," he said slowly. "That, my friend, will get you locked inside a rubber room."

She had no doubt about that at all. And it explained why he felt so free to talk about his "differences." "Are you really a wolf?"

He nodded.

"Then how can you be human?"

"We're a different breed than your people. My race was created about nine thousand years ago when my great-grandfather decided to save the lives of his sons by magically splicing their DNA with a few choice animals. Thus we were born. One son made two half-blooded creatures. One that held a human heart and one that held an animal heart. I'm directly descended from the animal."

"So you have the heart of a wolf?"

Again, he nodded. "And the morals and the self-preservation instincts of one too."

"Do you ever wish you were human?"

"No, never. Why would I?"

And yet she sensed he was hiding something. There was a lot more to his feelings than he was willing to admit and it was obvious he didn't want her to delve into it.

So she changed the subject. "Does it hurt when you change forms? Is it like the movies where you get all hairy and bones crunch?"

He snorted at that. "No. That's strictly a Hollywood dramatization. Since we're born of magic, for the most part we wield it painlessly. I feel about as much pain transforming as you did when we bopped from Talon's cabin to my bike. All you get is a little electrical frizz going through you. It's actually kind of pleasurable if you do it right."

"It must be neat to be able to do all that." She tilted her head, squinted her eyes, and looked at him.

"What are you doing?"

"Trying to imagine what you would look like as a wolf."

"Pray you never find out."

She stepped back from him. "You know, I think you guys really get off on scaring people."

"Sometimes we do."

Not willing to investigate that any further, Sunshine continued to wait.

Unfortunately, Cameron didn't show.

Vane tried to get her to go back to Talon's but she refused. "Maybe he's just late. Maybe he had a meeting or something. I can't just leave."

Vane gave a low, very wolf-sounding growl at that and took up a seat behind her stand, leaning back against the black iron fence while she sat on her stool, hawking her wares and sketching.

The afternoon dragged on, but nothing happened.

Cameron still hadn't shown up.

Selena left at four for a brief break.

Vane was now sitting on the curb behind her. His long legs were stretched out on the street, and he had them crossed at the ankles. He was leaning back on his arms. The position pulled his cotton T-shirt tight over his impeccable body.

"You do this every day?" he asked.

"Pretty much."

"Man, this is boring as hell. What do you do to keep from going insane?"

"I usually sketch or paint, and before I know it, the day has passed and it's time to go home."

"Well, I don't get it."

People who weren't artists never did.

"Hi, Sunshine, you got anything new?"

Sunshine turned to see Bride McTierney approaching

her on the opposite side of the cart. A tall, plus-sized type of voluptuous, Bride had the face of one of Botticelli's angels. Her hair was so dark an auburn that it appeared black unless Bride was outside. Then it was a deep luminescent red. Bride usually wore it up in a clip with tendrils of it falling around her face.

A real sweetheart, Bride was one of her regular clients. She'd even taken some of Sunshine's paintings and used them in her boutique.

"No," Sunshine said, "sorry. I haven't been painting the fantasy or Jackson Square stuff lately. I've mostly been working on commissioned pieces."

"Rats, I just moved into a new apartment and was hoping you'd have something to make the drab walls tolerable."

Sunshine frowned. Bride had loved her place on Iberville. "Why did you move?"

"Taylor doesn't like coming all the way into the city at night so I thought it would be easier if I lived closer to where he works."

"But *you* work in the quarter."

"I know. It's one of the sacrifices we all have to make for love." She offered Sunshine a smile, but Sunshine could tell it was only a façade.

That was exactly what Sunshine was afraid of.

Why was it always the woman who had to sacrifice for love? Just once, couldn't a guy do it instead?

Bride sighed. "Give me a call if you paint anything new that I'd like, okay?"

"I will. By the way, you're looking really good. Have you lost weight?"

Bride beamed. "I'm down to a size sixteen. But I have to tell you that I am starving *all* the time."

"Yeah, but you're a knockout."

"Thanks. Taylor signed me up for an aerobics class at his club that meets four times a week and that helped to get a lot of the weight off."

"You don't sound like you enjoy it very much."

Pain darkened Bride's eyes as she averted her gaze. "I just hate having to put on sweats and then walk into a room filled with size-two women in leotards—like they really need those classes. It makes me want to head to Krispy Kreme even more than the diet does."

Sunshine laughed. "Tell me about it. I personally don't think they should make anything except gunny sacks for anyone under a size ten."

Bride smiled again. "Speaking of dress sizes and skinny women, I guess I better head back to the shop. You take care, okay?"

"You too."

Bride wandered off in the direction of her store.

"Who was that?" Vane was now standing up, staring after Bride with a hungry glint in his eyes.

How did he do that? The man, or rather wolf, moved with an eerie silence.

"Her name is Bride McTierney. She owns a boutique over on Iberville."

"She's . . . very nice."

Sunshine was amazed he thought so. Most guys were intimidated or just plain turned off by Bride's height and Rubenesque build.

Vane looked as if he had just seen a supermodel in the flesh.

Now this could be good . . .

He blinked and returned to sitting on the curb.

"You know, I could introduce the two of you."

He looked up at her, then glanced away. Still, she had glimpsed the regret in his green eyes.

"Wolves don't socialize with humans. You guys tend to freak out when you learn what we are. Not to mention, your females are rather frail. I don't like having to hold back for fear of bruising or killing my partner when I mate."

"And people think I speak my mind. Jeez. You will just say anything, won't you?"

"I told you, I'm not human. I don't share your inhibitions."

She supposed that was true enough. But it was a pity. Bride could use a man who accepted her as she was and didn't put her on strict diets and exercise regimes all the time.

"So," Vane said after a few minutes. "What's between you and the Celt? Are the two of you just casually carnal or is there something more?"

"Why are you asking?"

"Because you've asked me for a full bio. I figure turnabout is fair play."

Sunshine sat down next to him. "I don't know. When I'm with Talon it's like we fit. Like he's a part of me that I didn't know I was missing until I found him."

"Does he feel the same way?"

She sighed wistfully. "Who knows? With him it's hard to tell sometimes. I'm not really sure that *I* am the one he loves."

"True. Emotions don't appear to be his strong suit. Still, you must mean a lot to him for him to call me in."

"How do you figure?"

"Going against Acheron's orders isn't a smart thing for a Dark-Hunter to do. That man has life-and-death control over them. Secondly, Talon was willing to barter with me to keep you safe. Again, not a smart thing to do."

"Why, you're not going to hurt him, are you?"

"Not at the moment, but when you consider the danger my people live in, obligating yourself to a Katagari Slayer is one step away from blatant stupidity."

"A what Slayer?"

"The real term for what I am."

Sunshine frowned at him. "Okay, and what exactly is a Katagari Slayer?"

"Someone who kills without remorse."

A chill went down her spine and yet she found it hard to believe he could be capable of such a thing. He was feral, no doubt, but he didn't seem completely without a conscience in spite of what he said. "Would you really do that?"

"Baby, I would kill my own mother and not think twice."

She remembered what her grandmother had said about his siblings. "Yes, but would you kill your brother or your sister?"

He looked away.

She nudged his shoulder. "You're not as amoral as you pretend, Vane Kattalakis. I think there may be more human inside you than you think."

Sunshine returned to her cart and sat on her stool. She continued to scan the people around her, but as the sun set and Cameron didn't show, she saw no one who even remotely seemed threatening.

Well, no one other than her guard.

Talon was up and dressed before sundown. He was pacing the floor of his cabin, dying to leave and find Sunshine.

Anxious, he dialed Vane.

"She's still alive and unharmed," Vane said without greeting. "Sunshine," he called, "it's the Celt wanting a little reassurance that I haven't eaten you or anything."

Talon rubbed his head at Vane's odd humor as he waited for Sunshine to reach for the phone.

"Talon?"

"Hey, baby, you okay?" Talon asked, instantly relieved to hear her smooth Southern drawl in his ear.

It was the most blessed sound he'd ever known.

"I'm fine. Absolutely nothing has happened. It's been really boring today. Except for Vane. He's interesting in a very Cujoesque sort of way."

He smiled. His mood was instantly lighter just knowing she was okay. "I'll bet. You be careful and I'll be out there as soon as I can."

"Okay. See you soon."

His heart clenched as she made a kissing noise to him,

then handed the phone back to Vane. Gods, how he loved that woman.

"Ahh, Tally, me lub you too."

"Shut up, crotch-sniffer. You're not allowed to make lovey noises at me, only my honey is."

Vane snorted. "You know, I'm really going to make you pay one day."

"Yeah, I'll bring along a few extra kibbles for you."

Vane laughed good-naturedly. "For that, swamp rat, you owe me an extra nice plate of prime rib."

"You got it. How are you doing, by the way? You holding on to your human form without any problems?"

"I'm just peachy. Even managed to keep most of my clothes on and everything."

"Yeah, you do that. Don't want your scrawny body making my Sunshine go blind or anything."

"Trust me, if she hasn't gone blind looking at your fat, hairy ass, mine's not going to hurt her any."

"Hairy? Excuse me, but you definitely have me confused with your brother."

Vane laughed again.

"Seriously, though, the sun'll be down in about fifteen minutes. I'll head out immediately."

"I'm holding down the fort, Custer. Don't worry."

"Thanks, Bull. See you in a bit."

Talon hung up and waited until he could feel the tingling on his skin that always alerted him that the sun was gone and it was safe to leave.

It was about forty-five minutes after dark when Sunshine asked Vane to walk the short distance around the corner to the Coke stand and get her something to drink.

He balked, but she finally convinced him that she would still be in full sight and wouldn't wander off until he returned.

As soon as he got in line, she heard Selena's low whistle.

"Now that man looks scary with a capital S. He has serial killer written all over him."

Sunshine turned to see an extremely tall, dark-haired man rounding the corner. The horses that lined Decatur Street snorted and pranced uneasily as he passed by them.

It was as if they sensed something evil about him.

He looked so incredibly sinister that her stomach drew tight. "Should I call Vane back?"

"I don't know." Selena got up from her card table and moved to stand beside Sunshine. "If he makes a move on you, I'll grab him and you scream."

"Okay. Maybe he'll just keep on walking right past us."

He didn't.

He glanced at her cart as he came even with it, then paused.

Sunshine's gaze fell to the vicious-looking silver claws on his left hand.

He didn't speak a word as he approached her cart. She swallowed and instinctively moved closer to Selena. The man would be incredibly handsome if he didn't look so ferocious.

She exchanged nervous looks with Selena.

His dark, deadly gaze was focused on the bowls she had fashioned after a Greek design she'd seen in a museum catalog. With a gentleness she wouldn't have thought him capable of, he ran his hand over a red-figured bowl.

A flash of longing darkened his eyes, as if the design brought back some bittersweet memory for him. "You make these?"

She actually flinched as his intense black gaze met hers. He had a deep, provocative voice that was so heavily accented, it took her a minute to understand his question. "I do."

"Nice work."

She couldn't have been more stunned had he taken a gun out and shot her. "Thanks."

When he reached into his pocket, she braced herself to

scream for Vane until she realized he was just pulling out his wallet. "How much?"

"What are you doing here?"

She looked past the man to see Talon approaching. His long, angry predatorial strides brought him to her side. Fast.

"None of your friggin' business, Celt," the stranger growled.

"Get away from Sunshine, Zarek, or I swear I'll put you down."

Zarek tucked his wallet back in his pocket and turned to face Talon. "Try it, Celt, and I'll have your heart in my fist."

Talon lunged and shoved him back.

Zarek swung at him, but Talon ducked and shoved him again.

Vane came out of nowhere to break them apart. "Hey, hey, hey!" he snarled at Talon, forcing him away from Zarek. "What is this about?"

"I better not ever catch you around her, Zarek. I mean it."

Zarek flipped him off with his claw, then turned around and stalked angrily toward the Presbytere building.

Sunshine was terrified as she saw the wild look on Talon's face. He really looked like he could kill someone. "Talon?"

"Stay back," Vane warned. "You okay, Celt?"

Talon couldn't respond. All he could feel was the rising fury inside him. The demanding, hot need he had to rip Zarek to pieces.

The moment he had seen Zarek, his mind had flashed back to Zarek in the alley with his victim.

God help the man if he *ever* attacked Sunshine that way. He'd kill him regardless of the consequences.

Without comment, Talon pulled Sunshine against him and held her there. He fisted his hand in her hair, inhaled her warm patchouli scent, and just reveled in the peace he felt while holding her.

"You were supposed to be watching her, Vane," he snarled at the Were-Hunter.

"It was just Zarek, Celt. Calm down. He wasn't doing anything but looking at her dishes."

"He could have hurt her."

"But he didn't."

"Yeah, and you're damn lucky for that."

Zarek was still fuming as he made his way down Pirate's Alley.

When was he going to learn? Every time he had tried to help someone, it had always turned around and bit him on his ass.

He'd recognized the woman the minute he'd seen her and was wondering why Talon had left her unprotected.

He clenched his teeth. "Fine. Let her die."

What did he care anyway?

As he neared the end of the alley, he stopped. A foreign, cold sensation ran over him. It was one he hadn't felt since the night he'd crossed over from human to Dark-Hunter.

"Zarek."

He turned to see none other than Dionysus before him. The Greek god had his short brown hair impeccably combed. He wore a dark tweed jacket over a navy turtle-neck and looked like some kind of high-paid corporate raider.

"If you're going to blast me, Dionysus, have at it."

Dionysus laughed. "Please call me Dion. Dionysus is just so passé."

Zarek stiffened as the god neared him. The power of the being was undeniable and it caused the air around him to sizzle. "Why are you speaking to me?"

Dionysus indicated the Pedestrian Mall with his thumb. "I overheard your little exchange with Talon. I was thinking we could make a deal, you and I."

Zarek scoffed at the very idea. "That would be like making a pact with Lucifer."

"Yes, but I don't smell like sulfur. And I happen to dress better. Luc always looks like a pimp." He offered Zarek a cigarette. "Go ahead, have one. It's even your brand."

Zarek took him up on it and eyed him suspiciously as he lit the cigarette. "So what's the pact?"

"Simple. I have a boy in town who is doing some favors for me. You ran into him last night. The one who looks like your boss."

"Yeah, I know the bastard. I owe him too."

"I know. It was unfortunate that the two of you met like that. But if you can put aside your anger, I think you'll like my deal a lot better."

"And that is?"

"My boy needs a few things. Now we could kill you, but I'm thinking a man of your 'special' abilities and skills would be better on our side than drifting through eternity as a disembodied Shade." Dionysus paused.

"Keep talking."

"All I need is for you to not hunt. Go home like Acheron wants and stay there until Mardi Gras. During my celebration, Styxx will be in touch. Help him with the final preparations and I will give you what you want most."

"And what do I want most?"

"An end to your suffering."

Zarek had to give the god credit, he knew what to offer, all right. "You're not trying to trick me, are you?"

"I swear by the river Styx that if you assist us, I will put you out of your pain. Completely. No tricks. No loopholes. One blast and you're beyond even death."

"And if I don't?"

Dionysus smiled evilly. "Hades has a nice corner of Tartarus waiting for you."

Zarek took a drag on his cigarette and laughed darkly. "Like that scares me. What's he going to do? Tear the flesh off my body? Break my bones? Better yet, why not hold me down and stomp on me until I bleed or make me shovel shit? Oh wait, been there, done that, and got the videotape."

Dionysus's green eyes blazed. "I can't believe Artemis lets you live."

"I can't believe you're a god with no better threat than that. But don't worry," he said as Dionysus looked like he was ready to strike. "I hate these assholes anyway and couldn't care less how many of them you turn into Shades."

The god calmed down instantly.

"I take it you know my cell number?" Zarek asked.

Dionysus nodded. "We'll be in touch."

"Fine. I'll see you Tuesday."

At Talon's insistence, Sunshine packed up her cart and let the men wheel it back toward her art gallery. But as they started away, she stopped them.

"What are you doing?" Talon asked as she opened up the small side door on her cart.

"Nothing."

He frowned at her as she pulled out the bowl Zarek had been looking at. She handed it to Vane. "Would you mind taking this to Zarek for me?"

Talon was aghast. "What are you, insane?"

"No, Talon. That man is in a lot of pain. I think he could use an act of kindness from someone."

Vane scoffed. "What he could use is a good butt-kicking."

"Vane, please." Sunshine urged him to take it.

He did, grudgingly. "Okay, but if he throws it at me, I'm going to want some compensation."

She kissed him on the cheek.

"Lame compensation, but in the presence of Talon, I'll settle for it."

Vane took the bowl and headed off down the street.

She turned back to Talon who was still frowning. "Zarek will slam it against a wall and break it the first chance he gets."

"I don't think so. Even if he does, I can always make another one."

He helped her lock up her cart and then led her back out to the street. "You have such a generous heart."

"That's what they tell me. So, shall we go hunt for Styxx?"

"Hell, no. I'm not going to chance you getting hurt."

She growled at him. "Listen, my grandmother said something to me this afternoon. She told me to follow my heart tonight. I don't know what she meant by that, but I trust her. She is an extraordinary psychic. Everything she has told me has come true."

"Look, Sunshine, I can't help what she said. I just know that I'm not willing to let anything happen to you. When Nynia died, I was so lost and cold, and I haven't been warm since. Not until I felt your hands on me. The only way I've been able to cope without you is to bury what I feel, but I can't seem to do that anymore. When I'm with you all I can do is feel and need."

"That's how I am too."

"So where does that leave us?"

"I don't know, Talon. I wish I did."

Talon put his arm over her shoulder as they walked back toward the square. He noticed other couples around them.

How he wished they could be a normal, happy couple with no worries other than a mortgage payment.

But it wasn't meant to be.

Camulus was playing with both of them and Sunshine was going to get hurt.

Talon only knew one real way to protect both of them.

"So where are we going?" Sunshine asked.

"We're going to see a god about a miracle."

Chapter 15

Ash ground his teeth as Artemis ran her hands through his long, blond hair. He shuttered his eyes as he watched her draw a lock of it between her fingers and flick the curl back and forth with her fingertip.

"I have to go," he said.

She pouted seductively, running her graceful hand down his bare chest, her fingernails gently scraping his skin. "I don't want you to go."

"Release me, Artie. I have to find Styxx before he hurts anyone else. He almost killed Zarek last night."

"Who cares? Zarek is better off dead."

"That can be said for most of us."

She painfully raked her nails down his arms, which were secured to her bedposts by a pair of soft golden cords. "I hate when you talk like that. You're so ungrateful after all I have done for you."

Oh yeah, she had done so much *for* him. More like *to* him and very little of it had been kind or enjoyable.

"Don't make me break your restraints, Artie." If he used his powers to untie her "special" cords, it would send a signal through Olympus alerting the other gods of his presence in her temple. Anytime he "visited" her, his powers were seriously restricted. He could do paltry parlor-type tricks such as open doors or dress and undress, but anything more than that would be picked up by the Olympian gods and would cause them to investigate the unknown source of power.

That was the only thing Artemis feared.

"You'd like that, wouldn't you? To have Zeus or one of the others find you in my bed?"

"Then let me go."

The golden cords unwrapped themselves from his wrists. Ash sighed as he moved his arms for the first time since dawn and let the circulation travel back into his hands.

A wave of exhaustion hit him, but he shook it off.

As usual, Artemis hadn't let him sleep at all while he'd been with her, and he'd now been awake for two days straight.

He was so tired, he wanted nothing more than to sleep.

"Oh, guess what I found out for you," Artemis said. "My worthless brother, Dion, has hooked up with yours and with the Gaulic war god, Camulus, in a bid for power. Is that a goof or what?"

Acheron froze. "What did you say?"

"Dion and Cam think they can retake their godhoods and they're using your brother as their ringleader. Can you say, rockball's chance?" She laughed. "Just imagine, a forgotten Gaulic war god, my brother, whose only claim to fame is sucking down wine and getting laid, and your brother, whose only good mark is he happens to look like you. And they think the cabbage can lead them to glory." She snorted, then laughed again. "I can't wait to see what these losers have planned."

Acheron stared at her. She might underestimate their abilities, but he had a sneaking suspicion of what they intended to do.

On Mardi Gras, the barrier between this world and the one where the Atlantean Destroyer was held would be thin.

There could be only one reason for them to have Styxx in on their plans . . .

They wanted to release the Destroyer and the only way to do that would be by killing Ash.

One way or another, Ash was going to make sure it didn't happen.

Come Mardi Gras, they all had a big surprise coming.

They had no idea who and what they were dealing with. The Destroyer was far beyond their ability to command or control. Once unleashed, she was the most merciless ancient god imaginable. One who had slain every member of her own family. Afterward, she would have destroyed the entire earth had she not been stopped and imprisoned.

If Camulus and Dionysus thought to bargain with her after they killed him, they were pathetically mistaken.

He almost smiled at the thought of them trying to reason with her. Mardi Gras night would be interesting, no doubt.

"By the way," Artemis said as she reclined naked on the bed and ran her bare foot up his spine in a long, cool caress, "your children have been very bad while you were here."

Ash stopped rubbing his wrist and looked at her. "What do you mean?"

"In direct disobedience to your orders, Zarek was out and about earlier this evening, and he and Talon got into a fight in the French Quarter."

Anger rushed through him. "What? When?"

"About two hours ago."

"Dammit, Artemis," he snarled. "Why didn't you tell me?"

She shrugged and ran her hand over her naked breasts in an effort to draw his attention to her. "I liked you where you were and I knew if I told you, you'd leave."

Ash glared at her. Her selfishness knew no bounds. Angry at her, he snapped his fingers and returned his clothes to his body. He made his hair black and grabbed his backpack up from the floor.

"I hate that hair color on you," she said petulantly, zapping his hair back to blond.

He stiffened. "Yeah, well, the only color I hate more than blond is auburn." He made his hair black again, then zapped hers to a matching shade.

Her furious shriek echoed through the temple as Ash mentally commanded himself back to New Orleans.

Sunshine felt an adrenaline rush as they approached the biker bar at 688 Ursulines Avenue. It was the best place in town to come meet friends, eat good food, and find all kinds of fun things to do.

"You didn't tell me we were going to Sanctuary."

Talon frowned. "You know about Sanctuary?"

"Honey, there's not a single woman in this town who doesn't know about Sanctuary, Land of the Bodacious Gods. Heck, me and my girlfriends want to get together and vote Mama Lo an award for her policy against hiring any man not seriously buff."

She noted the offended grimace on his face and couldn't help laughing. "Not that you're not buff. You can certainly hold your own against the Sanctuary Hotties. But face it, haven't you ever noticed that this place is like Hooters for women?"

"No. I can honestly say that I've never noticed how good-looking the men at Sanctuary are. Nor have I ever cared."

The outside of the club was a typical New Orleans building that had been constructed in 1801. The brick was a rust color and a huge sign swung over the old-fashioned saloon-type doors. It showed a full moon rising over a hill where a motorcycle was parked and proudly proclaimed this place as Sanctuary, Home of the Howlers—the Howlers being the house band for the club, and a mighty fine-looking group of men they were too.

The bar was open twenty-four hours a day, seven days a week, and was owned by the Peltier family. The owner, Mama Lo, had eleven studly sons who again warranted the woman an award for beautifying the city.

Each one of them was a prime male specimen guaranteed to make a woman pant.

Dev Peltier was at the door as they entered. A regular

bouncer, he was one in a set of identical quadruplets. Sunshine had never met a woman who didn't want to take one of the quads home. For that matter, they wanted to take them all home and use them as matching bookends in the bedroom. Only it wasn't books her friends wanted to sandwich between the quadruplets.

Dev had a pair of piercingly blue eyes and long, wavy blond hair that fell to the middle of his back. The only way she knew it was Dev as opposed to one of his brothers was the bow-and-arrow tattoo on his arm.

She paused as she realized it was identical to the brand on Talon's shoulder.

"Hey, man," Dev said in that shivery-hot, deep accent that was a cross between French and Cajun as he caught sight of Talon. The two of them did a high-five shake. "Where have you been?"

"Out and about. You?"

Dev gave him a wicked grin. "Mostly in and out."

Talon laughed. "I'm not going there."

Dev looked at her and winked. "Hey, little Sunshine, why you hanging out with this loser? You lose a bet or something?"

"Or something," she said with a smile.

"You know Dev?" Talon asked her, his body going rigid as if the thought made him jealous.

"Yeah," Dev answered before she could. "She comes in all the time. Her and Aimee play pool in the back."

"You come here alone?"

Sunshine shoved Talon playfully on the shoulder. "Would you stop? You're not my father and no one bothers me here thanks to Dev and his brothers."

"That's right, Talon, you know my policy. No one harasses a woman in Sanctuary unless she wants to be harassed."

"The exception being Aimee," Sunshine couldn't resist adding. The only daughter in the massive Peltier clan, Aimee couldn't get near a man without one of her brothers or her enormously tall, well-muscled father having a stroke.

"Double damn straight." Dev inclined his head to the coffin that was kept in the corner of the club right as you came in the door. "That's the last moron who asked my sister out."

Talon laughed again. "There's another place I don't want to go to. I'm looking for Eros, has he been in here yet?"

"Upstairs by the storeroom playing poker with Rudy, Justin, and Etienne."

"Thanks." Talon led her through the front half of the bar where tables and booths were set up for eating. The place was rather crowded tonight and the music from the Howlers was loud and thumping.

"Hey, Talon," Sunshine shouted in his ear. "Why do you and Dev have the same bow-and-arrow mark on your bodies?"

He glanced back to where Dev stood at the door. "Dev thinks it's funny that he bears the mark of a . . ." His voice trailed off, but she caught his unspoken meaning by the glint in his eyes.

The bow mark must be the signature sign of a Dark-Hunter. "Is he one too?"

"No, he's another *breed* entirely."

Understanding ripped through her. "A breed like Vane?"

He paused and lowered his head so that he could speak without being overheard. "Yes, and at the same time, no."

So he must be a were-beast of a different sort. "Does this mean his entire family is able to change . . ."—she shifted gears as a patron came too close—"their clothes to something entirely new?" she finished.

He nodded.

Wow! Who knew? An entire were-family ran one of the most popular places in town. Very chic.

Talon straightened and headed for the back where the pool tables were kept. There was an ornate pine staircase that led to the area above, where additional tables were set up for people to eat and watch the band as they played below.

Even the upstairs area was packed tonight.

Without stopping, Talon led her past the patrons and headed for the last table on the left, which was set in a corner.

Five people sat at it and four of them were playing poker. Etienne Peltier was leaner than his older brother Dev, but no less muscular. He had shoulder-length, straight blond hair and a face that could only be called angelic. But as Sunshine had learned on more than one occasion, the devil himself resided in that handsome body. No one wanted to cross Etienne.

Rudy St. Michel sat next to Etienne. Average in appearance, he looked like the typical New Orleans drifter with long black hair, and colorful tattoos covering every inch of visible flesh. He'd started working here about a year ago and was responsible for the arcade games downstairs.

Another bouncer, Justin Portakalian, had his back to the wall and one long, leather-encased leg stretched out over a wooden chair as he handed two cards over to Rudy. He was as gorgeous as any of the Peltiers, with medium-length, dark brown hair and hazel eyes that glittered with malice. At six feet six and with a bad attitude that redefined the term, he was someone Sunshine had always tried to avoid. He didn't talk much and had tossed her last boyfriend through the back door. Literally.

She'd also heard a rumor that Justin was fresh out of prison for murder, and something about his deadly demeanor added quite a bit of credibility to that speculation.

The other two people she didn't know. One was a blond biker who held a beautiful, barely dressed redhead on his lap. He looked up, saw Talon, and the smile faded from his lips. "What are you doing here, Celt?"

"I need to talk to you."

"Can't you see I'm winning?"

Talon looked at the poker chips by his elbow. "Yes, and I can also see that you're cheating."

"What?" The other men were suddenly animated.

"Talon, you dick!" The blond cleared his throat. "He's just kidding. Give me a minute, okay?"

Rudy snorted at Justin and Etienne as he adjusted the five cards in his hands. "I don't know why you guys are bitching. Both of you cheat too."

Etienne smiled that charming devil-may-care smile while Justin passed a less than amused glare at Rudy.

The blond biker started away from the table, then hurried back and grabbed up his cards.

"Just in case," he said to the others.

As soon as the blond stepped back to them, Talon introduced them. "Sunshine, meet Eros and Psyche."

Sunshine looked at them curiously. "They just think those names are cute, right? They're not really Eros and Psyche."

Eros gave her a peeved stare. "Why is she talking to me?"

"Cupid," Talon said, a warning note in his voice. "Play nice." He turned to Psyche. "Would you please do me a favor, Psyche, and keep Sunshine occupied while I deal with your husband?"

"Sure, hon." Psyche draped her arm over Sunshine's shoulders. "Come on, let's go see what kind of trouble we can get into downstairs."

Sunshine followed Psyche to the ornate staircase that led to the floor below, not far from the stage. The whole area was crammed with dancers and people who wanted to hear the Howlers sing, and with women who wanted to ogle the gorgeous band members.

She and Psyche went over to a pool table where a guy named Nick Gautier was playing a game with Wren, one of the Sanctuary busboys. Wren was a quiet, shy type who had an aura around him that said he would rather be invisible. Still, there was something dangerous about him. Kind of like he would gladly fight anyone dumb enough to disturb his introverted space.

His dark blond hair was long, and he wore it in a style that wasn't quite dreadlocks, but something not far from that either. His eyes were so pale a gray that they looked almost colorless.

As for Nick Gautier, Sunshine had met him here a few times. His mother was one of the cooks and he often came in for dinner and to play a quick game of pool with Wren.

"Hi, ladies," Nick said with his light Cajun drawl.

Psyche took the cue from his hand. "Rack your balls, Nick. We want to play."

Nick laughed. "Psych, one thing a woman should never tell a man to do is rack his balls."

Ignoring him, Psyche looked over to Wren. "You don't mind, do you?"

Wren shook his head no and handed his cue to Sunshine. Without a word, he quickly vanished into the crowd.

"I didn't mean to disturb you guys," Sunshine said to Nick.

"Ah, don't worry about it. Wren and I play a lot. He needed to get back to the kitchen anyway. You ladies want something to drink?"

"Beer," Psyche said.

"Water."

He nodded and left.

Sunshine watched as Nick navigated the crowd. She turned back to Psyche. "So you and Eros come here a lot?"

She nodded. "I've even seen you here a few times. You usually hang out with Aimee and some black-haired chick."

"Trina."

"That's her."

Psyche grabbed the cue ball and lined it up. "Yes," she said as she took her shot, sending six of the balls into pockets. "I'm a goddess and Eros is a god."

"How did you know—"

"I'm a goddess. I can hear every thought in your head." She smiled at Sunshine while she chalked her tip.

"That's a really uncomfortable fact to know."

"Isn't it, though?" Psyche blew across the tip, set the chalk aside, then knocked three more balls into the pockets. "And because I know what you're thinking, the answer is yes."

"The answer to what?"

"Whether or not Talon loves you."

Sunshine grimaced as Psyche sank the rest of balls on the table. "I don't know. There are times when I get the feeling he can't tell me from Nynia. I think he loves her more than me."

Psyche racked the balls again. "No offense, but that's stupid. You and Talon are soulmates. He will always love you no matter who or what you are. You, my friend, could come back as a humpback whale and he would love you. He can't help it. The two of you are destined for each other."

"Yeah, but—"

"There are no buts, Sunshine." She moved to stand in front of her. "I am the goddess of souls and soulmates. Unlike the other Olympian gods, I know when I see two people who were created for each other. If both you and Talon died tonight and were later reborn at polar ends of the earth, sooner or later the two of you would reunite. That's the schtick with soulmates. Alone you can survive, hell, you can even be with other people, but neither of you will ever be complete without the other." She glanced upstairs where they had left the guys. "You two can fight this all you want. But all you're going to do is make yourselves miserable."

She patted Sunshine's shoulder. "I know you don't believe me. I know it'll take time before you accept it. And that being said, the problem with your relationship isn't whether or not he loves you. It's that he can't afford to even think that thought."

"Why?"

"Because the minute he does, Camulus will kill you. Talon knows that. He will not let himself love you for fear of your dying again."

Sunshine swallowed at her words. Everything kept coming back to that one irritable and irritating Celtic god. "Is there any way to get around Camulus?"

"Maybe."

"Maybe? That's the best you can do?"

"Hey, it's better than no."

True, but still she wanted more hope than that.

"And what about Artemis?" Sunshine asked. "Even if we get past Camulus, what about her?"

Psyche twisted her cue in her hands as she thought about that never-to-be-forgotten fact. "She's tricky. With her you have to negotiate very carefully."

"So it's possible I could talk to her?"

"It's possible."

Sunshine's mind whirled at the thought. Could there really be hope for them?

Talon led Eros into the storeroom and shut the door. Quinn Peltier had soundproofed the room a few decades back to ensure that the Peltiers and other select friends could have emergency privacy if they needed it.

Originally, the room had been planned as a holding place in the event one of them accidentally turned into a bear while the club was occupied, but over time it had come to serve as a convenient place for one of the brothers to take a willing woman should they have an itch that wouldn't wait.

But that was another story.

Talon switched on the dim overhead light and faced Eros. "I need a favor."

"Favor, hell. Didn't you know that I'm supposed to vaporize any Dark-Hunter who gets near me?"

Talon looked at him drolly. "I'll remember that the next time you want to borrow poker money from me without Psyche knowing."

Eros smiled good-naturedly. "Good point. Okay, what can I do you to?"

Talon hesitated. Silently, he prayed Eros would give him an answer other than the one he feared.

"Do you know the Celtic god Camulus?"

Eros shrugged. "Not really. He runs with Ares, Kel, Ara, and those other war gods. Being the god of love and lust, I don't tend to associate with them. Why?"

"Because I was cursed by him and I wanted to know if

there is any way for me to break the curse."

"Honestly?"

"Yes."

"Most likely not. War gods as a rule aren't real forgiving. It kind of comes with the whole mass-destruction mentality. But it depends on what you did and what he used as a curse."

"I killed his son and he has forbidden me to ever love a human. When I do, he kills them."

"Ooo," Eros breathed. "Sorry, man, but something like that, you can hang up an out clause. Vengeance runs deep in the bones of the war gods. Now, if you had the blood of a god in you, you might have some leverage. Do you?"

"No. I'm fully human, blood-wise anyway."

"Then you're totally screwed."

Talon clenched his teeth at the truth, even though he wasn't surprised by it. He hadn't realized until then that he had started to see a future for him and Sunshine.

That in the back of his mind there really had been hope. But it was futile.

"There's no way to keep Sunshine."

He hadn't realized he'd spoken aloud until Eros said, "If you love her, then I'm sure she'll pay for it."

Talon braced himself for what he had to do. Even though it tore his heart out and made him want to cry. He knew he had to do this.

It was the only way to protect her.

"Fine, then. I have one last request."

Eros gave him an understanding look. "You want me to shoot you guys with the lead arrow to kill your love."

He nodded.

Eros pulled his bow necklace from around his neck and made it larger.

Talon grabbed his hand as he aimed it at him. "Not yet. Okay? I just want a little more time with her. Can you wait until midnight?"

Shrinking the bow back to necklace size, Eros nodded and patted Talon on the shoulder. "Love bites, man. Believe me, I know."

Talon thought about Psyche and he felt a twinge of jealousy. "Yeah, but you got to keep your love."

"True. I'm damn lucky in that department." Eros shifted as if something had made him uncomfortable. "Where do you want me to shoot you?"

"Someplace that won't hurt."

Eros rolled his eyes.

Talon answered seriously. "The club Runningwolf's. I'll have her there at midnight."

Nodding, Eros took two steps away. "I'll see you at midnight."

"Thanks, Eros. I owe you."

"Yes, you do."

Talon inclined his head in mutual understanding. Now he was indebted to Vane and Eros. At the rate he was going, he was likely to lose a whole lot more than his soul before all was said and done.

He just prayed that in the end, Sunshine didn't lose her life.

But he wouldn't think about that now. All he had was a few more hours to spend with the woman he loved.

He wanted to enjoy what little time they had before she learned to hate him.

Talon left the room and stopped as he caught sight of Sunshine downstairs playing pool with Psyche.

She was so beautiful there. The stage lights played off her midnight-black hair. And her lush, sweet body . . . It was perfection.

Sunshine was everything to him.

Talon's thoughts scattered when he realized that a thin man of average height was talking to Sunshine and she didn't look happy about it.

Suddenly, their conversation escalated into a verbal fight. Sunshine was animated as she poked the man with her finger and pushed him back.

Psyche put her cue down and stepped between them.

Talon saw red.

Without thinking about the patrons or anything other

than Sunshine, he placed his hand on the banister and swung his legs over and dropped to the floor below.

The people downstairs gasped and scattered.

Pain shot up his leg and worsened as he took a step. Talon didn't care. The only thing he saw was Sunshine's distressed face. The only sound he heard was her angry voice.

"How could you do this, Jerry, you snake!"

"I told you before, Sunny, everything's fair in business."

"But he was *my* client. I sat out there all day today waiting on him to show."

"Yeah, well, you snooze, you lose."

"Here's another saying," Talon said, grabbing the guy and turning him to face him. "No one messes with my girl."

Sunshine froze at the look on Talon's face. It was truly scary. He stared at Jerry as if he were one inch away from making Jerry fillet.

"It's all right, Talon," she said, not wanting him to get into trouble or, worse, arrested for beating the slug.

She could tell by Jerry's expression that he was dying to say something snide, but the sheer size and ferocity of Talon kept his lips sealed.

She took Talon's arm. "C'mon, babe, let's go."

Talon really wanted to tear the guy apart. How dare he steal Sunshine's client from her? He knew how much it meant to her.

His anger snapped and hissed, straining against the control he was using to keep it leashed.

"Who is this dick?" Talon asked Sunshine.

"I used to be her husband, what about you?"

Talon's eyes flared. "Ditto."

Jerry couldn't have looked more shocked had Talon actually hit him.

Talon looked at Sunshine. A part of him felt extremely betrayed that she had dared marry someone else. It didn't matter that she'd had no idea about their past life together. It still hurt.

Her eyes apologized to him. "I was going to tell you."

"When, Sunshine?"

She turned and glanced at Jerry. "You're such a jerk. I can't believe I was ever stupid enough to marry you."

She started through the now silent crowd.

"Hey, Sunny," Jerry called after her. "Make sure you go to Fallini's sometime and admire my work. Remember when you look at it that the best artist won."

Talon saw the tears in her eyes.

His temper exploded.

Rotating his shoulders, he turned and slugged Jerry so hard that he was knocked off his feet. He landed with a solid thump on the pool table, sending billiard balls rolling and bouncing.

Several members of the bear clan cursed as cameras flashed.

"Way to keep a low profile, Celt," Justin said snidely from beside him.

Talon ignored the panther. He took Sunshine's hand and led her through the crowd.

Nick met him and Sunshine at the door. "Man, Ash is going to flip when he finds out about this. I can't believe you pulled something like this with a Mardi Gras crowd to witness it. You're worse than Zarek."

"Just make sure you clean it up."

"Clean it up, hell. Do you know how many cameras just caught your stunt-jump from upstairs? My mom now thinks you're on the drugs she suspects Kyrian sells. We're screwed. My life is toast. I'm about to get lectured about working for drug dealers . . . again. My mom, bless her heart, is so goofy, she doesn't even realize she works for bears. I'm so screwed."

"Don't worry about it," Dev said as he joined them. "We have your back, Celt. Cleaning up indiscretions is our specialty. No human here will remember it tomorrow and we'll make sure none of the electronics show anything either. Everyone will be ticked off that all they got for a picture was a big black blob."

"What about me?" Nick asked. "I don't want any of your mind-meld stuff."

"I said humans, Nicky."

Nick looked extremely offended.

"Thanks," Talon said to Dev.

"Any time. I'll see you tomorrow for Mardi Gras."

Talon inclined his head to the bear and led Sunshine outside even though his entire leg felt as if it had been broken by the jump.

Once they were on the street, he confronted her. "You were married?"

"It was seven years ago, Talon. I was young and stupid."

"You were married," he repeated. "To *him*."

Sunshine took a deep breath and sighed. "Yes."

"I can't believe this."

"Oh, c'mon, Talon, give me a break. Don't hold something against me when I had no idea you even existed. If anyone has a right to be mad, I think it should be me."

"Excuse me?"

"Selena told me about you and your rep, bud. How you've pretty much laid every woman in New Orleans. You want to tell me about that?"

"That was different."

"Why? Because I'm a woman? You knew I wasn't a virgin, Talon. What did you expect?"

Talon didn't know. But then, it didn't really matter.

After tonight, she'd hate him anyway. The last thing he wanted was to spend the evening fighting with her. This was all the time they would ever have.

"Okay, Sunshine. You're right. I'm sorry."

Sunshine was stunned. This was the first time she'd ever known a guy to cave so easily. "Are you really?"

"Yes," he said, his eyes sincere. "I don't want to fight, okay? Let's just forget about him and go eat."

She lifted his hand to her lips and kissed his knuckles. "Sounds good."

As they walked to a small café on Iberville, she noticed he had a slight limp. "Are you okay?"

"Yeah, I just twisted my leg when I jumped over the railing," he said. "Whenever I get mad, I tend to lose my Dark-Hunter powers, and without them, my body becomes human."

"Do you need a doctor?"

He shook his head. "As long as I stay calm, it should heal while we eat."

Talon kept her close to him the entire time it took them to reach the restaurant and be seated. He memorized everything about her. He would always remember her like this and those memories would live inside him right along with the ones of her as Nynia.

Or would he lose those memories when Eros shot him?

Would his mind somehow distort them so that he couldn't love her anymore?

His stomach knotted at the thought. What would it be like to not even have the comfort of his memories of Nynia and Sunshine?

To not remember the softness of her touch, the smell of her patchouli on his skin?

The way her eyes lit up every time she looked at him?

Grinding his teeth, he tried not to think about that, or to feel the pain in his heart.

This wasn't about him and what he stood to lose.

This was about her.

He had to do this for her.

She sat in the booth across from him, her head bent while she ate. The candlelight reflected the darkness of her hair, making her skin a creamy tan. A creamy tan that made his mouth water for a taste.

Talon watched the graceful gestures of her hands as she cut into her garbanzo bean salad and ate it. He loved those long, tapered fingers. Loved teasing them with his mouth, feeling them on his body.

"What made you want to be an artist?" he asked.

"I love working with my hands."

He reached across the table and took her left hand into his. He studied the delicate curve of it, the way it felt so dainty in his palm. "You have such beautiful hands."

She smiled and squeezed his with hers. "Thank you. They're the most valuable thing an artist can ever have. I used to have nightmares that something would happen to them, a severe scar or burn that would prevent me from ever using them, for pottery or drawing again. Art is my life. I don't know what I'd do if I couldn't create."

Talon closed his eyes as agony washed over him. His emotions swirled, but he forced them down. He had to.

The clock was ticking for them.

Sunshine fed him a bite of her salad and he did his best not to cringe.

"Why aren't your eyes amber anymore?" she asked.

He swallowed his bite and took a drink of wine. "Part of the whole Dark-Hunter package. We're turned into predators so that we can track down and kill Daimons. Our eyes become black and dilate a lot more than human eyes so that we can see in darkness."

"And your fangs? Do you use them to suck blood?"

He shook his head. "No. Blood has never been to my taste. The fangs are just part of the package too."

"And do you like what you do?"

"There are times when it's fun and challenging and times when it's kind of boring. For the most part I don't mind."

She seemed to accept that.

She ate for a few minutes before she spoke again. "Talon, why did you give up your soul?"

He looked away. In his mind, he could see that day so clearly. He had been lying on the altar, his hands tied above his head, his chest bare and marked in blood with the sacrificial symbols. It had been a cool day, and every member of his clan had been there.

Dressed in black robes, the Druid priest had looked down upon him and smiled cruelly.

"Seize Ceara."

His cousin's words had rung in his head. It had taken a full minute before he understood what was going on. Horrified, Talon had watched his men grab his sister's arms.

"Speirr! Help me, bràthair, *please!"*

He had fought against the ropes until his wrists had bled and stung. He had screamed out for them to release her.

Like a caged animal, he had tried to reach her.

Over and over, she called out to him.

"It's the will of the gods that you both die for what your mother did."

His cousin had sunk his dagger deep into Ceara's heart.

She had looked to Talon, her eyes terrified and tear-filled as she struggled to breathe.

Worst of all, he had seen the disappointment in her eyes. She had believed in him, trusted him to protect her.

The men had released her and she had stumbled to the ground, landing on her hands and knees.

"Speirr?" Her voice had trembled as she reached a bloodied hand out toward him. *"I don't want to be dead,"* she whispered, her voice that of a child.

Before his eyes, she had died.

Panting in fury, he had let his battle cry roll out and then he had cursed them all. He had called down the wrath of the Morrigán and she had ignored him.

It was Artemis who had answered his cry for vengeance.

The last thing he'd seen was the Druid holding his head back and then making the savage cut across his throat.

Talon breathed deeply in and out and he sought to bury those memories. That was the past and now he had Sunshine to watch out for.

"It was youthful fury," he said with a calmness he didn't feel. "I had lost so much in such a short time—my aunt, my uncle, you, and our son. After I lost you, I walked around cloaked in grief. I struggled to make it through every minute of every day. The only thing that kept me going was knowing that the clan and Ceara needed me.

"When the Druids came to me and said that I would have to give up my life to the gods to protect the clan, it was actually a relief. I didn't think twice about allowing them to place me on the sacrificial altar."

Talon ground his teeth as he saw his sister in his mind again. The way she had looked that day. "Ceara was weeping, but she was trying to be strong. Everything was going as it should, until Murrdyd turned on her and told my clansmen to seize her. He said we both had to die to appease the gods."

"Was that the truth?"

"No. He wanted to be king. He needed both Ceara and me out of the way since we were legitimate heirs. I can understand his wanting me killed, but he didn't have to kill Ceara. It was the injustice of it that I couldn't stand."

She placed her hand over his. "Baby, I am so sorry."

He squeezed her hand as he blinked against the agony he felt. The only comfort he had ever known in his life was the touch of this woman. "So were they in the end."

"What did you do?"

Talon cleared his throat as he tried to squelch the memories of that night. The regrets. He had been like a single-minded monster raging through his village.

The only thought on his mind had been reaching his cousin.

Making the bastard pay.

"I went through the village killing every man who came between me and the ones who had killed Ceara. The women and children fled while I fought my way to Murrdyd. After I took my vengeance on him, I burned the entire village to the ground."

"And you've been serving Artemis ever since?"

He nodded.

"Have you ever met her?"

"Just the one time when she came to bargain with me for my soul. She met me in the nether region where a soul gets trapped after it leaves this world, but has yet to travel to the next."

"You haven't seen her since?"

He shook his head. "We're not allowed to have contact with the gods. They see us as an abomination."

"But what about Eros?"

He took a deep breath and felt a twinge of humor at the thought of the fun-loving, irreverent god of love. "He's a little different. For some reason, he likes hanging out with us."

Sunshine considered his words as they finished dinner. Poor Talon. He had been through so much pain. So much grief.

To some extent it bothered her that he was still confusing her with Nynia. They might share a soul, but ultimately, they were two entirely different people.

Not that it really mattered. So long as he was bound to Artemis and cursed by Camulus, he could never be free. He could never have a future.

While she'd talked to Psyche, the goddess had told her how to summon Artemis.

Sunshine really wanted to have a nice chitchat with that goddess and see if maybe Talon could earn his freedom again. If she accomplished that, then maybe they could do something to stop Camulus as well.

After they paid for dinner, they left the restaurant and headed for her father's club.

Sunshine didn't know why Talon wanted to take her home, but she snuck them in unnoticed so that they could have a little more time alone.

Talon led her to the dance floor.

Sunshine had never realized before just how hot a man could be when he danced. Personally, she'd always thought most men looked rather goofy.

But not Talon. He was the sexiest thing she'd ever seen in her life.

When the song ended, Talon urged her to introduce him to her father and brother. They were sitting nearby, going over paperwork and accounting stats for the club while Wayne helped them.

"Hi, Daddy, Storm, and Wayne."

They looked up and smiled until they saw Talon behind her.

"Sunshine, are you all right?" her father asked.

"I'm fine. I just wanted you to meet Talon. Talon, my father, Daniel Runningwolf."

Talon offered his hand, but her father declined.

"I'm a shaman and can't touch you."

Talon nodded at him with a look that said he understood. "Sorry, I wasn't thinking."

Wayne excused himself.

After he left, her father's dark brown eyes glittered

harshly as he swept his gaze to Sunshine. "Starla didn't tell me your boyfriend was soulless, kitten."

"She probably thought you'd flip out. Are you?"

"Yes."

Sunshine quickly sought to change the subject. "How's Mom, by the way?"

"She's fine. What about you?"

"I'm fine, Daddy. Don't worry."

"I'm your father, Sunshine. Worrying about you is my full-time occupation."

She smiled at him. "And you 'do it very well."

Still, he looked less than appeased.

Talon stepped forward. "Daniel, could I have a word with you?"

Sunshine frowned at the ominous note in Talon's voice. Her father's eyes narrowed even more before he nodded subtly. "Sunshine, stay with Storm."

She watched as the two of them drifted off and a wave of terror crashed over her. Something was definitely wrong.

Talon led her father to another corner of the bar. He glanced over to Sunshine and his heart wrenched.

"What is it you want with me?" Daniel asked.

"Look, I know you don't like me."

"Don't like you? You're a soulless killer. Granted, you do it protectively, but it doesn't change the basic fact that you are no longer human."

"I know that. It's why we're here. I'm going to release Sunshine into your protection tonight. There are some people who are out to harm her and I would really appreciate it if you watched out for her. I'll be staying nearby, out of sight, until after tomorrow night just in case the thing after her tries to take her again."

"From what my wife tells me, Sunshine won't let you leave her voluntarily."

"In another four minutes, she won't ever want to lay eyes on me again. I promise you."

He frowned. "What do you mean?"

Talon cleared his throat as he glanced to the large Bud-weiser clock on the wall over the bar.

Their time was almost up.

Damn you, Fates.

"Nothing," he said quietly. "Just take my word for it, your daughter is yours."

Daniel nodded.

As Talon walked back to Sunshine, his entire being ached. He couldn't stand the thought of what Eros was about to do. It cut him on a level so deep it was unfathomable.

But it had to be done.

They couldn't be together. It was foolish to think otherwise.

He had to do this to save her life.

From the corner of his eye, he saw Eros appearing in god-form. Invisible to humans, the god of love was easily discernible to Talon's Dark-Hunter senses.

"You sure?" Eros's voice echoed in his head.

Talon leaned over, kissed Sunshine gently on the lips, and then nodded.

He held her face in his hands, and stared at her brown eyes, waiting for the moment when they would turn dark with hatred. Waiting for her to stiffen and curse him.

Eros raised his bow up and shot it straight into Sunshine.

Talon swallowed as painful expectation tore through him.

Goodbye, my love.

She grimaced at him. "Ow! Talon, did you hit me?"

He shook his head and waited for the hatred to come into her eyes.

It didn't.

Seconds ticked by slowly as her frown deepened.

"I don't feel right." She rubbed her heart where Eros had shot her.

Then, amazingly, she looked up and focused her gaze on Eros. "Cupid?"

Eros looked around nervously. "You can see me?"

"Well, yeah," she said.

Eros shifted and looked a bit green.

Talon frowned as a bad feeling went through him. "What happened, Eros? Why doesn't she hate me?"

Eros looked even more uncomfortable. "You two wouldn't happen to be soulmates, would you?"

"Yes," Sunshine answered. "Psyche said we were."

Eros gave a sheepish grin. "Oops. I think I need to have a talk with my wife. Damn, she should have told me."

"Oops?" Talon repeated. "Eros, *oops* better not be in your vocabulary."

Eros cleared his throat. "No one told me you two were soulmates. See, this"—he held up his bow—"only works on lust and infatuation. Soulmates are a whole 'nother ball game. That kind of love, I can't kill. Nothing can."

Sunshine gaped as she understood what was going on. In that moment, she wanted to strangle Talon. "You tried to get him to make me hate you?"

Now Talon looked as sheepish as Eros. "Honey, I can explain."

She glared at him as rage rocked every particle of her body. "Oh, you're going to explain all right. How dare you try to monkey with my mind and heart? I don't appreciate your doing something so underhanded."

"Sunshine," her father said. "He's right. You can't have a future with him. He's not human."

"I don't care what he is. He and I have something to- gether and I can't believe he'd do something like this."

"I forbid you to see him anymore." Her father's tone was stern.

She turned her anger toward her father. "And I'm not thirteen. I don't care what you forbid or not, Daddy. This is between me and him."

"I will not watch you die again," Talon said slowly, stressing each word.

"And I will not be manipulated. Nor will I just give you up."

Talon turned and stormed out of the club, his emotions churning. He couldn't do this. He couldn't.

He had to let her go.

It was for both their sakes.

Without looking back, he went to his motorcycle. He got on it, but before he could kick-start it, Sunshine grabbed his arm.

"You're not going to get rid of me like this."

He bared his fangs at her. "Do you not understand what I am?"

Sunshine swallowed. Suddenly everything Psyche had said made sense to her. He wasn't Speirr, the leader of his people. The frightened little boy who had turned his heart to stone in order to live. The man who had stolen Nynia's heart and then claimed her when no other would have.

This was Talon, the Dark-Hunter who spent eternity protecting strangers from the dark evil of the night.

She loved him even more.

He made her heart sing. Without him, she couldn't even imagine her future.

She didn't know how to conquer everything that stood between them, but he was worth fighting for.

"I know what you are, Talon. You are the man I was born to love. The *only* man I was born to love."

"I am not a man. Not anymore."

"You are mine and I will not let you go without a fight."

Talon didn't know what to do. The tone of her voice tore through him.

He wanted to crush her to him and hold on to her forever.

He wanted to push her away and curse. To make her hate him.

She stepped into his arms and kissed him deeply.

Talon groaned at the taste of her. Although he knew he shouldn't, he pulled her across his bike and started it, then headed off into traffic.

His love and anger roiling, he drove them out of the city, all the way to the edge of his swamp. The entire time the scent and feel of her permeated him, making his emotions even more volatile. Her body was pressed so close to him that it was all he could focus on.

Her warmth, her love.

He had to have her.

Unable to stand it, he pulled up into the woods and turned the engine off.

Sunshine was partially afraid of the feral look of him as he stared at her.

His eyes were blazing with fire and passion as he seized her and kissed her roughly.

His hunger tore through her, incited her. She wrapped her arms around his shoulders as he leaned her back over his gas tank.

She'd never seen him like this. It was as if all his emotions were out of control, as if he were living only to touch her. He kissed her neck and face as his hands loosened her blouse so that he could cup her breast in his hands.

He was wild and untamed and it seemed to her that he had more than two hands. It was as if he were touching her all over at once.

She wanted him desperately. Wanted him with the same need he had for her.

She kissed his lips, rubbing herself against his swollen groin as she pulled his T-shirt off, over his head. She ran her hands over the wide expanse of his chest, feeling his muscles bunch and flex.

He shoved her full skirt up over her hips.

"I need you, Talon," she whispered.

Talon wanted to possess her. Every part of him screamed out for it. He'd never in his entire life felt like this. He had to get inside her. Had to touch her. Had to feel her hands on his skin, her breath against his neck.

It was a need so powerful that it shook him.

She fumbled with his fly before she unzipped his pants, freeing his erection. He trembled as she sheathed him with her hands.

He choked at how wonderful her hands felt on him. "That's it, Sunshine," he breathed against her hair. "Bring me home."

She arched her back and gently guided him into the wet heat of her body. Talon growled ferociously at the feel of her.

Like an animal, he made love to her furiously.

Panting and weak from desire, Sunshine clutched him to her as he thrust himself against her until she was dizzy with pleasure. For the first time since they had met, he didn't hide his fangs from her. He let her see him as he really was.

Let her know the untamed beast that inhabited this man's body.

Their gazes locked, she watched the ecstasy on his face as he rocked himself between her thighs.

She cupped his face in her hands, mesmerized by the man and the predator he was.

All her life she'd heard tales of immortal beings, of vampires taking possession of their victims.

Tonight, she wanted to be his.

Talon was out of control with her. He knew it. His emotions surging, he couldn't think. He could only feel. She was his focal point. His everything.

Her scent permeated his head, covered his body, heightening his senses.

He heard the blood rushing through her veins, felt her heart pounding against his chest. The heat of her soft, feminine skin sliding against his.

Take her!

It was a feral command.

Primal.

Demanding.

Had he been in his right mind, he would have controlled himself. As it was, he couldn't.

Now, he was the beast that stalked the night. His only thought having her, he slid himself deep inside her and then he sank his fangs deep into her neck.

He felt her surprise for only an instant until complete sexual ecstasy tore through them both.

Their bodies and minds were united. Joined.

He felt every thought in her head. Every emotion. Every fear. Every joy.

He saw inside her heart down to her fear that he didn't love her as much as he loved Nynia. That he would never love her as much. He felt her hopelessness and her determination.

Most of all, he felt her love.

Growling fiercely, he let her essence wash over him. Let her seep into every corner of his being. There were no more secrets between them. No more places to hide.

She was as bare to him as he was to her.

And her love for him was the most incredible feeling he'd ever experienced.

Talon thrust himself in deep as his head and body exploded. Their orgasms were so fierce that he couldn't keep the motorcycle upright. Before he knew what had happened, they were lying on the ground, still entangled as his sense returned to him.

Sunshine stared up at him in the moonlight, her clothes disheveled and her face adoring.

In her mind, she could still hear his thoughts. His fear of losing her, his need to protect her.

She saw his guilt that he had allowed his sister to die. His need to right the wrong that had been done to Nynia.

The sadness and grief that lived inside him as constant companions.

Most of all, she saw his need to hold her. His need to not fail her.

She felt his power and strength, which were unlike anything she had imagined. He was a predator.

And he was the man she loved. One who loved her and one who was willing to do anything for her.

Even give up his own life.

"I love you, Talon," she breathed.

Talon couldn't believe what he had done as he brushed his hand against her neck and removed the telltale signs of blood. Her taste permeated his mind, his senses.

Zarek had been right, that was the most incredible high he'd ever known. And now that he'd seen inside her heart . . .

Gods, what had he done?

In one moment of careless passion, he had sown the seeds of both their destruction.

Chapter 16

Talon took her back to the cabin, but he didn't speak to her. He wasn't sure what to say.

She didn't seem to mind the fact that he'd bitten her, which was a very good thing.

But he couldn't get it out of his mind.

Her taste.

Her feelings.

Her love.

It would haunt him forever.

Sunshine went to the bathroom to freshen up while he turned on his desk lamp.

A few seconds later, someone knocked on the door.

Talon pulled his srad from his boot. Visitors didn't come often to his house.

"Who is it?"

"It's Ash, Celt. Don't have a coronary."

"Is it Acheron or Styxx?"

"It's T-Rex and I'm not wearing sunglasses."

Prepared for a trick, Talon opened the door carefully. It really was "old spooky eyes" and he didn't look pleased.

"What are you doing here?" Talon asked.

"Fighting Daimons. What about you?"

He caught the sarcasm and the condemnation in Ash's voice. "There were Daimons here? Where?"

"They attacked the Katagaria den and I went to help Vane and Fang."

Talon winced at the news. He should have been here to help fight. Damn, he'd screwed up royally. "Are they okay?"

"No. Their sister and her pups were killed in the fighting."

Talon's heart clenched at the news. That was one pain he knew all too well. The brothers would be devastated over her loss. "Man, I'm sorry."

"So, where were you?"

Before he could answer, Ash answered for him. "Wait, I know this one. You were at Sanctuary showing off your powers to a busload of Japanese tourists who were armed with digital cameras and camcorders. Congratulations, bud, we just went global."

Talon covered his face with his hand. "Oh jeez, are you serious?"

"Do I look like I'm kidding?"

No, he looked really pissed off.

"I can't believe this," Talon said.

"You? You can't believe this? I'm the one who has to go to Artemis to save your ass. She was freaking out over Zarek, now how the hell do I explain to her that Mr. Cool-Calm-and-Collected was doing his impression of Spider-Man in a bar loaded with tourists and ended up as the main feature on Tokyo news as what's wrong with American culture?

"Question. How many rules *did* you break in less than a minute?

"Worst of all, I now have Nick calling me up, wanting to know why he has to keep everything secret while you guys are running around exposing yourselves at random. The little prick even wants a raise because he can keep a secret while none of you can."

"I can explain."

"Okay, I'm waiting."

Talon tried to come up with a reason for what he'd done. There wasn't one.

"Okay, I can't explain. Give me a minute."

Ash narrowed his eyes. "I'm still waiting."

"I'm thinking about it."

Sunshine came out of the bathroom, then blanched as soon as she saw Acheron. She grabbed one of Talon's staves from the wall and went after him.

Acheron caught it in his hand as she swung it for his head. "Hey!"

Sunshine turned to Talon. "He's the one who kidnapped me!"

"I did not," Acheron said huffily as he tugged the staff from her grip.

"This is my boss, Sunshine. Acheron."

She formed a small O with her mouth. "Vane said you two looked alike. He wasn't kidding. Although now that I'm a bit calmer, you don't really look like him that much. He was scary, but you . . . you're *really* scary."

"If I had more time, I'd feel complimented." He handed the staff to Talon. "Outside, Celt, so we can finish our talk."

Talon didn't like being ordered about, but in this case he had no choice.

He had truly messed up and Ash had a right to vent.

Talon had put all of them in a very bad situation.

He went outside to stand on the dock where Ash was waiting with his hands on his hips.

Ash's face was mottled by fury. "You know, I've had a *really* wonderful night tonight. I got to tell Kyrian and Julian that Valerius is in town and spent, oh I don't know, three, four hours trying to keep them from going after the Roman. Then, just when I could relax and do my job, I find out there are Daimons in the swamp and no Talon to kill them. And why wasn't Talon here? Because Tarzan was swinging off a balcony to save Jane from Cheetah.

"Now all I can do is stand here and say, next fiasco, please, right this way."

Talon glared at him. "You don't have to be so sarcastic. I know I screwed up, okay?"

"No, *screwed up* is getting caught without your pants in

Sunshine's apartment. This is a little bigger than just screwing up."

"I'm not going to apologize for what I did."

A tic beat in his jaw as Ash glanced away. "There are a lot of things that are still up in the air about tomorrow night. A lot of unknown factors. What we *do* know isn't good.

"I have Julian and Kyrian, who want to put Val in a pine box. Val, who doesn't want to lift a finger to help anyone not descended from the Romans. Two pissed-off wolves who are going to want revenge over what happened tonight. Zarek, who is mental on his best day, and who is currently wanted by New Orleans' finest. Nick screaming that he's quitting because he's tired of cleaning up after psychos. An angry goddess who is going to want everyone's head over this. And the only Hunter I have who is reliable is you."

Ash paused and gave him a stern glare. "And buddy, no offense, but you haven't been reliable in days."

"I'm okay, T-Rex."

"No, Talon, you're not. You were swinging from the rafters and punching out innocent humans because of Sunshine. You risked not only yourself, but all of us and the Peltiers just to protect one woman from hurt feelings. Where was your head?"

Anger tore through him. "I'm not a child, Ash. I know how to prioritize."

"Normally, you do. But you're thinking with your heart, not your head, and that will get us all killed. We're Dark-Hunters, Talon, we don't *feel*."

Any other time, he would agree with that, but at the moment Talon was feeling a whole lot of frustrated rage. He didn't need this lecture. He knew the risks and the dangers even better than Ash did. He more than understood everything at stake.

"I've got it under control."

"Do you?" Ash asked. "Because from where I'm standing, you don't. You have directly disobeyed me when I told you to keep Sunshine here. You have made pacts with the Katagaria and with Eros, and that's not your place. You don't make those kinds of obligations, Talon. Have you *any* idea how that can play out?"

"I had to do it. I have to protect my wife. I don't care what it costs."

"Your wife?" Ash shook his head. "Talon, look at me."

Talon did.

Ash stared at him intently, his gaze cold and unfeeling. "Your wife is *dead*. She died fifteen hundred years ago and was buried in your homeland. Sunshine isn't Nynia."

Talon roared with his anger and pain. It wasn't true. Sunshine was his wife. He felt it. He knew it. She was all that mattered to him.

All that mattered.

Before he could think twice, he attacked Acheron. He caught the Atlantean's throat between his hands and shook him, trying to make him understand.

"She's not dead!" he snarled. "Damn you, she's not dead."

Ash broke his hold and used his powers to immobilize him.

Talon hissed and snarled as he tried to break free, but it was useless.

And in that moment, he realized just how far gone he really was.

I've attacked Acheron.

The thought sobered him. Ash was right. If he didn't calm down and get a hold of himself, he could get them all killed.

All of them.

Ash took a deep breath and released him. "Talon, you have a decision to make. Dark-Hunters don't have wives. We don't have families. At the end of the day, we have no one but ourselves. Our responsibility, our *only* responsibility, is to the humans who can't protect themselves from the Daimons. You've got to get your head straight."

"I know." Talon breathed raggedly.

Ash nodded. Then his eyes turned a strange, deep silver.

"Tell me what you want to do. Do you want me to petition Artemis for your soul?"

Talon thought about it. Right now, he stood on a precipice that he had never thought to face. Not once in his entire Dark-Hunter existence had he ever dared to dream Nynia would be back.

That she would . . .

He closed his eyes and winced.

Nynia wasn't back. Acheron was right.

Nynia was dead.

The woman in his cabin right now wasn't his wife.

She was Sunshine. A vibrant, caring woman who had fire and spunk.

She might have his wife's soul, but she was someone else. Someone he didn't want to live without.

Someone he didn't dare keep.

He felt as if his heart were being shredded. Sunshine was human. In time, she could forget him and have another life. Someone else to love.

The thought pierced him, but he had to do this.

Either way, he would lose her. At least this way, she stood a chance for happiness that wouldn't kill her.

"No," Talon said quietly. "I don't want to reclaim my soul knowing that I'll lose Sunshine to Camulus's wrath. I don't want my freedom at that cost."

"You sure?"

He nodded, then shook his head no. "Honestly, T-Rex, I'm not sure about anything anymore." He looked at him. "Have you ever loved anyone?"

Acheron met his gaze stoically, and didn't respond to the question. "You know, the thing about life and love is that they are both ever-changing while people seldom are. If you know this woman and you really love her, isn't it worth the chance for freedom to have her?"

"But if I lose her . . ."

"That is an *if*, Celt. It seems to me the only certainty is if you don't at least try, then you will definitely lose her."

"But if I let her go, she'll at least be alive."

"The way you've lived since the day Nynia died?"

"That's not fair."

"I'm not paid to be fair. I'm paid to kick Daimon ass." Acheron let out a tired sigh. "You know, I met a wise man centuries ago in China who said to me, 'He who lets fear rule him, has fear for a master.' "

"Confucius?"

"No, Minh-Quan. He was a fisherman who used to sell what I'm told was the best *zong zi* ever made."

Talon scowled at the unexpected comment. That was the thing about Acheron, you never really knew what you were going to get out of him.

"You're a strange man, Acheron Parthenopaeus. Tell me, what you would do if you were me?"

Acheron folded his arms over his chest. "I would never presume to be anyone other than myself, Talon. I'm not the one who has to bear the consequences of your actions. That's for you, alone, to do."

Talon sighed. "Is it possible to fight a god and win?"

His eyes turned dull. Talon watched him curiously. There was something in Acheron's past that his question brushed on. Something deep and dark, judging by the look on Acheron's face.

"Celtic and Greek gods are very much like people. They make mistakes. And those mistakes are what will either make us or break us in the end."

"You're sounding like an Oracle now."

"Scary, isn't it?"

"Not scary, just irritating." Talon started away from him. "Talon."

He stopped and turned back to face Acheron. "To answer your question. Yes, you can win battles with a god. But it's much easier to negotiate." Acheron's tone told him that he spoke with the voice of experience.

"How do you negotiate with a god who wants you to suffer for all of eternity?"

"Very carefully, little brother. *Very* carefully." Acheron

glanced away, into the swamp. "You know, I think you may be losing sight of something really important."

"And that is?"

"Very few of us are ever given a second chance to reclaim what we've lost. If Nynia came back to you, maybe there's a reason for it."

Acheron unfolded his arms. "You have my number, Celt. If you change your mind about the petition, let me know. But you need to make your decision fast. I need your mind clear by tomorrow night."

"Why are you giving me a choice when you didn't give Kyrian one? You petitioned Artemis and gave his soul to Amanda without his knowing it."

Acheron shrugged. "Kyrian didn't have a choice to make. Without a soul, Desiderius would have killed him. Your life isn't in danger if you don't get your soul back, Talon. Just your heart is. And as you well know, you can live without your heart. But do you really want to?"

There were times when he seriously wished Acheron was the twenty-one-year-old snot-nosed kid he appeared to be, and not an eleven-thousand-year-old wise man.

This was definitely one of those times.

"I'm going to take Sunshine back to town with me."

"No," Talon said automatically. "She stays here so I can protect her."

"It wasn't a question, Celt. You need time away from her to think. Time to clear your thoughts before tomorrow night."

He started to argue, then realized Ash was right.

He was going to have to let her go anyway. He might as well do it now.

It would be easier for both of them.

"Okay, I'll go get her."

Sunshine knew something was wrong the minute she saw Talon come through the door.

His face was haunted, his eyes dark.

"What happened?" she asked.

"Acheron's going to take you back to your loft." His voice was so dispassionate that it made her stomach tight.

"I see. And do you agree with him?"

"I do. I think it's for the best."

But she didn't want to go. The depth of how much she wanted to stay startled her. "I see."

Woodenly, she started gathering her things. But inside, inside she was dying.

Talon couldn't stand seeing her like this. He wanted to grab her and run away to a place where no one could find them. To hold her safe.

The only problem was, no one could hide from a god.

Sooner or later, Camulus would find them and then she would die.

He took her backpack as she reached for it. "I've got it."

She nodded, her eyes bright and shiny.

Neither one of them spoke as he led her outside to where Acheron was waiting. He handed her backpack to Ash.

"It's, uh . . . it's been fun, Talon," she said. "Will I see you again?"

He looked at Ash, who watched him with an arched brow as if he wanted an answer to that one himself.

"No," he said slowly.

She cleared her throat, but didn't speak. Instead, she walked over to Acheron. "I'm ready."

Ash stepped back and let her lead the way to the catamaran. "Celt," he said, "if you change your mind about our discussion, call me."

Talon nodded.

His heart breaking, he watched Sunshine strap herself in. Ash started the boat and then headed them out into the swamp.

It was over.

She was gone.

I am Darkness. I am Shadow.
I am the Ruler of the Night.

I, alone, stand between mankind and those who would see mankind destroyed. I am the Guardian.

The Soulless Keeper.

Neither Human, nor Apollite, I exist beyond the realm of the Living, beyond the realm of the Dead.

I am the Dark-Hunter.

And I am Eternal ... unless I find that one pure heart who will never betray me. The one whose faith and courage can return my soul to me and bring me back into the light.

If not for Camulus . . .

"Not all of us are given a second chance to reclaim what we've lost. If Nynia came back to you, maybe there's a reason for it."

Aching, he turned his back on the sight of Sunshine leaving him and walked back into his cabin. He shut the door and looked about.

There was so much emptiness here now that Sunshine was gone. She had filled his home with happiness. Most of all, she had filled *him* with happiness.

His gaze fell to her pink cosmetics bag on his desk. She had forgotten it along with her hairbrush and hair ties.

Poor Sunshine, she was forever forgetting things.

"Speirr?"

He turned sharply to see Ceara beside him. "*Lurach,* are you here to judge me too?"

"*Nae,* my *bràthair,* I am here only to speak with you."

"About what?"

She reached out for him and then dropped her hand when she remembered they couldn't touch. "I just wanted to tell you before I leave that I have agreed with the god Bran to be reborn."

Talon's lungs seized.

He couldn't move.

He couldn't breathe.

Ceara gone?

Nae! The word tore through him.

She couldn't leave him. Not now. Not after all this time. She was the only solace he had left to him.

And at the same time, he couldn't bring himself to say that to her. To let her know how much he wanted her to stay.

How much he *needed* her to stay.

If he did, she would do as he asked and give up her future . . .

He could never be so selfish.

"What made you agree to it finally?" he asked, taking care to keep his voice level and smooth.

"It is time, Speirr. I want to live my life again. To find all the things I didn't have the last time. Love. Children. Even a job and a mortgage."

He couldn't smile at her attempt at humor, not while the pain inside him was so raw. So debilitating.

But he knew in his heart that she was right. It was time she had the things that had been denied her all those centuries before.

He wanted her to have all that and more. She deserved every happiness life could bring her. "I will miss you."

"And I shall miss you too, my *bràthair*."

He offered her a smile that he knew was hollow. "I wish you all the best, *lurach*. I send my heart with you."

"I know, Speirr. I love you too, but you have Nynia now. You won't be alone without me."

Yes, I will. Because I can't keep her either.

He nodded stoically. "I'll always remember you, Ceara."

Her eyes sad, she sighed regretfully. "I had best be going. Goodbye, Speirr."

Talon choked on his goodbye. He couldn't say the word. It hurt too much to say it. Saying it would make it real and he desperately didn't want this to be real.

He wanted this to be a bad dream he could wake up from.

But it wasn't. It was real. All of it.

Sunshine was gone.

Ceara was gone.

He had no one.

Feeling forsaken, he watched Ceara fade out of the room. His heart shattered, he sank to the floor on his knees and did something he hadn't done since the day Nynia had been buried.

He cried.

In his mind, he could see his father cut down by the Saxons while the boy, Speirr, had kept his mother and sisters safe from the murderous warriors.

He saw his mother and sister sick from a ravaging pox. Saw him working for Gara as hard as he could while the old woman took pleasure in making him suffer. At night, he'd cared for his sisters. And during those last few months of his mother's life when she'd been too ill to care for herself, he'd taken care of her too.

He saw Ceara as an infant who had been inconsolable as he tried everything to care for her. He remembered Gara turning them out into the dark night while they had no place to go.

It had been snowing that night too, and all he could think of was keeping his sister alive.

She was all he had.

And so he had carried her through the snowstorm while she screamed and howled. Through the leagues of frostbitten land until he had found his mother's people.

For his sister, he had begged and pleaded and allowed them to beat him until he couldn't stand.

He had never asked anything for himself.

Not until he found Nynia.

He had taken her and made her his, and by his own stupidity he had lost her.

They could never be together. Never.

I am solitude.

I am sorrow.

Talon bellowed in anger.

Suddenly, something to the right of him caught his attention. Talon frowned.

There was something sticking out from under his bed.

He moved toward it and pulled it out.

His heart stopped beating. Then it began pounding.

Sunshine had left them for him. There were three paintings of his cabin and dock and the view from his porch.

He stared at the vibrant, crisp colors that captured the scenery in the light of day.

They were beautiful, but nowhere near as beautiful as the woman who had given them to him.

A woman who had given him the greatest gifts of his life.

He found a note sandwiched between two of the paintings. Opening it, he felt his stomach knot.

> *This is the swamp as I see it, but what I can't capture on canvas is you as I see you.*
>
> *No brush or paint will ever show the hero that you are. It will never be able to portray the sound of your voice when you whisper my name. The way my skin tingles when you touch me.*
>
> *The passion of you inside me.*
>
> *I love you, Talon. I know that I can't keep you. No one can ever tame a wild beast.*
>
> *You have a job to do and so do I. I only hope that when you think of me, it'll bring a smile to your face.*
>
> *Love always,*
> *Sunshine*

He reread the note four times.

For centuries, he'd loved Nynia. But what he felt for Sunshine was so much more.

"Yes, you can win battles with a god." Acheron's words hovered in his mind.

Talon drew a ragged breath.

Yes, he could win. He would go out tomorrow night and take care of Mardi Gras for Acheron.

But once it ended . . .

He was going to summon Camulus and end this once and for all.

By Wednesday's dawn, either he or Camulus would be dead.

Chapter 17

Sunshine wasn't sure what to make of Acheron as they entered her loft. He was lean and humongously tall, and those eyes of his . . .

She shivered.

Something about them made it seem like he could see straight through her. Like he could hear every thought she possessed.

She dropped her backpack beside the couch and watched him walk a circle around her loft, as if making sure no one was in here, and yet she sensed it was more habit than a real need he had to verify that they were alone.

He had such a deadly, graceful swagger. A predator's lope. There was something intrinsically sexual about Acheron. Something compelling, seductive. Just being near him made her want to reach out and touch him.

It was as if he were putting off powerful pheremones, and at the same time, she was scared of him. He was like a lethal, beautiful animal in the wild that part of you wanted to cuddle, even while the other part of you knew he was just as likely to rip your arm off as he was to cuddle back.

He was magnetic and fierce and he made her want to run for the door.

When he spoke, the powerful sound of his voice made her jump, but what struck her most was how erotic his voice was. It was so deep that it rumbled and every syllable he spoke went down her spine like a seductive caress. She'd never been around anyone whose entire body and character appeared to have been made for no other purpose than to entice women sexually.

Boy, did it ever work.

"Your brother, Storm, is below, cleaning up. You might want to have him spend the night with you."

"How do you know Storm is below?"

"I just do."

She frowned—he was even more eerie than her grandmother. "Why aren't you staying?"

"Do you want me to?"

No, not really. But she didn't want to offend him. "You probably have things you need to do."

He gave her a tight-lipped smile that seemed to indicate that he had heard her real response. "Then, good night, Sunshine."

He started for the door.

"Acheron, wait."

He paused and looked at her.

"Am I doing the right thing by letting Talon go?" she asked. "You need him, right?"

His mercury eyes seared her. "I think you need to listen to what your grandmother told you, Sunshine. Follow your heart."

"How did you know about that?"

He gave her a hint of a smile. "I know lots of things."

This was a very spooky man. She wondered if he was a missing member of the Addams family.

Acheron turned on his heel and walked out her door.

Sunshine stood there for several minutes, debating what she should do about Talon.

But in the end, she knew what her heart demanded she do . . .

She'd asked Psyche if it were possible to summon a goddess. She wasn't sure if Psyche had been honest, but there was only one way to find out.

"Artemis," she said out loud. "I summon you to human form."

Nothing happened.

There was no sound, no great flash of light.

Nothing.

Depressed, she started for her bedroom.

"Who are you? And why have you called for me?"

She froze at the sound of the peeved, thickly accented voice behind her.

Turning around, she saw an incredibly tall, beautiful woman standing by her sofa. Artemis had long, curly auburn hair that spiraled around the face of an angel and vibrant green eyes that didn't look happy to be here.

The goddess was dressed in a long, white sheathlike dress and stood with her hands on her hips.

"Are you Artemis?"

"Gee, let me think. Did you call for Artemis or for Peter Pan?"

Well, Artemis was definitely *not* a late-night person. She gave a whole new meaning to the word *cranky*. "I called for Artemis."

"Then since I'm not dressed in green and have the body of a woman and not some prepubescent boy, I guess I must be she."

"Are you always this irritable?"

"Are you always this stupid?" She crossed her arms over her chest and gave Sunshine a withering glare. "Look, little human, I have no patience for you. You're not one of my subjects and that medallion around your neck greatly offends me. So tell me what you want so I can tell you to go bugger off."

This was not looking good. Talon's boss-lady was a serious bitch. "I wanted to ask you if I could get Talon's soul back from you."

She cocked her head at the question. "You mean Speirr of the Morrigantes? The Celtic chieftain I snagged away from the Morrigán?"

"Yes."

"No."

"No?" Sunshine asked in disbelief.

"Is there an echo? No, human, his soul belongs to me and you can't have it."

"Why not?"

"Because I said so."

Sunshine was aghast. Furious at her too. Artemis would never be voted Miss Congeniality. The goddess needed some personal-relationship seminars. "Well, that just makes it official then, doesn't it?"

Artemis arched a haughty brow. "Little girl, have you any idea who or what you're dealing with?"

Sunshine took a deep breath and prayed for patience. She couldn't afford to lose her temper with the person who happened to own Talon's soul. Not if she wanted it back.

Not to mention the small fact that as a goddess, Artemis could probably wish her dead if she made her mad enough.

"I know, Artemis. I'm sorry. I don't mean to offend you. I am in love with Talon and I want us to have a future together. I would do anything to keep him with me. Can you not understand that?"

Artemis's face softened a degree, as if she could relate. "Yes, I understand."

"Then can I—"

"The answer is still no."

"Why?"

"Because nothing in this world is ever free. If you want his soul back you have to earn it or pay for it."

"How?"

Artemis shrugged. "*You* can't. You have nothing I want or value, therefore you have nothing to barter with."

"Oh, come on, are you serious?"

"Deadly." Artemis flashed into vapor and vanished.

Ugh! Sunshine wanted to throttle the woman. How could she be so selfish?

"Artemis!" she called out before she could stop herself. "You seriously suck!"

Closing her eyes, Sunshine sighed. What was she to do

now? There was no way that selfish heifer would ever let go of Talon's soul.

What were they going to do?

Amanda Devereaux-Hunter woke up at seven-thirty in the morning. She glanced absently at the clock and closed her eyes, then jerked to full alertness as the time dawned on her.

It was seven-thirty A.M. and her infant daughter, Marissa, hadn't awakened for her five o'clock feeding.

Not quite panicked, but definitely concerned about her baby, she got up and went to the nursery in the room beside hers.

As she neared the crib, her heart stopped.

It was empty.

At only three weeks of age, there was no chance Marissa had gotten up and walked away.

Oh God, it was Desiderius!

He'd come back for them!

Terror gripped her at the thought. Ever since she and Kyrian had defeated that monster, she'd had recurring nightmares of him returning from the dead for vengeance against them.

"Kyrian!" She raced back to the bed and woke her husband.

"What is it?" he asked grumpily.

"It's Marissa. She's gone."

Kyrian sat up, fully alert now. "Gone where?"

"She's not in her crib. I don't know where she is."

He sprang from bed and grabbed his pants from the floor. Without waiting for Kyrian, Amanda ran through the upstairs, her heart pounding.

Where could her baby be?

The thought of losing her child was her worst nightmare.

She dashed down the stairs to see if the front door was open. If maybe someone had come in and taken her.

As she started into the living room, Amanda pulled up

short. Shocked to the core of her being, she focused her gaze on the most unbelievable sight she'd ever beheld.

Acheron lay on the leather couch with Marissa cuddled contentedly on top of his muscular chest, up under his chin.

A pack of diapers was on the coffin-shaped coffee table along with an empty bottle of formula.

Relief and disbelief flooded her simultaneously.

When she had first met Acheron a little over a year ago, he had been the most terrifying thing she'd ever seen. A man possessed of incredible powers and contradictions, she had no doubt he could wish all of them into oblivion and yet there he lay with her infant daughter cradled tenderly in his huge hands.

"Is something . . ." Kyrian's voice trailed off as he, too, saw them.

She looked up at him over her shoulder. "I didn't know Ash liked babies."

"Neither did I. The uncomfortable way he's been behaving with Marissa in the house, I just assumed he had no use for them."

Kyrian was right. Ash had done nothing but avoid being around Marissa as much as possible. Every time she cried, he actually cringed and made a hasty exit. Amanda would never have guessed that he would actually tend her daughter.

Crossing the room, she reached for the baby.

Ash came awake with a look so feral and fierce that she stepped back with an audible gasp.

He sat up on the couch, but didn't move farther.

He blinked as he saw her and Kyrian.

"Sorry," Ash breathed. "I didn't realize it was you."

"I was just going to take her off you."

He glanced down at Marissa who was still sleeping within the shelter of his hands. "Oh. I must have fallen asleep while I was burping her."

He handed her to Amanda and the way he did it told her a lot. Acheron had an expertise that said he'd handled a baby more than just a few times.

"I hope I didn't scare you," he said apologetically. "She was crying when I came in and I went upstairs to make sure she was okay." He looked strangely pale, as if the thought of a baby crying was somehow painful for him. "Since the two of you were still sleeping and I was up, I figured I'd give you guys a break."

Amanda bent over and kissed him on the cheek. "You're a good man, Ash. Thanks."

A pain-filled look crossed his face as he pulled back from her. He got up from the couch and picked his backpack up from the floor. "I'll go on up to bed."

Kyrian stopped him as he started for the hallway. "You okay, Acheron? You look kind of shaken."

Ash laughed at that. "When have I ever been shaken?"

"Good point."

He clapped Kyrian on the shoulder. "I'm just tired."

"Yeah, I was wondering where you spent yesterday. You never came back here to sleep."

"I had something to take care of. Something that wouldn't wait."

Amanda sighed. "You know, Ash, one day you're going to have to learn to confide in someone."

"Good night, Amanda," Ash said. He inclined his head to Kyrian and headed for the stairs.

Amanda joined her husband as Acheron vanished upstairs. "I can't believe you've known him for twenty-one hundred years and you know so little about him that you can't even tell me his real hair color."

He shrugged. "Ash is so self-contained and -controlled that I doubt if anyone will ever know anything about him other than his name."

Sunshine lay in her bed long into the morning, remembering the sound of Talon's deep, even breaths while he slept.

She remembered the way he liked to keep his knee snuggled high between her thighs and his arm draped possessively over her chest with his left hand buried in her hair.

How she missed him.

Then, her thoughts drifted into the past. Far into her other life . . .

"Don't go, Speirr. There is evil in this. I know it."

Angry, he'd jerked his arm free of her grasp. "They murdered my uncle, Nynia. Cut him down before my eyes. I will not rest until I have vengeance."

As Nynia, she had been too afraid of losing him to press the matter. She'd always deferred to him in all things. He was her husband. But in her heart, she'd known he was about to set matters into motion that could never be reversed.

And she had been right.

Just as she knew somehow tonight would settle everything one way or another.

What if she lost Talon?

She couldn't bear the thought of it any more than she could bear the thought of living out her life without him.

She glanced around her loft, at all the familiar things.

Since the day she'd divorced Jerry, all she had wanted was her career, her art.

Now, alone with her stuff, it just didn't seem quite so important to her.

Her art didn't hold her at night. It didn't make her laugh or seduce her. It didn't make her body burn with desire or shiver with orgasms.

It didn't punch Jerry in the nose for being a jerk.

Only Talon did that.

Only Talon *could* do that.

Her eyes fell to the Snoopy dispenser as tears welled up. "I can't let him go."

If only she knew how to keep him.

Zarek sat in the darkened corner of the living room, listening to the city outside awaken. He should be sleeping, resting up for the night that was to come, but he couldn't seem to find the peace he needed.

His phone rang.

He answered it to find Dionysus on the other end.

"Are you ready for tonight?"

Zarek took a drink of vodka before he answered. "I'm always ready to cause trouble."

"Good. Since Talon is now on to Styxx, it requires a little more effort for tonight's preparations. I'll need you to get Sunshine away from the Celt and bring her to me. She has to be in the warehouse by eleven-thirty. Now rest and be ready to kill Talon and Valerius."

That he could do with no problem. "What about Acheron?"

"Leave him to us."

The phone went dead.

Zarek tossed his cell phone aside and returned his attention to the vodka. He'd already drank three-quarters of it. It was a pity Dark-Hunters couldn't get drunk. For that matter, they couldn't even get numb. The only induced pleasure they could take was human blood.

Closing his eyes, he remembered the woman he had tasted last night. Now she had been full of passion. Laughter. Even love. And there for a short time he had felt something other than the pain that cocooned him.

He leaned his head back against the wall and finished off the vodka, letting its smooth taste burn down his throat.

And as he sat there, alone, he couldn't help but wonder how Sunshine would taste . . .

Talon got up alone to the smell of turpentine on his sheets. He should have washed them, but he couldn't bear the thought of losing that last bit of her.

He wanted his Sunshine. He needed her.

And she was lost to him forever.

Sighing, he got up, showered and dressed, then headed into the city.

Tonight everything would be decided.

As soon as the sun set, he rode his motorcycle to Sanctuary where Ash had told him to meet everyone.

Instead of meeting them in the bar itself, he went to the building next door that was also owned by the bear clan.

Attached to the bar by a locked door in the kitchen, the other building was where the bears and certain were-members of the staff lived. The house was equipped with a makeshift hospital, complete with a doctor and a vet.

Sanctuary was more than just a bar. It was a safe haven for any Dark- or Were-Hunter who needed aid.

By the time Talon was admitted into the drawing room of Peltier House, the Peltier quadruplets had already been dispatched to patrol the Mardi Gras crowd for Daimons.

Julian and Kyrian were locked in a holding cell upstairs where Mama Lo Peltier was guarding them until morning. Even in the drawing room, Talon could hear them threatening to kill Valerius, who stood by the fireplace with a sneer on his face.

Nick sat in a stuffed chair, munching a bag of potato chips, and Eric St. James sat on the couch, staring into space.

Almost thirty years old, Eric looked a lot younger. He had long black hair and was another one of the goth contingency.

He'd come into their community as a second-generation Squire, but preferred Dorean Status, meaning he didn't serve one particular Hunter. He served anyone who needed him.

"Acheron, you better let me out of here," Kyrian shouted from upstairs. "Do you hear me?"

"Sounds like I missed a party," Talon said to Ash, who was standing with his back against the far wall.

"You have no idea. I decided it was best to keep Kyrian and Julian locked up until morning. I already called and told Amanda and Grace not to worry about them."

"I really wish you would let them out," Valerius said to Ash.

Ash didn't bother to comment.

Instead, he stared at Talon. "You almost look normal tonight. Are you going to stay that way?"

"I told you I could contain myself." So far, it was working.

Talon was at peace with the fact that come the dawn he'd be having it out with Camulus.

When Ash stepped forward to speak, it dawned on Talon that Zarek was nowhere to be seen.

Was he upstairs too?

"Where's Zarek?" he asked Ash.

"I have him guarding Sunshine."

Now that destroyed his calm.

"Like hell!" Talon roared.

"Trust me, Talon. I believe in Zarek to do the right thing."

Talon's response was emphatic. "I don't trust him. At all. And after this, I'm not sure if I trust you."

"Enough of the bickering," Ash said. "Just do as I told you and everything should work out."

"Should?" Talon asked.

When Ash spoke, there was an odd note in his voice that made Talon wonder how much more Ash knew than he was telling them. "We have predestinies, Talon, but human will can circumvent them. If everyone does as I've instructed, then things should work out the way they're meant to."

Talon clenched his teeth. "And if we don't?"

"We're all screwed."

"Gee, Ash," Nick said sarcastically, "you're just so damn comforting."

Ash gave him a wry look. "I try to be anyway."

Nick's answer was flat. "You fail admirably."

Talon was still stewing.

Ash spoke to all of them. "What I need everyone to know is that we have a truly sinister night ahead of us. It seems Dionysus and Camulus have combined their forces to try and get themselves reinstated to their full godhoods."

"How are they planning on doing that?" Valerius asked.

"The two of them aren't strong enough to do it on their own. They need the power of a third god to aid them."

"What god?" they all asked simultaneously.

"Apollymi."

"Who the hell is Apollymi?" Talon asked. "I've never even heard of her."

One corner of Ash's mouth turned up wryly. "She's an old god who dates back to my time. One who has powers over life, vengeance, and death. The Atlanteans affectionately referred to her as the Destroyer."

"Is she like Hades?" Valerius asked.

"Oh no," Ash said ominously, "this god makes Hades look like a Boy Scout. Apollymi finishes off her victims with an iron hammer and commands an army of malformed demons.

"The last time someone freed her, plagues and suffering permeated the world and she sent Atlantis straight to the bottom of the sea. She headed across Greece, laying waste to the entire country, and setting them back culturally thousands of years before she was finally returned to her holding cell. The Destroyer will unleash holy hell on this earth. Starting with New Orleans."

"Oh goodie," Nick said sarcastically. "I just love knowing about these things."

Ash ignored him.

"So how do they intend to free the Destroyer?" Talon asked.

Ash took a deep breath. "The only way to do that is with the blood of an Atlantean."

"Your blood," Talon said. It was a given, since Ash was the only Atlantean left alive.

Ash nodded. "At midnight, the threshold between this plane and the one where she lives will be thin enough to breach. If they unleash her . . ."

"Anyone else have an ulcer?" Nick asked.

Talon ignored his question. "How do we stop them?"

"With a lot of faith and by doing exactly what I tell you to do."

Nick snorted at that. "Does anyone other than me think that Ash is being just a little too vague about all this?"

Everyone except Ash raised their hands.

"You're not funny," Ash said to them.

Ash looked to Valerius. "I need you on the streets with the Peltiers. At eleven-thirty, Dionysus is planning to unleash his Daimons on the population in order to distract us. Slay any of them you find.

"Nick," Ash said, "I want you and Eric ready to mobilize if you're needed."

The Squires nodded.

Ash put his sunglasses on. "Talon, you stay with me. You and I are going after Dionysus and his crew."

"Just out of curiosity," Talon said, "how do you know all this?"

Ash ignored him.

"All right, children," Ash said, "head out and guard the streets."

"Just one question?" Eric asked him.

"Sure."

"Maybe I'm being dense but why are these guys after power now? Why didn't they do this last year or at some other time? Why wait?"

Ash's answer wasn't comforting in the least. "This isn't the first time they've tried to take their powers back. This is just the best shot they've had at succeeding."

"Okay," Eric said slowly. "So what happened to their powers to begin with?"

Talon answered for Ash. "When a god ceases to be worshiped, their powers diminish. If a god is defeated by another god, then a chunk of his powers is absorbed by the victor and he loses his ability to regain his former position."

Eric nodded. "Okay, one last thing. What happens if they do regain their powers?"

Ash looked away. "Let us hope we don't find out."

"Why?"

"Because according to Atlantean myth, the Destroyer is supposed to be the one who will bring about Telikos—the end of the world. No doubt Dionysus and Camulus are thinking that Apollymi will be so overcome with gratitude when they release her that she won't think twice about joining them and sharing her power with them.

"What they don't know is that there was a really good reason why Apollymi was imprisoned by the Atlantean gods. Even the other gods feared Apollymi's wrath, and in the end, she killed them all. Whatever we do, we can't ever let her escape. If they free her tonight, everything you know about this existence will change. *Everything.*"

"Gotta love saving the world," Talon said. "Another day in the life."

Ash took a deep breath. "And on that note we have things to do."

Talon nodded, but in his heart, he wished he could see Sunshine one more time.

He didn't want to die without seeing her face again.

Duty, how it reeked.

Valerius headed out first.

Talon, Nick, and Eric went out through the back door with Ash pulling up the rear.

As Ash left the house, the back door slammed shut, catching the tail end of his long black coat.

Ash jerked to a stop and cursed.

Nick howled with laughter at the sight of Acheron trapped. "Don't it take the bad-ass right out of you?"

Ash arched a brow.

The door opened by itself, freeing his coat, then it slammed shut again.

Nick sobered instantly. "And that puts it right back in you."

Ash ruffled Nick's hair like an older brother. "Watch our backs and soothe Amanda's nerves until Kyrian returns."

"You got it."

Ash and Talon left the ornate courtyard and headed into the crowd of tourists and locals who were as thick as fog.

There were hundreds of people out. Hundreds who had

no idea that the very fate of the world rested in the hands of the two men dressed in black who were making their way slowly through them.

Two men who were tired tonight. Weary.

One because he had long ago ceased feeling anything except the heavy burden of his responsibilities.

Ash wanted nothing more than one single day to just lie down and rest. One day to find a moment's worth of comfort.

He'd spent eternity waiting for a second chance.

Waiting for an escape from the wreckage of his past and the damnation that made up his future.

Tonight, he had to face his brother for the first time in eleven thousand years.

The two of them had never been on equal footing. Styxx had hated him since the moment of his birth.

For Ash, this was going to be a long, long night.

Talon's thoughts were on Sunshine. On the gentle curve of her face. The beauty of her touch.

Was she in her loft painting?

Was she thinking of him?

"I love you." Her words tore through him.

Talon clenched his teeth, wishing he were touching her. Hoping that at the end of this night she would be safe from Camulus forever.

"Faith, Talon," Ash said as if he knew his thoughts.

"I'm trying."

Talon took a deep breath.

His death didn't concern him. It was Sunshine he couldn't allow to die. Right or wrong, he would see this through, and come morning she would be safe.

No matter what it took.

Chapter 18

Sunshine followed Zarek's directions to the Warehouse District, but getting there in the heavy traffic wasn't easy. They probably could have walked faster.

Normally the traffic wouldn't have bothered her; however, Zarek wasn't exactly friendly, and between his sour mood and the drunken revelers on the street who kept staggering out into the road, her nerves were pretty much fried.

She wasn't really sure why they had to go out tonight, but Zarek had assured her that Ash wanted her moved for safety's sake.

He'd promised her that Talon would be able to fight better knowing she was hidden away from Camulus and Styxx.

"So how long have you been a Dark-Hunter?" she asked, trying to do something to ease the tension between them.

"You don't care, so why do you ask?"

"Well, you're just Mr. Warm and Fuzzy, aren't you?"

He looked at her coldly. "When you kill things for a living, it tends to take the warm and fuzzy right out of you."

"Talon isn't like that."

"Well, bully for him."

She growled as she slammed on the brakes to avoid hitting a man dressed up like a bull. He pounded on the hood of her car and yelled, then dashed across the street.

Sunshine moved forward again, even more slowly,

through the bumper-to-bumper traffic. "You don't like Talon, do you?"

"Wish him dead every time I see him."

She frowned at Zarek's blasé tone. "I can't tell if you mean that or not."

"I mean it."

"Why?"

"He's an asshole and I've had enough assholes in my life."

"Do you hate Ash too?"

"Baby, I hate everyone."

"Even me?"

He didn't answer.

Sunshine didn't bother him after that. There really was something spooky about Zarek. Something cold and unreachable. It was as if he took pleasure in the fact that he shoved everyone away from him.

At least twenty minutes passed before Zarek shocked her by asking a question of his own. "You love the Celt, don't you?"

"Yes."

"Why? What is it about him that makes you care for him?"

She sensed Zarek was asking something much deeper than that. It was as if the concept of love were so alien to him that he was struggling to make sense of it.

"He's a good man who makes me laugh. He looks at me and I melt all over the floor. When I'm with him, I feel like I can fly."

Zarek turned his head away from her and watched the Mardi Gras crowd outside.

"Have you ever been in love?" she tried again.

Again, he didn't answer. Instead he directed her to a warehouse on St. Joseph Street.

The place was dark and forbidding. "Is this where we're supposed to be?" she asked.

He nodded.

She parked in an alley behind the building, and they left the car.

Zarek led her in through a back door and up a series of stairs. He opened a door at the end of the hallway and let her enter first.

Sunshine stepped inside. At first glance, she thought the tall blond man was Acheron with a new hair color. But when she saw Camulus standing by his side, she knew it wasn't.

It was Styxx who was standing between Camulus and a brunet man she didn't recognize.

Sunshine turned to run.

Zarek closed the door ominously and took up a blocking position before it. The look on his face told her that he had no intention of letting her pass through him.

"Come in, come in, said the spider to the fly," Camulus said.

Sunshine lifted her chin as she faced the men. Camulus was extremely handsome, but he had a smile that was pure evil.

Even more so than Zarek and that was hard to accomplish.

The man she didn't know was humongously tall with light brown hair and a goatee. He had an extremely refined, well-bred look to him.

"I'm going to take a wild guess that you are Dionysus," Sunshine said, remembering what Selena had once told her about the patron god of Mardi Gras.

He smiled as if flattered she knew him. "Guilty."

Camulus let out a long breath. "She's so bright. It's almost a shame to kill her. But . . . oh well."

"You can't hurt her," Zarek said from the door. "You promised me she wouldn't be harmed if I brought her here."

"So I lied," Dionysus said. "Sue me."

Zarek started for the god, but Sunshine stopped him. She wasn't really sure why she did that, it just seemed as if he were the closest thing to an ally she had in that room.

She turned back to Camulus, knowing exactly how he

planned to hurt Talon tonight. "I'm not going to let you kill me in front of Talon."

They all laughed. All except for Zarek.

"You can't stop us," Camulus said.

Zarek glanced down at her, then did a double take as his dark gaze fell to her necklace. "Uh, gods, I think you've forgotten something."

Dionysus curled his lip. "We forget nothing."

"Oh, okay," Zarek said sarcastically, "then you must already know that she wears a Marking Medallion."

They sobered instantly.

"What?" Camulus snarled.

Sunshine pulled her grandmother's necklace out of her shirt and held it up to them. She couldn't really believe it might help her, but hey, anything at this point was worth a try. "My grandmother said that the Morrigán would always protect me."

Camulus cursed. "Oh, this ain't right." He cursed again.

"This thing really works?" she whispered to Zarek.

"More than you know," he whispered back. "He can't kill you without making the Morrigán angry."

"Well, who knew?" she said, amazed by the knowledge. "Cool."

"Yup," Zarek concurred. "Better than a cross with Dracula."

She beamed. "Does it work against Dionysus too?"

He nodded.

Oh, this was good. Very, very good. "Okay, then, let's talk."

"Talk about what?" Dionysus hissed.

"Not you. Him." She indicated Camulus with a nod. "I want to talk about Talon's curse."

Camulus's eyes blazed at her. "What about it?"

"I want you to lift it."

"Never."

She held her medallion out to him. "Do it or . . ." She gave Zarek a sideways glance. "Does this have any power to hurt him?"

"Only if he hurts you first."

Damn. What kind of protection was that? She needed to have a talk with whoever came up with these things.

A calculating glint lightened Camulus's eyes. He sighed as if bored. "Oh well, since I can't kill you, I guess I'll have to content myself with killing Talon instead."

Terror consumed her. "What?"

Camulus shrugged nonchalantly. "It's rather pointless to let him live happily ever after with you when my intent was to make him suffer. Since you can't die, he'll have to."

Her hand shook as she held the medallion in her suddenly sweaty grip. "Won't Artemis be mad if you kill one of her soldiers?"

He looked at Dionysus, who burst out laughing. "Artemis, darling that she is, would most definitely care. However, she won't start a war with the Celtic pantheon over it. Unlike me, Cam is safe from her wrath."

"Doesn't it just reek?" Camulus asked. His happy smile belied his dire words.

Sunshine wanted to cry. This couldn't be happening.

By saving herself, she had condemned Talon to die.

No! She couldn't let this happen. "Okay, there has to be another way."

Camulus narrowed his eyes as if thinking about the matter. "Perhaps there is. Tell me, Sunshine. How much does Talon's happiness mean to you?"

"Everything," she said sincerely.

"Everything. Well, that certainly is a lot." His look turned steely cold, frightening. "Does it mean as much to you as your own soul?"

"Sunshine," Zarek said. "Don't."

"You, heel," Dionysus snarled.

Zarek cracked his knuckles. "Don't tell me what to do. I don't like it."

Sunshine ignored them. "What are you saying to me, Camulus?"

He tucked his hands into his pockets and acted as cool as someone chitchatting about the weather, not sealing the fate of her immortal destiny. "A simple trade. I lift his curse. You give me your soul."

Sunshine hesitated. "That seems easy."

"It is."

"So what are you going to do with my soul once you have it?"

"Nothing at all. I'll keep it with me, just like Artemis keeps Talon's."

"And my body?"

"A body doesn't need a soul to function."

Zarek put a hand on her shoulder. "Don't do it, Sunshine. You can't ever trust a god."

"Sure you can," Styxx said. "Trusting them is the best thing I ever did."

"I don't know," she breathed, searching her heart and mind, trying to decide what she should do.

Acheron and Talon stood on the crowded street. There were people everywhere, most of them drunk as they celebrated Mardi Gras.

Talon did a double-take as a man danced by him wearing a large diaper and a fake pair of gold wings. His long blond hair was tied back in a gold cord and he held a crossbow in one hand and a bottle of Jack Daniel's in the other. Drunk, the man was arbitrarily shooting his golden arrows at the people he passed by.

"Eros!" Talon snapped, grabbing the bow from him. "What are you doing?"

"I'm celebrating."

Acheron raked a less than amused stare over Eros's "costume." "What's with the get-up?"

Eros shrugged. "If you can't beat them, join them. They expect Cupid in a diaper, so here I am. Cute Cupid in a diaper." He threw an arm over Talon's shoulders. The god was so drunk he could barely stand on his own. "Hey, I found out something interesting. Dion has teamed up with another god for tonight's festivities. And would you believe, it's the same guy you were asking me about? What's his face, Camululu?"

Talon went cold at the name. "Camulus?"

"Yeah, *him.* I heard Dion saying they were going to party with your woman and that the psycho Hunter from Alaska was going to hand her over to them."

His blood boiling, Talon pushed Eros away and started back toward his car.

Acheron grabbed him. By the look on Ash's face, he could tell this was nothing Ash didn't already know. "Talon . . ."

"You knew!" Talon snarled at the betrayal. "How could you?"

Ash gave him a hard stare. "It's all right, Talon."

"Like hell it is." Rage gripped him hard. How could Acheron have betrayed him like this? How could he have turned Sunshine over into the hands of a man he knew was going to give her to the one god who wanted him punished?

"Damn you, damn you straight to hell!"

He punched Acheron in the jaw.

Ash took the hit without flinching, but when Talon moved to strike him again, he caught his hand. "This isn't accomplishing anything."

"It's making me feel better."

Ash grabbed him by the shoulder of his leather jacket and held him immobile. "Listen to me, Talon. The only way to save the two of you is to maintain your grip. Trust me."

"I'm tired of trusting you, Ash. Especially when you won't return it. Tell me what's going on here and why you sent Zarek to her knowing he was going to turn on her."

"It's the way things are meant to be."

Rage rolled over him. He wasn't some child to be lectured to about fate.

"Who the hell are you to say that? You're not a god, even though you pretend to be one with your vague-ass comments and spooky powers. You don't know the future any more than I do." Talon snarled at him. "If she dies, so help me, I'll kill you."

"Listen to me, Celt," he said sharply. "If you want to break Camulus's curse, the two of you have to confront him together tonight. This is the only shot you'll ever get to break free of him."

Talon didn't like any of this. Damn Ash for his secrecy. "Where are they?"

"They're in a warehouse. If you'll calm down, I'll take you to it.

"The night is far from over, Talon. Look inside you and find the peace you used to have. If you don't find it, you've lost even before you start to fight."

Talon did it, but it was hard. Nearly impossible. But he had no choice. He had to rein himself in or he would be useless to Sunshine.

When his head was clear, Acheron let him go.

"Maintain." The voice seemed to come from inside Talon's head.

Ash placed a hand on his shoulder.

One instant they were on Bourbon Street, the next they were outside a warehouse.

"What did you do?" Talon asked, wondering how many people had seen them vanish.

"I'm doing what I have to. Don't worry, no one saw us leave or arrive. I don't make those kinds of mistakes."

Talon hoped so.

Ash held the door open for him and Talon led the way into the building.

They were halfway through the main room when something akin to lightning flashed from upstairs. Screams rent the air.

Talon lost his calm as he sprinted for the stairs with Ash hot on his heels.

They rushed through a door and were almost run over by Zarek who was covered in blood and carrying Sunshine in his arms.

"What the hell?" Talon asked, terrified by the sight. "What happened to her?"

Before Zarek could answer, the door was blown from its frame.

"Run!" Zarek shouted.

No one had a chance. A swarm of hideous winged demons flew into the room. Talon cursed. He'd never seen anything like them. They were the color of rust and screeched like banshees as they flew at them.

They had three barbed tails that they wielded like whips.

Acheron held his hands up and blasted them with electrical energy. They recoiled, but kept coming.

"Get Sunshine out of here," Acheron ordered.

They headed back to the stairs only to find Daimons coming up from below.

Talon tossed two srads, taking out four of the creatures, but it didn't even slow them down. "We're surrounded."

Acheron spoke in a language Talon couldn't understand. The demons paused and flew around as if dazed by his order.

"It won't hold the demons for long," Ash shouted, his voice barely discernible over the ethereal flapping of wings and claps of thunder.

Ash threw his hands up and the Daimons ran into what appeared to be an invisible barrier between them.

Talon led Zarek down the hallway, hoping to find another way out of the building.

He shoved open a door to a smaller room.

"I think she's dying." Zarek's voice sent an electric chill through him.

"She's not dying."

"Talon, I think she's dying," he repeated.

The demons forgotten, Talon took her from Zarek's arms and laid her carefully on the floor.

Her face was so pale that it shook him.

"Sunshine?" he breathed, his heart pounding. "Baby, can you look at me?"

She did, but instead of the vibrancy he was used to seeing, he saw pain and deep regret.

"You're free, Talon," she whispered. "I made him break the curse."

"What?"

"She traded her soul to Camulus so that he would set you free." Zarek curled his lip at him. "I told her not to do it, that it was a trick. She didn't listen and as soon as she agreed, the bastard blasted her."

Talon choked. "No!" he roared at both of them. "Sunshine, why?"

"He said he would kill you. I thought he would just take my soul, Talon. I didn't know he would do this. I didn't know he couldn't take possession of my soul without killing me first."

Talon tore the medallion from Sunshine's neck. "Damn you, Morrigán," he shouted, throwing it against the wall. "How could you forsake her too?"

She pressed her cold hand to his lips, "Shh, baby. Don't say that. It's my fault."

"I told her there's always a catch. But she didn't ask the right questions."

Tears flowed down Talon's cheeks as he watched her struggle to breathe. Over and over in his mind he remembered every moment of their time together, both in this life and her previous one.

He saw Sunshine's bright, tender face the first time they had made love. Saw her wrestling for her easel with Beth.

Heard her singing "Puff the Magic Dragon" as she doodled.

He took her hands into his and kissed them, with their smell of paint, turpentine, and patchouli. Hands that created breathtaking works of art.

Hands that could tear him apart with a simple touch . . .

"I'm not going to lose you again," he breathed. "Not like this."

Zarek came forward. "What are you doing, Celt?"

"Get away from me."

Talon placed his hands over her chest wound and closed his eyes. He forced himself to calm down, forced his emotions to leave him, and then he summoned his Dark-Hunter powers, and let them wash through him. His immortal strength flowed, surged. It swelled up and moved from his hands into her body.

His arms burned as he, in turn, absorbed her injury into his own chest.

Normally, it would hurt when he did this. Tonight, the pain was crippling because this wound wasn't a small injury.

It was mortal.

Gasping from the wrenching agony of his heart being pierced, Talon fell back, away from her.

Sunshine lay still, waiting for the pain to return.

It didn't.

Afraid she was already dead, she reached up to touch her chest where Camulus's blast had struck her. There was no longer a wound there.

"Talon?" She sat up to see Zarek staring at him.

"Oh God, no!" she shrieked as she saw Talon lying on the floor, bleeding. She scrambled to his side and pulled him into her arms. "What have you done?"

"He took your injuries into his own body," Zarek explained. "Now, instead of you dying, he will."

"No, Talon, no! Please don't die," she begged.

"Shh," Talon said quietly. "It's okay."

Ash came running through the door, took one look at them and cursed. "What happened?"

"The Celt absorbed her injuries." Zarek's voice was scarcely more than a whisper and filled with disbelief.

Something struck the door. Hard.

"Don't worry," Ash said. "I have a shield on the room. The gods can't pop in here until they breach it."

"Yeah, but at the rate they're going, they'll have the door knocked down any second," Zarek said. He pushed Ash toward Talon. "Go, get him out of here. I've got your backs."

"You sure?" Ash asked.

Zarek nodded.

"So help me, Slave," Dionysus snarled from the other side of the door. "I'll see you obliterated for this."

Zarek laughed coldly. "Come get some."

Ash opened the door on the opposite side of the room.

Sunshine was terrified. She didn't know what was happening. She still couldn't believe Zarek had turned around and helped them. Nor could she think past the sight of Talon covered in blood.

Everything was happening so fast that she wanted to run away and hide. But she couldn't.

Talon needed her to be strong for him and she refused to fail him.

As she started away from Zarek, he called out to her. "Hey, Sunshine?"

She looked back at him.

"Thanks for the bowl." Then he turned around to wait for the gods to break through Ash's barrier and the door.

Amazed by his actions, Sunshine ran to help Ash carry Talon down the hallway and into the last room on the left.

Ash laid him carefully on the floor, then used his powers to seal the room.

Sunshine's hand shook as she knelt beside Talon. He was pale and trembling. His entire body was coated with sweat and blood. "Hold on, baby," she whispered, not sure if he could even hear her now.

"He's immortal, right?" she asked Ash. "He'll be fine."

Ash shook his head. "His heart is pierced. When it stops beating, he'll die. Again."

His face grim, Ash looked up at the ceiling. "Artemis!" he shouted. "Get your ass here, right now."

A flash of light almost blinded Sunshine as the goddess appeared beside her.

Artemis gave Acheron a furious glare. "What is your problem?"

"I need Talon's soul. Now."

She laughed incredulously at him. "Excuse me, Acheron, but you haven't paid the price for it."

"Dammit, Artie, he's dying. I don't have time to nego-tiate."

She shrugged. "Then heal him."

"I can't and you know it. It's a mortal god-bolt wound. I'm not allowed to interfere with that."

Sunshine felt an electric ripple flow through the room.

Rage darkened her sight as she stared at the selfish goddess. Sunshine started to lunge at her, but Ash caught her and pulled her back.

Sunshine trembled in fear and anger.

"Give it to me, *now*." Acheron's deep voice sounded like thunder. "Do it and I'll give you a week of total submission."

A calculating gleam darkened Artemis's eyes. "Give me two."

Sunshine saw the fury and resignation on Ash's face. "Done."

Artemis held her hand out and a large maroon stone appeared in her palm.

When Ash went to take it, Artemis pulled it out of his reach. "You will come to me at dawn."

"I will, I swear it."

Artemis smiled in satisfaction, then handed the stone to Ash. Ash returned to Talon. Then, he met Sunshine's gaze. "Sunshine, you're going to have to take this into your hand and hold it over the brand mark until his soul is released back into his body."

She reached for it, but Talon caught her wrist. She hadn't even known he was still conscious until she felt his weakened grip on her arm.

"She can't, Ash."

"Talon!" she said, angered that he was stopping her. "What are you doing?"

"No, Sunshine," Talon whispered, his voice strained. "If you take that, it will scar your hand. It could leave you unable to draw or paint ever again."

Her greatest fear.

She looked into Talon's pain-filled eyes.

Her greatest love.

There was no contest.

She grabbed the stone from Ash's hand, then cried out as it seared her flesh.

"Watch Talon's eyes." She heard Ash's voice inside her head. "And for Zeus's sake, please don't let go of his soul. Focus . . ." She did and the pain lessened, but still she could feel the fire of the stone searing her hand.

Time stood still as she stared into Talon's jet-black eyes. Memories of this life and of their former one merged in her mind. She flashed back to her own death, to Talon holding her close.

She leaned down and kissed him. "I'm with you, love."

Talon took his last breath and relaxed. Her own heart stopped beating as raw terror consumed her.

Please, please, let this work!

Ash placed her hand over Talon's bow-and-arrow brand mark. Slowly, the heat faded and the stone turned dull in color.

Still, her hand burned.

When it was completely cold, she dropped the stone and waited.

Talon didn't move.

He didn't breathe.

He lay there, completely still and unresponsive to her.

"Talon?" she asked, her entire body shaking with the fear that he was gone.

Just when she was sure he was dead, he drew a deep breath and opened his eyes.

Sunshine let out a joyful cry as she saw his amber eyes. She hugged him close as the door behind them flew open.

The Daimons, the demons, and the two gods spilled into the room. There was no sign of Zarek anywhere. She only hoped they hadn't killed him.

Talon jumped up and put himself between Sunshine and the others.

Ash rose to his feet, ready to fight.

"It's midnight," Dionysus said with a laugh. "Let the show begin."

The demons moved aside and out of their midst appeared Acheron's "twin."

"Hello, Acheron," Styxx said in a tone that was neither kind nor welcoming. "It's been a while, hasn't it? Eleven thousand years or so?"

Talon held his breath. He couldn't believe what he was seeing.

He had suspected as much, but now the reality of it came crashing down on him. Ash had had a twin brother all this time.

Why had he hidden it? And how could Styxx still be alive and not be a Dark-Hunter too? It didn't make sense.

Styxx approached Acheron.

"Stand down, Styxx," Ash said sternly. "I don't want to hurt you, but I will if I have to. I won't let you release her."

Styxx met Talon's gaze and laughed. "It's like some bad soap opera, isn't it? Good twin, bad twin."

His furious gaze returned to Acheron. "But then, we're not really twins, are we, Acheron? We just happened to have shared the same womb for a while."

Styxx moved to stand behind Ash who tensed noticeably. It wasn't like Ash to allow anyone to do that to him and yet he appeared to be frozen by some unseen force.

Styxx was so close to him that barely a hand separated them.

They didn't touch.

Styxx leaned forward to speak in a low tone near Ash's ear. "Shall we tell him who the good one is, Acheron? Should I tell him which of us lived his life with dignity? Which of us was respected by the Greeks and Atlanteans and who was laughed at?"

Styxx reached his hand around Ash's neck and placed it in the exact spot where Ash's scar often resided.

He pulled Ash back against him so that he could whisper in Ash's ear in a language Talon couldn't understand.

Ash panted as if in the throes of a nightmare.

His eyes were haunted and glazed, his breathing ragged. Still he didn't move to break Styxx's hold.

Talon watched, unsure of what he should do. Surely Ash could handle this. He'd never known of anything Ash couldn't handle.

"That's it, Acheron," Styxx said in English, between clenched teeth. "Remember the past. Remember what you were. I want you to relive it all. Relive every foul thing you ever did. Every tear you made my parents weep for you. Every moment I had to look at you and feel ashamed that you bore my face."

Talon watched as tears filled Ash's eyes and he trembled. He didn't know what secrets Ash hid, but they must be hideous to affect him like this.

Personally, he didn't care what Ash had done in his past. For fifteen hundred years, he had never known Ash to be anything but caring and decent.

Secrets or not, the two of them were friends.

"Let him go," Talon ordered.

Styxx cocked his head, but he refused to release Ash. He tightened his grip on Ash's throat. "Do you remember when Estes died, Acheron? The way my father and I found you? I have never been able to forget it. Every time I have ever thought of you, it's the image I have. You're repulsive. Disgusting."

"Kill him," Dionysus ordered, "and open the portal."

Styxx didn't seem to hear him, his attention was fixed on Ash.

Camulus started toward them with a dagger. Talon rushed him and they fought for the weapon.

The demons attacked as Styxx continued to taunt and insult Ash.

"Kill him, Styxx," Dionysus ordered again. "Or we'll miss the portal."

Styxx pulled a dagger out from underneath his coat.

His fight with Camulus forgotten, Talon tried to reach them.

But he couldn't make it.

Styxx raised his hand and sent the dagger straight into Ash's heart. He buried it all the way to its hilt.

Ash gasped and arched his back as if something had possessed him. The dagger shot through the air, bouncing off a wall above Dionysus's head. Light poured out of the wound, then seared it closed.

In the next instant a shock wave went through the room, knocking everyone off their feet. Styxx was hurled to a far corner while the gods were pinned to the ground.

Acheron rose from the floor, to hover spread-eagled several inches above it.

Unable to stand upright against the unseen force, Talon crawled to Sunshine and held her close so that he could protect her from whatever was happening.

No one could stand. Not even the gods.

Lightning bolts shot through Acheron's body, blowing out the windows and the lights. Electrical energy snapped and hissed all around. Acheron laid his head back as bolts of light pierced his eyes and mouth. They seemed to shoot through him and then out, into the room, emitting bright flashes of light.

The Daimons and the demons exploded in one bright flash.

A winged dragon seemed to come out from under Acheron's sleeve and wrap itself around him as if it were protecting him.

Or perhaps devouring him.

In all his life, Talon had never seen anything like this.

"What the hell is that?" Camulus asked. "Styxx, what did you do?"

"Nothing. Is this from the portal opening?"

"No," Dionysus said. "This is something else entirely. Something no one told me about." He looked up at the ceiling and shouted, "Artemis!"

Artemis appeared and was immediately pinned to the floor with the rest of them.

Talon tightened his grip on Sunshine, who clutched him fiercely as she trembled against him.

Artemis took one look at Acheron and her face went flush with anger. "Who's the idiot who pissed off Acheron?" she demanded.

The two gods pointed to Styxx.

"You fools!" she snarled. "What were you thinking?"

"We needed to kill an Atlantean to raise the Destroyer," Dionysus said. "Acheron's the only one left."

"Oh, you are so stupid!" Artemis snapped. "I knew your plan had to be a bad one. You can't just kill him with a dagger. In case you haven't noticed, he's not human. Where was your brain?"

Dionysus curled his lips at her. "How was I to know your pet was a god-killer? What kind of idiot ties herself down to one of his kind?"

"Well, gee, what was I supposed to do?" Artemis shot back. "Hook up with Mr. All-powerful God-killer or get myself a Mardi Gras float and hang out with him?" She pointed to Camulus, who looked extremely offended by her comment. "You're such a moron," she said to her brother. "No wonder you're the patron god of drunken frat boys."

"Excuse me," Talon snapped at them. "Could you gods focus for a sec? We have a bit of a situation here."

"Oh, shut up," Dionysus snapped. "I knew I should have backed up when I ran you over."

Talon's jaw went slack. "That was you who hit me with the float?"

"Yes."

"Damn, boy," Camulus said to Dionysus. "You've fallen a long way down. Yesterday Greek god . . . today incompetent float driver. Sheez, and I hooked up with you? What was I thinking? Artemis is right, what kind of idiot picks a float to mow a guy down so that he can go home with his dead wife? You're lucky you didn't kill him then and blow the entire plan."

"Hey, have you ever tried to drive one of those things? It's not exactly easy. Besides, he's a Dark-Hunter. I knew it wouldn't kill him. I just needed something that would hurt him enough to make her take him home. Need I remind you that it did work?"

Artemis growled at them. "You're so pathetic. I can't believe we share a common gene between us."

Shooting a nasty glare at her brother, Artemis struggled against the invisible force that held them down. Like the rest of them, she couldn't reach Ash.

"Acheron!" she called. "Can you hear me?"

Disembodied laughter filled the room.

Ash leaned his head forward and more lightning flowed through him. The dragonlike beast tightened its grip around him and hissed a fiery breath at the goddess.

Artemis tried to climb up his leg, but she was forced back, away from him.

"You know, folks," Camulus shouted. "The idea was to kill Acheron, free Apollymi, and reclaim our god status. Not piss him off and end the world. Personally, I don't want to be ruler of nothing. But if someone doesn't stop this guy, that chant he's making is going to undo life as we know it and un-create the world."

"What are we going to do?" Sunshine asked Talon.

Only one thing came to his mind.

He had to bring Acheron to his senses.

Talon kissed her lips, then moved away from her. He hadn't gone through death to get her back, only to lose her now.

He summoned his remaining powers and allowed them to cocoon him. He no longer had his Dark-Hunter immortality, but he did retain all the psychic powers that had been given to him.

Hopefully they would be enough.

He rose slowly to his feet.

A lightning bolt came at him.

Talon deflected it. He moved slowly through the maelstrom until he reached Ash's side. So long as he stayed calm, he seemed to be shielded from Ash's wrath.

"Let it go, T-Rex."

Ash spoke to him in a language he didn't understand.

"He says to back off or die," Styxx translated. "He's summoning the Destroyer."

"I can't let you do that," Talon said.

The laughter echoed again.

Wanting to distract Acheron from what he was chanting,

and not knowing anything else to try, Talon rushed him.

He caught Ash about the middle and knocked him to the floor. The dragon arched up, shrieking.

Talon ignored it as he slugged Ash.

Sunshine held her breath as she watched the two of them fighting. The entire building felt as if it were going to break apart.

The floor beneath her shook.

They were locked together like two great primal beasts and the fate of the world lay in who would win and who would lose.

She whispered a prayer as she watched them, awed by the morbid beauty and grace of their battle.

Zarek came through the door, bleeding, and was immediately thrown backward, against a wall.

Artemis tried again to reach Acheron and again he tossed her back while he fought with Talon.

"I'll give the boy credit," Camulus said. "He always was a fighter."

Talon stopped fighting as he heard those words.

"You never could learn your place, Speirr. You never knew when you should just lay down the sword and play nice."

Camulus had been right. Up until now, Talon had never known when to fight and when to withdraw.

Being calm was what had allowed him to reach Ash.

Then, he remembered what Acheron had said to him on the night he'd become a Dark-Hunter. *"I can show you how to bury that pain so deep inside you that it will prick you no more. But be warned that nothing is ever given freely and nothing lasts forever. One day something will come along to make you feel again and with it, it will bring the pain of the ages upon you. All you have hidden will come out and it could destroy not only you but anyone near you."*

He wondered now who those words had really been meant for. Him or Ash?

He looked up at Acheron and saw the fury of the man who was attacking him. This was what Ash had meant that night.

Both of them had kept such a leash on themselves for so long that their fury blinded them to reason. It made them attack when they needed to withdraw and rethink the line of battle.

Closing his eyes, Talon summoned the soothing calm, as Acheron had taught him.

Ash rushed him again.

This time, instead of fighting, Talon embraced him like a brother.

Possessed of a strength and power Talon had never known before, he cupped Ash's face in his hands and tried to make his old friend see him.

Ash's features were no longer handsome or human. They were those of a twisted demon. His eyes were blood-red and yellow, and there was no mercy in them. They were cold. Vicious.

The colors swirled and danced like fire.

Talon had never seen anything like this before.

Who knew Ash had this kind of power?

But he had to stop him.

One way or another.

"Acheron," he said calmly, slowly. "Enough."

At first he didn't think Ash had heard him. Not until Acheron turned his head to see Sunshine on the floor.

"Talon," he rasped hoarsely. Ash's eyes flickered, then he looked back at Talon.

Suddenly, another shock wave shot through the room, this one in the reverse direction from the first. It was as if the unleashed power were drawing back into Acheron.

The dragon shot up toward the ceiling, then vanished.

Ash's features transformed back into the face of the man Talon had known these centuries past.

Ash blinked his now silver eyes and looked around as if he were waking up from a nightmare.

Without a single comment, Ash stepped away from Talon, wrapped his arms around his chest, and walked across the room as if nothing had happened.

As he passed Artemis, she reached for him, but he dodged her touch and kept walking.

Artemis turned on her brother with a snarl. "Just you wait till Dad gets his hands on you."

"Me? He knew what I had planned tonight. Wait until I tell him about Acheron!"

Artemis curled her lip. "Oh, shut up, whiny boy." She held her hand out and zapped him out of the room.

Styxx shrank back as Artemis turned her gaze to him.

"You," she said, her tone thick with loathing.

Styxx gulped audibly. "How can you protect something like him? After I died, I was sent to the Elysian Fields while he was—"

"No concern of yours," she said, interrupting him. "You and your precious family, you turned your backs on him and condemned him for something that wasn't his fault."

"Not his fault? Please." Styxx tried to say something more, but his voice vanished.

"That's better," Artemis said. "Funny, the two of you sound alike and yet *you* whine. Thank Zeus, Acheron doesn't have that repugnant quality. But then, he was always a man and not a sniveling little child."

She backed Styxx against the wall. "I can't believe you. I gave you a perfect existence. Your own island, filled with everything you could ever desire, and what did you do? You've spent eternity hating Acheron, plotting ways to kill him. You don't deserve mercy."

"You can't kill me," Styxx squeaked out. "If you do, Acheron dies too."

"And I curse the day the Fates bound your life force to his." She narrowed her eyes at him as if she wanted nothing more than to splinter him where he stood. "You're right. I can't kill you, but I can make living a worse hell than anything you can imagine."

"What are you going to do to me?" Styxx asked.

She smiled evilly. "You'll see, little human, you'll see."

Styxx vanished.

Artemis turned to face them. She took a deep breath and seemed to calm down exponentially.

"Take care of your soul, Speirr," she said to Talon.

"Know that it was purchased for you at a very dear cost."
Then she too vanished.

That left them alone with Camulus.

"Well," Talon said to the Celtic god. "It appears your
friends have abandoned you."

Camulus sighed. "What a pity. Excess, War, and Destruction. Together, we would have had a high time on
earth. Oh well. I shall just have to content myself with
taking her from you again. After all, she gave me her soul
and now I wish to claim it. And of course, the fun thing
about souls, they can only be claimed from a dead body."

Camulus started for her.

Talon pulled his srads out ready to do battle.

Out of nowhere, a bright flash lit the room. It faded into
a form that was almost as dear to Sunshine as Talon's.

"Grammy?" Sunshine asked in disbelief.

Her grandmother stepped between them and Camulus.
She faced the Celtic god with a stern glower. " 'Fraid not,
hon. You don't own bupkis."

Camulus was aghast at her appearance. "Morrigán?
What are you doing here? This doesn't concern you."

"Oh yes, it does." Her grandmother transformed from a
little old lady into the beautiful war goddess Talon had met
in his days as a mortal man.

Talon went cold.

Sunshine sputtered. "Excuse me? What is this?"

Her grandmother looked at Sunshine apologetically. "I
didn't mean for you to find out this way, Little Bit, but
Acheron and I had to stop them from unleashing Apollymi.
And to get Talon free, we needed the two of you here to
face Camulus."

Talon gaped.

Ash had known all about this? Why hadn't he told him?

The Morrigán turned back to Camulus. "Sorry, Cam. For
once *you* forgot to read the fine print. You agreed with Bran
to let Nynia be reborn to mortal parents for your scheme.
You never specified that her grandparents be mortal too.

"Since I couldn't help Speirr escape your curse and his

bargain without declaring war on you and Artemis, I figured the least I could do was return his wife to him in the body of someone you couldn't touch. Nynia now reborn as Sunshine is flesh of my flesh, blood of my blood. When Speirr drank from her neck, he took my blood into him and now he, too, has my protection."

Camulus cursed.

Her grandmother wrinkled her nose. "It just reeks, doesn't it? You can't kill her or him unless you want to fight me."

Talon exchanged a stunned look with Sunshine.

"One day, Morrigán. One day . . ." Camulus flashed out of the room.

The Morrigán took a deep breath, then turned around to face them. "Congratulations, kids."

"I'm free?" Talon asked, still unable to believe it.

The Morrigán nodded. "With your Dark-Hunter powers intact."

Sunshine hesitated. "Is he still a Dark-Hunter?"

"No," her grandmother said. "Artemis released him from his vow when she gave up his soul. Once psychic powers are bestowed on someone, they remain with them forever."

Sunshine smiled. "So he can go out into daylight now?"

"Yes." The Morrigán looked suddenly uncomfortable. "By the way, there's something I need to tell you two."

"What?" they asked in unison, both of them afraid of what she might say.

"Because of the way our pantheon works, the two of you are . . ." She bit her lip and wrung her hands.

"We are what?" Talon prompted, terrified of what was coming next. When dealing with a god, one could never be too careful.

"You're immortal unless you renounce it."

Sunshine blinked. "What?"

Her grandmother cleared her throat. "You and your brothers were born immortal, sweetie. It's why you still look like a baby even though you're pushing thirty."

"Does that mean Mom's immortal too?" she asked.

"No. Since your father isn't, she decided that she would

give up her immortality to age with him. But since it was my blood that gave her immortality, it was passed on from her to you and then from you to Talon."

Joy ripped through Talon. "You mean I never have to watch her die again?"

"Never. Not unless you choose to."

"Oh hell no," Talon said, laughing.

"I figured as much." The Morrigán stepped back. "Well, I'm sure the two of you have a lot to do. Like plan a wedding. Go make lots of babies." She took their hands into hers and then pressed them together. "I expect a large number of great-grandkids from you two."

The Morrigán vanished, leaving them to stare at each other in wonderment.

Sunshine licked her lips as she stared up at him. She couldn't believe everything that had happened tonight.

Most of all, she couldn't believe she had Talon for her own. "So what's our first course of action?"

That familiar look came into his amber eyes. "Try to make a baby?"

She laughed at him. "Sounds good, but it'll probably take us the rest of the night to get back to your cabin."

"True, but your loft isn't that far away . . ."

Sunshine smiled. "No, it isn't."

He kissed her hand and then led her from the room.

They left the building and blended into the monstrous crowd of Mardi Gras celebrants who were heading home. Sunshine's heart was light as they walked hand in hand, until they reached the street.

Gasping, she pulled Talon back as a giant float narrowly missed him. Then she burst out laughing. "What is it with you and the Mardi Gras floats?"

"It's not the floats, love, it's you. Whenever you're around, everything else fades from my notice."

She bit her lip impishly. "You keep talking like that and I'll definitely take you home, lock you up, and throw away the key."

"That's fine with me, just make sure you're naked when you do it."

Chapter 19

Zarek watched as Talon and Sunshine vanished into the crowd. He was happy for Sunshine, but he couldn't understand what the two of them felt for one another.

He'd never known any kind of love.

"Fuck it," he snarled, limping away from the building. He needed to get back to his townhouse.

"Dionysus will be coming for you."

He paused at the sound of Acheron's voice behind him. "So?"

Ash sighed as he drew near. "Can we not have a truce?"

Zarek scoffed at the thought. "Why? Mutual disdain suits us so well."

"Z, I'm too tired for this. Give me something to use with Artemis. Something that will make her want to give you another chance."

Zarek laughed bitterly. "Yeah, right. After what I saw in there you don't honestly expect me to believe that she pulls your chain, do you? How stupid do I look?"

"Things aren't always what they seem."

Maybe, but Zarek wasn't willing to give on this. He'd screwed himself royally tonight. The moment he had turned on the gods, he'd known they would make him pay.

Not that he cared.

Let them come for him.

"Look," he said, turning his back to Acheron, "I'm tired

and hungry, and I just want to lie down until my injuries heal, okay?"

"Okay."

Zarek paused as a group of college students stumbled past, laughing and teasing each other. He watched them curiously.

They turned a corner and vanished.

He looked around at the drunken tourists and locals who were screaming and cheering. It was almost one A.M. now and still the city was alive and vibrant even though the crowd was being told to disperse.

"When do I go back?" Zarek asked, dreading the answer.

"Tomorrow. Nick'll be by to pick you up about two. He'll have a tinted van that can get you out to the airstrip without exposing you to daylight."

Zarek closed his eyes and winced as he thought about returning to Alaska. A few weeks more and spring would arrive.

He'd be housebound again.

A flash to his left caught his attention. Three seconds later, a Daimon came running through the crowd. The Daimon flashed his fangs and snarled at Zarek as if he had no idea who or what he was facing.

Zarek smiled evilly, anticipating what he was about to do.

"What are you?" the Daimon asked when he failed to scare or intimidate him.

Zarek quirked his lips. "Oh please, let me give you the job description. Me, Dark-Hunter. You, Daimon. I hit, you bleed. I kill, you die."

"Not this time." The Daimon attacked.

Acting on instinct, Zarek caught him in the throat and used his claw to kill him.

The Daimon evaporated as Valerius came running up through the crowd.

The Roman was breathing hard and had obviously been chasing after the Daimon for some distance. Valerius looked at Ash and inclined his head, then he glanced to Zarek and froze.

Zarek met his shocked gaze without flinching. As per Ash's orders, he had shaved his goatee off.

Recognition darkened Valerius's eyes as he stood there without blinking.

Zarek gave him a wry smile. "Surprise," he said quietly. "Bet you didn't see that one coming."

Without another word, he headed off into the crowd, leaving Valerius and Acheron to their own ends.

Epilogue

Brothers. The word hung in Valerius's heart as he stared at the marble bust in his foyer. It was the face of his father.

It was the face of his brother.

Zarek.

Pain racked him as he stood there trying to reconcile the past with the present. Why had he never seen the resemblance?

But he knew. He'd never really looked at Zarek before tonight.

A pathetic lowborn slave, Zarek had been so far beneath his notice that he had barely glanced at the boy.

There had only been one time in their lives when he had truly seen him.

He couldn't remember now what Zarek had been beaten for. For that matter, he couldn't even remember which of his brothers had committed the deed that had caused Zarek's punishment. It could just as well have been his misdeed as that of one of the others.

He only remembered that it was the first time he had recognized Zarek as a person.

Zarek had been lying on the cobbled floor, clutching his arms over his chest, his naked, scarred back bloody and torn.

What had struck Valerius most was the look on Zarek's

face. The boy's eyes had been hollow. Empty. Not a single tear was evident.

Valerius had wondered at the time why Zarek hadn't cried at such a harsh beating, but then it had dawned on him that Zarek never cried.

The wretched slave had never uttered a single word while they beat him. No matter what they said or did, the boy just took it like a man, with no sobs, no begging. Just hard, cold stoicism.

Valerius couldn't fathom such strength from someone who was younger than him.

Before he realized what he was doing, he'd reached out and touched one of the welts on Zarek's back. Raw and bleeding, it had looked so painful that he tried to imagine what it would feel like to have *one* such wound, much less an entire back full of them.

Zarek didn't move.

"Do you need . . ." Valerius had choked on the last of the sentence. He had wanted to help Zarek up, but knew they would both be punished if anyone saw him do such a thing.

"What are you doing?"

His father's angry voice caused him to jump. "I-I-I was l-l-looking at his back," he answered honestly.

His father had narrowed his eyes on him. "Why?"

"I was c-c-curious." Valerius hated how he always stuttered around his father.

"Why? Do you think it hurts him?"

Valerius had been too afraid to answer. His father had had that dead look that often came into his eyes. A look that meant the kind, loving father he knew was gone and the brutal military commander was there instead.

As much as he loved his father, he feared the military commander, who was capable of most any act of cold-blooded ruthlessness, even against his own sons.

"Answer me, boy. Do you think it hurts him?"

He nodded.

"Do you care if it hurts him?"

Valerius had blinked back his tears before they betrayed

him. The truth was he did care, but he knew his father would fly into a rage if he ever dared breathe that aloud. "N-n-no. I don't c-c-care."

"Then prove it."

Valerius blinked, suddenly afraid of what that meant. "Prove it?"

His father had retrieved the whip from the stand and handed it to him. "Give him ten more lashes, or I will see *you* given twenty."

Heartsick and with his hand shaking, Valerius had taken the whip and delivered the lashes.

Unused to wielding a whip, he had missed Zarek's back entirely. His lashes landed on Zarek's unscarred arms and legs. Virgin flesh that had never been beaten before.

For the first time Zarek had hissed and recoiled from the lashes. So much so that the last lash ended up cutting across Zarek's face, right below his brow.

Zarek had screamed, cupping his eye as blood poured from between his dirty fingers.

Valerius had wanted to vomit as he heard his father praise him for blinding the slave's eye.

His father had actually patted him on the back. "That's it, my son. Always strike where they're most vulnerable. You'll make a fine general one day."

Zarek had looked up at him then and the emptiness was gone. The right side of his face had been covered in blood, but with his left eye, Zarek had conveyed all the pain and anguish he felt. All the hatred that was directed both inward and out.

That look was seared inside Valerius to this day.

His father had beaten Zarek again for the insolence of that glare.

No wonder Zarek hated them all. The man was entitled to it. More so now that Valerius knew the truth of Zarek's parentage.

He wondered when Zarek had learned the truth. Why no one had ever told him.

Angry, Valerius gripped the stone bust of their father.

"Why?" he demanded, knowing he'd never have an answer now.

And right then he hated his father more than ever. Hated the blood that flowed through his veins.

But at the end of the day, he was Roman.

It was his heritage.

Right or wrong, he couldn't deny it.

Lifting his head high, he retreated from the foyer to his bedroom upstairs.

But as he ascended the steps, he lashed out one last time.

Turning around, he kicked his leg out, catching the pedestal.

The bust of his father toppled against the stone marble floor and shattered.

NEW ORLEANS, THAT AFTERNOON

Zarek leaned back as the helicopter took off. He was going home.

No doubt he would die there.

If Artemis didn't kill him, he was sure Dionysus would. Dionysus's threat rang in his ears. For Sunshine's happiness, he had crossed a god who was sure to make him suffer even worse horrors than those in his past.

Zarek still didn't know why he'd done it, other than the fact that pissing people off was the only thing that truly gave him pleasure.

His gaze fell to his backpack.

Before he knew what he was doing, he took the handmade bowl out and held it in his hands.

He ran his hands over the intricate designs that Sunshine had carved. She had probably spent hours on this bowl.

Caressed it with loving hands . . .

"They waste their time over a rag doll and it becomes very important to them; and if anybody takes it away from them, they cry . . ."

The passage from *The Little Prince* ran through his mind. Sunshine had wasted much of her time on this and given him her work. She probably had no idea just how much her simple gift had touched him.

"You really are pathetic," he breathed, clutching the bowl in his hand as he curled his lip in repugnance. "It meant nothing to her and for a worthless piece of clay you just consigned yourself to death."

Closing his eyes, he swallowed. It was true.

One more time, he was going to die for nothing.

"So what?"

Let him die. Maybe then he would find some kind of solace.

Angered at his own stupidity, Zarek splintered the bowl with his thoughts. Pulling out his MP3 player, he scrolled to Nazareth's *Hair of the Dog*, put his headphones on, and waited for Mike to lighten the windows of the helicopter and let the lethal sunlight in on him.

It was, after all, what Dionysus had paid the Squire to do.

TARTARUS

Screams surrounded Styxx, piercing the blackness. He tried his best to see something and saw only the strange pinpoint ghost-lights of eyes that were desperate to be of use.

This place was cold. Icy. He felt his way along a craggy rock only to learn he was encased in a small, six-by-six-foot cell. There wasn't even enough room for him to lie down comfortably.

Suddenly, a light appeared beside him. It faded to form a young, beautiful woman with dark red hair, fair skin, and the green, swirling eyes of a goddess. He knew her instantly.

She was Mnimi, the goddess of memory. He'd seen her likeness countless times in temples and on scrolls.

She held an old-fashioned oil lamp in her hand as she studied him closely.

"Where am I?" Styxx asked.

Her voice was faint and gentle, like a breeze whispering through crystal leaves. "You are in Tartarus."

Styxx swallowed his outrage. When he had died aeons ago in ancient Greece, he had been placed in the paradise of the Elysian Fields.

Tartarus was where Hades banished the evil souls he wished to torture.

"I don't belong here."

"Where *do* you belong?" she asked.

"I belong with my family."

Her eyes were tinged by sadness as she regarded him. "They have all been reborn. The only family you have left now is the brother you hate."

"He is not my brother. He was *never* my brother."

She cocked her head as if listening to something far away from them. "Strange. Acheron never felt that way about you. No matter the times you were cruel to him, he never hated *you*."

"I don't care what he feels."

"True," she said as if she knew his innermost thoughts, as if she knew him better than he knew himself.

"Honestly, I don't understand you, Styxx. For centuries, you were given the Vanishing Isle as your home. You had friends and every luxury known. It was as peaceful and beautiful there as the Elysian Fields, and yet all you did was plot more vengeance against Acheron. I gave you memories of your beautiful home and family, of your peaceful and happy childhood to comfort you and instead of gaining pleasure from them you used them to fuel your hatred."

"Do you blame me? He stole everything from me. Everything I ever hoped for or loved. Because of him my family is dead, my kingdom gone. Even my life ended because of *him*."

"No," she said softly. "You can lie to yourself, Styxx, but not to me. It was you who betrayed your brother. You and your father. You let your fear of him blind you. It was your own actions that condemned not only him, but yourself as well."

"What do you know of it? Acheron is evil. Unclean. He defiles everything he touches."

She danced her fingers through the lamp's flame, making it flicker eerily in the darkness of the small cell. All the while her eyes burned him with their intensity. "That is the beauty of memory, isn't it? Our reality is always clouded by our perceptions of truth. You remember events one way and so you judge your brother without knowledge of how things were to him."

Mnimi placed a hand on his shoulder. The heat of it seared his skin and when she spoke her low tone sounded evil, insidious. "I am about to give you the most precious of gifts, Styxx. At long last, you will have understanding."

Styxx tried to run, but couldn't.

Mnimi's fiery touch held him immobile.

His head spun as he rushed back in time.

He saw his beautiful mother lying on her gilded bed, her body covered in sweat, her face ashen, as an attendant brushed her damp, blond hair from her pale blue eyes. He'd never known his mother to appear more joy-filled than she did that day.

The room was crowded with court officials and his father, the king, stood to the side of the bed with his heads of state. The long, stained-glass windows were open, letting the fresh sea air offer relief to the heat of the late summer day.

"It is another beautiful boy," the midwife happily proclaimed, wrapping the newborn infant in a blanket.

"By sweet Apollymi's hand, Aara, you've done me proud!" his father said as a loud jubilant shout echoed through the room. "Twin boys to rule over our twin isles!"

Laughing, his mother watched as the midwife cleaned the firstborn.

It was then Styxx learned the true horror of Acheron's birth, learned the dark secret his father had hidden from him.

Acheron was the firstborn son. Not him.

Styxx, who was now in Acheron's infant body, struggled to breathe through his newborn lungs. He had finally taken a deep, clear breath when he heard a cry of alarm.

"Zeus have mercy, the eldest is malformed, Majesties."

His mother looked up, her brow creased by worry. "How so?"

The midwife carried him over to his mother, who held the second-born babe to her breast.

Scared, the baby wanted only to be comforted. He reached for the brother who had shared the womb with him these past months. If he could just touch his brother, all would be right. He knew it.

Instead, his mother pulled his brother away, out of his sight and reach. "It cannot be," his mother sobbed. "He is blind."

"Not blind, Majesty," the eldest wisewoman said as she stepped forward, through the crowd. Her white robes were heavily embroidered with gold threads, and she wore an ornate gold wreath over her faded gray hair. "He was sent to you by the gods."

The king narrowed his eyes angrily at the queen. "You were unfaithful?" he accused Aara.

"Nay, never."

"Then how is it he came from your loins? All of us here witnessed it."

The room as a whole looked to the wisewoman, who stared blankly at the tiny, helpless baby crying for someone to hold him and offer him solace. Warmth.

"He will be a destroyer, this child," she said, her ancient voice loud and ringing so that all could hear her proclamation. "His touch will bring death to many. Not even the gods themselves will be safe from his wrath."

"Then kill him now." The king ordered his guard to draw his sword and slay the baby.

"Nay!" the wisewoman said, halting the guard before he could carry out the king's will. "Kill this infant and your son dies as well, Majesty. Their life forces are combined. 'Tis the will of the gods that you should raise him to manhood."

The baby sobbed, not understanding the fear he sensed from those around him. All he wanted was to be held as his brother was being held. For someone to cuddle him and tell him that all would be fine.

"I will not raise a monster," the king said.

"You have no choice." The wisewoman took the baby from the midwife and offered it to the queen. "He was born of your body, Majesty. He is your son."

The baby squalled even louder, reaching again for his mother. She cringed away from him, clutching her second-born even tighter than before. "I will not suckle it. I will not touch it. Get it away from my sight."

The wisewoman took the child to his father. "And what of you, Majesty? Will you not acknowledge him?"

"Never. That child is no son of mine."

The wisewoman took a deep breath and presented the infant to the room. Her grip was loose, with no love or compassion evident in her touch.

"Then he will be called Acheron for the river of woe. Like the river of the underworld, his journey shall be dark, long, and enduring. He will be able to give life and to take it. He will walk through his life alone and abandoned— ever seeking kindness and ever finding cruelty."

The wisewoman looked down at the infant in her hands and uttered the simple truth that would haunt the boy for the rest of his existence. "May the gods have mercy on you, little one. No one else ever will."

MOUNT OLYMPUS

As Ash approached Artemis's sacred temple, he opened the oversized double doors with his thoughts.

With his head held high, he gripped the padded strap of his black suede backpack and forced himself to walk through the ornate, gilded doorway into Artemis's throne room where she sat listening to one of her women play a lute and sing.

Nine pairs of feminine eyes turned to stare at him curiously.

Without being told, her eight attendants gathered their things and rushed from the room as they always did at his appearance. They shut the door discreetly behind them and left him alone with Artemis.

Vaguely, Ash remembered the first time he'd been allowed inside Artemis's private domain on Olympus. As a young man he had been awed by the intricately carved marble columns that framed the throne room. They rose twenty feet from the marble and gold floor under his feet up to the domed gold roof that was intricately embossed with wildlife scenes. Three sides of this room had no walls. Instead, it looked out over the perfect sky where white, fluffy clouds floated by at eye level.

The throne itself wasn't as ornate as it was comfortable. More an oversized chaise longue that could easily double as a bed, it occupied the center of the open room and was covered with lush, decadent ivory pillows with gold tassels and trim.

Only two men had ever been allowed to set foot inside this temple. Artemis's twin brother Apollo and him.

It was an honor Ash would gladly have ceded.

Artemis was dressed in a sheer white peplos that left her lithe body all but bare to his gaze. The dark pink tips of her breasts were hard and puckered against the gauzy material, and the hem of it rose high on her legs, showing him a glimpse of the dark auburn triangle at the juncture of her thighs.

She smiled seductively at him, bringing his attention back to her perfect, beautiful face. Her long, auburn curls seemed as iridescent as her green eyes while she watched him with fascinated interest. She lay on her side, her arms folded over the high back of the chaise and her chin resting on the back of her hand.

Taking a deep breath, Ash closed the distance between them and stood before her.

Artemis cocked a finely arched brow as she gazed ravenously at his body. "Interesting. You look more defiant than ever, Acheron. I see no proof of the submission you promised me. Do I need to revoke Talon's soul?"

He wasn't sure she had the power to do such a thing, but then, he wasn't willing to chance it. He'd called her bluff before and had lived to regret it.

He shrugged his backpack off his shoulder and dropped it to the floor. Then he removed his leather jacket and draped it over the backpack. Falling to his knees, he placed his hands on his leather-clad thighs, ground his teeth and lowered his head.

Artemis unfolded herself from the chaise and approached him. "Thank you, Acheron," she said breathlessly as she moved to stand behind him. She ran her hand through his hair, turning it golden blond and freeing it from its braid so that it spilled over his shoulders and chest.

Artemis brushed the hair on the left side of his neck aside, exposing the flesh beneath it to her gaze. She dragged a long fingernail down his bared skin, raising chills over his arms and chest.

And then she did the one thing he hated most of all.

She blew her breath across the back of his neck.

He fought down the urge to cringe. She, alone, knew how and why he hated that sensation. It was a cruel thing she did to remind him of his place in her world.

"In spite of what you might think, Acheron, I derive no pleasure from making you bend to my will. I would much rather have you here by your own choice—the way you used to come to me."

Ash closed his eyes as he remembered those days. He had loved her so much then. Had ached any time he was forced to leave her side.

He had believed in her and had given her the one thing he had never given anyone else—his trust.

She had been his world. His sanctuary. At a time when no one would acknowledge him, she had welcomed him into her life and had shown him what it was like to be wanted.

Together, they had laughed and they had loved. He had

shared things with her that he had never shared with anyone before or since.

Then, when he had needed her most, she had coldly turned her back on him and left him to die painfully. Alone.

She had spurned his love that day and had proven to him that in the end, she was just as ashamed of him as his family had been.

He meant nothing to her.

He never would.

The truth of it had hurt, but after all this time he had come to terms with it. He would never be anything more to her than a curiosity. A defiant pet she kept around for her own amusement.

Again in a gesture she knew he hated, Artemis knelt at his back, her knees brushing gently against his hips. She ran her hand over his shoulder, and then down the intricate bird tattoo on his arm.

"Mmm," she purred as she nuzzled his hair with her face. "What is it about you that makes me want you so?"

"I don't know, but if you ever figure it out, let me know and I'll be sure to stop it."

She sank her fingernails deep into his tattoo. "My Acheron, ever defiant. Ever vexing."

She ripped open his T-shirt and removed it from his body.

Ash held his breath as she pulled his back to her front and hungrily skimmed her hands over his bare chest. As always, his body betrayed him and reacted to her touch. Chills ran over his skin and his gut drew tight as his groin hardened.

Her hot breath fell against his neck as she ran her tongue along his collarbone. He leaned his head to the right to give her more access to him while she unlaced his tight leather pants.

His breathing ragged, Ash clutched his hands against his thighs and waited for what was to come.

She freed his swollen shaft and sheathed it with her hands.

Her tongue teasing his neck, she ran her right hand upward to the tip of his manhood where she stroked him until he was so hard for her that he hurt. He moaned as she dipped her other hand down and cupped and stroked him from underneath while her right hand continued to tease him.

"You're so large and thick, Acheron," she whispered hoarsely as she used her fingers to coat him in his own wetness so that she could stroke him even faster. Harder. "I love the way you feel in my hands."

She took a deep breath in his hair. "The way you smell." She nuzzled his shoulder with her face. "The sound of your voice when you say my name." She ran her tongue across his shoulder blade back to his neck. "The way your cheeks mottle whenever you exert yourself."

She nibbled his ear. "The look on your face when you release yourself inside of me."

She brushed her breasts against his spine so that she could whisper her next words in his ear. "But most of all, I love the way you *taste*."

Ash tensed as she sank her long canine teeth into his neck. The momentary pain turned quickly to physical pleasure.

Reaching over his shoulder, he cradled her head to his neck and rocked himself against her hands as she stroked him even faster than before. He felt her and her powers flowing through him, uniting them even closer than the intimacy of sex.

His head swam until he could see nothing. All he could feel was Artemis. Her demanding hands on him, her hot, living breath against his throat, her heart pounding in time to his.

They were synchronized. Her pleasure was his and, for this moment in time, they were one creature with one heartbeat, bonded on a level that transcended human understanding.

He felt her desire for him. Her need to possess every part of his mind, body, and heart. He felt as if he were drowning. As if she were pulling him far away from him-

self, into a cold, dark cell where he would never again find his way back.

He heard her whispering to him in his mind. *"Come for me, Acheron. Give me your power. Your strength. Give me all that you are."*

He fought against her intrusion, and as always, he lost the battle.

In the end, he had no choice except to give her what she wanted.

Ash threw his head back and roared as his entire body shook in complete orgasmic ecstasy. Still she drank from him, taking his essence and powers into her own body.

He was hers. Regardless of what he might think, want, or feel, he would always belong to her.

Panting and weak from her possession, Ash leaned back against her and watched as a thin trail of blood ran down his chest . . .

Epilogue

THREE MONTHS LATER

Sunshine smiled as she carried her small box of oil paints into the living room. She'd been intending to take them to her new studio that overlooked Talon's swamp, but as soon as she had caught sight of her husband hanging her paintings of his old cabin up on the wall, she'd stopped.

He didn't seem to know she was there. He had the hammer hanging out of his back pocket as he lifted the framed landscape and placed it on the wall.

As soon as the two of them had emerged from her loft after Mardi Gras, Talon had decided to build them their own house.

Together, they had designed every detail. An extremely large computer room and a garage to accommodate his toys, and an open, airy studio for her art. They even had a game room with shelves that displayed his massive collection of Pez dispensers. Snoopy took a prime location in the center of the middle shelf.

But her favorite room was the small one that adjoined their master bedroom suite. The one that would hopefully be a nursery someday.

"Did I get it centered?" he asked, surprising her that he knew she was standing behind him.

"Looks good to me."

He glanced at her over his shoulder and caught her gazing at his nicely shaped rear.

"I was talking about the painting."

"And I was talking about your butt, but the painting looks all right too."

He laughed as he neared her and took the box out of her hands.

He brushed his hand though her hair and gave her a light kiss. Sunshine reached around his hips and gave a tight squeeze to his heinie.

"You keep doing that," Talon said throatily, "and we won't get any more unpacking done today."

She gave him a devilish grin. "That's okay. It's not like we don't have the rest of eternity to move in."

"Well, in that case . . ." He set the box down and scooped her up in his arms.

Sunshine laughed as he headed toward the indoor pool. "Where are you taking me?"

His look was purely sexual. "To the only room we haven't broken in yet."

"You are insatiable."

"I know. Evil to the core."

As they passed the dining room, she made him put her down long enough to grab a small, wrapped package.

Talon frowned, then he tossed her over his shoulder and sprinted with her to the back of the house.

Sunshine was still laughing when he laid her down gently next to the pool.

"What's this?" he asked after she handed him her gift.

"It's a housewarming present for you."

He opened it to find an Eddie Munster Pez dispenser.

A wide smile spread across his face. "I can't believe you found one."

Sunshine lifted his scarred right hand and kissed it. Then, she turned it over in her hands and studied the swirling design of the burn.

The first thing Talon had done when he had taken her

to her loft had been to remove the scar from her hand that
she had received from holding the medallion.

Now that scar resided on his hand instead of hers.

"I love you, Talon," she whispered. "More than you will
ever know."

He fingered her cheek with his left hand as his amber
eyes scorched her with their sincere intensity. "I love you,
too, Sunshine. Thank you for your strength and for giving
up soy products."

She laughed at that, then kissed him passionately.

Talon stepped away from her as he caught sight of the
box she'd brought in a few minutes ago. It held a collection
of things they had packed up from his desk, including the
box that held Nynia's torc.

"I've been meaning to do something." He removed the
torc from around his neck and placed it with Nynia's.

Sunshine frowned as she watched him slide open the
door to the back porch that looked out over the swamp.

"What are you doing?"

"I'm putting the past to rest. As much as I loved Nynia,
I love you more and I never want you to doubt whose eyes
I'm looking into when I make love to you."

He drew back to toss the torcs.

Sunshine grabbed his hand. She knew exactly what those
torcs meant to him and what he was doing for her.

Kissing his lips, she took them from him. She pulled
back with a smile. "I will never doubt you, Talon."

She took his torc and returned it to his neck.

He smiled tenderly, then placed the other one around
hers.

Her skin tingled from the feel of his hands on her collarbone.

Staring into his eyes, she remembered the night she'd
met him. The sight of the float running him over.

Even though she should hate Dionysus for all he had
put them through, she couldn't.

After all, had the incompetent god backed up, her story
would have had an entirely different ending.